Don't get lost in ~~our~~ Shadows

THE SHADOWBORN SERIES

AN OMNIBUS: BOOKS ONE TO THREE

ERIN O'KANE

Don't get lost in the Shadows

CONTENTS

Note from the Author	v
PART I Hunted by Shadows	1
PART II Lost in Shadows	215
PART III Embraced by Shadows	413
Acknowledgments	669
Also by Erin O'Kane	671

The Shadowborn Series Omnibus: Books 1-3
By

Erin O'Kane

Copyright @ 2021 Erin O'Kane

The Shadowborn Series, an Omnibus, books One to Three

First publication: 2021

Editing by Elemental Editing & Proofreading

Proofreading by Bookish Dreams Editing

Cover by HQ Artwork

Formatting by Kaila Duff

All rights reserved. Except for use in any review, the reproduction or utilisation of this work, in whole or in part, in any form by any electronic, mechanical, or other means now known or hereafter invented, is forbidden without the written permission of the publisher.

This is a work of fiction. Any resemblance to places, events or real people are entirely coincidental.

Published by Erin O'Kane

Erin.okaneauthor@gmail.com

Author Note

This book is an omnibus and as such is made up of three books. These books were originally published in 2018 and 2019, and have been re-edited slightly, but the story has remained the same. Exclusive bonus scenes have been written for the purpose of this omnibus.

This book is dedicated to the whole team of people behind me, be that family, friend, someone directly involved in getting this book published, or my readers.

I've really enjoyed re-visiting Ari's world again, and I hope you enjoy the stories just as much as I did writing them.

All the best,
Erin xoxo

Prologue

"Little wolf."

Fear pulses through my body at the sound of his singsong voice, my inner wolf screaming to be let out. My heart pounds against my chest as I look around the dark, dingy room for a way out—trapped. My dirty, unwashed hair clings to the tears rolling down my seven-year-old cheeks.

I hear footsteps making their way towards me. I would have known it was him by the sound of his shoes clipping against the floor, even without him announcing his presence with his favourite chant. As the sound of his feet get louder, so does my breathing. I know all too well the fate that awaits me on the other side of the door.

"Run, little wolf."

My fists clench as I fight the change, my nails digging into my palms as they transform into claws. My skin tingles. I don't need to look to know that fur is sprouting along my body. Closing my eyes, I force my wolf to back down, knowing that turning into my other form is exactly what *he* wants.

Keys clank in the lock, and the door squeaks as it's pushed open. Shadows creep into the room, almost seeming to crawl towards me. I force my weak, battered body to stand up, glaring at my tormentor as he fills the doorway.

"Hello, little wolf."

Chapter One

17 YEARS LATER

The myriad of sounds and smells of the hospital batter my heightened senses as I walk into the emergency department. The fluorescent artificial lighting above irritates my eyes, and the whining and whirring of the multitude of machines make it difficult to focus on what the portly, sweaty man in front of me is trying to tell me as he flags me down. Don't even get me started on the various scents and odours that are overwhelming my enhanced sense of smell. It may be early in the morning, but it's still just as busy here. It's enough to make most shifters turn tail and run, excuse the pun. But not me. I work as a nurse in A&E—or the emergency department, as the Americans call it. I've lived here for six years now, and I still can't seem to lose my Briticisms. I love working here, being surrounded by the chaos and mayhem, at least, human-Ari does. I can feel wolf-Ari cringing at the assault on our senses. She's been getting more and more agitated recently. It's been too long since we last shifted.

It's dangerous for a shifter to ignore their inner animal for too long. Suppressing these instincts tends to have disastrous consequences, both for the shifter and those who happen to be nearby when they lose control. Thankfully, this is rare, but working as a nurse, I've seen my fair share of rogue shifter injuries. Not that humans are privy to this kind of knowledge, they only know them as unfortunate and horrendous muggings or animal attacks. Even now, I can feel my wolf eyeing up the man in front of me. My eyes wander to his neck where I can see his pulse fluttering rapidly under his skin.

He would be easy prey. Having consumed one too many pies, he would be slow, and he would be no match for my superior strength... I shake my head to get rid of these thoughts and force a smile instead, pretending to know what he's been going on about. These humans are so slow to communicate what they want, like they have all the time in the world. All I would need to do is jump forward and snap his neck, and bang, life over.

Now, now, Ari, stop looking at the nice humans as prey, I scold myself. That would be a spectacular way to lose my job and reveal the existence of shifters to the human world. Not to mention being hauled in by ASP—the Allied Supernatural Protectors—who are our version of the police. They govern us and make sure we keep the peace and, most importantly, don't reveal ourselves to humans. I have a good setup here, so I'm not prepared to blow my cover by going feral.

A sudden quiet catches my attention and brings me back to where I am—at work, behind the nurses' station, staring at the man in front of me. Seeing the expectant look on his face, I know he's asked me a question, and I haven't got a clue as to what it was. *Way to go, Ari*, I rebuke myself again. I seem to be doing that a lot lately, talking to myself. Perhaps I should get out more. Thankfully, I'm saved from answering as an announcement comes from the overhead speaker system.

"Trauma call, adult male trauma. ETA five minutes. Trauma team to resus one please."

Making my hasty, half-hearted apologies to the startled man waiting for my answer, I hurry over to resus station one, waiting to be briefed. Anticipation and excitement run through me as we're given our roles for the upcoming trauma patient. This is what I've trained for and what I love doing, the adrenaline pumping through my body as I mentally go through the emergency procedures in my mind I may need for my patient. Hearing someone call my name, I look up and smile as I see who's walking towards me.

"Good evening, Dr. Daniels." Beaming at the handsome doctor, I lean against the trauma desk, already anticipating his expression at my choice of greeting. I was right.

"You know I hate it when you call me that," he replies, but the smile on his face takes any sting from his words. Eric Daniels is gorgeous with his blue eyes, short blond hair, and dazzling smile. It's no wonder he's a hit with all the ladies. Gorgeous, kind, *and* a doctor? He even has me eyeing him up when no one's looking. I grin at his comment, and he takes a step towards me and places his hand on my arm, his face lighting up at the physical contact. The smile drops from my face as I take a small step away, feeling guilty when I see a brief look of hurt flash across his eyes.

So what's the problem, you ask? A gorgeous man who has a good job and is interested in me sounds like a win, right? Problem is, he's one hundred percent human, and I can't date a human, even if I'm pretending to be one. We met at one of my crazy housemate's parties, where she forced the two of us together with a quick, "Have you met Ari?" before disappearing into the crowd. She's always trying to set me up, and Eric is just one of the latest men she's deemed suitable. Victoria Smith, or Tori as I know her, is my best friend and flatmate. Being a witch, she blends in well with humans, given the fact that she is one, albeit with a few extra...abilities. Typically, shifters don't get on with other supernaturals, preferring to stick with our own kind, but we hit it off straightaway. Knowing what I am, she should know better than to keep trying to set me up with humans, yet she can't seem to help herself.

Focusing on the task at hand, I try to centre my attention on the briefing, acutely aware of Eric standing next to me. My senses are heightened, his scent more inviting than usual. Maybe Tori's right, perhaps it *has* been too long since I've gotten laid, and a tumble in the sheets with Dr. Gorgeous wouldn't do any harm, right?

As if he can sense my thoughts, I feel Eric's attention turn to me. Thankfully, the paramedics burst into the trauma room, and controlled chaos commences as people fill the trauma bay. A brief fight with my wolf begins, as it does with all major trauma cases such as this. I'm a wolf, after all, and when the smell of blood fills the air, it makes her restless. She wants out, especially when I haven't shifted for so long.

Pushing my instincts aside, I home in on my patient, my attention fully on him as I focus on my job of keeping him alive. My sensitive hearing can pick up his gurgling wheeze from here. I'm positive it's a punctured lung. Continuing my assessment of the patient alongside the medics, I pass on my judgements to Eric, who agrees without question. He knows I know my stuff, and I have yet to be wrong about a diagnosis. Nurses often have an intuition about patients, and thankfully, that's what I'm able to pass my abilities off as. Minutes elapse, although it may be hours since time passes strangely in emergency situations. Finishing my primary survey, I lift the patient's arm to get a better look at his side, but I pause when I see strange bruising. A sense of worry fills me at the unusual location of the injury.

"Dr. Daniels, I think he's wounded on his back as well," I inform him, keeping my voice calm despite the sense of urgency I'm feeling.

With the help of the team, we're able to lean the patient to one side so we can look at his back. Cursing comes from the nurses on my side of the patient, but I pay them no attention, my gaze fixed on the patient's mutilated back. My wolf rushes to the surface, demanding to be let free. *Protect, find, kill, run.* Her demands pound though my head, each one louder than the last. My bones ache at the force of her trying to shift, my front teeth elongating into sharp points as I grasp the bed in front of me, the fabric tearing under my grip.

"Ari." I jerk my gaze up to the person trying to gain my attention—Eric. Taking a deep, steadying breath to keep my wolf under control, I step back from the patient, pretty sure my already unusual eyes are softly glowing with my wolf this close to the surface.

"Go take a break," he orders, his tone not giving me any choice other than to obey. But his eyes are soft, understanding. Shaking my head, I walk away. I don't have time to think about Eric right now, so for once, I do as I'm told.

My steps are hurried as I walk to the ladies' changing rooms. The door slams into the wall behind me in my rush, but mercifully, there's no one else in the room. Bracing my arms against the sink, I look up into the mirror above me. My amber eyes are reflected back at me, made even more unnatural by the supernatural power that is making them glow softly as my wolf prowls under my skin. A shudder racks my body as my wolf tries to force the change again.

My mind soon returns to the patient and his mess of a back, to the symbol that had been marked—no, fucking *carved* into his flesh. The very same symbol I have tattooed on my upper back, just over my spine and between my shoulder blades. The symbol depicts a wolf howling to the moon, covered in shadows, representing the pack it belongs to.

I place my shaking hands into the sink and let the cold water wash over them before splashing some onto my face. *Calm the fuck down, Ari. Think.* I pace the room. This isn't just a random shifter attack, not with Shadow Pack's symbol carved into a random human's back. Were it any other pack's symbol, I could rule it out as some sort of punishment—shifter justice is brutal. But why would a human be carved with the symbol of a pack that is over three thousand miles away in England? That of my former pack. There's only one conclusion.

With a deep breath, I look at my reflection again as I admit to myself what I've feared since the day I arrived in the U.S.

They've found me.

Pushing aside the rising feeling of dread, I walk to my locker where I've stashed my personal belongings. I shake my hair out of its hospital required ponytail, letting the brown and gold strands fall across my face, creating a shield between me and the rest of the world.

Right, that's enough of the pity party, I think to myself, never being one for self-pity. If I'm going to get out of this, I need to be strong, not falling apart in the locker room of the hospital.

Pushing away from the locker, I open it, pulling my mobile phone from my jacket pocket. Seeing a message from Tori, I tap on it and frown. She doesn't usually text me when I'm at work unless she wants me to pick up takeout on the way home. A woman after my own heart.

Tori: So that was weird. Some hottie just came to the apartment asking after you. He felt like a wolf to me. Had that growly, alpha feel to him. I kept it vague, saying you were out.

Shit. I keep my distance from shifters, and I certainly don't give any of them my address. Tori has this built-in sense where she can get a 'feel' of someone and their supernatural abilities, and so far, she has never been wrong. If Tori says there's a wolf asking after me, then I believe her. Running my hand through my hair, I sort through my options. There's protection around our flat, and as long as he isn't invited into the house, he shouldn't be able to get in, so she should be safe. Picking up my phone again, I send a text to Tori.

Me: Don't let him in, I'm not expecting anyone. Just stay alert. Any bad feelings from him?

Almost immediately I get a reply, and I smile as I read the message, imagining her expression as she was writing it. Tori can always make me smile, even when she's not trying to.

Tori: Girl, I wasn't born yesterday. Besides, you would have told me if you were expecting *that* piece of hotness. No, no bad feelings. I would have blasted him to next Tuesday if he had. I didn't get much of a feeling off him to be honest.

Me: Thanks for having my back, Tori. I'll pick up Chinese, my treat.

Tori: You know the way to my heart <3

Laughing at her message, I feel some of the tension leave my body. This mysterious visitor can't be from Shadow Pack if he doesn't have any malicious intent. Anyone from the pack would be radiating bad feelings if they came for me, and Tori would have picked up on it and warned me. So who was this mysterious 'hottie' who was asking after me?

Hearing the emergency bell ringing brings me back to reality. Right, I'm still at work. I'm not in immediate danger, and I'm not going to let those bastards from Shadow Pack intimidate me and ruin the life I've worked so hard to build here. Walking back over to the mirror, I pull my hair into a ponytail, pleased to see that my eyes have returned to normal. I'll need to be careful though, I can almost see my wolf prowling under my skin. I smile at myself in the mirror, nurse Ari is back. Rolling my shoulders and holding my head high, I walk out into the emergency department. Patients to save, wolf butts to kick. Just another day in my crazy life.

Chapter Two

I shoulder my way into the dingy club, making my way through the crowds on the dance floor as I head towards the bar. It's always busy here, even on a weeknight. Thankfully, once I make it through all the sweaty, dancing bodies, there's a stool at the bar that is unoccupied.

With a grateful sigh I sink into it, feeling the tension of the day ease out of my bones. What a night. After the shift I've had, I deserve a drink, but that's not the only reason I am here tonight. I take a moment to look around the bar. It looks like it used to be a nice place, but years of misuse have left it needing some TLC.

The patrons don't exactly help the image. This particular establishment caters only to supernatural beings. The world that we live in is not as simple as the humans like to believe it is. Werewolves, vampires, fae, witches, and demons? All real, not to mention the hundreds of other creatures that roam the streets. We're not like the movies portray us. The moon doesn't force me to shift, and vampires are not all gorgeous, otherworldly beings—they are dead, after all. Werewolves are just one of many types of shifter, we just happen to have the largest population. We don't all live in harmony —there is always a blood feud going on between several of the races —but this bar is one of the neutral territories in the city where everybody is able to mingle freely. There is still a lot of prejudice, though, and you can almost see the divide in the room between the magic users and other supernaturals.

Now, I know what you're thinking: why would a person who's determined to stay as far away as possible from other shifters be sitting in a supernatural bar? Unfortunately, it is necessary to show my face occasionally, even for a lone wolf like me. The powers that be at ASP expect us to make appearances. If we don't, they start poking their noses where they don't belong. If you want to stay off their radar, you have to act like they expect you to. So for me, that means showing up at the occasional bar, as would be expected for a young unmated shifter, and keeping out of trouble. Plus, places like this are great for finding out information and listening to gossip.

"Wolf girl, haven't seen you here for a while."

I spin on my bar stool. I know that growling voice, and only one person would dare call me 'wolf girl.' Trying to hide a smile, I scowl at the towering wall of muscle in front of me.

"Garett, what have I told you about calling me that? Or shall I refer to you as 'grizzly' again?" I retort, addressing the bear shifter in front of me.

Laughing, I watch as he starts to pour my usual. Like his inner animal, he's huge, his muscles almost bursting out of his white shirt as he moves around behind the bar. My eyes drop to his ass, and let me tell you, in his tight black jeans, it's a sight to behold. Turning around, Garett raises his eyebrow at me as I'm caught in the act, then he smirks as he places my beer on the counter in front of me.

"Like what you see, sweetness?" Flipping him off, I take a sip of my cold beer, trying to ignore the blush that covers my cheeks.

Laughing, Garett turns to serve a willowy fae at the other end of the bar. Man, I really need to get laid. But he is the closest thing I have to a friend in the shifter community, and I'm not going to ruin that by jumping his bones.

The club is crowded, people are pushing for a space at the bar and trying to get served, all except for a clear circle of space around me. I smirk into my beer. This is another reason I came to this particular bar—no one is going to mess with someone who has a grizzly bear looking out for them.

Falling into my thoughts, I take a sip of my drink, not really paying attention to the people around me until I feel a tingle race down the back of my neck. Someone's watching me. I slowly sit up straighter in my chair, trying not to tip them off that I know I'm being watched. My wolf pushes to the surface, wanting to protect me. An uneasy hush falls near me as the supernaturals closest to me feel my power start to emerge. They may not all be shifters, but they can feel the waves of alpha strength rolling off me.

All shifters are born with a certain amount of power, and within a pack, our ranking is determined by how strong that is. Certain shifters will be powerful enough that they can claim positions within the pack, such as beta or gamma, the second and third in command after the alpha. Some of these shifters will have alpha power, which means they have the potential to become head of the pack. This is why I stay away from most shifters, as I am unusually strong for a female shifter. I happen to have alpha power, although I've never wanted to claim that responsibility. This puts a target on my back, either because I'm a threat that needs to be taken out, or I'm viewed as a prize for the strongest male to win. That doesn't work with me, hence the lone wolf attitude.

The people nearby start shuffling away from me, aware something is happening, even if they're not sure what that is. Garett stalks towards me, frowning as he scans the bar, looking for the threat that has sent my senses into overdrive. His shoulders are tense, and he braces himself against the bar, leaning towards me. His eyes widen with surprise when he feels a wave of my power as he moves his gaze from the crowd to study my face.

"When was the last time you shifted?" he asks. "I know you don't like doing it, but you're putting yourself and everyone around you in danger. Plus, you're putting off my customers." He says the last part with a sly smile to take the sting out of his reproach, although his posture is still tense.

This is a long-standing argument of ours. The tingling has stopped, so whoever it was has moved on, most likely because of the scene I unwittingly caused. I close my eyes, calming myself. *I am in charge, I am in control, I am not in danger.* Opening my eyes, I see Garett's look of concern quickly turn to amusement.

"Want to get naked together?" he asks with a grin, although I'm sure I hear a note of worry in his voice. Shifting is something he's been trying to convince me to do more often, and he tries to hide it under smiles and jokes because he knows it makes me uncomfortable, but I know he worries about me.

Laughing at his comment, I roll my eyes and take a sip of my drink to hide the blush that's covering my cheeks.

"Oh, Garett, how could I say no to such a proposal?"

Garett and I have shifted together on occasion. I may distance myself from other shifters, but at a base level, wolves are pack animals. It feels good to rub my fur against someone else, even if that someone is a massive, seven-foot bear. Garett may look ferocious in his animal form, but really, he is a fuzzy, overprotective mother hen. He may play it off like he wants to see me naked, but his first instinct is to protect me. Plus, his favourite hobby seems to be making me blush. I place my beer back on the bar, running my finger through the condensation forming on the glass as I muse over today's events.

"Garett, have you heard of any...unusual attacks on humans recently?" I sense him pause, and I glance up to see him frowning before he continues polishing the glass in his hand.

"What kind of attacks?" he asks, his voice low as he glances around the bar, eyeing the goblin on the stool closest to me. I sigh.

"A human turned up at the hospital today barely alive, and he had a pack symbol carved into his back," I tell him quietly, aware of how many supernatural ears may be listening.

Garett instantly stiffens, his eyes briefly flashing amber as he fights his bear for control. His gaze flicks to my shoulder as if he can see the tattoo between my shoulder blades. While shifting doesn't require a person to take their clothes off, it is easier to shift naked, so he's seen my tattoo on several occasions.

"Any particular pack symbol?" he inquires, his voice deeper and more gravelly than it had been a moment earlier. He tries to pass it off, but I know what he's asking.

I nod, verbal confirmation not necessary for the direction of his thoughts. He crushes the glass as his control slips, the sharp shards exploding from his hand and covering the bar. I raise my eyebrows at him as I see blood dripping from his fist, gesturing for him to let me have a look at the damage he caused. Garett doesn't know the specifics of what happened between me and my pack back in England, but his suspicions make him very protective of me. I shake my head as I look at his fist. Had he been human, he would have needed it to be cleaned and stitched up, but being a shifter, he's protected from infection and would be healed within an hour. I pluck out a few pieces of embedded glass, raising my eyebrows at his noises of complaint.

"You grizzlies are so easy to rile up," I tell him with a small smile, letting go of his fist.

The bleeding has already stopped. He looks at me with a serious expression, leaning closer.

"If they have found you, you will need protection."

My inner wolf does not like the comment. Hell, I don't like that comment, not when we have proven that we can protect ourselves just fine. I've managed on my own for six years, and for eighteen before that in the hellhole that my former pack had called 'home.' I'm just about to whoop his ass and give him a piece of my mind when I feel a strong presence behind me.

"I guess it's a good thing I'm here then," a deep, velvety voice remarks. I grudgingly look over my shoulder at the person invading my space. Usually, I would be kicking serious butt if someone snuck up on me like this. However, I know that voice all too well.

"Oh God. What did I do to deserve you being here?" I groan, cursing my luck and putting my head in my hands on the bar.

I'm a nurse, I save people's lives on a daily basis, so why do the gods seem to hate me so much? Despite me wishing otherwise, I feel his presence moving closer as he takes a seat in the vacant bar stool next to me. My 'piss off' vibes must not be clear enough tonight. Throwing a glare at the imposing werewolf next to me, I look back at Garett, who's watching the both of us with an amused smile. There are only a handful of reasons why Alexander Parker, beta of the local wolf pack, would be here sitting next to me. Judging from Garett's relaxed posture, he obviously isn't concerned for my welfare. He wouldn't let me get hurt in his bar. Besides, I stay as far away from the Moon River Pack as possible.

"Why is he here? Can't I get any peace in this city?" I complain before standing up to lean over the bar, taking a bottle of whisky. I'm going to need something stronger than beer to get me through tonight. What I haven't anticipated is how far away the bottle is, requiring me to lean far enough that my mid-thigh length skirt rides farther up my leg. I hear a very appreciative male hum behind me, and I immediately straighten, catching said beta staring at my ass.

"Really?" I raise my arms in an 'are you serious?' gesture.

Alex has the audacity to shrug, a small smile tugging at the side of his mouth, not in the slightest bit ashamed at being caught ogling me. Glancing over at Garett for support, I glare at him as he raises his hands in a 'not my issue' gesture before heading to the other end of the bar. I don't miss the look he gives Alex before he leaves though, nor Alex's respectful dip of his head. Shaking my head, I turn my attention back to the bottle in my hands and pour myself a generous glass of whisky. Men are weird.

"Ari," he starts, the hair on my arm standing on end and my breath catching at his deep voice saying my name as he pulls his bar stool closer to mine.

Traitorous body. I turn and finally give him my full attention. He hasn't changed since I last saw him. The stubble across his lower face frames his jaw, emphasising his model-worthy cheekbones. His face has a raw, unmistakable masculinity to it, making him annoyingly handsome. Enviable long, dark eyelashes frame his piercing grey eyes, and his dark hair falls in waves to just above his shoulders. Perfect for gripping on to. *Whoa, calm down, girl.* My eyes flare gold as my wolf walks under my skin, making all of my baser urges come to the surface. Of course Alex notices this, his eyes glinting with a hunger I'm all too familiar with seeing in the eyes of male shifters. Ignoring him, I continue my assessment of his body, passing his broad shoulders and sliding my gaze down his chest. His loose T-shirt can't hide the muscle under there, the fabric straining against his biceps as he leans towards me, his gaze intense. Even sitting, I can tell he is tall, making me feel petite, which is a feat in and of itself since I stand just under six foot.

"What do you want, Alexander?" I ask, forcing my eyes away from his body, which is taking considerably more effort than I care to admit. Taking a swig of my drink, I savour the burn of the whisky, focusing on the comforting feeling rather than the sizzling power that is radiating from the male next me. He leans closer to me again, placing a hand on the bar, knowing better than to touch me right now. He may make my wolf want to rip his clothes off and have her wicked way with him, but he would be foolish to touch a shifter this close to losing control.

"Come to Moon River Pack," he says, his tone not leaving room for debate. He is used to being obeyed.

This is not the first time Moon River Pack has tried to get me to convert, nor the first time Alex has asked—although it has been a while since the alpha stopped sending eligible bachelors to try to convince me. I thought they finally got the message, but apparently not.

"Let us protect you."

Oh, hell no. I slam my glass onto the bar, albeit maybe a little harder than necessary, and push to my feet.

"I don't need anyone to protect me. Especially not some male who feels he has some claim over me," I bite out, my voice more guttural than it had been previously.

Tasting blood on my lip, I know my fangs have descended. My wolf is just as pissed off as I am at the insinuation that we cannot protect ourselves. This is just one of the many reasons why I can't stay in a pack. I am too dominant for most shifters, and I'm not content to be some trophy mate for those who wish to dominate me.

Striding away from the bar, I'm aware of how quiet it is, as many have turned to watch the scene unfold. I see Garett glaring daggers at Alex, but he makes no move to defend my honour, knowing it wouldn't end well for him. I snort. Useless males. I'm getting out of here before I tear into someone, literally.

"Ari, wait. We need you."

I come to a stop, and a frustrated sigh passes my lips. It's not so much the words that make me stop, but the hint of desperation in his tone. Part of me wants to tell Alex to go fuck himself, but the other part of me wants to hear him out. It would take a lot for a male such as Alex to come to me for help. However, I really, *really* don't want to get involved in pack politics. Ever since I arrived in America, I have tried to have as little involvement in the local pack as possible. I followed protocol and presented myself to the pack council within twenty-four hours of arrival in the city. I then politely but firmly told them I did not wish to join the pack, that I wanted lone wolf status. The alpha knew that forcing me to stay wasn't in anyone's best interest and granted my request. He seemed kind. Alex's older brother had been beta at the time, though I don't remember his name. What I do remember is that he stood up for me when some of the higher-ranking wolves wanted to stop me from leaving.

I think again about turning Alex down, but a part of me—the damaged, broken part of me—reminds me that I have some atoning to do. That if someone needs help and I can offer it, I have an obligation to do so. With a groan, I turn to him, pointing my finger at him accusingly.

"I will give you ten minutes to tell me your problem. After that, I'm out. Oh, and you're buying the next drink," I order as I stalk towards the bar, ungracefully throwing myself back into my seat and gesturing a smirking Garett over to get our drinks.

Fifteen minutes later, I'm sitting in a booth, pressed up against six feet something of sexy werewolf, uncomfortably trying to pay attention to what said werewolf is telling me. Alex suggested a quieter spot to discuss 'pack business,' and insisted I sit next to him so he could speak quietly. Personally, I think he just likes to be close to me. Our power levels must be similar, as I can feel my wolf pushing for dominance against the waves of alpha power that are rolling off him. I keep my eyes on the glass of whisky I have been nursing since we sat down. I can't possibly make a rational decision when I am this close to shifting. Fishing my phone from my skirt pocket, I push it across the table.

"Give me your number. I'll think about it and get back to you." There is no room for compromise in my voice, and I think he can sense that. He doesn't push the matter, merely entering his number and nodding to me before leaving the booth.

Once he has gone, I feel like I can breathe again. I may not like the guy, but I have to admit he is one sexy male. I mull over what he revealed to me. His pack is having problems carrying pregnancies to full term, or even conceiving in the first place. Turns out their pack medic was killed in an attack last year. Even I had heard of the attack. It was a massacre on a scale that made ripples in the supernatural community. It even made it to the human news, although they were under the impression there had been a large fire that had killed sixteen people at the local woodland retreat. After that, the pack had attempted to recruit me again, which I politely but firmly declined.

And now they are trying again, but this time they want me for my nursing skills. It helps that I'm a werewolf too, they won't trust anyone who isn't. Not that I know how I can help them. Sure, I have completed my emergency birthing training as all nurses do, but I don't know the slightest thing about pregnancy health—I'm not a midwife! But apparently, I'm their best option. I think it has more to do with the fact that I am a strong female with lots of power, as I can't be the only available nurse in the shifter community. What Alex doesn't know is that he has played right into my soft spot—I'm a sucker for protecting those weaker than me.

I throw back my glass, savouring the burn of the whisky as it glides down my throat. I send Garett a quick text letting him know I'm going for a run. I stand up and throw a mock salute in his direction, gesturing to my phone as I walk out of the bar. I don't want to talk to anyone right now, I just need some space, and I know he would make me wait for him so he could go with me. I snort to myself at this thought and step out onto the dark streets. I don't need anyone's protection.

Chapter Three

Even this far away from the city, I can still hear the noise from the streets thanks to my enhanced hearing, although I don't have to walk too far into the trees before the sounds fade. I look around at the silent trees surrounding me as I make my way towards my favourite spot to shift. This land is unowned by any of the various packs, so not many shifters come here, and it's far enough away that humans rarely visit either. I walk for about half a mile before I find the right place. Striding up to a twisted old tree, I kneel down beside it, running my hand over its bark before I find the natural crevice where I store my belongings. I learned the hard way that clothing often goes missing if you leave it unattended in the middle of the forest. Unhurriedly, I strip from my clothes, as only someone who is confident in their body can. There is no room for squeamishness in shifter packs. I'm no Greek goddess, and I eat far too many doughnuts to have a truly flat stomach, but I have an athletic physique from a rigorous training regimen, so I know I look good, both naked and fully clothed. Even the scars covering my skin aren't enough to make me ashamed of my body. I stash away my clothing and other belongings and walk a little farther into the forest.

Closing my eyes, I search for the source of power that resides inside me and reach for my wolf. I open my arms wide, like I'm about to embrace a close friend, and I coax my wolf to the surface. The shift is not pleasant, pain pulsing through my body as my bones shift. This is the price I pay when I don't shift often enough to satisfy my wolf. I drop to my knees, and a cry of pain escapes my lips as I let the shift take over my body completely. The process takes a minute or two, but it feels infinite. I really shouldn't go so long between shifts. Finally, the pain recedes, and I open my eyes, my heightened sight easily allowing me to see in the dark.

I push up onto all fours, shifting my paws in the dirt and stretching my body from snout to tail. With a feeling of freedom, I race deeper into the forest, the trees becoming a blur as I zip between them. I have a bittersweet relationship with my wolf, but this feeling *almost* makes everything worth it.

I savour the rush of the wind through my fur, feeling invincible as time seems to melt away. After a while, I pad to a stop near a small stream, lapping at the water eagerly. As I drink, I look at my reflection. The same amber eyes stare back at me, and my brown-gold fur is thick and healthy looking. Like in my human form, I'm tall for a female wolf, and my powerful back legs make me fast and strong. I take another drink from the water, and I realise the forest has gone quiet. Sure, it's nighttime and I'm a predator, so wildlife tends to disappear, but my hearing can pick up sounds from over a mile away, and I know this silence is unnatural.

My body tenses as I hear a twig snap about ten meters behind me. I discreetly sniff the air to see if I can scent who is stalking me without tipping them off that I know they are there—wolf. Alex said Moon River would leave me alone until I responded, so unless they're defying their beta, this is a wolf from a different pack. The wind shifts, bringing the scents closer to me. Scratch that, more than one wolf. Five, if my senses aren't betraying me. I internally curse myself. I should have picked up on this earlier. If I shifted more often and my skills were not so rusty, they never would have been able to sneak up on me.

Turning to face my stalkers, I sink into a defensive stance, my hackles raising. Five male wolves of various sizes face me in a loose semicircle. I don't recognise any of them, although the one in the middle keeps grabbing my attention. He's a brute, both in size and by the power rolling off him. He has dark grey fur, but his most noticeable features are the scars that run from his mangled left ear across to his snout. While I believe I'm stronger, he has the advantage of numbers.

I think I should give them a chance and not assume they are here to attack me. I mean, sure, they snuck up on me in the dark, but they may just want to talk. The large one in the middle snarls and takes a menacing step closer, the other wolves following his lead. Okay, so they aren't here to talk.

I growl as my lips draw back over my teeth, baring my fangs, my fur standing on end as my ears flatten against my head, ready for them to attack as I wait to see what they plan to do. I need to even the numbers if I'm going to stand a chance. At a growl from the grey wolf at the front, the two wolves at the edges break off from the group to circle around behind me.

My wolf is not happy with this at all. A strong wave of power surges through me, almost knocking me off my paws. I can see when the wolves sense it, as they come to a stop. The grey wolf's gaze narrows on me as he growls a command to approach again. The wolves do as ordered, but much more hesitantly. I grab onto the alpha power running through my bloodstream and push my intent into it, commanding the wolves to stop, bow down to me, and stay.

Immediately, two of the wolves drop, whining in the process. The two wolves flanking the grey wolf stumble as my command weighs heavily on them. Though they don't possess alpha power, they are possibly beta or gamma in ranking. Grey continues to stalk towards me, my command slowing his steps and making him more cautious. I may be stronger than him, but he has more practice at this than me.

Shit.

I turn on my heels and bolt as fast as I can from my pursuers. I don't care where I'm going, I just know I need to get away. I can hear more than one set of paws behind me, and glancing over my shoulder, I see Grey and one of his betas, while in the distance the other beta is stumbling to his paws, fighting my command. I face the direction I'm running in. I need to pay attention, and I need a plan. I may be fast for a female, but there is no way I can outrun a full-grown alpha male wolf.

I have more tricks up my metaphorical sleeves, but I won't use them unless there is no other choice. I've been running from my demons for the last six years, and I swore I wouldn't use that power again unless my life depended on it.

Hot, searing pain flares in my right flank as I'm bitten. I turn and fiercely bite the closest thing to me, which turns out to be Grey's shoulder. We tumble to the ground in a tangle of claws and teeth as I slash at his belly. He growls at me, letting go of my flank. I back away from him with a limp, trying to keep the weight off my back leg. I see his shoulder is oozing blood, which fills me with a sickening sense of satisfaction. The other wolf that was chasing me stalks closer, trying to get around behind me.

Growling, I dart forward, slicing my claws across his face. While I am distracted, Grey pounces on me, pinning me to the ground and biting into my shoulder, mirroring the wound I inflicted on him. I howl in pain as he bites me, pain and blood loss making my vision dim. I can feel the other wolves begin to creep closer, and I know I have lost this fight. Realising I have no other choice, I close my eyes and will that dark little piece of my power to come forward, and I become shadow.

I stumble in my shadow form towards Garett's bar. At some point within my shadow form, I have changed back to human, although

I'm not sure when. My wounds and the fizzling adrenaline in my system are making me dizzy. I'm not sure why I even came here, or when I decided that Garett was my 'in case of emergency' person, but I know deep in my bones he will help me. I wait in the dark alley by the employee entrance, knowing he will be leaving soon. It must be about four in the morning, and thankfully, it's quiet out, just a few drunks milling around. I collapse against the wall, letting it take my weight. The dripping sound of my blood should concern me, but there are worse things out here to worry about than werewolves, and I can't find the energy to care. At the sound of a door opening, I look up. I've never been more glad to see Garett in all my life.

"Garett," I call out, surprised at how weak my voice sounds. He looks up, immediately alert, confusion clouding his features as he looks around the dark alley.

"Ari?" he asks, taking a step in my general direction.

I wonder at his confusion and realise I'm still in my shadow form. He can't see me. I close my eyes again, and with colossal effort, I focus on pulling the darkness back inside my body. I let out a small cry of pain, falling to my knees at some point during the process. I know it has worked when the pain hits me at full force and I hear Garett swear, his large form filling my vision.

"Hey, Big Bear." I smile up at him as he runs his hand gently through my tangled locks.

He swears again at my affectionate tone, and glances at my very naked body covered in blood. I hear a menacing growl coming from him, and I glance at his face, seeing his eyes are glowing, indicating that his bear is close to the surface as he looks around the alley for my assailant. I should probably be worried that I am inches from a shifter who is close to losing control, but I know he won't hurt me. I gently place my hand on his chest to gain his attention and frown when I see blood caking my skin, transferring to his shirt with my sluggish movements.

"Oops, I've stained your shirt. I'll have to get you a new one," I tell him. Or he could just take his shirt off, I wouldn't mind.

I giggle at this thought, then I let my head rest against his chest in exhaustion, the events of the evening catching up with me. I should probably be worried. I *never* giggle, but the giddy feeling of being safe and protected is making me act strange. Or it could be the blood loss.

"Ari, forget the fucking shirt. I need to get you somewhere safe, but this is going to hurt like a bitch. Are you ready?" My bear has a potty mouth tonight. I should get him a swear jar for Christmas.

Fighting another giggle, I nod, reaching up and running my hand through his messy hair. He shifts his arms around me, picking me up and cradling me against his chest. I cry out, I was not prepared for the jarring movement. My vision dims as I feel Garett pick up his pace, trusting that he will take me somewhere safe.

"I've got you, Ari, you're safe."

I think I can hear Garett talking to me, saying sweet things that no one has ever said to me before. It's nice. Shame it's probably just a hallucination. As unconsciousness comes to claim me, something keeps repeating in my mind, an uneasiness I can't seem to shake. The satisfaction in the grey wolf's stare chases me into the darkness. It was almost like me shifting into my shadow form was what he wanted all along.

Chapter Four

I wake up to someone stroking my hair. It's a nice but unfamiliar feeling. I smile and arch my back into the warm body behind me. It's been too long since I shared a bed with anyone. A warm hand presses against my stomach, pulling me closer, and I find that someone is *very* happy to see me this morning. I rack my brain to try and recall the events that led to this situation. How have I ended up in bed, naked, with a stranger? At least I hope it's a stranger. Oh please, God, let me not have slept with my ex. Or worse, Dr. Eric Daniels. If I sleep with him, I want to be able to remember it.

I attempt to move my body, preparing myself for the worst. I go to look at the male pressed to my back when I feel a hand move on my leg—on my other leg, from an angle that does not match the body behind me. Unless I've slept with Mr. Fantastic, which I doubt, there is more than one person in bed with me.

Jolting up from the bed, I hear some very disgruntled male voices as I break free. I stumble to one knee, cursing in pain as my legs give way. Spinning around, I look across the bed to see four confused and blinking males—all of whom are totally naked.

"What the fuck?" I practically screech before realising I'm just as naked.

I reach across and snatch the bed sheets away from them, covering myself but exposing the men on the bed in the process.

"Will someone please tell me what the fuck is going on? And put some clothes on!" I order. It's seriously distracting with all their naked glory on display.

"I told you she would be pissed off." Relief fills me when I hear Garett's comforting voice, and I attempt to push to my feet.

I don't know why, but right now I need his arms around me. I can't explain these emotions rushing through me. As if he can read my mind, he comes to me, wrapping his arms tightly around me, which I'm thankful for because my legs aren't cooperating right now. I bury my face in Garett's chest as I struggle to remember the events of last night. I hear some shuffling around from the comfort of Garett's arms as the men move from the bed to put some clothes on—at least that's what I hope they are doing. Usually, I would be guarding my back—that's rule one, after all—but I know Garett will handle that for the moment and won't let anything happen to me.

"Will you please explain what is going on? And why the fuck did you bring me here?" I ask, pulling away from his chest, pissed off once again.

I hate being in situations where I don't know what's going on. It makes me cranky. Besides, I just woke up in a bed full of naked men, and I have no idea who they are, so I have the right to be a bit pissy. From the scents surrounding me, I know Garett has brought me to the Moon River Pack. I've not been in this room before, but it smells like them. Wolf packs have a distinct smell, almost like a bond that links them together. Each individual has their own scent, but it gets overlaid with their pack bond. Besides, this is the closest wolf pack for miles.

Why he decided that this was the safest place for me, I don't know. I try to stand again, but the ache in my legs slows me down, causing me to hiss in pain as I stumble back to the bed, still trying to keep my dignity by clutching the sheet. All but one of the men has moved from the bed, the last languishing with a smile in my direction, stretched out like a cat. He crawls closer and rubs up against me, the stubble of his jaw scraping over my skin as he nuzzles the crook of my neck. If he had been in wolf form, he would have been scent marking me. My eyebrows rise in shock, and I shoot a questioning look at Garett just as the man tries to crawl into my lap. I forgot how touchy-feely shifters are.

"Okay, I'm out," I state dryly as I push to my feet, looking in vain for my clothing.

I don't do well with physical contact, especially from people I don't know. I'm dimly aware of Garett's rumbling growl as he stalks closer to place his hand on my arm, halting my search.

"My God," I say. "You shifters are so touchy." I shake him off just as a figure enters the doorway. "Oh good, another person to make this shitty morning even worse!"

"Everybody out, give us some privacy. Sebastian, please show some restraint and find Ariana some clothing." I look at Alex's intimidating frame in the doorway, and I'm not surprised that they are doing as ordered.

The male from the bed, who I'm assuming is Sebastian, gets up to leave, but not before sending a wink in my direction. Pouting at Alex, he exits the room. Garett crosses his arms and stays put, thank goodness. Now it's just the three of us, and I feel like I can breathe again. I shoot both of the men a dirty look before leaning against the nearest wall as I wait for answers.

"Ari, sit down, you're not fully healed yet." Giving Garett the stink eye, I do as he suggested, sitting primly at the end of the bed, very aware I am fully naked under the sheet that is tightly clasped around me.

I may not be ashamed of my body, but I have scars that tend to invite questions I would rather avoid today.

"Come on, Ari, don't act like I betrayed you. Where else could I take you?" he questions imploringly, sinking to his knees in front of me. "I was going to take you to the bear commune, but you were shifting in and out of shadow. I didn't think you would want them to see that, and I was terrified! Why didn't you tell me you were Shadowborn?" Garett asks quietly, but I stiffen at his words.

Shadowborn are rare, even within the supernatural community. With the ability to turn into shadow, they are notoriously trained and used as assassins. In their shadow form, no one is safe from them. Being impervious to injury while in this form makes them difficult to kill, which puts a target on their back. Only a handful are born every century or so, and they tend to be killed off early in life before they learn to master their skills.

The Shadow Pack was named for their high percentage of Shadowborn, but I was the only one in the last hundred years. What might seem like an honour has only resulted in pain and suffering my entire life. Born into a pack that believes females are only good for breeding and have no place of power within the pack, my childhood was especially rough. Trained to be strong in body but weak in mind, they didn't anticipate the strength of my alpha power. I had to wait until I was eighteen until I could make my escape.

Shuddering away from my dark memories, I focus on Garett who's still kneeling in front of me, and I feel uncomfortable at the look of concern on his face. We are friends, and sure, we have flirted on and off for years, but just in a friendly way. While we talk, we have never broached the issues around my old pack or what brought me here, but he knows it wasn't pleasant. Tori knows what I am. Not because I told her, but because her powers revealed to her that I was something 'other,' and she guessed. I was so shocked when she flat-out asked me that I couldn't hide the surprise on my face. Most Shadowborn learn not to advertise what they are if they value their life.

"I'm fine," I mutter, as I survey my legs. They were shredded last time I saw them, and my shoulder felt like it had been used as a chew toy. Now they ache, but only in a muted way, like a shadow of the pain I should be feeling. Tight, shiny pink scars crisscross my legs, the stage of healing much further advanced than I had expected. Shifter healing is more evolved than that of our human counterparts, but with the extent of my injuries, my wounds should not be at this stage already. I glance up, my expression of surprise clear to see, and I raise a questioning eyebrow to Alexander, who is silently watching us with his arms crossed.

"We healed you. You were losing too much blood. We nearly had to amputate your leg. Which we would have done too, but your bear here wouldn't let us." Garett half-heartedly growls at this comment, and I have never been more thankful for his friendship.

Forgetting I'm supposed to be pissed off at him, I lean forward and bury my face into the crook of his neck. Gratitude floods my body. I'm overwhelmingly grateful that my friend is always looking out for my best interests. I don't deserve someone like him in my life.

"Thank you," I whisper quietly before pulling away in confusion, only just registering what Alexander said. "Healed me? You have a witch? I thought you needed a nurse?" I ask, puzzled.

That's why they wanted me here, after all. Only beings who possess magic, such as witches and sorcerers, can 'heal' people. Over one hundred years ago, it would be uncommon for there *not* to be a witch in a pack, but it was almost unheard of nowadays. Prejudices run strongly in the supernatural community just as much as in the human world.

I watch as Alexander shakes his head, his shoulder-length hair catching my attention. I have always liked guys with longer hair, more to grab onto. *Down, girl.*

"No, we don't have a witch," he answers with scorn, and I raise my eyebrows at his tone, wondering what he would say if he found out that I live with a witch. I'm sure it would piss him off, so I store this bit of information away for later.

"Do you know nothing of being in a wolf pack? I thought you were raised in a pack. Surely being a lone wolf for a few years hasn't made you forget everything about your kind."

My back stiffens at his comment and I glare at him. How dare he comment on my upbringing like I'm a disgrace to shifter kind? A cold fury fills me, my wolf urging me to bare my fangs and make him sorry for taking such a tone with me. Instead I go still, and even Garett has the good sense to look worried. He knows I'm sensitive about my past and that I never, ever talk about it. I answer Alexander with a tone that could cut ice.

"I was raised in isolation. Sorry I don't meet your expectations." The growl in my voice is enough to put anyone off from asking more questions. Except Alex doesn't get the hint.

He nods to himself, almost in confirmation, his expression deadly calm. "Is that where your scars came from?"

I give him an 'are you serious?' look, but keep quiet. I can't believe the audacity of this guy. First he insults my upbringing, and then he has the cheek to ask sensitive questions he has no right to ask. I decide not to answer him, he doesn't deserve a response. He hasn't earned my trust to know about my personal life. Garett, however, has no problem talking to the asshole leaning against the doorframe. Rising slowly from his crouched position in front of me, he walks menacingly towards Alexander.

"Don't talk to her like that," he says calmly, like he would when he was addressing one of his difficult customers mouthing off in the bar, but I can see the tension across his broad shoulders.

Pissing Garett off is likely going to end in someone having broken bones, none of which would be his own. I've seen it in the bar before. Like the calm before the storm, he'll be quiet and reasonable until you push his buttons a little too far. He's always been protective of me, and I'm still not used to it. It can be suffocating. I've done a pretty decent job of taking care of myself thus far. I glance down at my newly scarred legs again and pause. Perhaps a little help every now and then isn't so bad, right?

Alexander pushes away from the doorframe, giving zero fucks that an almost seven-foot shifter is bearing down on him, excuse the pun. I feel the alpha power rolling off him, and I have no idea why Alexander is beta of this pack and not alpha, because this guy is *strong*—possibly even stronger than me, not that he will ever know that thought crossed my mind. Coming chest to chest with Garett, they square off against each other and I feel I should step in. With a weary sigh, I stand and walk over to the two infuriating shifters, which is harder than it sounds when you have a limp and are clutching a bed sheet.

With careful movements, I take the end of the sheet, secure it under my armpit, hoping it will stay put, and stretch my arms to push on their chests, trying to separate them. Of course there is no way a female shifter is going to be able to push two fully-grown male shifters. Neither of them pay attention to me, the bastards.

"All right, boys, handbags away," I tease, trying to lighten the mood.

At this exact moment, the sheet that has been tasked with protecting my modesty betrays me, dropping to the floor and exposing every naked inch of me. Internally, I curse. Externally, I let a blank expression cross my face and try to keep my body relaxed, as if I haven't a care in the world. Shifters are used to nudity within their packs, so this shouldn't bother me. Of course, *now* I have the men's attention, both of whom have taken a step away from each other.

Men! I raise my eyebrow at them and place my hands on my hips. Alexander is in the process of running his eyes up and down my body, an approving smirk on his face. Garett has the decency to look embarrassed and takes his leather jacket off and hands it to me. I place it over one shoulder, but I refuse to hurry into it because Alexander is attempting to make me feel uncomfortable with his obvious perusal of my curves.

"Like what you see?" I retort before stalking back to the bed.

I may have added a bit more sway to my walk than usual, so sue me. I shrug Garett's leather jacket on, and it falls to mid-thigh. I pull it closer around me, enjoying the feel of the leather on my bare skin. Garett's scent surrounds me, a woodsy outdoors smell that makes me feel safe. I decide to keep the jacket for myself, he is going to have to fight me for it. With a small smile, I plonk myself ungracefully back on the bed, crossing one ankle over the other. Now that the situation has been defused—thanks, nudity—I look to Alexander for an explanation.

"Shifters heal better when they have physical contact with other shifters, and it works best with skin-to-skin contact. You needed to heal quickly if you wanted to escape permanent injury. It required four of our wolves to heal your injuries."

My eyes widen as I realise I must have been more seriously injured than I thought. That explains the puppy pile I woke up in the middle of.

"Why were they all male? I am not prepared to work for a pack where women are not considered equals," I insist.

I may have come from a pack that was frowned upon for its harsh methods, but I know it's not the only one that considers women unequal or only there to boost the alpha male's powerbase.

Alexander shakes his head, a smile on his lips as he does so. "Nothing of the sort. Our gamma is a female, and the alpha's wife has just as much authority as he does. They are a true mated pair, so their power levels are equal."

I raise my eyebrows at this.

Mated pairs are uncommon, and the chance of finding the one you are destined to be with is rare. You don't see it often, especially when about fifty years back, the rate of these pairings dropped even further. Some theorised that because our numbers had dwindled so much through hunters, the chances of meeting our true mate had dropped even further. It is said that once you accept the mate bond, you are equal in power and can access the other's strengths.

Alexander clears his throat, bringing me back to the conversation at hand.

"No one was forced to help heal you. We asked for volunteers, and there were quite a few who offered. Although, I think the prospect of spending the night with a beautiful naked woman helped." He ends this last part with a smile that makes me feel a bit flustered.

I lean back on the bed, the leather jacket rising up my thighs, and I can feel the eyes of both men in the room on me. It's quite a sensual feeling, the worn leather brushing my naked skin, the only barrier between the heated gaze of two very good-looking men watching my every move.

"So what happens next?" I ask, startling both guys.

Alexander gets a contemplative look on his face, and I know exactly where his thoughts have gone.

"Mind out of the gutter, Alexander," I scold, but I say it lightly so as to take the sting out of my words.

This pack has helped me, hell, they might have even saved my life, whether I like it or not. I owe them. Owing a wolf pack and not paying up never ends well for the debtor, whether that debt is money or a favour. I'm not well off—I work as a nurse, for heaven's sake—but I have some savings I managed to 'acquire' when I left my old pack, so if it is money they want, I may be able to cough some up. It is the favours I am more worried about. Although, with Garett here, I doubt he will allow them to demand anything too serious.

"Call me Alex," he says. "I hate being called Alexander. Besides, before I explain anything, the alpha wants to see you."

Those six words send shivers down my spine, and not the good type of shivers. These are caused by fear. *The alpha wants to see you.* My breathing picks up as memories engulf me.

Darkness surrounds me. Some people are afraid of darkness, but when it's all you know, it becomes comforting. Harsh artificial light fills the room, causing me to hiss with pain and cover my eyes with my dirty hands.

"The alpha wants to see you."

I dread these words. Nothing good ever happens when he wants to see me. I stumble to my feet, my legs shaking from lack of use. I try to exercise in this dark cell they call a room, but if I make too much noise, they come check on me, which I try to avoid. They don't train me anymore, not since I tried to escape. No point training someone who won't do as they're ordered.

I take a few steps forward, squinting against the light, and glance at my pale hand. I'm so thin that my bones are protruding from my skin, and you can tell I haven't been out in the sunshine for too long. My nails are dirty and chipped. He won't be pleased. He likes the women of the pack to look presentable and neat. Seen but not heard.

The guy who was sent to get me shoves me, and I stumble into the wall. I think he just meant to push me along, but the lack of food and sunlight has made me weak. I glare at him, and he has the decency to look nervous. I see my reputation still precedes me. Straightening up as much as I can, I step out into the hallway to meet the alpha.

Tearing myself from the memories, I become aware of someone calling my name. My eyes refocus, and I find myself staring into Garett's caring eyes, grounding me to the here and now. He must have been the one calling my name.

"Ari, you're safe here. The alpha won't hurt you." Alex's voice reaches me, and I look over Garett's shoulder to see he has moved away from the wall and is standing behind Garett.

He turns to look at Garett, his voice turning harsh, revealing his anger. "What the hell happened in her previous pack that going to see the alpha would make her react like this?"

"She'll be okay in a minute. Look at her eyes, she is back now. When she's ready to talk, she will," Garett replies. His eyes hold sadness as he watches me, but right now, I can't comprehend the meaning behind it.

I pull away from Garett and groan. When I arrived in the U.S. and my flashbacks first started, Tori forced me to see one of the supernatural doctors in the city. They say I have post-traumatic stress disorder, PTSD, where something will trigger me and send me back in my memories. Thankfully, it doesn't happen often, but I always feel like crap afterwards. I don't have time to deal with my many issues right now. I need to pull up my big girl panties and go face the alpha.

"Right, someone get me some clothes. Let's go see the big guy."

Chapter Five

I glance around the compound as they lead me to see Alpha Mortlock. The compound holds the guise of a woodland retreat, with the main offices being based here. I know what you're thinking—a big, macho werewolf pack running a woodland retreat? Well, they have to earn money somehow. It works well for them. It's far away from human society, they have private space where they can shift without fear of being seen, and they rake in the money. This compound is mainly where they run their other businesses from, but they do have a couple of wooden cabins for supernatural guests. Their other compounds are branded as a luxury and open to the humans at an exorbitant fee.

The atmosphere seems relaxed, and the people I've passed so far seem happy and well looked after. Everyone we have come across has nodded respectfully to Alexander, or Alex, as he wants to be known as, and only sent questioning glances towards Garett and me, not a glare in sight. I imagine it's not every day that a new wolf and a bear shifter wander through their private compound. Alex wanted Garett to stay behind, which resulted in another argument. Sebastian, the overly friendly naked guy from before, arrived at this point with some clothes for me, which were almost a perfect fit, showing he has a good eye. The argument ended pretty quickly once I stood up and dropped the jacket to the floor to get changed. Sebastian made a comment about helping me into my clothes, which had Garett growling at him. My grizzly bear is grouchy today.

I glance behind me at Garett and catch him looking at my ass. I snag his gaze and wink at him. My ass does look great in these jeans, and the tight black strappy top reveals just enough to show my assets nicely. My wink has the desired effect as he smiles at my cheeky gesture, but I can still see the tension in the way he holds himself. He seems to have calmed down a lot, although he must be feeling out of his depth in the middle of all these wolves. I turn to face forward and see Sebastian walking in front of us. Seems he's also going to see the alpha too.

"Hey, Sebastian?" I call. He turns his head and smiles widely at me. "Can I call you Seb?" I ask. He's way too touchy-feely, but I like him, and I feel like I'm going to need a friend here.

"Darling, you can call me anything you like," he replies with a wink.

I chuckle, trying to rid myself of this uneasy feeling as we get closer to the main building. I smile as I feel the sunshine on my skin and take a deep breath of fresh air. As we approach the main building, I think back to when I first came here.

I stare at the large compound in front of me. The expensive wrought iron gates guarding the land are intimidating, but they give the impression of an expensive retreat—which, in a sense, I guess it is. Anxiety attempts to overwhelm me. I try to push it down as I press the button on the intercom built into the wall, requesting an audience with the alpha. The gates squeak as they open, setting my already fried nerves on edge. The wheels of my suitcase clack on the road as I walk towards the main house and glance around, taking in any and all escape routes. They are based in the middle of the forest, log cabins are dotted around and a couple of larger buildings surround the main house. My inner wolf is close to the surface. She hated the plane ride and the feeling of being trapped thousands of feet up in the air. I need to let her out, but pack protocol states we present ourselves before we change. Any shift by an unregistered wolf is regarded as an insult or a threat, both of which are dealt with swiftly and brutally.

I am nervous. I have finally escaped the cruel and dictatorial thumb of my pack, and without so much as a 'Welcome to the U.S.,' I have to present myself to the local pack like some sort of prize. I bristle at the thought. I have fought my entire life for freedom, but even in America I'm trapped within shifter rules. The pack will want to keep me—I know they will—but I'm not prepared to let that happen. I know how they will see me—a young, skinny, unmated female with a whole load of alpha power, covered head to toe in bruises and scars. Even if they were cold-hearted bastards and ignored their instincts to protect, they would see the benefit of having that much power around. I feel my limbs begin to shake, and I tell myself it's from exhaustion, not fear. If they were human, they might see my small frame, thin from years of malnutrition, and believe this. I can lie to myself all day, but shifters will be able to smell my fear.

I stop a few meters from the main building, and I decide in that moment that I will not let fear control me any longer. I will no longer let others dictate my life. I will no longer be a victim.

Closing my eyes, I push away all of my insecurities and fears. My wolf agrees with me, and I feel a surge of strength come from her. We are strong. We can protect ourselves. This is the closest thing to harmony that I have ever felt with my wolf. Opening my eyes, I grab the handle of my suitcase and step through the front door to face the alpha.

Alpha Mortlock looks just the same as he did six years ago when I first met him. He is handsome, with short, sandy blond hair, and looks to be in his late thirties, but I am pretty sure he is near seventy. We can thank our shifter genes for our longer lifespan, which extends to around one hundred and forty, and we stay looking youthful for most of our lives.

We were supposed to be meeting in his office, but Alexander had some quick words with Seb as I was getting changed, and the next thing I know, we are meeting in the living room in the main house. I have a sneaky suspicion that Alexander is trying to make the alpha seem more approachable after my little episode down memory lane. It's thoughtful, but unnecessary.

Mortlock and a beautiful woman, who I'm assuming is his wife, are waiting for us in the communal room. They rise from the soft-looking leather sofas, and Alpha Mortlock takes a step towards me, holding his hand out slowly for me to shake. I turn to glance at Alex, raising my eyebrows in question. What on earth has he said to these people? They are treating me like I'm about to bolt from the building. I straighten my shoulders before turning back to the alpha and shaking his hand firmly. I'm no shrinking violet. I'm also not the frail, malnourished eighteen-year-old I was the last time he saw me.

"Ariana, good to see you again, although I wish it was under better circumstances. Welcome back to Moon River Pack. This is my mate and wife, Lena." He gestures to the woman just behind him, who is beaming at me. "You've met my beta, Alexander, and this is my gamma, Isa."

A tall, broad woman peels away from the wall she was leaning against. Her muscles almost put Garett's to shame. Note to self—don't piss her off. Although, with a name that literally means 'strong-willed,' I wouldn't expect anything less. Walking towards me, she reaches for my hand, gripping it tight in a death grip of a handshake. I force my face not to show pain and meet her steely gaze, mirroring her tight grasp. She smiles slightly at this small display of dominance and slaps me on the back hard enough that I take a small step forward.

"I like her. She can stay," the mountain of a woman states in a thick German accent.

I hear a small whistle of disbelief and glance over my shoulder to see who is making the noise. Seb is watching the exchange with his mouth open in shock.

"I have never seen Isa smile. Ever. What did you do? Did you break her?" he mock-whispers.

The smile drops from Isa's face as she glares at him, promptly causing Seb to mime zipping his lips as he takes a step back into the corner. He may act like everything is a joke, but I don't miss the slight paling of his skin. I smile to myself. I can see why she is the gamma of this pack, and I am pleased to see such a strong-willed female in a position of power. The structure within a wolf pack will always have an alpha and a beta, who is the second in command and acts as a protector of the pack. The role of gamma isn't always adopted within packs, depending on the alpha. Some believe keeping too many powerful wolves around is risky. Their primary role is as an enforcer within the pack. Moon River Pack didn't use to have a gamma. I guess this role was introduced after Alex's brother, the previous beta, was killed.

"Alpha Mortlock, Lena, pleased to meet you," I say formally with a bow of my head, my British sensibilities kicking in.

I may not have been here in six years, but I haven't forgotten the manners that we pride ourselves on. I also don't want to piss anyone off within the first ten minutes of being here, so I need to be on my best behaviour. Lena, however, doesn't feel restrained by these formalities and jumps forward, embracing me in a tight hug. God, these shifters are so affectionate! I'm pretty sure no one notices me flinch as she throws herself on me, and I awkwardly pat Lena's back as she hugs me. I'm really not a hugger.

Even Tori and Garett know not to touch me without making their intentions obvious. There have been many occasions where I have nearly thrown someone across the room for simply touching my arm. What can I say? They shouldn't sneak up on me!

Right, that's enough physical touch from strangers for one day. I pull away from the woman latching onto me, although trying to remove her arms is like trying to pull off a squid. I glance around the room for help and see Alexander frowning at me. Guess I wasn't as stealthy at hiding my flinch as I thought.

"Please, no formalities. Welcome to the pack! I'm just so pleased that we have another strong female joining our ranks! Maybe we can finally get Alex paired off!" she tells me excitedly.

I am still awkwardly trying to remove myself from her grip, sending pleading looks for help towards Seb, and the traitorous little wolf just sniggers at me, enjoying my discomfort. I freeze as her words fully register. *Welcome to the pack.* What the actual fuck?

"I'm sorry?" I ask, my voice coloured with disbelief.

I must not have heard her properly. I did not sign up to join another pack. No. Nadda. Hell no. I am not prepared to sign my freedom away, and I will not be tricked into joining a pack. I start looking around the room for a way out. I will need to avoid Isa, knowing I won't get past her. I look to the other side of the room where Alexander is standing against the wall by the window. If I'm quick, I can get past him and jump through. I shift my stance, and the tension in the room rises. Isa's and Alexander's positions change to match mine, their limbs poised and ready to attack. Lena realises she has committed some faux pas and takes a step back, glancing to Alpha Mortlock uncertainly.

"Ariana, before you flee from the room and make my beta chase after you, let's chat. It seems there has been a misunderstanding." Alpha Mortlock's calm voice evaporates the tension in the room, and everyone resumes their previous positions.

Except me, of course. I look at him, my distrust clearly written on my face. I look over my shoulder to Garett. He shrugs at me, leaving the decision up to me. He wouldn't have brought me to these people unless he trusted them to some degree. I nod sharply, deciding I will hear them out. Mortlock takes a seat and gestures for me to do the same. Lena sits next to him, still looking upset that she's offended me. I'm surprised she is so...nice. Nice people don't tend to last long in positions of power within the shifter world. I perch on the edge of the seat, ready to spring to my feet at a moment's notice.

"Ariana, we would like you to join our pack. Alex has already told you that we need you here to help us, but we would like to extend the offer indefinitely." I'm already shaking my head before he's finished his sentence. Alpha Mortlock tilts his head in question. "Is joining our pack so bad? Do you really want to stay a lone wolf? Never to settle down and feel safe among your own people?"

I sigh. Of course I don't want to be a lone wolf. Shifters belong in a pack, it's part of our nature. All I have ever wanted is to feel safe, welcomed, and maybe even loved if that's possible in this cruel fucking world. What he doesn't realise is that I have only ever experienced the worst of my people. My darkest moments have always been at the hands of my pack, my so-called 'family.' Besides, I am fine on my own. I don't need anybody else. I have Tori to watch my back, and I watch hers. That's what friends do. We take care of each other.

Shit. Tori.

Fuck. I am a terrible friend. She is probably going nuts that I didn't come home last night. You do not want to piss off a witch, especially not one as powerful as Tori. I'm lucky she hasn't tracked me down with a location spell and dragged my ass back to the apartment to explain. I need to get hold of my phone and call her before she blows a gasket.

I also need to make a decision. Alpha Mortlock is watching me expectantly, and Lena has a hopeful look on her face. To turn down a pack, especially when you owe them your life, is a bad idea.

"When you've been through what I have, it makes it difficult to trust others. My pack caused me nothing but pain. I don't mean to be disrespectful, but I cannot join your pack," I tell him. I even let some warmth back into my voice so he knows I am sincere.

"But you were attacked, and you won't be safe on your own. They will probably keep trying. We can offer you protection."

Damn, he does have a point. I may even have to admit to myself that I need help this time. Not that I will ever admit to such a thing out loud.

"I won't join the pack, but I will help in any way I can. I can come back each day for three months, which should give you time to find another nurse. I'll have plenty of protection that way while I'm working here and on my own. My apartment is warded, so I will be safe at home, and I can protect myself otherwise."

The hospital is not going to be pleased with me. I can only offer to stay for three months because I can't afford to take any more time off. I am lucky that today is my day off anyway. As if he could read my mind, Alex pipes up from his corner of the room.

"We will sort things out with the hospital and reimburse you for your loss of earnings."

Mortlock nods in agreement, running his hand through his neatly trimmed beard. "You are also invited to stay here while you are working for us. We have accommodations attached to the medical room. We will need a nurse around the clock."

I shake my head. I said I would help, not give up my independence. With a sigh, the alpha nods his head wearily and stands, looking at those around the room.

"What is said now within this room is to remain a secret," he commands, his alpha power strong in his words. It's so strong, I'm not even sure if I could resist his order. Alpha power works a little like a vampire's persuasion, and if you're stronger than the alpha giving the order, you can fight against it. If you're not, then the alpha's word is law.

He looks back to me, and I'm on alert at the expression on his face. "You're Shadowborn," he says. "We will keep your secret, but in return, you must let us train you, both in human form and wolf form. I will not have an untrained Shadowborn on the streets."

Hmm, so someone has told him I'm Shadowborn. Or he was there when Garett brought me in and saw me shifting in and out. The last part of his comment sounds a little like a threat, and my hackles rise, but I don't disagree with him. I would rather train elsewhere, but even I have to admit that I'm a liability at the moment. Once I've used my shadow abilities, it's always harder for me to control it for a while after. Bollocks. I realise too late that I'm being backed into a corner. I grumble and look over at Garett, who I see has a resigned look on his face.

"I hate to admit it, Ari, but I don't think you have much of a choice," he tells me, and I remember the conversation we had earlier.

I don't want this pack knowing about my abilities. The fewer people who know, the better. Besides, my shadow powers are unstable at the moment. I sigh again. I seem to be doing that a lot.

"Agreed," I tell Mortlock, leaning across to shake his outstretched hand, although I can't help but feel like I have signed my freedom away.

Chapter Six

"He said what?" I ask, dumbfounded, as I stare at the bundle of pink fabric in Seb's arms. I gingerly pluck at the offending item as if it's diseased to see if it really is what I think it is. Yup. It's a fucking dress. A pink, frilly, afternoon tea type dress. I throw the ridiculous garment onto the bed in disgust. I've found that I slip back into calling Alex by his full name when he's pissed me off. Now is exactly one of those times.

"You can tell Alexander to shove this right up his—"

"Is wearing a dress really that big of a deal? I don't get the problem," Garett, the traitor, points out.

I spin around and glare at him hard enough to let him know he is in the doghouse. Sorry, the bear house. Wait, bear cave? Oh, whatever. I'm pissed off at him.

"Oh, Ariana, can I see you in your sexy nurse's uniform?" Seb asks with a smirk as he stalks towards me, a predatory gleam in his eyes.

"No, you can't. I'm mad at you too. And stop calling me Ariana, it's Ari," I order, my frustration coming through as some of my alpha power slips into my comment. I see Seb stop in his tracks, his eyes widening slightly as his knees buckle under the force of my order.

"Shit. Seb, I'm really sorry." I'm a terrible friend, if that is even what we are. I need to get my shit together.

I didn't realise how low down in the pecking order he is. He's so confident that I assumed he was reasonably dominant. Not strong enough to have a position of power, but not one of the weaker wolves. He certainly doesn't look physically weak. He stands just slightly taller than me, with messy blond hair, and he looks like he could star in a movie. I'm talking Zac Efron looks, ladies. Yes, even werewolves go to the cinema. He also looks like he spends a fair amount of time working out. His T-shirt, which is straining against his muscular shoulders, proves this. I guess looks can be deceiving. Even his vanilla scent is mouth-watering.

His head is bowed, his breathing quickened, and I kneel next to him, feeling like the worst person in the world as I place a hand on his shoulder.

"Seb, I am so sorry," I apologise again when he lifts his head to look at me. His pupils have dilated, and a look of pure arousal shines brightly in his eyes. I raise my eyebrows.

"You kinky little shit. That turned you on?" I query, rocking back on my heels, torn between feeling uncomfortable and amused. I settle on amusement and stand up with a slight laugh.

"I thought I'd upset you!" I accuse, still smiling as he stands from his crouched position. "I'm still not wearing that dress though," I argue, trying to change the subject.

I look over at Garett. He does not look amused at the whole exchange. In fact, he's scowling at Seb. Such a grumpy bear. Rolling my eyes, I walk over to him and lean against the wall.

"Has anyone found my phone yet?" I ask. I really need to call Tori. I'm worried she is going to bring down hell on the pack—quite literally—if I don't speak to her soon.

"I think Alex was looking into it. They are trying to locate where you left your clothes in the woods, but they were shredded by the wolves that attacked you." Garett pauses meaningfully before looking back at the dress on the bed. "Which is why I don't understand why you won't wear the dress."

I scowl, my temper beginning to rise once again. "I am not wearing that bloody dress! I will go to the social naked if I have to. I don't care what they say. The Queen of England could order it, and I would happily commit treason to get out of wearing that thing," I rant.

Okay, so maybe I'm going a little far, but I'm not going to be paraded around this pack at the social this evening dressed up looking like a meek little wolf in a pretty pink dress, like I'm some prize to be won. I'm already regretting the deal I made with Alpha Mortlock. What I didn't realise is that I'm now expected to attend the pack socials, the first of which is this evening, when I will be formally introduced to the pack. Lovely.

Garett shifts against the wall next to me, and I can see from the corner of my eye that he wants to comfort me, but knowing my aversion to touch he changes his mind. He must have decided against arguing any further about the dress, knowing I'm not going to back down on this one. Good decision, buddy.

"I like seeing you in that jacket," he tells me, changing the subject, his voice lower than usual. I look down at the jacket in question. It's the one he gave me earlier, and it makes me feel safe so I've decided to keep it whether he likes it or not. I'm starting to feel uncomfortable again. All the startling admissions from this afternoon have put me on edge. I don't know how to respond to this, and I start to pull away, my walls stacking up brick by brick. He must have sensed this, as he stiffens next to me.

Thankfully, I'm saved from answering as Alex walks through the door with my phone in his hand, plus what looks like a woman's shirt and a smart pair of jeans.

"God, never thought I would be saying this, but I'm glad to see you," I blurt out. I don't seem to have a filter today, but what I said is true. Not only does he have my phone, but he has also saved me from responding to Garett. Hopefully, I can cover up my slip of the tongue by grabbing my phone from his hands, although a glance over my shoulder at Garett's expression tells me otherwise. And if that isn't enough, his next comment tells me I've fucked up.

"Now that I know you're safe, I'm going to head out. I'm not really wanted here anyway."

I flinch like he's hit me, which I immediately regret. Why am I so worried about what he thinks? If he wants to leave, then that's fine, I don't need him here. He brought me here when I was in need, but I'm fine now, his obligation to help me is over.

Garett cuts off my internal battle by striding over and enveloping me in a bear hug. Idly, a part of me wonders if this is where the term 'bear hug' comes from as my arms slowly come up and return the embrace. He gives great hugs. I immediately feel a little better, although I'm not going to admit that to anyone.

"I didn't mean it like that, Ari. I think we just... A bear shifter does not belong with a bunch of wolves." Pulling back, he meets my eyes. "I'm needed with my people. Call me if you need anything, okay?" At this last part he gently holds my chin, not letting go until I nod at his request.

He looks to Alexander, and they do that male communication thing where they nod and grunt at each other. Whatever was communicated seems to be acceptable to Garett because he turns back to me and kisses my forehead gently before walking away.

"Well, that was dramatic," Seb comments and I glare at him, about to respond with a snarky comment, when my phone buzzes in my hand. I completely forgot I even had it, what with Garett distracting me. I quickly put in my passcode and grimace at the screen. Seventeen missed calls and twenty-six text messages, the last of which reads:

Tori: Call me now, or I am summoning some hellhounds and coming to get yo' ass.

Oh shit. I'm in big trouble. I scroll through the other messages. Most of them are from Tori, although I'm surprised to see a few are from Eric, which get increasingly concerned as I didn't reply. I send off a quick response.

Me: Hey, Eric, sorry for the late reply, something came up. I'm fine, taking a break from the hospital for a while. I'll see you soon though.

With a sigh, I look over at the men still in the room, Alexander propping up the wall in the corner, and Seb lounging on the bed like he owns it.

"I need to call my friend. This may take a while," I warn, hoping to try and get some privacy, but no, they just nod and stay where they are. Sighing again, I dial Tori's number.

After what feels like the longest phone call in history and many assurances to Tori that I'm okay and not being held against my will, I hang up. Trying to convince my overprotective witch best friend that I'm not being held captive turned out to be a challenge.

"But you have never wanted anything to do with the local pack before. I can keep you safe. I'll magic up a few 'friends' to keep you protected. We don't need them, Ari."

Her words are true, and I don't doubt that she could keep me safe. The problem? That would require dark magic, and Tori walks a very fine line with her magic already. I don't want to be responsible for pushing her over that line and turning her dark. Not to mention that using that kind of magic would bring ASP down on us like a ton of bricks. No, this is the best solution for the moment. I will work here and travel back to the apartment at night. I will only shift when I'm on Moon River territory, as per their suggestion, and I will shift as little as I can get away with.

Glad that conversation is over with, for now at least, I glance down at my phone and see another message from Eric. Frowning, I click the message.

Eric: Are you safe? Do you need protection?

Well, that's confusing. I might have accepted the message if he was just asking if I was safe. I did disappear off the radar, after all. But to follow it up with 'do you need protection?' Does he know more than he let on? He's human—Tori would have told me otherwise—so why is he asking if I need protection like he knows what's been going on? Could he be one of the few humans that knows?

I send him a message in return.

Me: I'm safe. What do you mean by protection?

He replies almost immediately.

Eric: Look, can we meet up? I have something I need to talk to you about.

I sigh, rubbing my eyes. Why can't anything be simple? I'm about to reply when Alex comes stalking over, eyeing my phone.

"Everything okay?" he asks. Having eavesdropped on my entire conversation with Tori, he obviously wants to know what is going on in my text messages too. Nosy wolves.

"Yeah, just another complication. It's fine. What are you still doing here anyway? Don't you have important beta business to attend to?" I question with a little more snark than I intended, my eyes flashing with frustration.

Alex doesn't miss a thing and raises his eyebrows at my lack of control. Luckily for him, he doesn't mention it. Seb, on the other hand, has no problem making comments.

"Ari, they are going to rip you to shreds if you can't control yourself tonight." Great. However, he is right. I need to get control of myself.

"Come on, Sebastian, let's leave Ari to get ready for tonight," Alex says as he goes to leave the room. Just as he is turning away, I remember something from my conversation with Tori.

"Oh, Alex, did you or one of Moon River Pack go to my apartment the other night?" They must have been one of the 'hotties' Tori kept referring to, trying to make the best of the situation and hook me up with someone. My stomach sinks a little as he shakes his head.

"No, we were ordered to stay away. The first contact we have had with you was when I spoke to you at the bar the other night."

Shit. So who was this mysterious shifter that had turned up on my doorstep? Like I don't already have enough to deal with.

Alex is still waiting at the door expectantly for Seb, who shakes his head as he gets up and starts looking through the wardrobe in the borrowed room, muttering something about 'helping' me get ready. I share a bemused look with Alex and wave him out of the room. I'd hoped for a bit of quiet to sort through my thoughts. I'm so used to being by myself that having all these people around me, who actually *want* to be around me, is a little overwhelming. But as Seb picks up the horrendous pink dress from earlier and models it against his muscular chest, making me double over with laughter, I find myself thinking that perhaps that isn't such a bad thing.

Chapter Seven

Turns out that Seb's idea of helping me to get ready is very different from my idea. However, I have never laughed as much as I have in this last hour, my cheeks aching from smiling too much. I don't make friends easily. Sure, I can talk to people at work and care for my patients and their relatives—building a rapport is important in my profession—but in my personal life, I like to keep to myself.

I'd always been alone until Tori came barrelling into my life, and I couldn't have turned away her friendship even if I wanted to. She's like me, isolated and different from her kind, which is why we stick up for one another. She is the closest thing to family I have.

Garett is the only other person I would consider a true friend. We met when Tori was taking me 'out on the town' at the start of our friendship. I was still bewildered by the large city, with all the sounds, smells, and people. It was so different from the small British town where I grew up, not that I had seen much of it, having been kept in isolation for so long. Having only just turned eighteen when I flew to America, I had not tasted alcohol before. Turns out the rules in the shifter community are more lenient than the American laws on alcohol. As shifters, we have a higher tolerance and it takes much more to get us drunk than humans. What I wasn't warned about was the fae drinks. Those are lethal. Feeling high as a kite after my first one and just about to accept a second from a very attractive Summer Fae, Garett intervened, saving me from a nasty headache and some very unpleasant side effects. I later discovered that fae drinks bring our animals closer to the surface. Problem with that? It leaves shifters stuck in half-animal forms. Not nice.

Ever since that night, a tentative friendship developed as he helped me adjust to being a lone wolf in the city, showing me the best places to shift. Tori is amazing, and I will always be grateful to her for what she has done for me, but she isn't a shifter. She will readily agree with this and is always trying to get me to expand my social circle.

Seb pulls me out of my musing by wolf-whistling as I stand in front of the mirror. I glance across at my new friend and grin. He has a way of making me feel at ease. Sure, he flirts like it's going out of fashion, but I know he won't push me for anything like so many male shifters do. There are also no domination battles with him, he doesn't care I'm stronger. Glancing back to the mirror, I focus on my reflection and have to agree with him. I don't look half bad. I've settled on wearing the smart jeans and shirt that Alexander brought in. The jeans fit well, showing off my legs and ass nicely, with some little black boots that Seb stole from somewhere. The top is a white, oversized women's shirt, which cinches in at the waist with a small brown belt. With the top two buttons undone, it shows off a little cleavage, and the belt accentuates my shape nicely. After I showered, I left my hair to air dry, so it falls in natural waves to just below my collarbone. I don't have any makeup with me, but I rarely wear any, so I don't feel like I'm lacking anything.

Turning around, I smile at Seb and walk to the bed where I left Garett's leather jacket. Picking it up, I slide my arms into it as I walk towards the door, feeling comforted as the leather surrounds me.

"You can't wear another man's jacket to a shifter social," Seb says. "Especially not a bear shifter. They'll think you belong to him."

I stop in my tracks. "I don't give a flying fuck what they think. I don't belong to anyone. Not Garett. Not the pack," I fume, my walls slamming back in place. I hadn't even realised I had let them slip. I need to be more careful. Seems I can't escape from judgemental shifter thoughts.

"Whoa, girl. I wasn't saying you were." His smile fades as he senses my frustration, and a small part of me misses his happy-go-lucky expression. "I'm just telling you what they're going to think if you walk into your presentation to the pack wearing the jacket of a bear shifter. You may not like it, but gossip travels fast, and you're a powerful, unattached, unmated female. People are going to want to know you, and if you go barrelling in there in that jacket with the 'fuck off' expression you currently have on your face, it is not going to give a good impression," Seb explains, walking slowly towards me with his hands out to the sides like he is taming a wild beast. Maybe that's what I am.

"What impression do I want to give them?" I ask tentatively. I don't even know. I'm in uncharted territory here. I don't want to join this pack, but I have an opportunity to interact with my own kind. "I don't have the best track record with packs," I say, not liking how vulnerable my voice sounds.

Without a word, Seb walks up to me and wraps his arms around my shoulders. I stiffen immediately at the sudden contact, not moving, not even breathing as I suppress the urge to fight. Seb must feel it, but he doesn't mention it, just rubs my back softly. I relax ever so slightly into his arms. This is...nice. I breathe in his vanilla scent.

"Just be yourself. Give the pack a chance. They're a good bunch."

I feel his voice rumble through his chest where my hand rests. His T-shirt is thin, and I can feel his muscles shift as he rubs my back. I move my hand slowly over his chest and relax further into the embrace. I freeze as I feel a hardness press against me. Seb clears his throat and shifts his weight slightly, and I bury my face into his chest to prevent him from moving away, worried I'm going to lose a friendship that has only just begun.

"I could really do with a friend right now, Seb," I mumble into his chest.

Pulling away from me, he gently takes hold of my chin and lifts it so my eyes meet his. They are soft, understanding.

"And that's exactly what you've got." He winks at me, his usually cheeky expression returning to his face. "I can't help it when I've got a beautiful woman pressed up against me."

I laugh and step away from him, feeling reassured, although I'm not completely sure what just passed between us.

Reluctantly, I pull Garett's jacket off and drop it on the bed. I may not be trying to make a good impression here, but I shouldn't actively try to piss them off.

Straightening my shoulders, I prepare myself for what I may face this evening. Thankfully, my wounds are pretty much healed, so other than stiff legs and a sore shoulder, you wouldn't know I had been so badly injured only the night before. All thanks to a naked puppy pile of guys. Who'd have thought it? Confident, strong, but non-threatening is the look I'm going for. Let's hope it works.

"Let's do this."

Chapter Eight

In the middle of the compound, just behind the main house, is the 'hang out,' the building where they hold the socials. As we walk into the large lodge-type building, I see a room off to the left that is full of comfy looking sofas and beanbags in front of a large flat screen TV, with a couple of pool tables at the back of the room. Inside the main room, there's a bar to one side—I'm guessing I'll be spending a lot of my time there. There are tables set up all along one edge of the room, all of which are overflowing with food. The middle of the room is empty, I'm assuming for mingling and dancing, as I spy a DJ in the corner.

This seems more like a party than the social I was imagining it to be. The only socials I've been to in the past are pack meetings, where everyone sat in silence listening to the alpha. Those were certainly never anything to look forward to, whereas the atmosphere here is electric, and there's an excited feeling coming off the pack members who walk past me. There are a few curious looks, and a couple appraising glances, as if to gauge my strength, but nothing threatening and no fearful gazes. Very different from what I'm used to.

The room is starting to fill now, the buzzing of voices rising in volume. The sight of smiling faces and hugs of reuniting friends and family makes a small part of me ache. I haven't felt that part of me in a long time. I push it away. I am fine. I have Tori and Garett. I don't need this.

As if sensing my walls reinforcing and the bricks recementing, Seb grabs onto my hand with a smile and pulls me through the crowd. I see a blonde blur before something barrels into me hard. Almost as quickly as it happens, Seb is wrestling with a small, very excited child.

"Is this her? Is this her?" she asks, barely able to control her excitement before escaping from Seb's arms and launching herself at me again.

I barely catch her in time and laugh at the giggling child in my arms. I raise a questioning eyebrow at Seb. It's clear they're related. They both have the same, messy blond hair and crystal-clear blue eyes.

"Jessica, you must stop throwing yourself at people, even if they are your brother's friends. I swear, one of these days..." An exasperated voice trails off behind me, and I turn around to see an older version of the little girl in my arms.

A little plump, with a large bosom, she looks like all the mums in the storybooks I used to read when I was a child before I was removed from the schooling system. So this must be Seb's mum. And the squirming child in my arms must be his sister. Giggling, Jessica jumps out of my arms and runs over to her mother, talking around a hundred words a minute about Seb's 'new friend.'

I look over at him, smiling at his expression as he watches his younger sister and mum.

"So you told your family about me. Don't you think we're moving a little fast in our relationship?" I say with a teasing grin. After all, we only met this morning—with his naked body curled around mine. Ahem. I hope he left that part out when he spoke to his parents.

"What can I say? I wanted you to meet them. They know you're here to help the pack and wanted to meet you," he says with a grin, and then leans forward like he's sharing a secret. "You're a bit of a celebrity. We never get new wolves here."

Fantastic.

I see Alpha Mortlock and Lena step up onto a small stage at the front of the room, Lena gesturing for me to join them. I glance back to Seb and his family.

"Off you go, dear. We will be here once you're done. We can chat more then," Seb's mum tells me with a smile while trying, and failing, to tame Jessica's wild hair.

Seb nudges my shoulder and motions for me to head to the front of the room. Internally, I sigh. Here we go.

Around me, people move out of my way, allowing me to walk to the front. Alexander and Isa are there too, the latter of whom nods her head to me in greeting. I'm unsure where to stand, acutely aware I can cause grave offence if I position myself in the wrong place. If I were to stand before Alex or Isa, I would be disrespecting them by saying I think I'm stronger than both of them, whereas if I automatically place myself at the end, I would be saying I'm weaker than them. As an outsider to the pack, it's not clear where I should be, as I don't really fit in anywhere.

Thankfully, Alpha Mortlock saves me from having to decide as he calls me up onto the stage.

"Good evening, Moon River Pack. It is wonderful to see so many of you here tonight. Tonight is a special occasion, as we welcome a guest to our pack." There is a ripple of noise from the crowd, and I can guess it's because I've been named as a guest and not a new pack member.

"Ariana here will be our new nurse for a few months. She will be travelling here to care for you, so I ask that you show her the same respect as any other member of the pack. She is under pack protection, so any threat to her life is a threat to all of us. Is that understood?"

His last statement is said with the power of the alpha behind his voice. I notice several heads bow low and a chorus of "Yes,

Alpha" can be heard from the crowd. At this confirmation, Alpha Mortlock smiles, the tension in the room dropping.

"Then make her feel welcome. Maybe we can convince her to join us. Now, enjoy and have fun!" he says with a wink towards me. I smile back at him and step off the stage with a sinking feeling in my stomach. He has voiced his intentions to the whole pack, he wants me to join, which means that this is not going to be easy.

Isa walks up to me and gestures to a line of people waiting to meet me. And so it begins. I look around for Seb, but I can't see him anywhere. Alex appears next to my shoulder, so I'm surrounded by the beta and gamma of the pack. Appearances must be kept, I guess.

"If you're looking for Sebastian, you won't see him for a while. You're to meet the strongest, most important members of the pack," he informs me. I just look at him, gobsmacked.

"Bullshit," I reply loudly, startling both Isa and Alex. "Being important has nothing to do with power." Bloody pack politics getting in the way. "Where is he?" I demand. Alex places a placating hand on my arm, and I glare at it.

"You won't be helping him by doing this. You'll be putting a target on his back."

I growl quietly under my breath, my frustration causing my control of my power to slip, making the wolves near me pay closer attention. I have just announced how powerful I am, and now I have them eyeing me up like I'm a shiny new toy. *Suck it up, Ari. You can't change centuries' worth of pack politics overnight.*

And so begins the tedious procession of all the 'important' members of the pack. Thankfully, there aren't too many of them, and I find myself actually liking a few of them. We reach the end of the line, and I sigh with relief. Maybe I can go and enjoy myself now. Isa stiffens and mutters something under her breath in German, which I'm pretty sure is a curse word. I follow her gaze, and it's all I can do to stop my jaw from falling open.

Stalking towards me like I'm his next meal is the most

gorgeous man I've ever seen. He must be just over six foot, and he looks like he was a warrior in a past life. He has a vicious scar that runs down the side of his face, which only adds to the impression, and his stormy grey eyes stare out at me. His face is set in a frown, his lips tight as he moves closer to me, and I get the impression he doesn't smile all that often. I can think of a few activities that could change that... *Behave, Ari! Not the right time or place.*

Unlike the others, I can feel the alpha power rolling off him, and I'm unsure why Alpha Mortlock would have such a strong wolf here who wasn't in a position of power. He feels dangerous. If I know what's good for me, I need to stay away from him. Unfortunately, my wolf thinks the opposite. I feel her brush up against my barriers, pushing our power out to meet his. I see his eyes widen as it hits him, stopping him in his tracks. His face twists into a snarl.

"Stay away from me, Shadowborn. Nothing good can happen from having you here," he spits out before spinning on his heel and leaving the hall.

Well, that was pleasant. I look to Isa, who is shaking her head, then over to Alex, who looks like he is having to stop himself from following the rude stranger.

"That's Killian. I would avoid him if you can," is all the explanation I get from Alex before he walks away. I guess I'm going to have to do my own research there then.

Isa makes her excuses and walks over to a group of other shifters who are talking loudly in German.

I look around me. Everyone is with their friends and family. They all seem...happy. For the first time, I feel lonely, like the life I lead may be lacking. I never knew what that was before, but maybe this is it.

Pushing these confusing feelings aside, I use this time to find Seb. He is in the corner of the room with a plate piled high with food, chatting to one of the men from this morning. Seb's mother, who I have learned is called Gloria, is sitting at one of the tables watching fondly as Jessica plays with some of the other children. I sit with her and she smiles at me, patting my hand.

"How are you finding your first pack social?" she asks with a knowing look on her face.

"A little overwhelming, to be honest. There are so many people here, but it's not what I expected. Everyone is happy," I comment as I look around the room, taking in all the sights.

Raising her eyebrows, Gloria tilts her head as she looks at me, her eyes seeing more than I would like.

"Why wouldn't they be happy, dear? They are safe and protected here, surrounded by those who love them."

"That must be nice," I reply quietly. I don't really mean to say it out loud, and I say it more to myself than to Gloria. However, I see her nod to herself, like she has come to a conclusion. I lean back in my seat, watching those around us. Seb keeps glancing at me when he thinks I'm not looking.

"So, what's the deal with Killian?" I ask Gloria. She seems like the kind of woman who would know everyone in the pack. Seb wanders over with his friend, and they pull up chairs next to us.

"He's complicated, that one," she replies with a sigh. "He was alpha of one of the largest packs in New York. There was an attack on his pack," Gloria explains, her voice heavy with sorrow. My eyebrows raise as I lean back in my chair. I remember hearing of that attack several years ago—it was brutal. I thought the whole pack had been wiped out.

"He screwed up," a voice spits, and glancing to the side, I see it's Seb's friend. "He's the reason that his pack's dead. There was some sort of agreement with Alpha Mortlock, and he allowed him to come here. Fucking bad idea, if you ask me. He's a cold bastard who doesn't belong here."

His view seems kind of harsh, but I see Seb nodding. That explains why someone who is so strong isn't in a position of power. I can't imagine how difficult it is to go from being the alpha of a successful pack, to an outsider in a pack that doesn't really want you there. Well, I know all about the outsider part.

"He's okay. Bit of a bastard, but considering what he went through, I can understand that. Steve's right, though, he doesn't fit in here, and he makes no effort to. I would try and stay away from him if you can," Seb offers, gesturing to his friend.

I look at the guy next to Seb—Steve, I'm assuming. Steve uses our eye contact as an excuse to start a conversation.

We spend the next ten minutes or so chatting about the pack, the social, and what I enjoy doing outside of work, until the DJ starts playing music. Several couples go up and begin dancing, and I notice Alpha Mortlock and Lena dancing near the front. Seb drags me to my feet, pulling me onto the dance floor, ignoring my protests.

Despite what I thought, I find I'm actually enjoying myself. I have a dance with Seb, Gloria, and Jessica, a couple with Steve, and even one with Alpha Mortlock. I just finish a particularly vigorous dance with Seb that has me in fits of laughter—his dance style is... unusual—when I bump into Alex. I literally fall into his arms.

"You don't have to throw yourself at me to get me to dance with you," he comments with a grin.

"Yeah, you wish, Casanova. Since when do you dance? I've seen you propping up the wall over there like it couldn't stand on its own. I thought you were allergic to fun?" I tease.

It's true though. So far this evening, I have only seen him watching everyone else, always on duty. He leans in closer to me as the DJ changes the music, a slower song coming on. People around us couple up and start to slow dance. Placing his hands on my lower back, he pulls me so I'm almost pressed against him. I place my hand on his chest to stop our bodies from touching. He uses this as an invitation to start moving us to the music. I'm really not a dancer, so it's more of a sway than anything else.

"So you've been watching me then," he says softly in my ear, although it sounds more like a statement than a question.

I snort. Of course I have been watching him. He makes me nervous.

"Don't flatter yourself, buddy. I watch everyone." And that's the truth. In fact, I'm watching everyone as we dance now, taking in details, looking out for anyone who's paying too much attention.

Alex raises his eyebrows and stops dancing.

"Do you always push everyone away or is it just me?" he inquires. His tone is soft, like he is asking a normal question, but his body language is tense.

I stare at him, gobsmacked. Whoa, where the hell has this come from? I do my best fish out of water impression, lost for words.

"And are you always this rude?" I finally retort, feeling my temper rise as we stare at each other.

Alex has obviously reached his limit, and without a word, he turns and leaves the room. It's at this point that I notice the room has gone silent. Everyone has stopped to watch the show.

"Wow, Ari, you sure know how to liven up a party!" Seb comments loudly, causing chuckles around us. Thankfully, people start dancing again, only throwing me curious glances rather than full-on stares.

Pulling me to one side, he puts an arm around me and lowers his voice.

"You okay?" he queries, and I hate the look of concern in his eyes.

"I'm fine, Seb," I say, shaking his arm off before grabbing his hand. "Let's go dance."

The next hour or so I spend dancing to try and forget my embarrassing moment with Alex. I don't want to think about it now, or about the reasons why Alex might care if I let people get close to me. I have a couple of drinks, and Gloria keeps trying to feed me. Jessica seems to have taken a liking to me, and the rest of the pack seems to dote on her. To be honest, it's easy to see why. Wolves have always been protective of their young, but happiness just seems to shine from her. One of the grumpy pack elders is currently having his shoulder-length hair braided by her, and although he's scowling, I think he secretly likes it.

I'm chatting with one of Seb's friends when a heavy hand grips my shoulder. Startled, I spin to face the person touching me, a snarl on my lips. A tall male puts his hands up in a peaceful gesture, but his smile is anything but nice. Something about him makes me uneasy, although I can't put a finger on what it is about him that makes me feel this way.

"Hey there, pretty lady, no harm meant. I just want to talk with you. Care to dance?" he asks, and I get the feeling he's used to getting his way. Normally, I would never give this kind of guy the time of day, but I've agreed to try and integrate into the pack while I'm here, so reluctantly I nod.

Ignoring his outstretched hand, I walk onto the dance floor, waiting for him to join me. He immediately pulls me in close, and my hackles rise as I push back against his chest a little to gain some space. Presumptuous much? I study the man before me. He's good looking, I guess, but he's full of himself, which is a major turn-off.

"So, what is someone as strong as you doing with the runts of the pack?" He removes his arm from my lower back and gestures towards Seb, Gloria, and the group of shifters I have been spending the evening with. "You should be spending your time where you belong, with the strongest of the pack. With a male who can keep up with you."

Nope. I know what I promised the alpha, but I am not putting up with an attitude like that. I may have just met those people, but they have already shown me more kindness in the last few hours than I've experienced in my life. Grabbing onto his shirt, I pull him closer, obviously startling him with my show of strength.

"Listen, shit for brains. If the strongest in the pack are anything like you, I want nothing to do with them. No one tells me where my place is. Those people over there that you talk down about? They have treated me better than anyone ever has, and they are probably more decent than you could ever hope to be."

So maybe I'm a little strong with my words, but every single one is true. I shove him away from me and start to walk back to Seb and his friends. Limp dick obviously doesn't get the message though, as he grabs my arm and spins me around.

"Now listen here, you little bitch—" He starts, his face getting red with rage, obviously not used to being spoken to that way. I interrupt him, putting an end to his useless tirade with a low blow.

"Did you not hear me? Leave me the fuck alone. I would rather eat garbage than spend another minute with you."

I probably shouldn't be provoking a shifter who's shaking with rage, but I won't let people talk about my friends that way. I catch myself at the use of the words 'friends' and realise it's true. In such a short space of time, I have come to appreciate the familial group I've spent time with today. Walking away, I see the gratitude on Gloria's face, although when I look at Seb, he seems worried.

"Ari," he warns, before a deafening roar fills the room, filling me with dread. That's a sound I know all too well. Someone just lost their temper and the battle with their wolf.

"I challenge you!" is bellowed across the room, and for the second time that evening, everyone goes silent. I turn around to see who's been challenged, but the lead in my stomach already knows.

Panting like he has just run a marathon is the supreme dickhead who felt he had a claim on me. His eyes, glowing an unearthly green, have turned fully wolf, and at the end of his fingers, his nails have turned to claws—sharp, wicked-looking points that can slice open a person in seconds. Claws that are aimed right at me.

Oh shit.

Chapter Nine

Mutters and whispers fill the air around me, and I hear mentions of 'not allowed' and 'guest.' Dread fills my stomach. I may not know much about how packs work, but even I know that formal challenges can't be turned down. If I forfeit, then I'm subjected to the same punishment as losing a challenge—death. That is not an option for me. I've overcome too much to get to this point only to have to give it up all because I have damaged some idiot's pride.

Seb pulls me from my thoughts as he pushes through the crowd and tries to stand in front of me.

"Marcus, you can't challenge her. She's a guest of the pack," he states, and I can hear the fury in his voice, which is very out of character from the usual fun-loving Seb that I've come to know.

Turns out that dickhead, or Marcus as he is apparently called, doesn't like being told what he can and can't do. Snarling, he leaps forward, slashing at Seb with his semi-turned hand, slicing his razor-sharp claws across his chest. I hear someone cry out—I think it's Gloria, but in my rage-filled mind I'm not sure, since my focus is entirely on Marcus.

Stepping in front of a crouched Seb, I move into a protective stance in case Marcus dares to attack him again. I have hurt many in the past, more than I care to think about, and I promised myself that I would never hurt anyone again when I left my old pack. I'm trying to make a better life for myself, to atone for the actions of my past, which is why I took a vow to do no harm when I trained to be a nurse and help people for a living. But right now, all I can think about is the fact that this bastard has hurt someone I care for. A little part of my mind is wondering how these people have wormed their way into my heart so quickly, so easily, but I push that aside, needing to concentrate on the dickhead before me.

My wolf rushes to the surface, and I feel her walking under my skin. We're in complete agreement for once, wanting to protect Seb and make the bastard that hurt him pay. Mutters fill the room again as our power fills it, pushing against each other. Some of the weaker shifters are forced to their knees, a few even bursting into their wolf form, and they crouch against the floor in submission against our warring energies. The power is so thick in the room, you could choke on it.

"I accept," I announce in a voice that I hardly recognise as my own as I take a step towards him.

"Ari, no. Don't do this!" I hear Seb's pain-laced plea.

I glance over my shoulder at him, not trusting Marcus enough to turn my back on him. Seb is leaning against one of the chairs, Gloria and a couple of other shifters with him. I can see that the wound isn't too deep, since it has stopped bleeding already. He should heal quickly, although, since it's been caused by another shifter, it will probably scar. My nursing side is satisfied that he'll be okay while I deal with this threat. I smile in what I hope is a reassuring way, but I'm pretty sure it appears as a grimace before I turn back to the problem at hand.

I'm still not fully healed from the attack last night, and here I am about to engage in a challenge to the death with a fully-grown male shifter. I must be out of my fucking mind.

I hear a commotion, and when I look over to where the sound is coming from, I see Alpha Mortlock moving through the crowd.

Looking furious, he storms towards Marcus, grabbing him by the shoulders as if he's going to shake some sense into him.

"How dare you issue a challenge to a guest? You know the rules. Rescind your challenge immediately," he orders, the full power of the alpha evident in his command.

Man, I wouldn't want to be Marcus right now. I can see his face contort in pain as he fights against the order, his muscles trembling. He may be strong, but he's not alpha strong. A sliver of hope flares to life as I think there may be a way out of this. I'm not scared, but I'm practical, and entering into a fight you're not sure you can win is foolish. Wolf-Ari does not agree, and I know she wants to rip Marcus to shreds. But thankfully for me, right now I'm in charge of this shit show.

However, that sliver of hope is shot down by Marcus' next comment.

"Too late, Alpha. She already accepted," he grinds out, a grin of sick satisfaction across his smarmy face.

Alpha Mortlock turns to me, his face grim. "Is this true?" he asks, his voice resigned.

I nod. Some of the wolves who have gathered around Marcus are shouting out that now that I have accepted the challenge, the alpha has to honour it. I guess Marcus has his own cheerleaders. I nearly smirk at the image of the large, buff shifters in little cheerleading costumes. *Come on, brain, not the right time. Focus.*

Alpha Mortlock sighs and nods towards Marcus. He turns to address the crowd.

"Marcus of Moon River Pack has challenged Ariana, lone wolf and guest of Moon River Pack. As the challenge has been accepted, I have no choice but to allow this to proceed. But I do not condone this and there will be consequences," he says sternly to the watching shifters, a wave of his alpha power backing up his words.

The crowd erupts into shouts, many, I am pleased to hear, who are protesting the challenge.

"Enough! I have made my decision," he hollers before walking to me. Pulling me aside, he lowers his voice. "Do you know the rules? You know what you're getting into?"

I nod. Anyone in the pack can issue a formal challenge. Usually, it's used when a shifter wishes to change their station, because they want a higher role within the pack. Shifters can also issue challenges to someone they believe has wronged them, however, as a fight to the death, it's not something that happens often. You wouldn't challenge someone for crushing your roses, for example. Apparently, it's against the rules to challenge a guest, but once the challenge has been accepted, it cannot be overturned, not even by the alpha—who knew? No weapons are allowed other than claws or fangs. Most fights begin in wolf form, but some prefer to start in human form.

"Prepare yourself," he says loudly to everyone, but I feel like he's directing this comment at me.

The crowd steps back, creating a loose circle around us, with me at one end and Marcus at the other. A group of people has formed at his end. I assume they're his supporters, given the sneers and growls they're throwing my way.

I hear a commotion behind me and turn to find I have a large group of people who have come to support me or offer me words of guidance, some of whom I have never spoken to before. A small part of my heart hurts at this show of community, that people who I don't even know are willing to support me through this. I do notice Alex hasn't returned to the room, and a part of me is disappointed. Gloria pushes through and places a hand against my cheek.

"You show that nasty brute," she remarks, which brings a smile to my face.

I take a step forward into the makeshift ring and start shrugging off my top, indicating that I will start in wolf form. I don't trust myself to shift quickly enough if I need to later on in the fight. Alpha Mortlock barks out for everyone to turn while I shift. As one, the whole room turns, all except Marcus, who smirks at me, crossing his arms and daring me with his eyes to strip in front of him.

Fuck him. Standing tall, I remove the rest of my clothes, meeting Marcus' eyes as I do it. I will not let him make me feel ashamed or cowed into covering myself. I am not his victim. I am no one's victim. Once I finish undressing, I crouch and call my wolf to the surface. She rushes out all at once, ready for justice.

The shift takes longer than I would like, unpractised as I am since I'm still avoiding shifting unless absolutely necessary. Once I'm in wolf form, I get to all fours and snarl at Marcus, who smirks and bursts into wolf form within twenty seconds, not even bothering to take his clothes off. Show off. The crowd turns back around, and I feel the anticipation, which is thick in the air as they watch the two of us. However, I feel more nervous tension in the room than I was expecting, and I almost wonder if they are worried about my well-being.

I can hear Seb's voice as he demands to be let closer. I'm distracted, and I turn to look at him, my desire to check he is okay overwhelming my need for revenge. Marcus uses this moment of distraction to charge at me.

Fuck, he's big!

Thankfully, this should make him slower, and I dart out of the way, snarling at him as he flies past me. I lower myself into a defensive position as he circles me. He goes to attack my right, so I instinctively move to the left, unfortunately realising too late that he's tricked me, and I dive into his jaws. With a sickening crunch, his teeth sink into my already injured shoulder. I howl in pain as he shakes his head, his fangs ripping into the newly healed muscles and tendons. With a final shake he lets go of my shoulder, sending me flying into a table. Pain flares through my back at the impact, although compared to the agony of my shoulder, it's nothing.

I haul myself to my feet, limping as I try to avoid putting any extra weight on my injured shoulder. Distracted by the pain, I don't see Marcus until it's too late, and he bites down on my hind leg in the exact place where I had been injured the day before. I snarl as his plan becomes clear. The bastard is deliberately aiming for places he knows are going to cause me the most pain. He's playing with me, trying to maim me and cause as much agony as he can before he makes the killing blow. I turn, my leg slicing more in his jaws as I swipe at his belly with my claws. I also manage to bite down on his flank in the process, causing him to let go of me and retreat to the other side of the ring.

I try to back up and feel my legs give way. I shouldn't be fighting this soon after being injured. Besides, I'm not exactly the best at fighting in my wolf form. My wolf whines in pain, and I hear a scuffle behind me as Seb demands that this be called off. I hear shouts of agreement and calls of this being 'inhumane.' Surprise shoots through me. This pack acts very differently from what I expected. Alpha Mortlock looks on, but he is unable to intervene now. He has to stay impartial, although I can tell he wants to wade in and stop this.

"Get up," someone commands.

I turn my head, my ears flat against my skull, my lips pulled back over my teeth in a snarl. If I wasn't in so much pain, I would be surprised that Killian is crouched next to me. He is sneering at me, looking at me like I deserve the treatment I'm receiving, but I see something like fear in his eyes. I must be delirious with pain. I growl at him, telling him to back off.

"Useless," he spits at me, causing anger to swell inside me. Can't he just leave me alone?

"Do you want to die? No? Then get. The. Fuck. Up," he commands, his alpha power flowing through me, giving me strength. I'm so tired, but he's right. That pisses me off. I am not going to die here today, especially not at the jaws of a scumbag like Marcus.

Pushing up on trembling legs, I turn to face Marcus. It was foolish letting my guard down. He could have attacked me. Luckily, he's struggling as well, but I'm losing energy fast and I need to end this quickly.

"Use your brains. You couldn't have survived this long as a Shadowborn without them," Killian chides.

I don't understand why he's helping me. I'm pretty sure he can't stand the sight of me. But the anger that fills me at his comments pushes away the fog of pain that is making it difficult to think. Perhaps that was his plan after all? I don't have time to think about it, though, as Marcus prowls towards me again. I start to analyse the wolf in front of me and play over the last few attacks. I need to look for his weaknesses.

"Show him what happens when you fuck with a Shadowborn," Killian whispers, and my wolf agrees with him.

I go into a defensive stance, favouring my uninjured leg. Marcus picks up his pace, running towards me with his jaws wide. I stay still. Just as he is about to attack me, I see it—he's left his neck undefended.

I pounce with a growl and lock my teeth onto his neck. Twisting, I pull him down, and with my fangs in his jugular, he has no choice but to follow me. I twist again so I'm on top. I have the upper hand. All I need to do now is squeeze, but I hesitate as a memory surfaces.

His eyes widen as my jaws tighten against his neck. So young. He doesn't deserve to lose his life.

"Ari. Do it. Now." A crack of a whip in the background makes me flinch, his voice echoing in my ears. I bite down, quickly and without mercy. I feel his neck break under my fangs and watch as the light leaves his terrified eyes. They stare at me, and his last word echo in my ears. "Why?" And I know this day will haunt me.

I hear him step closer, his shoes clicking against the floor, and I flinch as his hand falls on my shoulder.

"Well done, little wolf."

I shudder as the memory overcomes me. I hear my name being shouted and yells to end it. I glance down and see fear in Marcus' eyes. He closes them as he prepares to lose his life.

No.

My wolf fights against me, but in this I am absolute. I will not take another life. Closing my eyes, I summon my human body. Crouched and naked, I place my human hand onto Marcus' bleeding neck. I squeeze enough that he opens his eyes. They widen in shock. Before he can get any ideas, I call my shadow form, not to change fully, not enough for anyone else to see, but enough to scare the shit out of Marcus.

"Do you concede?" I ask, my voice more wolf than human. I shift only my hand so it sinks slowly into his neck, then I reform it enough so he can feel the pressure there.

He nods, eyes wide.

"Stay down," I command, putting my full alpha power into my voice.

He whines. I stand as well as I can on my injured leg, not ashamed of my nakedness.

"I will not kill him," I say to Alpha Mortlock, but also loud enough that the rest of the pack can hear me.

The alpha nods at me, announcing my victory. All of a sudden, it's over, and I'm surrounded by people congratulating me, checking my wounds, and admiring my decision. All of this passes in a blur as my mind is elsewhere and my body goes through the motions. I look through the crowd, searching for someone who wasn't there. It's not until I can't see him that I realise I am disappointed that Alex isn't here to congratulate me. It isn't until I'm escorted from the hall that I realise Killian is no longer in the room either.

Chapter Ten

For the second morning in a row, I wake up with Seb's naked body pressed up against me, but probably not in the way he hoped when I insisted he share my bed. Alpha Mortlock wanted to use his puppy pile method again, but I refused, and in my pain-addled state, I hadn't let anyone close to Seb. He'd protested, saying he was fine, but until I was able to check him over and see for myself, I wouldn't let anyone near me to look at my wounds.

I spent the night with him wrapped around me, unable to sleep, twitching at every sound in the unfamiliar room. I don't know why I'm acting this way with Seb, but something about him sets off my protective instincts. At some point, I must have fallen asleep, as I wake up with his arms around me. I stay still so I don't wake him. It's nice being held purely because someone wants to hold me. There is nothing in it for him other than for comfort.

He moves in his sleep, and I feel his erection pressed up against me. This wakes me up fully. It also wakes up my lady parts, making me squirm. *Now is not the time, traitorous body.* I can feel Seb wake up, as he nuzzles his face into my neck. I can also feel when he senses my arousal, damn that shifter sense of smell. Taking a deep breath, which comes out as a predatory growl, he runs his hands over my hips. I arch back into his body, unable to stop myself from reacting to his touch. We're in dangerous territory here. It would be so easy to cross that line. All I need to do is roll over and kiss him.

I stop moving. All my past romantic dalliances have been just that—dalliances. They're great, but they all come to an end very quickly. Am I willing to lose this new friendship because I'm horny and can't keep it in my pants? Considering my reaction last night when Seb was hurt, I'm going to say no. We may not have known each other long, but my protective instincts are on overdrive with him, and I'm not sure I can cope if anything happens to him.

Seb, having felt me freeze, also stops, waiting for my lead, but I can hear his heavy breathing behind me. I scrunch up my eyes. I can't believe I'm turning away a gorgeous guy who obviously wants to spend the morning getting to know me in the biblical sense.

"Seb," I say with a sigh, regret clear in my voice.

He instantly rolls away from me, and I look over my shoulder to see him getting out of bed and pulling on his jeans. Panic surges through me, and I bolt upright in bed, the covers falling around my waist and exposing my chest.

"Wait, where are you going?" I ask.

He turns and smiles at what he sees. "I'm going to take a cold shower. It's rude to have a hard-on around your naked friends," he replies with a wink.

Relief fills me, and I lie back in the bed with a laugh.

Now that I'm alone, I think over the events of the night before. I roll my shoulder. It's sore and stiff, but when I look at it, I just see the slightly raised pink skin of new scars. I look at my legs, expecting to see mangled skin, but I'm greeted with the same sight as my shoulder. New scars to add to the collection. It's a good thing I'm not vain. I've never been bothered by my scars. They show a battle I've lived through, and they are the marks of a survivor. I wouldn't say I'm proud of them, and I don't go out of my way to show them off, but I'm certainly not ashamed of them.

I muse over the fact that I'm healing so quickly. Sure, we have fast healing times, but injuries caused by other shifters take longer to heal, and considering the damage that was done, especially as it was a previously wounded area, I should be in far worse shape than I am. Seb's injuries practically healed before my eyes during the night as I watched him sleep. Perhaps it is due to our friendship. Does the healing thing work better with people you are close to? I'll have to ask Alex next time the growly beta decides to show his face.

Urgh. The thought of having to leave this room and face everyone after last night is not something I want to deal with. Marcus is going to be a problem. The challenge is a fight to the death for a reason. Wolves can't stand a challenge to their honour, and Marcus is too much of a dick to let it stand that a woman defeated him. I've literally been on pack grounds for twenty-four hours, and I'm already causing problems. I'm not blaming the pack. Other than a few exceptions, they've been nothing but welcoming, which is a massive blow to the feels. I hadn't expected the kindness shown by complete strangers to an outcast like me.

And now I have to go out there and help them, heal them. I feel their expectations on my shoulders like a heavy weight. It was okay when they were just nameless, faceless patients that I was dealing with, but now I know them, and even in this short time, I've begun to care for them. I can see that if I stay here for much longer, they will begin to care for me too. My breathing speeds up. Nothing good happens when people care for me. Tori is safe in the apartment, and she has friends who would care for her. Garett can look after himself, and I've purposely kept my distance up until now to keep him safe. Seb blindsided me with his instant friendship, but he is safe within the pack.

Now I have a whole group of people who are seeping their way into my cold, shrivelled little heart.

Jumping to my feet, I feel my battered body protest at the speed of my movements, but I ignore it, pushing down the rising panic in my chest. Hurrying to the side of the room where I discarded them last night, I start hastily pulling on my clothes. I need to get out of here, I need space.

Glassy dead eyes stare back at me as I remove my jaws from around his neck.

I shake my head to clear it from the memories trying to flood my brain, but it creeps in again.

I step away from the freshly dead body, look behind me, and jump from the corpse that lies next to me. Rather than a nameless body, I see the corpse of little Jessica. No—this isn't real. I didn't know Jessica then. I step back and startle as my foot touches a hand. Spinning around, I howl in grief as I look at the body of the boy I just murdered. It's not the nameless boy I played with, the boy who gave me comfort—it's Seb. His face is twisted, as if in terrible pain.

"It's your fault I'm dead."

I spin, my heart rate spiking in panic as I try to find who spoke. My eyes widen as I take in the room full of bodies—Alex, Tori, Seb, Gloria, and members of the pack whose names I don't even remember, all dead.

"Ari."

I snap out of my twisted flashback as I step back into a solid wall. Except walls aren't warm, and they don't wrap their arms around you. I stiffen, ready to break free of my captor's arms, until I take a deep breath. The scent of the woods and the sweet smell of brandy reach me—Alex.

"Ari, breathe," he orders.

I do as commanded, trying to slow my breathing now that I know what happened in my 'memory' wasn't real. We stand there for a long while, his strong arms holding me up, and I try to ground myself. The words 'they're alive' keep running through my head, my mantra to keep myself in the here and now.

"You want to tell me what's going on? I came to see you, and I could sense your panic through the door. I thought something happened," he admits, and the tension in his voice makes me frown.

I turn my head a bit, and I see the door is now hanging off its hinges. He literally ripped the door off to get to me. Too much. This is too much.

I pull from his arms, gathering up my meagre belongings that have been strewn around the room.

"Ari, what's going on? Where are you going? If it's Marcus, he's been banished. You don't have to worry about him anymore."

I shake my head. Marcus is the least of my worries right now.

"I just need some space. I'll be back. I just need time, okay?" I blurt out, not looking him in the eye.

I hear him sigh, and out of the corner of my eye, I see him nod.

"Tell Seb I'll see him around," I say before I start walking out of the room.

This place is like a bloody maze. I walk around the back of another building, looking for my car so I can get the hell out of here. Several people have tried to stop me to talk about last night, but I have just smiled tensely at them and walked on.

"Where the hell do you think you're going?" I hear shouted angrily at me.

I spin around and see a fuming Killian striding towards me. My temper boils, although my wolf perks up at the sight of him. *Down, girl.*

"And how is that any of your fucking business?" I demand, close to losing my temper. I am not in the mood for Mr. Dark and Moody to grow a conscience.

He snarls at me, and I can see his wolf is as close to the surface as mine, our alpha powers rubbing up against one another.

"It matters to me when you lose control and kill all of the wolves here. You're a fucking mess. It's a surprise you've survived this long as it is. You need to get yourself under control before you cause any more problems," he goads.

But he's right. I am going to get these wolves killed. I see a brief flash of panic in his eyes as he realises he isn't going to get the reaction he wanted. I turn away, my heart heavy, and restart the mission of trying to find my car.

"You're going to get yourself killed," he states. His voice is tinged with sadness as he says this.

I spin around, my temper flaring again. Why does he care if I get myself killed or not? He's made it clear that he thinks I'm a danger to everyone around me. He clearly hates Shadowborn, so shouldn't my death please him?

"Why do you care what happens to me?" I demand, fire back in my voice.

A look of confusion greets my question, like he doesn't have an answer. This disappears as his face hardens.

"Take your break. Once you've gotten over your pity party, come back and I'll teach you how a real wolf fights."

I snort at his comment, flipping him off as I turn away, and stalk towards where I'm sure my bloody car is. What a dick. But as I finally find my car and haul myself into it, I realise my heart isn't quite as heavy as it had been when I first left the house.

Chapter Eleven

I send Tori an SOS text and hightail it to the only place I can think of—Garett's bar. It's only eleven am, so the bar is dead when I walk in, there are only a few alcoholics nursing their morning drinks in the corner.

Garett is standing behind the bar, looking gorgeous in his tight uniform shirt and jeans. He smiles widely when he sees me, but this quickly turns to a scowl when he notices my slight limp and the look on my face.

"Someone hurt you," he states, his voice like granite, cold and hard.

I sigh, sliding onto my favourite bar stool, my body protesting.

"I was challenged last night," I explain.

Cue lots of cursing and male grumbling. I watch in silence as Garett fights his bear for control. It's quite a sight to see. He slowly, quietly, places the glass he was polishing onto the bar, bracing his arms against the bar like it is the only thing keeping him up. I reach across and grab the glass he was polishing, leaning over the bar to pour myself a whisky. Sure, it's early for a drink, but cut me some slack—it has been one hell of a morning.

While I nurse my drink, Garett gets a co-worker to cover the bar. Walking up to my side, he grabs my hand and pulls me along behind him.

"Come," he demands.

I follow him, not about to argue with a bear this close to losing control. I follow him up the stairs at the back of the bar, leading up to the apartment he rents. It's handy living just above your workplace.

Pushing open the door, he holds it open for me. I duck under his arm and head into the apartment. It's nice in here, homey. It's not a large apartment, but it's big enough for Garett. I look around the room. I haven't been up here in a long time, but it looks the same. I walk over to the fireplace and there is a picture frame that takes a place of pride. I pick it up and surprise flashes through me as I realise it's a photo of me. I remember that day. Tori had decided she needed to get to know my 'bear friend' better and had organised a picnic for the three of us. It had been a great day, but I don't remember this photo being taken.

I turn around to ask Garett where this came from, but I stop at the expression I see there.

"Explain," he orders, his voice more bear than I've ever heard it.

So I do. I tell him about the events of the previous evening, I even tell him about me fleeing from the compound this morning.

"I just... They're all depending on me. I'm not good for any of them. It was okay when I didn't care for them or them for me. But now it's different. Everything's happening so fast! I already got Seb hurt. I'm going to get them all killed. I'm not good enough," I blurt out, all my pent-up feelings coming out in a rush.

"Ari, stop."

I look up, swallowing at the sight before me. Garett is looking at me in a way I've never seen before. He prowls towards me, and I step back until I'm pressed up against a wall. He keeps walking until he is a hairsbreadth away from me. Placing his arms on the wall on either side of me, blocking me in, I have no choice but to look up into his eyes. They're pure bear at the moment, glowing back at me with his supernatural power. Seeing Garett like this awakens a different part of me, overshadowing my despair. Arousal spreads through me, and Garett makes a satisfied rumble as he scents it.

Pushing his hips up against me, I can feel his own arousal, hard and unyielding. My wolf, the hussy, is eager to reciprocate, and I feel her walking under my skin. My eyes mirror his own.

"Never think that you aren't good enough. You are more than enough."

He lowers his head. I can see in his eyes that he is waiting for me to make a move and that he would back off if I asked him to. I shouldn't cross this line, he's my friend, but I need this comfort right now. Sure, I have an attraction to another guy—ahem, a couple of other guys—but I need this physical comfort, and I know Garett will do anything to protect me.

I lean forward, capturing his lips with my own. He groans into my mouth, and we kiss, slow and unhurried, as his hands begin to explore my body. I run my fingers over his chest, scraping my nails gently over his nipples as I trail them down towards his jeans. He bites my lower lip, pressing me further into the wall. I run my hand over the bulge in his jeans before slipping them into his waistband. He isn't wearing underwear. *Fuck.* Feeling the velvety smoothness over the pure hardness of his cock is doing all sorts of things to my hormones, sending a shock of pure desire right to my core.

"I knew it!" someone shouts, causing me to jump. I shouldn't have let someone sneak up on us. I let my guard down, got distracted because I felt safe, but I know that voice, so I don't bother to whirl around and attack like I normally would.

Garett groans, dropping his head to my shoulder, but he makes no effort to move. Standing on tiptoes, I peek over Garett's bulk and see a very smug Tori standing in the doorway. I pat at Garett's chest, signalling him to let me out. When he doesn't move, I duck under his arm, and he just rests his forehead against the wall in defeat.

Noticing Garett's demeanour, I raise my eyebrows at Tori, a smirk crossing my face.

"Bloody hell. Look what you've done to him," I remark as I embrace Tori. I hadn't realised how much I needed this until her arms were wrapped around me.

Tori laughs, returning my hug tightly, holding on for a fraction longer than our usual slap on the back. Neither of us acknowledge it, we just pretend that we're two normal friends that hug.

"Girl, this has nothing to do with me and everything to do with your months of holding out on him." Releasing me, she saunters up to him and pats him on the shoulder. "Poor baby," she coos.

My mouth drops open in mock outrage at her comment. Garett turns from his position against the wall and smiles at Tori. He doesn't try to hug her like I did, knowing she has just as many issues over being touched as I do.

"Hey, witch," he calls out to her affectionately as he walks over to the sofa. I can't help but notice that he discreetly tries to reposition himself as he sits down.

Tori walks towards the doorway where she left some bags, which she now brings over to the coffee table in the middle of the living room. Sitting opposite Garett, she begins unpacking the bags which, it turns out, are full of takeout.

"Months," she says.

I make an ungraceful sound, which sounds suspiciously like a snort, still stuck on her comment about finding the two of us getting hot and heavy against the wall. "This was a completely spur-of-the-moment thing. We were just letting off some tension after everything that happened. You know. Stress," I ramble. My voice sounds unconvincing, even to me. "It's not going to happen again."

It wouldn't. No matter how much my wolf wanted to howl at that thought. Garett wouldn't just want a tumble in the sheets, he would want more from me than that. He wouldn't be able to help himself. It's in his nature to be protective.

I see Garett look up at my comment and the brief flash of hurt in his eyes before he goes back to helping Tori unpack the food.

"Uh-huh," she comments, not for a minute sounding like she believes me. "Now will you stop deluding yourself and sit your ass down. The food is going cold. The food you promised to bring me *two nights* ago." She glares at me as she says this.

I cringe, knowing I'm in the wrong here. Bad friend award goes to me. It's not a good idea to piss off a witch, especially when it involves food.

I perch sheepishly on the end of the sofa next to Garett, the only other available seat in the room. I don't want this to be awkward because I couldn't control my hormones. Besides, Garett deserves someone way better than me. For a start, I'm a wolf. He wouldn't ever be able to have a family with me. I'm not sure I would even want to start a family. I struggle to look after myself, let alone miniature versions of me.

I shudder at the thought. I wouldn't do that to him. Garett would make a good father, with his own cubs. He wouldn't have that with me.

Not to mention I'm a hot mess. I don't mind a one-night fling, but a relationship is a whole new ball game. Within the supernatural community, we are much more open and liberal with sex. We aren't squeamish about these things.

With Tori, Garett, and now Seb, I have all I need. A small part of me starts to call out that maybe that's not enough anymore. I crush that voice. I have all I need.

"I'm sorry, Tori, I've been a terrible friend. I just got so caught up in everything..." I trail off, feeling guilty.

If I weren't so used to looking out for myself, I would have thought to call her sooner. A normal, undamaged person would have done that.

It was a big shock to me when I first realised that another person cared for me. Our first major fight had been when I stayed out with a cute fae and ended up on a little jaunt to the fae realm. It had taken me a day and a half to find the portal back to the city. I found Tori pacing the apartment in tears. It had left me bewildered that someone would be so upset because they were worried about where I was. I instantly went on the defensive, convinced she was mad at me because I had been out with a fae. I think it was a shock to Tori as well that she cared enough about someone that she had become so worried. Her past was almost as dark as mine.

I look up as I hear a rustling noise, a large grin spreading across my face.

"I was going to eat these in front of you and not let you have any as punishment for putting me through hell. But I can't stay mad at that face," Tori teases, handing me a bag of doughnuts.

I greedily grasp the doughnuts, clutching the sweet balls of heaven to my chest. I'm not a possessive person, but you better not even think about messing with my doughnuts.

"I love you," I tell her around a mouthful of the divine confections.

She just laughs, knowing me well enough not to question the fact I'm eating dessert before the main course. Garett watches with a shake of his head, but I spot the small smile that crosses his lips.

"Right. Enough stalling. Tell me what's been going on," she demands.

I know better than to push her. With a sigh, I explain the craziness of the last few days.

When I finish retelling my story, Tori looks thoughtful. Pissed off, but thoughtful. Garett, on the other hand, looks ready to tear into someone. He's heard this all before, but listening to it again has set him off. He's pacing up and down the room, beginning to give me a cramp in my neck from where I've been watching him.

"Alexander promised me you would be safe there. I never would have left you there if I thought you would have been in danger," he spits out, his voice tight with anger. His green eyes flash as his bear pushes to the surface. I'm surprised by his show of rage. He usually has very tight control over his bear, but the last couple of days, I have never seen him closer to losing control.

"Well, I doubt he knew some asshole would challenge her. Besides, what idiot would accept that kind of challenge?" Tori comments, throwing a glare in my direction.

"I thought I had no choice but to accept!" I say indignantly.

They both ignore me and continue to talk about me as if I'm not here. I decide to ignore them in return and tuck into the food. I'm not going to let good food go to waste.

The rest of the morning, we go over my options, and we decide I will continue to go to the Moon River Pack on a daily basis to work as a nurse as agreed, and I shall return home to the safety of my apartment every day unless the threat from the Shadow Pack increases.

Garett is not impressed and argues every step of the way. If he had his way, he'd make me stay here so he could 'look after' me. Infuriating man.

Tori is just getting ready to leave. She has some explaining to do to her boss—she did ditch work to come and see me here, after all. Slinging her bag over her shoulder, she comes over to give me a hug.

"Oh! Before I forget, you remember McHottie? The guy who turned up at the apartment asking after you? Well, he was on the doorstep again this morning. He's getting a bit pushy. I told him you'd moved out," she tells me with a wink before walking out the door, waving to Garett as she leaves.

Who the hell is this guy? Besides, how does he know where I live? I'm not sure Garett even has my home address. It's my sanctuary.

"McHottie?" Garett asks in a barely controlled voice.

"Whoa, down boy. Some stranger turned up at the apartment asking after me. Seems he tried again today." I shrug this off as if it's nothing.

In reality, my mind is spinning, but I have too much to think about already. Garett must sense this as he stalks towards me with a low growl, backing me against the wall again. My body reacts, arching into him as a bolt of desire fills me. I see his pupils dilate as he watches my reaction to him. Lowering his head towards mine, he stops an inch away from my lips.

"Move in with me. Let me keep you safe."

I instantly go cold, all hints of desire gone as I stiffen in his arms. As I raise my eyes to meet his, I know my gaze is steely.

"Really, Garett?" I push past him, possibly a little harder than I needed to as I see him stumble a little.

I'm fuming at Garett, but mostly at myself. I should have seen this coming, I never should have kissed him, but I can't help but play with fire. However, I have never been the most tactful.

"Why the hell would I move in with you? Just sit in your apartment forever and let you fight my battles for me? What is it with you males thinking I'm so weak? I. Don't. Need. Protecting!" I shout at him, my anger getting the better of me.

I can see I've upset him, but I can't seem to stop myself.

"I'm just trying to help you, Ari. Why are you so stubborn? When will you learn that accepting help is not a sign of weakness? If you keep pushing, one of these days, you're going to look around and there will be no one there. What the hell happened to you to make you such a bitch?" he retorts, his own pain clear to see on his face.

I flinch as if he's hit me. It might have been better if he did, bruises will heal. These types of wounds take much more time to recover from. Bitch. I've been called worse, but never by Garett. My eyes sting, not from the harshness of his words, but from the fact they're true. I will myself not to cry as I pull on my shoes, which I'd kicked off earlier, and hurry towards the door. I see my phone vibrate and flash up with a message. Grabbing it, I tap out a quick reply and shove it in my back pocket.

"Ari, I'm sorry. I didn't mean it. Please, don't go." Pain and desperation sound in his voice, making me pause.

I stop in the doorway, indecision warring within me. If I leave, then everything that he accused me of is true. But I can't stay, and I certainly can't move in with him. Not because of what he said, it just isn't an option for me, and he won't understand that.

I feel him step up behind me, close enough to touch, but not daring to. With my heart in my chest, I make the decision for him and turn around, burying my face in his chest. My hands come up and clutch the fabric of his shirt.

"I'm sorry. I know I can be a bitch. I just... It's always been just me. I've learned not to trust anyone until I moved here and met Tori. And then before I knew it, you came into my life whether I wanted you to or not, and I've come to trust you as much as I do her. It just takes a long time to bring down walls like that," I mutter, my words muffled by his shirt, but I know he hears me as he relents, sighing as he wraps his arms around me.

"I know, Ari, I'm sorry I pushed you. I know you're not ready," he soothes, running his hands through my hair. "Will you stay, just for a bit?" he asks, and I can hear the fear in his voice. The worry that I will walk out that door and not come back.

Leaning away, I smile at him, hoping it conveys my affection towards him as I slowly shake my head. That is not a good idea. Besides, I have someone I need to meet before I head back to the pack. His smile is resigned, and as he leans forward, brushing a soft kiss across my forehead, I can see the pain in his eyes that I am causing him.

Not wanting to drag this out any further, I head towards the door, stopping briefly once I reach it to throw a saucy smile over my shoulder.

"You're still the first person I'd call if I want to get sweaty and naked," I tease, echoing the words he said to me in the bar the other night.

My comment works, and he laughs, nodding at me before shooing me out the door.

Chapter Twelve

Sitting in the busy coffee bar, I stare into my coffee, watching the steam eddy across the top of the liquid as I think over the events of the day. I feel bad about how I left things with Garett, but where he was going with his feelings and declarations was a place I was not ready to travel. Hell, I might never be ready for that. I'm too broken and damaged for someone as perfect as Garett. I'm mean, rough around the edges, and have a tendency to push people away when I don't feel safe. Garett is the opposite. Not to mention the fact that I can't seem to control my panties around Alex. Or my closeness with Seb.

I sigh. What a mess my life has become. This is why it was easier not to have any friends. The only person I had to worry about hurting was myself.

I'm so caught up in my musings that I don't notice that someone has approached me until the seat opposite me squeals as it's pulled back. With a start, I look up into the smiling face of Eric Daniels.

"You look like you've had a rough couple of days," he comments, and I smile, rolling my eyes at him.

"You really know how to compliment the ladies, Eric," I tease, chuckling as he realises his faux pas.

He looks like he is going to say something but changes his mind. "I'm just going to get a coffee. Can I get you something?" he inquires.

I shake my head and watch as he walks over to the counter to order his drink. Now I know what you're thinking. What on earth am I doing in a coffee bar in the middle of the city meeting Dr. Hotstuff? This is exactly what I want to know. When I checked my phone earlier in the day, I found several messages from him, each one sounding more desperate, until he finally asked me to meet him here. Apparently he has something he needs to tell me. I wonder what it is and what is so urgent that it has pulled him from work. I feel unsettled and grouchy not being able to go to work. I worked damn hard to become a nurse, and now I am being stopped from doing that by supernatural bullshit. I sigh, running my hand through my hair. That's not true. I will still be able to help people, those people just happen to turn into wolves.

While Eric is standing at the coffee bar, I can't help but admire his looks. His tousled blond hair and dreamy, baby blue eyes are the perfect match for his boyish good looks and beaming smile. He has the kind of face that puts you at ease with a smile, which helps with his profession, not to mention that he's a brilliant doctor. Wearing his smart blue trousers and short-sleeved white shirt, he has most of the ladies in the shop admiring him, not that he seems to notice.

I think back over our friendship. We work well together, and outside of work we've hung out a couple of times, always with Tori present. But if I'm honest, I have always pushed away any of his attempts to take our friendship further. Part of this is because he's human, but I can't keep hiding behind this excuse anymore, especially if what I suspect about him is true. He knows too much about the supernatural—he must have known a shifter, perhaps dated one. His past comments and actions over the last year are starting to make more sense now. At the hospital, when the patient came in with the carving on his back, he knew when to get me out of the room before I lost control. But the real reason is because he wouldn't just be a one-night stand. I can see a future with Eric and that terrifies me. I also know he would want more from me than a 'friends with benefits' arrangement. So I've kept him at arm's length.

I pull myself out of my thoughts as I see Eric walking back over to our table, a coffee in one hand, and a plate with an iced doughnut in the other. Eric sits with a sweet smile, but my attention is on the doughnut. His amused chuckle drags my eyes off the doughnut, reluctantly, to his smiling face. He pushes the plate towards me.

"This is for you," he tells me, his eyebrows raising as I immediately reach forward, shoving the heavenly cake into my mouth.

I've already eaten half of it before I smile at him, pretty sure there's icing on my face, but I don't care.

"You shouldn't have, I'm trying to watch my figure," I joke as I inhale the rest of the doughnut. I'm licking the icing off my fingers when I see he looks nervous. "Man, it must be bad news if you're buying me doughnuts," I say in a teasing voice, trying to ease some of the tension from his shoulders.

He laughs at my comment but doesn't relax at all. Instead, he looks even tenser. Shit. My comment must have hit a mark. What on earth is he going to tell me?

"Ari, how are you? You haven't been at work. Where are you staying at the moment?" he asks in a rush.

Whoa, question overload. I raise my eyebrows at him and take a sip of my coffee as I digest his questions.

"I'm fine, I just needed some time off work. I'm staying with a friend. Anyway, how did you know I wasn't staying at the apartment?" I ask, starting to get frustrated. Since when did this become an interrogation?

"I stopped by the apartment a couple of times and knew you weren't there," he tells me, looking down into his coffee cup, distracted.

I put my coffee cup down and stare at him, not sure I'm hearing him right.

"You stopped by the apartment?" I ask. Also, what did he mean by saying he knew I wasn't there?

"Well, since that guy keeps turning up at your apartment, I wanted to check that everything was okay," he continues.

At this point, I don't think he is fully aware of what he is saying or the hole he's digging. I've never seen Eric like this. He's usually so calm and composed, but here he is, rambling and unable to meet my eyes.

"Eric, what the hell are you on about? What's going on?" I've had enough. I want answers and I want them now. He grimaces, and I feel my frustration ease. Leaning forward, I place my hand on his. I don't like seeing him like this. I may have been keeping my distance, but we're still friends. I think.

Eric looks at my hand on his and his face turns into a grimace once again. I'm starting to think it's me and go to pull my hand away until he grabs it with his other hand, holding mine in place.

"Ari, you're in danger."

I go still at his words, running my eyes over the man in front of me. My inner wolf comes to attention, assessing the situation for the supposed danger, and my senses go into hyperdrive. I look around the coffee bar, trying to discreetly sniff the air for any potential threat. I can't smell anything unusual. In fact, the only thing that I can really smell is Eric. Okay, I know that sounds weird, but he has always smelled interesting to me, sweet and rich like honey, different from any other scent I have smelled before.

"What do you mean I'm in danger?" I ask, keeping my tone of voice low, although it doesn't hide the slight growl that slips from me.

Eric looks at me, and I'm hit with the full force of his stunning blue eyes, but even those aren't enough to distract me today.

"I've been hearing things. I have...friends. People are after you.

Dangerous people. I think you should lay low for a bit," he tells me earnestly, his grip on my hand tightening a bit as he leans towards me. "I have a safe house, you could come and stay with me. I'll look after you."

I pull my hand away and look at him incredulously. Is this guy serious?

"What is it with people asking me to move in with them today?" I rant, well and truly fed up. "And what do you mean you've been hearing things? Who are these friends? How do you know all this stuff?" I am practically spitting this at him as I try to keep my voice low, my anger making my words clipped and harsh.

My wolf doesn't like this. She wants me to fight or run and is pushing for control. I shove her back. I can handle this. I am in control here.

"Ari, I know what you are. I know you're a werewolf."

And with that little bombshell one of the baristas comes over to the table to ask if we have everything we need, flirting to the max with Eric. Ever the gentleman, he's politely trying to get her to leave, his eyes only leaving mine for a few seconds before darting back. Normally, I would find this amusing, but not today. I snap my head towards the simpering woman and narrow my eyes.

"We're fine. Thanks," I bite out.

She raises her eyebrows at me, and with another look at Eric, she leaves the table. She probably thinks I'm a jealous raging bitch, but I really don't care. I have bigger fish to fry.

"Explain," I order, not in the mood for this run around anymore.

Eric sighs, running his hand through his neat hair, messing it up in a way I've not seen before. It suits him. *Focus, Ari, now is not the time.*

"I've been part of the supernatural world all my life, so I know what you are. I know you're a lone wolf and you live with a witch—who has great protection on your apartment, by the way. I've been hearing some things that worry me. Things about you. I don't know what you've done, but you have pissed off some pretty nasty people," he explains.

I lean back in my chair and think over what he is saying. Is he guarding his words because of where we are, or because he's hiding something? He's telling the truth, that much I can tell, but he isn't telling the whole truth.

"Shadow Pack?" I ask. It has to be, but I need to know for sure.

He nods his head, his eyes worried. Dread fills my stomach. They really have come for me.

"They are my former pack, back in England," I mumble, and understanding fills his eyes.

"The patient that came in the other night with the symbol..." He pauses but doesn't need to explain anything further, we both remember only too well. "Was that Shadow Pack?" he finally asks, and I just nod. Guilt fills me that this was done to an innocent because they were sending me a message. The brutality of it was just a hint at how far they could go.

"It's not just Shadow Pack. You've also started to attract some other attention. There are some dangerous people in this city. Let me help you, Ari, please."

I rub my hand across my face, thinking through everything I've learned. Something about what Eric said is bugging me, but I can't think why. Wearily, I take a sip from my coffee, hoping the caffeine will give me inspiration. He seems to know too much for a human. Even if he has been brought up by supernaturals, no one would tell a human this sort of thing, unless he was dating someone who knew this information.

Unless he was a supernatural. Son of a bitch.

A deadly calm fills me. I place my coffee cup back down on the table gently and look up at the lying, traitorous man I started to call a friend. He can see it in my eyes, and he has the decency to look nervous.

"Ari, I—"

"What are you?" I demand, not giving him the chance to finish whatever his excuse was going to be.

"Ari, I'm human, I just know—" I cut him off again, anger practically vibrating through my body as my hands start to shake.

"Do not lie to me," I snarl, my fury wild and difficult to contain, and I realise why he picked a public place to meet me. I force myself to calm down. "What. Are. You?"

He isn't going to answer. I can see it in the way he is looking at me. Well, I'm done. I push away from the table, my cup spilling in the process, covering the table in leftover coffee. I am halfway across the shop when he calls my name.

"Ari. Wait. I'm sorry, I'll tell you," he calls, his voice sounding tired and defeated.

I let him sweat it out for a moment before nodding and walking back to my seat. I try to keep my distance. Eric has broken my trust, and it will take time for him to earn it again.

"I'll listen, but you have to tell me the truth," I tell him, and my heart hurts a little at his expression. Like I have promised to give him all his hopes and dreams.

"I don't know how to do this," he admits, and I understand that. If I suddenly had to admit I was Shadowborn, I wouldn't know how to do it either. When you've been hiding something for so long, it's difficult to break that habit. Doesn't mean I forgive him though. I stay quiet as he's working through what he wants to say.

"There isn't really a name for what I am, but the closest thing is an incubus," he finally tells me, not meeting my eyes, his voice barely above a whisper.

"Wait. Isn't an incubus a sex demon?" I ask. I've never met one before. In fact, I didn't think they really existed. I've only ever heard stories about them. Suddenly, I'm glad I didn't let my hormones get the better of me. He grimaces and shakes his head.

"No. Well, some are. Not me." He sighs, running his hands through his hair again. "I feed off energy like an incubus, but I feed off pain."

Shock fills me. He feeds off pain...

"How does that work? Where do you feed?" I ask, a sinking feeling filling my stomach. My suspicions are confirmed when he looks up at me guiltily.

"Where is the place where people feel the most pain?" he questions as disgust fills me. "I only feed a little off each person, not enough for them to feel anything but slightly tired. I only feed deeper off those who are already dying."

I feel like I'm going to vomit. Anger fills me at the thought of him feeding off my patients.

"You are a doctor. You signed a Hippocratic oath to 'do no harm.' How could you?" I demand, staring at him like I've never seen him before.

It is the ultimate betrayal of trust to harm a patient. I don't care what he says about only taking a little of their energy. He has done so without gaining consent, which in my mind is assault. Those patients come to the hospital and place their trust in us to care for them. The idea that a being who can feed off of pain has been working in the hospital fills me with anger and disgust. The fact that it's Eric makes this all the harder.

"Wait, how did I not know you were anything other than human? Even Tori thought you were human," I ask, confused. Not much slips by Tori.

Eric sits silently, looking pained as I speak.

"I'm very old, I can hide my presence."

I blink at him. For him to be able to do that he must be *old*, like five hundred years plus.

"Ari, I don't hurt anyone. Besides, I have to feed to live. Many of my kind like inflicting pain on humans and then feeding off it. I would *never* do that. I work as a doctor because I want to help people, not because I can feed off them. It just has the added benefit..." He trails off at my expression.

"I have to go," I say, as I pick up my bag, pushing my seat back.

"Ari, please don't go."

I stand with a sigh. Why are things never easy?

"Eric, I have somewhere I have to be. Besides, I can't be around you right now. I need to think. You lied to me, but worse, you put patients in danger. I'm not sure I can forgive that," I tell him honestly.

He nods, looking resigned, almost like he expected my response.

"I understand that. Just, stay safe, okay?"

I don't answer him, just give him a slight nod before walking out of the coffee shop. I don't look back at him. I just walk to my car and begin the journey back to the pack compound.

Chapter Thirteen

I park my car behind one of the main buildings at the pack compound. I place my head on the steering wheel and close my eyes. I just need a moment to myself to think through everything I've learned.

Eric is an incubus. A fucking pain-eating parasite who has been feeding off my patients. I should have known. Maybe I could have done something. I sigh with frustration. What could I have done? Told my boss? I would have been thrown into the psych ward before you could say werewolf.

My silent breakdown is interrupted by a loud bang on my car. Jerking up, I glance around for the cause of the noise. There, standing at the bonnet of my car, is a very pissed off looking Killian. Arms crossed, he looks like he's about to burst out of his shirt with a flex his muscles. His scowl makes his features look harsh, especially with the scar that runs down the side of his face. He strides to the side of my car and yanks open the door.

"Glad to see you got your lazy ass back here," he spits out, glaring at me with enough hatred that I wonder what I've done to personally offend him so much. "Training room, ten minutes," he orders, before turning on his heel and striding away from me. Nope, I think he is just a dick.

I was planning to go back to the medical wing, look over the supplies, and try to get my head around how things are run here, but I guess that's not going to happen now. I haul myself out of the car and walk towards where I think I remember the training room is.

"Again!" Killian barks at me for what feels like the thousandth time this afternoon.

I growl under my breath as I pick myself up off the mat where I had been thrown, brushing down my leggings in the process. *Stay calm, Ari. Patience is a virtue.* Or so I keep reminding myself. I would say I'm a pretty patient person—my job makes that a necessity. However, Killian seems to be an expert in pushing my buttons. Walking around me in a circle, with that look on his face, he looks like he has just stepped in something unpleasant rather than being in the middle of training me.

First, he had me running laps around the compound until I fell to my knees feeling like I was going to throw up, shouting insults at me all the way around. After that he had me boxing and weight training. He's been in a foul mood all afternoon, but he seems to have cheered up a bit. Unfortunately for me, this is because we are fight training, which means he gets to throw me around.

"I've never seen a more lazy and out of shape wolf in all my life," he tells me, disdain dripping from his words.

I try not to let him get me angry. At the challenge he helped me, encouraged me. Sure, he did it by insulting me, but he helped more than anyone else did. Being alpha of another pack meant that he didn't have to follow quite the same rules as everyone else. I hoped after the fight that he would have thawed out a bit, after all, we're similar, and neither of us belong here. However, I find myself disappointed. He's treating me with as much disdain as when he first met me. Sure, he seems to be rude to everyone, but he seems to have taken a particular dislike to me.

I face him again, dropping into a defensive stance. He has been trying to teach me basic self-defence. As it turns out, I'm useless in close combat, as Killian has delighted in telling me all afternoon. He walks up behind me and wraps his arms around me in a bear hug. I drop my weight and try to kick my foot back around his leg as instructed. In theory, I should be able to use his weight against him and throw him to the ground. In practice, I can't get him to go down.

"Twist your upper body more. You haven't hooked your leg properly," he scolds, his mouth close to my ear. I can feel his breath against my skin, and it distracts me.

He growls and shifts his weight. He moves his hands, and before I know it, I am thrown across his body and I land on the mat with a thud.

"Useless! Why the fuck should I bother teaching you?" he shouts at me, twisting his body so I'm pinned to the floor. "Fight me! Get up!"

I struggle in my position on the floor, but he's too heavy, and I can't get out of his grip. I try to kick him, but he pins my legs down with his.

"Pathetic," he scolds, lowering his face towards mine. His eyes have shifted so I'm staring at his wolf. I can feel his alpha power rising, pushing against my own. His voice has lowered when he speaks again. "Pathetic," he repeats, but I stop seeing his face as I'm dragged into my memories.

"*Pathetic,*" *the voice sneers at me.*

From my position where I'm pinned to the floor, I can only see his face, and his dark eyes pierce me with his sick gaze as it rakes over my body. His eyes are so dark they're almost black. I'm too weak to fight back—months of being locked in the dark and being underfed will do that to you.

"Do as we say, and we'll let you rejoin the pack. You will get regular meals again. You can see the sun. And once you have proved your loyalty to Shadow Pack, we will start training you again."

I am still being punished for when I tried to escape nearly six months ago. Since then, I've been locked in the dark cell they call my room and only given enough food to keep me alive. The only time I have been permitted to leave is to see the alpha, like now. All these meetings go the same. I'm dragged before the alpha and the elders, and ordered to use my Shadowborn powers at their discretion. I refuse, and then get punished and dragged back to my 'room.' If I'm particularly unlucky, I will get brought to the alpha alone. Without the elders to hold him back, the punishments are always significantly worse.

Today is like the other days. The alpha is stalking around the back of the room, watching as his young beta, Terrance, pushes me around and 'teaches me my place.' I look up at Terrance and spit at him.

"Fuck. You," is the only response I give them.

My head snaps to one side as I'm backhanded for my comment. Terrance's hands move from my shoulders to my neck. My heart kicks into overdrive as my airway is cut off. I know he won't kill me —they need me—but that doesn't stop the panic as I can't catch my breath.

"Terrance," the alpha calls. Immediately the pressure from my throat is removed and I can breathe again. I lie on the floor, gasping, as Terrance walks towards the alpha. "Ariana, I have a different proposition for you."

I know I am in trouble since he's used my name. Usually I am just 'the Shadowborn' or 'girl.' I prop myself up on one elbow and look towards the alpha and the elders.

"Terrance has offered to mate with you. Now that you're nearly eighteen, you need to be mated. We can't have a female running around unmated. You will be given space and a small measure of freedom, food, and we will even begin your training again. I'm sure that under Terrance's...guidance, you will become a valuable member of our pack."

I feel the blood draining from my face as he speaks. I think my life is bad now, but under Terrance's 'guidance,' it would be ten times worse. Guidance my ass. I would be under his control, and that's what they want. At the moment he can't be alone in a room with me, because of what I am and pack rules. As soon as we are mated, there will be nothing to stop him from doing whatever he wants. What I don't understand is why they're asking.

"Never," I rasp out, my throat raw after the abuse it's just been put through.

The alpha's expression never changes, but I can see by the way his body stills that I have pissed him off. Terrance looks like he wants to strangle me again. The alpha nods at him, and with a sick smile he walks up to me, kicking my arm out from underneath me. I fall to the ground with a cry and he straddles me again, pushing me into the ground as his hands circle my neck. He leans down so his mouth is next to my ear.

"There is only one way out of this, Ariana. You will be mine," he whispers, his breath hot against my tender skin.

I realise now why they told me. They weren't asking. The alpha was warning me that things could get much worse if I didn't do as they said.

Hands tighten around my neck again and I gasp for breath, my vision starting to dim around the edges. A small part of me hopes Terrance will take it too far, that he will kill me in his anger.

"Pathetic."

"Ari!"

I can hear my name being shouted. Why are they so loud? My head is pounding.

"Ariana, snap out of it!" the angry voice continues, but I'm sure I hear a tinge of worry hidden behind the growl.

"What did you do to her?" a familiar voice shouts, although I'm not used to hearing him sound so mad. What's his name again? A gentle hand touches my arm, and a warm vanilla scent surrounds me. Seb. I feel my body relax a little. He won't let me get hurt. I don't know where that assumption came from, I've known him less than forty-eight hours, but somehow, I'm sure I'm right.

"We were practising some self-defence moves and she just went stiff in my arms. I let her go and she went limp, staring at the ceiling. Then her eyes closed, and she started shaking like she was scared. She kept whispering a name. It was like someone was hurting her," the voice continues, softer now as he explains. Killian, I realise, although I've not heard his voice so soft before. Sounds like he actually cares. Ha!

"She gets flashbacks. Something must have triggered her," Seb mutters as he gently lifts my upper body into his lap.

Cracking open my eyes slightly, I see a worried Seb looking down at me. A cute smile crosses his face when he sees me awake.

"Hey, beautiful," he says, which makes me smile.

I'm aware of movement down by my feet, and I glance down to see Killian staring at me, his eyes glowing as he fights his wolf, his hands balled into fists at his sides.

"Flashbacks. Like memories. You mean this happened—" He cuts himself off, a growl reverberating through his chest. He holds his arms open and gestures for Seb to pass me across to him.

Seb looks down at me and then back to the angry alpha.

"Give her to me," Killian growls, and I can feel the power in his words, but I also hear an undercurrent of something that sounds like concern in his voice. I must be hearing things.

Seb is try to fight against the order, but there is no use. Even I would struggle to fight an order from someone as powerful as Killian.

I'm passed over to Killian, where he cradles me in his arms. I would protest, but I'm too exhausted, my breathing still coming in rapid gasps. I find that I don't have the energy to care whose arms I'm in. We stay this way until Alex comes storming into the gym. Killian's face is set in a turbulent scowl as he holds me, like he's being forced to care for me, but the whole time he's been slowly stroking my back, trying to calm my frantic breathing. I even tried to get up once and was growled at so fiercely that I decided to stay where I was. I'm not even sure I would have been able to break out of his grip. Eventually, my breathing settles and I become mortified at what's happened. Thank God no one else witnessed me having the flashback. It's bad enough that Killian saw it and the bastard felt compelled to comfort me. Face red, I try to sit up.

"Killian, I'm okay now. You can let me up," I tell him.

He just growls at me half-heartedly and tightens his grip.

"Bloody alpha male babies," I mutter under my breath, and smirk as he hears me and bares his teeth at me.

To be honest, although I bitch and moan, I feel safe in his arms. His alpha power calls to mine and calms me. If we didn't drive each other crazy, we would probably make a good match. Maybe in a different world that would work.

"What happened?" Alex demands, storming into the room, and I fight back my groan. I can hear anger and frustration in his tone. I'm not surprised. I have been nothing but trouble since I got here.

"She had a flashback, and now Mr. Macho Alpha over here won't let her go," Seb informs Alex, not worried about the backlash from Killian now that Alex is here.

Killian growls at both men as they try to get closer, sounding more wolf than man. His stance changes as he tries to put himself between Alex and me while still keeping me in his lap. I glance up at him and see his eyes have turned fully wolf. What the hell is going on?

"Killian, let go of Ari, I'm here now," Alex comments, and he comes closer.

What is it with these guys wanting to hold me? I am perfectly capable of getting up and walking, I'm not bloody injured. It's embarrassing enough having a flashback without it setting off their protective instincts.

Werewolves are naturally very protective of their pack and those they consider family, but I've literally just walked into their pack. Besides, Killian isn't part of this pack either, so I don't understand where his protective behaviour is coming from. Seb seems to be behaving himself, but as one of the 'lower' pack members, those instincts won't be as strong. His feelings towards me are his own, not some wolfy bullshit. The stronger the wolf, the stronger the instincts.

Killian growls louder at Alex, so fiercely that it causes the beta to stop in his tracks. He looks across at Seb, who also looks pale at this point. I thought it was from all this alpha power floating around in the air, but with the looks they are giving each other, I'm not so sure anymore.

"Mine," says a guttural voice from above me as arms tighten around me.

"Um, excuse me?" I retort, looking up at the alpha.

I hear Alex curse under his breath as he crouches down to our level like he's trying to tame a wolf cub during their first shift. What the hell does he mean by 'mine'?'

"Seb, go get Alpha Mortlock. And Isa. We may need their help," he instructs, not taking his eyes off Killian, as if he's afraid what he might do if his back is turned. "Ari, just stay still. I know this will be difficult, but try keep your mouth shut."

I'm just about to protest when the angry werewolf holding me snarls again. Alex spreads his arms wide in a placating gesture.

"Killian, I'm not going to hurt her, but you need to put Ari down."

I hear running footsteps and glance around to see Alpha Mortlock hurrying over, his eyes widening at what he is seeing.

"What happened?" he demands of Alex, who stands up and walks over to the alpha.

With their voices low, I can't hear much of what they are saying, only snippets. Seb is looking at me worriedly, but he smiles at me when he sees me looking at him, trying to comfort me as always. If anything, this makes me feel worse. Something is definitely wrong.

"Have they mated?" I hear Mortlock ask, which has me jerking in Killian's arms.

Fuck this.

"Mated?" I shout, ignoring the growl coming from Killian.

I jump up out of his hold, even though he tightens his grip on my arms to keep me close. That's going to bruise. Right now, all I care about is getting out of his arms. Killian comes towards me like he is going to grab me again, so I drop into a defensive position.

"Mine," he growls again.

I've had enough. I jump forward and punch him in the face, hard enough to make him take a step back. Stunned, he stares at me for a moment until I see his eyes start to turn back to normal. Hand on his jaw, he narrows his eyes at me, his hurt and anger clear to see before he glares at Alpha Mortlock and storms out of the room.

I spin around to look at the stunned males behind me.

"Will someone please explain what the fuck just happened?"

Chapter Fourteen

We're back in the family room of the main building. Alpha Mortlock and Lena sit on one of the leather sofas, the latter wringing her hands as she watches me pace up and down the room. Alex is in his usual place to the alpha's right, propping up the wall with arms crossed and a scowl across his face.

Isa walks into the room and heads straight towards me. With a hand on my shoulder, she takes me to the side, lowering her voice as she looks at me seriously.

"I hear you have problems with a man," she tells me in her thick German accent. "Would you like me to pummel him?" she asks sincerely.

I raise my eyebrows at her, struggling not to laugh at the gamma offering to beat up Killian. Now that is a fight I would pay to see. A warm feeling fills my chest, and I realise with a shock that it's the feeling of belonging. I look at the woman in front of me in bemusement. When did she start considering me as someone she would protect? Because that's exactly what she's offering by threatening to beat up Killian.

"Is Killian not part of the pack? Does he not get protection?" I query. Surely she's not being serious.

With a wink, she chuckles softly. "Men who think women

cannot look after themselves deserve being shown otherwise," she tells me conspiratorially.

I let out a stunned laugh. I like this woman.

"I'll keep that in mind, Isa. Thank you," I reply, and I hope she knows from my tone how much her comments mean to me.

Isa nods her head in acknowledgement and goes to take her spot behind the alpha. I resume my pacing until Seb walks in and wraps his arms around me. I go still at the sudden contact, but as soon as I smell his sweet scent and know it's him, I relax in his arms. I'm glad he's here, although I would have insisted had the alpha not invited him. I'm not sure when it happened, but Seb is part of my little family now.

"Ariana, please take a seat. We have a lot to discuss," Alpha Mortlock says, bringing my attention back to the room.

I give Seb a grateful smile and squeeze his arm affectionately as I pull out of his arms. Walking towards the other leather sofa, I sit down so I'm facing the alpha and his mate. I expected Seb to sit next to me, but I can't see him. Spinning in my seat, I see him standing by the door. I raise my eyebrows at him and gesture to the seat next to me. He widens his eyes at me and looks over to Alpha Mortlock like he's asking for permission. Mortlock nods and Seb comes and sits next to me with a smile. I struggle not to sigh at this show of pack politics. Just because Seb's not as strong as the others in the room does not mean that he should be standing on the sidelines. Sure, Mortlock is much more lenient than other alphas, from my limited experience, but this still frustrates me.

Mortlock looks around the room and clears his throat.

"Now that we're all here, we can get started," he announces. Guess that means Killian isn't part of this discussion.

I haven't seen him since he skulked off after the showdown in the gym. What the hell was all that about anyway? Anger, frustration, and a little bit of fear are all running through me, and I have to take a deep breath to calm myself.

"Ariana, how much do you know about mated pairs?" Alpha Mortlock asks me.

I feel the blood drain from my face and can feel all eyes in the room on me. I stand up, my fight-or-flight instinct kicking in. This cannot be happening. Especially not with an asshole like Killian. I'm planning my escape from this room for the second time in less than a week when someone takes my hand. Jerking my head down sharply, I see that it's Seb.

"Ari," someone calls, and I look across the room to see Alex walking towards me. "It's all right, let's work this out together." His voice is soft and rings with honesty. He's never spoken to me like this before.

I turn and focus on Seb's face. There's nothing there but worry for me. He nods and gently pulls at my hand to get me to sit again. I slowly sit back down, fighting my natural response to bail on situations like this.

"Mating is for life," I say, finally answering Mortlock's question. I don't know much, but I do know this.

The alpha nods his head in acknowledgement of my response, and my unspoken fact that I know next to nothing about the intricacies of pack life.

"Any shifters can choose to form a mating bond, but as you said, these are permanent and for life. These should not be rushed, and we don't see these often, as most shifters tend to use the human form of bonding and commit to marriage instead."

I nod to show my understanding, not quite sure how this relates to me.

"True mated pairs are a different ball game altogether. We don't see these often anymore, but a true mated pair is when two shifters are drawn to each other and are destined to be together. They are your perfect partner." Mortlock stops at this point and smiles at Lena, takes her hand, and places a kiss on the back of it. I can see the love the two of them share from here.

"The bond, once accepted, is also for life," he continues.

I latch onto this piece of information. I have a bad feeling about where this conversation is going.

"So the pair bond is not inevitable? You don't have to accept?" I ask, a note of desperation in my voice.

Mortlock sighs and looks back at me, shaking his head. "No, the bond has to be accepted by both shifters. It doesn't happen often, but there are records of rejected bonds. But once the bond has been triggered, it's very difficult to resist. If the bond is accepted, the shifters will have access to each other's power," he finishes.

"Okay, so why are we having this conversation?" I question a little bluntly. I know it's rude to talk to the alpha that way, but my nerves are making me feisty. A little part of my brain is screaming at me that I already know, that I just don't want to admit it, but I silence those thoughts.

Mortlock pauses, looking like he really doesn't want to be having this conversation.

"Killian is showing signs that you might be his true mate." I go still as he continues. "The overprotective behaviour, not letting another male close... It's all behaviour ingrained in us to make sure another male doesn't mate with our true mate. When the bond has been accepted, this will calm down. It never goes away, but it gets easier." He smiles at me in a way that says he understands. I'm sure he does, but I don't like that he keeps saying 'when,' like I'm just going to accept the bond.

"But I don't feel anything!" I practically shout. Surely if we were a mated pair I should be feeling this 'bond' as well.

Mortlock shoots me a look like he doesn't believe me. "You don't feel drawn to him in any way? Your powers don't call to each other?" He shakes his head slightly, not waiting for my answer. "Even if this was true, the bond often takes time to grow. Killian's was triggered at the thought of others hurting you."

I run my hands through my hair, trying to take in the overload of information.

"So why isn't Killian here? Why is it just me having this

lesson?" I inquire. Where is that bastard anyway?

Mortlock sighs and looks at Lena as if searching for strength.

"Killian is having a difficult time accepting all of this." I'm about to protest at this comment when he continues. "He had a mate before. Julie. They loved each other and decided to take the mating bond. He was alpha of another pack..." Alpha Mortlock pauses and runs his hand over his face, his tone weary. "He made a bad decision, and there was an attack on his pack. Everyone died, including Julie, and the bond was broken. I've never experienced it, but I'm told it's like a piece of your body is ripped open and the wound never heals. For him to now find he has a pair bond...well, I can't imagine all the thoughts running through his head right now. Just give him time." His voice is rough as he talks.

A lot more of his behaviour makes sense now, and I definitely understand his attitude. I can't imagine the pain of losing someone you are bonded to. Even my shrivelled, broken heart can understand the heartbreak of losing someone like that. If I lost Tori, Garett, or even Seb, I think I would break. Then to find that he has a true mate as well, it would be like rubbing salt into his wounds. Fate is cruel.

"So what happens next?" I ask, a little subdued from the turn of conversation.

Alpha Mortlock shrugs, and a slight smile graces his lips.

"That is up to you, like I said. You don't *have* to accept the bond. I would suggest that you don't rush anything, either way."

I nod at his sage advice. It may be my first instinct to push the idea of a bond away and flee immediately, but perhaps it's time to stop running. I'm still not accepting the bond, but I'm starting to feel like I might be a part of something here in the pack, and I find I'm reluctant to leave it before I've even properly started.

"So when can I start in the medical wing? I'm beginning to feel twitchy not being at work," I say with a small smile, focusing on the familiar rather than the unknown, pushing all thoughts of mates to the back of my mind.

I expected the alpha to smile, but instead, he looks weary, rubbing a hand over his face. Lena leans across and takes his hand, stroking it to comfort the alpha. The image makes me smile, the large alpha receiving comfort from his small female mate. Equals.

"I was hoping you could start immediately. I was coming to find you when Seb came to get me. One of the pups is very unwell. She developed a fever, and we thought it would pass, but she's taken a turn for the worse," Mortlock explains.

I jump to my feet, the need to see this child increasing as he speaks. I feel guilty that I've kept a child who needs my help waiting because of my freak out with Killian.

"What are we waiting for? Let's go."

I brush hair from the little girl's forehead. She has a fever of 39C, or 102.2 Fahrenheit as it is here—I still can't get used to that. I look down at the sick child. Lottie, her parents told me her name was. She is a little younger than Jessica, only six years old. Her mother hasn't left her side since I arrived, holding her hand and talking to her the whole time. It's dark outside now, but I'm not sure what the time is. I've learned a lot about Lottie in that time. She likes to climb trees and wrestle with the other children. She often gets into trouble for getting into fights when sticking up for the smaller wolves. She's going to be strong when she grows up.

Alpha Mortlock took me straight to her after a quick trip to the medical building for some supplies. Seb has been running things back and forth to the medical building for me, since she's too unwell to move and a human hospital is not the place for her. When the alpha came to check on how things were going, I pulled him aside and told him he needed to get a doctor here. I can't be here twenty-four seven, and if someone else becomes unwell, I would struggle to spread myself between my patients. I also need a doctor, as nurses can't give medications that aren't prescribed, and I don't want to lose my licence. In an emergency, I can give fluids, which is what I did, but there is a limit to what I can do. The alpha reluctantly agreed with me and managed to borrow a doctor from a local pack who came over and prescribed some IV antibiotics. Lottie's mother broke down at seeing her little girl hooked up to machines, but I explained that she had a severe infection and this would hopefully allow her to heal quicker.

The doctor left a couple of hours ago, and Lottie's condition has stabilised enough that we can move her to the medical building. Her temperature has lowered now, and she's even woken up enough to complain that she's hungry. A nurse from another pack attended with the doctor and agreed to stay the night to keep an eye on the little girl.

I hear the door open and look over my shoulder to see Alex. I look across to the other nurse, who nods at me, letting me know she's got this. I leave the little girl's side and walk over to Alex.

"How is she?" he asks quietly, glancing over at Lottie.

The pack is struggling with one of their pups being so unwell, being fiercely protective of their young.

"She's stabilised now. She'll be running around causing havoc again before you know it," I tell him with a tired smile.

"When was the last time you took a break?" Alex asks with a frown.

I shrug. I've lost track of the hours. I yawn as I pull my phone from my back pocket, surprised to see it's ten o'clock in the evening. I see a text from Tori telling me she'd seen my message that I'm not going home tonight. When I saw how poorly Lottie was, I decided it would be best for me to stay onsite. It's been a long day. Alex gently puts his hand on my arm and starts to pull me towards the door.

"Come on, come with me," he instructs softly. I look over my shoulder at the little girl and her mum, not wanting to leave them. "Nurse Beth has everything under control. Besides, there's a rotation to keep an eye on things. One of us will be here constantly."

I frown at him. "You didn't do that when I was looking after her," I comment.

"While we trust the alpha's word that Nurse Beth can be trusted, we take looking after our young very seriously and aren't going to risk that. We trust you," he says simply. That warm feeling in my heart heats again, and I have to look away from the expression in his eyes, not quite ready to acknowledge what I can see in them. I glance over at Lottie, and Beth smiles at me.

"Don't worry, Ari, I'll watch her," she assures me, and I can hear the sincerity in her words.

I smile at her and cast one last look towards Lottie before turning back to follow Alex.

"Ari, wait!" a voice calls.

I turn to see Lottie's mother, Mary, just before she wraps her arms around me, hugging me tightly. I startle slightly at the sudden contact, but I relax and hug her in return. We don't say anything, we don't need to, her gratitude shines through her eyes. She squeezes my hand before going back to her daughter's side.

I look back at Alex who's smiling at me. "What?" I ask him, raising an eyebrow in question.

"Nothing. Come on," he tells me, taking my hand in his as he leads me from the room.

I'm so shocked he's holding my hand that I don't think to ask where we're going. I debate pulling my hand away, but it feels nice. I pull a face at that thought. Since when have I gone from groaning when I see Alex to liking the feel of his hand in mine? I pull my hand away. Spending all this time with the pack is making me soft. I expect Alex to say something about the space now between us, but instead, he smiles his understanding. It's unnerving.

"Where are we going anyway?" I inquire, as I notice we are walking towards the woods.

He grins, and this worries me. No good can come from a smile like that.

"We're going for a run. It's time to shift."

Chapter Fifteen

I'm leaning against a tree with my arms crossed, pretending that the sight of Alex shirtless in front of me isn't affecting me at all. My wolf, on the other hand, has no qualms about letting him know she likes what she sees, pushing against me for control.

"Remind me again why we're doing this?" I ask, trying, and failing, to keep my eyes on his face and off his toned body.

"Because you need to learn to shift properly so you can control your wolf better. She's constantly pushing for control because you suppress her. She *is* you, yet you seem so disconnected," he explains. "Besides, we'll be having a pack run soon, and you'll be expected to take part. I thought you could use the practice." I'm about to argue at his statement, but he just raises his eyebrows. "Watching you shift at the social was painful. Do you really want to go through that process again?" he points out.

Fine. He isn't wrong. Besides, the thought of having to shift in front of the whole pack, again, makes my blood run cold. Maybe I do need the practice. Wait, what does he mean watching me shift was painful? I didn't see him there at the challenge, and everyone turned their backs. Sneaky bastard.

Sighing, I move away from the tree and start removing my

clothes, turning slightly so I'm not facing Alex full on. Out the corner of my eye, I can see Alex doing the same.

"So why isn't Seb or someone doing this with me?" I query. I still don't feel fully comfortable around Alex yet, although he is growing on me. *Like mould,* I think dryly.

"Your wolf is so suppressed, I wasn't sure if Seb could handle you if you turned on him. I didn't think you would want to risk that," he tells me, and I agree with him.

I'd never forgive myself if I hurt Seb. Not that I ever would, but Alex is right. I can't always control my wolf, especially once I've shifted. I hadn't thought about the possibility that I could hurt Seb. In my old pack, I was only ever surrounded by powerful wolves, as they never risked putting me with the weaker wolves in case I escaped.

I push down my jeans and underwear, bending slightly to take my feet out of the legs. I can feel Alex's hot gaze on me, and it does things to me that I would rather not acknowledge. I straighten up and look him in the eye, so I see the moment he senses my arousal when his eyes flash, his wolf making his feelings clear.

"Are we doing this or what?" I ask, trying to ignore the predatory look on his face.

I see him struggling to take his eyes off me as he nods.

"Okay—" He stops to clear his throat, which makes me smirk. "Okay, shift, show me how you do it," he orders.

I roll my eyes at the order and kneel on the ground. I close my eyes and go to the place where my wolf resides inside me. I coax her forward, and she rushes to take control. The shift hits me hard, making me fall to all fours. I grunt at the effort of it, my body screaming out as the shift takes over. I'm aware of Alex moving to my side, kneeling next to me.

"You're fighting her, like she's a separate part of you. Welcome her. You are one," he tells me softly, encouraging the change.

I try to focus on his words, and after what feels like a lifetime, the pain ends and I open my eyes again.

I raise my muzzle and look around me, jumping back in shock that a human man is crouched next to me. I leap into a defensive position, baring my fangs in warning. He puts his hands out to the side. I don't think he means me harm.

"Easy, Ari. I'm not going to hurt you. You know me," the human tells me.

Ari's the human who shares my body, and I can tell something is different. She's given me more control this time. Usually, she's controlling my actions and my thoughts. It's exhausting. I sniff the air and realise the human is right, I do recognise his scent. Alex. I sit on my hindquarters and watch him, my head tilted to one side.

"All right, all right." He laughs at me before getting onto his hand and knees.

I watch as he changes to a large black wolf with white dotted up his front legs and the tips of his ears. He makes it look effortless. I hope human Ari is paying attention. That is what we could have if she stopped fighting me. Wolf-Alex turns his large head to look at me, and a playful gleam enters his gaze. Giving me a wolfy grin, he shifts his weight, and I know he's going to pounce on me. I shift into a defensive position before darting to the side of him just as he leaps towards me. I race off deeper into the woods, aware of him on my tail.

This goes on for a couple of hours, chasing each other and playing. This is nice. Other than shifting with bear-Garett, we don't play in this form, and never with another wolf before. Our pack was cruel, especially in this form. I stop for a drink at a small stream, drinking my fill after running around. Wolf-Alex is doing the same next to me. All of a sudden, he jumps me from the side, play biting at my ears. I growl, but softly, so he knows I'm playing. He has me pinned to the ground, and I can see when something changes in his eyes. Human-Ari and I are so shocked by what we see that human-Ari gains the upper hand and shifts.

The shift back to human is quick, and I find myself still pinned under Alex's wolf. He winks at me in a very un-wolflike manner before shifting back to his human form. I groan as his full weight falls on me, and I am about to complain until I see his look of arousal, which has me stilling. So I can see what he is doing, he moves towards me slowly, lowering his lips until they are an inch from mine. I blame the adrenaline from the shift for what happens next.

I surge forward from my position on the ground and crush my lips to his. With a masculine groan he returns my kiss, rough and urgent, like he's wanted to do this for a long time. My hands go up to his head, twisting into his shoulder-length hair. His hands roam along my body, and I can feel his arousal pressed against my leg. I hear a howl in the distance, and I'm startled away from him. What am I doing?

I push him away, our breathing heavy as we try to untangle our limbs. I climb up from the ground, looking anywhere but at the evidence of his arousal, and start searching for where we left our clothes.

"Are we going to talk about this?" Alex asks from the ground, propped up on one arm. His tone sounds resigned, like he already knows my answer.

"Nothing to talk about," I tell him, forcing my voice to sound cheery.

I thank the gods when I find my clothes, hurrying into them, and I throw Alex's towards him.

"Put some pants on. You're distracting," I say, trying to make my tone teasing.

I hear him sigh before the telltale sound of someone getting changed reaches my ears. I make sure I'm facing the opposite direction, uncertain if I can stop myself from touching him if I see him naked again.

"Bye then. Thanks!" I call out before I hurry off towards the medical building, frustration and shame chasing at my heels.

I don't sleep well that night. My thoughts are running riot through my head, along with worry for Lottie. I stopped by the room she was staying in to check on her and found her and her mother fast asleep. Nurse Beth informed me her temperature has dropped further, and she's responding well to treatment.

I kissed Garett *and* Alex today, not to mention Killian showing signs of having a true pair bond with me. And there was Seb... Now, this is why packs were messy. I don't want a relationship with *anyone*. Besides, Alex was probably just feeling high off our run and the kiss didn't mean anything. Killian certainly doesn't want anything to do with me. He couldn't get away from me fast enough once he'd snapped out of his protective daze.

I look in the mirror in the borrowed bedroom that I'm staying in and sigh at the grey circles under my eyes, proof of my restless night. I brush an invisible piece of lint off my white shirt and black jeans, pulling my hair up into a loose bun. I'm planning on spending the morning in the medical room, so I need to be dressed sensibly. It's strange not wearing scrubs.

Walking downstairs, I head to the treatment room where Lottie's staying and am greeted by an animated little girl talking a hundred words per minute. Lottie's mother comes over to me with a beaming smile on her face.

"She is so much better, thank you!" she says, her eyes wet with unshed tears.

I smile, pleased to see Lottie has responded so well to treatment. I take her vitals and am happy to see they are all normal. I turn back to Mary.

"She can probably go back to your cabin today, but she will still need antibiotics. One more via IV, which I'll give now, and the rest can be taken orally." I turn to look at Lottie and put my stern face on. "But you can only go if you promise to rest up for a few days, deal?" I ask, knowing what her reaction would be.

She frowns as she thinks over her options before she nods and gives me a smile.

"Okay, I promise!" she replies happily.

I go to prepare the last dose of IV antibiotics and get a handover from Nurse Beth. She's going back to her pack tonight, so I want to know any details that might be important once she's gone.

Two hours later, I'm cleaning the treatment room now that Lottie's gone home. I was given a list of home visits that will need to be done at some point either today or tomorrow. Mostly older wolves or younger children, just to check in on them. I have one pregnant wolf to visit as well. I'm just getting a bag of equipment ready to go out on my visits when I hear the door open again.

"One second!" I call out, as I finish wiping down the desk.

I look up and am surprised to see Garett standing in the doorway with an odd look on his face.

"Garett!" I say, ridiculously happy to see him.

I walk straight up to him and take him by surprise by wrapping my arms around him. He lets out a shocked grunt and wraps his arms around me in return.

"How come you're here?" I ask, pulling back from his chest to look up at his face.

"Tori told me that you were staying here last night, and I wanted to make sure you were okay. I bumped into Sebastian, though, and he told me about Killian." Frowning, he scans my face. "Were you going to tell me about him?" Garett inquires, his voice getting louder as his frustration rises, his hands at his sides as he tries to stay calm.

I sigh and gesture for him to follow me, walking out of the treatment room and upstairs to the room I've been staying in. I let him walk in before I do and shut the door behind me.

"So that's it then? You bonded with him? Your 'true mate.'" He practically spits the last words at me, his body shaking with rage. What's happened to my kind, sweet Garett?

He strides forward and wraps his arms around me. I'm confused by his change of attitude until I hear him inhale and I realise he isn't hugging me.

"Did you just sniff me?" I shout, pushing him away from me. "Do you even know me, Garett? Of course I haven't bonded with him." I feel sick with my anger as I glare at my friend. "In fact, I nearly knocked him out when he tried that macho alpha bullshit on me!"

I'm fuming as I pace up and down the room, trying to cool my temper. I can't believe Garett thinks I would just accept a mating bond with someone at the snap of their fingers. Or that he would sniff me to see if my scent has changed through bonding or sex. Was my word not good enough? He's never treated me this way before, it's one of the reasons I love spending time with him. He's safe and doesn't impose shifter bullshit on me, at least, he didn't until today.

"Why does this even matter to you?" I shout, my anger at him for not trusting me making my words harsh.

"Because I love you!" he roars.

I stare at him, frozen in place at his admission. My mouth drops open, but I have no idea how to respond.

"Wh—I... Huh?" I stammer, eyes wide.

I can see the moment he realises he's made a mistake and rapidly tries to calm himself down. He knows I have a tendency to run after dramatic declarations or when I can't deal with my emotions.

"Ari, wait," he says, hurrying towards me, even though I haven't moved.

I don't think anyone has ever loved me before. The love that

Tori and I have for each other is different, and even that took me a while to understand. But a love like what Garett is proposing is something I never thought I'd get to experience. Never thought I'd want to experience.

He backs me up against the wall and places his hand gently on my cheek.

"Ever since I saw you, when you first came into my bar, I knew. You were so tiny, and you had this hollow look in your eyes like you couldn't trust anyone. Then when you were around Tori, you smiled, and I knew I was doomed." His thumb strokes my cheek, his eyes scanning my face for a reaction. "I tried to tell myself you needed a friend, and as you grew into the person you are now, I could see the fire in you, the passion to do good and not to let your past hold you back." I find myself watching his lips as he speaks.

No one has ever said things like this to me, and I know he is telling the truth. Garett has always been there for me. A protector, a friend, and now, if I let him, a lover. He loves me. The fractured, broken me. I don't know if I'm capable of loving someone in that way.

I can feel him watching me, and I flick my eyes up to his. He looks hungry.

"Fuck it," he says under his breath, and leans forward to press his lips to mine.

It's like a dam breaks, and I push forward, deepening the kiss as I wrap my arms around him. His lips match my greedy kisses, pressing me back into the wall, reminding me of our kiss yesterday. His mouth leaves mine and kisses a trail along my jaw and down my neck. His hands slide up my shirt and roam up to my breasts, his fingers gently tweaking my nipples. I moan and press myself against him, gasping as I feel his cock straining against his trousers. I slide my hand inside the front of his tight jeans and grab onto his cock, his breath coming out half gasp, half groan. I run my hand up and down and enjoy the contrast between the velvety softness of his skin on the solid hardness of his arousal, especially when he calls out my name like a prayer. I thread my other hand through his hair and pull his head back from where he is still kissing my neck. His neck arches, and I can see he's getting off on the pain from me pulling his hair—kinky. With an evil smile, I pull his lips to mine, enjoying the feeling of his cock twitching in my other hand.

"Bed. Now," I order, my wolf adding our power to the command in agreement.

I feel a brief shock of surprise at her approval. Garett is a bear shifter, after all, and while it still happens, interbreeding is frowned upon. I push these thoughts away as Garett lifts me up. I wrap my legs around his waist as he carries me over to the bed. With me in this position, my intimate parts are pressed up against his cock, and I wiggle my hips as he walks, savouring the masculine groan that passes his lips. He drops me down, and I pull myself up the bed.

Pulling his shirt over his head, Garett drops it to the floor and pins me in place with his eyes. Climbing onto the bed, he crawls towards me, a slight predatory growl emitting from deep in his chest. I admire his thick muscles and the way they bunch as he moves. I run my hands over him as he reaches me, only for him to pin me down. I wrap my legs around his waist and twist us so I'm on top. His eyes burn with desire as I straddle him, moving my hips as I feel him straining against his trousers.

"Too many clothes," he comments, his voice deep with passion.

I give him a wink and crawl off him, standing to remove my jeans and underwear. I turn away from him as I do this so he gets a view of my ass as I bend over. Spinning back towards him, I see that he's now naked, his clothes in a forgotten pile on the floor. His cock stands proudly, his hand wrapped around it as he strokes it leisurely with an adoring look on his face. I stalk towards him, slowly unbuttoning my shirt as I go. I reach up behind my shirt and remove my strapless bra, leaving the top in place, unbuttoned. Looking like a man starved, he reaches towards me, pulling me on top of him. Laughing, I push up onto my hands so I can look down at him. His pupils have dilated, and I can see his bear is close to the surface. He leans forward and kisses down my collarbone until he gets to my breasts, taking one of my nipples in his mouth while his other hand comes up to tweak the other. I throw my head back, a satisfied sigh leaving my lips. Desire shoots straight down to my core. Straddling him again, I feel his cock press against my inner thigh. His free hand strokes down my side and over my hip. When he finally reaches where I want him, I let out a moan, his thumb flicking over my clit in lazy circles. I run my hands over his strong shoulders and back, my nails dragging across his skin as his fingers slip inside me. I cry out as they fill me, my nails digging deeper into his skin as they start to pick up a rhythm. His breath catches as I move one of my hands to his cock, slowly pumping it with my hand as I rub my thumb over the top of him, enjoying the way his breath hisses out from behind clenched teeth.

"Ari," he warns me.

Rising up onto my knees, I guide him to my entrance, crying out as I sink down onto his cock, savouring the slight burn that comes from being filled completely. I hear him curse under his breath as one hand comes to my hip, the other cupping my cheek as he watches me. I start to rock my hips, my hands gripping his shoulders as I move. Moving his hand from my cheek to my clit, he starts circling it again, and I lose myself in the rhythm of our movements, all of which are controlled by me.

I tend not to sleep with more powerful shifters, as they are dominating, whereas I can take more control with weaker shifters. With Garett, I don't feel like I have to fight to be in control. He's just interested in making sure I receive pleasure—which means I get to set the pace.

I look at his face again and the look of pure desire has me crying out as my orgasm hits me. I feel myself clenching around him as he finds his own release. The feel of him coming inside me is almost enough to make me orgasm again. He pulls me towards him and kisses me, gently this time, as he runs his hands over my arms and back.

I climb off him, groaning slightly as he slides out of my body. Sex is messy. They always leave that bit out in the romance books. I go to leave, but Garett pulls me back onto the bed. I laugh as he climbs over me, kissing me in a way that makes me want to pin him to the bed and demand he fuck me again. But with a sigh, I roll out from underneath him. I have work to do. I stand up and throw a wink at Garett before scooping up my discarded underwear and heading to the bathroom, the ache between my thighs the telltale sign of good sex. I pull the door closed behind me to clean myself off.

Once I'm done, I pull my underwear back on and do up my bra, deciding to leave the shirt unbuttoned. I open up the bathroom door when I hear a loud slam. I spin to the source of the noise and see Killian in the doorway, a look of pure rage on his face as he takes in the scene before him. Looking like he's going to shed his skin and turn into his wolf, he takes a menacing step towards Garett, who's jumped off the bed and dropped into a fighting stance.

In a voice more wolf than human, Killian snarls, "What the fuck have you done to my mate?"

Anger instantly fills me, killing my buzz. Oh, for fuck's sake.

Chapter Sixteen

"Killian, what the fuck do you think you are doing?" I shout, completely pissed off and mortified that he has barged in on us.

At the sound of my voice, his head whips around to look at me, and then he seems to calm a little. He takes a step towards me, and I get a good look at him for the first time since yesterday. His eyes are wide and glowing, fully consumed by his wolf. His chest is heaving like he ran here, and from the state of his clothing, I think he has. He has bits of branches and undergrowth caught in his clothing like he's been hiding out in the woods, which, for all I know, he has been. Now that he's seen me, I can see the moment he gives into his instincts as he starts stalking towards me.

"Killian, stop," I order, my power filling the room with my frustration.

I shift my weight and my open shirt moves, grabbing his attention. His eyes narrow on my exposed skin, halting his movements. All of a sudden, I can feel his power rushing to meet me as he darts forward and pushes me up against the wall and buries his nose into the crook of my neck, growling as he does so.

"I can smell him on you." I can feel the vibrations of his

growling voice through my body from where he is pressed against me. A sick part of me is turned on by his behaviour.

The other part is just pissed off. I shove against his chest to push him away. To my dismay, he only moves back a couple of inches and looks like he's going to come closer again.

"Keep your hands off her." Garett's deep voice fills the room as he comes closer, his eyes flitting from me to Killian.

I appreciate Garett hanging back, allowing me to deal with this. He knows full well I can hold my own, and that I don't deal well with controlling behaviour. He also knows I will kick his ass if he comes swooping in to the rescue like a knight in fucking shining armour when I'm perfectly capable of whooping Killian's butt. Killian, on the other hand, has a different idea.

His head turns sharply to stare at Garett, his teeth fully exposed in a snarl, and I can see the tips of his canines have lengthened into fangs. Dropping into a fighting stance, he charges Garett, leaping towards him at the last second and shifting into wolf midair. The sound of ripping clothes and snarling animals fills the room as Garett shifts to protect himself.

Normally, I would say that a large bear shifter would beat a lone wolf shifter in most fights. However, Killian is huge. I have never seen a wolf so big before. The snow-white tips of his ears almost reach my shoulders. I briefly admire the fact that he is a fine specimen of wolf. I don't think I have ever seen a pure white wolf before. That admiration is quickly washed away by the fact he's being a possessive, idiotic dickhead. He's also more dangerous as he is caught up deep in his instincts to protect his 'true mate.'

I'm pulled from my musings as Garett roars in pain, my eyes zeroing in on the large claw marks that have cut him across his chest. This is ridiculous. I pull on my discarded jeans and quickly do up my shirt. Me walking around half naked is not going to help anything.

"Guys, knock it off!" I shout, trying to push some of my power into my voice.

They both ignore me and continue fighting. Garett is up on his two hind legs, swatting at the large wolf, trying to pounce when Killian gets too close. Killian has a couple of lacerations on him, but he is carrying on like he can't feel them. Perhaps he can't, given how worked up he is. Garett, however, lets out a pained roar as the wolf bites his front paw hard, causing the bear to retreat. Enough is enough.

I jump forward and try to put myself between Garett and Killian. Bad idea. Killian spins towards me, locked so deeply in the fight he doesn't realise it's me. He leaps towards me, teeth bared, and I know I'm about to get bitten. Garett roars again and swats me out of the way, taking the bite that was meant for me. The strength of Garett's push sends me flying into a chest of drawers. The pain running through my arm where I hit the furniture makes me want to cry out. Flashes of white fill my vision as the pain threatens to overwhelm me. I look at my arm to see it's bleeding, and a glimpse of protruding bone tells me I've broken it. I hiss out a curse and bind my arm with whatever I can grab of out of the chest of drawers. I know if I cry out, or if I stay for long and the boys scent my blood, it will distract them and make them sloppy. I don't want either of them to die today, so I need to do something about it. I'm also pretty sure I'm going to pass out soon, so I need to get help.

Gritting my teeth, I stand up and make my way to the door, trying to avoid the two ferocious shifters who are circling around the room. I exit and hurry down the stairs as quickly as my legs will carry me. I have to lean against the wall when I reach the bottom as the room begins to spin, my vision starting to blur. I look down and see I have left a trail of blood. Shit. They may be neck deep in fighting, but if Killian gets caught up in bloodlust, he will track me down. Pushing away from the wall, I stumble through the building, shoving the door open and running towards the main house. I can't see anyone around. Bloody typical. Usually I'm tripping over people, and now I can't find a single person when I need them. I continue to jog, my steps becoming more of a stumble as the main house comes into view.

"Ari!" a happy voice calls out.

I spin around and see Seb walking towards me with a large smile on his face, until he sees me cradling my arm and the state of my once white shirt. I'm sure I look a sight, and from Seb's horrified expression, my guess is correct.

"Ari! What happened?" he calls out as he runs towards me, catching me as I stumble forward.

"Get Alpha Mortlock! Killian and Garett have shifted and are fighting," I say, my words tumbling out in a hurry.

"Shit! Where are they?" he asks, frowning as he looks me over.

"My bedroom," I say, and I see a look cross his face.

Had the situation been different, he would have made a remark, but I watch him push his jokes aside as he nods solemnly at me and runs back towards the main building.

I turn around and begin the journey back to the room, hurrying as quickly as I can—which, in my current state, isn't very fast. By the time I make it to the top of the stairs, I can hear pounding footsteps running towards me.

"Ari, stay back. I'm afraid your presence is only going to make things worse," Alpha Mortlock says, his face looking apologetic but firm. He is not going to let me in that room.

"No way, I need to check if Garett is okay," I bite out, but my voice comes out weak.

Alex walks up to me. I didn't even see him arrive, but he puts his hand gently on my cheek, bringing my eyes up to meet his.

"Ari, you need to take care of yourself. Both of those men are going to need you later, and you can't help them if you're passed out." His comment is reasonable, and it makes me groan.

He takes this as acceptance that I'm not going to barge into the fight and follow the alpha into the room. I get a glance of shattered furniture and hear lots of growling, but I don't see either of the shifters. A gentle hand touches my shoulder, and I look around to see Seb smiling softly at me.

"Come on, Ari, let's get you taken care of."

I follow him down the stairs and into one of the treatment rooms. Thankfully, Nurse Beth hasn't left yet. Her eyes widen as she sees me. She hurries over and gestures for me to sit on the examination bed.

"My God, Ari, what happened?" she asks, unwrapping my arm and sucking in a deep breath as she takes in the damage.

I explain in as little detail as possible what happened, keeping out the part where Garett and I had sex, but Seb wiggles his eyebrows at me so I know he has an idea as to what we had been up to.

Several stitches later, my arm is bound up and suspended in a sling. My shifter healing has already started to kick in, and I should be good as new by tomorrow. Nurse Beth has to leave, but she is going to send over a colleague to help us out while I'm injured. I lean against the counter in the treatment room while Seb tries to make me smile by telling me pack stories.

"—and then Alex came running in, looking like he was being chased by death hounds, and had to explain to his older brother why Elder Smith was so furious," Seb tells me between bouts of laughter.

I have to say, hearing stories about a young, impulsive Alex is taking my mind off of the current situation a little. I fight to keep back a smile at the image of the current pack beta acting so recklessly.

"What happened to Alex's brother?" I ask. I remember meeting him when I first presented myself to the pack.

Seb sighs and rubs his hand across the back of his neck like he is uncomfortable.

"Do you remember the attack on the pack?" he inquires, to which I nod in response. It's the reason I'm here, after all. Their last medical staff members were killed in that attack. "Well, Mark was killed during that. He was our beta at the time. It was an assassination rather than a random attack. ASP tried to play it off as a random rogue attack, but they hit us hard by aiming for specific pack members—our medical team, both our gamma and our beta, a couple of the elders. Alpha Mortlock and his mate were targeted, but the alpha managed to fight them off." Sorrow laces his voice.

"When the previous beta died, Alpha Mortlock suggested Mark for his beta. No one challenged it. Mark was a good beta, he was always fair. Alex was always the more powerful of the two, but he was younger and more reckless. When Mark died, Alex stepped into the position. There were some who weren't happy with that, but they knew they wouldn't be able to beat Alex in a challenge. The death of his brother changed him. Gone was the carefree Alex that I grew up with."

I let myself digest this information. It explains some things about Alex, like why one minute he's flirting and teasing me—a glimpse of the old Alex—and the next he is the serious beta of the pack. I feel for him that he had to grow up too quickly. I know how that feels.

There is a pause in the conversation, and I notice that the upstairs has become much quieter. There is no snarling or growling from the fighting shifters. That has to be a good sign, right? Seb realises I'm distracted and goes to make us some coffee. I'm staring at the clock on the wall when Alpha Mortlock walks into the room, his face weary. I push off from the counter and race to his side.

"Is everyone okay?" I demand in a hurry.

"Nothing that a few hours' worth sleep won't sort out. I think their pride has been injured more than their bodies. Garett is pretty torn up over your arm though," he tells me, his face grim. "Let's go over to the gym. We need to sort this out, and I think it's best if we do so where there is some space in case someone gets riled up again."

I nod in agreement.

An hour later, I am pacing the gym as I wait to get the answers I need. I would prefer to do this without an audience, but the alpha insisted. The alpha, Lena, Alex, and Isa are here, along with Seb, Garett, and Killian. Even Nurse Penny is here, tending to Killian's wounds. She is the nurse sent to relieve Beth from the other pack.

Garett is leaning against the gym wall, avoiding my gaze. At first, I thought it was because he was angry with me, but when I saw the look of anguish in his eyes, I knew it was because he's feeling guilty. I should probably feel bad and go to comfort him, but right now, I can't process what I'm feeling. Besides, it will not help the situation for me to be comforting Garett when Killian is snarling at any man that comes near me. I look across at the idiot and see he's staring at me again. Tearing his gaze from me as if it's agony to do so, he snarls at Nurse Penny, who is trying to tend to his wounds.

"I give up!" she proclaims as she pulls away from the surly shifter. Turning to the alpha, she shrugs her shoulders. "He won't let me treat him. All of his wounds will heal by themselves," she explains and packs her equipment.

"Thank you, Penny. Please go back to the medical room in case anyone else needs you. We will call down if we need you here again," Alpha Mortlock instructs.

She nods like she was expecting this, but a slight look of disappointment fills her gaze. I bet she was hoping she would get to listen in and report back to her alpha. Suspicion creeps in. I will be keeping an eye on her. Mortlock meets my eyes and nods in agreement, his thoughts matching mine. Smart move to send her away.

"I can smell the bear on her," Killian growls as Nurse Penny leaves, and I fight the urge to smack him.

"Who I fuck has nothing to do with you, Killian," I retort, anger fuelling my words.

This guy really gets on my fucking nerves. I don't know what it is about him that gets under my skin so much. My wolf can't decide if she wants to fuck him or fight him. Maybe both? *Focus, Ari!*

Killian jumps up from his chair and starts to stalk towards me, a challenge in his eyes. Alex and Isa jump forward to stop him from reaching me.

"You are my mate, it has everything to do with me," he growls out, his voice dropping to the point I think he is going to lose control to his wolf.

Alpha Mortlock is by his side, talking low into his ear, trying to calm him down. Garett has moved away from the wall, and from his rigid stance, he looks about one comment away from shifting as well.

"I am not your fucking mate! Just because some stupid instinct is telling you we 'belong together' does not make it true! I have not accepted the bond. I don't even know you!" I spit. My wolf is pushing against my control, and my grip on my power has diminished, filling the room with alpha power.

I can see how it is affecting Killian. His power meets mine in a rush, brushing up against me almost in a caress, feeding my power rather than fighting it. Killian's front teeth lengthen, and he takes another step forward, pushing past Alex and Isa, forcing them both to take a step back. The beta and gamma share a look. That on its own should have me worried, but I am so deep in my frustration and anger that it doesn't register.

"Are you really telling me you can't feel it? You can't feel our bond?" His words come out as a caress, his voice almost a purr as if he knows the answer already.

I want to snarl at him and tell him I feel nothing, but that would be a lie. His power does call to me. Most alpha power is rough and fights for dominance, but Killian's feels like it is supporting me, making me stronger. It makes my power want to do the same, and that terrifies me. I'm about to lash out, out of panic, when Alpha Mortlock turns to look at me.

"Ari, pull back, you are not helping the situation by throwing around your power," he says calmly.

Had it been anyone else, it might have felt like he was scolding me, but I know he's just being truthful.

"Killian, you need to calm down. Ari is safe. You need to fight your instincts so we can sort this out. You're stronger than this, my friend," he says softly, and I can see this reaches Killian.

He blinks, and I can see him trying to fight against his instincts, his muscles trembling. Tearing his gaze away from me, he takes deep breaths to try and regain control.

By some unspoken signal from Mortlock, Lena steps forward, wringing her hands as she comes under the gaze of us all.

"Ari, something obviously occurred between you and Garett. What I am sure you don't know is that Killian would have been able to feel your... arousal through the bond, which is what caused him to snap," she explains to me.

That clarifies why it looked like he had run into the room. Because he could feel me fucking another man. My face burns red as embarrassment fills me. Fan-fucking-tastic.

"So Killian is going to know every time I sleep with someone?" I ask bluntly, and Killian's head whips towards me. "How can I stop it?"

"The only way to stop this is to accept the bond. It is highly unusual for someone to sleep with someone else when they have found their true mate," she says, igniting the anger in me once more.

"I can sleep with whoever I want! I don't care what some 'bond' says," I retort, and Lena takes a step back at the venom in my words.

I will not be made to feel guilty for sleeping with Garett. Alpha Mortlock snarls slightly at the threat to his mate before regaining his composure with a slight cough.

"Oh no! I didn't mean it like that, Ari. I just meant that once the bond has made itself clear, the two don't usually *want* to sleep with anyone else. It usually takes *years* to get past the urge to only spend time with your true mate. If you don't accept the bond, those feelings will eventually disappear, but it takes time," she hurries to inform me, wanting to make sure I understand she isn't judging me.

"But I don't want a mating bond!" I cry out.

"You think I want this?" Killian demands, pushing past Alex and Isa as he stalks towards me.

Garett snarls, and Killian bares his teeth at him.

"Don't push me, bear," he spits out, his temper barely under control. He comes within an inch of me, his eyes piercing, pinning me to the spot. "I had a mate. What we had was real. This 'true mated pair' business is bullshit. You think I want to be mated to an uncontrolled Shadowborn who barely knows how to summon her wolf? I don't." His voice starts off harsh, but towards the end, frustration laces his tone. "But then why can I not seem to control myself around you?" he asks, but I know the question isn't directed at me.

His hand comes up to cup my cheek, and I can't stop myself from leaning into the warmth of it, my wolf practically purring inside my chest. What the fuck is going on with me?

Chapter Seventeen

It was decided that we all needed some time to cool off and figure out what everyone involved wanted. I hadn't paid Alex much attention, but I felt his eyes on me the whole time, and I couldn't help feeling like I'd let him down. Garett agreed not to discuss Killian's attack on him with his pack. The last thing any of us needed was an all-out war between the bears and Moon River Pack.

He almost caused a fight when he was saying goodbye though. Prowling towards me, he pulled me into his arms and kissed me soundly before walking out to the sounds of Killian's growls. He wanted to stay, but it had been decided that was not the best idea while Killian was still fighting for control. I would be having words with him about his predatory behaviour another time. It was out of character for him, but I didn't want to mention it in front of everyone after Killian wounded his pride.

The next couple of days fell into a bit of a routine. I arrive at the compound and check on my patients. I then have an open clinic for anyone to come and ask for advice about various ailments. I'm glad to throw myself into work, into something familiar, as it means I'm too busy to think over everything that's happened in the last few days. I'm not ready to deal with that just yet. In the afternoon before I leave for the day, I train with Killian. Isa is now helping with my training, since it was thought it would be best for me to have a sparring partner and someone who could break up any fights between the two of us. Isa is a much harsher sparring partner and fighting with her is like trying to throw a brick wall. Thankfully with her around, there have been no further 'incidents' between Killian and me. Once I finish with training for the day, tired and sore, I head back to the apartment where Tori grills me on what happened that day. She's even started to eat popcorn while I'm filling her in, telling me my life is far more entertaining than any soap on TV.

I'm not sleeping well. At night, when I no longer have anything to distract me, my thoughts keep me awake. Garett has been calling me, checking I'm okay and that Killian is staying in line. I know he wants to be with me and that he's fighting against his nature to stop his bear from tearing down the compound to find me. I don't regret that we slept together, but it makes it much harder to sort through my feelings for him. I like him, I do, and I can't ignore that my feelings for him are more than just friendly, but I am scared to take things further. While bears do take mates, like with wolves, it isn't all that frequent. But when they find a partner, they tend to stay together for life, and I fear that's what Garett will want from me. I know I should ask him, but I'm scared of the answer. I don't know if I can be that person for him.

Not to mention Killian. Even if I weren't psychologically screwed up, that would throw a spanner in the works. I also can't deny that I do feel something when I'm around him, but is that just because of the bond? Just some wolfy voodoo that's forcing us to feel something for the other? I'm not even sure I like the guy, let alone want to bond with him.

Alex is also another problem I keep pondering. When we kissed in the woods, something just clicked. It felt right when we were in our wolf forms. I've gone from despising the guy to wanting to fuck him. But if I push further, my four am thoughts whisper to me that it's more than that.

Then there's Seb. Sweet, loving Seb, who always manages to put a smile on my face. He hasn't treated me differently at all or tried to make me feel guilty about what has happened. And as hard as I fight it, I keep finding myself watching him. I'm developing feelings for him, and I don't want to—I don't want our friendship to change in that way.

My alarm clock blares to life, and I sit up in bed to switch it off. I was already awake anyway. I go through my usual routine and get ready for the day, throwing on some loose clothing. Thankfully I've fully healed now, so getting into clothes that fit isn't an issue anymore, but I asked Alpha Mortlock to provide me with a uniform so it felt more like a job. I need to keep that distinction. This is just a job, and my life will return to normal once it is all over, right? We still haven't gotten to the bottom of the Shadow Pack. There have been no more attacks, and no one in the supernatural community has heard anything—except for Eric and his mysterious 'friends.' I sigh as I pick up my phone and see another text from him. He's backed off a lot since our last chat, but he's been sending me updates. A large grey wolf with a scar on its face, who doesn't belong to any of the local packs, has been seen prowling around the city.

"Well, that's a coincidence," I mutter dryly to myself.

I'm still no closer to working out what I'm going to do about them. Since I've been training, I can feel myself getting stronger, but I certainly can't take on a whole pack. A little part of me whispers that I could if I accepted my Shadowborn abilities, but I push that part deep, deep down and carry on getting ready for the day.

My morning flies by with check-ups and walk-in appointments. Lottie has fully recovered, and her and her mother visit me every morning with a fresh batch of muffins. I keep telling them they don't need to, but secretly, I love it. I've been seeing Sarah, the pregnant shifter, regularly as well. Her pregnancy seems to be coming along well, but now she is thirty-six weeks and will be delivering soon.

Shifter pregnancies are similar to human ones, however, most shifter babies arrive after thirty-seven weeks. Don't ask me why, I never studied supernatural births. Female shifters also experience a strong desire to nest just before they give birth, so Sarah has been busy cleaning her cabin and getting it ready for the baby. The father, Rubin, is always nervously pacing the room when I visit. The one time Seb came with me, Rubin chased him out of the house, his protective instincts on overdrive. This is an understandable reaction for our kind, especially since Moon River has been having problems with expectant mothers carrying pregnancies to term, or problems with the birthing. Alpha Mortlock pulled me aside one morning and told me there have also been issues with fertility as well. In fact, the last litter of healthy pups was born over two years ago. This makes me nervous, and I have requested Nurse Beth to put me in touch with a supernatural midwife. Mortlock won't be happy, but he will have to put up with it. Babies are not my specialty, and he knew that when he took me on.

I am just wiping down the examination room surfaces when I hear a cheery call of my name.

"Ari, hello, dear!"

I turn and smile at the happy woman walking into the room.

"Gloria, how are you? I don't think I've seen you since the social. How's Jessica?" I ask, my smile wide and genuine.

I surprise myself when I realise I've missed her. I only met her once at the social, yet I feel connected to her through Seb. She makes me feel like I'm welcome, even though I have caused so much trouble in her pack.

"I'm fine, dear," she replies as she takes a seat in the room, her eyes running over me. "But how are you? Have you been sleeping?

You look exhausted," she comments, concern crossing her delicate features.

For once, I find I'm not annoyed by someone 'mothering' me. In fact, I find myself smiling at the older woman, knowing she's just looking out for my best interests.

"I'm fine, Gloria, pleased to be doing some good again," I tell her with a smile, gesturing to the treatment room.

I hadn't realised how much of an effect not being able to practice would have on me, or how much nursing is ingrained into my identity.

"Seb told me about what's been going on with Killian and the others." Damn, I was hoping to avoid this conversation.

I sigh and am hesitant to meet her eyes, worried what I might see there. When I do, however, all I see is understanding, not even a flicker of disappointment.

"Last week was eventful," I tell her, and she chuckles at the understatement.

"So are you going to mate with Killian?" she inquires, getting straight to the point. That's one of the things I love about Gloria—no messing around! She calls it as she sees it.

I bite my lip. I really don't want to be having this conversation. If I say it out loud, it makes everything so much more real. Tori knows the basic details, but she doesn't understand pack politics. She thinks I should just sleep with all of them, no strings attached, but I know that won't work. There are too many alpha males with delicate egos, and if I were to sleep with Killian, I don't think we would be able to deny the mating bond. Not that I even want to sleep with him. *Liar.* Okay, so maybe I do? Gah! Too many feelings. Half the time, I don't know whether I'm coming or going!

"I don't even know him! Why should I tie myself to someone because some supernatural bullshit has decided that we belong together? Why can't I decide for myself? He certainly doesn't seem to want to bond, he hates this!" I share, and I see her nod her understanding.

"Okay, so Garett then. What's happening there?" she prompts, watching me intently like my body language is telling her more than my words.

I feel a wave of sadness fill me at the change of topic. I miss Garett, but with everything going on, I feel it's best we have some distance from each other. He agrees with this, although I know he's struggling, his instincts telling him that he should be with me. Not necessarily even because he loves me, but because he's my friend and he's worried about me. He knows how I'm struggling with everything and wants to help me.

"I don't even know. We're taking some space from each other while this is going on. I miss him though." Growling, I throw my hands up in the air. "Oh, what a mess! I don't know what to do. I don't want a relationship with him—I'm not ready for that, and I know that's what he wants," I rant, my thoughts flying around my head.

"And Alex, I know there's something going on there." She chuckles and raises an eyebrow. "Oh, come now, don't pull that face at me, I know these things," she chides as I make a face at the topic.

"We kissed when he took me for a run," I admit, looking down at my nails as I avoid her gaze. "He's so hot and cold though. One minute, he flirts with me, and the next, he's distant."

Gloria nods through this and tilts her head to one side.

"Do you know about his past?" she asks, and I nod. Seb filled me in only the other day. "Since his brother died, he changed. Some for the better, but he's distanced himself from us and doesn't seem to know how to enjoy himself anymore. He doesn't think he deserves to. When you're around though, I can see a bit of that playful little boy that used to cause havoc in my kitchen with Seb."

She pauses to let this information sink in. I take my hair down from the professional ponytail I'd put it up in and run my hands through it, trying to order my thoughts. In the end, I groan and put my face in my hands.

"What a mess. I don't know what I'm going to do. How do I choose between them when I don't know what I'm feeling? Do I even want to choose? I don't want a relationship," I mutter from behind my hands.

I hear footsteps and then a gentle hand touches my back, rubbing in small circles to comfort me.

"Why don't you want a relationship?" she queries softly, her hands keeping up the gentle caress on my back.

I bite my lip. How much do I tell her? I'm not sure I'm ready to face this.

"I—" I stop, my voice croaky. Clearing my throat, I start again. "I loved once. I was young. It was more infatuation than anything..." I'm rambling. *Stop, Ari, focus.* I take a deep breath. "My old pack was harsh, their rules definitive. He was the only one to show me comfort, and he was punished for it. It was forbidden, and he was taken from me." I stop, my eyes burning.

I squeeze them shut, pushing the memories away. Flashes of his face pass through my mind, and I shove them away, deep down. Not today. I can't think about him today.

"Relationships only end in pain and loss. Everyone will be taken away from me eventually. Tori and Garett are only in my life because they made such a nuisance of themselves and were so persistent that I didn't even notice when they went from acquaintances to family." I open my eyes, and I'm sure my pain is clear on my face from the expression Gloria gives me.

"Besides," I mutter, my voice dropping as I admit to my true reason, "I'm not good enough. I did some terrible things when I was in my last pack, things that you would hate me for. I'm broken because of it. I can't inflict that on someone." I'm whispering by the end of my confession.

I'm afraid to meet Gloria's eyes, as I am sure she will hate me for what I have told her. She will not want me anywhere near Seb. My fears are met when her hand stops its slow circles on my back.

"Were you forced to do these things? Did you choose to do them?" she asks, her tone neutral, hiding her thoughts from me.

"No, I didn't want to do them! I fought against it, but I wasn't strong enough. It doesn't matter though. I still did them. I'm just as evil as the ones who made me do it." Despair fills me, and I'm sure the pack is going to learn how broken and twisted I truly am.

My eyes fly open as arms come around me tightly, and I stare down at Gloria in shock, who is hugging me fiercely, tears glistening in her eyes.

"I'm so sorry you had to go through that, and that you've felt this burden. You're not evil. You had tough decisions to make and you survived. You work so hard to help others. You deserve a chance to feel loved." She releases me from her arms and looks up at me, a small smile on her lips. "And if that happiness is with more than one person, then so what?"

I stare at her in disbelief. Is she really suggesting getting into a relationship with more than one guy? Alphas will struggle to share and would never accept a bear into that mix. My head is spinning with the possibilities.

"Oh, don't look so shocked. It's not uncommon for female shifters to have more than one partner. It just doesn't happen as often as it used to. But now that our numbers are so low, who knows what may happen in the future? Besides, each of those men can offer you something different. Perhaps they can help heal you. Now." She pauses, and I look up at her in expectation. "What about Seb?" she asks, her tone gentle and without an ounce of judgement.

"What about him?" I counter, guilt filling my voice and my face flushing red, giving me away.

"I don't think anything has happened between you yet, but Seb can't stop speaking about you. After he's seen you, he bounces around like when he was a pup at Christmas. I know he cares for you, and I personally would love to welcome you into our family as one of our own. But I just ask you, please don't hurt him." Taking my hands in hers, she meets my eyes. "Don't lead him on. If you have feelings for him, then by all means, but he isn't as strong as the alphas that are vying for your attentions. Please keep him safe," she implores earnestly before embracing me again, kissing my cheek, and walking out of the room, leaving me standing there speechless.

Chapter Eighteen

My training session with Killian comes around all too quickly. They're going well, I'm progressing fast, but sooner or later, I'm going to have to start training in my wolf form, and I've been dreading this. Isa is the only one allowed to spar with me, because when we tried with Alex being my sparring partner, Killian nearly ripped his head off when he flipped me. He still has to fight his instincts, and I can hear snarls coming from his end of the gym when I'm pinned to the mats.

I walk into the gym and see him lifting weights in the back corner. His loose tracksuit bottoms do nothing to hide his muscular legs, and he's shirtless, the muscles in his arms and upper body cording as he lifts the weights.

"Personally, I don't tend to go for skinny guys. I prefer mine more muscular." Isa's voice comes from behind me, making me jump.

She smirks as my face flushes red at having been caught staring. I follow her into the room but can't help looking over at Killian. I can't believe Isa thinks he's skinny. He is more muscular than most football players. I dread to think how big Isa's men are.

We start warming up, and Killian walks over, wiping his forehead with his towel as he does so.

"Decided to show up?" he asks me, his eyebrow raised.

"Of course I did. Why wouldn't I? I've been here every day this week," I reply indignantly.

"You made such a fuss yesterday that I thought we might have broken you. Delicate little princess." He smirks. He knows I hate it when he calls me that.

"Stop being such a dick, Killian. Let's get this over with," I say tiredly.

He frowns as he looks me over, noticing the dark rings under my eyes. "Why are you so tired? Are you not sleeping?"

"Since when do you care?" I retort, no venom in my voice. I actually want to know the answer.

He goes still and looks me over again, an expression I can't describe passing over his face.

"I do care. I just wish I didn't," he answers quietly before walking to the edge of the mats. "Right, stop standing around. Get to it!" he shouts, back to his dickish self.

Isa has been looking back and forth between the two of us, and if I wasn't so thrown by Killian's comment, it might have been comical. Raising an eyebrow, she wisely doesn't comment, and instead starts running through one of our warmup drills.

The first hour of training goes as usual, but because I'm so tired, I keep making mistakes.

"Come on, Ari, even a five-year-old could get out of that hold," Killian calls from the side of the mats.

I'm pinned to the floor once again, and my temper is starting to rise. I should be used to his taunts by now, and I have to admit, he isn't as harsh as he used to be, but lack of sleep is making me cranky.

Isa lets me out of the hold, and I push from the ground angrily. Killian watches my display of temper in silence, his arms crossed with a contemplative look on his face.

"Let's change this up. Shift into wolf form," he shouts out.

My head whips around to look at him, my body stiffening up at his command. "No," is all I say.

"I said shift," he snarls, our tempers setting each other off.

"And I said no. I will not shift." Not today, not when I am in this mood and not in front of Killian.

"What is your problem? I thought you Shadowborn relished that opportunity to shift and show off your powers? *Shift*," he orders again, embedding his alpha power into his words.

My knees buckle, but not from his power. Memories flash before my eyes, and I am dragged under.

"Shift." The command comes at me again.

I shake my fifteen-year-old head, but not out of teenage attitude. I stare up at the alpha and bare my teeth.

"No." My voice croaks and my body aches from the punishment I received earlier in the week.

The fact that my shifter body had not yet healed my wounds just goes to show how badly they beat me. After I tried to escaped with Zack's help, they held a much tighter leash on me, and the beating I received when they dragged me back was the worst so far. Had I been human, I would have died. Now that Zack was dead, I had no one to tend to my wounds under the cover of darkness. My heart threatens to break at the thought of the only wolf who ever showed me kindness losing his life because of me.

A boot kicks me in the back, and I cry out as I fall forward before pushing myself up onto my knees, glaring at the alpha and my tormentor. I don't care how much they beat me, I will no longer do as they ask. Any misplaced loyalty to them was lost the moment they killed Zack.

"I said shift," the alpha repeats, his voice full of alpha power.

I fall forward onto all fours once again as his power forces the change in me. He doesn't need to raise his voice, his power will make me do as he wishes. I know resisting is futile, but I can't just roll over and do as he says, so I fight it. The change is painful, and once again, I hate that he has this power over me, that I'm a wolf, a predator, but I can't stop him from controlling me.

Eventually, I find myself looking at my paws, panting, and I hear him walk forward. He drops his hand to the scruff of my neck, and I flinch as he pats me.

"Well done, little wolf. I have a job for you."

I come back around to Killian calling my name, his hands on my shoulders as he anxiously looks at me. Wait, Killian looks anxious? Scratch that, now that he's seen me come around, his expression has dropped back into his customary scowl, but I can see the worry in his eyes.

"What happened? What triggered you?" he asks, but I get the feeling he already knows.

"You trying to force me to shift," I mutter, running my hand across my face.

I only notice then that my hands are shaking. Killian notices too and swears under his breath.

"Isa, we're going to stop for the day. Ari, come for a walk with me," he tells me, and his tone sounds resigned.

Isa looks between the two of us again like she can't decide what's happening or whether to allow this. This time, it does make me crack a smile.

"Go, I'll be fine," I say. "If he tries to seduce me, I'll just hit him over the head like you showed me," I tell her with a wink.

This makes her laugh and she walks out of the gym, leaving just me and Killian. I turn to look at the shifter and find him putting on a shirt. Shame. He catches me looking and raises an eyebrow at me again, desire heating his eyes before he shuts it down. I just shrug.

"So where are we going?" I inquire, hoping my nerves at being alone with him don't come through in my voice.

"Into the woods. Come," is all he says before walking off.

I can't help but wonder if this walk is going to be anything like the last time I went into the woods with a shifter, when I ended up making out with Alex. Part of me hopes so.

"Why are we here?" I ask as we stare out at the trees.

Killian has brought me to a small clearing in the middle of the woods. We're close enough that I can still hear the hubbub of the main house, but far enough away that no one will be able to overhear our quiet conversation. I'm sitting on a log, watching the small birds hunt for grubs in the undergrowth. Killian is sitting on the other end of the log, and I can feel that his gaze keeps landing on me.

"We need to talk. About the bond. And about you," he tells me, and I sigh.

This is another conversation I really don't want to have, but he's right—we do need to talk. We can't keep avoiding the issue.

"Fine. What do you want to know?" I ask, finally meeting his gaze.

"Why do you keep rejecting the bond?" he questions, and I hear a slight note of vulnerability in his voice.

I'm surprised, and I'm sure it shows on my face. "Are you saying you want this bond? I thought you hated me!" I state incredulously. I can't get a reading on this guy!

Frustration fills his face, and he pushes away from the log, prowling through the clearing. If I didn't know he was a shifter, I would still be able to tell he was something *other* with the power rolling off him. His sharp features almost make him look fae.

"I don't hate you! I hate what you are!" he snarls as he paces.

I feel like he has poured a bucket of ice over me. Shadowborn.

Even when I feel like I'm making a life for myself elsewhere, it still follows me. I can never escape it. I stand up stiffly, trying to hide the hurt from his comment.

"Well, I can't do anything to change that. I hate that you're such a bastard, but that's not going to change either. Guess both of us are going to be disappointed," I retort and spin to leave the clearing.

I'm not going to sit here and listen to him insult me. I thought we were going to chat and finally work out what's going on, but it seems I'm going to be disappointed. I hear Killian's footsteps pause as he curses under his breath.

"Ari, wait. I'm not doing this very well. You rile me up, and I forget what I'm trying to say," he admits.

I turn around and raise my eyebrow at him and his shitty apology. But I can see from his posture that he is not used to doing this. Sighing, I sit back down and look at him expectantly.

"I'm not going to apologise for being Shadowborn," I tell him, my voice strong on this point. I wish I hadn't been born this way, but there's nothing I can do to change that.

"I know. Let me try and explain." He sits back down on the log and turns so he is facing me. "I was mated before. Julie and I chose to be bonded, and I meant those vows when I took them. We loved each other. She was kind and gentle and never had a bad word to say about anyone." His voice is soft as he tells me about her, and I realise I've never seen him like this.

"A couple of wolves from another pack came to petition for a secure place to stay. Something was off about them, but I decided to offer them a place in the pack against the judgement of my beta and gamma. They didn't really fit within the pack, and several members came to convince me to ask them to leave. I declined. I was trying to be more accepting." He huffs a laugh, but there's no real humour in his voice, only pain and self-loathing. "A month later, there was an attack on the pack during the night. Someone had let them into the compound and told them where to strike to cause the most damage. It was a complete slaughter," he says, his voice hard.

He stops and takes a deep breath, his hands clenching together, and I have to fight the urge to stroke his back in comfort. I can feel his wolf trying to take over, and I swear I can see his claws pressing against the skin on his knuckles as he fights for control.

"I ran back to our house and found one of the wolves I granted a place of safety within the pack at my bedside. His hands were wrist deep in my mate's stomach as he pulled her apart bit by bit. He was Shadowborn and half in his shadow form at the time. Julie hadn't even heard him coming." His voice is soft, broken, and I can see unshed tears in his eyes.

I go to place my hand on his arm, but his gaze sharpens.

"That is what was off about that wolf. He was Shadowborn. He infiltrated my pack, betrayed us, and then killed them all. I managed to kill most of them, but I have a feeling they left me alive on purpose. As a message."

He turns to look at me now, and his eyes soften a little as he looks at me, although I still feel the anger within him.

"That's why I knew you were Shadowborn. I also had some training from my predecessor on how to teach them. We had a Shadowborn in our pack about one hundred and fifty years ago, so we pass the knowledge down in case another is born." He seems to realise his use of the present tense and lets out a tired sigh. "Not that I have anyone to pass that knowledge to anymore. My pack is dead."

He shifts his weight on the log and turns to face me fully, his knee bumping against me as he runs his eyes over me again, taking in every detail.

"Fate has a sick sense of humour. I had a mate, and that love was real." He emphasises the last word, like he's trying to convince me. Like somehow, this bond between us takes away from the love he felt for her. "And now it's brought me to you, the very same kind that killed her. You're nothing like Julie. I shouldn't want anyone else." He pauses, and I can hear the self-loathing in his voice. "But I feel complete when you're around, like I might have a reason to still be alive. When Julie and the pack were killed, I wondered why the world was so cruel. I should have died with them. Protecting them."

My heart breaks for him as I feel his pain as if it was my own, and I understand him a little better.

"Since then, I have been living a half-life, not truly belonging." His eyes flit across my face. "Perhaps fate led me to you so you could mend the rift in my heart." His words are soft, uncertain, like he's laying his heart out for me to see.

Oh shit. I stare at him with wide eyes and panic. Jumping to my feet, I start pacing in front of the log, needing to work off some of this nervous energy. He can't possibly think I can fix him. *Me!* I let out a slightly manic laugh as I pace.

"I am the most broken person here!" I practically shout at him, my nerves getting the better of me.

My fight-or-flight instincts are screaming for me to leave, but I know I can't get out of having this conversation.

"I'm not a good person. I don't belong anywhere. You said it yourself, I'm nothing like Julie! I've killed. The things I was made to do should make you want to kill me. Hell, I probably deserve to be ripped to shreds! What I don't deserve is a fated mate!" My voice is loud, and I can hear my panicked breaths coming out fast. I'm sure my eyes are bright with tears that threaten to fall. All my carefully built walls are being torn down by these guys and leaving the scared, damaged little girl that is hiding behind it exposed.

Killian watched my breakdown in silence, but now he stands and prowls towards me. I can't work out what is in his expression, but he doesn't look like he is going to kill me like I suggested.

"Ari." He pulls me to a stop when he gets close enough. Putting his hand on the tops of my arms, he looks me in the eye. "I have my dark side too, things I am ashamed of. I know you are different from the Shadowborn that killed my pack, and I know I don't always show it very well, but I don't blame you for things you were forced to do. Perhaps we were brought together to help fix each other. I don't belong anywhere either. I don't have a place here, and I don't have a place to call home, and I didn't expect to have that again after I lost Julie. But when I'm with you, that feels like it could be a possibility again."

Huh. Who knew Killian had a romantic side?

"I know it's not going to be easy, but I'm working on my prejudices. Sometimes, I see your strength and it scares me, but I've seen how you push yourself to help others. I know you're not like him," he tells me, raising one of his hands to cup my cheek.

I take a deep breath and fight the urge to lean into his hand as I gather my thoughts and brace myself for the backlash of what I'm about to say.

"I do feel drawn to you. Your power speaks to me, and I feel connected to you, somehow, in a way I never have before. But I'm also drawn to Garett and Alex, and even Seb. I don't know if I can commit to this bond when I have feelings for other people as well. There is something deeper going on here." I bite down on my lower lip as I wait for his response.

He pulls away and is silent for a while. A frown mars his face, making his scar look more severe.

"I don't like it. It goes against who I am," he tells me, and I brace myself for rejection. "But I have decided to trust my instincts more. I should have trusted them that night the Shadowborn asked for shelter, and I didn't. My instincts are telling me this is right." He pauses again and paces the clearing.

I can tell he's struggling with this, and the fact he is even considering giving us a chance makes me see him in a different light. I can't deny that I have feelings for him any longer, and it seems he has come to the same conclusion.

"So, if you are saying you're being pulled towards these other men as well as me..." His voice trails off in a growl as he fights against his instincts. "Then I will trust you. Just don't expect me to be happy about sharing you."

With that shocking declaration, he leans down and smashes his lips to mine. His lips are firm, and as I open mine to kiss him back, he bites down on my lower lip, making me gasp. He pulls away, and I can see the lust in his eyes, his alpha power rising and coaxing mine as they push against each other.

"I've been wanting to do that for days," he growls out before stalking to the main compound.

I stand, dumbstruck, as I watch him walk away, my hand going to my bruised lips. My wolf is demanding that I follow him and finish what he started, but I know I won't be able to stop myself from claiming him. I take a deep breath to calm myself. *Take things slow, Ari.* I shake my head and let out a small laugh. What an afternoon. I start the walk back to the medical building. Time to get back to work. But first, a cold shower.

Chapter Nineteen

I'm standing by the front gates of the compound, my foot tapping excitedly, as I hear the sound of a car coming along the driveway towards me. The black limo turns around the corner, and I press the buzzer to make the electric gates open, allowing the car entrance. Normally, the limo would take guests to the main house, but I'm so excited to see the limo's passenger that I took the short walk down to the gate. The backdoor flings open, and the car screeches to a halt. I laugh at the disgruntled expression of the driver as Tori leaps out of the back and throws herself at me.

It's been a week since that disastrous training session with Killian, and it was decided that it was best for me to stay on the compound. Not for any 'mating' reasons, but because mysterious attacks on shifters have started happening. They've not been linked to the Shadow Pack, but it was decided it would be best overall. And with Sarah about to give birth at any moment, I wanted to be available for when that happened.

Tori understood and even agreed with the reasoning behind me staying here, but I've missed my best friend. I offered to try to get her a room here, but she declined, saying the attacks were only on shifters so she'd be safe. Besides, her magic would protect her. I managed to convince her to come to the compound for the weekend though. She's been bugging me to introduce her to my 'hot shifter boy toys,' and there's a pack social tonight, so this is the perfect opportunity.

Getting her officially invited was easier than I expected. There's a lot of animosity between wolves and witches from a feud that spans back generations. The two species used to work together in harmony. Each wolf pack had a witch who would work to protect and heal them. One witch was not able to save an alpha's mate and was killed as a result. The witch councils then recalled their members from all packs. Even if they didn't want to leave, they had no choice. This resulted in the death of many sick or injured wolves who were no longer protected. The wolves have never forgiven the witches for this, and the witches never forgot the slight against their fallen sister. I saw this myself when I asked Alex whether they had a witch working for the pack. Some packs have moved past this and have covenless witches working for them, but this isn't common.

Which was why I was surprised when I requested that Alpha Mortlock allow Tori to come and stay, and he agreed. I was even more surprised when he suggested she come to the pack social. This was a time for family and togetherness. To invite a witch to this makes a statement. It's raised my opinion of him even more. Alex wasn't too happy, but he trusts my judgement of people and knows I wouldn't invite Tori if I thought she would harm anyone here.

I focus on a squealing Tori and hug her back tightly. We wave the limo on. It'll take Tori's bags to my room, where she will be staying while she is here, but we'll walk from here.

"Come on, I'll show you around," I tell her with a grin on my face.

We leisurely walk up to the main house in the centre of the compound, arms linked as Tori talks excitedly about everything she's been doing this week. She's told me all this in our nightly phone calls, but I'm enjoying spending time in her company so much that I don't mind.

"Girl, I can see why you're staying here—this place is huge!" We've reached the main house by now, and I'm showing her over to the medical centre. A couple of people have already stopped to greet us with warm smiles. "And there is plenty of eye candy to keep you entertained. Not that you need any more men to add to your harem!" she jokes, and I nudge her, hissing at her to keep her voice down. But I can't help but laugh. I haven't realised how much I've missed having her around.

I keep the tour of the medical building brief before taking Tori up to my room. There are a couple of guest rooms up here, but she'll be staying with me.

"It's a slumber party like you see in the movies!" She laughs and jokingly throws a pillow at me.

I throw it back at her, laughing. Neither of us have ever had a slumber party, our childhoods not allowing for it. After a bit more messing around, I help Tori settle in and we decide to start getting changed for the social, which starts in an hour. I watch Tori as she pulls on a white playsuit with a little black belt. The colour shows off her beautiful dark skin, and the belt accentuates her generous curves. Her mixed heritage has blessed her with gorgeous curly dark hair that I've always been secretly jealous of.

"So," she begins, looking at me through the mirror as she adjusts the belt on her outfit, "any updates on Killian?"

I sigh and walk towards the wardrobe where I'm storing my clothes. I pull out a simple red blouse with a plunging neckline and hold it against myself, looking in the mirror.

"I don't really know, Tor. He takes every opportunity to touch me, especially when the others are around, but as soon as we're alone, he bolts. He's so on and off, it's giving me whiplash," I say, before shaking my head and pulling off my top.

I pull the shirt on and do up the buttons, smoothing down the fabric as I look in the mirror. It shows off my figure nicely, with more cleavage than I would normally show. Flicking my eyes down, I take in my tight jeans, which I know make my legs and butt look good.

"What do you think? Too much?" I ask, biting my lower lip as I wait for her response.

"Girl, you look hot! You're going to have those guys fighting over you by the end of the evening," she says approvingly.

Snorting, I shake my head. "That's the problem, I don't want them fighting over me!" I protest.

"Whatever you say, Ari," she replies, her tone clearly saying she doesn't believe me as she rolls her eyes.

I sit in front of the vanity mirror and start putting on my makeup, paying more attention to it than I usually would. Pausing as I look at my reflection in the mirror, I wonder why I'm making more of an effort tonight. I tell myself it's because Tori's here and it's nice to dress up.

We joke and gossip for a bit before there is a knock on the door.

"Come in!" we both chorus, throwing a grin at each other as we do so.

Seb walks in and leans against the doorframe as he takes us in, whistling appreciatively. A sultry grin spreads across his face.

"Be still my beating heart. You both look beautiful this evening," he greets us smoothly.

Tori grins and pretends to fan herself, loving the attention.

"Now who is this piece of hot stuff? I wouldn't mind a roll in the sheets with you," she comments with a cheeky grin. Typical Tori.

I feel a rush of jealousy run through me at the comment, but I can't really blame her, Seb is looking fine this evening. His dark blue shirt is tight against his muscular torso, the colour showing off his tanned skin.

"I would be only too happy to oblige your wish," Seb replies, a teasing glint in his eyes as he stalks towards Tori.

I know they're only joking, and that Seb can't resist flirting with everyone and anyone, but jealousy fills me again and a wave of possessiveness makes me walk forward and place my hand on his shoulder.

"Tori, this is Seb. Seb, Tori," I introduce them, my voice tighter than I intended.

Tori raises her eyebrows at me, and Seb takes my hand, grinning as he squeezes it gently. Damn, guess I didn't hide it very well. I have no right to be possessive of him. We're nothing but friends, but seeing the two of them flirting like that stirred something inside me. Pushing it aside, I give them an apologetic smile.

"Ready to go meet the pack?"

As we walk into the hub, I can't help but remember the last pack social I attended. It started out great, and I found that I actually enjoyed myself. Until Marcus, the dickhead, spoiled the whole thing by challenging me. Thankfully, nothing has been heard from him since he was banished. There was a little backlash from it—a few of his friends had chosen to leave the pack—but apart from that, things settled down quickly.

I take Tori to the front of the room where Alpha Mortlock is waiting with Lena, Alex, and Isa. I smile at them and pull Tori to my side.

"Alpha, Lena. This is Victoria Smith, Tori, my best friend," I introduce formally.

Alpha Mortlock smiles at me before nodding towards Tori. Lena is beaming and practically oozing happiness.

"Tori, welcome to Moon River Pack. You are a guest here, and I hope you will be made to feel welcome by me and my own," he replies back formally. "Which coven do you belong to?"

"None. I'm a bit of a misfit and don't really fit with any coven," Tori replies happily. She's proud of her differences and always describes the covens as nosy bitches.

Mortlock and Lena laugh and nod. "I think you will fit in well here then," Lena offers with a smile towards me. I roll my eyes but give her a small smile so she knows I'm not offended by her joke.

Alpha Mortlock stands up on the stage and begins welcoming everyone to the social. Alex pulls me aside and whispers to me.

"I've hardly seen you all week, Killian always seems to be with you. How are you?" he asks quietly. I can tell there's more he wants to say, but he doesn't have time. "I've got to go on stage, but save me a dance later, all right?" he requests with a wink before walking off.

"What was that about?" Tori whispers to me, and I shush her since people are looking our way. I'll fill her in later.

"You've probably already heard, but we have a guest on the compound. Before the gossip starts spreading, she *is* a witch, but she's been approved by me to be here," the alpha announces. There are several mutters in the crowd to which he now speaks.

"She's like family to our honorary packmate, Ari, so I expect you to show her the same respect. Know I would not allow anyone here who wishes us harm. Ari vouches for her, and I trust that." His alpha power settles over us as he speaks, making it clear how serious he is. Then, like a switch has been flipped, he smiles, his whole face lightening. "Enjoy your evening," he announces before stepping off the stage with Alex and Isa in tow.

I remain where I am in shock. Since when did I become an honorary member of the pack? For him to announce that he trusts my judgement in front of the whole pack is a big deal. Not to mention I notice many in the crowd nodding in agreement when he mentions my name. I'm blown away by this show of support. Many of the pack had become friendly with me during my time here and my daily visits, but I hadn't noticed they were slowly accepting me as one of their own.

I snap out of my stupor when Tori pulls on my arm. I smile at her and start guiding her through the crowd.

"Come on, I want to introduce you to some people," I tell her with a wide smile.

An hour or so passes with lots of laughter and food. Gloria immediately takes to Tori and welcomes her with a large hug. Tori is just as shocked at the instant acceptance as I was when I first met Gloria, having never had a mother figure growing up. Seb introduces her to all his friends, and even Alex comes over for a chat. I can't see Killian, but I know he's around here—something tight in my chest tells me he is close. This new development started yesterday, like some sort of freaky homing beacon.

"Miss Tori, may I trouble you for a dance?" one of the young shifters asks Tori. Mark, I think his name is.

Tori smiles widely at him and takes his hand, walking out onto the dance floor. I struggle to hide my smile. Mark doesn't know what he's in for. Tori's dance style is...eccentric.

I'm sitting with Gloria and Jessica, watching Seb chatting with his friends. Jessica's sitting in my lap, making me braid her hair when Alex comes over.

"Ari, I've come to claim my dance," he says with a smirk, holding his hand out.

Jessica jumps out of my lap, and I stand, taking his proffered hand. Butterflies dance in my stomach, and I wonder why I'm so nervous about dancing with Alex. At least it's a lively song and we won't have to slow dance. As if he can hear my thoughts, the DJ changes the song, a slow tempo filling the air. I glare over in his direction. Typical. Alex pulls me closer, a smug smile on his lips as he holds me close to him. Suspicions rise.

"Did you have anything to do with the song change?" I ask, raising my eyebrows.

"I have no idea what you're talking about," he says with mock innocence.

Yeah right. I snort, shaking my head as he starts leading me in a slow dance. After a while, I lose myself in the rhythm of the movement and rest my cheek against his chest. He hums happily, pulling me a little closer.

"Ari," he begins, and I look up to see he's anxious. "I've got something that I need to tell—" He is cut off when a looming shadow appears over my shoulder.

"Can I cut in?" a voice asks, the tone more a demand than a question.

I know before I turn around that it's Killian from the little spark in me that has lit up. Alex is stiff in my arms, and I know he's agitated.

"We are in the middle of something," Alex tells him, his tone firm as his arms tighten around me.

"I'm sure that can wait," Killian replies, his voice deep, and I feel his power start to rise. I'm worried that the two of them are going to start a fight in the middle of the social. Time to defuse the situation.

I turn around and look at Killian, crossing my arms as I stare at him expectantly.

"Do we have a problem here?" I ask in a tone to match his.

"It's fine, Ari, I'll catch you later," Alex mutters, and I know he must be swallowing his pride to back down to Killian.

Alex stalks off, and I turn to glare at Killian. He puts his arms around me, and I ignore the feeling of wholeness as he starts moving to the music.

"What was that all about?" I question, my tone demanding answers.

"Alex and I had words. We have come to an agreement," he states, not even having the decency to look embarrassed at his behaviour.

"What type of agreement?" I ask through gritted teeth. Wait. "Do I even want to know?"

"Probably not." He shakes his head, a small smile playing on his lips.

We spend the rest of the dance in silence, but it's a comfortable silence, even though I'm still annoyed at him. I know shouting at Killian isn't going to get him to change or apologise, so there is no point. Unless he really pisses me off, that is. Once the dance has finished, he walks with me back to where I was sitting.

The rest of the evening passes quickly with laughter and happiness. I don't see much of Tori, who spends most of the evening on the dance floor in Mark's arms. When I finally retire to my bed, Tori doesn't join me. Instead, she decides to warm someone else's bed.

Chapter Twenty

Tori slinks back to my room at around ten the next morning, looking like the cat who got the cream.

"Good night?" I ask with a sly grin as I wiggle my eyebrows.

She laughs and nods, her cheeks heating in a blush. My mouth drops open at the sight. Tori never blushes.

"Oh my God, you like him!" I accuse as a large grin spreads across my face.

Tori groans and face-plants on my bed, grabbing a pillow and throwing it at me.

"Yeah, and if you tell anyone, I'll turn you into a frog," she threatens half-heartedly.

"So tell me all the details," I demand, needing to know what had kept my friend's attention all night.

"We didn't sleep together, if that's what you're asking. We just stayed up and talked all night... Okay, maybe a lot of kissing, but we didn't move past third base," she tells me with a laugh, the blush spreading farther across her cheeks.

We spend the next hour giggling and gossiping like schoolgirls as we get ready for the day. I love spending time with Tori like this, and I can't remember the last time we did.

"So, Ari..." I turn from the dresser where I'm brushing my hair to look at her, raising my eyebrow. I know that tone of voice, it means she wants something. "I know we were going to spend the day together, but do you mind if I spend some time with Mark?"

My heart sinks a little. I was hoping to spend the day with her. I arranged for Nurse Beth to come to the compound so I could have some time off with Tori. But looking at her face, I find I can't tell her no. She looks so excited. I smile and nod.

"Oh, all right then. But I'll see you this evening, right?" I say, trying to keep my tone light.

"Of course! What are you going to do with yourself?" she queries, and I know she feels guilty from her uncertain tone.

I think about it, a whole day to myself. "Don't worry about me. Enjoy yourself."

I get a sense of déjà vu as I sit in the coffee shop, waiting to meet Eric. Just after Tori left to see Mark, I was pondering what to do with my unexpected free time when I received a phone call from him. He sounded pretty rough and had practically begged me to meet him. I'm still mad at him, but being the bleeding heart I am, I caved and agreed to see him.

I take a sip of my latte as I glance around the shop. It's a Sunday morning, so it's reasonably busy. The hum of conversation in the air and the chink of china cups settles me with its normalcy. I like coming here, or at least I did before everything kicked off with the packs. I like watching the humans go on with their day-to-day lives, oblivious to everything that's going on around them.

The bell above the door chimes to announce someone has entered the coffee shop, and I glance up. Someone is hurrying towards me and throws themselves into the chair opposite me. I raise my eyebrows in question until I realise that the person is Eric. He looks appalling. His usually neat hair is all messed up, and he has a couple of days' worth of stubble on his usually clean-shaven face. But the thing that shocks me the most is how pale and gaunt he looks. Dark circles mar the underside of his eyes, and he looks like he hasn't slept in a week.

"Eric, what's happened to you? Are you all right?" I ask, concern lacing my voice as I place my hand on top of his. What on earth has happened to make him look like this?

He sighs and rubs his hand across his face, looking like he's going to just fall asleep where he's sitting.

"I'm fine, Ari, it's you I'm worried about," he replies as his eyes run over me hungrily.

"What do you mean? I'm fine, I'm staying with a local pack that's keeping me safe," I tell him, confused at his fear for my well-being. "What's happened to you?" I question again. I may be pissed off at him, but I still care for him.

"Look, it doesn't matter about me. There are some really dangerous people looking for you." His voice has increased in volume with his frustration, and I glance around the room to make sure no one is obviously listening.

"You told me this before and nothing has happened—"

"No, Ari, listen to me. Something is about to happen, something bad. You need to leave the pack and run," he urges, leaning out of his chair and grasping my hand like it's his lifeline.

I snort at his comment. I'm not running, not after I've built a life for myself here and am just starting to feel like I fit in. There is movement around me, but I'm focusing only on our conversation.

"I'm not running anywhere. What do you know about the pack? You need to tell me—" I'm cut off as a shadow crosses the table.

I look up and see two tall men in suits. They both look like they've walked off a fashion runway. The one closest to me smiles, and it's the kind of smile I would expect if a crocodile could grin, the one that makes you want to run.

"Ariana Blake. We're from ASP. You're going to need to come with us."

I'm in deep shit.

My eyes run over the small interrogation room I'm currently sitting in. It's like every cop movie I have ever seen, and if it weren't me who was in trouble, I would find it amusing. At least I'm not in cuffs. I look around the sparse room. A two-way mirror fills one side of the room, and the table and chair I'm sitting at are plain. A recording device sits at one end of the table. I lean back against my chair and try to think of a way out of this. The issue is that I don't know why I have been brought in. Is this the threat Eric came to warn me about?

The sound of the door opening brings me out of my thoughts. The two men from the coffee bar walk in, their black suits accentuating their forms. One is a little taller than the other, but other than that, the two could be related. Both have black hair, although the taller one has stubble and his hair is longer. The shorter of the two is clean-shaven, and although his eyes are grey like his partner's, his are softer. They both sit on the opposite side of the table, and the taller of the two clears his throat.

"I am Ryan Cross, and this is Aiden Cross. We are agents for ASP, and we have some questions for you," Ryan tells me, his eyes running over me as he speaks.

I nod in response to what he is saying. Same surname. I'm right—they are related somehow. If I know what is good for me, I will keep my mouth shut and just respectfully answer their questions and be out of here in no time.

"You are a hard woman to get a hold of. I have been trying to find you at your workplace and your apartment for a while now. Your roommate told me you moved out," Ryan tells me.

Well, that explains who has been coming to the apartment. Tori's instincts reckoned they didn't mean me harm, so this should be interesting.

"So which one of you is the good cop?" I ask. Apparently, I

don't know what's good for me. I nod toward Aiden. "I reckon you're the good cop," I drawl before looking to Ryan, who has a slight smile across his handsome face. "Because you have bad written all over you," I say as I lean back in my chair.

"Please don't mistake us for human police, Miss Blake. We don't follow the same rules as them and are not restricted by human squeamishness. We will do what we need to do, to get the answers we need." He finishes on a slight growl, his smile still in place.

I am not impressed by his show of dominance, but he has just confirmed he is shifter. Their scents are off, and I can't quite tell what they are, but now I know what Agent Ryan is—wolf. Which means that's what Aiden is too. Although, that doesn't feel completely right. Frowning, I look across at Aiden, who has yet to say anything. I lean forward and take a sniff, not embarrassed in the slightest, before leaning back in my seat once I pick up his scent and look between the two of them.

"Bird? How can you be a bird shifter when he is a wolf? You're related, right?" I ask, briefly forgetting my current position.

It should be impossible for them to be related if they are from different shifter species. Some shifters choose to mate with a different race, but they have never been able to produce offspring, interbreeding doesn't allow reproduction. The two agents look at each other with a smile like they are sharing a joke with each other.

"Cousins," Aiden confirms, speaking for the first time since he entered the room, his voice soft and quiet.

"But that's impossible," I argue. They must be lying, although I should be able to tell if they are lying.

"You would know about impossible," Ryan says, before leaning towards me, his eyes predatory. "For example, a Shadowborn being born and surviving under the radar for twenty-four years, six of those years right under our nose here in the U.S.A."

Shit.

I raise my eyebrow and pray they don't hear my heart rate spike or see the bead of sweat that's threatening to roll down the back of my neck. They can't know for sure, otherwise I wouldn't be sitting here with them like this. They would have killed me on the spot.

"That is impossible, Agent Cross. I've heard there hasn't been one of those in over one hundred years, plus they don't tend to live long. I don't fancy meeting one, to be honest. I hear they're pretty nasty," I say with a shrug, trying to keep my tone light.

"We have been informed that you're a Shadowborn. Do you know a Marcus Oswald?" Ryan challenges, and my blood goes cold.

Bloody Marcus. For fuck's sake, I knew I should have killed him. However, he may have given me an out.

"I wouldn't believe anything that scumbag says. He challenged me while I was a guest at Moon River Pack. I won and chose to spare him." I see both their eyebrows go up when I mention I spared Marcus. "He was then banished from the pack for challenging a guest. I haven't seen him since. He's sore I got him kicked out and is now out to get me." The two shifters exchange looks. They can sense I'm telling the truth, every single word ringing true. "I can't believe the bastard came running to you guys." I shake my head, disgusted he ratted me out.

"He didn't come to us. He's been selling the information to anyone with a bit of money. We picked the information up from one of our usuals who'd overheard a conversation between him and a member of the Shadow Pack."

I freeze at the mention of my old pack. Their sharp eyes pick up the movement, but neither of them points it out. He just simply continues.

"One of their members has been skulking around the city causing problems. We would have brought him in, but he always seems to disappear every time we turn up. Remind me, Ariana, you were from Shadow Pack originally, right?" he asks, his nostrils flaring as he scents my fear.

What was Marcus doing talking to Shadow Pack, and why were they still here? It's not like them to hang around. They're usually all action. The fact that they are holding back makes me more nervous.

"If you're in danger, we can offer you protection," Aiden offers. Definitely good cop.

I find this odd. If they think I'm Shadowborn, why are they offering me protection? I'm getting confused, and frankly, it's giving me a headache.

"Look, boys, what's going on? Why am I here?" I ask, trying to keep my tone even.

"We want to hire you. We need someone with your...abilities," Ryan answers, and I lean back in shock.

ASP wants a Shadowborn. I don't even want to think about what they would use those powers for, but ASP doesn't have the best reputation. Ryan was right when he said they weren't the human police. They govern themselves and make their own laws. They're known more for 'shoot now, talk later,' and their justice is brutal, even for shifters.

"I'm not Shadowborn," I proclaim.

"Liar," Ryan retorts. Damn shifter senses!

"Do you have any proof?" I counter, knowing they don't, as they would have used it against me already.

Both agents look at each other, and I know they have nothing against me. I smile and push up from the table.

"It's been wild, boys, but I have a busy afternoon ahead of me, and I need to get going." Both agents stand with me, Ryan with a pissed off look on his face and Aiden seeming like he wants to say something else. A thought occurs to me. "Oh, my friend from the coffee bar?"

"We sent your friend on his way. We don't want to involve humans in our business," he says, confirming my suspicions that even ASP doesn't know what Eric is. Hell, if ASP doesn't even know what he is, there's no way I was going to, so this makes me feel a little better. A hand stops my path to the door when it lands on my shoulder.

"Will you consider our offer?" Ryan inquires, his hand tightening on my shoulder.

"I'm sure a Shadowborn would love to join your team. Shame that's not me," I tell him, giving him a simple smile.

Ryan growls at me and stalks from the room. What did he expect? That I would jump on his offer? I've been hiding who I am all my life. It's the only reason I'm still alive today. I shake my head at him and go to walk away. Aiden stops my exit with a gentle hand on my elbow, lowering his voice to the point where I have to strain my ears to hear him.

"Protect your pack. Something is coming."

My eyes widen at his warning. I don't bother to explain that I'm only a guest and I don't belong with the pack. I nod and hurry out of the room. I need to get back and speak with the alpha.

"Ari, the offer of protection is still there. Shadowborn or not," he calls out.

I smile at him gratefully over my shoulder, hoping he can tell how appreciative I am at the warning.

"I'll keep that in mind!" I call back before hurrying out of the building. He may be wrong, but Eric said something about the pack earlier as well. I need to warn them. Too much has been happening around the city for this to be a coincidence.

Chapter Twenty-One

I toss and turn in bed, my thoughts stuck on the events of the day. I requested a meeting with Alpha Mortlock as soon as I got back to the compound. They wanted it to be just the alpha, beta, gamma, and me, but I insisted that Seb and Killian be included, because I wanted them to know everything. Everyone was quiet while I explained, except for Killian and Alex, who growled when I told them that ASP had taken me in for questioning. Even Mortlock bared his teeth when he heard this. Apparently, if ASP takes a shifter into custody, they have to allow the alpha of that pack in the interrogation room. However, ASP doesn't need to do this if the suspect is a lone wolf. There's a grey area when it comes to guests of a pack. But Moon River believes that the alpha should have been present, especially in my case. I'm still blown away that they care enough to help fight my battles, I hadn't even thought of calling the alpha to help me.

I sent Eric a simple message letting him know I was safe and with friends, as I know he would be worried about me. Rolling over for what feels like the fiftieth time, I hit my pillow to make it more comfortable when I hear an odd sound, like footsteps, but many of them. I rack my brain. As far as I'm aware, there isn't a pack run organised for tonight, and I'm sure I would have been told if there was. I get up from my bed to walk to the window.

Yes, it's definitely footsteps I hear. Suspicion start rising through me as I reach the windows, squinting my eyes I gasp as I see around twenty wolves I don't recognise running through the compound. I hear a scream coming from the other side of the main house, which has me running for the stairs.

I sprint down the staircase and rush through the front door of the medical wing. There are wolves everywhere, and it's difficult to tell who's who in the dark, especially since I haven't seen many of the pack in wolf form. I'll have to do this off scent alone, which is going to make it difficult for me. I don't want to harm anyone from Moon River, and I'm going to have to get close to smell which pack they belong to.

A loud howl rings through the compound, which has my hair standing on end along my arms. The howl is quickly met by others as I hear people shouting as they wake up to chaos. A trio of wolves runs past me, and I know it's the alpha, Alex, and Isa. I've seen Alex in wolf form before, but I am still surprised by how big he is. He certainly rivals Mortlock in size. Alpha Mortlock has fur like my wolf, but while mine is more bronze, his is darker brown mottled with black. He has a vicious snarl on his face as he dives towards some of the enemy wolves. Isa is large in her wolf form, but slimmer and leaner, her grey fur slightly longer than the male wolves. Alex barks at me as they race past, and I'm sure it's an order to shift.

I feel a pang in my chest, and I know Killian is looking for me. My heart is torn. I want to go with Alex, but I need to know Killian and Seb are safe. Not to mention Gloria and my patients. I try to calm my mind, my wolf going into overdrive wanting to protect those who are *ours*.

I decide to ignore that little thought for now. Since when did I become so possessive?

"Ari!" I spin, finding myself in Killian's arms, my face buried in his chest.

I take a deep breath, inhaling his scent. Only then do I realise he's doing the same, his face nuzzled into my neck.

"It seems the warning was true," Killian tells me as he pulls away just enough to look at me.

I go to reply, but a loud growl has us turning towards the woods. A large grey wolf that I recognise is stalking towards us, his muzzle pulled back into a snarl. I curse as I see the long scar running down the wolf's face.

"It's the same wolf who attacked me. Guess we know who's behind this attack now," I tell Killian, but I'm not sure he's listening, his attention on the wolf in front of us.

The grey wolf snaps his teeth in my direction, and Killian growls loudly, his body shaking as he fights his wolf.

"I know this bastard," Killian grits out, his voice barely human, and I know he is close to losing control. "Protect the others. I've got this."

Jumping forward, Killian changes mid-air into his beautiful white wolf. I can't help but admire him for a few seconds before a scream cuts through my daydreaming. As I run towards the sound, I can't help but think it's not a coincidence that the two wolves I just left both have similar scars across their faces.

I fight against my wolf. I need to stay in control in case anyone gets injured. I rush around the corner when I see Seb backed up in front of one of the cabins in wolf form. Fear and anger rush through me. I've not seen Seb in his wolf form before, but somehow, I know it's him. His fur is an auburn colour, and he is much smaller in stature than the other wolves. He has two large wolves snarling at him and a bite on his front foot. I step closer and finally lose control of my wolf when I hear screaming inside the cabin—Jessica. My wolf rushes to the surface, and I don't hesitate to let her take over as we become one.

I barely notice the sting of the change, adrenaline pumping

through me. My change is fast, quicker than ever before, but I don't have time to think about that now. My thoughts and my wolf's are the same, finally in sync, neither of us is fighting the other. Our need to protect is running fiercely through our veins.

Seb is still facing off with the two stronger wolves, refusing to back down. Pride runs through us, my wolf seeing Seb in a different light. I snarl as I stalk up behind the other wolves, causing them to turn their backs on Seb, thinking me the bigger threat. I don't give them a chance to strike me, darting forward and latching onto the bigger one's neck. I catch him by surprise, and as I bite down and twist my head, I hear a sickening crack of the bones in his neck. A life taken so quickly, but I don't have time to think about that. I turn to fight the other one, but Seb is already attacking him. He may be smaller and not have as much power, but he's been training for years and currently has the upper hand in this fight.

Another scream from inside the cabin has me running towards the sound. I know Seb has this. Jessica needs my help. I run up the stairs and through the broken doorway, freezing at the sight before me.

"Ari!" a small, frightened voice calls out to me.

Jessica, Lottie, and the other pack children are cowering in one corner, huddled together, with Gloria pinned to the ground by a wolf double her size.

"Ah, little wolf, you've finally arrived," Alpha Black says as he pushes away from the cabin wall where he had been leaning. I struggle to calm my breathing. I need to change back to human form. I need to be able to talk. I take a deep breath through my muzzle and pull my wolf towards my centre. The change back to human is easier than it's ever been. Perhaps my wolf can sense my urgency.

I stand, seeing that someone has left a long coat by the doorway. Bloody considerate of the bastard to leave me clothes. I'm surprised. I thought he'd love me being vulnerable, standing naked in front of him. I pull the coat on and scan the room, trying not to grimace at the fact that the coat smells like *them*. I realise now why they left the clothing. They're trying to prove ownership of me. I want to throw off the coat, but I have more pressing matters. I glance around the room again. The children seem frightened but unharmed. Gloria is motionless but breathing. I think she's unconscious until I see her eyes flutter.

"Gloria, are you okay?" I call, not moving from my defensive position.

"Hello, Ari, dear. I'm fine. Keep the children safe for me," she replies. Even in a life-or-death situation, she is still caring for others, but I can hear the fear in her voice.

There are four members of Shadow Pack in the room—two grunts I don't recognise, Alpha Black, and lurking in the corner of the room is Terrance, my childhood tormentor. I realise that someone else is here as he walks into my field of vision. I don't know how I missed him. Grinning at me like he's won the lottery is Marcus.

"You fucking traitorous piece of shit. You would betray your pack like that? Attacking those who are your kin?" I ask incredulously.

"They stopped being my kin when they sided with you, you bitch," he snarls, losing his composure. Terrance places a hand on his chest in warning.

The alpha clears his throat, pulling my attention back to him. I bare my teeth at him in a snarl, anger filling me.

"Why the fuck are you here? What do you want?" I demand, my fury fuelling my words.

Alpha Black's knowing smile drops into a frown as though he is disappointed in my question.

"Oh, Ariana, you know better than that. We're here to take you home," he tells me, ending his statement with a smile like we're a having a happy family reunion.

That sounds like him. He came to get me, but he has to cause as much pain and suffering in the process. I think this is a little dramatic for the likes of Alpha Black. Usually, he goes straight for the jugular, unless there is something in it for him.

"That place was never a home, and if you think I'm going back with you, you're delusional. Especially after you have hurt my friends."

"That is no way to speak to your father," the alpha comments lightly, and I shake my head angrily, spitting at his feet.

"You lost all privilege of me calling you that the day you tortured me to access my powers," I fume, mourning the childhood I never had.

His expression turns into a frown. His eyes flick over my shoulder, and I'm made aware of someone standing in the doorway behind me—Killian. The alpha turns to look at Terrance before turning back to me.

"Aren't you going to greet your mate?" he goads, trying to make me slip up and make a mistake.

Killian growls and goes to step forward, but I block his path with my arm.

"*I* am her mate," Killian growls, but he doesn't make a move towards the others, instead trusting my judgement and standing by my side.

Alpha Black raises his eyebrows in surprise. Terrance has pushed away from the wall and looks like he wants to tear into Killian.

"My, my, you have been busy. Our little wolf is full of surprises," the alpha remarks, his tone even so I can't tell what he's thinking. "I'll cut you a deal, Ariana. Come with us, and I will call off the attack."

It sounds like a genuine offer, but I know that nothing is ever that simple with Shadow Pack. I would rather die than go back, but I'm also not prepared for my new family to get hurt any further because of me.

"Don't even think about it," Killian growls in my ear. I turn my head toward him slightly, my eyes staying on the alpha and Terrance.

"Killian—" I begin before he cuts me off.

"That self-sacrifice bullshit is exactly the type of thing you would do. Remember, I can feel your intentions. Besides, I don't trust this bastard to honour his word."

I nod. He's right. Damnit.

There are suddenly lots of loud noises outside of the house. Killian spins and snarls at something behind him. He races out the door, bursting into his wolf form mid-air.

"That's our cue to go," Alpha Black states.

Terrance stalks towards Gloria and kneels down next to her. Meeting my gaze, he stares at me with a sick smile on his face that I recognise all too well. I start moving before I even realise what I'm doing. My shadow powers are pushing at me to let them out, but I fight against it. I don't know if I can control it, and I don't want to hurt the children. But this is a mistake that will haunt me—I'm too slow.

Partially shifting his hand, he slices his claws through her neck. Everything moves in slow motion. I see her look at me before her eyes widen as she gasps for air.

I wordlessly scream and run at Terrance, pummelling my fists into him, not aiming for anywhere in particular, just trying to cause as much damage as possible. I'm so focused on Terrance that I don't hear someone come up behind me. Something sharp stabs me in the shoulder, but I ignore it, until my vision goes blurry and my arms become weak. I fall to the ground, my body numb. The last thing I see before my vision goes are Gloria's wide eyes, her hand stretched towards me. Blackness encompasses me, and I can feel myself being lifted. A mournful howl is the last thing I hear before unconsciousness claims me.

Chapter Twenty Two

"Why didn't you save me?" Gloria asks, her neck wound gaping as she looks up at me from the ground. Betrayal and disappointment are clear in her eyes.

"You let me down. Now Jessica has to grow up without a mother because of your incompetence," she continues.

I shake my head in denial, even though every word she says is true. I did let her down. I should have acted sooner. Poor Jessica is never going to speak to her mother again, and Seb... My heart clenches. How can I ever look him in the eye again?

"Seb is going to hate you for letting me die," she says, as if she can read my mind.

"Gloria, I'm so sorry. I will take care of them for you. I'm so sorry," I repeat, my heart breaking at the glazed look in her eyes.

Chemicals burn my nose, irritating my sensitive sense of smell. My brain is foggy, and I'm struggling to make sense of where I am. Flashes of Gloria's distraught and disappointed face float through my mind as I try to comprehend what is going on. I jerk upright as a stab of panic runs through me. Gloria.

My vision swims, and I throw my arms out to steady myself, my hands connecting with cold concrete walls. My breathing picks up as I try to focus, the dream playing through my thoughts. I hiss in frustration as my memories evade me and look around the room to try and make sense of things. *Think, Ari. Focus on what you do know as opposed to what you don't.*

At this point, it seems obvious that I was drugged, given the foggy state of my brain and the unknown location I'm currently in. Looking around the room, I try to take stock of all the details. I'm alone in a small, undecorated room with a single bulb hanging from a fixture above me, the dim lighting not quite permeating the corners of the space. I'm on the floor with a plain blanket thrown over me. It's cold in here, and I get the feeling we're underground. My wolf agrees with my assessment, we are far from the moon. This is not Moon River property, and I can't pick up any smells over the stench of cleaning chemicals, which have undoubtedly been used to wipe away any trace of who was previously here. This tells me that whoever brought me here went through a lot of trouble to hide their tracks.

I try to keep my thoughts clear, but the dream keeps creeping back in, and I can't shake the deep sadness that's running through me. I try to run through the last thing I can remember. I was woken up in the middle of the night…screams…the sound of feet running…paws…Killian…Seb. An attack on Moon River Pack. Everything comes back to me in a flash, and blinding grief hits me and threatens to overwhelm me. Gloria is dead. Shadow Pack killed her.

I don't know how to deal with this vast feeling of loss and grief, especially as I'm in unknown territory—I assume at the hands of Shadow Pack, given the circumstances of my capture. I do the only thing I know how to do—I channel the dark anger that lurks at the centre of my being, and I let it overcome me until my thoughts are quiet, focusing purely on my hatred for Shadow Pack. Seb's face flashes in my head, and I use it to fuel my anger. I can't think about how distraught he will be over the death of his mother or the fact I couldn't stop it, as it might threaten to break me.

I push up from the cold ground with shaky limbs and pace the sparse room I've been placed in. The metal door looks solid, it would need to be to hold in a shifter. I run my hands across it and test the handle—locked. No surprise there. I run my hands along the walls and count my steps from one side of the room to the other. I need to know everything about this room if I stand a chance of escaping. Unfortunately, I've been kept in rooms like this before, so I know the drill. A flashback threatens to overcome me, but I force it back with the cold rage that has taken over.

I'm not sure how long I've been here. Time passes strangely in captivity. The sound of footsteps alerts me to someone coming my way, and the sense of déjà vu makes me want to laugh. They've done this on purpose, most likely to 'teach' me my place. I lean against the wall in the far corner, crossing my arms as a key turns in the lock. A familiar figure fills the doorway, and I smirk in a way I know will piss him off.

"Hello, Terrance. Fancy seeing you here."

Terrance throws me a look of disdain at my smirk and greeting, probably disappointed I'm not cowering in the corner. Sorry, mate, you picked the wrong girl. I smile, a sick part of me pleased that I have, on some level, messed up his little fantasy of getting me back. A cold glint enters his eyes as he smiles back at me, but it's not a friendly smile. It's the evil kind of smile you would expect from a psychopath.

"Let's see if you're still smiling after what we have planned for you," he tells me as his eyes run over me.

I just arch my eyebrow at his comment. Other than that, I don't move a muscle. I know they killed Gloria to try and weaken me, but what they don't realise is that they've pushed aside my soft human feelings. Only anger reigns here now. If he's disappointed at my lack of reaction, he doesn't show it as he gestures, and four unknown lackeys fill the hallway behind him. Even if I weren't still feeling the effect of the drugs, I would have struggled to fight against four shifters of this size, and whatever they used on me is silencing my connection with my wolf and my shadow powers feel far away. They corner me in the small room, and I snarl at them as they reach for me. I punch at the guy closest to me and manage to throw the next guy who grabs my shoulder. Turns out my repetitive training with Killian did some good after all. However, eventually they overpower me and drag me from the room, Terrance following behind with a sick smirk on his face.

Pain racks my body as I shift positions on the hard floor, but I refuse to let out a moan of discomfort. I'm not sure how long I have been here, but I have endured five 'questioning' sessions so far, which is their bullshit name for torturing me for information.

All of the sessions go the same. They drag me into another room where they beat me until Terrance is happy. He then takes over, asking me all about Moon River Pack, trying to work out my connection with them, who my friends are, who I care for, and his biggest question—whether I have mated with anyone. He wants to know if Killian's claim is true. My scent has changed and it's driving him crazy, but I don't smell like Killian. If we had truly mated, he would have been able to sense the bond. Once they realise physical beatings aren't going to make me talk, they move onto psychologically hurting me. Talking of how he killed Gloria, how weak she was and that she deserved to die. How her kids would be motherless because I wasn't strong enough to save her. This is nothing that I don't already know, but it's starting to get to me.

I try to keep my wall of anger strong, but the pain and lack of food is making it hard for me to keep my resolve. The fact that they keep me drugged is also not helping. It's smothering my senses, and I keep thinking I can hear Killian's voice in my head. I know it's a hallucination, as he's being nice to me, telling me it's not my fault and to stay strong. I keep getting this annoying pulling sensation deep in my chest every time I feel like giving up and just giving into the pain. It feels like a kick in the chest. Had I not been so drugged, I might have paid more attention to it, but right now, I just put it down to being in so much pain that I'm feeling things that aren't real.

The sound of footsteps alerts me to my daily wake-up call. I push up from my curled position on the floor and lean against the wall, not strong enough to stand. The door opens, and I smile up at my tormentor.

"Hey, Terry! Ready for my daily dose of torture?" I mock him.

Something I've learned is that he hates it when I talk to him like this. It drives him mad that I'm not treating him with the respect he feels he deserves from me. It makes the beatings worse, but an angry, out of control Terrance is better than the sick, calculating Terrance that I know all too well.

"Bring her," he tells the guys behind him, ignoring my comment, but I can tell it got to him by the tic in his jaw.

I smirk and try to push down the feeling of dread that's rising up in me as they drag me to the room I have affectionately started calling the torture chamber. I refuse to admit it, but the moments when I am alone in my cell, I have begun to feel numb, the pain filling my every thought, and as much as I try to push it away, grief and remorse have started to press against my wall of anger. As much as I hate Terrance and his abuse, it helps to fuel my anger, even if only while I am in this room.

I'm dumped unceremoniously onto the same chair in the middle of the room. The room is a little bigger than the cell I am kept in, but it is brightly lit and painted all white. It must be a bugger to keep clean, seeing as I keep bleeding all over it, and the sharp smell of cleaning chemicals tells me I am right. The biggest difference between this room and the one I'm kept it is that one wall is filled with a mirror I am pretty sure is a two-way mirror. I wave at the mirror, before grimacing at my appearance—not pretty. I haven't seen the alpha since I was brought here, but I'm pretty sure he has been watching from behind the mirror. Someone is controlling Terrance and stopping him from going too far.

"Morning, Terry, what's the plan for today?" I chirp, enjoying the snarl that lets me know my comment has hit its mark. He really is easy to annoy.

He looks over his shoulder and nods towards the mirror before addressing the lackeys filling the space.

"You can go," he orders them. They glance at each other before nodding and leaving the room.

Hmm. That's different. Different makes me nervous.

"Today is going to go a little differently," he tells me, echoing my thoughts as he paces up and down the room.

"Tell me about Moon River Pack," he orders. The question is the same as usual, and I ignore him.

I look back into the mirror and shake my head at my bruised face. My hair hangs dirty and unwashed, and even in my drugged state, I almost don't recognise myself. I look down at my nails and tut at the broken, dirty state I find them in.

"I need a manicure," I mutter to myself.

The blow to my face takes me by surprise since I was looking down. Oh, the punishments are starting early today. Lucky me. I look up at Terrance's face as he looms over me.

"I said things are going to be different today," he spits out as his anger overtakes him. I watch as he tries to push it away and straightens up, a worrying gleam entering his eyes.

"There is no point in fighting it anymore, Ariana. Alpha Black has given me permission to mate you. You are mine now. You just need to agree to the bond."

I snort and roll my eyes.

"You really know how to proposition a girl, Terrance. You didn't seem to understand when I said no before, but I will say it again. Hell. No," I calmly reply.

Internally, I am filled with dread, but I'm pleased that my voice doesn't betray that fact.

He has the audacity to laugh at me as he starts to pace the room again, his gaze running over me. The look in his eyes makes me feel sick, and I have to fight to hide the shudder that runs through me.

"You think you have a choice in this?" He laughs again, turning and stalking towards me. "I know you have people you care about in Moon River. I will train that out of you. You belong to me now. If you agree to play along and behave, then I promise not to go back and slaughter the rest of the pack."

I feel like I have lead in my stomach and have to fight against the urge to vomit. Visions of Shadow Pack slaughtering my friends and the pack fill my mind with fear. I can tell when he senses my internal panic, as his smirk gets wider.

"I will never submit to you," I snap at him, watching as his smirk changes to a snarl. I'll never trust his promise not to hurt them. He would probably hunt them out of spite.

"You think this is bad?" His laugh makes me want to shudder, but I try to hide the reaction. "Things can get so much worse for you."

He hits me again, and the force has me falling to the floor. He pins me in place, and I fight under him as he forces my shoulders onto the ground.

"That boy you care for, the one whose mother I killed? He will watch as I mate you and we seal the bond with our bodies. And that bear you slept with? Oh yes, I know all about him. I can smell him on you. He will be the first to die, but not before I make him watch the bonding too," Terrance threatens me, his voice thick with desire as he talks about fucking me in front of my friends before killing them.

"You really are one twisted bastard," I spit. His words have refuelled my anger as I struggle under him, causing him to refocus on keeping me in place.

He ignores me and reaches for his belt, filling me with horror.

"Let's get some practice in, shall we?" he says as he removes his belt, releasing my shoulders as he straddles me and works at his clothing.

This is a totally different type of torture I was not prepared for, and it threatens to crack my wall of anger. He's about to hurt me in the most intimate way, and panic claws its way through my body.

"Fight it, Ari! Snap the fuck out of it and fight him!" hallucination Killian orders.

He may just be a figment of my imagination, but he's right. I won't let Terrance take that piece of me without a fight.

I start thrashing with renewed vigour, clawing at his arms and biting any piece of him that comes too close to my face. Swearing, Terrance stops undressing to pin me down once more. Shouting out a name I don't recognise, he struggles with holding me down until I hear the door open and one of the lackeys from before lumbers in.

"Hold her down," he orders with a snarl.

The guy does as he's told, forcing my shoulders onto the ground as Terrance reaches forward, ripping my top open and causing buttons to fly across the room. Even the evil lackey looks disturbed.

"Um, sir? Alpha Black said not to—" he begins before he is cut off.

"Shut the fuck up and hold her down!" Terrance practically screams, and the lackey pales but nods at the order from his beta.

"Terrance, don't cross this line," I tell him, pleased that my voice doesn't show the terror that is running through me.

His hand gropes my breast as I struggle against their holds. Terrance leans over me, pressing his face against the side of mine so I can hear his rapid breathing in my ear. His erection is pressed against my stomach, and he grinds against my body.

"I will make you forget about them. Eventually, you will only think of me. I will kill anyone who dared touch you," he whispers into my ear, his breath hot against my skin.

Anger takes over my body, filling me with a deadly calm I have only experienced once before.

"Hold on, Ari, fuel that anger. We're nearly there," hallucination Killian orders me.

I do exactly as he tells me, my body stilling. I feel Terrance relax his weight over me, thinking I have given in to his sick groping of my body.

"Didn't your mother ever tell you that no means no?" I whisper into his ear before rearing up and smacking my head into his.

Leaping off me, Terrance clutches his head as blood streams from his broken nose. I ignore the pain I inflicted on myself, focusing on the anger running through me. Remembering Killian's training, I twist my body, trying to get out of the lackey's hold on my shoulders, using his shock and weight against him. With him now on the floor, I straddle him and brace my weight against his shoulders before he realises what is going on. I place my hands on his neck and twist, hearing the sickening snap of his neck. His eyes go wide before his body goes limp beneath me.

I push myself up on shaky legs before turning to look at Terrance. He is staring at me in shock, his hands still on his profusely bleeding nose. I take a step towards him before I hear shouting in the distance. Terrance swears and spins on his heel, sprinting out of the room and down the corridor. I curse and try to follow him before reality hits me at what just happened. I was nearly raped, and I just killed a guy. I try to focus on my anger again, but reality is taking over. I stumble out of the room towards the sounds of fighting before pausing at the end of the corridor. I have no guarantee that whoever is fighting Shadow Pack is any more on my side than Terrance was. Thankfully, I am saved from making that decision as a furious Killian rounds the corner.

"Ari!" he shouts, his voice cracking as he runs towards me.

He goes to touch me, but I flinch away from the sudden contact. He stops in his tracks as he registers my ripped shirt and my reaction to being touched. I can see him vibrating in fury as he comes to conclusions about what happened to me.

"Killian, now is not the time. We need to get her out of here." Seb's voice fills the corridor, and I look around to see my friend.

I have never been so glad to see my guys—well, two of them anyway. Seb looks at me like he wants to embrace me, but I can tell he is trying to give me space. Besides, Killian would probably blow a gasket if he touched me right now. I'm surprised at how he is talking to Killian, though, and even more surprised when the stronger shifter nods stiffly in agreement.

"Can you walk?" Killian asks me softly.

I nod, wanting nothing more than to surround myself with my guys, but not now, not here, while I still have the impression of Terrance's hands on my body. They lead me down a series of twisting corridors until we come to a larger room, which is full of bodies. Alex is in the centre of the room, panting as he breaks one of the lackey's necks and drops the body to the ground. He looks up as we enter the room, and an emotion I don't recognise fills his face.

"Ari," is all he says before he notices how I am cradling my body. His face hardens before he and Killian nod at each other. I don't know what they're communicating to each other, but I just want to get out of here. I can hear fighting in other rooms, so I assume other members of the pack are here, which means that Moon River Pack is at risk.

"Please, can we just go home to the pack?" I request, and I see their faces soften.

"Killian, Seb, can you take her back? I'll finish up here," Alex tells them.

They both nod, and Seb offers me his hand. Killian looks like he is about to protest, but when he looks at me, his expression softens, as if he can see that I need this small act of comfort right now. I take Seb's hand, and they silently lead me out of the building. I numbly walk over to one of their cars and climb in, dimly wondering when the pack had become home.

Chapter Twenty-Three

I scrub at my skin, trying to get the feeling of Terrance's hands off my body. The water of the shower is nearly scalding, and it does nothing to help the pain of my bruised and cut body, but this is something I need to do to feel sane. Tori is waiting on the other side of the bathroom door for me while I shower. When we got back to the compound and the boys walked me to my room, I burst into tears when I saw her sitting on my bed. She gently wrapped her arms around me and shooed the guys away. Killian protested but didn't dare piss off a witch.

My skin is raw and red from standing under hot water for such a long time, and I turn off the shower with a sigh. The room falls silent, and I numbly pat myself dry, trying to avoid the worst of the bruising. A soft knock comes from the door, and I pull on an old pair of Seb's PJ bottoms and a soft T-shirt of Killian's that they left for me to change into. They knew I had clothing here, but all of it was too tight to wear comfortably while I am so bruised. I inhale the scent of the guys, and it makes me feel stronger. The knock comes again.

"Ari, are you okay in there? The guys want to see you." Tori's soft voice reaches me.

I look at myself in the mirror and shake my head. I look broken.

When did I become this person? I open the door and smile at Tori, my gut clenching at her gentle smile.

"Let's go face the music," I tell her before striding out of the room—well, as well as someone as hurt as me can stride.

Once I reach the bottom of the stairs—with lots of swearing, mind you—I come to a stop as I see everyone gathered in the medical office. My office. I walk slowly into the room and take stock of who is here. Alpha Mortlock and Lena are here, along with Alex and Isa. Killian looks pissed off in the corner, but my eyes are drawn to Seb, who looks different. He is radiating more power than I have ever felt from him, not as strong as the others in the room, but enough to make me stop in my tracks. He is smiling at me, but I can see he is grieving deeply for the loss of his mother. Guilt hits me, and I wonder what the result of this meeting will be. The attack was my fault, after all. If I wasn't here, then Shadow Pack would have left them alone and Gloria wouldn't have been killed.

"She's blaming herself for the attack," Killian growls out from the corner.

Everyone's eyes flick to him, then back to me, wearing varying looks of shock and anger on their faces. How on earth does he know that? I thought my poker face was pretty good. I can feel the anger and frustration rolling off him, and a part of me wants to go over and comfort him. I push that away. Now is not the time.

"Ari—" Alpha Mortlock begins before Alex strides forward, a look of anger on his face.

"Why the fuck would it be your fault? Don't let those sick fucks make you think that any piece of this is your fault," he shouts.

I raise my eyebrows at his outburst, rarely seeing this much emotion or anger from Alex. What is winding him up so much that he would lose his usual professional cool? I have seen him playful and flirty, but never this angry.

"If anything, it is my fault," he says. "I'm the protector of this pack. As beta, it's my job to anticipate threats like this. You even warned us, and I still let it happen! Because of my failings, they killed Gloria and the others. They took you, and I couldn't find you!" he continues, his voice breaking as he finishes.

Ah. That's why he seems so angry. He's blaming himself. A feeling of belonging and a warm emotion I don't have words for fill me at his words. Alpha Mortlock places a hand on Alex's shoulder in comfort, but Alex's eyes are glued to mine.

"I thought we had lost you. They hid all traces of where they had gone or where you were," he says brokenly.

"He is right, Ari, you are not to blame. Nor are you, Alex. This was the sick minds of the Shadow Pack," Alpha Mortlock tells us, and I hear the truth in his words. He fully believes what he's saying. He doesn't blame me. A weight I didn't realise I'd been carrying lifts from me, and breathing feels a little easier.

"There was magic involved in getting Shadow Pack out of the compound." I spin around at Tori's voice.

I still wonder how she is here. I haven't had the chance to ask her yet. She walks farther into the room and puts her arm around me as she leans against the counter, giving me comfort with her touch.

"When you disappeared, Alex called me to see if I could help." I glance over at Alex in surprise, knowing his feelings around witches. He was civil with Tori when she visited, but I knew he was uncomfortable around them. He must have been desperate to find me to contact Tori. "I went to the place you were taken and tried a tracking spell. I used everything I know, and I couldn't find you. You know me, Ari, tracking spells are my thing!" she states earnestly, and I can tell from her voice she is feeling guilty that she couldn't track me.

"I eventually did a spell that proved magic had been used, but I couldn't break through it, which means that a strong witch or warlock is involved," she concludes, and the others nod in agreement.

"What we need to work out is why a witch or warlock would

help Shadow Pack. And where have they gone now?" Alpha Mortlock asks, looking to me for inspiration.

"As far as I know, they never had any contact with any magic users while I was held captive with the pack." My guys flinch at the mention of my abduction. "But I wasn't exactly privy to that kind of information," I state, running my hand though my damp hair in frustration.

I bite down on my lip and look up to meet Alpha Mortlock's eyes, dreading this question. "Did we lose anyone else? What happened?" Out of the corner of my eye, I see Seb flinch at the unmentioned fact that his mother had been killed.

The alpha sighs and nods, pulling Lena closer into his side, her arm wrapping around him. Her eyes are red and puffy, like she'd been crying.

"We lost a couple of our wolves during the attack, along with Gloria. We also lost a wolf when we managed to track you down. Although their deaths are a tragedy, it could have been much worse. Thanks to your warning, we were more prepared," he tells me, his voice soft as he talks of the dead.

"We killed all of the shifters in the building you were in except for the beta—Terrance, is it?" Growls filled the room at his name, surprisingly not just coming from me. The loudest one comes from Seb, who looks like his wolf is going to burst out of his skin.

Alpha Mortlock nods in agreement at the frustration in the room and keeps a wary eye on Seb as he continues.

"Unfortunately, he escaped. We're not sure how. We suspect magic was involved. We also couldn't find the alpha."

I curse at his words. They won't give up trying to get me. The best thing I can do is to leave so these guys don't get hurt any more. I know they don't blame me for what happened, but that doesn't stop the fact that as long as I'm here, Shadow Pack will keep attacking.

"No." Killian's deep voice reaches me as he slowly walks

towards me. His body is tense, and as he approaches me, he keeps his movements slow, like he's worried he might startle me.

He places a hand on my waist and looks deeply into my eyes. I should feel crowded and want my space, but it feels right, him comforting me.

"You can't leave. You belong here with us. Do you want to leave?" he inquires, his tone demanding, like he needs to hear the answer.

I pause before I reply, admitting to myself what I have been trying to ignore for the last month—I have felt more at home here with the pack than I have ever felt before, even living with Tori. The acceptance from the pack has made me care for them, and I can't imagine not seeing them all again.

"No. I don't want to leave." My declaration rings around the silent room.

The sounds of relieved breaths fill the room, and I see several smiles, including one from Alpha Mortlock, who is being hugged by a beaming Lena.

"There is always a place for you here, Ariana," he tells me warmly. I wince slightly at his continued use of my full name. Only Shadow Pack calls me Ariana, all my friends call me Ari. I will have to have a word with him about it, but now is not the time. I hate to break the somewhat happy mood, but it's important.

"But how can I stay? Shadow Pack will keep coming for me. I can't put those I care about in danger over and over again," I admit as I look around at those faces who have earned a place in my heart. I pause and frown. Someone is missing.

"Where is Garett?" I ask. I would have thought someone would have called him to tell him what had happened, even if they hadn't called him to help find me. I know the pack's relationship isn't the smoothest with him, but they accepted he was important to me and should have informed him of something like this.

The mood in the room changes, and the grim looks on their

faces have me straightening and pulling away from Killian and Tori.

"What are you not telling me?" I question, my tone harsh with my worry.

"We tried to get in touch with him after you were taken, and we couldn't find him. We contacted his pack, and they haven't heard from him since yesterday. They're looking for him," Tori replies, and I'm glad it is her who breaks the news to me.

Worry fills me, and I try to calm my thoughts. We don't know for sure that he has been taken. He is strong and would put up one hell of a fight. Sometimes, Garett goes off the grid for a day or two—something about being one with nature. It's a bear thing.

"Okay, so what happens next?" I ask, clamping down on my fear for Garett. As soon as Tori and I are alone, I will get her to track him.

"Now we grieve our dead. Then we plan. Moon River does not just take an attack lying down. We demand justice." Mortlock's voice is firm as he says this, and I can feel his alpha strength fill the room. There is nodding from the others in consensus.

Everyone in the room breaks off into small groups, chatting quietly amongst themselves. People start to leave, and Alpha Mortlock comes over and looks like he wants to place his hand on my arm but changes his mind.

"Are you okay?" he asks me, his eyes scanning me, taking in my bruised appearance.

"No," I answer honestly. "But I will be," I say with a small smile.

"You know where I am if you need anything," he offers with a small nod before leaving the room.

Tori leaves with a small wave, gesturing that she is going back up to my room, leaving me alone with my guys. Well, all of them except Garett. My heart clenches at the thought of him missing. Killian notices and comes over to me, placing his hand on my cheek gently.

"He will be okay. And if he isn't, we will find him," he vows.

This is a different side of Killian I've never seen before, softer, kinder. I look into his eyes and can't stop myself as I lean forward and place a tender kiss against his lips. He freezes in shock before kissing me back, a slight groan leaving him as he presses against me.

The sound of feet moving towards me has me pulling away as I see Alex standing next to us. He places his hand on my shoulder, rubbing it gently with his thumb.

"Killian's right. If anything has happened to him, we'll help you find him," he tells me, and from the sincerity in his tone, I know he means it.

I look between the two men giving me comfort and raise my eyebrows.

"We came to an agreement," Killian informs me, answering my unspoken question, his voice gruff as his eyes run over me again.

"What kind of agreement?" I ask warily, confused.

"When you were taken," Alex explains, "we realised you were important to us and that we couldn't lose you. We then realised you care for each of us, Garett included, and that any of us fighting over you is going to hurt you. We agreed that's not what we want and we would no longer fight over who you care for."

I am gobsmacked, and I look between the three of them before my gaze lands on Killian.

"Wait, you agreed to this?" I ask, shocked that my alpha wolf would fight against his instinct and the bond to agree to this.

He nods slowly, reluctantly, as he looks from Alex to me.

"I don't like it, and it won't be easy, but I never want you to be hurt again, especially when it is my behaviour that is hurting you," he answers, and I feel my eyes well up.

I look across at Seb. My funny, caring Seb. He is standing by himself on the other side of the room, and I realise the guys included him in the group of those I cared about. Seb and I hadn't explored that part of our relationship, trying to keep things strictly as friends, even though our feelings may have wished otherwise. I walk over towards him, unsure how I feel about all this, especially as Alex has apparently shared he has feelings for me.

"You agreed to this too?" I ask Seb softly, wincing slightly at the pain in his eyes.

"I'm not assuming anything. None of us are. If you don't want a relationship with any of us, that's fine. We are not trying to push anything on you. But we also want you to know we won't fight it. I don't know what might happen between us, but I know I feel more for you than I ever have with anyone else, and I am sick of fighting it," Seb tells me, his voice stronger and more confident than I have ever heard it. "Mom wouldn't have wanted us to pussyfoot around our feelings," he adds, his voice heavy with grief.

"Seb," I start, my heart heavy. "I am so sorry about your mum." I break off, my voice tight, and I see his eyes fill. "If you blame me for not being able to save her, I understand. I feel the same," I tell him quietly, feeling as though my heart is breaking as he turns away from me.

His eyes shoot back up to me at my comment, his brows pulled into a frown. He turns so he is facing me again and walks towards me, backing me into my desk. Placing his hands on either side of me, he traps me so I have nowhere to look but into his gorgeous eyes.

"You are not to blame. Never think that again. Do you hear me?" he demands, and I silently nod at my suddenly dominant Seb.

At my agreement, he leans forward, placing his hand on my jaw, and firmly pulls me towards him like he is going to kiss me. My emotions are a mess and I know there is a chance I might regret this later, but right now, all I want is Seb's lips on mine, even though I know the other guys are watching.

"Ari!" Tori's panicked voice has me jerking away from Seb as she thunders down the stairs, my phone grasped in her hand.

The guys around me are instantly on alert and surround me as if to protect me. I push past them to get to my best friend.

"What is it? What's wrong?" I demand as I hurry towards her, my stomach dropping as I see the picture that has flashed up on the screen.

I turn away from her and lean against the wall for support as panic threatens to overwhelm me. Seb hurries to my side, placing a hand on my shoulder as Alex takes my phone from Tori, his face paling as he sees the graphic picture that has been sent to me before passing it to Killian, who snarls in response.

"They have Garett."

Chapter Twenty Four

The next few hours pass in a blur of arguing and planning, but we are finally on our way to find Garett. I wanted to go alone, as the message had stipulated, but was quickly shot down. Now, I'm sitting in my car with Seb and Killian, with Alex at the wheel.

"This is probably a trap," I mutter as I stare out of the car window.

They refused to let me drive, protesting that I was too injured. They all wanted me to stay behind, stating that I was what Shadow Pack wanted and they didn't want to risk them getting me. I had swiftly informed them that I would be going, and if they somehow left me behind, I would just follow them. If they were looking for backup from Tori, they were disappointed, as she had just shrugged and told them I would find a way to get there anyway so they might as well take me. Isa and several of the pack defenders had wanted to come along. Even Alpha Mortlock had wanted to help, which warmed my heart. Eventually, it was agreed that the pack couldn't be left undefended in case this was a trap, especially so soon after the last attack. Besides, the alpha is needed with his grieving and vulnerable wolves.

"That is exactly why we didn't let you go alone," Alex retorts as he drives towards the address sent to me.

The message contained the address where I was to meet them, specifying that I was to go alone and that they wanted me in exchange for Garett. A second message had shown a graphic photograph of Garett, who had clearly been beaten. I try to control my breathing as the image flashes through my mind again, trying to contain my anger.

"They probably won't expect you to bring us. From what you have told us about Shadow Pack, they isolated you and made you distrust anyone. You've always been a lone wolf because of it, so they are hoping you'll run straight to them and sacrifice yourself for Garett without saying a word to us," Seb says from his seat next to me in the back of the car, his hand in mine.

Annoyingly, what he is saying makes sense, as that is exactly what I was going to do. If I'd seen the message before Tori, I would have snuck out on my own and done exactly that. Killian snorts from his seat and turns to look at me over his shoulder.

"We all know you're the self-sacrificing kind. Do you really think we would let you go on your own?" he asks as I gape at him in offence.

"I am not the 'self-sacrificing' kind!" I retort, having no idea what they are insinuating. "I run away from every situation that makes me uncomfortable," I continue, not sure why I'm saying any of this out loud.

Alex looks at me through the rearview mirror and gives me a slight smile.

"You only run away from commitment. If someone is in need, you would sacrifice yourself for them," he tells me firmly, and I realise there is some merit in what he is saying.

"You accepted the challenge to defend me at the pack social, and you ran into a fight without thinking to protect Jessica, even though you knew there would be dire consequences for you. Plus, you're a nurse. I would call that self-sacrificing," Seb chips in with a squeeze of my hand.

Huh, maybe they are right. I chew on my thumbnail as we get closer to the abandoned warehouse I have been directed to. I know, cliché, right? The plan for us is to abandon the car a few miles out. The guys will shift into their wolves downwind and follow behind as I walk to the warehouse in my human form. They debated about this, but I argued that Shadow Pack will probably be watching out for me, and if they walk in with me, they could do something to harm Garett. Seb was the one who suggested that they should follow behind in wolf form to make sure I wasn't ambushed. I tried to convince him to stay behind. I'm worried he is going to get hurt against such dominant wolves, but Alex spoke up for him and said he should come. He has been different since the attack, quieter, but more than that he *feels* different, stronger, more powerful.

I glance over at him, worry gnawing in my chest. He feels my gaze and turns to smile at me. It's a soft smile meant to comfort, but I see the grief in it, and there is a new hardness about him.

The car pulls to a stop, and I take in a deep breath, calming my nerves and calling up the anger that has been boiling in me since the attack. I must now put on a mask. This is nothing new for me, but this time, I must convince Shadow Pack that Garett is nothing more than a possession, taken without permission, that I am now here to reclaim.

The woods are silent, save for the sound of my feet against the ground. I can't see or hear the guys. They have done a good job of silently tracking me. If I didn't know they were following me, I wouldn't know they were there. The abandoned warehouse is in front of me, and I look around for any signs of movement. This is an odd place for a warehouse. It must have been a privately owned building, as no company would store their merchandise out here in the middle of nowhere.

Keeping my steps strong and my shoulders back, I make sure I appear confident as I stride towards the old building. A feeling of foreboding hangs over me, and I can't shake it. I know we are walking into a trap, and I can only hope that Seb is right and they will be expecting me to come alone. Chemicals burn my nose and obscure my senses as I try to pick up their scents. I can hear shuffling and some low murmurs coming from inside the building, so I know several people are inside.

As I step over the threshold, a tingling sensation runs across my body. Shit. I've just set off some sort of magical ward. If I was human, I wouldn't be able to feel it, but anyone with supernatural blood would be able to feel that. Dread lines my stomach, and I turn to face the doorway I just walked through. Reaching out my hand, I curse as it hits an invisible barrier, confirming my suspicions. Once someone has crossed the ward, they cannot leave unless the one who controls it allows passage or dies. Meaning I'm trapped. It also confirms that Shadow Pack has no intention of letting Garett go, even if I comply with their whims. I suspected as much, but it's still a blow to my stomach.

"I can hear you, little wolf. Come in," Alpha Black calls.

Fighting against the urge to turn and run, I straighten my back and walk down the corridor into the main room of the warehouse. It's a large and mostly empty room, filled only with people and a single chair in the centre. There are about a dozen wolves in the room, one of which is the traitor Marcus. The alpha and Terrance are standing by the chair, and I meet their smirking faces, keeping my eyes away from the slumped figure on the chair. I want to run to Garett, fall to my knees, and beg for his forgiveness. The nurse part of me is desperate to assess his injuries, worried about his laboured breathing. However, I can't show any of that. Any sign of affection will be viewed as a weakness, and I can't let them see how I care for him, as they will use that against me.

"Let's get this over with, shall we?" I state, looking over my enemies with a coldness in my eyes I rarely let show.

I see some of the wolves in the room flinch under my gaze, but if it affects the alpha or Terrance, they don't let it show. In fact, the alpha's smirk grows, as if he knows I'm putting on a front.

"Are you ready to come home with us and take your rightful

place among us?" Alpha Black asks. A knowing look has entered his eyes, and it is making me nervous.

"I'm here to reclaim what you have taken from me." I keep my voice firm and nod toward Garett.

I still keep my eyes off him, although the temptation to look, just to check that he's okay, is almost overwhelming. Especially because at the sound of my voice, he's been trying to lift his head, making pained noises and struggling against his bonds. I know he's trying to get to me, to protect me from these monsters who call themselves family. I know I'm going to have to say and do things in this room that will hurt him, but my main priority is keeping him safe, and I hope he understands that.

"You expect me to believe you have no feelings for this *bear*?" Alpha Black questions with a laugh and a shake of his head.

His tone makes it clear what he thinks of me sleeping with a different race of shifter. Terrance has a similar disgusted expression on his face and is looking at Garett with hate in his eyes. It's not hard to guess that Terrance was the one to dole out Garett's beating. Another reason for me to kill the bastard. My wolf growls in agreement, eager to tear him apart for all he has put us through.

I feel a shudder run through me as magic brushes over my skin as my guys pass through the magical barrier. Part two of our plan has begun. Three snarling wolves dart into the room and start attacking the shifters. They would have felt the ward on their way in, so they will know we have to kill whoever controls the ward if we have any hope of leaving here alive. We may be outnumbered, but we have surprise on our side.

The shock on Terrance's face is almost comical, and the alpha looks impressed.

"I'm surprised at you, little wolf. You accepted help. Perhaps the lone wolf is ready to settle down after all. I guess it's a good thing I installed the wards then." He smirks.

I shrug my shoulders. None of this is news to me. I suspected he wouldn't just let us walk out. The magic had been a surprise though.

"I knew this would be a trap. Not even you travel without backup, so why shouldn't I?" I ask with a shrug, trying to ignore the snarls and growls coming from the fighting wolves around me. Terrance has joined in the fight now. I don't like that he's out of sight, but I keep my eyes trained on the alpha. "So, you have a mage doing your dirty work now?" I query, keeping my voice even.

"I bought the wards off a mage. He didn't even know what they were for," he answers with a shrug.

This puts me at ease a little. Mages have the power to put certain spells into objects or paper. For example, a ward spell like the one used here could be put onto paper to be activated in the desired place at a later date. The thought of Shadow Pack having direct access to a mage was a worry, so the fact he probably just bought this on the black market, while surprising, is not as disastrous. I am surprised that Shadow Pack is buying spells from mages though. Alpha Black is more racist towards other supernatural races than most shifters. I guess he takes a break from being a bigot when it suits him.

I start taking small steps towards the alpha. We need to wrap this up quickly. Killian and Seb are covered in bite wounds, and Alex is cornered by two smaller wolves—Marcus is one of them—but the room is littered with the bodies of Shadow Pack. I'm so focused on the alpha that I fail to realise that Terrance is about to grab me until it's too late. Caught in a bear hug, I try to struggle out of the hold using the technique Killian taught me, but I can't shift my weight.

"Call off your wolves," Alpha Black demands.

He may have me trapped, but as I look around, I see we have the upper hand—we're winning. Killian has killed his opponent and is now helping Alex finish off the two who had him cornered.

I laugh, which turns into a grunt as Terrance squeezes me harder, but I find that I don't care what they do to me. As long as my guys get out of here, Shadow Pack can do whatever they like. Huh, guess I am self-sacrificing after all.

"We will kill your *precious bear*," Terrance whispers cruelly into my ear.

My stomach twists, but I know that was their plan anyway. I try to keep my face neutral, remembering the role I am playing. I attempt to shrug, but it's difficult with my arms trapped by my sides.

"I don't trust you. Plus, I told you. I don't care. I just came to retrieve my property." The words burn my mouth as they come out.

I know I've made a grave mistake when the alpha smiles at me. I know that smile. It's a cold, evil smile, like he is going to enjoy this moment.

"Then you won't care if he's dead or alive."

The world slows down, and before he has even finished his sentence, I'm on the move. Calling down to the dark part of my soul, I bring forward my shadow self. I let go of the hard-earned control that usually keeps that part of me on lockdown and let her take full control. With all my inhibitions gone, my shadow self acts faster than those in the room can blink.

My body ghosts out of existence, slipping from Terrance's hold, darting forward to the alpha. We watch as his hand slowly moves towards Garett's exposed neck with a blade he must have had concealed somewhere. I grip the knife, and my body returns solid as I twist the knife from his grip, slicing across his neck. I watch numbly as my father's blood covers me and he falls limply to the floor.

"Ari..." Garett's broken voice breaks me out of my stupor.

I spin around and drop to my knees in front of him, placing my hands on his face, needing to feel him, to know he's okay. I press my forehead to his, relief spreading through me. Suddenly, a sharp pain shoots through my head and a wave of dizziness nearly knocks me to the ground.

I've gone too deep, let go of too much control. There's a price to be paid with Shadowborn powers. I can feel the Shadow Dimension tugging at my soul. I don't know what will happen on the other side. Grief surges through me at the thought of losing the guys just as I am beginning to acknowledge that there may be something worth fighting for.

"I love you, Ari," Garett whispers tiredly. I hear the love in his voice even after everything that has happened.

My heart warms, and I find I don't mind sacrificing myself if it means that Garett and the guys are safe.

"I love you too," I whisper to him, my eyes filling with tears. I lean forward and press a kiss to his lips.

With a cry, I feel my soul being ripped from my body as I fade into the Shadow Dimension.

For an odd moment, I seem to hover above myself, and I get one last look at the people who have become everything to me in such a short span of time. The last thing I see is my lifeless body with the guys running to surround me and Garett, who's still restrained to the chair screaming my name.

Now all I know is darkness.

BONUS SCENE

A scene from Killian's point of view when he realises that Ari is his true mate.

Killian

"Again!" I demand, watching Ari scowl at me from her place on the floor, causing my insides to twist. "I've never seen a more lazy and out-of-shape wolf in all my life," I continue to shout, my face twisting into a mask of disgust. Ari pushes up from the ground and takes her defensive position, the look on her face making her feelings for me perfectly clear. I know that I am being harsh, and a little part of me is screaming at me to knock it off, to stop hurting her. But if she is hurting, then she will know where she stands, she won't try to get close to me. I can't deny the pull I feel towards her. I shake my head and lift my lip in a snarl.

I can't afford to think that way. My heart belongs to my mate, Julie. The ever-familiar pain of losing her rips through me. They say that time helps heal all wounds. That is a lie, this is a wound that will never heal, the pain is just something that becomes part of your life. When I first lost Julie, it was like the oxygen had been taken from my lungs, every living moment was painful. Not only had I lost my mate, but I lost my pack as well. The pain was almost enough to consume me and almost did. It was only my desire for revenge that kept me going. That, and the fact that if there is a Heaven or Hell, I knew that when I died, I wouldn't be joining Julie and my pack in eternal rest. I would be going to Hell where I belonged.

I step up to Ari and position myself in an offensive stance like I have been doing for the last twenty minutes. For a Shadowborn, she's useless at protecting herself. How she has managed to survive this long, I have no idea. *Shadowborn*. Just thinking the word makes my wolf bristle and push to the surface, demanding to be let loose. If it wasn't for this annoying pull that I feel towards her, I would stay the hell away.

I place my hands on her, ignoring the small thrill that runs through me at touching her. My eyes run up her body, and I tell myself that it is because I am checking her stance and not the way that her curves are shown off in her workout gear.

"Twist your upper body more. You haven't hooked your leg properly," I whisper in her ear, but she has gotten distracted again. How is she ever going to protect herself if she can't even manage this?! A growl escapes my lips at the thought of someone attacking her. I am so shocked at this thought passing through my head that in attempt to clear it, I twist my body and throw her to the ground again. She lands on the floor heavily, and I spin and pin her to the ground. *Come on Ari, fight me! Prove me wrong, throw me off.*

She stares up at me, her face frustrated. Frustration I can work with. I remember her at the fight at the pack meet the other day, it wasn't until she was angry that she started fighting like she actually *wanted* to win. Fine, if getting her angry is what it takes to make her take this seriously, then that is what I will do.

"Useless! Why the fuck should I bother teaching you?" I shout, seeing her face twist. "Fight me! Get up!" I bellow. I see her try to fight me, her small form twisting and thrashing underneath me, but she can't shift my weight. Fine, if I have to play the bad guy to keep her safe, then that is what I will do. My wolf agrees, we need to keep her safe. I shake my head at that thought as if to clear it from my head.

"Pathetic." I lower my face to hers, and my wolf pushes to the surface. Being this close to her awakens something inside me that I haven't felt since before Julie was killed. No! I cannot feel this way about a Shadowborn. My anger at myself and my traitorous feelings rise, along with my alpha power. "Pathetic," I sneer again, but I'm talking more to myself at this point rather than Ari.

Something about my words must have reached her, as I see her eyes widen slightly before she goes limp beneath me. I stare at her body for a moment in shock. She starts shaking, and this is when the panic begins to rise within me.

"Ari?" I call, reaching forward and shaking her shoulder. She cries out at my touch, and I whip my hand away as if I have been burned. What the hell is happening?! She cries out again as if she is in pain.

"Ari!" I shout. What have I done? "Ariana, snap out of it!" I shout, my voice filling the hall, my concern for her making my voice harsh.

The doors slam open, and I glance over to see Seb walk in, his usual jovial expression falling as he sees Ari twitching on the ground under me. I hurry off her and kneel by her side as he runs over, placing his hand on her arm.

"What did you do to her?" he shouts. I've never seen him so angry, and I have to fight with my wolf not to tear into him and discipline him for speaking to me that way. I glare at him before my eyes fall back to Ari, she seems to be waking up now, which helps ease the panic within in me.

"We were practising some self-defence moves, and she just

went stiff in my arms. I let her go, and she went limp, staring at the ceiling. Then her eyes closed, and she started shaking, like she was scared. She kept whispering a name. It was like someone was hurting her." I spit the last words out.

"She gets flashbacks. Something must have triggered her," Seb mutters, his attention fully on the woman he is lifting into his lap. Ari opens her eyes fully and smiles weakly up at Seb.

"Hey, beautiful," he says with his own beatific smile.

An anger and jealousy like I have never know fills me until Seb's words register with me.

"Flashbacks. Like memories. You mean this happened—" A growl cuts off my words, ripping from my chest. I am more wolf than man right now. I need to protect her. I need her in my arms right fucking *now*. My focus is narrowed just on Ari and the male hands that are touching her. I hold open my arms, gesturing for Seb to pass her to me. I don't trust myself to get any closer, and I am fighting every instinct that wants to tear Seb limb from limb.

"Give her to me," My voice is more animal than human. I can see that Seb wants to fight my order, and part of me wants him to so I can fight him. I see the moment that he realises this flash through his eyes before he sighs and passes her over to me.

As soon as she is in my arms, my eyes widen as a powerful rush runs through my body. My breath is taken from my lungs like I have been punched in the chest, and I feel the moment that the true mated pair bond settles over me, connecting me directly to her. I try to fight it, but it's a losing battle. My wolf howls within me as we are consumed completely by the bond.

I'm aware of other people entering the room, but my focus is locked on her. I am acting like a love-struck pup, but my wolf is fully in control, the bond riding me hard. I stroke my hand up and down her back, needing to help calm my mate, who looks two seconds away from freaking out. She speaks to me, but in this state, I can't understand her.

Someone tries to walk towards us, Alex, I realise as I flick my eyes up at the approaching threat, growling in response, my arms tightening around my mate.

"Mine." The word rip out of me.

"Killian, I'm not going to hurt her, but you need to put Ari down," Alex says to me as he crouches down near us, his arms wide. I hear the words, but I struggle to understand them. They want to take Ari from me. I growl again fiercely. My gaze shoots up as someone runs into the room. Alpha Mortlock. My friend. I growl as he tries to come closer. He stops, taking a step back. I can feel Ari getting distressed through the delicate, not yet accepted bond between us. I look down at her again, pulling her even closer to my chest.

Ari struggles in my arms with a strength I didn't know she possessed, throwing herself away from me. My wolf howls at the loss of contact between us, my body jerking as he tries to take over. I stalk towards her, needing my mate in my arms.

"Mine," I remind her. She. Belongs. With. Me.

I can see the moment that she has had enough as her face tightens and she leaps forward, smacking me in the face.

The hit is enough to stun my wolf, bringing me back in control. I stare at her, stunned that she punched me, bringing my hand to my aching jaw. That's my girl. My mate.

Fuck.

I look across at Alpha Mortlock, hating the sad look that is crossing his face. Glancing back at Ari, I feel the need to pull her into my arms rising again. I can't be here right now.

I spin around and march towards the door with more than just my jaw hurting.

What the fuck am I going to do?

LOST
IN
SHADOW

SHADOWBORN SERIES BOOK TWO

ERIN O'KANE

Prologue

Her eyes are the first thing I see, and my heart aches. Her beautiful amber eyes stare back at me. The rest of her face comes into focus, and I start to notice details about her, like the fact she is biting her lip. She only does that when she's unsure, not that she would admit it.

Pain flashes through my skull, and my vision shakes, the image of her fading. No! I need to talk to her, find out what's going on. The image strengthens again, and I can fully see her. I take a step toward her, I need to know she's okay, my hand reaches out so I can touch her, but passes through as if I don't exist.

She looks lost, her arms hugging her chest as she glances around the sparse space. Turning from me, she starts to walk away, and my heart squeezes painfully as she does so.

"Ari!" I shout out, my voice breaking from the concern that has been building within me.

She stops in her tracks and tilts her head as if she heard me. Turning, she stares directly at where I'm standing. I'm not sure she can truly see that I am standing there, but her eyes bore into me.

"Help me," she pleads, her voice raspy.

Pain fills my head again, and I cry out, collapsing to my knees.

I wake up on the cold floor of my apartment, my head reeling from what I just saw, pain pounding through my temples. What the hell just happened?

Chapter One

Turns out that eternal damnation is really boring. I have no idea how long I've been here for, it could've been hours, or it could have been days for all I know. Glancing down at my watch, I roll my eyes as I see it has stopped working, typical. Nothing is ever easy.

I look around again at the mostly empty landscape I'm stuck in, the forest at my back is the only thing to be seen. Everywhere I look, a grey hazy fog fills the air, covering the land around me, obscuring my view of the forest, allowing me to see no farther than the tree line. I stand at the fringe of the forest and turn to look at the trees towering over me, their dark gnarled branches making the whole place look creepy. Coupled with the fog, it isn't exactly welcoming. Behind me is a vast empty grey space, where nothing ever seems to move or change.

I walk along the edges of the trees again, the fog rolling against my skin and making small eddies as I move. I haven't ventured into the forest, and I don't think that I will just yet. It makes me feel uneasy, and a place deep within me is warning me not to venture in too far. Turning away, I take up my place back in the vast void of nothingness, dropping to the ground and laying on my back, staring up at the equally grey sky.

I wonder how I ended up here. I know that Shadowborn appear here when they die, but I don't feel dead. However, I must be if I'm here, in the Shadow Dimension, or Shadow Realm, as it's known. A place where bad Shadowborn like myself end up if we don't learn to control our powers. It's not a very well-known fact that Shadowborn fight against our nature on a daily basis, and if we're not strong enough, we're consumed by that power and our souls get called back.

We're a rare breed, with the ability to make our bodies *become* shadow, blending in wherever darkness exists. Historically, we have been used as assassins, which is why we often don't live past childhood, as we're killed off. Or, if we're untrained, we end up being pulled back to the Shadow Realm. I don't know much about Shadow Law, but I was told that when we're born, our souls come from Shadow, which is what gives us our abilities. Some say that the Shadow Realm reclaims our souls when we die.

I've been running from my powers my whole life. My old pack, the Shadow Pack, was cruel and tried to beat me into submission, but I managed to endure, escaping to America when I was eighteen. Recently, a local pack I'd been staying with was attacked, and I used my powers to save the men that I'm close to. I knew I was toeing a line, using too much power after keeping it suppressed for so long, but I was desperate. If I had to do it again, for them, I would.

But I have to say, I hadn't expected death to be like this—an unending nothingness. As I glance up into the bleak sky, I wonder how the guys are getting on. I have a lot of time for reflection here, and loneliness has started to set in, which surprises me.

I've always found comfort in my own company and have lived as a lone wolf for the last six years, until Alex from Moon River Pack marched into my life. I needed protection, no matter how much I proclaimed otherwise, and they needed a new nurse.

The pack overwhelmed me after so many years of avoiding them, but they were welcoming and they all seemed to thrive off each other's company, making it difficult not to enjoy spending time with them. I guess you never know what you're missing until you have it. But now, it's been taken away. I sigh, running my hands through my hair.

Tori, my best friend, was one of two people that I considered family before all this happened. She adopted me as hers when I arrived in the US from England, back when I fled my old pack. I'm not the only one with a dark past, and we bonded, became each other's family, not needing anyone else. Until I met the guys that is. I'm still not sure what it is I feel for them, but they've forced a way into my heart, whether I like it or not.

A stirring in the distance rouses me from my musing, my heightened senses on alert. To my right, the grey fog is moving and the area is brighter, like it's creating a pathway. Well, this is different. Standing up, I hesitantly walk towards it, I have no idea what is happening or if I should be following this unknown 'path.' Aren't you supposed to avoid walking into the light? What do I do?

Closing my eyes, I try to focus on my wolf and the power that resides within me, my instincts have never let me down so far. My problem is, I often don't *listen* to those instincts. My wolf has been very quiet since I've been here, and I find that I miss her presence. It's like missing a part of yourself. I hadn't realised how much a part of me she was. I've always had a love-hate relationship with my wolf, like a sibling who's annoying as hell but one you couldn't live without. I can still feel her, but it's like our bond is muted. I open my eyes again and watch the swirling, misty path. My instincts are telling me to follow it, and for once, I decide to listen. I've already lost everything, what's the worst that can happen? I stand up and start walking slowly towards the light. A strange feeling comes over me the farther I walk, like opposing forces—one pulling me towards the light, and the other holding me back. Indecision wars in me, do I stay or keep going?

Determination fills me, and I push forward, following the tugging sensation. The light is so bright, I have to close my eyes as it becomes blinding. I start to hear voices, but they're muffled, so I can't make out what they are saying. The light is still too bright for me to look around, but the voices are getting louder, until suddenly, I know who's speaking.

"Why hasn't she woken up yet?" Killian's angry voice makes my eyes shoot open.

I'm back? My eyes flash around the room, my heart filling with an emotion I can't place as I see all of my men in my bedroom at Moon River Pack. I start to cry out, my emotions making it difficult for me to express my feelings in words, and I go to step forward when I notice a figure in my bed.

I stop in my tracks. It's not just any figure. It's me.

I peer around the room again, dread filling me before I stare back down at myself. I look like I'm in my shadow form, so while no one else can see me, I'm still able to see my body, some weird quirk of being a Shadowborn. I try to take a step towards my form in the bed and the guys, when something brings me to an abrupt stop. Frowning, I glance around and see that I'm standing in shadow against the back wall of the room, and a sinking suspicion fills me. This suspicion is confirmed when I try to take a step directly into the light, and I feel like I've walked into a wall. I'm trapped in the shadows.

I gaze over at my prone form again, horror filling me as I see my wasted body. My skin is pale and I've lost weight, looking like I've been unwell for a long period of time. This has never happened before, when a Shadowborn uses their shadow form, their whole body turns to shadow without a trace, like they were never there. Yet my body is lying there, telling a different story.

"We don't know, Kill, but you getting angry and smashing things is not going to help." Alex's voice stops me from staring at my body and has me looking around the room again.

Killian is pacing the room, and his long silvery blond hair is a mess, like he's run his hands through it multiple times. His usually clean-shaven jaw is covered in stubble, and he looks like his wolf is about to jump out of his skin. I can feel his alpha power from here. He bares his teeth at Alex in a snarl, but it lacks the usual harshness that I'm used to associating with Killian. He appears genuinely worried.

Movement next to the bed has me turning my gaze to the other guys. Garett is sitting up by my head and is brushing my hair gently, my usually glossy golden-brown locks looking dull and limp in his large hands.

"We need to stay calm, shouting is not going to help Ari. If you want to fight, take it out of the room," my bear shifter says, his voice quiet and gentle, despite his words, his eyes never leaving my still form.

I shouldn't be surprised that Garett is here, since he's always had my best interests at heart and has been my protector since I arrived in this country. He was the only other person besides Tori that I considered family before the pack barrelled into my life. But as a bear surrounded by a wolf pack, he must be feeling outnumbered here.

On the other side of my body, holding my limp hand, is Seb. My heart breaks a little at his broken expression as he gazes down at me. He's smaller than the other guys in the room and is physically less powerful than them, but his happiness is what draws you to him. Not to mention his model worthy looks and boyish charm. I almost don't recognise him.

"You're talking like she's ill and will get better. She has been like this for two weeks and is wasting away! Her soul is gone! She sacrificed herself for us, and now she's *gone!*" Killian's words are harsh and get louder as his pacing becomes more erratic, his voice breaking on his last word.

This seems to trigger something in Seb, and my gentle wolf does something I never thought he would. He pushes up from his place at my side so fast that his chair falls back with a bang. Killian stops his pacing and turns to look at Seb with a look of shock, not from the sudden loud noise, but the burst of power that's coming from him.

"Do *not* talk about her that way. She *will* be back." Seb's voice is low, but laced with a power that I've never felt before.

Despite his show of power, Seb has always been one of the lower-level wolves within the pack...or so I thought.

There's a hierarchical system within most shifter communities, with an alpha, beta, and gamma at the top. All shifters are born with a certain amount of power, and someone may be born with alpha power but never actually become an alpha. Alex is an example of this, being in the position of beta but possessing bucket-loads of alpha power. You can't change your level of power, you're stuck with what you're born with. However, the pulsing waves of power coming off Seb are new. The powers coming off of him are the strength of a beta, which shouldn't be possible. The guys share a look of concern as Seb's power fades, and he turns to look at my prone form again, returning to my side, holding my hand once more.

I watch the four of them, surprised that they're all in the same room and not tearing into each other. Alex pushes away from the wall where he'd been leaning to walk closer to Killian.

"Killian, you mentioned before that you'd been trained by your previous alpha about Shadowborn, did they mention anything about this?" Alex probes. I can tell he wants to demand the answers, but in the mood Killian's in, that would be a bad idea.

"Don't you think I would have said something already?" he retorts with a slight snarl, and his pacing picks up speed as he runs his hands through his long hair.

Alex, to his credit, doesn't rise to the comment as many alpha level wolves would.

"Tell us what you know," he responds calmly, although I can tell from the slight tick in his eye that Killian's behaviour is bothering him.

"Shadowborn come from shadow. They have the ability to

become shadow, but it comes with a cost. If they are well-trained and strong-willed, they can control the shadow, if not, *it* controls *them*. We all know that Ari hated her abilities and refused to use them," Killian explains, and a hush falls over the room as they take in what he's implying.

"The stronger the Shadowborn, the worse the potential consequences, which is why it's essential they're well-trained. I assumed Ari was weak because I never saw her use her powers, until the night of the rescue." Killian stops pacing and leans against a wall, sliding down it until he's sitting on the ground, staring up at my body.

Garett lifts his gaze from my face to look across at Killian, his hand still playing with my hair.

"I've never seen anything like it before. One minute, she was there, and then she was gone. In that moment, she was strong. She didn't look like the shadow was controlling her. It was only after that asshole, Black, was dead that it happened." He looks down at me as his voice quiets and a sorrow fills his eyes. "She looked scared, but like she knew what was going to happen. Like she was accepting what was happening. Then she was gone," Garett chokes out.

The urge to go to Garett and wrap my arms around him is so strong, it's like a physical pain within me, and the sorrow and anguish in his voice is tearing at me. I try to step forward, fuck the Shadow Realm and its claims over me! I push against my invisible bonds and try to force my way farther into the room. Pain rips through my body, and I'm thrown back into the darkened corner with a cry.

Panting from the effort and with pain zipping through me, I glance back up at the guys. All of them are the same, except for Killian, who's looking into my corner with a confused expression on his face and his hand rubbing at his chest as if it hurts. I freeze, does he know I'm here? Shaking his head as if to clear his thoughts, he sighs, running a hand over his handsome features. The scar down the side of his face looks stark in this light, and his severe frown doesn't help with the rough warrior look he has going on.

"From what I was told, weak Shadowborn who can't control their powers, or those who use too much, can get consumed by them. I saw it once, but their body went with them, they were enveloped by the shadows and they never returned." Killian pauses, his face twisting into a pained expression before he continues. "Which is why I don't understand why her body is still here."

I push up from where I'm curled up on the floor. Fuck this. It's time for them to know I'm still here, haunting their asses. I lean forward, growling as the pain starts spreading through my body, tingling at first before becoming blinding as I push harder against my shadowy cage. My wolf shifts inside me for the first time since I was taken by the shadows, and I urge her to help me. With her strength, I'm able to take a step before I feel shadowy tendrils start to wrap around me and tug at my body, trying to pull me back to the Shadow Realm. I shout in frustration and throw everything I have into staying, but I can feel that it's not enough.

"No! I'm still here! Help me!" is my last desperate cry before, with an almighty tug, I'm pulled away once again from the guys I call family.

Ari's usually beautiful face is twisted into a painful grimace.

Shadows twist up her arms and legs, claiming her like a controlling partner, pulling her back into the darkness. I can feel her pain, her panic and frustration as she tries to get away from the inevitable.

I watch in horror, unable to do anything, as she fights for the upper hand and is beaten.

The last thing I hear is her voice.

"No! I'm still here! Help me!"

My breath comes in pants, and my body is stiff from lying on the floor. The vision plays over in my head again.

I push up from the ground with shaky legs and run my hand though my hair. These visions have been coming more and more frequently. This is all I can think to call them—visions. Something is going on, but I can't figure it out.

I need to speak to a witch. They aren't very forthcoming to those who aren't their kind, but luckily, I happen to know one. Plan made, I release a breath I didn't know I was holding.

Ari is alive, but trapped.

I have to help her.

Chapter Two

Son of a bitch, that hurt. Lying back in the dull grass of the Shadow Realm, I stare up at the blank grey sky and wait for the pain to leave my body. Well, that went great. Twisting a piece of grass through my fingers, I think back over what just happened.

Somehow, I managed to get back to the real world, but in my shadow form. No one had been able to see me or sense me, except for the weird moment where Killian seemed to look towards me. I would expect this in my shadow form, except my body had been left behind and I was unable to control my powers. As Killian had explained, Shadowborns usually just cease to exist when they are overwhelmed by their powers, their souls claimed by the shadow. So, how have I ended up stuck half in the real world and half here in the Shadow Realm?

My body has been in the real world for two weeks, without my soul. So this means I can't be dead, right? Sure, I looked pretty terrible, but I'd seen myself breathing and dead people don't do that. Although, I'm not sure how well a body can survive without its soul for that amount of time. I have to figure out a way to get back. I have unfinished business to deal with before the shadows can take me. Specifically, the men I've left behind.

Garett, my bear shifter and protector. Along with Tori, he's the closest thing I had to family here in the US. I've known him for years, although I only recently found out that he's been in love with me for most of that time. Well, that's what I keep telling myself anyway. I've been pushing away any romantic intentions from him for a while, telling myself it was just harmless flirting until recently, not ready to get into a relationship or wanting to ruin our friendship. Shifters are touchy and overly flirty by nature, and I'd convinced myself those lingering touches were just part of that nature. I finally gave into my suppressed feelings for him and had sex with him. I know I hurt him when I tried to push him away, not willing to admit to my feelings like he had. The only love I've ever known had either been a lie or lead to pain. I've been used and betrayed most of my life, so giving up that kind of control and allowing someone to care for me, to love me, was difficult for me to allow. When I pushed him away after we slept together, I knew I'd be causing him pain, but I thought I was saving him. I have done terrible things, and he deserves better than me. I finally realised how I felt about Garett when he was taken by my former pack and tormentors, the Shadow Pack. Only when I'd truly believed that Garett was going to be killed, did those feelings to make themselves clear to me.

I've learnt the hard way that love and trust are only something that will end up hurting you. The Shadow Pack had taught me that, my supposed family being a perfect example of this. Alpha Black, the Alpha of the Shadow Pack, being my father and behind my torment. As such, it takes a lot for someone to earn my trust. Garett has proven himself over and over again, but now I can finally see that. Just as I'm taken away from him.

Killian has been a constant source of surprise for me. Dark and brooding, he's an alpha male with trust issues nearly as bad as mine. He was the leader of a prosperous pack until he trusted the wrong people, and then the entire pack was killed by a Shadowborn. Lost and with nowhere else to go, he found refuge with the Moon River Pack. Although his alpha power was strong, he didn't choose to fight for the leadership of the Moon River Pack. Instead, he chose to remain separated from the others, living half a life as he mourned his mate and pack that were brutally taken from him. Then I came barrelling into his life, disrupting the solitary existence he'd created for himself.

It's safe to say that we didn't get along, and we still argue like cats and dogs. I smile when I think of how he would react to me calling him a dog, then I stop myself. Why am I feeling warm and fuzzy when thinking of Killian? The most stubborn and overprotective male I've ever met? Is it because I've come to truly care about him, or is it because of our 'true mated pair' bond that was triggered not long ago? This rare bond is only triggered when you've found your soulmate. Things got very complicated as Killian fought off his prejudices against Shadowborn and the protective instincts the bond ignited in him. Especially because although I feel something for him, something that seems to be growing, where I shouldn't want to be with anyone else, I can't deny my feeling for the others.

Cue Seb. My adorable, flirty friend who welcomed me into his family with open arms. This is exactly what we were, friends, until he was threatened at a pack meet and I realised that my feelings went deeper than just that. I'm still not sure what I feel for him, but seeing him standing up for me and fighting to protect his family, even though he knew he was the weaker wolf, made me, and my wolf, realise we couldn't live without him.

I wonder what Seb is up to now. Probably bugging the hell out of Alex. I sigh as my thoughts turn to the beta. There's always been sexual tension between us, and perhaps that's all there is and a good shag is all I need to get him out my system. But a part of me says there's more to it than that. However, he's confusing. His moods go from hot to cold, giving me whiplash. One moment, he's the pack beta, the protector and enforcer who takes his role very seriously. The next, he's playful and flirty, which makes me wary about taking things any further with him. Who is the real Alex?

I sit upright with a sigh. I've gone from no love life to this complicated mess. A humourless laugh leaves my lips, and I absent-mindedly start braiding my shoulder-length golden brown hair. If I ever leave this place that is. My twisted love life is probably the least of my worries.

Uneasiness fills me, the skin on my arms breaking out into gooseflesh. I feel my wolf sluggishly stir within me, trying to assess if there's a threat. I lean forward, straining my ears for any unusual sounds in this usually silent, unmoving place. My eyes scan the unchanging horizon, looking for the cause of my discomfort. I stand, not feeling safe for the first time since I arrived here. Sure, I have felt a range of emotions, from pissed off to mournful, but I've never felt scared here, just accepting of my fate. After all, I've always known that a happy ever after was never in the future for me. Slowly circling around, I come to a stop, facing the dark, dead forest, and a feeling of dread overtakes me as I stare into the trees.

Although part of me is screaming not to, I start walking slowly towards the towering trees. Something is tugging me, like I have no control over my legs and a ghostly tether is reeling me in. My wolf, feeling my fear, seems to wake up and starts to fight for control of my body to pull us away. It's no good, however, and I can feel her getting weaker the closer we get to the forest.

We reach the edge of the tree line, and I'm able to force my body to a stop as the invisible power wanes, and I strain against the imperceptible bonds that anchor my feet to the ground. The feeling of dread hits me again as I'm forced into the forest, and I get the feeling that I'm being toyed with. They allowed me to stop at the edge of the plains because *they* allowed me to, not because of any strength of mine. An eerie fog begins to fill the woods, twisting around the dark, almost black bark of the trees. It's cold, which is strange, as there is no weather here, nothing changes. The farther I'm pulled into the forest, the more I get the feeling that I'm being watched, but when I look, all I can see are the towering trees. I don't know how long I've been walking when a movement draws my eyes. At first, all I see is what looks like the flickering of shadow.

I would have written it off as my overactive imagination if I didn't sense the malice pouring from that direction. My body comes to a stop, and I find I'm in control of myself again. A spine-tingling noise that sounds suspiciously like a howl splits the air, making my metaphorical hackles stand on end. Delving deep, I try to rouse my wolf and discover my connection with her is all but gone. I curse. Looks like I'm on my own. A thought crosses my mind that shocks me. I'm like a human, with no access to my Shadowborn powers and no wolf. In a twisted turn of fate, I got what I wished for—to be human. Stupid Ari.

The shadows flicker again, and I realise they are forming into a humanoid shape. It seems to focus on me and starts taking predatory steps in my direction. Don't ask me how a shadow can focus on someone, but this being has its sights set on me. Falling into a fighting stance, I try to remember my training from Killian—look for its weaknesses and use them against it.

The shadowy being pauses, watching me, and I can't help but feel like it's amused at my show of defence. Then a feeling of someone dragging an icy finger down my back alerts me to the arrival of another shadowy bastard. Throwing a look over my shoulder, I see that I'm right, and in unison, they step towards me with eerie synchrony.

"Join us." A hissed voice fills the air around me, coming from every direction. It's not loud, but it seems to fill the space.

I shudder, the voice reminding me of every horror movie I've ever watched. I look from one of the shadows to the other and see a third has decided to join the party. Well, that's just great. I put on what I like to think is my politest face and give them an ironic smile.

"That's very kind, but I'm going to have to say no," I reply, starting to slowly back away from the three beings.

I have no idea which direction I've come from, as they all look the same, and spinning to look at the bastards stalking me has thrown off my sense of direction.

"Join usss," the voice demands again, the tone the same but louder this time.

They're persistent, I'll give them that.

"I don't think you understood me, but I'll say it again. Hell. No."

Way to go Ari, just piss off the ghostly guys who have seemingly led you into the middle of a haunted wood. It's difficult to tell from their expression, seeing as their faces are made of shadow, but I get the distinct impression that I've upset them. Their fluid movements become stiffer and more aggressive looking as they stride towards me.

"You can come willingly or we will make you," the voices state, making me shudder. I don't doubt that they could drag me away, despite being made of shadow. "We will feed on everything you are, every good piece of you, until only the darkness is left. We shall enjoy it, we have not fed for a long time." The united voice fills the air again, coming not from one of them, but *all* of them.

This doesn't sound like a fate I want. I'm starting to get pissed off now. Some bloody man is always trying to claim me or possess me, even in the fucking Shadow Realm, it's the same.

"Well joke's on you, asshole. There's nothing good left about me," I snarl with a feral grin.

If I'd hoped that the shadow figures would be put off by my show of aggression, I would've been disappointed. In fact, the feeling of malice increases, but I can't help but feel like the figure directly in front of me is amused. I stand my ground as they start to float towards me, their forms flickering in and out of shadow. My fear spikes, and I feel a pang, as I realise that neither my wolf nor my Shadowborn powers are reacting to my panic. I truly am on my own.

The first shadowy form launches itself at me, stopping my internal panic and making me focus on the fight. They are fast, faster than most shifters, and I thank my lucky stars that even though my wolf isn't responding to me, I still have my supernatural speed. Ducking the arm thrown towards my face, I counter with a punch towards its head, only for my fist to go straight through its form. *Fuck!* If I can't touch it, does that mean that it can't hurt me? A sharp burning sensation flares up my arm, and I glance over to see a wicked pair of talons gleaming from the hand of the second shadow, who has now joined the fight. Guess that answers that question, they seem to be able to materialise parts of themselves at will.

Now with two of them attacking me, I have to focus purely on defence, ducking and weaving the dagger like claws being aimed at me. I try to use some of the self-defence moves Killian taught me, but they are no use on someone who doesn't have a solid form.

I can't defeat these guys, not here, and not with this many of them. They only showed up once I entered the tree line, if I managed to get back, would they be able to follow me? Deciding it's better to try that than end up skewered on their talons, I start to back up. Ducking another swipe to the head, I spin on my heels and run back the way I came. They don't make a sound, but I know they're following me. I can't help but look over my shoulder to see what's happening behind me. Two of them are following me, and the one who first appeared is standing still, watching me as I run away.

I face the way I'm running, trying to throw off the sense of satisfaction that I felt from the shadow. I have to focus all of my attention on avoiding obstacles as I jump over fallen logs and duck low branches, my breath ripping out of me in harsh pants. Death by being mauled from shadow beasts is not the way I want to go.

A pulsing light catches my attention and I hurry towards it. Shining through the thick, dark branches of forest, it barely lights the area, but I see it as a beacon. Nearly sobbing in relief as I see the edge of the tree line, I hurl myself forward. Just as the light comes within touching distance, something sharp drags down my arm, a searing pain following in its wake. I can't hold back the scream that tears out of me, but I keep running, trying to keep my footsteps sure as I hurtle through the forest. I can feel my energy draining, my arm is throbbing now and I clutch it to my chest, feeling the blood run through my fingers.

The creatures behind me give a chilling howl to which is met by more howls in the distance. There are more of these things and I need to get out of here, *now*. The light flashes again, and I don't know if it's just my pain muddled brain, but I know I have to make it to the light. I risk a look over my shoulder and wish I hadn't, the two monsters following me are just behind me and gaining ground by the second. I throw the last of my energy into reaching the light, I can almost feel it on my face.

I make it back into the grey fields and stumble to a stop as I hear snarls and growls behind me. Turning to look, I see the two creatures, their bodies of shadow twisting and churning as if connected to their agitation. The leader lifts its arm to point at me, its sharp claw extended. The arm shudders and the creature looks like it's in pain, but it holds steady.

"This is not the end. We will have you," it hisses, and I know those words will haunt my dreams. Well, they will if I ever get back to the real world where I can actually dream.

The beacon of light that guided me out flashes brightly again and the creatures scream, finally disappearing into the trees and out of sight. I walk a few steps farther away from the trees before collapsing onto the ground, adrenaline and the pain from my wound finally winning out. I turn my arm and grimace at the sight that greets me. There are three slashes, the longest running from the top of my arm to my elbow. They aren't particularly deep, but they are seeping blood. This could be bad news for me, as I don't have anything to clean the wound and it could easily become infected. Vaguely, I wonder if it's even possible to catch an infection in the Shadow Realm and if this wound will show up on my physical body. I take the bottom of my shirt and tear it, attempting to make a makeshift dressing. Finished with my task, my attention is drawn by the light, which is now moving in my direction. I try to stand but find I don't have the energy, so I settle for frowning.

I don't think it means me harm, but as it gets closer, I can see the outline of what looks like...a man.

"Stop, don't come any closer," I demand, pleased that my voice doesn't show my exhaustion.

To my surprise, the light does as I said, and I get the impression he's amused.

"You have just made my existence all the more interesting," it says before disappearing.

What the hell is going on? A wave of exhaustion hits me, and I'm dragged under, my arm throbbing in time with my heartbeat.

I'm back at the Moon River compound again, in my corner of shadow. I don't know how I got here, but I didn't get tugged like I did last time. I passed out in the Shadow Realm, and then I was simply here. I'm alone in the room with my body and Killian. He's staring at my still form, and I can almost feel his angst and tension. He's sitting in the chair next to my corner, close enough where I could almost touch him, but I know my hand will just go through him.

"Hey man. How's it hanging?" I ask, tipping my head to him in greeting. I know he won't respond and that he can't hear me, but I need to talk to someone after my attack. "I've had a shitty day, and I never thought I would say this, but I'm glad to see you," I admit, leaning against the wall and glancing over at my body.

I frown as I do, taking in the room. My hair is longer, and I look...thinner? I turn to look at Killian and see his hair is longer too, and he also has the beginnings of a beard on his usually clean-shaven face. I have to admit that it suits him. He's also wearing different clothes, and the bed sheets have been changed.

"How long have I been gone?! I only saw you guys this morning!" I whisper shout, not sure why I'm whispering. After all, the sleeping body is me and no one can hear me anyway!

Killian suddenly stiffens in his seat, his eyes narrowing as he tilts his head back and sniffs the room, his supernatural senses picking something up. For a second, I wonder if it's me he can sense, and a thrill of hope fills me, which is quickly dashed as he stands up and hurries to my body's side. Of course, he can't sense me, I'm a shadow.

"Alex!" Killian roars, something akin to panic in his voice as he stares down at my body.

Soft murmurings from downstairs, which I hadn't even registered before, stop, followed by hurried footsteps pounding up the stairs.

"What's happening?" I hear Alex's voice before I see him, his muscled form filling the doorway, a look of concern creasing his features. His eyes narrow as he takes in the scene in the room, his nostrils widening as he also scents something.

"Is Ari okay?" Seb's voice comes from behind Alex, and I can see him trying to squeeze into the room.

Killian is crouched protectively by my body, his hand on my arm as he examines something carefully.

"She has a wound. It wasn't there before, it just appeared." His voice is tight, his words clipped. I guess that answers my question.

Swearing under his breath, Alex comes closer to my body, only to stop when Killian growls at him, his protective instincts riding high. Keeping very still, Alex glances over his shoulder at Seb, who is watching with a resigned look on his face, making me wonder how often this happens.

"Seb, grab Alpha Mortlock and Nurse Beth." His words are soft, but the command is obvious. After Seb leaves the room, he turns his attention back on the alpha wolf who's being greatly affected by the mating bond. I'd not accepted the true mated pair bond before the attack on the pack, but we had agreed to get to know one another.

We don't know why I don't experience the pull of the bond as much as Killian does, but I can't deny that I am developing feelings for him and the other others.

"Killian, I need to see Ari to be able to help her. You're not the only one who cares for her, brother." Alex's voice is still soft, but his words are firm, reminding me once again why he's pack beta.

Alex actually has the potential to be an alpha, the power flowing strongly through his veins, but he has no desire to challenge Alpha Mortlock for the position or start a pack of his own. I was also born with alpha power, not that it has ever done me any favours, having been born into a chauvinist pack.

A shift in the room brings my attention back to what's going on by the bed. Killian has moved, so he's sitting up by my head, and tension ripples through his body as he watches Alex with narrowed eyes. Alex is gently extending my arm, and the whole room erupts into growls and snarls as the wound is exposed. Seb comes into the room, looking graver than I've ever seen him. I miss my happy-go-lucky Seb.

Alpha Mortlock walks into the room, followed by Isa, his gamma, and Nurse Beth, who had been helping out with the pack before the attack. The pack is very protective, and they were wary of allowing outsiders onto pack land, so I'm glad they've allowed her to stay and help. Alpha Mortlock looks around the room before his gaze lands on my body, his face turning grave as he sees the wound on my arm.

"What happened?" he asks, coming closer to have a better look but wisely staying a respectful distance from Killian, who still looks like he may snap at any moment.

Killian tears his eyes away from my prone form and looks at the alpha, confusion and what could be pain flashing in his eyes.

"I was sitting with her when I felt like I'd been punched in the chest. Then I felt panic like I've never known before. I realised it wasn't coming from me, but from Ari. I can feel it down the bond." His eyes fall back to my body, his words rough with unshed emotions. "Then I felt this pain, a blinding pain. I didn't know what was going on until I smelled the blood coming from her. That's when I shouted for Alex," he concludes, a sort of hopelessness settling over him.

Nurse Beth approaches my body slowly, looking to Killian and Alex for permission to start examining me. They both nod and she starts a thorough examination. Seb, Alex, and a reluctant Killian leave my side to give her space. They stand by the door together, positioned so they can still see my body.

I'm blown away by this show of support. More time has obviously passed here than it has in the Shadow Realm, so this vigil that they seem to be holding both flatters and worries me. What if I can't get back? Are they going to continue to pine for me? I'm sure that Seb and Alex could move on with time. Garett would mourn me, but he has his pack and Tori would look after him. Killian, on the other hand, is worrying me. I run my eyes over him, and he doesn't look well, his skin looks pale, like he hasn't seen the sun in a really long time. The grey bags under his eyes tell me he hasn't been sleeping, and he looks like he hasn't eaten a good meal in a while. When I first found out about true mated pairs, I did some research to see if there was a way out without accepting the bond. What I found during my reading was that often, when one of the pair died, the other died as well. If the bond had been rejected, then one wouldn't die from the loss of the other but it would hurt like hell. In the one documented case where one had died and the bond hadn't been accepted or rejected, like in the case with Killian and I, the shifter had fallen into a state of madness, eternally trying to find his missing mate.

"How has your research been going? Any news?" Alex's voice brings me back to the room, his question addressed to Isa, who's shaking her head, her expression dour.

"No. No one wishes to talk of the Shadowborn." Her thickly accented words are tight with anger.

"Then make them talk," Killian growls, his eyes flashing as his wolf pushes to the surface. Alpha Mortlock takes a step closer to Killian, placing a comforting but firm hand on his arm.

"Friend, I know you are hurting, and we will do whatever we can to help Ari, she's one of us now. She proved that after what she did for the pack, to save all of you. But we don't hurt others to get answers, we will not become like the Shadow Pack."

My respect for the alpha shoots up, and I am again reminded how different he is from my old pack that I grew up in. I'm also shocked at how much I'm affected by his proclamation that I'm one of them. I've never wanted to belong to a pack and fought fiercely for my independence for years. Even when I agreed to help them, it was reluctantly, only out of my sense of duty as a nurse to help those who needed it.

Nurse Beth stands from her place at my side and walks over to where everyone is gathered, and her face is a careful mask. Uh oh, I know that look and have worn it on many occasions when I had to break bad news to a family.

"Any news for us, Beth?" Mortlock asks, although from his tone, I can tell he's expecting bad news. Beth sighs and brushes a strand of hair back behind her ear.

"I've dressed the wound. I have no idea what caused it, but it looks like she's been slashed by claws. It's oozing a substance I've never seen before," she informs the group with a sigh, before glancing back at my body. "But she's getting weaker. Whatever you're doing to get her back, we need to be quicker. Her body is dying."

I feel the familiar tug of shadow around my body as the Shadow Realm tries to claim me once again. I don't try to fight it this time, and I watch blankly as the shouting in the room begins and Nurse Beth is escorted out of the room, while the others try to calm an irate Killian down.

I stop in my tracks as I realise I'm in a vision again.

Terrifying beasts of shadow stalk along a dark tree line, their wicked talons almost reaching the ground, and even from here, I can tell they are sharp enough to cut through flesh and sinew. Although their faces are in shadow, what I can see is terrifying.

My position in the vision changes until I'm looking at Ari. I've found I have no control over what I see or even what I'm looking at, only that the vision will show me what it wants me to see. Struggling against it only makes it more difficult on my human form when I wake up.

Ari is lying back in the pale grass of what I assume is the Shadow Realm. One arm is thrown over her eyes as if she's resting, and her other arm is stretched out to the side. I wince as I see the vicious wound there. It's oozing a blackish substance, and I can see black track lines coming off the wound as it spreads through her body.

One of the beasts howls, the eerie sound inducing a reply of howls farther in the distance.

"Don't you bastards ever sleep?" Ari shouts back at them, but her voice is weak, resigned.

I awake from the vision, my head pounding, and I know from the trickle on my upper lip that my nose is bleeding again. Ignoring all of this, I grab my phone from my pocket, dialling the number I have on speed dial.

"Hello? We need to move quicker, Ari's in trouble."

Chapter Three

The next few days fall into a dull routine. Although, it's difficult to keep track of time when there's no sunrise or sunset. I hadn't realised how much I'd miss something like that, or how much I would miss seeing the stars at night or the feel of the morning sun on my skin. I sometimes find that I get confused here. I forget who I am, and the only thing that helps me remember and stops me from going mad are my visits to the real world. I still have no control over them, but it breaks up the monotonous nothing of the Shadow Realm.

I'm back in my room at the Moon River compound, leaning against the wall as I watch Garett gaze down at my body. Killian is also still in the room. It seems he never leaves my side. Even though I'm glad to see them, I still don't know why I keep being called back here. I suspect it has something to do with the true mated pair bond between Killian and me, but I don't understand the timings of it. So far, the only connection I can make is Killian's presence.

"Any change?" Garett asks from his position at my side. His hand is twined with mine, and I find myself looking down at my shadowy form, wishing I could feel his touch.

"No. She's getting weaker, and the wound is spreading," Killian replies. He's actually sitting next to my shadow form, not that he knows it. He gravitated over here one day, and now whenever I arrive, I find him sitting here.

"Tell me about it." I join in the conversation, not that they can hear me, but it helps keep me sane. I glance down at my arm, which is now a mess of black veins running up and down my arm. I'm getting weaker by the day, and my visits are getting shorter. I've only been here for a few minutes, and I can already feel the shadows calling me back.

"Have you heard anything from Tori?" Killian's question grabs my attention. What does he mean by that? Garett shakes his head, and I feel a knot in my stomach.

"No. There's been no word from her. I even reached out to the witch community, but no one will speak to me." The frustration in Garett's voice is easy to hear.

Wait. What's happening with Tori? Why is Garett trying to talk to the witch council? I step away from the wall, feeling the shadows tighten their grip on me, becoming suffocating. I try to fight against the shadows, knowing it's futile but having to try anyway.

"You would've thought that the witch community would be concerned that one of their own is missing."

My world comes to a standstill at Killian's words, my shock causing me to stop fighting the shadows, and I'm abruptly pulled back into the Shadow Realm.

Tori is missing. The words keep running through my head. This news only fuels my anger and determination. I *need* to get out of the Shadow Realm. I pace through the empty field, restless after the revelation of my last visit. Closing my eyes, I try to focus, attempting to narrow down the place where my Shadowborn powers come from. I feel nothing, not even a stirring from my wolf, which is worrying me. I try again, digging deep, but I can only feel shadows, and every time I try to grasp them, they slip out of my grip. I scream in frustration.

"I have to get out of here!" I shout, knowing no one is going to answer me.

"Well, it's about time." A dry, drawling voice has me spinning around, only to be greeted by a man made of light.

I squint and bring my hand up to shield my eyes as I try to see the person before me. He dims enough so I can make out his frowning features, and I drop my hand, confusion running through me. Who is this? And wasn't I just trying to do something? I look around me for answers, my fuzzy head is making it difficult for me to think. My gaze is brought back to the man, and I frown again.

"Who are you?" I ask.

"We met before, don't you remember?" he asks, and I frown, shaking my head. You would think I would remember a man made of light.

"What is your name?" the stranger of light asks, taking pity on me.

I open my mouth to reply, only to find that I don't know the answer. I frown again, feeling panic rising through me. I look at the stranger desperately.

"Why don't I know that?" I demand.

"You've been here too long. I'm surprised you have lasted this long here. When I first met you, I thought that you had control over your powers, you were so strong. You survived the creatures in the forest! You couldn't have done that if you weren't strong," he says, his voice fading off with his thoughts, although I'm not sure if he's talking to me or himself.

I tilt my head at his words, confusion obvious in my expression.

"We've met before?" My voice is uncertain, and inside, I'm still reeling that I can't remember my name. I should know this, how could I forget who I am?

"Yes. Do you remember being attacked in the forest? Do you remember the light?" he questions patiently, like he's talking to a child. I frown, a vague memory of a pulsing light forms in my mind, and a stinging on my arm brings back the memory. I glance at my arm, the wound throbbing as if to remind me of what happened.

"The light." The stranger nods at my answer. I squint up at him, trying to make out his features, but the light is too bright for my eyes. "Who are you?" I ask again, needing some answers.

"I'm a friend, and I'm here to help," he tells me. I know he's avoiding answering my question, but I'm too caught up on his last words.

"How can you help me?"

"You're trapped here. I'm going to help you get back to the real world, and then I'm going to train you. Having someone with your strength untrained is just a waste. Besides, you're going to get someone killed. I'm surprised you haven't already," he continues, then mutters under his breath about irresponsible mentors.

Pushing to stand on shaky feet, I step towards him, my hope beginning to grow.

"How?" I challenge, my voice strengthening, my posture becoming stronger as I realise that I might be able to get my old life back. The man before me makes a face, as if annoyed at my demanding tone, but just shrugs.

"Close your eyes." I do as he says, which surprises me since I'm not usually so quick to trust strangers, but I know I'm not in a position to argue. "Look inside yourself for your shadow powers." Again, I do as he says, flinching as I feel his hand on my shoulder. My eyes shoot open, and I see that his eyes are also closed and he's frowning as a consciousness joins mine. "Concentrate," he commands, and I quickly shut my eyes again.

Focusing, I find the shadow within me, and what I sense shocks me. I usually keep a tight lock on my shadow abilities, and whenever I visualise it within me, it looks like a small, tight pulsing ball. Now it has spread, and shadow is coating everything, including my shifting abilities. No wonder I couldn't feel my wolf, she's being suffocated. I start to feel panicked, overwhelmed, until the presence on the edge of my consciousness chimes in.

"Stay calm. I was right, your powers are incredibly strong, but you've been here too long, it's eroding you and changing your abilities." I can sense his concern, and a sense of urgency fills me. "Imagine the light within you."

"I don't have any light, that has never been my power. I'm Shadowborn," I explain out loud, unsure how to communicate to the presence in my mind. I can almost feel him rolling his eyes at my comment.

"Did your parents teach you nothing?" I can feel his anger and frustration, and I push away the feelings that threaten to overwhelm me at the mention of my parents. He tries to calm himself as images pass through my mind, memories I would rather not relive. "I'm sorry," he replies, realising he's distressing me, and I sense him focusing on the task at hand once more.

"There can be no shadow without light, how do you control your shadow otherwise?" His comment astounds me.

"I try not to use it, and I force it to do what I want," I reply, and his mirth fills my mind.

"You have only gotten away with that for this long because you're so powerful. Imagine a bright light within you, it will be there, a small spark. Kindle that spark, make it grow and push back the shadows."

The presence from my mind disappears, and I open my eyes to see he has stepped back. He holds his hand out to me, and there's something small sitting in his palm. I reach out and accept it, holding the item up to inspect it.

It's a pendant, or to be more precise, it's an old golden coin on a delicate chain. I look back up at him with a raised eyebrow. I don't need to voice my question though.

"You will need training if you wish to stay in the mortal world. Use this coin to call me, and I will meet you here."

"How do I get back home? And how would I get back here?" The questions tumble from my lips in a hurry, since his form is fading and I know I have limited time with him left.

"Your shadow will lead you back here, if you don't control it, then it will control you, remember that. And you know how to get back, focus on that light, you already have a path home. The light is all you need, but your bonds will help you." And with those parting words, he fades into nothing, vanishing from sight.

I look around me dumbly, as if he might appear again. Glancing down at the coin in my hand, I let out a sigh. I guess I have to figure this out by myself then.

Light. It's as simple as that? Imagine a light? I snort and start pacing the empty space, running my hands through my hair in frustration. I take a deep breath and try to focus, eager to get out of here. Closing my eyes, I go to my place of power. When I get there, I'm left reeling from the shadow which is smothering everything within me.

Light. There can be no shadow without light. I fumble and grasp at my power, frustration rising as nothing materialises. I *need* to get back. The guys need me, Tori needs me. Some distant part of me wonders why I can remember their names and not my own, but I don't have time to dwell on that. I feel a throb within me as I think of the guys waiting for me. Killian keeping vigil at my bedside, Garett visiting and brushing my hair, updating me on what I'm missing, Alex looking after them all, making sure they are taking care of themselves, and Seb, my heart gives a painful throb at the blank look I last saw in his face, the prospect of losing me is causing him physical pain.

Focus, I berate myself, searching for the light within me again, thinking of the reasons why I need to get back. The nurse said that I'm running out of time, that my body is dying, is that why I'm forgetting who I am? Their faces flash through my mind again. A bright burst of light has my focus thrown out of my body, my awareness back in the plains of the Shadow Realm. I did it. Quickly closing my eyes, I concentration again, seeing a small ball of light within the mass of shadows. I try to grasp the light but fall back with a gasp as a burning sensation spreads through my body. Okay, so that didn't work. Anxiety starts to build within me. The words from the nurse running through my head.

Her body is dying. Her body is dying. Dying.

My breath begins to speed up, my chest tight as panic threatens to choke me. Stop. Think.

The light responded when I thought about the guys. I bring their images up in my mind, and the light starts to grow. It's not easy. Several times, I lose my focus and lose the light, having to start all over again. It's irritating, but I push those feelings aside.

Finally, the light within me is so bright, it's blinding and pushing to be released. I don't know what will happen if I let it loose, it feels like it's going to rip me apart, but the stranger of light said to follow it, that I had a path leading home. I don't have many other options. I release the light and tug at the knot within me, hoping it will lead me home.

Light fills my sight, and I know I'm in another vision. I'm beginning to tell the difference now. At first, it was difficult to tell what was real and what wasn't.

Ari stands before me, looking nervous, but a wave of determination and hope reaches me as she closes her eyes. I wait for a while, wondering what's happening as her face screws up in frustration.

Just as I think she's going to give up on whatever it is she's trying to achieve, her body starts to glow, softly at first, and then so brightly, I have to cover my eyes with my hand to protect them. Her shocked gasp has me opening my eyes, only to find her gone, not a trace of her to be found.

My breath is coming in pants as I push up from my crouched position on the floor, where I must have fallen when the vision overtook me. I think over what the vision has shown me before a grin spreads across my lips. I grab my phone and dial the number I've memorised.

"Hello?" the voice on the other end answers.

"She's back," I reply as I walk to the window, looking out at the city below me while I start to plan my next move.

Chapter Four

I groan as my body is racked with pain. Curling up on my side, I screw my eyelids shut against the bright light that's burning my eyes. Bloody hell, that hurts.

"Ari?" The shocked voice has me opening my eyes, seeing an unbelieving Seb at my side.

I'm briefly disoriented, as I'm not in my usual shadowy corner of shame. "Where am I?" I ask, my eyes roaming around the room, not having the energy to move any more than that. I only then realise I'm lying down, and not just that, but I can *feel* the bed beneath me and the heat of Seb's hand holding mine. My eyes shoot up to meet his shocked gaze before he bursts into a blinding smile.

"Kill, Alex! She's back!" I wince at his shout, the volume making my sensitive ears hurt. In fact, everything hurts. "You're back at Moon River Pack. You came back to us."

Seb's eyes line with unshed tears as he looks over me, like he can't believe I'm here. Frankly, I don't blame him. I don't quite believe it myself.

"Am I really here? This is real?" I question, hope burning in me and making my voice break. I don't think I could cope if this isn't real. Seb's about to answer, but thundering footsteps sound outside of the door before two dominating presences fill the room. Removing my eyes from Seb, I look over to the doorway and see a frozen Killian and Alex staring at me in shock. Alex is the first to break out of his daze, grinning at me before fishing his phone from his pocket, pressing a button before putting the phone to his ear.

"Garett?" I hear him begin before he walks down the corridor and out of hearing range to finish the call. I'm grateful that he would think to call Garett, knowing how worried he would be about me.

The annoying sensation that has been bugging me since I entered the Shadow Realm pulls at me again, and if I had the energy, I'd be rubbing at my chest. I feel a *tug* that has me looking at Killian. His eyes are locked on me with an intensity I've come to expect from him.

"Killian." My voice seems to break whatever spell he's in, and he strides over to me, an air of violence following him.

"Kill," Seb mutters, trying to stand and block his path to me, but Killian snarls at him, and a whip of his alpha power settles over Seb, forcing him to sit down. Seb fights against his magical restraint, his growl ferocious. I'm briefly surprised at Seb's show of dominance against someone as powerful as Killian, but I don't have time to dwell on it before Killian reaches my side. Dropping to his knees beside me, he grabs my shoulders and pulls me to him, smashing his lips against mine in a searing kiss. Stunned, I freeze in his grip before returning his brutal kiss, the feral side of me coming out to play. My desperation and fear of never seeing them again pushes to the surface, resulting in desperate, heavy kisses. A cough at the door causes me to pull away, and a slight growl comes from Killian with my actions.

"Oi, none of that alpha macho bullshit," I scold, leaning back against the pillows as Killian releases me with an eye roll.

Laughter reaches me, and I look around the room and notice it was Alex who coughed to get our attention.

"Yup, she's back all right," he says with his signature smile, his eyes sparkling with repressed emotions. "We missed you, Ari." My chest tightens at his confession. Of all of my guys, I'm the least close with Alex. I still don't really know what, if anything, is going on there, but I can't deny the attraction I feel towards him. He bugs the crap out of me, but there is something about him that pulls me to him, and it's more than just his looks.

I drop my head back on the pillow as a wave of exhaustion washes over me. I don't miss the look Seb and Alex share between them. Killian, however, hasn't moved his eyes from me since he entered the room, almost as if he's worried I might disappear again. Frowning, I wonder if that's possible. Could I get pulled back to the Shadow Realm?

"Ari, what's wrong?" Alex asks as he comes closer, perching on the edge of the bed. I shrug in response to his question, so much has happened that my mind is spinning. I'm just so tired. As if to prove my point, a yawn overtakes me. Pushing up from the bed, Alex gestures to the others.

"Let her sleep for a bit, she's exhausted. We can't do much until Garett gets here anyway." The suggestion has Killian frowning, and his gaze finally leaves me to stare at Alex.

"I'm not leaving her, she might go again." Killian's comment confirms my suspicions, and his voice firm, leaving no room for argument.

"She needs to rest, she can't with you staring at her," Seb pipes up, earning a snarl from Killian. Ignoring the overbearing alpha, he stands and goes to leave the room. It's obvious that Killian doesn't plan on leaving, based on his protective stance next to me, but Seb's right. There's no way I'll be able to rest with all the alpha power and frustration that's pouring out of Killian right now. It's too distracting. I rub the bridge of my nose as I feel a headache coming on.

"Seb, you stay, but you two can go downstairs and wait for Garett. Seb can keep an eye on me until then." Neither Killian or

Alex look pleased about being dismissed, but I hold up my hand to stop their protests. "Both of you are throwing out power. I can feel your frustration and I won't be able to rest like that." Looking suitably mollified, they nod and head towards the door. Killian stops and looks over me once more, before glaring at Seb.

"Call me if anything happens. I mean it." His last words end on a growl as Seb rolls his eyes, making a little shooing motion that causes me to chuckle weakly. Killian's eyes shoot to me when I laugh, some of the tension around his eyes easing a little at the sound, before he nods solemnly and leaves the room. So dramatic.

Alone in the room, just the two of us, I smile softly at Seb. I had an ulterior motive in getting the others out of the room. He's still sitting in the chair next to the bed, looking unsure what to do.

My soft, "Hey," causes Seb to smile back at me, and some of that innate cheekiness he has shines through his expression. I bite my lip, hesitating, before I ask, "Can I have a hug?" My words are spoken so quietly that he has to lean forward to hear me, and once he does, his small smile turns into a wide grin. He immediately moves over so he's lying on top of the covers on the bed. Facing me, he smiles again, his eyes sparkling with humour.

"You didn't have to disappear on us to get me into bed, Ari. All you had to do was ask." I snort at his comment. I missed this. As his arms wrap around me, I close my eyes, letting his warmth seep into me. I hadn't realised how much I needed this, the physical contact. Although the guys seem to have come to some sort of truce, I knew that asking Seb to hold me in front of the others would be pushing things and not fair to any of them. I shuffle closer, pressing my face into the crook of his neck, inhaling his sweet, almost vanilla like scent. His arm settles over my waist, and as he holds me close, I let myself relax in his embrace. I shift as the movement causes pain in my arm, something pulls at my memory, something I need to remember, but Seb starts running a hand through my hair, causing the thought to slip from my mind.

"Sleep Ari, I've got you." His soft voice lulls me towards sleep as a feeling of contentment fills me.

At first, I'm unsure if I'll be able to fall asleep. You're at your most vulnerable when you're asleep, and I've always done everything possible to make sure I'm not vulnerable—including sleeping alone. But I find that as I lay wrapped in Seb's warm embrace, his scent surrounding me, that I don't mind sleeping next to another person. I feel safe. While I listen to the steady rhythm of his heart beating, I finally let sleep pull me into blissful oblivion.

Whispered voices bring me back into consciousness, and I bury my face in the warm chest in front of me, trying to get back to sleep. I have no idea what the time is, but I'm too damn tired to get up.

"Guys, keep it down. You're going to wake her," a hushed voice scolds, rumbling through my body as it warns the whisperers by the door, and the room falls into silence in response. This doesn't last long though.

"How is she?" Garett's quiet voice reaches me. Wait, what's Garett doing here?

Come to think of it, where am I? Why am I in bed with someone? I groan as I push away from the person holding me, forcing my gritty eyes open. What I see has me frowning. Seb's lying on the bed next to me, on top of the covers with his arm draped possessively over my body. Alex, Killian, and Garett stand in the doorway, all peering in. If I wasn't so confused, it would be comical—three large men peeking through the small door frame.

"What's going on?" I ask, my voice husky from sleep.

The four of them share a look as Seb helps me into a sitting position so I'm leaning against the headboard of the bed. My tired, achy brain struggles to put two and two together. There's something I should remember, sitting at the edge of my memory. A sharp pain in my arm has me gritting my teeth and looking down in confusion, only for me to gasp in horror. My arm has dark marks running along the length of it, with a dressing covering a large part of my upper arm. I rip off the dressing and expose the raw wound below. The lesion oozes a blackish liquid, and spreading from the nasty looking gash are black veins that track up my arm and across my shoulder.

Like a thunderbolt, my memory returns—the Shadow Realm, the creatures, the man made of light, using my light to find the path home... I'm back.

I look around me frantically, my eyes catching on the men keeping watch. They can *see* me—I'm no longer trapped in the shadows. I can feel the cool sheets as I clutch them in my fists and the heat coming off Seb next to me. I release the sheet to raise a shaking hand in front of my face, turning it side to side. It's solid.

"Am I really back?" I whisper, not wanting to believe it.

"Ari." Garett's rumbling voice brings my attention to him, my eyes greedily running over his large muscled form like a woman starved. My words dry up in my mouth as he stalks towards me. I would never usually describe his walk as stalking, bear shifters are all muscle and raw power, but today, the look he has for me is purely predatory. Reaching the edge of the bed, he climbs onto it and crawls up towards me, and his large body hovers over mine so he doesn't hurt me. Seb has moved out of the way, leaning up against the wall next to the others while he watches the show.

As Garett presses his forehead against mine, I can see how hard he's fighting his bear for control. His eyes have changed, glowing softly as his bear comes to the surface. Bear shifters are very predatory and protective of their females. Even those who aren't their mates, or their direct family. Bear family groups often are made up of a mix, with many members unrelated by blood. It took me a while to realise that Garett considered us as his family. It should have been obvious, but I'm a little dense when it comes to belonging, my own family has well and truly screwed me up in that department.

I raise a hand and bring it to his cheek, his eyes locked on mine.

"You sacrificed yourself for me." His voice breaks on the last word and I can feel his body start to tremble. I don't respond, there's no point, my last words to him hanging between us. *'I love you.'* I had thought I was dying, and in that moment, as I was being pulled away to the Shadow Realm, it had been a worthy sacrifice. What had surprised me was the burning need to let him know how I felt before I was taken.

"Don't ever do that to me again." His voice is husky, and I wonder for a minute if he's going to cry. My strong, fierce bear shifter, on his knees before me, and it awakens something inside me. "I know you don't value your worth, but I do. We do. I don't think I could live through that again."

I'm left raw from his words. This is too much for me to process. My usual fight or flight response for this kind of situation starts to rise, but I have to fight it. I'm safe here, with these guys, my family. As if sensing my inner turmoil, Garett pulls his face away from mine, sitting back on his heels. He's still close enough to touch, and his eyes are watching me warily. I can sense the weight of the other guys' gazes on me as they wait for me to respond. I know this moment will define how we'll move forward from here, since there were a lot of unresolved issues from before the fight.

I take a deep breath and meet Garett's eyes. *Come on Ari, time to admit your feelings.*

"I meant what I said before I disappeared." *I love you*, I continue silently, and from the widening of his eyes, I know he got my message. I hear the others muttering, but I ignore them. All I can see and focus on in this moment is the look of heat and love radiating from Garett's eyes. It's as if we're the only two in the room, caught up in the pull we feel towards one another. When he surges forward, I eagerly meet him halfway as he claims my lips with his own. The kiss is powerful and raw, like he's trying to claim me and remind me why I should never leave him again. His hand cups the back of my head, keeping me in place, but it's gentle, like he's scared to hurt me. I return his kiss, pulling him closer to me as all my fear, loneliness, and regret come out in the process. I show him how much I missed him, how much he means to me.

A throat clearing brings our kiss to an end, but our eyes are still locked on each other, our breaths panting as a satisfied smile crosses his lips. I lean against the headboard of the bed and Garett sits next to me, his hand on my leg, as if he doesn't want to break the physical contact. Seb is watching us closely, arousal clear in his expression. When he sees me looking, he grins at me and winks, not at all ashamed that he's turned on from watching me kiss another man. I roll my eyes but can't help the little smile the crosses my lips. Kinky shit.

Killian looks borderline pissed off and bored, which I'm coming to learn is pretty standard for him. It's Alex's expression that surprises me most, the look of raw longing is obvious for me to see. He tries to hide it, his signature smirk quickly replacing it, but he wasn't quick enough. I need to spend some time with him to work out what's going on between us. But not now, I have enough going on without trying to figure that out as well.

"So, what happened after I...disappeared?" I finally ask, unsure how to phrase my question, but I need to know.

"You mean after you decided it was better to nearly kill yourself than let us deal with it?" Killian spits the words at me, the short leash on his temper finally breaking.

Wow. Harsh. I lean forward and cross my arms, my anger rising.

"They were about to kill Garett. I wasn't going to let that happen," I retort. I'm not going to let him make me feel guilty about my choices.

"So you just jumped straight to self-sacrifice? Without a thought about what that might do to us?" His words make me pause. In my panic at the thought of losing Garett, I hadn't thought of anything else, just that I needed to stop it. I'd accepted the darkness in that moment and didn't expect to survive it. But that hadn't mattered to me as long as the guys were safe. "What if one of us had done that to you?" he adds. I growl at that thought, my wolf finally making an appearance as she pushes to the surface. I don't need to look in a mirror to know that my eyes are glowing with her power. Killian nods at my reaction, gesturing towards me. "Exactly, that's exactly how we felt."

I lean back against the headboard again, feeling deflated. I'm too tired for this. Alex obviously notices and decides to take pity on me. He places a hand on Killian's shoulder, silently asking him to back off. For a second, I think Killian is about to protest as his eyes narrow at the hand on his shoulder, but he takes a deep breath and nods curtly at Alex.

"After you used your powers to kill Alpha Black, your father..." He pauses for a second, and I know that I'm in trouble for omitting that part of my history from them. "Everything went crazy. The rest of Shadow Pack ran. We managed to track down a few of them later, but Terrance escaped. He's now alpha of what's left of Shadow Pack." His words are harsh, like they hurt him to say. A pain runs through me at the thought of Terrance getting away, but I shouldn't be surprised, he always was as slippery as a snake.

"We thought you were dead, Ari." Seb's voice has me turning to look at him, the usual joker that I know and love is gone. "Killian went a little crazy and tore apart Marcus. Like, literally tore him to pieces." I frown at the crazy comment, but I can't find it in myself to be sorry that the pack traitor, Marcus, is dead. My only regret is that I didn't kill him myself.

"What do you mean he went 'a little crazy'?" I ask, making finger quotations for emphasis.

"We think it was the mated pair bond. You were here, but your...soul wasn't," Garett jumps in, struggling to explain what happened. "It made him go a little... Well, it took a long time for us to calm him down," he finishes, and I look over at said "crazy" wolf.

Killian is looking at me with narrowed eyes, like he blames me for his killing spree. I sigh, rubbing my tired eyes as I try to get my head around what they are telling me. I need a whiskey and a chat with Tori.

Wait, Tori. I rack my brain for why I suddenly feel anxious at the thought of my best friend's name. As I run my hand through my messy hair, I look around the room, and my gaze stops on the corner. I remember appearing in it when I was trapped in my shadow form. I think back to those times when I was brought here and gasp as I remember a conversation Killian and Garett had not long ago. They said they couldn't get a hold of Tori.

"Is Tori okay?" The guys share a look again and seem to be doing some sort of silent communication thing, it makes me nervous. "Okay, what's going on?" I ask, instantly getting worked up as the silence stretches on. "She's missing, isn't she?" I question, and dread lines my stomach as they all look at me in shock. This is one of those occasions when I wish I wasn't right.

"How did you know?" Alex asks, the guys looking like they all want to know that same thing.

"I think I...came back a couple of times?" They blink at me like owls before they all start talking at once. I hold my hand up for silence, my face scrunching at the sudden onset of noise hurting my pounding head. "It was like I was in my shadow form, but I couldn't get out of it, I couldn't touch or talk to you. Trust me, I tried." My tone is dejected, and I'm frustrated at my lack of control over my abilities. "I think something kept pulling me back, I had no control over it." I don't say anymore, but I have my own theories about what was bringing me back. My eyes fall on that reason, and he has a thoughtful look on his face, as if he might have an idea as well. "But that's beside the point. Where's Tori?"

Garett, who's still sitting on the bed next to me, takes my hand in his.

"We're not sure. She just disappeared, seemingly without a trace about two weeks ago. But don't worry, we'll find her." I can tell that not knowing Tori's location is affecting him too. He may not be as close to her as I am, but he still considers her a good friend. I don't doubt that he'll find her, but there is one thing that's bothering me about his statement.

"Wait, two weeks ago? How long have I been gone?"

Chapter Five

Two months. Two bloody months I was gone. After they had dropped that little bombshell, the guys had decided I needed more rest. No one had wanted to leave me alone in case I vanished again, so someone has remained with me constantly since then. The only peace I get is when I go to the bathroom. Overprotective shifters.

That was three days ago, and I'm about to go mad if they don't let me leave this bedroom. At first, I was flattered, but now I'm just grouchy. They left Seb here on babysitting duty today because they know I wouldn't shout at him, which is just unfair.

Deciding enough is enough, I swing my legs out of the bed and stand. This is harder than I would like to admit. My body feels battered and weak, which I guess it is after not being used for two months. The first time I had looked in the mirror, I wanted to cry. I'm not vain, but seeing my withered, pale body had been a shock. Garett had pulled me into his arms and reassured me that he still found me beautiful, which was sweet, but not comforting when I looked more like a seventy-year-old rather than the twenty-four-year-old that I am. It doesn't help that the wound on my arm is throbbing. It doesn't hurt as much as it did, but it's still a continual reminder of my time in the Shadow Realm.

Seb, who's rolling around on the end of the bed like a cat, sits up and frowns at me as I walk over to the wardrobe and start to get dressed. I don't want to admit how much effort it takes for me to put clothes on, and I'm certainly not going to let him know that.

"Where are you going?" he asks, walking over to me and helping untangle me from my jumper that I'm frustratingly caught up in.

"I'm going downstairs to carry on with my life. I'm not going to let any of this stop me. Shadow Pack may have taken away my childhood, but I'm not going to let them, or the Shadow Realm, take away the life I've built for myself here," I insist, tugging on my favourite jeans and rummaging through the drawers to try find a belt since they puddle around my waist. "I need to train, to get stronger, so we can find Tori."

I expect Seb to put up a fight, and for a moment, I think he's about to, until he realises it's futile and shrugs his shoulders.

"Okay." I grin at him and pull him into a hug, grateful that he's going to let me do this. My wolf wakes up with the close proximity to Seb, and a content rumble fills the room. Growing up, I always resented my wolf, and now I find myself lost at the idea of not having her. I'd hoped that once I'd settled, my wolf would wake up more, now that I was back from the Shadow Realm, but that hadn't happened. I've found that she only seems to react around the guys, which is both comforting and worrying. It's comforting since I know she's still there, but worrying as it makes me wonder if I can ever shift again without one of the guys being near. She has certainly made her choice clear though, she's chosen the guys as hers.

Seb stiffens in my arms and pulls back from my hug slightly so he can look me in the eye. I can see his desire, so I don't understand his reluctance to my touch.

"What's wrong?" I demand, fed up of them tiptoeing around me.

"You're so thin, Ari! I'm worried I'm going to hurt you!" he says and tries to untangle himself from my arms.

My wolf doesn't like the implication that she isn't strong. She rushes to the surface, and I now have Seb's full attention as my eyes start to glow, my alpha power rolling off me. I can't control it at this point, but I'm not sure I would want to even if I could.

"I'm not some fragile china doll." My words are quiet and come out as a purr as I push Seb up against the wall next to us. He gasps, and his eyes dilate with arousal. I lean forward, nuzzling my nose against the crook of his neck, inhaling deeply. Seb goes to say something, but I cut him off with a gentle bite on the side of his neck, right over his pulse point. He groans, and I feel his erection pressing against my leg. We both know that right now he could probably physically overpower me, but metaphysically, I'm stronger than him. I've never taken things this far with any of the guys before, aside from Garret, but the dedication they've shown when I was in the Shadow Realm, combined with nearly losing them, has revealed what's really important. Besides, wolf-Ari is running the show right now, and she wants Seb. We don't usually agree on much, and before the attack, I probably would have fought this, but I find that right now, I don't care. I nearly lost them all, and I'm not going to risk that again.

"Yes, Alpha," he groans, his voice breathy as he leans his head to one side to stretch out his neck, giving me greater access. This is a truly subservient move, and if he wasn't holding me up, I know he would be on his knees. I graze his jugular again.

"Don't call me that," I whisper. I'm not alpha here. I don't want to be alpha anywhere. I don't imbed any of my power into the command, but his body jerks like I have and his eyes widen. I can practically feel his desire rolling off him and it makes me feel powerful.

"Yes, Ari," he responds, his eyes dropping to the ground as I pull away to look at him. I snake a hand up his body and grip on to his hair, pulling his head back to raise his gaze.

"Look at me." Again, I don't use any of my power, although I so easily could. His eyes instantly snap to mine, and a heat that threatens to burn me lingers in his gaze.

"Do you want this? I won't force you." I continue to whisper, our eyes locked. I mean what I say, I won't use my power to force anyone. If we're going to do this, it has to be consensual, I need to be sure that Seb wants this as much as I do. A look of shock crosses his face, like he isn't used to being asked.

"Fuck yes. This is all I've wanted for a long time, but we shouldn't." His words are strong and sure, completely in contrast to his actions, and right now, I don't care about shoulds or should nots.

"Then prove it. Kiss me," I challenge, as I nibble along his jaw, letting my teeth scrape across his skin.

A slight growl leaves his throat as he raises a hand to my face, pulling me closer, and presses his lips firmly against my own. The kiss is hot, deep, and full of pent-up passion. I know he's just waiting for me to take the next step. Unlike the others, Seb won't push me. He'll wait until the end of the time for me to give him the word, and I need that. I might've even taken that step if it wasn't for a sound by the door, alerting me that we weren't alone anymore. A soft growl leaves my throat, my lips still pressed against Seb's. I know it's one of the guys, so I don't go on the defensive, but my wolf still isn't happy at the interruption.

"Don't stop on my account." Alex's voice greets me. While some might be sarcastic, I can tell from his tone that he means what he says.

Keeping my body pressed to Seb's and pinning him to the wall, I glance over my shoulder at Alex. He's leaning against the doorframe with his arms crossed, a lazy grin, and an intense gaze burn into me. There is no jealousy or judgement in his eyes, just rapt interest and lust. His erection is clear to see by the bulge in his jeans, which he makes no move to hide.

"You like what you see?" I ask with a purr, my wolf fully taking over, making my voice husky and sensual.

This is obviously the response he was waiting for, as he pushes away from the doorframe and stalks over to us. Standing just behind me, to the side so I can barely see him if I crane my head, he brushes against me. Leaning forward, he presses his lips to Seb's throat, his teeth mirroring the movements I'd been doing on the other side of Seb's neck just moments ago. My eyes flick to Seb, who has his eyes closed in a mixture of pleasure and pain, his desire palpable. A little grin crosses my lips before I start to kiss and nip along Seb's neck again. The tension in the room rises, and I have to say, I'm thoroughly enjoying being an Ari sandwich, with domineering Alex at my back and submissive Seb in front.

"Alex, is Ari awake?" Garett's voice floats up the staircase, and Alex lets out a sigh of frustration, dropping his head to my shoulder.

"Just as we get to the good stuff," he mutters under his breath before calling back, "Yeah, we're just coming down!" He pulls away from me and starts to walk towards the door, letting Seb and I untangle ourselves.

We straighten our clothes in silence and try to make ourselves look like we weren't one kiss away from a threesome. You might think the silence would be tense, but it's not, it's heated, and if either of them so much as looks at me, I think I might tear their clothes off. Taking a deep breath, I start to leave the room before Alex's hand lands on my arm. I don't turn to look at him, but I feel him coming closer to me.

"This isn't over." His breath tickles my neck as he whispers before leaving the room.

Something has changed between the three of us, and I'm not sure if it's for the better or if it will consume us all.

I need to clear my head. I've only just made it back and I'm trying to jump everyone's bones. I could blame it on my time in the Shadow Realm, but I don't think that's the case. This attraction has been building for a while. The Shadow Realm may not have changed me, but it's made me realise that life is short. Gloria had encouraged me to explore my relationships with these guys and insisted that I shouldn't be ashamed that I have feelings for more than one of them, even if one was her son.

Gloria. My heart throbs in grief as I remember the woman I was beginning to think of as a mother to me. I glance over my shoulder at Seb, the son she left behind. He hasn't been the same since she was killed, and not just because he was grieving. Seb is changing. As a submissive member of the pack, he was one of the lowest in terms of power. Somehow, Seb's power seems to be changing, growing.

Feeling my heavy gaze, Seb looks over at me with a questioning smile on his face. A tension hangs over him that wasn't there before Gloria's death, like he's carrying the burden of it. Which I guess he is. Now that Gloria is gone, Seb will be the sole provider for Jessica, his young sister. Not that Moon River Pack would ever let her be uncared for. Shifters are very protective of their young and often share the rearing of their children, but I know personally what it's like growing up without a mother.

"Ari?" Seb's voice brings me out of my musing.

"How's Jessica?" The smile drops from his face at my question, and the weight of responsibility settles over him again. I almost regret asking, but I need to know.

"She gets nightmares."

I nod at his words, not needing him to say anything else. It's not a surprise that she's having nightmares. No one should have to witness an attack like the one on Moon River, especially someone as young as Jessica. Guilt runs through me. I need to make sure I go and see her as soon as all this is sorted.

"Let's get this over with," I mutter and start heading downstairs, the guys following me. My legs feel weak, my muscles protesting after not being used for months, and I have to pause at the top of the stairs to catch my breath. I seriously need to get back in shape.

"Ari..." Alex's tone holds a warning, but I shake my head and ignore it. I can't stay in bed and let the others sort out my problems for me.

The gentle murmur of voices reaches me as I make my way downstairs, and I pause as a wave of alpha power washes over me. There are a lot of strong shifters down there. I walk into the communal room of the medical building where I've been staying, only to find everyone waiting for me. Expressions of disbelief, happiness, and relief greet me, causing me to stagger to a stop in the doorway.

I'd known people were fond of me in the pack, but the number of people stuffed into the room and the goodwill coming from them is overwhelming. Some of the most influential members of the pack are here, but to my surprise, many of the lower-level wolves are also present, many of whom have been my patients. The noise in the room rises as everyone starts speaking at once.

"Ari! You're back!"

"It's so good to see you!"

"What happened? Are you okay?"

Killian comes to the front of the room and stands before me, as if to protect me from everyone. Usually, I would scold him for the overprotective, possessive behaviour, but I'm grateful as I try to get my bearings. I have spent so much time on my own, not being seen, that I'm completely overwhelmed. I close my eyes and lean my forehead against his back, allowing myself this moment of weakness, not wanting to examine why this direct contact with Killian sends a jolt of happiness through me. A little voice inside protests that this isn't weakness, but I push it aside. I'll deal with that later. A cough comes from the corner of the room, and a familiar presence falls over me.

"Alpha Mortlock." Pulling away from Killian, I open my eyes and greet the alpha with a weak smile.

"Ari, it's good to see you with us again. We weren't sure you were going to make it, but your men never gave up hope."

Your men. I ignore the blush the coats my cheeks at his casual mention of my little harem, if that's even what it is. I look around the room, expecting judging stares, but I'm surprised to see several looks of approval.

"Thank you, Alpha," I reply respectfully with a dip of my head before glancing around at the full room again. "There are a lot of people here."

"You are popular within the pack. When they heard the news you were back, they all flooded here to welcome you," he says with a jovial smile. He makes it sound like I've been away on a holiday. His smile drops a fraction as he runs his eyes over me, taking in my thin frame and tired expression. "All right, everyone, let's leave Ari in peace to catch up on what's been going on." Grumbles fill the room, and he rolls his eyes, raising his arms in a 'hush' motion. "We'll have a pack meet and run tonight, you'll get your chance to see her then!"

Appeased, they begin to file out and several call goodbyes to me as they leave. Wow. How did this happen? Several months ago, I was living a quiet life as a lone wolf with my best friend. I was desperate to live independently from a pack, fiercely fighting for my independence, but now I seem to be at the centre of a pack, surrounded by people who really do care for me. The old Ari would bolt for the hills, and I'm not ashamed to admit that the urge to run fills my body. As if knowing what I'm thinking, Garett pads towards me, and I feel completed as he joins my side. He is my rock, my point of stability. Placing one finger under my chin, he raises it so our eyes meet.

"You okay?" he asks softly. I take a deep breath and let it out slowly, nodding at his question. I'm not sure that I am okay right now, but I will be. I don't say as much, but I know he understands. He brushes his thumb softly across my cheek before planting a gentle kiss to my lips. A small sigh escapes me as he pulls away with a quirk of his brow. His eyes have dilated, and although he tries to hide it, I can see him sniffing the air. He leans into me, sniffing along my neck before grumbling into my ear.

"I can smell your arousal. And theirs." His words are not accusatory or judgemental, only that, and the dilation of his pupils, gives away his own arousal. Okay, that's embarrassing. Does that mean Alpha Mortlock can smell it on me too? Everyone who had just been in here? Oh man. I'm now trapped between an aroused bear and a possessive alpha wolf. My wolf, the hussy, is perfectly happy to stay here, but human-Ari? Nope, not going there right now. I give an awkward laugh and push against Garett's chest. He moves back, but only because he lets me, we both know that if he didn't want to move, my little push wouldn't have done anything.

"Okay, simmer down, Grizzly. Anyone want to fill me in on what's been going on?" I use the same words that Alpha Mortlock had used. Something about them bugged me, like there was something I needed to know.

The two shifters surrounding me step away, and I take a deep breath, having a look around to see who is left in the room. Alpha Mortlock and his mate, Lena, are seated in one of the sofas, her hand in his with a beaming smile on her face. I'm still blown away that someone so *nice* has managed to stay in a position as high and coveted as the mate of the pack alpha. Although, I'd learned very early on that Moon River Pack was very different than the pack I was raised in. In Shadow Pack, even something as sacred as a true mated pair wouldn't be enough to stop someone from vying for the position.

The pack gamma, Isa, is standing just behind the alpha, her arms crossed as she observes the room for threats. This is the reason she's the gamma. In addition to being strong and earning the position, she is truly passionate about pack safety, even within the relative security of the pack grounds. Although when she sees me, a smile lights her face, transforming her as she walks over to me. If I didn't know better, I would have guessed she was a bear shifter from her stature alone, she rivals Garett in the muscle and bulk department.

"Ari." Her thick German accent makes me smile, I hadn't

realised how much I would miss hearing it, especially since we hadn't spent much time together. When had she become someone I cared for? She pats me on the back in a welcoming gesture.

"*Oomphf.*" I stumble forward from the strength of her greeting before she reaches out to steady me.

"Your body is weak," she states with a frown as she looks me up and down. I'm about to protest when a fond smile crosses her face, and she puts her arm around me in a semi-hug. This is the most affection I've ever seen from the mountain of a woman. "But your mind is strong, this is what counts."

"Thanks, Isa. I missed you too."

I can't stifle my laugh as I see Seb watching the exchange with his jaw hanging open. I guess I'm not the only one surprised by her actions.

"Wait. She hugged..." He grins and steps forward with his arms open wide. "Does that mean I can get a hug too, Isa?"

"No." The word is spoken bluntly, and Isa returns to her position behind the alpha, but not before I spot a small smile on her face. She quickly hides it, and I don't think anyone one else saw it. Perhaps I'm not the only one who's learning to open up.

Alpha Mortlock gestures to a chair, and I take a seat, grateful to be off my feet. I won't admit it out loud, but I'm exhausted. I guess being trapped in a different dimension for two months will do that to you. The alpha clears his throat, and the room goes silent, all eyes falling on him respectfully. Even Garett, who's come to sit on the arm of the chair I'm seated in, falls into attention as his hand drops from my shoulder where he was playing with a piece of my hair. As an outside shifter, he's expected to follow the rules of the pack that invited him here, but the familiar smile between him and Mortlock hints that they have a closer relationship than that. Seb sits at my feet, curling around my legs and pushing his head into my lap where my hands fall to rest on his shoulders. Killian comes to my other side and rests his hand on the arm of the chair, his hand brushing against mine. To anyone watching, it would look like the contact was accidental, but the predatory look in his eyes and the tug in my chest tells me otherwise. Possessive bastard. The guys can't seem to stop touching me, random little unnecessary touches, almost as if they are trying to reassure themselves that I'm really here. Alex takes his position behind the alpha, as expected, but his eyes are trained on me, watching my every move.

"Ari, will you tell us what happened?" the alpha asks, and it's a genuine question. I'm pretty sure that if I said I didn't want to talk about it, he would accept that. Another difference between the packs.

I take a deep breath to gather my thoughts, a lot of what happened in the Shadow Realm is fuzzy, like a dream.

"When they were going to kill Garett, I delved deep into my Shadowborn powers, deeper than I've ever gone before. I knew there would be consequences for using that kind of power, but I didn't care if it meant Garett would live," my voice is strong as I speak, growls filling the air at my admission. "I also knew that by killing the Shadow Pack alpha, everyone else would be safe. They threatened us. I'd revealed my hand by showing that I care for you all. Once they knew that, they were always going to go after you. I brought that upon you, so it was my responsibility to put it to rights."

The words tumble out of me, my emotions a mess. I feel guilt at what I put the guys through, but also because I was the reason they were attacked in the first place. The burden of keeping this responsibility falls heavily upon me. I feel multiple hands being laid on me, in comfort or objecting to what I was saying, but I hadn't finished.

"After that, I felt the pull of the shadows, and I knew it was time to pay for my actions. Both there in that warehouse and from before." I don't need to explain what I mean by that, they've all guessed what manner of deeds I was forced to do when I was part of the Shadow Pack. "And do you know what? As I was taken away,

I knew I deserved it." The weight of their stares has me looking into my lap as I talk, not wanting to see any judgement in their eyes.

The loud, unmistakable *smack* of someone punching a wall fills the room. Instinctively, I flinch from the noise before I hear the sound of footsteps storming out. I don't need to look up to know it was Killian, a slight ache in my chest lets me know of his anger as he strides away from me. Good. I probably deserve that anger, but I'm unused to Killian walking away. Usually, he would shout at me, yell and throw his alpha power around, so this change in character makes me nervous.

"Ari." The word is quiet but firm, and I look up at the person who spoke it. Alpha Mortlock looks as serious as I've ever seen him, and I brace myself for the backlash of my actions. "Let me make this clear once and for all. The attack upon this pack was the action of a sadist. None of this was your fault. If anything, we're in your debt. You've made a difference here, through your nursing and your interactions with the pack. We've thought of you as family for a while now, but let me remind you that there is a permanent place here for you in Moon River Pack," he offers.

My eyes widen as he speaks, and disbelief runs through me. I wait for the feeling of panic and pressure to begin at the thought of being trapped, but find that it doesn't appear.

"There's no need to decide now, and you're still welcome to stay here for as long as you wish if you choose not to join us, you will forever be a friend of the pack. But if you want it, there's a home here for you. You can live here in the medical building, or we will build you your own cabin."

My throat is tight, and I worry that if I speak, I'll start to cry. My eyes burn as I nod at Mortlock's sincere offer. I've never had anything that was truly *mine* before, so his offer means more to me than he knows. I won't make this decision now, but I have been offered something I never thought I might get—a place to belong. I'm aware of so many eyes on me. Yes, they are people I trust, but I'm unused to showing so much emotion. Sitting up straighter, I smile at Mortlock and push down on the rising emotions.

"Will you tell us what happened in this Shadow Realm?" Lena asks gently, as if worried the question will upset me. I can't help the smile that crosses my lips at this.

I sober as I think over what I'm going to tell them about what happened.

"You might want to take a seat," I say to Isa and the others who are still standing. "This may take a while."

I tell them about the Shadow Realm, about its lack of life and time, how I roamed for days unable to sleep, seemingly going nowhere. I tell them of the forest that exuded malevolence, the eerie pull that drew me into the dark trees, and the beasts that haunted it. I explain the wound on my arm, how, over time, it deteriorated my memory of who I was, how I lost my wolf, and the only thing that kept me going were my trips to see the men who grounded me. At some point during the explanation, Killian came back into the room, cradling his fist before coming to stand beside my chair, his glare was enough to stop anyone from even looking in his direction. I know they want to ask questions, but everyone is silent as I explain. Several growls fill the room when I speak of the stranger made of light and his promise to help me. This is the only time they interrupt me during my story.

"Who was this stranger? How was he in the Shadow Realm with you?" Garett leans forward with a frown. Shrugging my shoulders, I turn my face to see him.

"I don't know, but I felt like I could trust him. He didn't feel dangerous like the shadow beasts did."

"You can't trust him," Killian snarls as he stalks towards me, placing his hands on either side of the chair, bracketing me in. "Besides, it doesn't matter, because you're not going back. Ever." I narrow my eyes at him, my wolf perking up with Killian's proximity to us, but not liking the possessive way he's acting. My own power reacts to his, making the hairs on my arms stand up. I'm about to respond, undoubtedly causing an argument, but Alex clears his throat.

"Killian, now is not the time." His voice is soft, but something about it causes Killian to look over at Alex. They lock eyes for a moment before Killian concedes, shocking me again when he pulls away, stalking away to glare at me from the other side of the room.

I continue my story, and before long, I've finished, the room staying silent for a while as they digest what I've just told them. Looking around, I see concern and frustration on their faces. I clear my throat to gain their attention, a pressing need filling me.

"Will someone tell me what's been going on? Where's Tori?" As soon as I say her name, the alpha's face tightens and a sense of dread fills me. "What's happened?" I demand. I should really watch my tone when speaking to an alpha, but I don't care about the repercussions, I need to know.

Alpha Mortlock sighs and rubs his hand across his weary face.

"A lot has happened since you went away."

Chapter Six

I sit in silence as Alpha Mortlock fills me in on what's been happening over the past two months. Supernaturals are going missing. Witches, shifters, vampires, and even the fae haven't been spared. At first it started off small, some lone shifters or a renegade vampire that strayed too far from their nest disappearing, and then it got worse. Now bodies are starting to show up, but the bodies were only those of shifters. Mangled and mutilated, with the stink of magic in the air and runes carved into their carcasses. ASP, the Allied Supernatural Protectors, had been called in, but they don't seem too bothered. They're only interested in covering it up to stop the humans from noticing. This is causing unease in the shifter world. Various supernatural races are going missing, but shifters are dying, torture evident in the marks on their skin.

"What do the other supernatural races think?" I ask, disbelief obvious in my tone. Surely they can't be happy with their people disappearing? "It's only a matter of time before their bodies start showing up too."

"I spoke with Damon, so far, the only vampires to go missing were rogues, so they aren't taking action at the moment. In fact, the disappearances helped them out." Mortlock's tone shows his distaste at the actions of the Master Vampire.

Damon is in charge of the city's nest and is someone I've had the unfortunate experience of meeting. Yeah, I know, a vampire named Damon, more like Demon. Let's just say our interactions always end up with me threatening to kill him and just leave it at that. I shake my head, I shouldn't be surprised that Damon is revelling in a bit of death.

"What about the fae? The witches?" I ask, my throat tightening when I mention witches, Tori's face flashing in my mind like a beacon.

"The fae have gone underground and are refusing to talk to anyone, but so far, those who disappeared are wanderers, not belonging to any clan," Alex explains, his brow knotted in frustration. "The witches are also refusing to talk to us since Tori disappeared. They think she was taken because of her involvement with us."

Anger fuels me as I push up from my chair. "What? They're just using her as a scapegoat, they never cared for her. She wasn't part of any coven! They were afraid of her!" I exclaim, running my fingers through my abused hair. A thought comes to me, stilling my movements as I look over to the alpha.

"Wait. Could they be behind it? You said magic was involved." My thoughts run a hundred miles a minute, flashing through my brain as I try to piece this together. I remember Tori telling me that the last time she checked in with them, they threatened her, warning her that if she didn't join them that something bad would happen. Maybe they had finally done it. Besides, the only bodies showing up are shifters. Witches and shifters don't get on, and they make no effort to hide their dislike of us. My wolf stirs within me, finally making an appearance at the thought of Tori being taken. My eyes glow, and I feel my power rise as I get more worked up.

"Ari, those are very serious accusations. You can't say things like that without any proof. You could start a war. Besides, Tori isn't the only witch to go missing, others have too. Why would they harm their own?" Alpha Mortlock placates, but his voice is firm. Has he considered this as well?

I start to pace the room, my weary body protesting, but I need an outlet for my frustration before I do something stupid. None of this makes sense.

"The attacks on the shifters. Are they definitely related to the disappearances? Could this be Shadow Pack?" I ask. They wouldn't be beyond mauling innocent shifters to prove a point, especially after they lost what they wanted—me. When they took Garett, they had wards to stop me from leaving. Alpha Black said they bought them from a rogue, but I wouldn't put it past him to lie about that. Could they have a magic user helping them? Could it be that they're behind everything?

Mortlock sighs and runs a hand over his face, the frustration that Shadow Pack got away alive after they killed wolves here obviously wearing on him. Lena squeezes his hand in support, feeling the weight of his despair through their bond.

"There has been no sign of Shadow Pack since they took Garett, but it's a possibility."

"We think they're recuperating since you killed their alpha. We killed a lot of their wolves, so their numbers will be spread thin." Alex's eyes are trained on me as he says this, judging my reaction. Everyone has been toeing around the issue. It wasn't just the Shadow Pack Alpha that I killed, but my father. Does it make me heartless that I don't care? He had no right to call me daughter, he never cared for me as one, only as a weapon and a brood mare he could use.

"I've spoken with other alphas in the local area, they're all listening for word on the Shadow Pack. They know they're unstable, and since they attacked us unprovoked, the other packs are on alert. The bears, lions, and coyotes agree with us and are willing to help if we need it."

I take in the alpha's words, digesting them as I pace. "Help in what way? Will they fight?"

Mortlock looks around the room before his eyes meet mine. "At the moment, they're offering help with information and search parties only. But I think they would fight if we asked them to. I don't want to put strain on these newly formed relationships, we've only just started to work together." His words hold a warning. He would ask them to fight for us if we needed to, but only as a last resort.

I mull over everything that has been said before groaning and rubbing my hand across my face. God, my head hurts, and my arm is throbbing from the wound I got in the Shadow Realm. A large hand lands on my shoulder, and I lower my hand from my face and look up at Garett.

"Ari, come sit down. You're shaking." I look down at my body in surprise and see that he's right. A small tremor is running through my limbs. With a sigh, I allow him to lead me back to the chair I'd been sitting in. He moves to stand behind me and starts rubbing my shoulders, my muscles crying in relief as he works out the tension.

"So what about Tori? She's one of those who've disappeared?" I ask quietly, not sure I want to know the answer. Garett's hands still on my body, and I feel him sigh, the weight of her disappearance heavy on his shoulders. Walking around the chair to face me, he crouches so we're at eye level.

"We don't know for sure." I frown at his words. How can they not know? She's either missing or she isn't. I'm just about to ask this exact question when Garett puts a finger on my lips to silence me. "Let me finish. There's been no sign or contact from her for two weeks. I'd been speaking to her regularly with updates, and she'd been trying to find ways to get you back." He pauses to take a breath. "Last time I spoke with her, she thought she'd found someone who could help. I warned her not to trust anyone, but she waved off my concern. We haven't heard from her since. Both my pack and Moon River have sent out search parties, but there's nothing untoward and no signs of any magic like there've been at the other disappearance sites."

So either Tori has left of her own free will or we haven't found the place that she was taken from. I can tell the others are thinking the same thing from the grim expressions on their faces. Despite this, hope starts to grow inside me. Tori is one badass motherfucker and it would take a lot to overpower her, so maybe she's just holed up somewhere waiting for all this to blow over? Yeah right. Knowing Tori, she's right in the middle of the trouble, stirring up the fire!

I look up to meet Garett's eyes. "We need to find her, Garett." He nods solemnly at me, bringing his hand to my cheek.

"We will," he promises, and I trust him to keep his word. His expression is so earnest and pained that I want to kiss the lines of tension from his face. I lean forward to do just that when Alpha Morlock's voice calls my attention.

"Ari. We're having a pack run tonight, do you think you will be strong enough to attend? We could use something good to celebrate, and it will really please the pack if you could come."

"Are you ready?" Alex pokes his head around the door to my room. It's starting to get a little cramped with all four guys in here with me. Alex had left with the alpha after our meeting to take care of pack business, but the other three hadn't left my side since I woke up earlier. They even tried to come into the bathroom with me when I went for a soak in the bath.

I hadn't minded too much, trying to be understanding that they'd been really worried while I was in the Shadow Realm, but I put my foot down at that. I spent an hour trying to soak the numb feeling of the Shadow Realm from my body, but it still clings to me like a second skin. I felt it tugging at me, calling me back, but I focused on the light within me, still shining bright and keeping me here in the real world.

I nod and stand, my little posse doing the same, circling around me protectively. I sigh. They're going to have to get over this little insecurity before I go mad. I'm so used to being on my own that this feels stifling. Seb seems to understand and throws a meaningful look at Killian and Garett, before following Alex from the room. I can hear Seb chattering away, which makes me smile, grateful for the distraction. Garett sighs and comes to stand in front of me, pulling me to his chest. I automatically wrap my arms around his large frame in return, savouring this feeling of safety.

"I have to go, a bear has no place at a pack run." I'm about to protest when he shakes his head, a small smile on his face. "Before you get all indignant, I was invited, but I know it wouldn't be right. Besides, I should check in with my own pack, the alpha wants to see me." He lowers his face to mine and places a gentle kiss on my lips. I'm sure if Killian wasn't in the room, things would've gone further, but Garett isn't the kind to rub his affections for me in another man's face. Another reason why I love him.

Love. Huh, it's a funny concept being in love with someone. I meant it then and I mean it now, but I don't really know what that makes us or where we go from here. I guess that's a conversation that I have to look forward to…

I say my goodbyes to Garett and make my way downstairs. Killian follows broodily behind me. He's barely spoken to me since I woke up, but I can always feel his eyes on me. He's been favouring his other hand since his little outburst in the communal room downstairs earlier. I found out from Garett that when I was explaining everything that happened, he had lost his temper and punched the wall. When I asked why he did it, Garett and Seb shared a look and told me I would have to ask Killian.

Walking in silence, I glance over my shoulder and see him staring at me. I sigh and come to a stop at the bottom of the stairs, turning to glare at him.

"Are you mad at me for something?" I ask, placing my hands on my hips. His eyes narrow at my challenging words, and he bares his teeth at me in a snarl.

"Yes, I am." I take a step back from the venom in his tone before snarling right back at him, but this doesn't put him off. "You're reckless and impulsive. Do you have any idea what it would've been like for us if we lost you? And the fact that you think you deserved going to that hellish place?" He cuts off his words as I see him struggling with control over his wolf, the alpha power in the room stifling.

"But I'm Shadowborn, you hate us. You told me that yourself. You don't hate me, just what I am." I remind him of our conversation, of the issues he has accepting that we are fated mates, a true mated pair.

"And I told you that you are nothing like them. You were forced to do bad things by evil people. That doesn't make you bad. I've come to realise that." He takes a deep breath, his eyes running over my face. "You know how I told you that a Shadowborn killed my mate?" I still at his words, wondering what he is going to tell me, but nod anyway. "He had another wolf working with him, he was a sick, twisted bastard who enjoyed causing pain. Do you remember the wolf that killed Gloria, the grey one with the scar? The same one that attacked you before you came here?" Dread lines my stomach as he speaks, and I start to shake my head as two and two come together. "That was the wolf that attacked me, stopping me from getting to my mate. He scarred me to match him, so every day when I look in the mirror, I'm reminded of him and what he did."

We are both silent as the implications of what he's saying settles over me.

"Shadow Pack was behind the attack on your pack." It's not a question, but he nods anyway.

"Guys, are you coming?" Seb runs back into the house and comes to an abrupt halt when he sees us. "Oh... Um, awkward."

I roll my eyes at him and wait to see what Killian is going to do next. He rolls his shoulders and walks out of the door towards the woods. I stand unsure for a moment, before Seb and I follow him out. His admissions have me reeling, the implications of what he's saying are huge. I try to shake off the gloom of his revelation, I need to focus on the pack run.

Alex and Seb had tried to explain the pack run to me earlier, and while I had never been part of one, I had heard of them. It's a chance for the whole pack to come together and shift, running in the woods as a pack. Those who are ill, old, or pups, stay behind with a few of the pack protectors to keep them safe, but all others are expected to be present. It's an honour for a non-pack member to attend, so it's a big deal that both Garett and I were invited, especially seeing as Garett isn't even a wolf. I expressed my concerns about shifting. I struggled before, but now that my wolf is so quiet, I'm worried it will be even harder. Alex assured me that with the amount of power being raised from the whole pack shifting, I would find it hard *not* to shift.

The walk into the forest is quiet, but the farther we get, the more people we start to see with happy smiles on their faces, and a couple call out to us, waving and wishing us well. We enter a clearing where most of the pack is gathered, and excited murmurs fill the air as people greet family and friends. Several come over to us and ask how I'm doing, which humbles me. The alpha catches my eye, and if by some unspoken cue, the pack turns to look at him, a hush falling across the clearing.

"Tonight, we celebrate by coming together. This is the first pack run since we lost some of our own, but we will not let those heinous acts turn us towards hatred. Tonight, we honour those we have lost and celebrate those who are still with us." His eyes fall on me as he gives me a small smile. His gaze quickly moves away, but many people notice and turn to look at me, their own smiles lighting up their faces as they realise I'm here.

Without any further words, the alpha turns to his mate and they begin undressing each other. I look away only to see that many other couples are undressing each other too. Some are undressing themselves or little children, but I turn and see Killian staring at me. Not wanting him to get any ideas, I start to remove my clothes, fully aware of three sets of eyes trained on my exposed flesh. In my attempt to avoid looking at the guys, my eyes fall on a woman with three males all removing her clothing. No one seems to be batting an eyelid at the fact she has three males, so perhaps Gloria was right. The looks of adoration on their faces as they undress each other is intimate, and I look away, feeling guilty for intruding on their moment. A little part of me whispers that I looked away because I was jealous. I squash that voice.

Before she was killed, Gloria pulled me aside to give me some advice. I'd been conflicted about caring for so many people, especially after trying to avoid those type of feelings my entire life. She had seen how these feelings were tearing me apart and told me there was nothing to be ashamed of by loving multiple people. I am only just starting to accept that mindset, but it's still difficult for me to get used to.

I keep my undone shirt around me like a shield until the last moment, letting it flutter to the ground as I drop to my knees, calling my wolf to the surface. Eyes closed, I focus on where she resides within me. She seems distant, and I fight to pull her forward. I startle as I feel a hand on my shoulder, but I keep my eyes closed when I hear his voice.

"Stop fighting. Let go, she will come." Killian's tone is deep and rough, his wolf close to the surface, making him sound more beast than man. He's right though, and his nearness calls to my wolf. I take a deep breath and think back to when I had changed in these woods with Alex, how freeing it felt to give up my control to my wolf. It was difficult, the associations with my wolf had always been bad, and I had hidden that part of me for so long, only giving into my wolf impulses when I had to, that giving letting it happen willingly was hard.

The air fills with an unearthly power that has the hairs on my arms rising, and Alex was right, it pulls at my wolf, waking her fully and calling her to the surface. I drop my barriers and let her take control. For the first time, the change doesn't hurt, and with the guys around me, it feels like coming home.

The world always looks different from this angle, the sights sharper and the smells stronger. I look around and find that I'm surrounded by wolves of all different colours. Funnily enough, even though I've never seen most of them in their wolf form, I still recognise them. So when a small, ash coloured wolf comes charging towards me, yipping in excitement, I know it's Jessica. I crouch down into a playful position and let her tackle me to the ground, giving her wolfy kisses as I do. I hadn't realised how much I missed her, and I'm glad to see that she's just as playful as I remembered.

A wolfy snort brings my head around to see Killian's large, white wolf choking—no, laughing. Huh. I didn't know he could do that. I then realise he's laughing *at* me. Right. My wolf narrows her eyes, and we leap forward, barging our shoulder into him so he stumbles. It's my turn to start snort-laughing. I hadn't realised he would stumble, he's usually so collected and together that I assumed he would move out of the way. He gives me a playful growl before swatting at me with his front paw. I dodge it and run around to his other side, bumping into his other shoulder. As we continue to play, a feeling of elation fills me. Last time I shifted with Alex, my wolf had taken over and I had let her. This time it's different, we work together, there's no fighting for dominance, we are simply whole. It's harder staying away from Killian in this form, the bond is almost like a tether, pulling me towards him, begging me to accept it.

Seb and Jessica are playing together right next to us, and Alex trots over now that his beta duties are completed. He comes straight over to me, moving his muzzle to my shoulder like he's breathing me in, before pressing our foreheads together in greeting. I may be new to the whole wolf gathering thing, but this seems awfully familiar of Alex, like the greeting of a lover rather than a friend. I might have expected it from him if it was just the two of us, but with the pack around us, it's more of a statement.

    A bark from the alpha has our ears perking up, and as one, we start to run. The forest is full of the sound of howls and footsteps as we take off. I look around me and notice all the happy faces, even Killian looks happy in his wolf form. Seb is joking around and playing tricks on us, like the Seb from before, and Alex looks comfortable in his wolf skin, the only thing missing is Garett. Several members of the pack run up to me, brushing up against my side in greeting, and I race alongside them. I don't know how long we are out there for, but my heart is full of emotions I don't have names for, and I think I finally understand what it would mean to be part of a pack.

Chapter Seven

Sitting in a coffee shop on a Sunday morning with four guys who are vying for your affections should be nice, right? Well, it would've been had it not been for the wake-up call I had received, in the form of two hellhounds snarling in my face and dribbling acid drool onto my bed sheets.

I'd ended up in a puppy pile with a naked Alex and Seb after the pack run in the woods. We hadn't had sex, although I'm sure the guys wouldn't have protested, and I'm not even sure if Alex and I are in any place where we would have sex. Killian had been invited, and he had looked torn, but he just silently shook his head and walked back to his cabin on his own. After the high of running with the pack, I hadn't wanted that feeling of closeness to end, hence the puppy pile. It had been surprisingly comfortable, until the hellhounds that is.

At my yelp, the guys had instantly gone into attack mode, Alex snarling and pushing me behind him, Seb snarling in the corner, looking ready to change at a moment's notice. I pushed up from my place on the bed and reached forward for the collar on the beast, feeling a scroll attached there. I pulled it away, rolling my eyes at the theatrics as I read the message, although the feeling of relief and annoyance started to build up within me.

With a sigh, I got up and started throwing on clothes under the bewildered stares from the guys. I explained to them that this had always been Tori's way of summoning me. When she wanted me, she would send a snarling hellhound to fetch me. It takes a huge amount of effort for her to summon these and I'd always told her it was a waste of her magic, but she didn't care. Found it hilarious, her version of a joke, crazy witch. So, I called Garett and Killian, and we all got ready to meet Tori.

Which is why we are all sitting here in the human coffee shop. Her message had explained that she needed to get away from everything for a while and a 'friend' was keeping her safe. Tori didn't have many friends, and the fact that she had just up and left without so much as a word to Garett concerns me. She either knew this person and trusted them, or she was in danger and had no choice but to trust them.

We sit in a corner of the coffee shop we have commandeered as our own. Killian is sitting a little ways from the rest of us, scowling at anyone who comes close. Alex and Seb are sitting opposite me, chatting amongst themselves, but I can tell that they're on alert, their eyes flicking around the room looking for threats.

Garett had met us here, swooping me up into a fierce hug, burying his nose into my hair, breathing in my scent. I fight against the part of me that wants to pull away and tell him off for his possessive behaviour. I know how hard it must have been for him when I was in the Shadow Realm, not just because his shifter instincts would have been telling him to keep me close, but because he loves me. Not to mention my own instincts are screaming at me to keep him in my arms, to nuzzle into his warmth and strength.

Now, he sits next to me with my hand in his, calmly looking around as we wait for Tori. I know he's nervous though by the creases around his eyes and the way his foot is tapping softly against the floor. I stare into my coffee, trying not to let my mind run away with all the possible things that could've happened to her. The *ding* of the bell above the door has me looking up from my cup, only to see Tori standing in the doorway. I nearly shatter my cup as I drop it and jump up to my feet. The only thing that stops me from rushing to her is the iron grip around my arm and on my shoulder, preventing me from moving. Garett grips my right wrist, and I turn to glare at Killian, who stands just to my left with a tight hold on my shoulder, keeping me in place. I bare my teeth at him in a snarl until I realise that Alex and Seb are also standing and have moved closer, surrounding me in a semi-circle of shifters. Good thing the coffee shop was almost empty, because nothing about my guys look human right now, their auras are screaming supernatural.

"Ari." Tori's guarded voice has my eyes shooting up again, running over her to check for injuries. She's smiling, but she looks tired and wary of the guys in front of me. That's when I notice someone is standing behind her. He hasn't come into the shop yet, but I can see his outline.

"Are you going to let me in? It's freezing out here," a male voice complains.

I know that voice.

"Demon, what business do you have here?" Killian's voice is like acid. I push past him, and he drops his arm with a small snarl but doesn't take his eyes off the figure in the doorway.

"Eric? What the hell are you doing here?" I'm shocked, and my voice conveys that. Eric Daniels—or Dr. McHotty, as my brain fondly likes to call him—was my friend and work colleague at the hospital I worked for prior to tending the pack. I haven't seen him since before the attack on Moon River Pack, where he told me that he was actually a type of incubus. Not the sex feeding type like I had thought, but feeding off emotions, specifically pain. This threw a major wrench in our relationship when I realised he had been feeding off the pain of his patients. As a nurse, this was a massive moral issue, not to mention the fact he'd been lying to me. The whole time we'd known each other, I'd thought he was human and he had gone along with that, hiding this huge secret from me. He knew I was a wolf, thanks to his powers, specifically that I was

Shadowborn, but didn't trust me enough to tell me he was a type of demon. I should've been able to work out that he was something *other*, but the fact I couldn't means that he is either very old, powerful, or both. Nothing had ever happened romantically between us, and not because I didn't find him attractive. It's hard *not* to find him attractive with his short, neat blond hair and bright blue eyes like some sort of Scandinavian god. But I'd thought he was human, and there was no way I was going to have a sexual relationship with a human. I would destroy them with my supernatural strength. And that was all that would ever happen, because I didn't date, ever, sex was the only option.

"Ari..." Tori's voice brings my attention back to her, and I see that she hasn't moved from Eric's side. I look over the two of them, they aren't touching but they're standing close together. Tori looks unharmed, a little tired maybe, but given what's been going on, that's understandable. Eric, on the other hand, looks like crap. The last time I saw him, he looked bad, but he looks worse now, if that's even possible. His usually neat hair is long and uncombed, he has about a week's worth of stubble on his chin, and his eyes are red rimmed. His cheeks are hollow, and he looks like he hasn't slept in about a month. Our last conversation had ended early when I'd been taken away by ASP for questioning. I feel a twinge of guilt that I've not spared a thought for him since, especially considering how he looks right now.

My eyes slide to my best friend again, and I take a step towards her, only to be stopped by Killian's hand on my shoulder again.

"I don't trust the demon." His words come out as a growl, which I meet with my own.

"Kill, if you don't remove your arm, I will rip it off and shove it up your arse." My response must have surprised him, because he stops glaring at Eric to look at me with his eyebrows raised in shock. Alex and Seb snort out a laugh, and even Garett smiles.

"That's our girl," I hear Alex say quietly to Seb. Tension now broken, I meet Killian's eyes and give him a small smile.

"I know him, it's okay. I need to see Tori," I explain softly, just for him. I know the others can hear me, supernatural hearing and all, but I need him to hear me and understand that I've got this. His eyes narrow slightly, and for a moment, I think he's going to say no, but with the slight nod of his head, his grip on me loosens. I give him a small smile, knowing how difficult it is for him to give up control, and walk over to Tori. I get halfway across the room before Tori flings herself into my arms.

"Girl, you have a lot of explaining to do," she murmurs into my ear as she squeezes me tight. Her grip is crushing, but I cherish it. I thought she'd been taken and didn't know if I would see her again. I pull away and narrow my eyes at her comment.

"Oh, and you don't? And what was with sending the hellhounds after me?" I accuse, but I'm not really angry, and the smiles on both our faces are relieved. I pull her towards our table, gesturing to the guys. "Sit with us. You know the guys, ignore Killian, he always looks like that." I point to the scowling alpha next to me. "Be nice!" I order jokingly at him, and I hear him mutter, "I'm always nice," under his breath, which makes me smile.

I take a seat, pulling Tori down onto the bench next to me, where she lands with a thump, rolling her eyes at my roughhousing. I look up and see Eric still standing by the door, his eyes glued to my face, the expression on his face close to hunger. I clear my throat and wave at the chairs next to us.

"Eric, come sit with us, I want to know how you fit into all this," I offer. I'm not sure if I forgive him for lying to me, but if he truly helped my best friend, then the least I can do is hear him out. The chair next to me squeals as Killian sits and scoots it closer to me, boxing me in, and stopping Eric from getting too close. Alphas! So possessive!

"Ignore the alpha baby. That's Killian, this is Garett." I introduce the bear shifter to my right, and then gesture to Alex and Seb, who are sitting to my left on the other side of Tori. "And this is Alex and Seb." Eric glances briefly at the guys before his eyes come straight back to me, and I swear his pupils widen as his eyes lock with mine. He finally comes to join us at the table, taking the seat opposite mine, and inhales deeply as he sits. Wait. What?

"Did you just sniff me?" I blurt out before I can stop myself. I can almost *feel* Tori's eye roll at my question, but I ignore her.

Erin gives me a small, apologetic smile before clearing his throat. "Sorry about that. How are you Ari?"

"Yeah, tell us what happened," Tori chimes in, impatient as ever. It's my turn to roll my eyes as I look at her.

I spend the next thirty minutes filling them both in on how I ended up in the Shadow Realm and what happened while I was there. I don't tell them everything, like my apparent soul link with Killian, which seemed to bring me back to the real world. Eric may recently be my friend, but he broke my trust and his Hippocratic oath. I question if he can earn that trust back. I finish my story and lean back in my chair, looking at the two of them expectantly.

"Your turn."

Tori looks towards Eric and starts biting down on her lip, that's never a good sign, and why is she looking at him?

"So, after the attack on your pack, Garett called me and warned me about everything going on. I holed up in the apartment, which was the safest place for me since no one can break through those wards." I smile slightly as she speaks, proud at how strong my friend's powers are and how she owns it, no hint of bragging in her tone.

"The day you disappeared, Eric called me and told me something had happened to you and that I was in danger," she continues, glancing at the doctor. "I thought he was crazy. I tried to call you, but I couldn't get through. That afternoon, there was a knock at the door, which I ignored, then the door was blown off its hinges." I gape at Tori as she explains. What the hell kind of magic were they using against us? Something she says triggers my memory back to what the guys had told me when they were searching for her.

"But the guys said that they couldn't see any signs of magic. Surely they would have seen the door blown off?" I exclaim as I glance at the guys, who look equally as confused as I am. She furrows her brow as she thinks over what I said, before shrugging her shoulders like this is an everyday occurrence.

"Hmm, they must have used some sort of cloaking magic to hide it. I didn't recognise the witch who attacked me, she wasn't local. Anyway, they may have broken my damn door, but they couldn't cross the wards, so I climbed out the window and ran. Called Eric as soon as I was far enough away, then he came and picked me up and has been keeping me safe since then." I look between the two of them, trying to understand Tori's words. The fact that it wasn't a local witch would fit with what the guys were saying about the kidnappings, and since that's obviously what they are, there's no point in beating around the bush and calling them disappearances when it's obvious that people are being taken!

Something about what Tori had said doesn't sit right with me. I look across at Eric, meeting his eyes, which are trained on me once again.

"What I don't understand is how you knew she was going to be in danger. Why would you risk outing your secret to save Tori? You don't even really know each other."

"I warned Tori because I know she's like family to you. And the rest is more complicated," Eric explains, finally breaking eye contact and looking around the coffee shop. "I'm going to get a drink before I explain. Tori, you want something?" The two of them excuse themselves and go to order drinks.

I look at my guys with a raised eyebrow before looking pointedly back at the two at the coffee bar. "Do you think something is going on there?" I ask quietly, keeping my eyes on the two of them. Eric is acting oddly, not like the guy I used to know.

"Something's going on, but I'm not sure it's what you think it might be," Garett replies, and I look at him in question. He just shrugs his shoulders in a 'we will see' way.

"I don't like the way he looks at you," Killian comments, his voice more controlled than earlier, but his scowl is firmly in place. I roll my eyes at his comment, which seems to be a theme today.

"You don't like the way anyone looks at her," Seb quips, and Killian snarls lightly at him in response. I briefly look between the two of them, surprised by their interactions. Before the attack and Garett getting taken, if Seb had said something like that to Killian, he would have probably gone all alpha macho on him and demanded that he submit. But his response just now was almost playful, there was still a warning growl for Seb to remember his place, but nothing like it would have been previously.

I look back over to Tori and Eric where they are discussing something in quiet voices, quiet enough that even my supernatural hearing can't pick it up. Eric's gaze turns back to me, and our eyes meet again. He stills as he sees me looking at him, an unreadable look crossing his handsome features. With coffee in hand, they make their way back over to our table. Tori keeps shooting me looks out of the corner of her eye as she sips at her coffee.

"Okay, stop stalling. Eric, spill," I demand, fed up with all the secrets. With a resigned sigh, Eric puts his coffee cup down and fixes me with that piercing gaze again.

"Ari, you know I'm a type of incubus, that I feed from pain? It's very rare, but incubi have mates, and much like your true mated pairs, we have fated mates too. The mate bond has to be triggered by something, usually one of their lives is at risk for the bond to make itself known. Once the bond has been activated, the incubus will have visions of their mate. As some sick sense of humour from the creator, we can't feed until the bond has been accepted," Eric explains, his eyes finally leaving me to scan those sitting with us for their reactions. The guys look tense, and things finally start to make sense.

"You've met your mate. You've been getting visions, and that's why you knew Tori was in trouble. Is that why you look like you're starving?" I question bluntly. Tact isn't my middle name. As he nods slowly at my suspicions, a thought comes to me. I look at Tori in shock. "Tori is your fated mate?" I screech, my voice flying up a couple of octaves. Tori tries to hush me as people around the coffee shop glance over our way.

"No, not Tori." Eric's voice brings my attention back to him as a dawning horror settles on me. "You, Ari. You're my fated mate." My mouth drops open in shock.

Growls and snarls fill the air around me as three of my four guys react to this bombshell, even Seb looks unhappy. I can now understand why they wanted to meet in a public space. With the humans around, my guys have to be on their best behaviour and can't beat Eric like I'm sure they want to right now.

"How can that be true, Eric? How do you know?" My mind is reeling as I try to understand how this happened. Killian is my true mate according to our law, so I can't be Eric's fated mate too, can I? Fate has a wicked sense of humour.

"The visions we have are always of our fated mate, and you were in every vision, Ari. It's you. I feel stronger just sitting near you."

"Wait, so if I don't accept the bond, you'll what? Die?" Talk about putting pressure on a girl. "Eric, you lied to me! I can't just let you into my life with open arms. What the hell is fate playing at?" I exclaim, thoroughly pissed off. I feel the guys next to me relax a little as they realise I'm not going to go skipping off into the sunset with Eric.

"Ari, calm down, please. Let me explain. If I can be near you, I'll be stronger. You don't have to accept the bond, I wouldn't force that on you. But if you choose to push me away...well, I'll die."

"So what happens if I let you close to us, and I choose not to accept the bond?"

"As long as I'm with you, I won't die, but I will never be as strong as I was. With the bond accepted, I'll be stronger than I ever was before." His eyes are doing that intense focus thing on me again, and I groan as I drop my head into my hands. What am I going to do?

"I guess you better come back with us then," I finally reply, lifting my head from my hands as I hear the complaints from my guys. "Look, I'm not going to let him die! I don't know if I'll accept the bond, but I won't have my friend's death on my conscience just because I have commitment issues. Something's going on here. One fated mate is rare, but two? Plus, this link with the five of us? It's not exactly normal, is it?"

I sigh as a heavy sense of responsibility settles over me. If I reject Killian's bond, he will live a half-life, constant longing for me. If I reject Eric, he'll die, and if we don't complete the bond, he'll never return to his full strength.

"Let's go back to the pack, we need to have a chat with the alpha."

Chapter Eight

The next few days are difficult and full of tension. I've been trying to get stronger, training with the guys and ignoring the pulsing shadow within me. When I feel like it's going to take over, I look inside myself for the light that the stranger in the Shadow Realm had taught me about, reinforcing it and making it stronger again to chase away the shadow. I haven't gone back to the Shadow Realm, and I haven't used the necklace coin he'd given me. It had been buried in the sheets next to me, and I hadn't found it until I had gone to bed that day. To be honest, I had forgotten about it, and I hadn't told the guys about it either. I'm not sure why, but I've decided to keep it a secret for now. I know the irony behind my actions—I had been so cross at Eric for hiding things from me, and now I was keeping things from all of them. I will tell them when the time is right.

Speaking of Eric...

The guys have come to an uneasy agreement. The talk with the alpha had gone as well as it could've done. He granted Eric permission to stay in the medical building that I called my home for as long as I wanted him there, on the agreement that he wouldn't feed from anyone unless they granted him permission. He had looked at me when he said that part, which had made me roll my eyes. So far, only Seb had made the effort to talk to Eric, with Alex only talking to him when he absolutely had to. Garett hasn't been around much. He's been required to be at his own pack a lot recently. One of their bears went missing, and their mutilated body had turned up yesterday, so tensions are running high. I missed him, but I understood, and he called me every day to check that I'm okay.

Killian, on the other hand, was downright hostile towards Eric and seemed to see him as direct competition. Frankly, it was giving me a massive headache. At least Eric seemed to be looking better. While he can't feed directly until I have accepted the bond, he apparently gains some sustenance from being close to me. He hasn't had any further visions since I returned from the Shadow Realm, but he's promised that he'll let me know if he does.

I groan as I look over at the alarm clock on my bedside table, time to get up. I push against the arm draped over my stomach, laughing as it just pulls me closer into the muscular chest pressed against my back.

"Seb, we need to get up."

Ignoring me, he just buries his face into my hair, taking a deep breath as he relaxes into me. I wiggle my hips to wake him up, but just succeed in waking something *else* up. Groaning, Seb pushes up to me, pressing his now firm erection against me. I bite my lip to hide the smile that's trying to creep across my face. *Bad Ari, you don't have time for that.* I haven't had sex with anyone since I got back from the Shadow Realm, the closest I've gotten was that time with Alex and Seb just after I got back. However, someone had stayed in my room every night since, usually Alex or Seb. Only Garett and Seb had shared the bed for the night with me so far, apart from the occasional puppy pile. They're the only two I'm comfortable letting my guard down enough to sleep next to.

"I am up," he jokes, his voice low in my ear as he leans forward and gently nibbles on my lobe. With a soft growl, I sit up and spin so I'm straddling his lap, grabbing his hands, I pin them above his head and look down at him with a smirk.

"Huh. Because from here, it looks like you're pinned beneath me," I tease, keeping his hands pinned with one hand while I lean forward and bury my nose in the crook of his neck, breathing in his scent. I feel him shudder beneath me, and I pull back, seeing that his pupils have dilated and a look of hunger and arousal is clear on his face, but there's also something holding him back. "What do you want? Tell me." I try to coax it out of him. I watch as he swallows and makes a shallow laugh.

"I want you, Ari, completely. But it can't be me."

I release his hands at his words and sit back, still straddling him, but my confusion is easy to see. "What do you mean?"

"I'm low in the pack, in our group, whatever it is. If you have sex with me first, it will change things. The only reason they let me sleep in the bed with you is because they don't consider me a threat." I frown at his words. They make sense, but I don't want them to. I'm so fed up of shifter dos and don'ts.

"So, I don't get a say in this? I can't choose who I want to share my body with?" I growl, causing Seb to groan underneath me as my alpha power starts to rise with my frustration.

"He's right." Alex's voice from the doorway has me scowling over my shoulder at him.

"You have an uncanny sense of knowing the worst time to interrupt us," I mutter dryly as he stalks into the room uninvited. His eyes run over the two of us with heat and desire. Of all my guys, these two are the most open to sharing me, but it still surprises me that Alex is as open as he is. Especially when we haven't been intimate yet. I still don't even know what this *thing* is between us.

"The dynamic will change if you have sex with Seb before any of us with alpha power, whether you like it or not. But if you had sex with one of us and Seb was there, that's different. But don't let me stop you..." His eyes are predatory as they run over us, and I contemplate what he just said. I don't understand the distinction. So I can have sex with Seb, but only if I've slept with the others or he joins in?

My eyes run over Seb again, who is practically begging me with his eyes, before flicking back to Alex. I narrow my gaze at him before leaning in to kiss Seb. I keep my head angled so I can watch Alex as I do it, so I see the moment as he stalks forward and climbs up onto the bed behind me. He also straddles Seb, who's sat up so he's propped against the headboard. I continue to kiss Seb as Alex's hands land on my waist, sliding around so one hand is flat against my stomach, pulling me closer to him, and the other hand goes up to my right breast, squeezing it gently through the thin fabric of my sleep top. I growl into Seb's mouth at the action, causing him to groan.

A tug in my chest has me freezing and sitting upright. Alex's hands fall from me, and Seb has a questioning look on his face. That *tug* happens again, and I know Killian is behind it. I sigh and drop my forehead to Seb's in defeat. Whether he's doing it subconsciously or not, because of our bond, Killian seems to *know* when I'm getting hot and heavy with someone else. We need to figure out this bond business before it drives me mad.

"What's going on?" Alex asks me, still pressed up behind me. I glance at him over my shoulder and say one word as if it explains it all.

"Killian."

Alex sighs and climbs off the bed, leaning against the wall with his arms crossed, knowing he isn't going to get anywhere with me today.

"You need to sort out that bond." I nod in agreement, but I have no idea how I'm going to do that. I sigh again and climb off Seb, then walk to the wardrobe, selecting some clothes for the day. I haven't gone back to working as a nurse for the pack yet, so I just throw on my casual jeans and a loose white shirt.

"I'm gonna grab some breakfast, you coming?" I question and smile as they both nod. "Seb, you might want to put some clothes on first," I add with a wink, gesturing to his half naked form clad only in a pair of boxers. Laughing, he reaches towards where he had dumped his clothes the day before.

"I'll be down in a moment, you go ahead." I nod with a smile and head down the staircase towards the kitchen.

Walking into the room, I head straight to the row of cupboards across the back wall, pulling out bowls and boxes of cereal. Turning towards the island in the centre of the room, I jump a little when I see someone sitting there eating breakfast.

"Oh, hi," I say awkwardly to Eric, my arms full of cereal. He raises his eyebrows, a small smile on his lips.

"Is that all for you?" he jokes, pointing to the overflowing bundle of food in my arms. I chuckle and put everything down on the counter before heading to the fridge to grab the juice. Returning to the island, I look Eric up and down, he looks better today, healthier. He still looks gaunt, but then so do I. He's kept to himself while he's been here, but I see the hungry, lonely look in his eyes when I walk into the room. He looks like a man starving and I'm waving a buffet in his face. In a way, I guess I am by flaunting my relationship with the other guys in front of him but not letting him in, despite the bond calling him to me, that's exactly what I'm doing. I sigh internally. I really need to work out what's going on with us.

"Eric—" I begin, but Seb comes bounding into the room, flinging his arms around my waist and pressing a kiss to my cheek before helping himself to a huge overflowing bowl of cereal. Alex follows in soon after and quickly stops, looking between Eric and I, before raising an eyebrow as if asking *'am I interrupting,'* but I shake my head and offer him a bowl with a small smile. The moment is gone now, I'll speak with Eric later. To be honest, I'm not sure what I was even going to say.

We all sit in companionable silence while eating breakfast, and

I realise with a jolt how happy I am. This isn't a huge, momentous occasion, but in these little moments, sitting here with my guys, I'm content. If only Garett, Killian, and Tori were here, then everything would be complete. Tori had gone to a safe place after our meeting with the alpha. She wouldn't tell me where, she said it was better for no one to know, but she was checking in with me every day. To be fair, she was probably the safest of all of us, with her magic, she was one of the most powerful witches I had ever seen.

Just as we are finishing our breakfast, there is a slight ease in my chest, which lets me know Killian is coming closer. I'm in the process of getting his breakfast ready right when he walks through the door. I hold the plate out to him with a little quirk to my lips.

"Bacon sandwich, tomato sauce, brown bread," I greet him, and his surprised expression and little twitch of a smile causes my stomach to flip, stupid stomach.

"Oh. Thank you," he murmurs, surprised that I know how he likes his breakfast, making him short for words. He sits down in the seat I vacate and eats at his sandwich silently, while I putter around the kitchen with his eyes following me as I go. I can't quite decipher his expression, it's almost like a cross between confusion and indecision. I've just finished washing my bowl when I feel a gentle touch on my arm. I turn around and see it's Killian.

"Ari, can I talk with you a second?" he asks, strangely formal. I quirk an eyebrow at him but nod my agreement, gesturing for him to lead the way. This is obviously something he wants to say away from the others. He leads me into the sitting room, closing the door behind me so it's just the two of us. I lean against the back of the sofa and cross my arms expectantly. I don't say anything, I just watch him pace the length of the sitting room. Boy, he's wound up. He suddenly stops pacing and walks up to me, his hands are clenched into fists by his side, looking like he wants to touch me but is stopping himself.

"Ari, I want to take you out. On a date. With me. Tonight."

My mouth drops open. That was not what I was expecting him to say.

"Why?" I hadn't meant for it to sound so blunt, but the word bursts out of me. Killian is not a dating type of person, he's an all or nothing type of guy. I half expected for him to demand that I accept the mating bond between us like he had before the attack on the pack. He sighs and run his hand through his long pale hair, the scar on his handsome face a stark contrast to his light hair and skin.

"Because I'm trying to prove I'm not the alpha macho baby you keep accusing me of being. I need to show you that I may be a wolf, an alpha, but I'm also a man. I want you to get to know that man. I know we got off to a bad start, and that's due to my prejudices, I know that. If we are going to make the bond work, it needs to be about more than just sexual attraction." His eyes are locked onto mine as he says this, and damn, my wolf is responding to him being so close. I see the moment he smells my arousal, as his pupils dilate and a quiet, rumbly growl emits from his chest as he takes a step closer, boxing me in as he places his hands on the sofa on either side of me. I would usually object to being trapped, but right now, I don't care. He leans in slowly, as if expecting me to tell him to stop, until his face is close and he rubs his cheek against mine.

"You would like that, wouldn't you? My wolf speaks to yours. We could be great together," he whispers in my ear before gently biting down on the place where my neck and shoulder meet. My head drops back as a moan escapes my lips. "Will you meet me tonight?" he asks, one of his hands lifting up to cup the back of my head, guiding it up until our gazes catch. He presses forward so our lips connect in a powerful kiss. It's the type of kiss where you lose yourself, and for the first time, he isn't fighting for dominance, just meeting me kiss for kiss. He pulls away and presses his forehead to mine. "Say yes."

"Yes." The word is out before I can comprehend what just happened. His satisfied smile is all alpha, eyeing up his prey as he pulls away.

"Meet me outside at six," he orders with a wink before walking away.

Just walks away! Damnit! I'm growling to myself the whole hike up the stairs as I head for my room. It's time for a long, cold shower. Bloody alphas.

Chapter Nine

I spend longer on getting ready that afternoon than I would've liked. I don't even know why I was so worried about how I looked. After all, all of the guys had seen me at my worst, so it shouldn't matter what I look like tonight. At least, that's what I keep telling myself. Damnit.

When I walked back into the kitchen, Alex and Seb had smug, knowing looks on their faces, so I knew they'd overheard my conversation with Killian. I tried to ignore them and struck up a conversation with Eric until they managed to control themselves. The rest of the afternoon had carried on like the last few days, with gentle training with Alex to get my strength back up. My trip to the Shadow Realm had caused my physical body to weaken, and even taking the stairs caused me to become out of breath, which I hated.

Well, I say it has been gentle training...compared to what I had been doing previously, it's gentle. Laps around the Moon River compound until I feel like I'm going to vomit is part of my warm up, but I'm starting to feel like me again. I even popped in to see Mary this afternoon, who has given birth to a beautiful baby girl. It was ironic that I was brought in mostly to help with their birthing and fertility situation, and I'd actually been gone for the birth of their one pregnant female. It was lovely seeing her and the pup though, and her husband was completely smitten by his new daughter. She's going to have her dad completely wrapped around her little finger when she grows up.

As well as training physically, I've been trying to get a greater connection with my wolf. That was something I have always neglected. The love-hate relationship between my wolf and me is something I've always struggled with. It wasn't until I nearly lost that connection when I was in the Shadow Realm when I realised what I would be losing. Alpha Mortlock and his wife, Lena, have been helping me with this, trying to connect and strengthen that bond. It wasn't easy after over twenty years of pushing against it, but I knew I'd be stronger for it in the long run.

In fact, everyone has been helping me, even people from the pack I hadn't dealt with previously. They had seen the impact I had on the pack and how I had defended them in the attack and wanted to offer their assistance in helping me recover. I've had offers of clothing, yoga instruction, friendship, and more dishes of meatloaf than I can count. It also turns out that Seb is a fantastic cook and has been tasked with creating meals to strengthen me up. I've been struggling slightly, as at first, I felt so trapped, like my every move was watched. I wasn't even allowed to sleep alone, but the guys have managed to back off a bit, knowing I am mostly in control of my powers and not going to disappear on them again. The sleeping is still an issue, but I'll let that go, for now.

I look in the mirror and grimace at my appearance. I'm still so gaunt and pale, even the makeup I've put on can't hide it. With a sigh, I tuck a loose curl of my golden-brown hair behind my ear, scowling at it as it springs free again. A wolf whistle from the doorway startles me, and I spin to see the perpetrator. A grinning Alex leans against the doorway, his arms crossed as his eyes travel up my body. I grin back at him, rolling my eyes before patting nervously at my clothing.

"What do you think?" I tease, giving him a spin before posing like I'm on the runway. My tone was light, like I don't care what his answer is, but the nerves in my stomach tell a different story.

"Gorgeous, Ari. Killian isn't going to know what hit him." He smiles and walks up to me, his eyes still running over my body, making my blood heat. "You're wearing a dress. He's a lucky guy." Alex's words make me shake my head, I'm being stupid.

"You're right, I'm being stupid. I'm going to take it off and wear something more me." My words come out fast as I reach behind my back to undo my dress. Alex's eyes widen slightly at my sudden change of attitude and my flustered appearance.

"Whoa. Wait." He places his hands on my arms, stilling my movements. "While I don't object to you getting naked in front of me, what's caused this panic?"

His hands are still on my arms, holding them in place and keeping us close together, in fact, I'm almost pressed against him. I know I could move his arms away, but I don't. Instead, I look up at him, taking in his confused smile.

"This isn't me," I confess, looking down at the dress in question. "I don't dress up for guys. I don't care what I'm wearing. Why is this such a big deal to me?" I ask, but I'm not sure he has an answer for me. It's probably not even fair of me to ask him this. I know he wants to be with me, and here I am, asking him advice about another guy. "I shouldn't even be asking you this, I'm a terrible person. Sorry." Alex raises his eyebrows at my barrage of words. In the end, he just smiles at me and gently turns me so I'm facing the mirror again, stepping up close behind me, and he ducks his head so he can talk quietly into my ear.

"If you want to change, then change. But you look fucking hot. I would steal you from Killian if I didn't know that he'd fight me for you tonight. While I would, and I would fight for you, Ari, I don't like my odds against a true mate bond." His words are whispered and rough, his breath tickling my ear as he speaks, chasing away my nerves and replacing them with desire. I fought my whole life to be independent. People used to fight over me in my old pack, but not for *me*, for what I represent, for the power it would bring them. The thought of two alpha level wolves fighting over me should anger me, frighten me, but for some reason, it just stokes the fire of need that has been building in me since I came back from the Shadow Realm. His body presses firmer against my back.

"You like that idea? The thought of Killian and I fighting over you?" He drops his nose to the place where Killian had bitten me earlier, breathing in deeply. "I can smell him on you." His voice has dropped even more, and I know that if I looked at his eyes, they would be glowing with the power of his wolf. Strangely though, he doesn't sound angry, slightly possessive, but more turned on than anything. I store that thought away for later.

I can feel Killian coming closer through the tugging in my chest, I don't know if he even knows he's doing it, but he's calling to me, trying to pull me to him. The slamming of the door downstairs announces his presence before he starts stomping up the stairs towards me. Alex sighs, dropping his forehead to my shoulder, but makes no move to pull away from my body.

Through the mirror, I see Killian the moment he walks into the room. He pauses as his eyes run over us, taking in Alex pressed against my back, before he realises what I'm wearing. A hungry look enters his eyes, and for a moment, I think he's going to become angry with Alex being so close to me. Stalking towards us, my body stiffens as I expect him to grab Alex, but he surprises me by walking straight up to me. He stands in front of me, and his hands land on my waist, pulling me against him. I place one hand on his chest to balance myself, glancing up to judge his mood. His expression is blank, but I feel his indecision. I decide to take the lead, stepping up onto tiptoe and pressing a kiss to his lips. The tension leaves his shoulders, and a slight growl slips from his lips as he returns the kiss. Alex starts to kiss along the length of my neck, causing me to moan in pleasure.

Pressed between two hot werewolves, I feel like I may have died and gone to wolf heaven.

"Yes! Ari time!" Seb's happy exclamation jolts us out of our make-out session, remembering where we are. Both Alex and Killian half-heartedly growl at Seb, who just laughs in response. "Ari, will you just fuck one of them already? The sexual tension in this house is enough to choke on," he says with a wink before sauntering away from the room.

I just laugh at his antics and push away from the two guys crowding me.

"Okay, enough playing 'who can turn Ari on fastest.' I have a date to go on." I wink at Killian before sitting on the end of the bed to put on my black wedge shoes. They are high enough that they make my legs look great, but low enough so I can still run in them. Hey, a girl should always be prepared. I sling my black leather jacket over my arm and grab my handbag before standing up and walking out of the room, glancing back over my shoulder to see Killian and Alex talking to each other in low voices.

"You coming?" I ask, eyebrows raised, and Killian just nods before following me. I call out my goodbyes to those still in the house before being guided to a black convertible car. "This is yours?" I question, surprise lining my voice.

A smug look crosses his face before he opens the door for me. Hm, he really is on his best behaviour today.

I settle myself in the car as Killian makes his way around to the driver's side. I finally take in his appearance as he does up his seatbelt and starts the car. He's really scrubbed up for tonight, perhaps I wasn't the only one making an effort. He has on smart blue jeans, a crisp white button-up shirt, and a smart grey jacket. His long, pale hair is tied back, exposing his chiselled jawline all the more. As he pulls out of the driveway, I glance over at him again as a thought comes to me.

"What were you saying to Alex as we left?" I wonder, watching as a smile crosses his face.

"I told him I would win." I raise my eyebrows at the comment, not sure what he's referring to. "The 'who can turn Ari on the fastest?' game."

I chuckle, not expecting that response. Trust them to actually turn it into a game. "Oh right, and what did he have to say about that?" I shake my head at the two of them.

"He just said he doubted it," he answers, but I know from the smug smile on his face that isn't the end of the story.

"Spit it out," I demand, not sure if I want to hear what's coming next.

"I told him I would prove him wrong tonight." He glances over at me as he says this, his eyes landing on the stretch of thigh that's exposed from my dress.

"Oh," is all that I can think to say. I turn away to look out the window at the passing scenery, but really, it's to hide the smile that's threatening to break through and to stop the thought that passed through my head with his comment.

Bring it.

Chewing on my breadstick, I look around the smart restaurant Killian's brought us to. I don't know where I expected him to bring me for a date, but it wasn't an expensive, romantic restaurant. He booked us a quiet table in a booth, separated from the main part of the restaurant by a partition, with a private waiter serving us. He ordered for me, which had made me narrow my gaze at him, about to protest that I was perfectly capable of ordering my own food, but he had smiled at me and told me to trust him, this food was to die for.

The smile alone was enough to disarm me, I've never seen him smile as much as he has in the last hour. I hate to admit it, but if the rest of the food was as good as the starter I just devoured, then he would be right—the food was *amazing*. I take a swig of my wine, finishing the glass and placing it down on the table. Before I can even blink, the waiter has come forward and is filling my glass.

"Are you trying to get me drunk?" I tease, a small smile spreading across my lips. I don't usually drink much, it leaves you too vulnerable, but I decided that tonight I would have a little. It's a special occasion after all...

He just shrugs, and that small smile, almost a smirk, graces his lips, and his eyes have been locked on me the whole evening.

"You look...really good tonight." I almost drop my wine glass at his words, and I'm pretty sure my eyes widen in shock, if his amused expression is anything to go by.

"You're complimenting me now?" I'm dumbstruck, that's probably the kindest thing he's ever said to me. He looks slightly uncomfortable at my comment, shifting in his chair and pulling at his shirt collar like it's trying to choke him.

"I'm trying to make an effort. I know that I was...well, a dick." I smile at his understatement and roll my eyes at him, causing that little smile I'm beginning to love so much to appear. "I had to make a decision when you were taken, to decide if I could live without you. I decided that I could." I frown at his words, about to call him out for being a dick again, before he holds up a hand and hurries on. "Wait, let me finish."

I pause, taking in his expression, and decide to let him continue. Nodding my head slightly, he smiles gratefully and continues.

"I decided that I would be able to live without you, but that I didn't want to. I hated the fact that I hadn't even gotten the chance to know you better, or for you to know who I really am. The thing that ate at me the most was that I didn't want you go still thinking of me as a dick." I lean back in my chair, wine glass in hand as I listen to his words, completely disarmed. Whatever I was expecting him to say, this wasn't it. The sincerity of them hits me, his eyes willing me to understand what he's saying. "I'm rough, I often say the wrong thing, and I *am* a dick sometimes. I miss Julie, and part of me feels like I'm betraying her by even being here with you. It's not going to be easy, especially sharing you with the others." His voice deepens as he says this bit, but he carries on regardless. "But there is a reason we were brought together."

I'm silent for a while as I let his words sink in. Killian is just as broken as me, with a past almost as dark as mine. If anyone understands the demons that I fight, it's him. If he can get over his prejudices against Shadowborn, or at least try, then I should do the same with my fear of commitment, right?

"I'm not sure I can accept the bond. Yet. But I'm willing to try… whatever this is," I finally answer him, and I see the tension leave his shoulders as he dips his head in acknowledgement. He understands my aversion and isn't going to push me on it tonight.

"I'll find a way to convince you." His alpha confidence makes me roll my eyes, which just makes him chuckle. The rich sound makes the hairs on my arms stand up on end, and I find that I want to hear that sound again.

The rest of the meal passes in a blur, and he was right—the food was delicious. I get to see a different side of Killian this evening, a more relaxed guy who likes riding motorbikes through the woods, who likes woodwork, and whose guilty pleasure is listening to Jessy J. Not that he would ever admit it if I told anyone. Away from the pack, he's like a different person. The pack is a constant reminder of what he has lost, his pack and mate who were killed. An alpha without a pack, always feeling like an outsider.

We arrive back at the pack and park outside the medical building. I should start calling it my home, since that's really what it is, but something is holding me back. Home just sounds too permanent. I look across at Killian, whose eyes are tracking my every movement, every inch the predator.

"Thank you for tonight," I say to fill the silence. I had a really good time, and I don't really want this evening to end. This peace we have between us, I feel like it will end when we return to pack life. "Did you want to come in for a coffee?" I know I'm playing a dangerous game, but I can't seem to stop myself.

Killian is silent for a moment before nodding and getting out of the car, only to come around and open my door for me, offering me an arm to help me climb out. I accept it with a smile and head into the house, straight into the empty kitchen. Putting the kettle on to boil, I start busying myself by getting the cups and milk ready. I feel his eyes on me as I bustle around, and the room heats up with sexual tension.

I sense the moment he decides to make his move by the change in the air. The next thing I know, his body is pressed up against my back, pressing me into the kitchen counter, causing me to brace my hands on the worktop. His hands come to my waist, almost hesitantly, as he drops his mouth to my neck, kissing along my shoulder. My breath comes out shakily as I tilt my head back, giving him more access to my neck. I feel his erection pressed into my leg, and my wolf rushes to the surface as desire passes through our bond. When we're like this, it's hard to think what our bond would be like if we accept it fully, as this is only a fraction of how close we will feel once or if it's accepted.

I spin around in his arms so my back is pressed against the cabinets, and I put my hands around his neck, pulling him closer to me. Our mouths meet in a frantic kiss, the sexual tension from the evening finally boiling over. His hands explore my body, grazing my nipples, which are pebbled against the fabric of my dress. A shot of desire fires through me, and I dig my nails into his shoulders before biting down on his lower lip. A growl emits from his chest, and it only turns me on more. My hands drop to his jeans, and I try to work the buttons, desperate to feel him, but he stops me, his breath coming out in short pants.

"Are you sure this is what you want? I'm not sure I could stop myself from claiming you if we fucked. If I bite you when we fuck, then that's it, we'll be bonded, nothing can undo that." He looks like it's painful for him to say these words, but I appreciate him doing so. He knows I would resent him if we ended up bonded accidentally because I didn't know how it worked.

"I'm not ready to bond. But I trust you, Killian." I mean it. I'm not sure when it happened, but I trust that he won't seal us together until I'm ready to accept the bond. If. If I decide to accept the bond. *Keep telling yourself that, Ari.*

I take Killian's hand and lead him up the stairs towards my room, although now that the heat has been broken, I find myself becoming nervous. I mean, I'm no virgin, but Killian makes me feel like an inexperienced pup half the time. As if he knows what I'm thinking, he pushes me up against the wall as soon as we enter my room, pressing his nose into my hair, breathing me in.

"What's wrong?" he whispers, his voice soft before he nibbles on my earlobe.

"You make me nervous, like you're going to consume me," I admit, closing my eyes against the barrage of sensations.

"Open your eyes," he demands, and I obey. "Sit on the edge of the bed." I narrow my eyes at him. I don't usually like being told what to do, but my wolf is demanding that I follow these orders.

I do as I'm told, perching at the edge of the bed, watching as he prowls towards me and sinks to his knees before me.

"You have an alpha on his knees for you. I think it's you who is consuming me," he tells me before leaning in to kiss me. These kisses are slower and more passionate than the ones in the kitchen, but they build until I feel like I'm going to combust from need. Gently pushing against my shoulders, he gets me to lay back and starts kissing a trail along my body, sliding his hand up my leg and under the skirt of my dress until he reaches my centre, groaning when he realises I'm not wearing any underwear beneath it. Falling back to his knees, he gently pushes my knees apart until he presses his mouth against me. My head falls back as he starts licking, kissing, and sucking, while wordless cries and pants slip from my lips. Just as I feel myself building up to the point of orgasm, he pulls away, a smug smile on his face as I cry out at the loss of contact.

"No, not yet. I want you falling apart around me." He grins as he pulls me up to sitting, my legs automatically wrapping around his waist before he picks me up. He walks us up to one of the walls, leaning my back against it with my arms locked around his neck. I can feel the power in his muscles as he holds me up.

"You're a dick," I mutter, glaring at him as he teases me. Deciding to get back at him, I lean forward and bite down on his lip, dragging my nail over his shirtless back. Wait, when did he remove that? Growling, he fumbles with his jeans, finally freeing himself, all the while holding me up against the wall with his other arm.

I feel him pressing up against my entrance, and he shoves into me as he claims my lips. The feel of him inside me, so tight, is almost enough to send me over the edge as he pummels into me. He's rough, and as I dig my nails along his back, it only seems to spur him on more, growling and snarling from both of us filling the room. We bring out each other's inner animal, like when we're together, we don't have to keep our human appearances up, we can fully be who we are, beastly traits and all.

Being with him like this, I can feel the bond waiting to be claimed, like a dull golden thread between us, binding us. I know my wolf has taken over as my nails are longer and sharper, my senses stronger. I bring my mouth to his shoulder as he continues to pound into me, my pleasure starting to spiral up. My canines have lengthened, and I gently bite his shoulder. I feel him shudder beneath me.

"Ari, if you bite me now, you claim me. I won't be able to stop myself from claiming you back if you bite me now," Killian warns, his words rough as he fights against his instincts.

Part of me, the human part, hears what he says, but my wolf side is fully in control, and as he pushes me higher and I reach climax, I bite down on his neck. I feel him roar beneath me, finding his own release as he plunges his fangs into my neck. A blinding light fills my vision, and I feel as the connection between us is sealed before another wave of pleasure washes over the both of us.

As the surge of pleasure fades, our foreheads are pressed together and our breathing is rapid. A small trail of blood trickles down Killian's shoulder, and I'm pretty sure that my shoulder is the same.

Killian gently lowers me from his waist but steadies me as I lose my balance. His eyes are locked on mine, and a deep contentment is emanating from him, a gentle purring coming from his chest as he brushes a lock of hair from my face. His eyes drop to my shoulder, and he turns to walk to the small en suite bathroom.

"Let's get that cleaned up, mate."

Oh shit.

Chapter Ten

The gentle breathing of someone sleeping is the first thing I notice as I wake. There's the comforting weight of an arm around my waist and the warmth of a male body pressed against my back. Even if I didn't remember who was sharing my bed with me, the warmth within me tells me that the person cocooned around me is Killian. He makes a sound in his sleep and buries his face into my hair, inhaling my scent.

I glance at the clock on my bedside table, but I'm in no rush to get up today. A sense of trepidation fills me. I'm not sure I'm ready to face the consequences of the last few days.

After I accidentally claimed Killian and he had returned the claim, sealing us together and affirming our true pair bond, a kind of frenzy had descended upon us. We couldn't get enough of each other, the thought of even leaving the room and seeing other people had set off a jealousy in us both so strongly that we had been confined to my bedroom. We had fucked pretty much throughout the first day, and that's exactly what it was—fucking. Making love came later, that first day was wild and animalistic, scratching and biting, our wolves trying to assert their dominance. As we settled down, we took the time to get to know each other's bodies better.

I roll over in the bed and run my eyes over the man I'm now

bonded to. I've had a lot of time over the last few days to think over it, and my feelings are mixed. A slither of sunlight creeps in through a parting in the curtains and falls on Killian, lighting up his features. A feeling of contentment warms me as I watch him sleeping. I pull a face. Urgh, have I really turned into one of *those* people? Soppy has never been a word in my vocabulary.

"Stop staring at me." Killian's voice is deep from sleep, making me smile and roll my eyes in the process.

"I can't help it, you're pretty," I tease, and I mean it as I reach forward and play with a strand of his pale hair. He looks serene when he sleeps, all the stress and tension that he carries around with him falls away, and he just looks peaceful. He snorts at my comment and opens one eye, scowling at me.

"I think the bond has addled your senses, mate." My insides clench at his used of the term mate. He's been using it at every opportunity, as if he relishes being able to call me it. His words were teasing, but a frown mars my face as I remember that we're going to have to face the reactions of the others regarding our actions soon enough. The others must have realised what was going on since we haven't been bothered, and little food packages have been arriving outside my door so we haven't had to leave my room.

Killian sits up as he sees my frown, although he would've been able to feel my turbulent emotions through our newly formed bond anyway. He reaches for me and pulls me into his arms, pressing his forehead to mine as a sigh leaves his lips.

"Look, I know this isn't what we planned, but what's done is done, we need to make the best of this. The others will understand." I bite my lips as he finds the root of my worries. I can deal with the uncomfortable fact that I'm tied to Killian for life at a later date, what I'm most worried about is how the guys are going to take it. I think Alex and Seb thought this was inevitable. They're wolf shifters, they understand how the pull of the true mate bond is difficult to resist. Garett is the one I am most worried about. How is this going to work between us, between *all* of us? Is Killian going to feel more entitled than the others? I don't love him more than the others, hell, I don't even know if what I'm feeling *is* love. Is what I'm feeling for him just fate taking away my choices and deciding for me? No. Fuck fate. I acknowledge that what I have with Killian is intense and different, but I will not let that affect my relationship with the others.

Trying not to focus on that, I press a kiss to his full lips, paying particular attention to where his scar crosses his lip. I had spent one of the nights we shared together kissing along every scar on his body. He doesn't say as much, but I know his appearance bothers him. He hides behind it, this hard exterior, and I think he believes he deserves it because of his failings to his pack. I've been trying to convince him that his scars do not define him. Hell, I'm covered in scars, and they don't stop me. The look on Killian's face when he realised that the marks were scars inflicted from my old pack was murderous, and it had taken me a long time to calm him down, as the protective instinct from the bond was riding him hard.

He rumbles in satisfaction as my kisses become firmer, and I crawl into his lap, wrapping my arms around his neck. Damn, this bond is going to make it difficult to get anything done.

"We need to go speak to everyone," I say, but the bond is screaming out to me to stay here with my mate. Urgh. Mate.

We eventually manage to leave the room and make our way over to the main house where the alpha lives. Killian had grabbed hold of my hand as we walked over, and his eyes kept flicking to me. As we reached the main house, as if they knew we would need to see them, Alex and Seb appear in the doorway, Alpha Mortlock pushing past the two of them to walk towards us. I feel Killian tense up, and we come to a stop a few meters away from the house. I glance over at him and give his hand a gentle squeeze.

"Ari, Killian. Congratulations on your mating. It came as a bit of a surprise to us." Alpha Mortlock strolls towards us slowly, and while he's smiling and his words are genuine, he's carefully eyeing up Killian, trying to judge his reaction.

"Yes, it came as a surprise to us too," I joke and shrug my shoulders as if it was no big deal. I can feel Alex's eyes on me, and when I look his way, he looks concerned, like he wants to say something but thinks better of it. I just smile and shake my head, hoping my gesture reassures him for now, we can talk properly later.

Killian looks at me as I speak, and he visibly relaxes and even goes so far as dropping my hand and going forward to greet the alpha, shaking his hand and accepting his congratulations.

"Thank you, Alpha, your acceptance of our mating means a lot to us."

Movement from within the house brings my attention back up as I see a figure making his way to the door.

"Hey, Ari," Garett calls out softly, his expression wary, but I notice his despair as he sees Killian and I together.

"Garett!" I cry out. My happiness at seeing him must light my face, as his expression turns bright and he takes a step towards me. I start to hurry towards him when I feel an iron band clamp down around my wrist, halting me in my tracks. I look down at the hand wrapped around my arm and frown up at Killian, who's holding me in place. His face is set in a scowl, and his lips pull back over his teeth as he snarls, but he isn't looking at me. Garett's expression darkens as he takes a menacing step towards us, his bear coming to the surface as his power floats through the air.

"Let go of her." His already deep voice deepens as he fights for control against his bear.

"She's mine," Killian growls out. Oh no, not this nonsense again. I rip my hand out of his grip and glare at him, smacking him on the chest until he pulls his glare from Garett to look at me.

"Oi, Mr. She's Mine. *She* belongs to herself, we've spoken about this before. Get your possessive mate addled head out of your ass."

"Ari..." Alpha Mortlock warns, ready to pull me out of the way if Killian shifts, but I see his pupils start to return to normal at my insults. Huh, guess that works then. He nods curtly at me and takes a step away. Alpha Mortlock goes over and starts talking to him quietly, Killian nodding at whatever he's saying. I wait for a few moments to check that he's calm before turning back to Garett. He's staring at Killian, his arms crossed, until he feels my attention on him. He smiles at me and opens his arms wide. I hurry over and wrap my arms around him, breathing in his scent as he drops a kiss on the top of my head. Reaching down, he places a finger on my chin and brings my face up to look at him. His expression is serious, and I know what he's going to say.

"You have a mate now, huh?" I let out a sigh. I had hoped to enjoy a bit of time with my guys before all this got brought up, but there is no point putting off the inevitable.

"Yeah. We didn't mean to accept the bond. I'm sorry, Garett." I start to look away, not wanting to see the hurt on his face, but he stops me with his finger on my chin again.

"Don't be sorry, Ari, I'm not mad at you." He sighs and gives me a rueful smile. "I'm jealous. I wish it were me you bonded with. I always knew I was going to have to share you, but I always thought that we had a special bond. Instead, it's with that dickhead."

I can't help but laugh at his words and the annoyance in his tone.

"Garett, we don't need fate to tell us what can and can't be. You know I love you." Garett wraps his arms around me even tighter, holding me close to him as I say this quietly.

A loud snarl has me spinning around, and I see Killian being held back by Alpha Mortlock, who is frantically talking to him.

"How's that bond treating you, Kill?" Alex chimes in, snapping what little control Killian had left. In a flash of claws and fur, Killian shifts into his wolf form, snarling and growling at Garett, who happens to be behind me. Garett starts to lose control and pushes me behind him as he falls to his knees and shifts into his bear form. I'm always taken aback at how large he is in his animal form. I shouldn't be because of how large he is as a human, but he's even bigger as a bear.

"Thanks, Alex, that was real helpful," I drawl at Alex, who just winks at me.

"Will you three just fuck already? This is getting repetitive," Seb jokes, pushing his way towards me, wrapping his arm around me. I half-heartedly return his hug, but my attention is on the two shifters who are battling it out. I wince as Garett gets bitten on the forearm and start forward to step between them.

"Not a good idea, Ari," Alex says as he pulls me back. "They won't be able to stop themselves if you get between them, and then think how badly they will feel."

"They're going to kill each other!" I practically shout, as I wave a hand at the fight in front of us.

"They won't, and Alpha Mortlock will keep an eye on them. The last thing we need is a dead bear on our property," Alex jokes, but I just look at him horrified. "Okay, that was in bad taste."

"Ari, let's go inside, your presence is just making things worse," Seb suggests gently before slipping his hand in mine and pulling me away from the two shifters who have a piece of my heart.

You better not kill him, Kill. I will shred this bond if you injure him, I threaten down the newly formed bond. I'm not sure if he can hear my words or if he just gets a hint of my feelings, but I mean every word. I know Garett wouldn't kill Killian, he isn't the type of person. Fiercely protective of me? Yes. But he wouldn't kill him out of spite. Killian, on the other hand, is a wild card.

The two of them lead me inside the house and into the kitchen, where I find Eric at the coffee pot, with cups and a plate of doughnuts spread out before him. He smiles at me as we enter, passes me a steaming cup, and gestures to the plate.

"I thought you could use some caffeine." He grins when I sigh in appreciation as I inhale the smell of the coffee and reach forward for a doughnut.

"Oh, man, I love you," I joke before stuffing half of the heavenly doughnut in my mouth. Pausing, I realise what I just said before frowning at him. "I mean..." I try to explain around the doughnut, looking as ladylike as ever. Eric just laughs, his blue eyes creasing at the sides as he smiles, his eyes running over me.

"I know what you mean, Ari." He takes a sip of his own coffee before leaning back against the kitchen counter. "I haven't seen you in a while. I hear you've had an interesting couple of days." I run my eyes over him as I realise he's right, I haven't seen him in a couple of days. He doesn't seem to be too affected by being away from me. He obviously sees my inspections of him and smiles slightly. "Just being on the compound is close enough to you to sustain me." What is that supposed to mean? My raised eyebrow has him chuckling. "There is a lot of...sexual energy around you, and I absorb it without realising it. I still can't feed properly, but I'm not starving," he reassures me.

"How have you been?" I ask him, unsure how to move our friendship-slash-relationship any further. He must be lonely here, I haven't exactly been keeping him company, and being around all of my men in a strange pack can't exactly be easy.

"I'm fine, Ari. I've been keeping busy. The pack has been letting me work here as their doctor for the last few days, it seems they have an opening." He smiles at me, and I can see he is truly happy he can help out. I'm surprised that Mortlock is allowing him to help though, when it took so much convincing to get help from other packs when we needed a second nurse. I would have to speak to Alpha Mortlock later, but I know that Eric would never hurt any of the wolves here, and he is brilliant at his job. It's just his morals when it comes to feeding that I have a problem with. I smile at his comments, happy he has found purpose here, at least until we figure out what's going on between us.

There is a tension in the room that's building, and I look around between the three guys.

"Okay, what aren't you telling me?" I demand, placing my coffee down to cross my arms and glare.

"Perhaps it's best if we wait for the others to come back?" Seb suggests, trying to placate me, but I shake my head. I have a bad feeling inside, and I have a suspicion that it has to do with the disappearances.

"No, tell me now. Please." I look around at them and hear Alex groan before he pulls his phone out of his pocket.

"Killian isn't going to be pleased that we started without him," he warns, pressing something on his phone before he places it on the kitchen counter between us.

"I'll deal with Killian," I mutter as the phone rings and the loudspeaker fills the room with the tone.

"Hello?" Tori's voice saturates the room, and a part of me relaxes. I know they would have said something if Tori was in trouble, but now I can be sure she is safe.

"Tori, it's Alex. I've got Ari, Seb, and Eric here," he explains, and we all call out our hellos.

"Hey, girl! Ari, you have a lot of explaining to do." Her tone is jokey, but I know she means business, there is no getting out of telling her *every last detail*. "You always seem to miss all the action!" she comments, and I narrow my eyes at the guys in the room.

"Why? What's been happening?" I glance at Eric, whose expression is dark, but he doesn't give anything away. Seb is staring at Alex, so I turn my gaze to him, a questioning look on my face.

"There have been more disappearances. Two vampires, a fae traveller, a dwarf, and a troll." My eyes widen, five disappearances in three days. They're getting worse.

"How the hell did they take a troll without anyone noticing?" I demand, those guys are big and don't go down without a fight. I think over the disappearances again and frown. "No shifters this time?"

The mood in the room goes darker, but the tight knot in my

chest loosens as I hear footsteps heading towards the building. Killian and Garett are in human form as they walk in, a few cuts and bruises mar their faces and arms, but they don't look too badly damaged.

"What was that about the disappearances?" Killian asks, his voice rough from the recent shift. Alex fills him in on what they just told me as I run my eyes over the two of them. They seem calmer now, both of them keep shooting me little glances, and I keep seeing Killian's hands clench into fists as if he's stopping himself from reaching out for me. I appreciate him trying, since the bond is also urging me to be closer to him, touch him. It's taking a lot for me to resist, but we have a more urgent matter at hand.

"Shifters have also been taken, but like before, their bodies are showing up. At least some of them are. Over the last three days, ten shifters have disappeared the same way as before, and traces of magic and runes show they were taken by force, but only seven bodies have shown up. We don't know why only the bodies of shifters are coming back, nor do we know why supernaturals are being taken," Alpha Mortlock explains as he walks into the kitchen, catching the end of our conversation and gratefully receiving a mug of coffee from Eric.

"It's a message. It has to be. Are the bodies still mutilated?" I probe, grimacing as Mortlock, Garett, and Alex nod.

"A bear was taken from our pack, and I was asked to go look at the body. I found this carved into the base of his neck." Garett passes me his phone and shows me a photo. My coffee turns to lead in my stomach as I recognise the symbol, the same symbol as the tattoo on my back.

"Shadow Pack."

"We thought they were involved, we just didn't have any proof until now," Tori chimes in from the speakerphone. "We just don't know why they've started marking the bodies until now. I've been looking into the disappearance sites, and other than proving magic has been used, I'm struggling to track down the users. They have a very strong magic user, and they're blocking me," Tori explains, and I hear the frustration in her voice. She isn't used to being out powered.

"It's a message to me. Just like the human that was carved up and sent to my hospital. They want me." I sigh in frustration and rub my hands across my face. I feel multiple hands reach for me, and I'm grateful for the support without them fighting amongst themselves. "What about ASP? What do they have to say about this?" As our supernatural police force, they should be out there dealing with this. The faces in the room turn even darker, and Tori makes a rude noise down the phone.

"They aren't doing anything. They are trying to keep the shifter disappearances quiet, although they're looking into the other ones. It's causing unrest. There's talk of the alphas meeting up to discuss what we should do, since ASP clearly doesn't care about us," Alex spits out, and I look over to Mortlock for confirmation. His expression is heavy, but he nods in agreement.

"We must be careful not to rush into things we may regret in the future," he tells the room, but he seems to be aiming his words at Alex.

A sense of dread settles over me as I come to a realisation. ASP aren't going to help us, we are going to have to look after ourselves. Which means I have to be able to protect myself. Shadow Pack clearly isn't going to give up, and they're still after me. I have to embrace the part of me that I hate, the part they want me for, if I have a hope of surviving this. I sigh and clear my throat, getting the attention of the room, uttering words I never thought I would say.

"I need to go back to the Shadow Realm."

Chapter Eleven

The rest of that conversation in the kitchen of Alpha Mortlock's house went about as well as you can imagine. Lots of shouting and cursing had ensued. Killian had nearly started a fight with Alex, who was furious at the thought of me going back to the Shadow Realm. Not because Killian wanted me to go, but because Alex was trying to throw his weight around, demanding that Killian he had to stop me from going. Macho bullshit, which wound up an already tense Killian. Garett was trying to find out why I wanted to go back but kept being interrupted. Seb had just looked worried and sat back, watching the whole argument with a frown on his face. In the end, it was Eric who alleviated the whole situation.

"Ari, why do you need to go back?" Eric calmly asked. The others were still wary of him and his powers, so they paid him a wary respect that they don't seem to show to each other, treating each other more like brothers.

I then had to explain about the coin necklace the stranger made of light had given me in the Shadow Realm. The necklace that I had kept a secret until now. This had only started another argument. Nobody trusted the stranger, especially with my safety. They didn't trust or understand his motives.

Eventually, I'd convinced them that I was going.

Well, it was more of a, 'I'm going and you can't stop me,' but they know why I have to do it. I need to master these powers. I've been fought over, tortured, and abused for this power my whole life, and I've been running from it. I'm tired of it. I need to embrace this side of me, like I've embraced my wolf, if I'm to ever be free of the shadow that's been hanging over me my whole life.

They wanted me to wait until tomorrow before I went back to the Shadow Realm, but I don't see any point in putting it off, not when waiting could mean that another supernatural gets taken.

We're gathered in my room, with my guys and Eric around me, ready if I need them. This is more for their comfort than mine, since when I'm in the Shadow Realm, they won't be able to help me, but they can care for my physical body. I don't plan on being there long, but as we learnt from last time, time works differently there.

Walking up to my desk, I open the drawer and pull out the necklace that was given to me, placing it around my neck. I turn to look at the guys, there's no point in dragging this out, and I can already feel the pull of the Shadow Realm calling me. It's been getting louder and louder over the last few days, but I've managed to chase away the shadows. Now, I look inside myself at the light, which is holding the shadows at bay. Sending out a quiet call for help, I hope the stranger made of light hears my call and finds me in the Shadow Realm.

"Here goes nothing. I'll see you soon," I call out with a confident smile, before I shutter out the light inside me.

I'm instantly dragged away with a ripping sensation, and a cry of pain leaves my lips as I land in the Shadow Realm with a bang. I can still hear Garett shouting my name and Killian's roar of agony as I was ripped away, and they ring in my ears.

"Well that was dramatic. It seems to be a talent of yours," a familiar voice greets me.

My eyes fly open, and I see the stranger made of light standing above me. Although I can't see his features properly, I get the distinct impression that he's smiling at me.

"You came." It's not a question, but he nods anyway.

"You called, so I came." He holds his hand out towards me and helps me to my feet.

I look around and see that the Shadow Realm hasn't changed at all since I was last here, and the feeling of nothingness falls upon me, causing me to shudder.

"I don't miss being here." I wrap my arms around myself. It's not cold, but my memories of being trapped here fill my mind, and I miss the physical comforts of having my guys with me. "Nothing has changed."

"Well, that's not true now, is it?" he says with a nod to my chest, where a golden thread leaves my torso and trails behind me. I look at it with a frown until I feel a tug. Killian.

"The bond," I exclaim with clarity as I look back up at my guide. We'd theorised that the bond was the reason I kept finding myself back in the real world before, and now I guess we know for real.

"I think that bond, even though it was only half formed, was the only reason you lasted here so long on your own without training. You should always be able to find your way back now if you ever get lost in the shadows again."

We walk together in silence for a while as I take in the revelations of the day. He seems happy just to walk quietly and let me sort my thoughts. I look up at the stranger again.

"Who are you? I keep calling you the 'stranger made of light' in my head, but I can't keep calling you that. Yoda perhaps?" I joke, and I get that feeling that he's smiling again, despite me not being able to see his features.

"Hm, I like the idea of being Yoda, your wise and ancient teacher. Although, perhaps less of the ancient part, young student." I snort out a laugh at his joke, loving that he gets my *Star Wars* reference. "You may call me Em." I raise my eyebrows, not expecting that to be his name, but nod in agreement.

"Okay...Em," I begin, sorting through the list of questions in my mind. "You said I would come back here, how did you know?" He snorts at my question, his impression of an all-knowing, benevolent teacher disappearing in a moment.

"Because you have no idea how to use your powers. Sooner or later, you'd get into trouble and end up back here again. I told you to return here and call me because you need to learn to master your powers. You're incredibly powerful, but there are not enough Shadowborn around anymore to teach you, which is why I offered."

I come to a stop and stare at him in shock, the implications of what he's saying astounds me, although it probably shouldn't, given the circumstances.

"Wait, you're Shadowborn? How did I not know about you? I thought all the Shadowborn were dead." He stops in his tracks and turns back to look at me, and I get the distinct impression he's rolling his eyes at me.

"How do you think I got here or knew so much about your powers?" He sighs, as if what he's going to say next pains him, and takes a seat on the ground, gesturing for me to sit beside to him. "You're not the only Shadowborn, but the rest of us are in hiding. We didn't know that you existed. The Shadow Pack kept you hidden from us, and for that, we're sorry, we would not have let them subject you to those kinds of torture if we had known."

There are more Shadowborn, a whole group of them by the sound of it. The information is overwhelming, but hope starts to bloom inside me. If I can find them, they can train me to control my powers, make sure I'm not dangerous but a formidable opponent not to be messed with. I turn to Em, but he's already shaking his head.

"Where are you in the real world? I'll come find you and train with you..." My voice trails off, and I narrow my eyes at him. "You're not going to help me?"

"The others won't take the risk to meet you. You have some dangerous people after you, not just the Shadow Pack, and they've worked for centuries to stay hidden. Once things have settled down, perhaps then..." He trails off as he sees my cloudy expression.

They find out about me, give me a spiel about how they wish they'd known about me, would've helped me, and when they can actually help me, they won't take the risk. Won't risk *their* safety. Bullshit.

"Ari. I want to help you, I'm willing to help you, but I'm somewhere where you can't get to me. I'm not free to wander around as I wish, which is why I am meeting you here like this." I look away, contemplating whether or not to believe him, when I feel a hand on my knee. I look up and see that Em has dimmed his light enough where I can almost see his expression through the brightness. It looks full of regret.

"When the time is right, I will tell you where I am. Remember that trust goes both ways." I narrow my eyes at him as I mull this over. I'm putting a lot on the line here, but I have to trust that he isn't going to sell me out. I don't think he's doing this just out the kindness of his heart, there has to be something he's getting out of this, but I don't have much of an option and he's right—I need to learn, and there's no one else to teach me. I let out a sigh and nod, I guess that's the best I'm going to get out of him.

"Okay, Yoda, what's the first lesson?"

For what feels like five days, but must have only been about an hour, I work with Em on calling my shadow powers to the surface. Other than the time where I killed Alpha Black and the fight with Marcus at Moon River Pack, when I've used my shadow powers, they have taken over my whole body, enveloping me completely in shadow. Em has been trying to teach me to control it, making only certain parts of my body disappear. It's hard work, and I'm get frustrated that I'm finding it so difficult.

"Aarh! Why don't I *get* this?" I cry out as I force my body to reappear in front of Em, who's giving off a distinctly amused attitude. "Well I'm glad you're finding this entertaining," I snarl. Frustratingly, this is supposed to be *easier* in the Shadow Realm, and while I seem to have no problem calling my power forth here, controlling it seems to be the issue. No surprise there, control of my powers has always been my issue.

"Okay, Ari, that's enough for today. Try and practice calling the shadows in the real world as well. When you're ready to meet with me again, just wear the necklace and call out to me. I'll be here," he says before he disappears in a flash of light so bright, I have to close my eyes.

I slump to the ground with a sigh, what a day. Right, I guess I better try and get back home. Anxiety swirls in my stomach at the thought of being stuck here again, but I focus on what Em said, that as long as I'm bonded to Killian, I'll always have a way home. I focus on the golden line and tug, and at the same time, I find the light within me and will it to flare to life, banishing away the shadows.

I slam back into my body and cry out in shock. I look around and see that I'm in my bed, in a puppy pile of all my guys, and even Garett is curled up next to me. They are all shielding their eyes, as if I brought my light back with me.

"What the fuck?" someone mutters.

"Ari, you're back." Killian's rich voice rolls over me, and he nuzzles into my neck, the other guys call out my name softly and try to get closer to me. I glance over at the alarm clock and see it's one am.

"How long was I gone for?" I'm almost afraid to ask, but I need to know.

"You left yesterday afternoon, so you've been gone for about nine hours," Seb tells me, his hand rubbing up and down my leg, his voice groggy with sleep as he settles his head back on my hip.

"Anyone want to talk about the fact that Ari was a human flashlight just now, or deal with it in the morning?" Alex mutters.

"In the morning," come several replies, which brings a small smile to my lips. Garett sits up slightly and runs his eyes over me, checking if I'm okay.

"Are you okay?" he asks, and I just smile, then lean forward to press a kiss to his lips gently. He makes a happy grumble in his chest and returns the kiss.

"I'm going to take that as a yes." He winks at me before laying back down, pulling my back against his chest.

I know that in the morning, we'll need to deal with everything going on and what I learnt in the Shadow Realm, but for now, with my guys surrounding me, I feel safe and fall into a deep, dreamless sleep.

Chapter Twelve

The gentle sounds of the radio babbling away to itself fills the air as we drive from the compound into town. It's not a far journey, about twenty minutes, but I enjoy the quiet of the countryside for as long as I can before the outskirts of the city start to show. The silence in the car is comfortable, and Garett's hand on my thigh is soothing. I try not to let my nerves get the better of me as we drive towards the bear compound, which is based in the centre of the city. The alpha of Garett's pack, Alpha Philips, has requested to meet me.

Bear shifter packs run differently than the wolves. They tend to live in small family groups, as opposed to one big pack, but they're often nearby and work together closely. Garett, as an unmated male, lives alone and chose not to work within the pack, but regularly helps out and keeps in touch. This might have been why I liked him—he wasn't continually under the thumb of his pack.

I worry about why Alpha Philips might want to meet with me. Garett seems calm, and he wouldn't knowingly lead me into a dangerous situation. I'm looking forward to seeing where he comes from though. I've only ever seen his bar, and I won't lie, I'm curious to see more about him and how he grew up. As the countryside disappears and we enter the more built up areas of the city, I can't keep quiet anymore.

"So, what does the alpha want to see me about?" Garett chuckles at my question and gives my knee a squeeze.

"Ari, I've told you already. He just wants to meet you, he's intrigued by the woman who's keeping me away from the pack so often," he jokes, but I can't help feeling uneasy. He was very upfront with me that he was going to tell his alpha about our relationship, and it made me nervous. While mating outside of your shifter species wasn't uncommon, it wasn't exactly approved of.

We pull up outside of the gym the Long Claw Pack is based out of. The Long Claw Pack has a series of successful gyms throughout the country, but their headquarters is based here, and most of their pack business is also run from this location.

I take a deep breath and climb out of the car, it's time to face the music. Garett comes around to meet me and links our arms, guiding me inside the building. From the outside, the gym looks like an unassuming warehouse, and if it wasn't for the large sign outside on the wall stating 'LC Gyms,' then I wouldn't have known there was a gym here. The car park is packed, so they must gain a good number of customers. As we walk inside and I see all of the latest, state-of-the-art equipment, I can understand why it's so busy.

"Garett!" A pretty, well muscled lady calls out from behind the reception desk. Definitely a bear shifter with a build like that.

"Hey, Molly, I'm here to see Philips. Are my brothers here?" he asks, his voice relaxed and friendly as he slings his arm around my shoulders. The woman from behind the desk, Molly, eyes up his arm, and as her eyes slide to me, I expect to see some judgement, but instead, she just smiles broadly.

"Well welcome! It's nice to see you smiling, Garett. Philips will come join you in the training room. And of course, your brothers are here, they're always here," she jokes with an eye roll. Garett laughs and waves goodbye to her as he steers me through the large gym.

"I didn't know you had brothers," I comment lightly, and I don't know why it's bothering me so much that I didn't know about his family. I try to hide the fact that this annoys me, but he gives my hand a squeeze and his next response lets me know he's noticed it bugs me.

"I don't talk about my family much, don't feel bad. You'll get to meet them today, and you'll soon wish you didn't know about them." I laugh at his comments, feeling a little better, although I hadn't realised that I'd be meeting his family today. Perhaps I should've worn something a little nicer than my old jeans and turquoise knit jumper.

"Stop fretting over your clothes, you look beautiful," he says to me in a low voice and pulls at my hand, which I hadn't even realised was playing with the hem of my jumper. "This is why I didn't warn you that we might bump into them here. I didn't want you to worry." I'm about to retort when we round the corner and see the three biggest guys I have ever seen.

"Gare Bear!" one calls out as he sees us, his shout getting the attention of the other two, who are clearly brothers. My mouth drops open a little at the sight. One of them, the one who called out to us, is a little older, but the other two have to be twins, they look identical. It's obvious that they're all related to Garett, they all have the same bronze skin tone and shaggy brown hair, stubble covering their chins. The twins have green eyes, but the older brother has the same eye colour as Garett. While Garett is muscled, these guys are huge! I had thought that Garett was one of the biggest guys I've ever seen, turns out I just hadn't met his family yet. They drop the weights they were casually lifting with a bang and make their way over to us, their smiles huge as they see Garett's arm around my shoulders.

"Gare Bear?" I ask quietly, trying to stifle the grin that's threatening to burst out of me. His mouth twitches as he fights a wry smile.

"Yeah, I can't shake that fucking nickname."

I do laugh this time, trying not to let my nerves show as these huge bear shifters stalk towards us. Their grins are predatory as they come to stop a short distance away, eyeing me up and down before looking to Garett. He stiffens as they look me over, before giving them a terse nod. This seems to be some sort of signal they were waiting for, as they let out a whoop, then swoop in. Before I know what's going on, I'm swept into a bear hug, literally, before being passed on to another brother.

"Little sister! It's good to finally meet you!"

"Jake, you're hogging her! I want to meet her!"

"Back off, I haven't finished yet."

I struggle to work out who is saying what as I'm passed around the group, and a laugh escapes me.

"Guys, you're being too rough, back off." A deeper voice cuts through the chatter, and the twins roll their eyes before taking a step back, but their excitement is still clear to see in their movements. I realise the guy with the deep voice is the older brother as he takes a step forward and holds out his hand for me to shake. "I'm sorry about my younger brothers, they're like excitable pups. We have been waiting for a while to meet the wolf that has captured my brother's heart. I'm Max," he says, introducing himself, and I can't help but smile, he reminds me of Garett.

"Nice to meet you, Max. I am surprised to meet you though," I say with a pointed glance at Garett, who at least has the decency to look abashed.

"I didn't want you to worry," he explains before gesturing to his brothers, who are still jostling for who's going to hug me first. "They're a bit overwhelming. I thought it best to just rip it off, like a band-aid."

"Are you saying meeting us is painful?"

"We are a delight!" the twins say at once, before pouncing on Garett. At first, I thought they were attacking him, but at their laughter, I can see that they're just playing.

"Please excuse my brothers. Jake and Ben act like children, but they are actually older than Garett," he comments with a shake of his head, but his smile is fond as he watches his three younger brothers.

"Any other surprise family meetings I should be expecting?" I joke, but when he doesn't answer me, I turn away from watching Garett to look up at Max. His expression is a cross between amusement and pain. "No. No no no. If you tell me I'm meeting your parents—" I'm cut off mid threat as the backdoor slams open and a couple walk through.

"Garett! Son, it's good to see you!" an older version of Garett calls out as he and an older, happy looking woman bustle towards us.

"Nooooo," I groan quietly before throwing a death glare at Garett, he'll pay for this later. I can't believe he blindsided me into meeting his entire bloody family. I thought I was here to meet the alpha!

"Sorry, Ari, I didn't know they were coming." Garett breaks away from his brothers and puts his arm around me, pulling me in close as he whispers to me.

The couple stops a short distance from us and waits for some signal from Garett before they come forward. Garett's dad is the spitting image of him, just an older version with slightly greying hair, but still just as handsome. The woman at his side, who I'm assuming is Garett's mum, is a pretty woman about my height with gently greying brown hair and deep brown eyes. Her face is lined with laughter lines, and it's easy to see why with the amount she's smiling right now.

"Garett, honey. It's so good to see you!" she coos as she sweeps him into a hug. She may be smaller than him, but I have no doubt that she's fierce if you cross her. Never mess with a female bear shifter if you want to escape with your life, especially if her cubs are involved. Garett's smile is warm and genuine as he embraces his mother. His dad steps forward to greet him, and his mum turns towards me. Her happiness is easy to see in her eyes, and I can tell that she wants to hug me. I smile and take a small step forward, holding out my arms a little, and this is all the encouragement she needs to hurry forward and wrap her arms around me.

"Oh, it's so good to finally meet you, Ari. I'm Molly, Garett's mom, and that's Simon, his dad. I've never seen Garett so happy since the two of you mated." I stiffen at her words, but she doesn't seem to notice my sudden tension. "The two of you will join us for dinner tonight, right? I'll cook Garett's favourite!"

"Okay, Mom, we'll be there," he says with a smile, but he keeps shooting me worried glances out the corner of his eye, knowing something's bothering me. "Guys, we need to go meet with the alpha, we can catch up tonight, okay?" he tells them, before giving his mum another hug and patting his brothers and dad on the back. I take a step back and give them a little wave, needing a bit of space. His family is amazing, but they're a little full on.

"I'm sorry, Ari, I didn't know my parents would be here, my brothers must have told them that we were coming. Are you okay? I know they can be a bit overwhelming." He runs his hand along my arm, leading me towards the area where we are meeting the alpha.

"Your mum said we had mated. What did she mean by that? We haven't had a mating ceremony." My voice is deceptively calm, but my insides are a knot of tension.

There are two types of matings in the shifter community, true mated pairs and voluntary bonds. True mated pairs, who are like soulmates, your fated other half who you were designed to love. The most common form of mating in the shifter community is a voluntary bond, which is formed between two shifters, and once made, it's for life. While there is a connection between them, it's nothing like the power of a true mate bond. It is more like marriage, but it's not entered into lightly because the only way out of it is death.

Garett winces slightly but nods at my comment. "You're right. Within bear communities, we don't date. We only settle down with the person we intend to mate with. My family has assumed mating is our intention. I think they believe we're here to get permission from the alpha to confirm the mating."

I stop in the middle of the corridor and look him in the eye, shocked that they would believe this. They don't even know me, and they think we're getting mated? I have more than enough mates, I'm not going to jump straight into another mating.

"You're going to set them straight though, right?"

"Yes, of course," he assures me gently as he steers me towards a set of double doors, which I'm sure is the training room we were told to meet the alpha in. He's quiet, and I can tell something is bothering him. I wonder if I sounded too harsh. With a sigh, I pull him to a stop and force him to face me.

"Garett, what—"

"Garett! Come through! And you must be Ari, welcome to Long Claw!" a booming voice greets us. I guess this conversation will have to wait until later. Squeezing my hand, Garett leads me into the training room, and I gape at the huge open space. Mirrors line the room, and a large rack of weights is covering one wall, it's like a hard-core ballet studio. The thought brings a smile to my face as I imagine Garett and his brothers wearing a tutu. A gentle hand on my lower back returns me to the present, and I smile up at the alpha.

"Alpha Philips, it's a pleasure to meet you," I say as I hold my hand out to greet him. His large hand engulfs mine but he shakes it with care, and his smile in return is genuine and reaches his eyes.

I take a step back and run my eyes over the alpha. He has that typical bear shifter build, looking like he presses fire engines for fun and making most bodybuilders look like children in comparison. He appears to be in his late thirties, but shifters age well, so I place him to be in his late forties. His short, cropped dark hair has a military look about it, and his tank top shows off a myriad of tattoos across his upper arms.

He shuts the doors behind us and smiles at me again, gesturing around the room.

"This room is soundproof, so don't worry about anyone overhearing us," he says, and a nervous chuckle escapes my lips.

"Okay, that sounded a little like you plan to abduct me." Philips laughs, and Garett smiles as he runs his hand down my arm, trying to comfort me. I'm feeling a little overwhelmed from meeting Garett's family, and now his alpha is making a big scene about us not being overheard, it's making me flighty.

"Sorry if this sounds rude, but why am I here?" I cut straight to the point, wanting to know what the heck is going on. That would be enough for some alphas to discipline me, hell, Shadow Pack would have me whipped for a remark like that, but I get the feeling that Garett's pack is different. Philips tilts his head as if he's re-evaluating me before barking out a short laugh.

"You picked one with spirit, Garett. Good choice." I'm about to protest at being talked about when I'm right in front of them, but Philips turns to address me. "I had two reasons for bringing you here. First, I did want to meet the woman that Garett is so enamoured with. We have all heard so much about you, and what you did for him after Shadow Pack took him..." His voice trails off in a deep growl, which seems to fill the room. "You have earned our trust and respect. You sacrificed yourself for him, for a bear your pack had no ties to."

"I love him," I say with a shrug, the only answer I have as to why I did it. I don't need to go into why I would save someone as good as Garett, the guy who has tried to protect me since day one. Philips seems to understand this and just nods at my answer, accepting it as truth.

"Well, we wanted to extend our gratitude to you, and if you ever need us or you ever need somewhere to stay, you're welcome. You are part of Long Claw now." I stare at him in shock. This type of thing doesn't happen across different shifter species, it's unheard of. I glance at Garett, and even he looks shocked. I've gone from being packless to having two, one of those with the bears. My chest feels tight with all the feelings that are overwhelming me, and all I can do is nod at Philips and hope the gesture portrays my gratitude.

"Unfortunately, the other reason I needed to see you is less pleasant." Philips sighs and rubs his hand across his face, causing me to frown at his change in attitude. "As Garett has probably told you, one of our bears was kidnapped and the body was left at the spot he was taken from, mutilated with Shadow Pack's symbol. We have followed all the laws, we took this to ASP and let them handle it, even though our nature is screaming at us for vengeance. But going to ASP is not getting us anywhere, and now they are denying to return the body of our pack member. They refuse to give it back, we need to bury him properly, put him to rest, but they refuse. We will not stand for it. They have always been less active in investigating crimes against shifters."

Unfortunately, what he's saying doesn't surprise me. ASP are quick to investigate when the person committing the crime is a shifter, but their prejudices against us runs deep. I'd always hoped though, that if someone was murdering shifters that they would step in, especially seeing as other supernaturals are being affected. Instead, they're completely denying that shifters are being taken and killed. If they aren't careful, they will have an uprising on their hands, or perhaps that's what they want? It would give them an excuse to hunt us all down. I try to clear these dark thoughts away, they're not helpful.

"How can I help, Alpha?" I ask, wondering how I fit into this turn of conversation.

"The other alphas are going to be meeting to discuss this, and we wanted you to come as the peacekeeper."

I laugh at the alpha's comment. I know it's rude and I should be more respectful, but he really doesn't know me well if he thinks I can be the peacekeeper. I'm the opposite! I cause more fights than I fix!

"Hear the alpha out, Ari," Garett's quiet voice urges, but I can hear the smile in his voice.

"Ari, you have connections with not only the wolves, but the bears too. Plus, your best friend is a witch and you have an incubus living with you." I wonder where he got the information about Eric living with us, but I choose to ignore that for the time being and try to focus on the alpha's words. "You're living proof that we can intermingle and still thrive. Plus, you have extensive knowledge on the Shadow Pack. We know they're involved now, we just don't know how they fit in with all this. We need your help."

I close my eyes and rub the bridge of my nose as I think over his words. He's right—they do need to know more about the Shadow Pack, and it's a good idea for them to be united, sharing information. ASP clearly isn't helping them. But do I really want to get involved in politics when I have worked so hard to stay out of it? I blow out a deep breath and glance at Garett, who is smiling softly at me. I know he'll accept whatever decision I make and won't make me feel bad if I decide not to help. I bite my lip, knowing what I *should* do, but not wanting to do it.

"Okay, I'll help you."

The house we pull up in front of looks cosy and just like any other in this suburban area. It's two stories and has a neat little garden with colourful flowers lining the flowerbeds along the front of the house. I don't know what I expected, but this wasn't it. However, the more I look at it, the more I can imagine a little Garett and his brothers growing up here. I chuckle as I glance at him now. I guess I had expected a larger house after meeting his brothers earlier. I step out of the car and smile at Garett as he comes to my side, holding his hand out to me.

"Don't be nervous, they already love you," he whispers in my ear, pressing a gentle kiss to the side of my head. I smile at him and nod, but I can't deny that I am nervous. Throw me up against shadow beasts and evil alphas and I'm fine, but being invited to Garett's parents' house for dinner has me quaking in my boots.

Arm in arm, we walk towards the front door, and Garett knocks before letting himself in.

"We're here!" he calls out before helping me take off my coat and hanging it on the rack. After we met with the alpha, we went back to Moon River so I could get changed. There was no way I was turning up to Garett's family home in my casual jeans and jumper. This is the second time in a week that I've worn a dress, and I hope this isn't becoming a habit. I play with the skirt, feeling uncomfortable, but what else was I going to wear to meet his family? Seb and Alex had teased me all afternoon about being nervous. Garett, trying to put me at ease, told me that they'd already met me and couldn't care less what I was wearing as long as we were happy.

I hear cheerful chatter and laughter from within the house as a voice calls out to us.

"We're in the kitchen, love, come on through!" Molly shouts.

I look around the hallway as Garett leads me through the house. It's warm and cosy, and photographs of Garett and his brothers line the walls. Walking into the large, open kitchen, I can see where all the noise is coming from, and I grin at the scene in front of me. Simon and Max are setting the table, talking about some football game that had been on today. Molly was trying to serve dinner, and the twins kept stealing bits of food and garlic bread from the plates and generally causing havoc. I would've expected Molly to be shouting at them, but she's smiling as she scolds them. It's like I'm watching the happy family scene in one of those soap dramas. I've never once thought that something like this would be possible for me, but as Garett squeezes my hand and pulls me into the room, I wonder if it might be possible. Everyone turns around as we enter and calls out a greeting.

Chapter Thirteen

The meal was delicious, and the company was great. They're full on, but I haven't laughed that much in years. The twins are hilarious and seem to make it their life mission to cause chaos. Molly is lovely and keeps trying to find out more about me, but I manage to get away with saying as little as possible without seeming rude. Garett has been throwing me heated looks over the table all evening, and it's been boiling my blood. We are just finishing our coffee when Garett squeezes my hand under the table.

"Come back to my place tonight?" I whisper as we start gathering the plates to help clean up. Desire shoots through me, I know exactly what will happen if Garett stays with me tonight.

The rest of the evening passes quickly with hugs and goodbyes, as well as Molly getting us to promise that we'll come for dinner again soon. I promise that we will and surprise myself when I actually mean it.

The journey to the pack is full of heated glances, and once we have made it into the house, all pretence drops. Pressing me up against the wall, Garett presses his lips to mine and slowly devours me, our kisses deep and unhurried, his hands skimming up my body until one of them reaches my breast. I'm not worried that someone else might see us, even though I know for sure there are others in the house and we aren't exactly being discreet. I can hear them moving around upstairs and in the kitchen, but if anything, the risk of being caught only turns me on more.

As Garett is palming my breast, a spark of desire shoots straight to my core, making me groan into his mouth. A quiet growl filling the hallway alerts me to the presence of someone else watching, and the tug in my chest tells me it's Killian. I know Garett is aware of him too by the tension now in his shoulders, which are rigid under my hands. I pull my mouth from his and drop it to his neck, kissing along the line between his neck and shoulders, trying to kiss away the tension. I feel him fighting for control, knowing he wants to continue but is waiting to see what I wish to do. I raise my eyes and meet Killian's as I continue kissing Garett's neck, biting down gently, and I enjoy the hitch in his breathing. I need to show Killian that I am not going to stop just because he's here. He raises his eyebrow at me and a small smile crosses his lips, and I get an impression straight down the bond between us.

Challenge accepted.

He jerks his head towards the stairs and heads up without another word. Garett watched the whole exchange in silence with a small frown.

"Do you want me to leave you to it?" he asks, hurt and desire evident in his voice, and I know it's paining him to ask this.

I shake my head and kiss him firmly before pushing against his chest so he moves away, letting me move away from the wall. I grab his hand and start to walk upstairs, pulling him along behind me. Desire and confusion lines his eyes, but he follows me without question. We enter my room, and it's empty. I have no idea where Killian has gone, but right now, I only care about the guy in front of me. I pull him closer and start working on the buttons on his shirt, needing to feel his skin against mine. I groan as his shirt comes off, and I lean forward to kiss across the hard lines of his chest, nibbling along his collarbone until he's growling. He reaches up and rips along the seam of my dress, leaving me standing in just my underwear. I gasp, not used to this kind of behaviour from him. Killian, perhaps. But my gentle bear? Never, although I can't deny that seeing him worked up like this is sexy as hell. Pushing the strap of my bra over my shoulder, he starts kissing a line from my shoulder down to my nipple, sucking it into his mouth as his other hand moves to my other breast, causing my nipples to pebble under the attention. My hand drops to Garett's waistband, and I fiddle with the buttons until I'm able to free his rapidly growing erection, and groans slip from both our lips as I wrap my hand around him. Garett's groan around my sensitive nipple has my toes clenching as the vibrations cause little shocks of pleasure to run through me.

I'm so caught up in desire that I don't notice Killian is behind me until I feel him pressed against my back, running his hands over my hips and humming in approval. Garett tweaks my nipple, causing a little gasp to escape my lips before standing up and raising his eyebrows at Killian, who is possessively running his hands over my body.

"This isn't about us. This is about giving Ari pleasure," Garett demands. This is the first time I've seen him truly stand up to Killian, and it's fucking hot to watch. There is tension in the air, and it could go either way.

"Don't tell me what to do, bear," Killian retorts, but there is no real anger in his voice as he drops his mouth to my neck, biting down where he claimed me.

"Fuck!" I cry out, and waves of pleasure shoot through me as he continues to lick and suck on the claiming mark. I can feel the sly smile that crosses his lips against my skin. It's a possessive and dirty move to pull, seeing as he's rubbing our bond in Garett's face. Enough is enough.

"Right, we're doing this differently," I say as I push them both away from me, completely flustered that I have two smoking hot guys fighting over my body. I can't think with them both touching me. "Kill, if you can't play nicely, you can watch, and if you behave, you can join in later."

Killian bares his teeth at me in a snarl, his erection straining against his jeans as he goes to take a step towards me. He sees my gaze and stops moving before raising his eyebrows as a smirk crosses his face when he realises I mean business.

"Fine, two can play that game. Go ahead," he says, and I frown at him, wondering what he's up to.

I don't have much time to think about it as Garett puts his arms around me and throws me over his shoulder, causing a small shriek to leave my lips. Carrying me over to the bed, he gently places me down before lowering his body over mine. I can see he's pleased that I picked him over Killian, even if for the moment, and he's going to make the most of it. Garett is careful to keep most of his weight off me, so I'm able to reach into his underwear and stroke along the length of his cock. He presses kisses to my forehead before making his way down my body until he's at the waistband of my underwear, kissing along my body as he goes. Pulling away my knickers, he wastes no time and starts kissing my centre, gently at first, and then with more force. His tongue shoots out and flicks against my clit, causing me to jerk with pleasure under him. He chuckles, sending vibrations through me. A noise from the corner of the room has me looking, only to see Killian sitting in the corner with his cock in his hand, lazily stroking it as he watches Garett tongue fuck me. I hadn't realised how much of a turn-on it would be, and he knows it, if the grin on his face is anything to go by.

"Eyes on me, Ari, I want to see that pretty face as Garett makes you fall apart," he calls, and my eyes snap back to him as Garett slips a finger into my centre, causing my head to fall back with a moan. He eases another finger into me, and then another, timing his thrusts with his kissing and sucking against my clit. The pleasure builds within me, and I know I'm about to come, so I bring my gaze back to Killian. Seeing the look of pure need on his face as he strokes his cock is enough to bring me to orgasm.

As the waves of pleasure start to fade, Garett crawls up my

body and presses hot kisses to my mouth. I shouldn't still want them, but I do. Both of them.

"I need you. Fuck me," I demand, and I see the desire flare in Garett's eyes as a rumbling growl leaves his chest. I look across at Killian, and an idea comes to me. Positioning myself so I'm on all fours, I see Garett's eyebrows rise in surprise until I smile at him. He moves behind me and I feel him press his cock against my entrance.

"Killian. Come here." He scowls at me, not used to being ordered around, but he does as I ask. Making sure I don't lose my balance, I use one hand to grasp his cock, causing his eyes to roll back in his head, before taking him into my mouth. Garett uses my distraction and slips into me, causing me to groan around Killian's cock.

"Fuck, Ari, don't do that unless you want me to come already." Killian grabs a fistful of my hair and guides me. I expect him to be rough, but he's unexpectedly gentle. We fall into a rhythm, our pants and groans filling the room before Killian pulls away.

"No, I want to come inside you," he says, as he takes a step back, watching as Garett fucks me. Garett pulls out of me suddenly, and I make a noise of protest before he lays back on the bed and pulls me to straddle him.

"I want to see your face," he tells me breathlessly, and I can tell he had been holding on for this. I slide down onto his length and ride him hard, gripping his shoulders. The look of love that he has for me is intense, and it's not long before we reach our climax with a cry. I fall to the bed next to Garett and look over at Killian, who looks wrecked. I'm knackered, but seeing him desperate with need, I gesture over to him with a smile.

"About fucking time," he grumbles with a smile as he crawls up my body, pressing kisses to my claiming mark, instantly causing those delicious sparks of pleasure along my body again. I wrap my legs around him, and he pushes into me.

I expected him to be rough, since that's his style, but he takes his time, kissing and caressing me, all the while Garett lies next to me, stroking along my arms and legs. Killian doesn't rush, knowing that I'm a little tender, instead, he makes love to me until I'm gasping and shuddering in his arms, and I feel him finally allow his own release.

Collapsing in a mess of limbs, I curl around my two guys with a smile on my face as I fall asleep.

Chapter Fourteen

"You fucked both of them at the same time?" Tori screeches gleefully as we pick up our coffee order to go, her grin filling her face. The barista the other side of the counter nearly drops our coffee as he goes to hand it over to us. He re-evaluates me as his eyes travel up and down my body, a sensual smile appearing on his face. I snort out a laugh and nudge Tori in the ribs.

"Bloody hell, woman, you don't have to tell the whole city," I hiss, but I can't keep the traitorous smile off my face. I walk away from the counter, ignoring the appraising looks from the barista as I walk to where the sugars and stirrers are kept. A cackling Tori follows behind, finding my embarrassment hilarious. "Well, I'm glad you're getting some amusement out of this," I jibe, but I sling my arm around her shoulders to reduce the sting of my words. She just grins at me and shakes my arm off so she can start pouring sugar packets into her coffee. I shake my head at her in mock disgust as she proceeds to pour her fifth sugar into the drink.

"I still don't know how you can drink it that sweet. You've ruined it," I tease, scrunching my nose up in disgust. What a waste of perfectly good coffee.

This is the one thing that the two of us have always disagreed on ever since I moved in with her all those years ago. I still remember when I sat on her sofa and she told me I was moving in. I wasn't given an option, not that I had many other choices. I'd been sleeping on the streets those first few weeks, and I had bumped into Tori—quite literally bumped into her. She had taken one look at my scrawny body and feral appearance, and had taken me to a burger joint. I hadn't trusted her, hell, I didn't trust anyone, but I was starving and she was offering free food. She had explained what she was, and that she knew what I was, and that I was going to be staying with her. I can't tell you why I decided to trust her, but I just had this feeling, and that gut instinct had never lead me astray before. So, when I was sitting in her apartment as she was explaining how everything would work, she had given me a drink with more sugar than coffee in it. We had then bonded over our opposing views on coffee.

I shake my head as I watch her take a drink of the monstrosity she has created with a happy smile on her lips.

"I don't know how you can drink it like that." I frown, taking a sip of my own coffee, savouring the rich, slightly bitter taste. "Ahh, now this is proper coffee," I comment, grinning at her look of disgust.

"Stop stalling. Tell me, tell me, *tell me*," she chants, and I know she won't let this drop until I tell her all the gory details.

"Well, I didn't have sex with both of them at the same time... just one after the other...while the other was watching..." Tori's eyes get bigger as I continue to talk, her grin growing as a knowing look enters her eyes. "Okay, fine. I gave Killian a blow job while Garett was fucking me," I admit quietly, as we walk out of the coffee shop, my smile scandalous.

I almost can't believe it happened myself, but when I'd woken up this morning, they were both still sharing the bed with me, one on either side of me, with possessive arms thrown over my waist. I'd worried that Garett would have been upset about sharing me, but I pulled him aside this morning before he left to talk to him.

Garett steps out of the bathroom with a towel slung around his hips, water dripping from his hair and trailing down his body. I've never been jealous of a towel before, but I have a ridiculous urge to rip the towel from his body. I'm not sure what expression I'm wearing, but whatever Garett sees causes his eyes to light up as he leans against the doorframe, crossing his arms with a smile as I walk towards him. Pressing my hands to his bare chest, I let my fingers walk down to where the towel is knotted, hooking my fingers over the edge before gently pulling the towel a little lower. I glance up at him and smile at the look of utter adoration he's giving me. It makes my heart hurt a little, knowing that someone as good as Garett loves me, and I wonder what I did right to deserve it.

"Are you okay with everything that happened last night?" I ask softly. I'm afraid of the answer, but I have to ask. Seeing my face tighten with worry, Garett wraps his arms around me and pulls me in close to his body. I don't care that I'm getting wet, I'm just thankful he's holding me. He wouldn't do that if he was about to reject me, right?

"Well, it didn't exactly go how I had imagined it," he says wryly, making guilt course through me. "Killian isn't exactly my favourite guy, but I understand you guys share this bond. I'm not always going to want to share you, but it was unexpectedly hot." I pull away at his words so I can look up at him, gauging his mood. He's smiling, and I know he's telling the truth. Pushing up onto my tiptoes, I brush my lips against his, moaning as his hands drop down to my ass, picking me up as I wrap my legs around his waist...

"Earth to Ari!" Tori's amused expression lets me know I've been caught out having a sex daydream. "Man, here you are with your very own little harem and having sex with multiple guys each night, and my poor vagina is seeing less action than a nun. It's as dry as the Sahara down there—"

"Tori, will you stop talking about your vagina in public?" I laugh, not at all surprised with what she's saying. She doesn't seem to have a filter, and she certainly has no shame. Red-faced members of the public, who've obviously overheard what she was saying, are hurrying by with grins or looks of shock on their faces. "What happened to that guy from the pack. Mark was it?" I ask, ashamed to admit I'd completely forgotten about him until now. Tori had gone on a few dates with one of the lower-level wolves, and I know for a fact that they'd been sleeping together. With a dramatic sigh, she links arms with me as we walk down the street towards the park we had agreed to check out together.

"Oh, little Mark. I broke his heart, you know? You wolves are really possessive and overprotective. I just wanted some fun, but he wanted to settle down." She does sound regretful as she says this, but I know she can be quite harsh when ending relationships. Poor Mark.

"So what's going on with you and Eric?" She sounds hesitant as she asks this, and I narrow my eyes at her. "What? He's a good guy! You should give him a chance. He is literally starving while you're trying to make up your mind, but he's too nice of a guy to say anything."

I huff out a sigh, knowing that she's right, I just don't want to accept it.

"Don't I have enough guys without fate coming and messing with my life again?"

"So you don't have any feelings for him?" Tori inquires with a raised eyebrow.

"Well, no. I didn't say that. I don't know what I feel. I mean, sure, he's attractive, but I never thought that we could have a relationship, so it's weird to think about being in one with him now," I explain, biting my lip as I run through it in my mind. Eric has been the perfect gentleman since he arrived at the pack, and the guys seem to get on with him, except Killian, but that's no surprise. I can't deny that I'm beginning to have feelings for him, but how can I trust if these are my own feelings or just the bond we're supposed to share? I felt an attraction to him before, when I thought he was human, but had never thought that going forward with my feelings was an option for me.

We fall into silence as we mull over everything that's been said, the reason behind why we are both here weighing heavily on our minds.

We enter the park, and Tori glances around before nodding in a certain direction. We're in the park where the latest kidnapping happened. We received a call from the avian shifters' alpha this morning, telling us that one of their falcons had been taken and the body was dumped here in the early hours. The body had been mutilated again.

"Have you found anything? Are your bloodhound senses working?" I tease, knowing Tori hates it when I compare her to a magic sniffing bloodhound. Her rare ability makes her very useful for things like this, but she hates it when I use that analogy. She glares at me, pointing at me threateningly.

"If you don't cut it out with the dog jokes, I will hunt down another mate for you." Her tone is teasing, so I know I'm not really in trouble. I mock gasp, clutching at my chest. I don't think I could cope with another mate.

Following Tori to an open spot in the park, I watch her silently as she makes some sort of gesture with her hands and then drops to her knees, feeling for something on the ground.

"Tor, what are you doing?" I mutter under my breath and look around us, the humans are sure to start asking questions if two people are rummaging around in the grass.

"Relax, I placed a spell. The norms can't see us. Get down here, will you?" she instructs, and I roll my eyes as I crouch down to her level, looking at the plain grass, wondering what the hell she's looking for since it just looks like grass to me. It feels like a weird place for a crime scene, and although she has assured me that the humans—or norms, as she calls them—can't see us, it feels like we're exposed. Mumbling under her breath, she's frowning as she runs her hands over the ground.

"They have a really strong magic user," she mutters, her eyes narrowed as she continues whispering before sitting back on her heels with a smug grin. "But not as strong as me. Got ya!" Her face is lit up, but soon drops to a frown again as she looks at the ground. I look down at what has her attention and gasp, falling back a little when I see that we're surrounded by a ring of glowing, purple runes. I have the heebie-jeebies just looking at them, but Tori doesn't seem worried, so I guess they aren't dangerous.

"Chill out, Ari, they aren't active, the magic has been used up. This is just like a fingerprint. You can't use magic without leaving an imprint behind. I used my magic to make it visible," she says distractedly as she looks closer at the runes, running her fingers over them.

"Do you know what the spell was?" I ask quietly. I don't know why I'm whispering, but my hackles have risen and my wolf is prowling under my skin. I glance around us to check no one is watching. There are only a few people in the park with us, and no one seems to be paying us any attention. Tori's spell will stop the humans from seeing us, but any supernaturals walking by would be able to see what we're doing. Alex had wanted us to bring the others to make sure we were protected, but I had said no. Tori and I can look after ourselves, plus we're in a public place during the middle of the day.

"Hm, there are runes of holding, silence, and invisibility here. So they wanted to keep hold of the shifter for a while and make sure no one saw or heard anything. There are some more complicated ones I need more time to explore. I'll draw them and research them later."

"Can't you just come back?" I question, confused by her

hurriedly scribbling in a notebook she has produced with a flick of her hand.

"The imprint fades with time, which is why I said we needed to come here today. We needed to make sure we got here while it was still fresh," she explains, but I can tell she isn't really paying attention, her gaze firmly on the runes, which now that I'm looking at them, I can see that they are fading.

My wolf jumps to the surface again, ready to protect me, trying to alert me to danger. The hairs on the back of my neck stand at attention, and I know we are being watched. I try to glance around surreptitiously so not to give the game away, and out of the corner of my eye, I see someone just outside of the park, watching us. They aren't even trying to be inconspicuous, so I decide *fuck it*, I'm going to let them know I'm aware they are watching us. Turning to face the stalker, I glare at them before realising I recognise him. He was one of the agents from ASP that took me in for questioning, the one who warned me that my pack was going to be attacked. I don't remember his name, but he was the friendlier of the two agents. I narrow my eyes when he doesn't move, and he just keeps watching us. After a moment, he turns and walks away. I take a step forward to follow after him, needing answers.

"Ari, everything okay?" I glance back down at my best friend. I'm getting a bad feeling, and I can't just leave her here on her own. I grumble internally but smile at her anxiously.

"We were being watched, but they've gone now. Can we hurry this up?" I ask, watching as she looks around with a frown before nodding and closing her notebook, and it disappears again with a wave of her hand.

"Yeah, I'm done now anyway."

Standing up, she waves her hand over the ground and the glowing runes disappear.

"I'm going to drop the shield, so the norms will be able to see us. Just start walking like we were here all along," she explains in a low voice, as she links arms with me before snapping her fingers and pulling me into a walk. No one seems to notice anything, and the two of us talk about inane things just like two best friends walking together would. We leave the park and start heading down the street. We had planned to grab some dinner together and are now on the lookout for somewhere to eat. My appetite has soured after what we discovered and being watched, but I'm determined to enjoy my time with Tori. We see so little of each other now that I'm living with the pack and she's staying somewhere safe. We had decided it was best if I didn't know where she was staying, in fact, no one does. This makes me nervous, since I won't know where to go if anything happens to her, but it's safer that no one knows.

We walk through town towards the quieter, industrial area. It's a little-known secret that one of the best Italian restaurants in the city is out here, and while it's a little way out, it's worth the walk. The sun is beginning to set, but it's still bright enough where we can see everything, the view around us is bathed in a warm, orange glow.

"There's no way you can fit a whole slice of pizza in your mouth," I scoff at my best friend as we walk, my shoulders shaking with laughter. That laughter just increases at the indignant look on her face.

"Ari, my friend, you seriously underestimate me. I could totally —" Tori's argument is cut off when we hear a strange noise. Frowning, we stop walking to see if we can hear it again, glancing around us.

My adrenaline causes my wolf to perk up within me, putting me on high alert again. Tori looks green, like something is making her ill.

"Someone's using magic," she gasps out, like it's choking her. "Strong magic."

For a moment, I think they are using it on her. I've not seen her react to magic being used like this before, and it makes panic rise inside me. She points towards an alley farther down the road, and I realise she's showing me where the magic is being used. I strain my ears to see if I can catch anything, but all I can hear is our breathing and quiet footsteps as we creep forward.

As we reach the mouth of the alleyway, I look over at Tori. I want to tell her to go somewhere safe, but I know she would just be insulted, besides, she can probably protect herself better than I can with the amount of firepower she has with her magic. A feeling of menace is rolling from alley, and I know whatever is happening is evil. With a deep breath, I take a step into the alleyway and feel my stomach drop at the sight before me.

A male shifter is pinned to the ground by glowing spikes of what I assume is magic. I can see that he's screaming from the look of agony in his face and the way he's thrashing around on the ground, but no sounds are coming from his mouth. I remember what Tori said about the runes we found in the park, marks of silence and holding. They were keeping him silent while they tortured him, so no one heard him and came looking. Three guys surround the shifter, they're wearing cloaks with the hoods up like something out of a sick movie, but I can tell from the power coming off one of them that he's a wolf. Crouched over the poor male pinned to the ground, the shifter twists in his position, slicing into the bare chest of the male with his partially turned hand. As he turns, part of his face becomes visible, and a sick smirk greets me as he enjoys the screams of the shifter. I recognise that sick smile, I've suffered under the hands of that twisted fucker. Terrance. The now Alpha of Shadow Pack.

"Just do as we say, Ari. It's simple. One little job, and you can come and join us in the main house." Terrance's voice washes over me from where I kneel in the dark, grimy room. I've heard this all before, this little routine where he acts like what he's about to do pains him.

"I'll treat you like a princess, you'll have whatever you want. All the food you could eat. All you need to do is a little job for us." I

shudder at the mention of him treating me like a princess, I know how he treats his women. My stomach betrays me at the mention of food and growls loudly, twisting painfully, reminding me that it must have been at least a day since I last ate anything.

"I hate treating you like this." *Liar.* "Just say yes."

I usually just stay silent, but today feels different, maybe madness has finally hit me. I lift my head to look at him, the gentle shift of my body makes the chain around my ankle rattle. They don't usually chain me, but I tried to attack them last time, so this is my punishment. Terrance's face lights up as he sees me lift my head, especially when I give him a small smile.

"Go fuck yourself, Terrance." The words are rough and raspy. I haven't spoken to anyone in a while, so the words break from my dry throat. It's worth it for the look of fury that crosses his face though. He sighs and takes off his suit jacket, the one he always wears since he thinks it makes him look cultured. Rolling up his shirtsleeves, he walks towards me, fists raised. I know I'll suffer all the more for my remark, but I can't help it.

"I don't want to do this, Ari, but your actions force my hand." His regretful tone is ruined by the bloodthirsty look on his face and the eager anticipation that flashes in his eyes.

I'm dragged back out of the memory when Tori shakes my arm roughly. Now is not the time for a trip down memory lane. Rage fills me as I run my eyes over the bastard that made my life a misery, and my wolf pushes to the surface. I'm tempted to shift and let her tear through Terrance and the bastards torturing the poor shifter on the ground, but I don't know what effect the runes they've cast will have on me. Besides, my shadow powers might be more useful here. If I can control them, that is. One of the robed dickheads must sense we're here, as he spins around to face us, his mouth opening in a shout, no doubt to warn the others that someone's watching them. They're all looking at us now, even the poor sod pinned to the ground is straining to look at us, and even though his voice is silenced, I can see the words he pleads at us.

Help me.

I look at Tori, and I'm sure my expression matches hers. Fury like I've never known is etched across her face, and her eyes glow purple in what I know means she's about to let loose a whole bucketload of magic.

"Let's fuck shit up," she eloquently says before stepping into the alley, her hands now glowing with her unearthly power. Her hands flick, and I see the same circle of glowing runes surrounding the end of the alley where the shifter and his attackers stand. "Avoid stepping over the circle, the magic is still active," she grits out as I see her fingers moving in complex patterns. I have no idea what magic she's using but I trust her, she'll deal with any magic users. Terrance, however, is mine.

As if he can hear me, Terrance stands up and pushes back the hood of his cloak, a look of sick joy crossing his face. His hands are covered with the blood of the trapped shifter, and as he steps over the rune circle, I can smell it on him. He reeks of alpha power, blood, and fear.

"Ari, what a delight that you're here! I hadn't anticipated getting my hands on you today, must be my lucky day." Glee dances in his eyes as he steps towards me. There are flashes and bangs of magic being used around me, but when I glance over, I see Tori and one of the robed guys locked in a battle of wills, silently staring each other, only their lips and hands moving. The coward hasn't moved from his protective circle of runes, and I see that Tori is struggling to break through it.

I need to end this. I close my eyes and focus on that power within me, rage making it easier for me to find. I concentrate on my body and let the shadow come forward, making my body go invisible. I watch, with pleasure, the furious look that falls over Terrance's face, before his eyes light up.

"You've been working on your powers. You're so strong, fit to be the mate of the Shadow Pack alpha. Come home with me, Ari, see the world I'm creating for us."

I shudder at his voice and the implications behind what he's saying, he truly believes that what he's doing is right. A cry from Tori has me looking around, seeing her on one knee, with blood dripping from a wound on her shoulder. Her eyes flash red, and the air around her starts steaming as she calls her hellhounds to her.

I ghost toward Terrance, aiming right behind him so I can become corporeal behind his back. Just as I arrive behind him, the other robed dickhead who's been silent and unmoving until now steps into my path. I'm so focused on pushing back my shadow that I don't notice. Pain, light, and screams of agony reach my ears. I look around in shock, the alley is coated in blood, and Terrance has spun to look at me, his face glowing with adoration and glee. I look around me in confusion, what the hell just happened? I'm covered in blood, but I can't see any wounds.

Loud snarls fill the alley, and Terrance has the decency to look nervous at the presence of hellhounds. He runs back into the rune circle, nodding towards the magic user, who makes some gestures, causing a blinding light to cover them. Once the light fades, they're gone, including the shifter who was staked to the floor. Although I couldn't hear Terrance after he crossed the runes, his message was clear. *Soon*, he had mouthed to me.

Turning my attention to Tori and the two snarling hellhounds standing guard in front of her, I eye her for wounds. Other than being exhausted and having the wound on her shoulder, she looks okay. I know calling the hounds takes a lot of her energy, so she will have to wait a bit before she sends them back.

"What the hell happened?" I ask, slumping to the ground next to her, leaning against the wall of the alley.

"I was going to ask you the same fucking question!" she responds, gesturing to my blood-soaked body. "You disappeared, and then you reappeared behind dickhead number one, who I assume you knew. But then you fucking ripped the other guy apart when you reappeared inside him!" My eyes widen at Tori's explanation, and I look down at my body in disgust, now understanding what the strange bits stuck to me are—bits of body. I shudder. I didn't realise it was possible to reappear inside someone! I lean forward and vomit as reality sets in. I just killed someone. I keep vomiting until all that's coming out is stomach acid, burning at my throat, while tears stream down my face. I'm dimly aware of a hand on my back and Tori's voice in the distance. The only thought going through my head was the look of excited delight as Terrance realised what I'd done.

Like I am exactly the monster they hoped I would be.

Chapter Fifteen

I'm led into the shower of my en suite silently. I haven't said a word since what happened in the alley. Tori must have been talking to someone on the phone because before I knew it, I was surrounded by my guys. Apparently, they'd already been on their way, Killian had sensed we were in danger through the bond. There had been lots of shouting and panicking, and I was being touched all over by so many hands. I'd lost it a bit then, I didn't want anyone touching me. I was a monster and covered in the blood and body parts of the person I just killed. They've never seen me lose it like that before and were unsure what to do, just looking at each other with stunned expressions.

Eventually, I allowed Tori to lead me the to the car where she climbed in with me, her arms wrapped around me as she whispered nonsense in my ear. I don't remember the journey back, only that Tori held me. When we arrived at the pack, she remained with me, and now she's helping me into the shower. I'm still fully clothed when she turns the hot water on in the shower. She gets caught in the flow, but she doesn't look like she cares. Smiling at me sadly, she shuts the glass door and starts walking out of the room.

"Please don't go. I don't want to be alone," I whisper, barely loud enough to be heard over the spray of the shower, but I know she hears me as she turns back to look at me. She nods at me and steps out of the room, causing my heart to sink even more. Even she left me.

I lean my head against the cold tiles of the shower, taking deep breaths as I try not to think about what happened, about what coats my skin. I scrub at my arms, watching the water turn red. My scrubbing becomes more vigorous as I scratch at my arms, desperate to feel clean. I hear his screams in my head as I tear his body apart. I feel my stomach lurch as it tries to empty itself again, but nothing comes out, my retching loud in the empty bathroom.

The door opens, but I don't turn to look, I scrub at my hair. I can feel *bits* of him on me, evidence of my evil on my body for all to see. I hear the person removing clothing and feel a blast of cool air as the shower door is opened. I continue to scrub and pull at my hair, the tangles and knots making it painful.

"Ari. Stop. You'll hurt yourself." Seb's voice rushes over me. I close my eyes and press my forehead against the cool tiles again. Of all of the guys they could send in after me, they send Seb? My innocent, gentle Seb?

"You shouldn't be in here. I could hurt you." My voice is broken as I open my eyes and focus on the blood tinged water swirling around our feet.

"You would never hurt me, Ari," he says with such confidence that I look up, glancing over my shoulder to meet his blazing eyes. "Besides, I'm not as weak as I used to be." So it's not just me who noticed that then, these waves of power that keep emitting from him. "Face the wall," he commands, and it breaks through my painful fog of despair enough for me to raise an eyebrow at him. He lifts the bottle of shampoo that has appeared in his hands. "Face the wall," he repeats with a gentle push on my shoulder, some of that unnatural power filling the shower.

I do as he says and close my eyes when his hands touch my scalp. He gently works though the knots in my hair, not mentioning the blood or bits of gore that are stuck to it. I'm not sure how long we're like this for, but his gentle ministrations relax me enough that I'm feeling more like myself again. He guides my head so it's under the spray of the shower, and I sigh as his fingers run through my hair, making sure it's clean.

"We need to get you out of those wet clothes." His quiet voice has me opening my eyes, looking down at my body. He's right, the clothes are sticking to my skin from being under the water for so long.

With Seb's help, I strip from my ruined clothing, wincing at the feeling and trying to ignore the blood that drips from it as I peel it away. I hear a bottle open, and soon we are surrounded by the smell of jasmine from my favourite shower gel. I feel Seb's hands on my skin and relax into him as he works on my muscles, washing the carnage from me. His hands pause as his fingers brush the underside of my breasts, his slight growl filling the small space. I find that I want his hands all over me, to make me feel love, to help me stop feeling like a monster. Placing my hands over his, I guide them up so they are on my breasts.

"Ari..." His voice is strained, like he's trying to hold himself back.

I turn around so I'm facing him, realising for the first time that he's naked, and raise an eyebrow. His eyes are locked on my body, and I know he wants me. Without saying anything, I pull him to me, pressing our bodies together. Our kiss starts off gentle, like the Seb I know, nipping at my lips as his hands skim my body, exploring, but soon, the kisses become harder and more demanding. I meet him kiss for kiss, my hand dropping between us to his cock, pleased to find it hard and eager. His breath comes out in a hiss, and he pulls away and presses his forehead to mine, closing his eyes as if he's in pain. I use his distraction to stroke up and down his length, a growl leaving his chest and making me clench my thighs together in anticipation.

"Alex," he calls out, sounding torn as he continues to growl quietly. His power pulses through the room, it's odd, not natural, but it's heady and calling to me. Part of me wonders why he called Alex, but the rest of me doesn't care.

Alex pushes the door open and stops in his tracks when he sees us, his eyes widening as he feels a wave of power rolling from Seb. I start kissing along Seb's neck, causing him to spasm slightly, and he grabs onto my shoulders hard enough to bruise. I keep my eyes on Alex the whole time, his arousal obvious from seeing the two of us together like this. He starts peeling off his clothes and opens the door to the shower. I should be surprised, but I'm not. For some reason, Seb needs Alex here. I'd thought it was the whole, 'you have to sleep with the alphas first' thing, but I suspect it has something to do with all this extra power that's rolling off him. He looks like he's struggling to stay in control. Alex seems to see this too, since he takes a step closer, putting his hand on Seb's shoulder.

"Take a step back," he orders, some of his alpha power slipping in there. Seb's eyes narrow and a slight growl leaves his lips again, but he does as he's told, stepping back until he's pressed against the shower tiles. Alex turns to me, a gentle smile on his face as he brushes a strand of my hair behind my ear, leaning forward and pressing a kiss against my lips. Seb's snarl fills the shower, and Alex spins around with a furious look on his face.

"Do not snarl at your alpha!" he commands, and for a moment, I think he is talking about himself, until I realise he's pointing at me.

Seb bows his head under the force of the command, slowly sinking to his knees. I would have thought he was upset from his position, but I can see the gleam in his eyes and the way his cock sits proud. This is exciting him. Kinky little shit.

"Sorry, Alpha," he addresses me, glancing up before dropping his gaze back down. I go to walk to him, to pull him up, but a hand on my chest makes me stop. I look at Alex questioningly.

"Seb, show your alpha how sorry you are," Alex commands again, his voice harsh, but he's dropped his power enough that Seb doesn't have to carry out the order if he doesn't want to.

Seb, however, obliges, crawling forward on all fours until he reaches me, his hands sliding up my legs as he trails kisses along the way. Alex comes to stand behind me, pulling me against him and kicking my legs apart so Seb has better access. I gasp at Seb's first kiss against my core, his tongue running along my slit, then coming to rest against my clit, flicking it with a swipe of his tongue. If it weren't for Alex holding me up, I would have collapsed into a puddle on the ground. I moan as Seb slides a finger into my core and turn my head to lock eyes with Alex. A rumble of pleasure comes from Alex as he captures my lips in a searing kiss, keeping my body still as Seb worships me. Pulling away from our kiss, Alex looks down to see Seb watching us with undisguised desire in his eyes. He nods at Seb, who stands up and runs a predatory gaze over my body. I reach for him, wanting to run my hand over his cock again, but I don't get a chance before he's pressed against me, his cock nudging against my entrance. I feel him hesitate and pull back to look at me, a question in his eyes.

"If you don't fuck me, I will bite you," I tell him, half joking. As his eyes widen and heat up at my words, I wonder if I threatened the wrong thing. Seb would probably enjoy me biting him.

Thankfully, I don't have to say anything else as he thrusts up into me.

I wrap my arms around his shoulder as he pounds into me, our breath mingling as we kiss. I feel Alex harden behind me, his erection pressing against my back and his strong arms holding me in place. We fall into a rhythm, the hot water running down our bodies, my mouth tracking some of the drops of water along Seb's shoulder and collarbone, nibbling trails along it, savouring his moans as I bite him gently.

"Look at him, he's completely at your mercy. We both are," Alex whispers in my ear, his voice husky and soft, at odds to his hard body holding me firmly in place. He bites down on my earlobe at the same moment Seb slides his hand between us, pressing down on my clit in time to his thrusts. This sends me over the edge, pleasure making me cry out as I bite down on Seb's shoulder. I feel the moment he lets himself go, shuddering against me as he comes. When the pleasure started to wane, Alex releases me and starts running his finger along my skin, making patterns in the water clinging to my skin, kissing along my shoulder. His erection is pressed against me, and knowing that he had been there the whole time, holding me up while Seb fucked me, is a major turn-on. I wiggle against him, smiling at the growl that rumbles through his chest. Before I know it, both Seb and I have been spun, so Seb is pressed against the shower wall and Alex is pushed against my back.

"You want to play that game, huh?" He bites my earlobe again, and I arch against him. I shouldn't be this ready for him, but need is swirling within me.

"Fuck me," I demand, and I feel him moving his cock to my entrance, gasping as he fills me with one thrust. Seb makes a noise in front of me, and I meet his eyes, worried he will feel uncomfortable pinned against the wall while Alex fucks me, but his eyes are heavy lidded with satisfaction, and he's aroused by what's happening. Alex continues to pound into me from behind, his hand wrapping in my hair, pulling my head back as Seb starts to kiss along my skin, and his hand goes to my nipple that's now exposed since I arched my back into Alex. I feel my orgasm start to build again, and I look at Seb, love shining in his eyes as he smiles at me, pressing a kiss to my lips. Alex grumbles and pulls gently on my hair so my head twists to meet his kiss. This is enough to undo me, and I tumble into my second orgasm, gasping into Alex's mouth. He follows me over the edge, gasping with his own orgasm before resting his forehead against my shoulder. We stay there, pressed together under the hot water from the shower, for a while, our heavy breaths intermingling. We eventually pull apart and make use of the shower to clean ourselves off.

Later, we curl up on my bed, with Alex curled behind me and Seb in front of me, his head resting against my shoulder as he plays with a strand of my hair. Something has been bothering me for a while, and now that we're snuggled together, I can't fight the need to get it off my chest.

"You should hate me. I'm a monster," I mutter quietly, my face buried into Seb's chest as they curl around me. They're quiet for a moment, and I know they are thinking about what I did today, what I'm capable of, but their hands continuing to stroke patterns on my arms. Seb is frowning the whole time, and he pulls my gaze to meet his.

"We all carry darkness within us, and we don't judge you for what happened. We love you Ari, darkness and all."

Alex makes a noise of agreement before turning me around in his arms so I'm facing him, pressing a gentle kiss to my lips.

"Don't let them win. If you believe you're a monster, then Shadow Pack has achieved their goal," Alex says gently, but there's fire in his eyes. I frown as I digest what he said before meeting his gaze again and nodding. He's right, and I won't let Shadow Pack win.

For the rest of the night, they show me how much they love me, worshipping my body into the early hours of the morning.

Chapter Sixteen

Today is going to be full of meetings and me repeating myself for what feels like the hundredth time. Alpha Mortlock needs me to tell him what happened, and the other alphas have called a meeting. I'm surprised I was left alone yesterday evening anyway, given the seriousness of what happened. I found out at breakfast that the alpha had ordered I be left in peace last night, although this had caused a strain with the other shifter packs, since everyone wanted answers and were not prepared to wait. I'm filled with gratitude that Alpha Mortlock allowed me those hours to come to terms with what I did and what we saw. I think he allowed that time for Alex and Seb too, we all needed to be together last night. Apparently, Killian went a little crazy when he saw me covered in blood, not realising it wasn't mine, and had to spend some time in his wolf form to blow off steam.

I sit on the edge of the bed and try to tame my hair, the brush catching on the tangles and causing me to snarl at my appearance in the mirror. Seb is just walking out of the bathroom, a towel tied around his waist, and he pauses when he sees me struggling with the brush.

"Let me," he says softly, and he climbs onto the bed behind me, taking the brush and working gently through my hair. The movements are soothing, and I close my eyes as he works, enjoying his soft touch. "Perfect," he announces, and I open my eyes and smile up at him.

"Thank you."

There is a knock at the door downstairs, and I hear someone open it. Thanks to my supernatural hearing, I can hear the quiet greetings and the guests being led into the living room, so I know Alpha Mortlock, Isa, and Alex are downstairs. I knew this meeting was coming. Alex had warned me this morning that he would have to speak with Alpha Mortlock and that the other packs would need to know about what I saw. It affected us all, so it was only fair that we shared the information. The question was, how much is the alpha going to tell the other packs? The reason Shadow Pack is after me is because of my Shadowborn abilities, so do I reveal this to the shifter community? On a separate, selfish level, I'm also dreading admitting to the others downstairs what I am capable of, that I killed someone last night.

With a sigh, I push up from the edge of the bed and make my way downstairs, Seb following behind me. No point putting this off. As I walk into the room, I see everyone is here, Eric included, all except Garett, who's with his pack, explaining what happened to his alpha. Tori sits on one of the sofas and pats the seat next to her when she sees me.

"Good morning, Alpha Mortlock, Alex, Isa," I greet them and give a slight nod of my head before sitting next to Tori, who's smiling as she immediately wraps her arms around me. She stayed here in one of the spare rooms last night, wanting to be close to me. Her magic had been drained from calling the hellhounds, so I felt better knowing she was here, recovering. I pull away from her quickly when I remember her injuries, guilt running through that I could've forgotten.

"Is your arm okay?" I ask, pulling at her jumper to try and see the skin on her shoulder, but she laughs and bats my hands away.

"I'm fine, I used a healing spell when we got here," she tells me, and then matches my expression and boops me on the nose when she sees my frown. "No. Stop feeling guilty. You had your own issues going on. You don't have to be super Ari, saving everyone. You have to focus on you sometimes." I roll my eyes at her lecture, having heard it a hundred times before, and I know she's right.

"Ari," the alpha calls, and my gaze immediately goes to him. He's smiling at the two of us, and his expression looks apologetic, like he's sorry he has to break up our conversation, but I understand this is important. "Can you tell me what happened yesterday?" he requests, and the room goes quiet as everyone turns their attention to me.

"As you know, Tori and I went to look at the most recent disappearance scene yesterday." Nods fill the room and I glance at Tori to see if she's okay with me speaking of her involvement. She nods, so I continue. "Tori used her magic to find the scene and identify what magic is being used. We found runes to capture a shifter and keep them silent and invisible. Tori didn't recognise some of the runes and is going to look into them. When we were there, I felt someone watching us, and when I turned around, I saw someone from ASP staring at me. It was the same agent from before." There are growls and hisses of anger in the room, which causes me to stop. Killian is pacing up and down the room, his fists clenching and unclenching the whole time. Alex and the alpha are sharing a significant look, and Isa stays silent, but her expression is grim. Eric stays silent in the corner of the room, his gaze not leaving me, while Seb's upper lip is pulled back in a snarl. It's his reaction that surprises me the most. In a room full of dominant shifters, he would normally be quiet and subservient, but he looks like he's struggling to control his wolf. I glance at Mortlock and notice that he has seen the same thing I have. He meets my gaze and nods for me to continue.

"He left when he saw me looking at him. Tori and I then went to get some food, and on our way to the restaurant, Tori felt someone using magic, a lot of it. We followed it and found someone, a shifter, trapped in a ring of runes, pinned to the ground." I continue to describe the three robed people in the ring with him, how we couldn't hear and touch them past the runes. When I mention that Terrance was in the circle, I'm met with more snarls and growls. Even Eric looks affected by this piece of information, his expression becoming dark and his eyes turning black as unnatural power starts to emit from his corner of the room.

"Enough!" Alpha Mortlock commands, his power filling the room and grabbing the attention of the snarling males. "Ari is safe, she's here with us. We need to know the facts, so if you can't control yourself, then leave." He looks around the room, meeting the eyes of each of the guys, particularly Seb, who I notice is nodding his head in acknowledgement. "Ari, can you continue please?"

"Terrance tried to get me to fight him. The magic user in the circle started attacking Tori, so she was working on getting through the runes. I used my shadow powers to ghost past Terrance, and it worked, but when I tried to reappear behind him, someone walked into my path as I was reappearing, and I couldn't stop it." My voice goes quiet as I explain, until I finish and drop my eyes in shame, waiting for the judgement to come my way.

"You exploded a man with your power?" Isa's strong German accent greets me, and I look up to meet her usually stoic face, which is graced with a small smile. "I've met a few men that I have wanted to make explode in my time."

I snort out a laugh, unable to hold it back in my surprise, and Tori giggles beside me. The tension in the room has been broken, and for some reason, my eyes are drawn towards Eric, who has an understanding look on his face. I can tell there's something he wants to say to me, but not with everyone around.

"So what happens next? I assume we need to let the other alphas know?" I turn to address the alpha directly, since it will be his decision as to what we do next. Mortlock leans back in his seat and nods at me with a thoughtful expression on his face.

"I've already told them a little of what we know. They wanted to speak with you, but I told them you needed to heal after the attack. I've told them nothing of your Shadowborn abilities, and I'll leave it up to you what you say." My heart warms at the alpha's words, and he must see the surprise in my expression, because he frowns and gestures towards me. "Did you think I was going to make you reveal yourself? I won't ever force you to do that unless the safety of the pack depends on it, and even then, I would consult with you first. This is your decision, and I know it's not official, but you are part of this pack now, whether you admit it or not," he finishes with a little smile, and I have to fight the tears that threaten to fall. I nod at his words, not trusting my voice. Tori squeezes my hand, and I turn to her with a smile. She knows how difficult it is for me to open up to others and accept people into my life, so she understands this is a big moment for me.

"We have something else you need to know." Alex's tone is guarded, so I know it's not good news. I look over and see both the alpha and beta are frowning, as if they don't want to tell me. "The shifter that was taken was found dead this morning, just outside of their pack's boundaries. The words '*See you soon*' were carved into his back. We think they were aimed at you."

My vision spins, and my ears start to ring. I need to get some fresh air, so I get to my feet, it feels like the walls are closing in on me.

"Ari?" someone calls, but I'm so focused on getting out of the room that I don't register who it is.

"Give her a moment, she needs some air," a deep voice answers.

I hurry out of the room, blindly pushing at the front door before falling to my knees in the grass outside the house. I'm going to vomit. I lean forward and retch, my breakfast threatening to make a reappearance. Images of the shifter we were unable to save keep floating in my head, him mouthing the words *help me* over and over again. I groan, bringing my hands to my head as I take deep breaths. After a few minutes, the feeling of nausea starts to recede, and I realise someone is sitting with me, not touching, but close enough that if I were to reach back, our hands would be touching. I should have realised from the humming in my chest that it was Killian.

"I know what it's like to feel responsible for the death of others." His voice is deeper than usual as he remembers his pack and the fate that befell them. I turn to see him sitting on the steps leading up to the porch, looking off at the trees that border the house, but I can tell he isn't really seeing them. I reach out and take hold of his hand, knowing his guilt will always be a burden he carries around with him. He didn't kill his wolves, but he trusted someone who betrayed them, resulting in all but Killian dying, his mate included. He blows out a deep breath and turns to meet my gaze. I'm hit by the agony I can see in his eyes, and I crawl forward until our foreheads are pressed together. We don't always agree and we fight like cats and dogs, but Killian understands the dark part of me I fight with and the guilt I carry with me.

"None of it's your fault. Not that he walked into you reappearing, and not the shifter they killed."

"But if I'd told you guys the details sooner, we might have been able to find him, to save him!"

"The moment he was captured, his hours were numbered, you know that. The actions of the Shadow Pack, and whoever is working with them, are not your fault, nor your sole responsibility." I look away as he speaks, but he gently pulls my face back to look at him "You're part of the pack, even if we have to leave and create our very own pack with the seven of us."

"Seven?" I ask, confused. Had I adopted more people to my rapidly growing harem?

"You, me, Garett, Alex, Seb, Eric, and Tori." I blink at him in surprise, and he smiles at my expression, chuckling slightly.

"You included Eric and Tori?" I thought he hated Eric, since he ignored him all the time, often refusing to even acknowledge his presence in the room.

"Well, Eric is just as much a part of this as I am. Fate is bringing us together for some reason, we just need to figure out what." His expression has adopted his typical scowl, and his voice is resigned. There's the Killian I know and love. "And Tori is part of your family, so she's part of ours."

"You would accept a witch into our pack for me?" I stumble over the words *our pack* as I ask the question, gobsmacked he would do that for me. I don't want to focus on the fact that he's offering to start our own pack just yet. I'm not ready to think about that, but the fact that he *has* thought about it warms my heart.

"You don't get it, do you?" he questions, his voice teasing as he pushes to his feet and reaches his hand down to help me up. Standing, I look up at him, the confusion must be evident in my face as he just smiles and presses a kiss to my lips. It's not the searing, possessive kiss I'm used to from Killian, but a sweet peck on the lips that leaves me wanting more. He just smirks and walks back into the house. Bastard.

"What don't I get?" I call after him, but he ignores me and walks back into the main room. I'm about to follow after him and demand he answers me when Eric walks through the door with a steaming cup of coffee in his hands. His stunning blue eyes are kind and show empathy as he walks towards me.

"You've had a tough couple of days, I thought you could use this." He hands me the coffee, and I smile at him gratefully. I'm still not sure how he fits in with everything here, but I can't deny the pull I feel towards him. It's different than the feelings I have for the other guys. It's more like I *need* to be near him. With the true mated pair bond with Killian, it's a constant tugging sensation when we're apart, like he has a part of me and has taken it with him, making being apart difficult. Whereas with Eric, it's more like being with him soothes a part of me, being together just feels *right*.

I bring the mug to my lips and inhale the comforting smell of coffee, blowing on it before taking a drink. It's too hot to drink really, but I can't help but take small sips.

"Thank you. How are you?" I ask, feeling ashamed that I

haven't been asking that much lately, in fact, I've barely had the chance to talk to him since that day in the coffee shop, and guilt fills me. He smiles and gestures towards the house.

"I'm about to have a visit from a patient, I believe you know them already, do you want to assist me? I imagine you miss being hands on with your patients," he offers, and a smile lights my face. I do miss seeing my patients.

"I would like that." He nods at me with a smile, and we walk together into the house and through the corridor to the rooms in the back, which act as a medical practice. There are two examination rooms, as well as a room with a set of beds, acting as a small ward should we need it. Thankfully, since I've been here, we only needed to use that room once after the attack on the pack, and luckily, the injuries were only minor and we used it as a waiting room. Following Eric into one of the rooms, I'm surprised to see my name has been painted on the other door to the room I use as my consultation room. Sneaky buggers, I haven't agreed to stay here, but they have obviously decided that I will be. I smile and shake my head. Eric gestures for me to take the seat behind the desk as he moves around the room, getting it ready to see his first patient, before washing his hands in the sink.

"To answer your earlier question, I'm okay. Better since I moved in here and I can be close to you. But it's difficult not being able to feed." He meets my eyes, and I know what he's saying. I haven't accepted the bond with him, not yet. I struggled with the idea of Killian as my mate, and now Eric is supposed to be my fated mate too? It's a lot to comprehend. He hasn't once tried to make me feel guilty or force the bond on me though, which I appreciate, but I know we'll need to have this conversation sooner or later. I put my coffee mug down with a sigh and walk over to him, placing my hand on his arm.

However, as soon as I touch him, he gasps like he's in pain, his face twisting as he falls towards me. I reach out to try and catch him, but he knocks into me and we both fall to the ground. Pain flashes through my head when my skull smashes into the counter on the way down. Eric lands on top of me, his heavy weight pinning me to the ground. Usually, I would be strong enough to move him off me, but the whack to my head has my vision doubling. For the second time in the last hour, I feel like I'm going to vomit as I wait for the dizziness to recede.

"Eric?" I rasp out, turning my head to look at his face, which is close to mine.

His eyes are wide open, and his pupils seem to fill his whole eye until only black is visible, and all traces of blue are gone. His body is rigid, and a trickle of blood drops from his nose.

The scent of blood, both mine and his, fills the air, and I hear a commotion farther in the house as the shifters' sense of smell picks it up.

"Ari!" I hear someone shout before several sets of feet start running towards us. The door slams open, and Killian, Alex, and Tori come crowding into the room.

"Careful! Eric is having some sort of seizure!" I call out, worried they might accidentally hurt him if they aren't careful with him. Tori comes forward and crouches down to observe his face, looking solemn and nodding her head.

"He's having a vision," she confirms, and I scrunch up my face.

"I thought those stopped once he came to live with us because he's near me now? He knows that we're fated and I'm not in danger, so why is he having a vision?" Eric had told me how visions worked for incubi and their mates. Something triggers the bond, and they get visions of their destined mate. Once they meet them, the visions stop.

"That's what we thought too. Come on Ari, you're bleeding, let's get you up." She looks to Killian and Alex, who nod and come farther into the room. They help move Eric off me, picking him up and placing him onto the examination bed in the room. Tori moves forward to help me up, and I groan as I stand, putting my hand to my head. I wince as I feel a wetness running down my neck.

"Ari!" Eric shouts, his eyes wide in panic. The blue of his irises is back now as he frantically looks around the room for me. As soon as he sees me, he throws his legs off the side of the bed and tries to hurry to my side, although Alex has to grab him when his legs start to give way.

"Dude, just sit down for a second. Ari's fine," Alex tells him, helping him sit on the edge of the bed. Eric leans forward and put his head in his hands.

"Eric, are you okay? What happened?" I ask softly, not wanting to panic him again.

"I had a vision when you touched me." We had assumed that already, but he carries on before I can ask more. "It's unusual, because the visions usually stop when you find your mate, but then the bond is usually accepted straight away, so this is an unusual situation anyway. Further visions sometimes happen when your mate is in danger." He sits back as he says this, his entire focus on me. I take a deep breath before leaning back against the counter that is supporting me.

"So I'm in danger?" No surprise there, I always seem to be in danger nowadays. He surprises me when he shakes his head though, looking at the others around the room.

"We all are. They're coming for us."

"Us? You mean Moon River Pack?" Alex steps forward, a frown on his face as he tries to work out the threat. Eric just shakes his head again, looking like he's about to vomit.

"No, all of us. They are coming for all the shifters and those associated with them."

"Shit. Fuck!" Alex shouts. "Okay, Ari, are you okay here? I need to go speak with the alpha. Killian, can you come with me? I could use your expertise." Killian just nods at Alex's request before leaning over to me, placing his hand on my cheek, and pressing a gentle kiss to my forehead, then the two of them leave the room.

"I'll call Garett. I'll just be in the next room, you'll be okay?" Tori asks as she fishes her phone from her pocket. I nod, waving her away, my eyes still on Eric. He's eyeing me up like I'm his next snack, and my pulse speeds up. I don't think I'm in danger with him, but I'm suddenly reminded that he is a demon.

"Ari, we're all in danger. A fight is coming, and I need to be strong enough to help keep you and the pack safe. I need to feed." I frown at his words, about to say no, we would have to accept the bond for that, wouldn't we? He sees my hesitation and shakes his head, holding his hand out to me. "I know you're not ready to accept the bond, but if you let me feed from you, I'll be strong enough to help. Please." I walk over to him warily, and he raises his hand to the back of my head where I hit it from the fall. I wince when his fingertips brush it and stare at the blood on his fingers as he pulls his hand away.

"You are already in pain, I can use that. I don't want to push you, but I need to be at full strength or as close as I can get. Do you trust me?"

I look into his eyes, the eyes of a friend I've known and trusted for years. That friendship had been rocked by lies, but he's proven himself since. I bite my lip in indecision, but there isn't really an option. If him feeding from my pain is going to help protect others, then I'll do it. I nod, trepidation filling me as a small smile appears on his face.

"You will feel a bit of pain, but I can make it pleasurable," he whispers into my ear as he pulls me closer, placing one hand on my waist as the other comes up to touch the back of my head.

His fingers brush my wound, and I feel a sharp bolt of pain before a strange pulling feeling fills me. The pain starts to tingle, the tingle spreading all over my body as I feel Eric press up against me. Need overtakes me as arousal spreads through my body, and the pain becomes pleasure running all along my skin. I feel like I'm on fire, and I gasp as Eric presses a kiss to my forehead, the pleasure-pain intensifying. I'm not sure how long this goes on for, time loses all meaning as I become absorbed in the sensation. This could become addictive. Eric pulls away from me, and I gasp as the intense feeling leaves my body, leaving only a slight tingling running along my skin.

When I open my eyes, which I hadn't even realised I'd closed, I gasp as I look at Eric. He's practically glowing. He was good looking before, but his features have sharpened, making him even more handsome. His eyes *are* glowing, an eerie reddish glow comes from them as they focus on me. He raises his hand, which is glistening with my blood, and brings it to his lips, putting one finger in his mouth before sucking my blood from the appendage. I should be disgusted, but with the afterglow of whatever Eric just did to me, I find that it's a major turn-on. I take a deep breath and step back. I need some space from the handsome demon in front of me before I make a decision that I'll regret.

Chapter Seventeen

After Eric's vision and premonitions of an attack, it was more important than ever to meet with the other alphas. I feel responsible for what's happening. I know I'm not the one capturing, torturing, and killing these shifters, but somehow, the Shadow Pack are involved. Not to mention the message that was carved into the back of the shifter I failed to save. Although the guys say otherwise, I'll carry the weight of his death with me until the day I die. Knowing the Shadow Pack, they would have done that to him while he was still alive, just to inflict as much pain as possible.

The rest of the day is spent organising the meeting. Apparently, a meeting with all of the shifter packs hasn't been called in over twenty years, so getting everyone together is proving to be difficult. Old rivalries and disputes are getting in the way of the organisation of a peaceful meeting. The local lion pride doesn't trust anyone, and the only reason they agreed to come was because the alpha personally knows Alpha Mortlock. People seemed to think we were plotting for a war. This both helped and hindered our progress. The coyotes and the other wolf pack are eager to meet, since their losses are some of the highest. Some of the packs, such as the avian shifters and some of the collective groups of more uncommon shifters, like the otters and foxes, are more reluctant, as they don't have large protective groups like others do. I know we can count on Long Claw Bear Pack coming to the meeting.

Tori had been in touch with a couple of her friends in the witch community who aren't affiliated with any of the covens, and a few agreed to come to the meeting, just to listen. They were anxious because of the tension between wolves and the witches, but Tori assured them that they would be safe. Eric had even spoken with a couple of his demon friends who promised they would attend the meeting. Alpha Mortlock invited representatives from the fae and vampire communities, but we don't think they will come, since they believe issues such as these are below them. We warned them that they could be the next to experience the deaths.

The main issue causing problems is that although supernaturals from all species are disappearing, only the shifters are turning up dead after they had been taken. It's assumed that the others who were taken are also dead, but why were only the bodies of shifters being left?

That night, I'm surrounded by Seb and Alex in bed, who are wrapped around me, fast asleep, but I can't sleep. My thoughts keep going back to the shifter who was taken, and when I do finally fall asleep, I have dreams of being pinned to the ground as Terrance crouches over me, drawing runes into my skin as I scream. I wake up in a cold sweat, finding a blinking Alex and Seb looking around in confusion before realising the noise that woke them up was me. They try to comfort me, but in the end, there is no point in me staying in bed, so I get up, shower, and make breakfast for everyone. Eric is the only one awake this early in the morning, so we sit and talk about everything and anything to pass the time, as long as it has nothing to do with Shadow Pack or the meeting today. It's nice, and I get to know him a bit better other than as just a doctor or an incubus. But our time together is over too soon, as everyone starts waking up and joining us in the kitchen, and before I know it, Alpha Mortlock arrived with a grim smile and the words I had been dreading.

"It's time."

The location that had been agreed upon for the meeting was a large, empty warehouse. I'm starting to hate warehouses, since only bad things have happened to me in them, but it was one of the only places large enough and with no humans around to see us. Tori and one of her friends had already been to the building and warded it so if there are any humans around, they wouldn't get suspicious when they see lots of people arriving at the abandoned building. The last thing we need is for a bunch of humans to discover us having a meeting inside, plus we need protection. With this many shifters turning up in the same place, it makes us a target, especially when there are people who are trying to kill us anyway.

I walk inside the building and am surprised to see that it's been decked out inside like a meeting hall, and is more cosy than I'd thought it would be. The walls have been boarded and painted cream with wooden accents, chairs fill the space, and a table is laid out at the back with refreshments. I raise my eyebrows at Alex as we walk in, and he smiles.

"This is already a common meeting space for groups of shifters, just not usually *all* the groups of shifters. Besides, it's not a proper meeting without tea and coffee." I nod in acknowledgement of his comment, that makes sense. I knew there was some neutral territory in the city, I've just never used it before. The rest of the representatives from Moon River Pack file in behind me, and only the alpha, Alex, and Isa had walked in before me. Killian should've been next, but he insisted that we walk in together, Seb following in last. I'd objected, but Alex had told me about the importance of following protocol here. Seb insisted that he comes in last, explaining that he didn't mind, but it doesn't sit right with me, he is just as important as the others, and power levels shouldn't dictate that.

The bear pack is already here, and I immediately see Garett and his brothers standing next to their alpha. I want to run over and throw my arms around him, but I know that would be frowned upon. I've missed having my bear around, all of the problems recently had meant that he was needed back with his pack, which I understand, it's just not easy being separated. Alpha Mortlock starts to walk over and greets the bear pack warmly. Each alpha of the packs was allowed to bring their beta and gammas for protection, plus three representatives. Standing next to Alpha Philips is Garrett's oldest brother and another guy who looks like he belongs in a biker bar. In fact, all of the bears seemed to have that look about them. I'd have to ask Garett later if having long hair was a requirement for being in their pack. A small smile crosses my lips at that thought. Introductions are made, and I learn that the guy I've not met before is Kurt, the Long Claw beta. I turn to Max and raise my eyebrow.

"I didn't know you were the pack gamma," I say with a smile. His position means he's strong. I knew Garett was strong, and when I met the rest of the family, I had gotten the general impression that strength ran in the family, but I hadn't realised his brother was so strong. "You didn't tell me that your brother was the gamma," I accuse in a teasing voice to Garett, who just rolls his eyes at me.

"Oh, think you've picked the wrong brother now? Besides, I didn't even tell you I had brothers until the other day, are you really that surprised?" he teases. That's true. I stick my tongue out at him, and Alpha Philips chuckles before turning away with Alpha Mortlock, locked in conversation.

Some people might be bothered that they didn't know stuff about their partners, but honestly, I don't mind I only just found out. It's not like we have been dating and he was hiding me from his family. His family were fully aware of me, apparently, and things have only just recently settled down where we could begin exploring our relationship.

I glance around the room again, a lot of the shifter groups are here already, standing separately from each other. The alphas are obvious, not just for their physical stature, but the power that is coming from them. I shake my head slightly, everyone is posturing and on edge. We should be supporting each other, but instead, they seem alert, almost waiting for an attack from one of the other packs. I notice some of the alphas are greeting each other, old alliances, but there is a definite air of unease. I hope this meeting will help combat that.

Tori enters the building, and when I see her grin at me, I release a breath I hadn't realised I'd been holding. She looks fierce tonight, dressed in tight black jeans and a deep purple blouse that shows off her deep tan skin. To top off the look, she has on a long leather jacket that falls to her knees and black leather boots. She looks like she's come to fight. I raise my eyebrow at her outfit and grin, shaking my head slightly at her. She gives me an innocent look, and only then do I notice the guy following behind her, looking at our group nervously. He would probably look tall if he wasn't in a room full of shifters. The nervous glance at the wolves would have tipped me off that he's a witch, if it hadn't been for the amount of power surrounding him. Tori sees me looking and shakes her head just enough for me to catch. Okay, I would meet up with her about that later.

"Ari!" she greets, putting her arms around me in a hug. We'd only seen each other a few hours ago, but I know this is to show the others in the room that different races and species could get on.

"Hey, Tori. Who's your friend?" I pull away from the hug and smile slightly at the nervous guy standing behind her. Tori looks back and smiles at him, and gesturing him forward, she placing a hand on his shoulder.

"This is James. He's another rebel witch like me who doesn't fit in with the city covens," she says with a bright smile, and James finally cracks a grin. A tiny one, but it's a start. I'm about to ask the two witches about the protection they have put around the building when a commotion behind me catches my attention. I turn and see that Garett's brothers are staring our way, more specifically, at Tori. Max, Garett's oldest brother, looks like someone has just smacked him in the face with a shovel, and his brothers have frozen completely. It would be comical if it wasn't for the growl that starts emitting from Max's chest. I turn to look at Garett and start to worry when I see his stunned expression.

"Um, Garett, what's happening?" I ask quietly, and this seems to snap him out of whatever shock he's in. Cursing, he runs over to his brother and stands in front of him with his hand placed on his chest as if to keep him in place. Jake and Ben, his twin brothers, are completely still, their eyes locked on Tori. Garett starts talking to them in a quiet voice, and I can't make out what he's saying. Alpha Philips has realised something is wrong and strides over to the brothers, although after a moment of conversation, he pulls away sharply and stares at Tori before taking Garett's place and holding Max back. The growling in his chest has raised a level, and people in the room are starting to notice that something is going on. Garett jogs back over to us, a pained expression on his face as he reaches our sides.

"Tori, can you please take your hand off James?" he asks, causing me to look sharply at him. Tori, to her credit, does as he says, and the growling in the room gets noticeably quieter.

"Garett, what the hell is going on?" I'm trying to keep my voice low, aware we're surrounded with beings that have supernatural hearing. Garett sighs and glances between Tori and me, before rubbing the back of his neck.

"Tori has set off a mating bond with my brothers."

"Wait, what?" Tori demands before looking over Garett's shoulder at the guys who are staring intently at her. "How? I'm a witch!" Garett blows out a deep breath and shrugs.

"It's been known to happen. It's rare though," he explains, and I fight the need to roll my eyes. That's something I've been hearing a lot of recently. Tori keeps glancing over at Max and the twins, an intense look in her eyes.

"Is that why I feel like I want to fuck them here in the middle of the room with everyone watching?" Garett snorts out a laugh and looks adorably awkward at the turn of the conversation. "Is that what you feel with Killian all the time?" She shoots me a look and waggles her eyebrows at me suggestively. She's taking this remarkably well, which causes me to frown.

"Doesn't this bother you?" I ask, and I have to snap my fingers in her face to pull her attention back to me.

"I have three hot shifters who are made to fight for me, love me, and fuck me whenever I want. Why would I be bothered?" she retorts, her hands coming to her hips, and I have to laugh. When she puts it like that...

"Now is not the time for this. Just...stay with Ari, stay out of trouble, and we'll try sort this out after the meeting," Garett pleads, turning to walk back to his brothers before glancing over his shoulder at us again. "And please, to avoid any heads being ripped off, don't touch any guys." Tori just grins evilly, and Garett groans, knowing he has his work cut out for him this evening. Staying out of trouble has never been something Tori and I have been good at.

The room has filled up now, almost so much so that the separate groups have to mingle a little. I try to keep an eye on Garett and his brothers out of the corner of my eye. He's taken them to one side and is talking to them in a low voice. Their eyes are still locked on Tori, but they look a little more relaxed now. Tori keeps shifting her weight, her eyes repeatedly flicking to the bears, and I can't help the little smile that creeps onto my face.

"Welcome to having a mate," I say quietly, the evil little smile growing at her frustrated look.

"Does it always feel like this?" she mutters, shifting her weight again. "I feel like my vagina's about to explode." I snort out a laugh at her unexpected comment, and I know from the chuckles around us that the others heard her too.

"Yup. And I have five of them," I answer drily. She gives me a sympathetic look before her gaze is pulled back to the bears.

Alex walks over to me and places his hand on my shoulder to get my attention. I smile at him and realise he's in beta mode. There are two definite sides to Alex's personality—the fun, flirty side, and the serious beta, protector of the pack. He's standing tall, and his eyes are moving around the room, open but also on the lookout for threats. Alex, as well as pack protector, is my guide for the evening. I have no idea who most of the people in the room are, and as I have been asked to be a peacekeeper for the meeting, I need to know who everyone is.

"You see the group of shifters standing by the door?" He nods towards them discreetly, and I make a noise of acknowledgement. "Those are the avian shifters, they have always been a bit flighty, excuse the pun, so they will probably be the first to leave. I'm actually surprised they came, since they don't like to mix with others." On the way over, Alex had explained to me that the avian pack was made up of lots of different species of bird shifters, but they kept together in one larger pack for protection, since separately, there wasn't enough of them to form a strong pack. "There are representatives from different species here tonight. There is Trina, an eagle shifter who generally acts as alpha." He nods towards the group again, there are six of them, and I can instantly tell who Trina is. She's holding herself with more confidence, and a man stands behind her and is looking around like he's hunting for his next meal. A slight, pretty young woman stands next to Trina, eyeing everything nervously as if looking for all the exits. "Vlad, standing behind Trina, is a vulture, and the nervous looking woman is Amy, she's a sparrow." I raise my eyebrows at his explanations. I'm not at all surprised that Vlad is a vulture, he gives off a creepy scavenger feel, but I am surprised that a sparrow shifter has been included in the representatives. Shifters that are classified as prey tend not to mix with the predators, since generally, these shifter types are weaker and don't have as much power, so they avoid us.

Alex moves onto the other shifter groups around the room, coyotes, the other local wolf pack, and even the lions came.

Conversation in the room suddenly drops, and I turn to the door to see that Eric has arrived with a beautiful woman gliding in behind him. This woman oozes sex, everything about her screams it from her clothes, down to the way she walks. I would bet everything I own that she's a succubus, and I realise what Eric was trying to explain to me when he said he isn't a true incubus. Eric is good looking in an unearthly way, but this woman makes me want to rip my clothes off and throw myself at her feet. I notice that half the room is looking at her in disgust, and the other half in rapt longing, but the attention of the whole room is on her. From the look on her face, I can tell she's enjoying it. I raise an eyebrow at him, and he walks over to us, his features schooled into his professional doctor's mask, which I recognise from working with him at the hospital.

"Ari, this is Vella, she has come to listen and offer aid." I turn to look at the succubus, surprised she's offered to help.

"Welcome, Vella. The only aid we need at the moment is information, we aren't looking for a fight." This point was reiterated to the packs when we were arranging this meeting. This was an opportunity to share information and plan, strength in numbers. We are not trying to fight. There may come a point where that is unavoidable, but until then, we need to know what we are up against. Vella tilts her head as she listens to me talk, her black silken hair tumbling forward, covering her mostly exposed chest. Up close, I can see that her eyes are almost entirely black, making her appear more demon than human. She takes hold of my fingers and raises them to her lips, kissing the back of my hand. I stiffen and have to fight not to pull my hand away from her grip.

"This is a shame. They have taken one of my girls, and I wish to return the favour." Her voice is soft and sultry, and I see several heads turn to listen as she talks.

"I'm sorry they've taken someone from you. We'll try and aid you in finding her where we can." I gently pull my hand from her grasp. She turns to smile at Eric, and a small part of me wants to claw her eyes out for looking at him like that. I know it's stupid to feel this way, but I can't help the snarl that escapes my lips as she brushes her hand up his arm. Her eyes flick to me, and then back to Eric, her smile widening.

"You picked a strong heart mate, Eric," she says to him, and they walk away to greet the alphas in the room, Eric throwing me an apologetic look as they go.

"You know I didn't choose this, Vella," he responds quietly. I don't catch her response before Seb shudders.

"Well, she gives me the creeps," he declares loudly, and I can't help the laugh building up in me from escaping.

"Succubi and incubi are the same, which is probably why you didn't know Eric was part incubus, he doesn't give off that feeling. Although once they reach a certain age and power level, they can suppress that otherworldly feeling, most of them just choose not to," Alex explains with an eye roll.

I glance at the clock, it's nearly eight, the time we had arranged from the meeting. It had initially been agreed to meet during the day, but then the vampires wouldn't be able to attend, and it was decided that they should be given the opportunity to come, not that anyone thought they would show. The alphas of each group, and Tori and Eric, have all gathered at the end of the room, discussing how the meeting is going to be run. I'm standing with them, just outside of their little circle, alongside the betas, who are looking anxiously at their alphas. They must be finding it difficult to be in a room with so many potential threats to their leaders and not be right by their side. Max, the bear gamma and Garett's brother, is standing on my right, and although he's fighting to keep his eyes on Alpha Philips and on the lookout for threats, I can see his gaze keeps being drawn to Tori. Tori, on the other hand, looks focused, and I know it's driving Max crazy. If he knew Tori, he would've known from the way she's playing with the hem of her shirt that she isn't paying attention to anything that's being said, despite her nodding along in all the right places.

Alex is standing on my left, his hand keeps brushing mine, and at first, I thought it was by accident, but it's happened too many times now for it to be a coincidence.

The circle of alphas breaks apart, and I notice Alpha Mortlock look over for me. I'm just about to go over to join him when the doors open, and a group of shifters slink in. It's obvious they are shifters from their energy and the power they're throwing off, but I can't tell what type of shifters they are.

"They came," Alex comments, and his tone shows his surprise as the group positions themselves by the doorway.

"Who are they?" I ask, keeping my eyes on the group. They're shifty, and they're looking around like they are expecting us to attack them.

"They call themselves Pack Unite." I raise my eyes at the name, but he just shrugs. "They're one of the collective groups of shifters the alpha was telling you about. Murry there, the guys who's in charge?" He points to a guy who is talking quietly to the others, and they all seem to be looking to him for direction. "He's a fox shifter and he's the current alpha of the group. Next to him is Louie, a badger shifter, and Lottie, who's an otter shifter."

"How do they have an alpha of different species?" I can't even imagine how that works, as the power levels are different across species, not to mention the fact that alpha bonds don't work across species. I can feel the power of another species alpha and choose to submit because I know they are strong, but I won't be compelled to obey like I would a wolf alpha.

"They elect an alpha." My mouth drops open in surprise, that actually works? "They run as alpha for a set amount of time, and then another will be elected. It's the same with the avian shifters." I run what he's saying over in my mind, struggling with the idea of an elected alpha.

"So they're more like presidents?" I ask for clarification. Alex smiles and nods slightly.

"I guess, but don't let them hear you say that."

Everyone seems to have settled now that Pack Unite made their surprise entry, and I glance up when I hear my name called, seeing Alpha Mortlock gesturing for me to join him at the front of the room. I take a deep breath, time to get this over with.

Chapter Eighteen

As if by some unspoken signal, people begin to take their seats. I make my way over to Alpha Mortlock at the front of the room, my heart pounding at the thought of speaking before so many people. The doors open again, and three beings glide in. The room is filled with hissing and growling, and I realise who's entered the warehouse.

"They're not to be harmed, they were invited here," I say loudly, looking to the alphas to pass on the message. Some do so instantly, while others look dubious, but the hissing quiets down. I look across at the three strangers, vampires if their undead energy is anything to go by. They have the typical runway model looks with sharp features that vampires tend to possess, and if you have any doubt they're undead, the unnatural stillness they have about them is enough to convince you otherwise.

"Damon sends his best wishes," the leader says, and although he doesn't raise his voice, it carries across the room. He's tall, and his appearance would suggest he was originally from Scandinavia, with his blue eyes and cropped blond hair, his voice has a hint of an accent that could attest for this. The woman to his left is short, and you would be forgiven if you were to say she looked cute, especially since she's wearing a light blue dress that makes her look like a doll, but the hungry look in her eyes as she glances around the room takes away from that. Her crystal blonde hair falls in ringlets, only adding to the innocent doll-like look. I have to fight to hide the shudder that fills me as I watch her. The three of them move farther into the room, choosing to sit with Eric and Vella. It's only then that I notice the last woman with the newcomers isn't a vampire at all. Beneath her skirts are not two feet, but hooves. Now that I'm looking, I notice two very small horns poking out from the top of her long brown hair. Her facial features are human, but her eyes are lilac in colour and are rimmed with the longest eyelashes I have ever seen. She's wearing a floaty dress that falls to mid-calf, and her upper body is entirely human in appearance. I know from experience that below her waist, she will have goat legs. I had a fae phase when I first moved to the US, so I got um...well, acquainted with some of the local fae populations.

"She's a fawn," I mutter in shock, causing Alpha Mortlock to sharply inhale as he eyes up the new arrival. Her head flicks around to look straight at me, and I know she heard me. In fact, I now see the very tip of her pointed ears poking from the side of her hair. I nod respectfully at her, I don't want to piss off the fae. She turns back to her companions, and this raises a question—are the fae and the vampires allies? What does this mean for us? Looking around at the other alphas, I know they're thinking the same thing from their worried expressions.

I get a look from Alpha Mortlock, and I know this is my signal to begin the meeting, so I take a deep breath and look around the room. I have Killian on one side of me, and Garett on the other. There was a lot of debate about who would stand with me. I need to appear strong, so it was decided that Killian, as my fated mate and an alpha, would give the impression of strength to others who might think to threaten us. Killian also doesn't belong to any pack, and although he's staying with Moon River, he is a guest. Alex and Seb had wanted to stand with me also, but Alex, as beta for Moon River, needs to protect the alpha, and Seb would not be taken seriously as a lower-level pack member. Although it pains me, I agree that we need to appear strong. Strength is everything in the shifter community. Garett insisted on being by my side, and is a good choice since he isn't part of Moon River, so it makes us look more open to other packs, and being a bear also shows that different races of shifters can live together.

"Thank you for all coming today. I'm Ari, a lone wolf who's recently been staying with the Moon River Pack. I've been asked to be peacekeeper and run the meeting since I don't belong to any particular pack, but I have ties with many of the groups here tonight," I say, introducing myself, hearing some grumbles as I explain my ties to those in the room. I've chosen not to reveal my relationship status, but I will if it will help the course of the meeting. "We're meeting to discuss the recent disappearances and murders of supernaturals."

"Why are the bloodsuckers and witches here?" someone in the room shouts. "None of them are being murdered, only shifter bodies are turning up dead," someone spits, and I realise it's one of the lion shifters.

"We have lost people too, lion. We deserve to be involved in this meeting as much as you do," the blond Scandinavian vampire responds, he doesn't move a muscle, but his eyes flash with disdain at the shifters' comments, the only sign that he's bothered by what has been said. The lion looks like he's going to respond, if he had been in animal form, his hackles would have been raised, his whole body bristling with anger. This guy is out to start a fight, and I need to calm things down fast.

"We're all here because our people are being taken against their will. Just because only the bodies of shifters are turning up, doesn't mean that the others are still alive. Given the time that they have been gone for, it's unlikely that they still live."

There are grumbles around me, and I raise my hands to quiet them. I get some hard looks from the vampires, and I notice that the witch Tori brought with her has lowered his head. The fawn, however, is just watching me with an interested look on her face. She makes me nervous. I clear my throat and look around the room again. I'm no public speaker, and I'm sure there is a softer way to say this, but they asked me here because of my ties and people might trust me. "I know that's probably not what anyone wants to hear, but it's the truth. We need to work together to figure out what's happening." I glance over at Alpha Philips, feeling encouraged by his small nod. "Alpha Philips, how many bears have you lost?"

"Five have been taken, and the bodies of all five have returned mutilated. One was just a cub." His voice is calm, but I can see the rage in his eyes at the loss of his people. There are outraged calls at the fact a child was taken. Rage runs through me. I hadn't realised that *children* were being taken.

"How was a child taken?" someone shouts out. I had been wondering the same thing, but I wouldn't have asked it so callously. It's obvious that the bears are suffering from their losses. I see the alpha bristle, as does Max and the other bears. Even Garett looks ready to hit someone, but at a look from Philips, they all stay in place.

"The cub was with her mother at the time. We think that the mother was attacked, and the cub was taken as well."

We go around the room, and the other packs share how many they have had go missing. Over twenty-five have been taken, and all of them have turned up dead, traces of magic found at all of the scenes.

"Have these all be reported to ASP?" I ask, gobsmacked by the number of shifters taken. I hadn't realised it was on this big of a scale.

"Yeah, but ASP don't give a shit about us," someone shouts out.

"The only disappearances they've investigated are the vamps and witches. It's almost like they want a war on their hands," the alpha from the coyotes chimes in. He's been quiet up until now, and I can't help but wonder if that's exactly what ASP is after.

Based on the tension in the room and the hate towards ASP, they aren't far off from an all-out war.

"Ari, will you explain what you saw the other day, please?" Alpha Mortlock prompts, and I take a deep breath to explain. We had already decided that I was going to tell them everything about how I had seen the ASP agent while we were investigating and then about the attack. The only thing I left out was about how I had used my shadow powers and accidentally killed one of the cloaked guys. There's silence in the room until I finish my story, and then the room erupts.

"ASP must be behind it, they were watching you!"

"Why didn't you stop it?"

"Shadow Pack were involved! Weren't they behind the attacks on Moon River?"

Killian sighs behind me as we watch everyone shouting. "Quiet!" he yells, and everyone listens, turning to look at us. Many look ready to start fighting again, but no one dares antagonise Killian, knowing his reputation.

"Ari, weren't you from Shadow Pack?" the fawn asks in a crystal-clear voice, her eyes wide and innocent as she asks the question. The whole room turns from her to me with accusing expressions on their faces, and as they do, a little smirk crosses her lips before falling back into a perfectly innocent look.

I raise my eyebrows at her and continue addressing the room, heading off any more shouting.

"Yes, I was, which was why I was invited here. I know how they work and what their sick little minds are like." I turn around and lift the bottom of my shirt so they can see some of the scars on my back. "This is what Shadow Pack does to their pups. I was only six when I received my first punishments. I hold them no allegiance."

The room is silent after my admission, and several shifters in the room are looking at me with respect.

"Why would Shadow Pack be doing this?" the coyote alpha

asks again, and I see the intelligence in his eyes as he works through what information he has.

"Shadow Pack aren't clever enough to be doing this on their own. I believe someone else is behind this and they are using Shadow Pack to do their dirty work. Shadow Pack has their own agenda as well—me."

The room erupts into shouting again, but my attention is on the person who just entered the doorway in the back.

"What are we going to do?" someone asks, voices filling the room as people shout out ideas, but my focus is on the new arrival. They look around until their gaze lands on me.

"We should go to ASP again, show them how many shifters have gone missing now. Give them a reason to start looking." The suggestion comes from the corner of the room, and voices rise to offer solutions.

"We need to do this carefully, show ASP we're being peaceful, that we just want to stop our people from being taken." Alpha Mortlock's voice rises above the murmur of voices.

I narrow my eyes on the stranger, who glances down at his watch before looking back up at me, then mouths a word at me before silently slipping from the room again. I turn to look at Killian, who's glaring at the door where the person just left.

"That was the ASP agent who was watching me in the park with Tori."

Killian looks at me sharply.

"Did you see what he said?" he asks, a grim look on his face.

"He said '*Run*,'" I whisper, dread lining my stomach at Killian's nod. I turn to look around, my eyes locking with Alex's. He just sees the panic in my eyes when the doors at the back of the room slam open.

"Everybody stop! ASP officers! I said stop moving!"

The room erupts with snarls and a flurry of activity. Before I know it, I'm surrounded by my guys and the Moon River representatives, as well as Garett and the bear pack. Tori is by my side in a flash, Max and the twins surrounding her, glaring at anyone who comes close. The witch she brought with her, Eric, and the succubus, have joined us, forming a ring of supernaturals facing out at the threat.

The other packs have done similar things, surrounding their alphas to protect them. The room is suddenly swarming with officers, all holding up guns, aiming at the alphas in the room. The snarls and growls get louder as the leaders of the packs are threatened.

"You are breaking the law by organising plots against ASP. Those that leave peacefully now will be taken in for questioning before being released to their packs, you will not get into trouble as long as you comply," an ASP agent orders, looking around the room, his eyes landing on me. Many of the shifters move nervously from one foot to the other, particularly the avian shifters and the Unite shifters, who're eyeing the door. There's a moment of silence before a few break off and head for the door, being led away by a couple of agents. Growls and cries of "traitor" get shouted as they leave. I use this time to watch the agents here, none of them are the agent who had been watching us in the park, who appeared to be warning us. But why would he do that?

"No law has been broken here. We are just meeting to discuss the disappearances." Alpha Philips steps forward to explain, raising his hands in a placating gesture.

"Stop moving!" the lead agent shouts, his gun aimed squarely at the alpha.

"Yeah, the disappearances that you guys are doing *nothing about*," the mouthy lion shifter growls out, his body shaking with anger and the effort it's taking him to hold back his lion, stalking forward towards the agent.

Everything seems to go in slow motion then. Guns are raised towards the lion shifter, warnings are shouted, but the guns are shot before the warnings have even been finished. My eyes are trained on the lead agent, who's still pointing his gun at Alpha Philips, the glint in his eyes is almost feral, like everything he wanted has come to pass. Although the alpha hasn't moved a step, the gun is fired, going straight towards his heart. Without thinking I ghost forward, the shadows swallowing me and propelling me towards the alpha, pushing him out of the pathway of the bullet. I'm not quite fast enough and the bullet pierces his shoulder. He falls to his knees with a shout. That's when the chaos really begins.

The room is filled with snarling and growling, the sound of bones popping, and gunshots fill the air as shifters give in to their animal forms, attacking the ASP agents.

"Do not attack! Defend only!" Alpha Mortlock is shouting out to us as we pull back into a huddle. I look around to check that we still have everyone. Killian is next to me, watching the battle ahead carefully. Alex, Isa, and Seb are in wolf form, surrounding us and snarling at anyone who comes close. Eric and Vella are talking in quiet voices just to our right. Tori and James are standing close together, both of their hands glowing and moving in complicated patterns as they mutter under their breath, presumably working on some sort of protective spell. The bear pack has joined with us, and Garett is kneeling next to Alpha Philips, putting pressure on the wound, while Max, the twins, and the bear beta are surrounding us, facing out towards the threat.

"We need to get out of here," Killian mutters, ducking as a stray bullet whizzes past his head. "They aren't actively shooting at us at the moment because we aren't attacking, but I don't trust that lead agent." I agree with him, I saw the look in his eyes as he aimed at Alpha Philips.

I crouch down and look at the bear alpha's shoulder.

"Garett, can you move your hand please?" I ask, and the alpha moans as the wound is exposed. I can see the bullet, but there doesn't appear to be too much damage, and his shifter genes are already causing the wound the heal. "I need to get you back to pack land so I can get this bullet out. We need to go, and I'm going to need your people to help us. Do you trust us to get you out of here?" I move my gaze from the wound to his face, and I'm startled by his expression of trust.

"With my life." He nods at me before looking over at his gamma. "Max. We're getting out of here with Moon River Pack. Protect them like you would protect our own, we're in this together, got it?" Nods all around. The bear beta and one of the twins helps Alpha Philips up to standing. With a look from his alpha, the beta turns into his bear form. Eric comes to my side, his face grim. I look around and see that Vella is gone, and at my frown, he shakes his head.

"I can't hold Vella back. She's gone to hunt." Screams meet his words, and I glance over his shoulder to see an agent in Vella's arms, twitching in her embrace as she kisses him, his body shrivelling before my eyes. She drops his body with a satisfied look on her beautiful, gleaming face before she calmly stalks off to find her next victim. I shudder and look at Eric, feeling sick.

"I won't use my powers unless it's to defend myself or protect you," he tells me solemnly, understanding what I was going ask without me having to say anything.

"Right, we stick together, protect each other's back, but don't attack unless they attack you first. We don't want them having anything over us," Alpha Mortlock commands, his alpha power washing over us, and I'm reminded again why he's alpha of the pack. The screaming and snarling is making it difficult to concentrate, but we all nod, agreeing to the plan.

As a unit, we start making our way towards the exit. A couple of agents attempt to stop us, but the three wolves and the bear keep them away. As long as we stay together, we are strong and they can't stop us.

Almost as soon as I think that, I see an agent throw something towards our group and a sinking feeling fill me. Stun grenades. Devices that were developed to take out a group of supernaturals by stunning them and neutralizing their gifts.

"Stun grenades!" I shout and run towards Tori, tackling her to the ground. The others have supernatural speed, they can move out of the way fast enough, Tori on the other hand...

I look around us, dismay sinking in as I see we are now spread out across the large room, fighting our way towards the exit. Thankfully, no one is alone and they're working together to get out. I can see my guys trying to make their way back over to me, but there are too many people between us. I don't know where they're all coming from! They seem to be everywhere, and the warehouse looks like a battleground.

"Ari, are you okay? What the hell was that?" Tori's voice cuts through the haze, and I turn to look at her. She looks a bit bruised and battered, but okay, and it motivates me to get the hell out of here.

"Okay, I'm fine. Right, stay behind me. We're going to get out of here. Can you call your hellhounds?" I ask hopefully, but Tori just shakes her head at me, looking down at her hands in frustration.

"I can't access my magic, they've done something to nullify it."

"Shit!" I curse before nodding and helping her to her feet.

We start moving across the room, Tori holding onto the back of my shirt so I don't lose her, dodging bodies and people fighting as we go. I'm torn, I want to help the shifters here, but I don't have an alliance with them, and I could unknowingly start a war if I was to help one shifter group and not another. I hear a bear roar in pain and stop in my tracks, my heart stutters when I see Garett is okay, battling his way towards us, but his brother, Max, is in trouble, surrounded by several agents. Garett looks back over at me, and he's torn.

"Go! Help him!" I shout, and he nods before running over to help his brother.

We are nearly at the door when someone tackles me, sending me flying to the ground. Someone straddles my waist, and a fist flies towards my face, and I narrowly miss it by trying to twist away. I can't tell if the agent trying to pin me to the ground is a man or a woman, because of the balaclava type mask covering their face. I buck my hips to try and throw them off, and I manage to catch them off guard and scrabble to my feet. They jump up with speed only granted by being a shifter. My wolf pushes to the surface in disgust and rage. Gunshots and screams are filling the air, but I focus on my attacker. A shifter siding with ASP against us is enough to make me feel sick. Killian and Alex's training runs through my head as the agent tries to tackle me again and pin my arms. I raise my knee and smash it against their groin, realizing my attacker is a man when he groans and crouches forward to protect his now crushed nuts. Kicking forward, I knock him to the ground. I wait for a few seconds to see if he's going to get back up.

A shot nearby has me quickly standing to my full height, and I look around for Tori. She's staring at a bullet hole in the wall just to her left, before looking back at me, a nervous laugh escaping her.

"Fucking hell, that was close!" She steps towards me, and the agent I just fought sits up and aims a gun at Tori. Everything seems to move in slow motion again as I run towards Tori, except this time, my shadows don't respond to me. The gunshot goes off, shockingly loud, and pierces Tori in the forehead.

I watch as the shock briefly registers on her face, before her eyes go blank and her face drops. Her body soon follows, landing on the ground with a thud. In the background, I hear what sounds like bellowing, but all I can focus on is Tori's lifeless body. Something registers within me, and the world speeds back up to normal.

"No." I shake my head and run to her side, dropping to my knees. I can't look at the wound, if I do, I'll have to admit that Tori is dead. "No, no, no, no, no, this isn't happening," I mutter under my breath, my breathing becoming faster and more erratic as I try to take her pulse. Nothing. Not a single heartbeat. I finally look up at Tori's face and the tiny bullet hole in the centre of her head. I try not to look at the back of her head, but I can smell the blood, and I know it's pointless. Hot tears pool in my eyes, and a wordless scream rips out of my body, full of rage, hopelessness, and grief. I'm aware of my guys running towards me, my name is being shouted out, but all I can focus on is Tori's expressionless face.

"Target number four has been neutralized." The agent is far enough away that I shouldn't have been able to hear him talking into his radio over all of the noise in the room, but I do. His raspy voice snaps me out of my daze, and I stand up, my rage pushing me past grief into something else. I turn to face the man that murdered my best friend. I give into my wolf, letting her take over my body, and that dark shadowy place inside me begs to be let unleashed. I glance at Tori again, all traces of mercy wiped away at the sight of her body. I close my eyes and unleash the darkness within me, and in a whirr of shadows, claws, and fangs, me and my wolf tear the agent to shreds.

Epilogue

I know before I've even opened my eyes that I'm in the Shadow Realm. The lack of sound in the atmosphere around me is a dead giveaway, not to mention that my arm is throbbing from where the shadow beasts wounded me the first time I was here. I glance around dully, yup, nothing's changed. I close my eyes again, curling up on my side.

Tori's dead.

In the warehouse, my wolf form had become shadow, seamlessly using the shadows to ghost from place to place, ripping the agents to pieces. I know I should feel regret or remorse for killing them, but the only thing I feel is numb. I hadn't known that my wolf form and my shadow powers worked together. If only I had known that sooner, I may have been able to save Tori.

"I suspected I would find you here." Em's voice flows over me, but I don't open my eyes, I don't even move. "I'm sorry. I heard about what happened," he says quietly, and it's his tone that makes me open my eyes, not his words, but the pain and grief in them reaches me.

"How do you know what happened?" I ask, looking up at him from my curled position on the ground.

"You are tied to the Shadow Realm with your powers, as am I. I can sense when you use your powers," he explains, and I suspect he isn't telling the whole truth, but I don't have the energy to argue with him. Sighing, I push myself off the ground and look up at him again. His body is still in his light form, but he seems dimmer today, like the life has been sucked from him.

"You know that my best friend is dead?" My voice cracks on the last word. Although I can't fully see his features because of the light, I sense his empathy for me as he nods.

"Losing someone is never easy."

"Why are you here?" My words are quiet, lost.

"I wanted to check that you were okay," he's silent for a moment before he sighs and sits down in front of me. "And I have something to tell you." I look up at him expectantly, is now really the time? "You need some answers, and I can help. It's time to come and find me." I frown at him, wondering where this has come from all of a sudden. "It's to do with the disappearances and shifter deaths. But you're not going to like it, and it won't be easy to get to me." He rubs his hand across his face.

"Okay, where are you?" Perhaps if I can focus on something other than Tori's death, it will stop me from feeling like my heart has been ripped out of my chest.

"Don't get mad at me, just hear me out." I frown at his words, what is he talking about?

"I work for ASP."

The End

BONUS SCENE

The night Tori and Ari met

SIX YEARS AGO
TORI

I sink the shot and savour the burning sensation of the fae alcohol as it travels down my throat. I grin at the summer fae who is watching me with narrowed eyes. They say never challenge the fair folk to a drinking game, but I can't help it, I've never been one to turn down a challenge. Fae alcohol packs a punch, so I'll probably regret this in the morning, but thankfully, it takes a lot of alcohol to affect me.

"Garett, get us another one, will ya?" I call out to the cute bartender. The bear shifter and I have been acquaintances for a while now, and while he's attractive, I stay away from dating shifters, too possessive for me.

"Tori, you want to switch to the human stuff?" he asks, his voice might be rough and assertive, but I can see his concern for me in his eyes. Rolling my own, I shake my head, pushing the glass towards him again.

"Nah, I have a bet to win!" I reply with a grin, and although he doesn't agree with my choice, his lips turn up in a slight smile at my exuberance before filling my glass with the fluorescent blue alcohol. Turning a glare on the fae sitting next to me, he growls at them.

"If anything happens to her, I will rip you limb from limb," he threatens, and I watch as they pale and nod quickly in agreement. I grin at Garett and wink at him, there are benefits to having a bear shifter as a friend.

The bell above the bar door dings as someone walks in, and I freeze as a wave of powerful energy rolls over me. Turning on my bar stool, I search for the source of power and my eyebrows rise at what a see. A young woman, about my age, is walking towards the bar. Her face is set in a glare, and anyone who looks her way gets a snarl. Her expression may be fierce, but something inside her is broken. Her body is pale and thin, and she looks like she hasn't eaten a proper meal in years. Her hair is hanging limply around her shoulders, and I think that she could be beautiful if she smiled, but her severe expression gives off a *fuck off* vibe. The thing that attracts my attention the most though, is the energy she's giving off. She's a shifter, I can tell that much, but she's also *more*. I think I know what she is, but that could be dangerous for the both of us if I say anything.

I decide to just watch and stay out of her way, which is difficult when she takes the barstool next to me. Garett walks over, his eyes softening as he takes in her bedraggled state.

"What can I get you?" he asks, his voice bringing her eyes up as she assess him, as if to see if he's a threat.

"Just a glass of water," she responds, her British accent clear to hear. Huh, I guess it's not true what they say about Brits being polite. Garett nods and pours her a glass while running his eyes over her, a frown forming between his brows.

"Sure I can't get you any food?" I hear her stomach growl at his question, and her face goes blank for a second before she shakes her head.

She can't be serious, she looks like she's starving. I glance at the glass of water and a thought comes to me. This girl isn't going to accept any pity or food from me, so I've got to make her accept. A plan starts forming in my mind, and I try to hide my grin as I swallow back my shot. Turning to the summer fae next to me, I lean forward and press a kiss to his cheek before hopping off the bar stool and walking to the exit.

"Sorry, hun, I've got to go, we'll finish this up another day."

"Wait, you can't leave, we're in the middle of a challenge!" the fae sputters, outraged. Well, he'll be even more outraged when he realises I've been magicking the alcohol so it's essentially water. I grin to myself and flip him off as I step out of the bar.

I don't have to wait outside the bar for long before the girl leaves. Making sure I time it right, I hurry from the alley and smack straight into her.

"Oh my, I'm so sorry!" I cry out as I reach out to steady her. Growling at me, she takes a step back, swatting at my reaching hand.

"Watch where you're going!" she snarls, her eyes glowing with her inner animal, wolf I think. My powers are fairly good at sniffing out people's gifts, and she's screaming wolf.

"I'm really sorry," I say again, trying to sound like I mean it. "Look, let me make it up to you. I'm going to the burger joint around the corner to eat as much as I can physically stuff in my face, why don't I get you something?" I see her eyes narrow at me in suspicion, but I know she wants to say yes. Her stomach growling again makes the decision for her, and I nod as if she's answered me out loud.

"Good. Let's go!" I declare and start walking towards the restaurant, not giving her a chance to say no. I feel her hesitation, but I keep walking and smile the moment I hear her following me. When she reaches my side, I look over at her again. I don't know why I feel such a connection to this girl, it's not that I pity her, it's like I feel a kinship to her. Perhaps we share a similar history. I remember having the same lost look in my eyes not that long ago.

"What's your name?" I ask, not sure if she will answer me, especially as the silence stretches. Her eyes flick to me before going back to watching our surroundings.

"Ari. Yours?" I'm so surprised she answered me that I nearly stumble, but I manage to keep my footing.

"Tori," I reply, smiling again as a realisation dawns on me. "You know what, Ari? I think we're going to be good friends."

The barrier of distrust she holds around herself is going to take a lot to break through. I know she doesn't believe me when she rolls her eyes, but her lips twitch up into the semblance of a smile. I was right—she is beautiful when she smiles.

EMBRACED
BY
SHADOWS

SHADOWBORN SERIES BOOK THREE

ERIN O'KANE

Prologue

Killian

"Killian, you have to talk to her. She's tearing herself apart." My eyes narrow and dart to Garett as he comes to stand by my side. I want to snarl at him, say that I know, that I can feel her guilt and despair at the loss of Tori. But I don't, knowing he's struggling with this just as much as I am. Rubbing at my chest where the bond between myself and Ari seems to sit, I shrug in response to his comment.

"What am I going to say? You know I'm no good at this feelings stuff." The words are gruff and full of self-loathing at not being able to help my mate. I feel Garett's full attention turn from Ari to me, his hand landing on my shoulder in a brotherly gesture. If you'd have asked me a year ago if I would be having this conversation with a bear shifter, I'd have laughed in your face.

"You have a bond with her that I don't, you can reach through the pain and darkness and bring her back to us." His words hold a truth that gives me some hope.

Turning to look at my mate again, I feel my heart clutch painfully as we watch her training in the gym, her body flickering in and out of shadow as she runs through the obstacle course.

"It's not going to be easy. I know firsthand how tightly grief can hold you down." My voice is weary as I rub my hand over my face, none of us have been getting much sleep recently.

"Which is why you're the best person to help her through this," he responds, and we both fall back into silence as we watch Ari battle her demons.

Chapter One

Ducking, I bare my teeth at the invisible attacker as I weave through the obstacle course, my body ghosting in and out of the shadows. None of the imagined attackers have faces, just the black masks that the ASP agents use.

My body screams in protest as I push it to its limits, ignoring the pain, needing to get stronger, faster. I know I'm being watched, but I don't let that stop me, and I continue training until my heart is pounding in my chest and my legs feel like they're going to give way. Finally, when I can't push any further, I stop and roll my neck, stretching my weary limbs. Walking slowly to the corner of the room, I grab my drink bottle and towel from where I left them, taking a deep swig of water. Wiping my face and neck, I take some deep inhales to settle my breathing, glancing up as a tug in my chest alerts me to my mate prowling towards me.

Both Garett and Killian are walking over to meet me, the former has his usual tender smile, but there's a tightness in his eyes that makes me look away. I know he's worried about me, but he wants to talk about what happened, about Tori, and I can't deal with that right now. Looking over at Killian, I see he has his trademark scowl in place, although the corner of his lip twitches up into a semi-smile that I know is purely for me.

Pushing off of the wall, I meet them halfway, wrapping my arms around them both and silently pulling them into my embrace. Killian lets out a surprised grunt, but doesn't say anything, just nuzzling his face into my hair and inhaling deeply. We've discovered that the true mate bond seems to make our scents more attractive to each other, especially since I've allowed my wolf to take over more.

"Ari." Garett's deep voice rumbles through me, bringing my attention back to him. Looking up, I know what he's going to say from the look on his face, and I'm not ready to hear it yet. I place a hand on his cheek, guide his face down to mine, and press our lips together. I know he wants to pull away, to say what he's been trying to say for the last week since the attack in the warehouse, but he relents under my kisses, returning them softly. I feel Killian stiffen slightly from where he is flush against me, but he doesn't move away. Instead, he starts pressing soft kisses to my neck. Our kisses begin to heat up, causing a flash of desire to shoot through me. My wolf is demanding, and right now, she wants her mates. Sure, Garett might not officially be her mate, but she's claimed him as hers.

A throat clearing in the room has us pulling away from each other's lips, a guilty smirk on Garett's face as we turn to acknowledge the other person in the room. We're in the Long Claw training gym, and standing opposite us is Alpha Philips, the leader of the bear pack, who's wearing a knowing smile on his lips.

"Alpha Philips, it's good to see you again." I bow my head slightly to him in a show of respect, but he just rolls his eyes and strides up to me, pulling me into a one-armed hug. I can't help but notice that he looks at Killian before he touches me, checking that my mate isn't going to go all territorial and start attacking him. I hold back a snort, Killian knows better than to pull that kind of shit. Although I'm usually against being touched by people I don't know well, I'm starting to get used to the bear's touchy-feely attitudes. As he embraces me, a pang fills my chest at his affectionate gesture. With the amount of trouble I've caused his pack, he shouldn't be treating me like a daughter. My thoughts must be clear on my face, as he frowns at me when he leans back.

"Ari, we've had this chat already. You only saw me yesterday, you don't have to keep greeting me like that. You're welcome in this pack. You've done much for us, over and over again. When will you start to realise your own worth?" Pulling away from his touch, I shrug off what he's saying, trying to fight the uncomfortable feeling his words bring.

I know deep down that the attack wasn't my fault, except I can't help but feel responsible, so I'll keep helping them as much as I can to redeem myself. I feel like I've just about earned my place in the Moon River Pack, but that was after months of working there and the relentless efforts of the pack to encourage me to embrace their way of life, so it's going to take much more time until I feel like I belong here at Long Claw.

Garett must sense my discomfort and saves me from answering the alpha's question by asking about pack business. He's been splitting his time between being with me at the wolf pack and helping here after the loss of several pack members from the attack. He's barely set foot in his bar recently and has hired a young bear from the pack to oversee the running of it. He says he doesn't mind, but I know he misses it.

"How is Max? And the twins?" Killian asks, the change of subject causing a wave of sadness to wash through me. The alpha's face turns grave, and the air seems to deflate out of him as he looks at Garett. I turn to stare up at my bear and see that he's trying to keep his face neutral, probably so as not to upset me, but I can tell he's troubled.

"Garett? What's going on, is everyone okay?" My voice rises in pitch with my concern for his brothers.

Another reason I've been training here is so I can be close to

Garett's brothers. Just before the attack in the warehouse, Max and the twins found their fated mate, the bears' version of the true mated pair bond. I have no idea why fate was so cruel to let them find their mate, and then rip her from them so shortly after they'd met. Tori, my best friend, had triggered their bond, only to be killed during the attack. I haven't seen Max, the oldest of the brothers and the pack gamma, but I've visited the twins every day since. They've been...struggling.

Garett sighs before turning to look at me, his pain clear to see in his expression as he takes one of my hands in his.

"We didn't want to say anything, you feel guilty enough as it is, but they aren't getting better. I don't know what to do..." His voice hitches as he trails off. I've never seen this side of Garett before, and it makes me nervous. Killian's face is grave, and he steps forward and places a hand on the bear's shoulder in a comforting gesture.

"I know what it's like to lose someone so important to you. If I can help, then I will." His offer is genuine, and Garett nods his thanks to my mate.

"Thank you, Killian, we might need to take you up on that," Alpha Phillips replies. I look between the three of them, feeling frustration building in me as it becomes obvious I'm missing something.

"Will someone please tell me what's going on?" I demand, starting to lose my temper, my wolf walking just under the surface of my skin as my eyes glow with power.

Everyone looks uncomfortable, and eventually, the alpha nods and rubs the back of his neck.

"Max has lost control of his bear. Losing Tori has broken something inside him, and we can't reach him to bring him back to us," Philips explains, and I feel like I've been punched in the stomach. I've known Max wasn't fit for his duties as pack gamma, but I thought he'd taken off for a bit to get some space. I didn't know he's stuck in his bear form.

Killian's comment makes more sense now. He once told me how he lost control after losing his mate. When someone loses their fated mate, they not only lose the love of their life, but a part of themselves. The loss is so damaging to a shifter that they often die as well, or live a half-life, always craving something they can't have.

"No." The word bursts out of me. I won't let Max or the twins die because of this, even if it means I spend the rest of my life trying to make theirs more meaningful. They're my family, but I also owe it to Tori. "Let me see him."

"Ari, I'm not so sure that's a good idea—" Garett starts, obviously worried for my safety. But I can see he's torn, that part of him hopes, deep down, that I can help. I squeeze his hand and open my mouth to object, to say that I have to try, but Killian beats me to it.

"Let her try."

I spin around to look at him, shocked he's agreeing with this. Garett must be just as surprised as I am, judging by his expression. "Besides, we'll be there if we need to step in," Killian adds. His usual harsh expression is softer as he looks over at Garett, seeing the strain this is putting on him. I wonder at what point they went from adversaries to this kind of brotherhood. To be honest, seeing this more endearing side to Killian is making me realise that I still haven't scratched the surface with him. There is so much more to my grouchy mate than he lets people believe, his interaction with Garett only reminds me of this.

Garett and the alpha share a look before the latter nods and gestures for me to follow him. I hadn't expected to see him now, but there is no time like the present, I guess. My two men follow behind me as I walk alongside the alpha.

"Is this sort of thing common?" I keep my voice low as we work our way through the gym, not sure how much the other members of his pack know. Wincing, the alpha shakes his head.

"Yes and no. We haven't had a set of fated mates in years, none of the bear packs have, so I was ecstatic that the boys had found one. It was a bit of a shock that their mate was a witch, but I was happy for them," he elucidates before taking us down a corridor with a set of secure metal doors at the end. "For many bear shifters, our animals are very powerful and we can struggle to control them. Something as horrific as losing your fated mate is enough to let them take control."

Just before we reach the doors, Alpha Philips turns into a little alcove I hadn't noticed before. A floor-to-ceiling, one-way mirror fills the wall and, as I look in, I can't stop the little gasp that leaves my lips.

The inside of the room looks like it's been hit by a hurricane. The padded walls have been shredded, pillows and blankets are scattered around, their stuffing spread about the room like snow. In the middle of it all stands the biggest bear I've ever seen. I thought Garett was large in his animal form, but this is a whole new level. The bear has fur so dark, it's almost black, and standing on all fours, he's the size of a horse, with long, gleaming claws poking from his large paws.

"Let me in there." I can't seem to pull my eyes away from the bear in the room, but I can feel Garett stiffen next to me, wanting to protest.

"Are you sure, Ari?" Alpha Phillips asks. "You have nothing to prove, you don't have to do this." I can tell he's conflicted, but I meet his gaze and nod once.

"I do," I respond. I need to at least try.

Without another word, the alpha walks me to the door and presses a code into a pad. When the door opens, I hurry inside, and it closes quickly behind me, the lock reverberating loudly as I'm trapped inside the room with a feral bear.

The bear freezes, stopping his destruction as he lets out a heavy breath before turning to face me. He pulls his lips back in a snarl as he follows my movements with his gleaming, black eyes.

"Max. It's Ari, I'm here to help you," I murmur in a soothing tone, staying as still as I can. The last thing I want to do is antagonise a massive bear three times my size. He lets out a keening sound that's laced with pain, a sound I've never heard a bear make before. He suddenly shakes his head as if to clear a thought before his eyes narrow on me, and, with a bellow, he charges towards me.

Oh shit.

Chapter Two

I don't let myself think.

Instead, I trust my instincts, using my shadow powers to ghost to the other side of the room. His snarls fill the room, and I fight against the instinct to cover my ears as I turn to face the bear. He's looking around, searching for me, his nose raised in the air. Turning, he growls again as he spots me, and I notice any signs of the human part of him have completely disappeared.

"Hey, big guy, I need to speak to Max right now. You're safe, you both are, I'm not here to hurt you." Despite my thumping heart, I keep my words calm, trying to reach out to the man within. I'm dealing with the animal right now, but I need to speak to Max, to lure him to the surface so I can get him to shift back into his human form. My attempts at drawing Max out fails as the bear rears back, roars, and charges once again. Well, the calm and steady plan obviously failed. He doesn't want to give up control. I guess I'll just have to convince him then.

Using the speed gifted to me from my shifter genes, I dart to the side, trying not to rely on my shadow powers—they still aren't reliable and have been unpredictable. A massive paw comes swiping towards me, and I only narrowly avoid it by ducking quickly.

"Max, snap out of it!" I shout. There's no time to be nice, not when I have an eight-foot bear trying to kill me. "How's Garett going to take it if you kill me? Do you really want that, to put him through this too?" The bear pauses, and I have a moment of reprieve to back away, putting some space between us. Circling each other, I eye him for any signs of his human side surfacing.

"I'm sorry about Tori." My voice cracks on her name, and the bear snarls at me, flinching as if I struck him. "But I lost her too, and I'm not moping in my animal form. I'm trying to do something about it." There's a spark of awareness in his gaze a second before the bear roars, and I know I've pissed them both off. Fine, if I need to get him angry, then that's what I'll do. Shifting on my feet, I get ready for the attack I'm sure is imminent.

"I held her in my arms, but she was already dead. The bullet went straight through her head, and she didn't even see it coming." I spit the words out, my own anger growing inside me, wrapping itself around my heart. A single tear rolls down my face as the images of that night flash through my head. Something wraps around my arms and when I look down, I see I'm wrapped in shadows, embraced by them. At first, I think that I've turned into my shadow form, but I see the shadowy tendrils are actually manifesting around my body, flickering in and out of existence, pulsing with my anger.

Taking advantage of my distraction, the bear roars, a sound full of pain and rage. I snap my gaze up, watching as he charges towards me, but I don't move a muscle, meeting his furious gaze with one of my own. The impact knocks my breath from me, but it doesn't actually hurt much. Now standing over me, the bear presses his face close to mine as he growls, sniffing me. My scent must trigger something in him as I see a flash of recognition in his eyes.

"I'm going to get the bastards that did this, with or without your help. And when I find them, I'm going to tear them to shreds." I can feel my shadowy cloak pulse around me with my anger, and I'm pretty sure my eyes are glowing with the strength of my wolf.

She's with me, prowling under the surface of my skin in case I need her. We're fully in agreement right now. Someone needs to pay.

My stomach drops when I see anger twist the bear's face as he stands up on his back legs, his claws outstretched and ready to make a killing blow. I failed to reach him. I know I could turn into shadow, but something inside me is telling me to stay where I am. I close my eyes, listening to my instincts once again.

"I'm sorry. I loved her, and I know you would've too." The anger drains from me, my words soft.

I flinch as something heavy lands against me, but I'm not filled with pain like I had expected. Opening my eyes, I see Max's anguished gaze, so much like his brother's, that for a moment, I think Garett's jumped in front of me. Taking a deep breath, I realise that's not the case, his scent is different than Garett's, and looking closer, I see the differences I missed before.

"Max." As soon as his name leaves my lips, his face twists, and a tear drips onto my cheek.

"I nearly killed you." His voice is hoarse from lack of use. His eyes run over my face, like he's trying to be sure what he's seeing is real. After being stuck in his bear form for the better part of a week, I'm not surprised. The muscles in his arms bunch like he's trying to hold himself back, his jaw clenching as he fights for control.

"But you didn't." The simple words seem to register something in him as he relaxes slightly, his eyes closing as if he's in pain. I'm acutely aware that I'm lying underneath a very naked man who is almost pressed up against me, and I can feel frustration emanating down the bond from Killian.

"It hurts." The pain in his voice brings tears to my eyes. I nod, not looking away from the rawness in his gaze, even though I want to.

"I know," I whisper, "but we'll find the people that did this and make them pay. I don't know if ASP is connected to the disappearing shifters as well, but we'll figure it out. I need your help, and you need to stay strong for your brothers. Can you do that?" My voice gains more conviction as I speak, trying to give him a purpose, a reason to fight. When he narrows his eyes on me, I know I have his full attention, his gaze glowing black for a moment as his bear fights to take control once more.

"What do you mean? What's wrong with my brothers?" When he speaks like this, I can see why he's pack gamma. His authority rolls over me. I take a deep breath, feeling suffocated by the waves of his power as my wolf tries to show her dominance. Pushing her back down, I make sure to keep eye contact with him.

"They also lost their mate," I say gently, "so they're struggling too. They need you, they need their older brother, their gamma, to help them through this." He needs this motivation. The desire bears have to protect their own is a powerful thing, and I don't feel bad for using that to my advantage. Besides, I'm being truthful, the twins are struggling. He'll see for himself when he's fully in control. "Will you help me?"

He watches me for a few moments, his face thoughtful, before nodding and sitting back onto his heels and pushing up to stand. Leaning down, he offers me a hand and pulls me to my feet. He runs his eyes over me, and if it was anyone else, I would've felt that he was checking me out, but I know he's just ensuring he didn't hurt me.

"Sorry," he apologises softly, giving me a small, gentle smile. He doesn't explain what his regret is for, and he doesn't need to, so I just offer him my own slight smile. I feel a kinship to him, a connection that is only formed by losing someone. But I'm learning that there's a strength in that, and we'll survive it.

I glance towards the locked door as a feeling of impatience and frustration reaches me through the bond.

"We better head out there before my mate rips that door from the wall," I joke, smirking, even though it's not far from the truth. Max's smile drops at the word 'mate,' and I instantly feel bad. Good job, Ari. I open my mouth to say something, but he just shakes his head, the corner of his mouth turning up.

He walks past me towards the door, but pauses just before he reaches it, glancing at me over his shoulder.

"I won't forget what you've done for me or my family," he declares before knocking on the door.

I guess we just added a new member to our new little ragtag family. Last year, that thought would have terrified me, but now I feel a little part of me glowing.

Killian

I'm pacing in the alcove behind that blasted one-way mirror that's separating me from my mate. I can feel her anxiety down the bond, but mostly, I can feel her resolution. She *needs* to do this, which is why I didn't stop her earlier. I'm now regretting this decision, and my wolf is prowling within my mind, ready to spring into action if we need to protect her.

A pain in my hands has me glancing down. My palms are bleeding, my nails having punctured my skin. Watching Ari weaving around the room, trying to avoid a huge bear shifter, is almost enough to cause me to lose control.

Garett, Alpha Philips, and I now watch as Ari is pinned beneath the naked shifter.

"Her powers are growing." I don't turn from the window, keeping my eyes on my mate, but I nod in acknowledgment of Garett's words. He's right—she's getting stronger every day. It seems now that she's accepted her power, she isn't constantly fighting against what she is, *who* she is, and her abilities are coming to her more easily. She doesn't agree, she thinks she's still weak, that she can't control them well enough, but I think that's more out of fear of what she's becoming, or what she *could* become.

"I've never seen anything like it," Alpha Philips comments, and I have to agree.

I think back to the moment her shadow appeared in these training sessions, causing panic to rise within me, thinking she was being pulled back to the Shadow Realm. But I realized when she was taken from us before, I hadn't been able to see the shadows. This was something different. It had wrapped around her like a lover, caressing her skin.

When the bear charged to attack, I was ready to rip that damned door off its fucking hinges, but a feeling of calm and acceptance rolled down through our bond. Not her acceptance of imminent death, but trust in her powers to protect her.

My brave, foolhardy mate then faced off against the raging bear, looking like an avenging angel, her shadowy tendrils flaring out around her. She'd never been more beautiful to me than in that moment, darkness and all.

A deep breath beside me brings my attention back to the present, and I glance at my pack brother. I startle for a moment. When did I start thinking of Garett as pack? The old Killian would never have even considered being in a pack with a bear and certainly wouldn't share a mate with anyone else. I don't share well, I'm too selfish. But something about Ari has started to change that. I don't always like it, but Garett and the others offer me something I didn't think was possible after I lost Julie.

A family.

I place my hand on his shoulder, feeling some of the tension leave him as Ari and Max get to their feet. I know it's been difficult for him—keeping the news about Max from Ari. He's worried about his brothers, but he was trying to protect her.

"Your mate is incredible," Alpha Philips remarks as he turns towards us, shaking his head in amazement. I'm not sure if he's talking to Garett or me, but we both nod in agreement. Although, a part of me wants to turn on the alpha with my teeth bared and demand that he never speaks a word of what he's witnessed today, I push that instinct down. Ari likes this guy, and he has offered her sanctuary and help, so I don't want to jeopardise that. If Garett thinks he's a good guy, I'll have to trust that he's right.

The naked shifter is looking my mate up and down, and even though I know it's not in a sexual way, my wolf, along with jealousy, rises up. A quiet growl leaves my throat as I watch them.

"Can we please open the fucking door now?" I snarl, pacing the small space and turning my head side to side so I keep Ari within my sight.

"She's safe, my brother won't hurt her," Garett states with a slight smile, but he puts me out of my misery when he walks towards the keypad on the wall.

Apparently, this room is what they use when young bears change for the first time—their first shifts are renowned for being brutal. Bears are such strong animals that it can take a while to learn to control that spirit. But right now, I couldn't give a crap. I need to feel my mate in my arms.

A little burst of love reaches me through the bond, and I stop my pacing, a wry smile appearing on my face. This is Ari's way of telling me I'm being a territorial 'alpha male baby,' as she loves to call me.

A knock on the door arrives just as Garett punches in the code, and the door swings open to reveal Max.

"Brother," Garett calls out as he embraces Max. I shuffle from foot to foot, my patience waning, before I can wait no longer. Pushing past the two of them, I ignore the snort of laughter from the alpha and the 'asshole' comment Max throws my way as I stride over to Ari. My eyes roam over her body, looking for any damage, before meeting her gaze. With a small, tentative smile, she holds out her hand for me to take.

"Let's go home."

Chapter Three

As Killian's car pulls up outside Moon River Pack's medical building, he turns off the engine, and silence fills the space between us. I look up at the building I now call home, and a slight smile crosses my lips as the sound of people inside reaches us, particularly Seb's laughter. I'm not exactly sure when this place became my home, but I'm pretty sure it has something to do with the guys all claiming a piece of my heart.

I turn to look at one of those guys, only to see that Killian's eyes are already on me. Garett stayed behind with Max and the twins, and although it pains me that he won't be here with us tonight, I understand he's needed there. Killian looks relaxed as he leans against the driver's seat, but his stare is heavy.

"You scared me today." His voice is low and steady. "Seeing you in there against that bear made me want to tear that fucking door down." I wait for him to admonish me, my hackles beginning to rise at the thought of him not believing or trusting that I can take care of myself, but it doesn't come. I lean back and watch him, my eyes assessing for signs of anger, since he's been quiet the whole drive back.

"But you didn't." My words are careful, more of a question than a statement.

"No, I didn't," he replies, leaning across the centre console of the car so he's only inches from my face. "Because I knew you could handle yourself. Besides, I was there, so if you were ever truly in danger, I would've stepped in." I'm about to protest that I can, and did, handle it, but he stops me with a predatory kiss. I yield under his firm lips, kissing him back just as fiercely. If I'm truthful with myself, I find the thought of him watching, waiting in the wings, and ready to protect me if I needed him a huge turn-on. He growls into my mouth as I bite down on his lower lip, pulling his face away from me so I can see his eyes glowing with the power of his wolf.

"It was one of the hottest and fucking scariest things I've ever seen. My mate facing off against a shifter three times her size and coming away without a single scratch. I didn't know whether to storm in there and shout at you or fuck you." His lips meet mine again, and I practically crawl onto his lap, his words igniting something inside me. He pulls me close, so I'm straddling his lap. I thread my fingers through his hair, enjoying his moan as I tug on it and pull his head back. His hands move to my back, holding me in place as his erection presses against me through our clothes.

"You're magnificent." His words are breathless as he moves his hands up and down my back. I press kisses against his neck, gently nipping at his pulse point. His erection twitches against me, and with a smile, I nip at him again, enjoying being in control. He so rarely lets go. "Although, I can't guarantee that I won't tear that bear apart the next time I see him for daring to attack my mate," he growls out, cupping my face in his hands. He brings his lips down on mine, leading me in a powerful kiss before pulling back once again. "You're mine."

I'm trying to decide whether or not to kick his possessive ass or give in to him, when a knock on the car window startles us. We're so caught up in each other that we didn't notice someone coming up to the car. Pulling away from Killian, I look up to see a smiling

Seb waving at us with a smug look in his eyes. He obviously enjoyed having the opportunity to sneak up on us.

"Fucking pup," Killian mutters under his breath, and I can't help but laugh at how happy Seb is to see us.

Pulling open the door, he offers me his hand and helps me out of the car, wrapping his arms around me as soon as I'm standing.

"I heard the car pull up and I wanted to see you." His words are innocent, but the little gleam in his eye lets me know he knew exactly what was going on in the car. As if the fogged up windows weren't already a huge giveaway. Seb seems to get a kick out of doing things to piss Killian off, and surprisingly, Killian lets him get away with it. He'll act like he's angry, but I've felt a little surge of something down the bond on more than one occasion, something akin to belonging. Their relationship is more like a bond siblings would have, not that Killian would ever admit it.

Killian glares at Seb as he gets out of the car and adjusts his trousers, which does nothing to hide his erection pressing against the fabric. It's begging to be freed, and I can't decide whether to laugh or drag him into the nearest bedroom.

"Seems you got yourself a bit of a problem there," Seb comments with a raised eyebrow.

"It wouldn't be a problem if you hadn't interrupted us," Killian growls out, and although I know he isn't truly mad, he pushes a bit of his alpha power into the words anyway. Seb stiffens in my arms, and I feel that strange power start to build up in him.

Pushing back, I glance at Killian, who's watching Seb warily, darting his eyes between the two of us. The way he's looking at Seb, it's as if he's a threat, but Seb would never hurt me, right? Turning my attention back to Seb, I see his eyes are glowing slightly and fixed on Killian. But his eyes aren't the most surprising thing, no, it's the unearthly pulsing waves of power coming off of him. We know this shouldn't be possible. A werewolf is born with a level of power. Some have alpha power, which is stronger and makes the shifter capable of becoming an alpha, but this level of power is unchangeable. Somehow, Seb is changing. It shouldn't be possible, and it's worrying.

"Seb." Although my voice is quiet, it seems to jolt him out of whatever trance he was in, and his blinking, confused eyes meet mine. Killian gently takes my hand and tries to pull me away. Seb immediately releases me, backing up as hurt flashes over his features when he realizes Killian's trying to protect me from him.

"Kill, it's fine, Seb won't hurt me," I tell him firmly, confidently, but I have to admit that these little 'power surges' concern me.

"I-I'll see you inside," Seb mumbles, the light going out of his eyes as he turns and hurries inside.

"Seb, wait!" I call out, taking a step to follow after him, when I feel a hand tighten around my own.

"Leave him, give him some space," Killian advises before he pulls me into his arms. The benefit of our bond is that he gets glimpses of my feelings, and right now, I'm scared for Seb. Killian knows I'd never ask him to comfort me, but he also knows that's exactly what I need right now. With a sigh, I bury my face in his chest, inhaling his calming scent.

A few moments later, I hear a set of footsteps and move out of Killian's arms. When I turn to face the medical building, I see Eric approaching. Greeting me with a little smile, he leans against the doorframe, his arms crossed over his broad chest. Eric is the newest edition to our strange little family, and we're all still learning how he fits in with our group. We were friends for years, working together at the hospital, and sure, there was always chemistry there, but I thought he was human, so refused to take our relationship any further. Not long ago, he admitted what he really was, a type of incubus, and that I was his fated mate.

Seems that fate has a weird sense of humour.

Incubi discover their mates through visions triggered by some form of extreme event, and in our case, that 'extreme event' was me being stuck in the Shadow Realm. Once they discover their fated mates, incubi can't feed properly until the bond is accepted. Something we have yet to do. Since he's told me what he really is, he doesn't hide his presence from me anymore. I run my eyes over him, feeling his otherworldly power. Even half-starved, his power is phenomenal. I shudder to think how powerful he'll be if we complete the bond.

His white button-down shirt looks tight across his chest, and his smart, dark denim jeans hide muscular legs. When I bring my gaze back up, his blue eyes are twinkling slightly. He knows I was just checking him out.

Busted.

"I felt something out here, is everything okay?" He's still smiling, but I can hear the note of concern in his voice. Sighing, I walk up the steps to the porch and shrug my shoulders.

"Seb," is all I say. I frown when he nods, as if he was expecting that answer.

"I was going to ask you about his little..." He pauses to gather his words, a wrinkle appearing between his brows. "Power episodes," he finishes. I can tell he wanted to say something else, but he's holding back, which worries me. Taking a step closer, I put my hand on his arm, ignoring when his pupils dilate at my touch and the way his body seems to *hum* with energy.

"Do you know what's happening to him?" I try to keep my voice calm, quiet, since I don't want Seb knowing we're talking about him, but I can't help the feeling of urgency that fills my tone.

"Not really, but they feel a little like the bursts of power new demons go through," Eric explains gently, his eyes roving over my face. "The power doesn't feel like yours, or like any shifter, really. It feels more like raw energy."

Shaking my head, I look between him and Killian, my chest tightening at the unknown. "What does that mean?"

"I don't know, but I know some people I can ask," he offers, but I instantly don't like the idea. After the attack, we don't know who we can trust anymore. I go to speak when Eric steps closer, raising his hand to gently cup my face. "Don't worry, Ari, I'll be discreet."

His voice is soothing as he rubs small circles into my cheek with a featherlight touch. "I promise."

A warm feeling of wholeness builds within me at our touch. I've started to feel it growing stronger between us as we've gotten closer. I don't know if this is a result of the mate bond that's waiting to be completed, or if I'm genuinely developing feelings for him. Either way, being close to him feels right, much like the feeling I have with my other guys.

Nodding at his suggestion, I turn to Killian and take his hand. "Let's go inside," I suggest and walk past Eric to enter the house, ignoring the part of me that mourns the loss of his touch. If losing Tori has taught me anything, it's that I need to keep those I love close to me. I've spent so long pushing people away, but it's too late for that now. These guys, this pack, are family, and I'm not sure I would survive losing anyone else. My heart thumps painfully in my chest as the grief threatens to swallow me whole.

Feeling my distress through the bond, Killian squeezes my hand, pulling my gaze to his knowing eyes, which bore into me. I know he wants to talk about what happened, they all do, but I'm not ready. Instead, I train by day, work on getting stronger, and spend time with my guys at night. We've all grown closer in these last two weeks. I don't like them being too far away, and they help keep the nightmares at bay. I haven't been back to the Shadow Realm since Em's big reveal that he worked for ASP. I'm not quite sure how I feel about it, as I know there must be more to the situation, but I can't help feeling the sting of betrayal.

Laughter comes from the kitchen, which causes a little smile to touch my lips as we walk into the open plan room, seeing Seb and Alex behind the counters cooking dinner. Alex has turned out to be a surprisingly good cook, and the six of us have shared many meals together these last few weeks in this kitchen. Family dinners are quickly becoming a tradition.

"Hey, gorgeous," Alex calls out with a wink as he sees Killian and I in the doorway. Handing the spoon over to Seb, he walks over to me, places his hand on my waist, and presses a kiss to my lips. I'm not the only one who's decided to embrace our relationship, and Alex has been particularly forward recently. It's been a welcome change, as Alex's hot and cold yo-yoing had been giving me whiplash. The only downside is that Alex's more dominating attitude was rubbing against Killian's alpha side.

Killian stiffens next to me, his hand tightening around mine. Through the bond, I can feel he wants to keep Alex away from me, his wolf fighting to challenge Alex for dominance. I'm worried I might have to step in and say something, but a rumble through the bond stops me.

Stepping up next to me, Killian taps Alex on the shoulder. Body tense, Alex pulls away from me and looks at the alpha wolf with his eyebrow raised. He's expecting a fight.

"Don't I get a kiss too?" Killian's voice grinds out. I can't help the laugh that spills from my lips, and Eric and Seb join in. Alex rolls his eyes but cracks a smile, patting the other shifter on the back as he moves away.

"Sorry, man, I don't do alphas," Alex jokes before Seb bounds over to us and throws his arms around Killian.

"It's okay, Kill, I'll give you a kiss!" He clings on to the larger shifter like a baby monkey, laying noisy kisses on his face as Killian tries to dislodge him. He may look pissed off as he snarls and swipes at Seb, but he can't hide the little surge of feeling that shoots down the bond. Fun. Belonging. Family.

Smiling, I walk over to the dining table, where Eric is nursing a mug of coffee, watching the antics of the other guys. Alex has joined in, and him and Seb are now chasing Killian around the kitchen, making kissy noises at him.

"Ari, we need to talk." My gut clenches, not so much at Eric's words, but his soft tone. It's his doctor voice that he uses when he has to deliver bad news to patients. "It's about Tori's body."

I school my face into a careful, blank mask before facing him. The guys don't need to see how damaged I am or how difficult I'm finding everything. Everything I see or do reminds me of *her*. There's a tight, dark ball of rage inside that wants to consume me, urging me to find those who hurt her and destroy them.

Taking a deep breath, I meet his eyes and hate the sympathy I see there. It only lasts for a second before his expression changes into something else, an anger I rarely see from Eric taking over.

After the fight, we took Tori's body back to Moon River to prepare for the funeral. I'd been dreading it, not sure I could face it, but that day never came. Overnight, while I'd been in the Shadow Realm, her body had been stolen, and the only thing left behind was a circle of runes. Eric had gone silent when he saw them and told me he needed to do some investigating. Given the attacks and shifter disappearances, we assumed it was Shadow Pack that was behind stealing Tori's body.

The attacks on shifters have continued, but other races have started to disappear too. ASP made a big statement about how they were looking into it, and that we should leave the investigations up to them. But we still don't know how involved ASP is in everything. They lost the trust of the shifters when they attacked us in the warehouse. There have been rumblings of a rebellion, but Alpha Mortlock has been trying to work with the other city alphas to stop this. The last thing we need is an all-out war.

The noise of the others dims in the background, and I can feel as they draw closer, their hands touching my shoulder in comfort. Nodding for Eric to go ahead, I take a seat next to him.

"I'm not experienced with magic, but some of the runes left behind looked odd. So I did a little research, and then I realised what was bothering me about them. I recognised a few of them." I frown at his statement, trying to draw conclusions in my mind, but only coming up with more questions.

"I don't understand. You can't use magic, so how would you recognise them?" I ask, getting frustrated. I run my hands through my hair, turning to look at the others to see if they have any more insight. Feeling Eric's hand on mine, I face him again, startled by his intense expression.

"Because some of them weren't magic runes. They were demon marks." Silence meets his declaration before I choke out a startled laugh, throwing my hands up into the air in despair.

"So now I have fucking demons to worry about too? Shadow Pack is using demons now?" Fucking great. First magic, and now demons? I know nothing about demons other than what Eric has taught me of his people. How can I fight something I know nothing about?

"I don't know, Ari. It shouldn't be possible to mix magic and demon marks. They're completely separate magics and shouldn't work together," Eric explains, also sounding frustrated by this mystery we face. A dense sadness fills me as I realise that this means I'll probably never get Tori's body back, never put her to rest properly. I know she wouldn't care, but it feels important that we bury her. Silence fills the room as we all ingest the new information, the atmosphere heavy.

"What does this mean?" Killian questions Eric, and I feel his determination to keep me safe, to keep us safe, down the bond.

"If the demons are truly involved in this, it means we need to watch our backs."

Chapter Four

"Ari, please come in. Take a seat," Alpha Mortlock greets me as he gestures for me to enter the room. It's still early, but I needed to see him, and he instantly agreed when I called this morning. After a night of tossing and turning, I knew that we needed to have this conversation. Dreams had plagued me all night—demons taunting me as they stole my family, of Tori calling to me, begging for my help as I ran after her...but she was always just out of my reach.

I step into the house, and Alex, Killian, and Seb follow me, their large bodies filling the space and making the room feel small. I'd wanted Eric to come as well, but he declined, saying he had no place in the private wolf meeting about pack business. Garett was still with his own pack, but we spoke on the phone this morning. He'd sounded exhausted. The twins had a difficult night and tried to leave the compound to search for Tori. They couldn't seem to accept that she was dead and were starting to go feral. The situation with his brothers is wearing him down, and he feels torn between helping them and being with me. Thankfully, he's coming back to the compound tonight, so I'll be able to rest a bit easier since I'm constantly on edge when he's away from us.

Walking into the living room of the main house, I smile as I see

Lena walk in with a tray of coffee, enough mugs for all of us. Seeing my gaze, she smiles and shrugs her shoulders.

"I brought enough for all of your men. I wasn't sure who would be coming, but I knew you wouldn't be coming alone." She busies herself setting the mugs down, pouring coffee from the cafetière into each cup. I shouldn't be surprised at how accepting the pack is of me and my unorthodox relationships. They've been nothing but welcoming since I first met them, but it still takes me by surprise.

Alex shakes hands with the alpha and walks past me to help Lena. He places his hand on her shoulder, insisting that she sit down, before he serves us coffee. The beta serving us... This pack continually blows my expectations out of the water.

"Thank you, Alex, love." Lena places a motherly kiss on his cheek before walking over to the sofa where the alpha is watching us with bright eyes, taking his mate's hand in his own as she takes a seat.

I sit on the opposite sofa in the middle, with Killian on my left, while Seb chooses to sit at my feet, leaning back against my legs. There are plenty of other seats in the room and I want to protest, but he just smiles up at me as if he knows what I'm thinking. Returning his smile, I can't help but compare this to the first time I was in this room. The whole time I was here, I was searching for an exit, not trusting the alpha not to attack me, and I'd only sit on the arm of the couch, whereas now, I sit here comfortably.

Alex hands me a coffee, and I gratefully take it from him, breathing in the heady aroma. Once everyone has a mug, Alex takes the space to my right, nursing his own coffee as his spare hand comes to rest on my knee.

"How can we help you this morning, Ari?" the alpha inquires kindly, and I take a deep breath, reminding myself why I'm here.

"I have two things I need to speak with you about," I begin, dropping my gaze to my lap as the now familiar pain of grief wraps itself around my throat, making my voice tight. "I know I've been ignoring it, but I need to know what's been going on since the attack."

Feeling my distress, the guys start to comfort me. Seb shifts closer and wraps his arm around my leg. Alex reaches out and squeezes my hand where it rests on my leg, and Killian slides his arm around me, rubbing my shoulder.

I've been avoiding any meetings involving the other packs and news of ASP, focusing only on my training and my new family. But I know I can't continue to do that. Shadow Pack isn't going to go away, and with other supernaturals disappearing, things are only getting worse.

Alpha Mortlock sighs but nods in my direction, acknowledging how difficult this is for me, for us. "We didn't want to disturb you while you're grieving, but the situation is deteriorating, and we could use your help."

"What's been happening?" I ask with a frown, leaning forward as the alpha explains.

"As you know, ASP has now stepped in since other supernaturals have started to disappear. They have stayed suspiciously quiet about their attack on us, stating that they were carrying out routine investigations against conspirators against their organisation." Seb snorts at my feet, at which the alpha makes a noise of agreement.

"The agent I killed said that he had taken out 'target number four,' which means they were hunting her, and she wasn't the only one. Why was Tori a target?" My voice breaks on her name, but I hold the alpha's gaze.

"We don't know." His jaw clenches, and his eyes light with fire. "ASP is currently refusing to answer any of our questions, but we'll find out. I promise you this, Ari." His voice is strong and full of determination, and I find myself nodding in agreement. Whoever was behind Tori's death will pay for what they did.

"You said that things were getting worse. What do you mean? The disappearances?" Killian queries, also leaning forward, tension running through his body.

Mortlock sighs and rubs his hands over his face as Lena leans over and rubs his shoulders to help ease his tension. "There have been some killings recently, the bodies being left behind."

"Shadow Pack?"

"This isn't their usual pattern. Usually, they take someone and then leave their body, marked with their symbol. These bodies have been completely torn apart, missing limbs. So much so, it's been difficult to identify the corpses. They also don't seem to have been moved. It's like the killer stumbled across them and killed them on the spot." His words are troubling, and I don't hide the shudder that passes through me at the idea of more killers being on the streets.

"So, either Shadow Pack has changed their methods, or we have someone else killing supernaturals?" I muse, looking at my hands as I ponder the situation, wondering if ASP could be involved in any way. Although, it doesn't make sense for them to leave the bodies for anyone to find.

"There is something else different about these killings. Everyone who's been killed so far has worked for ASP or been associated with them in some way." My eyes dart up to the alpha's, and I know the guys are just as shocked as I am.

Silence fills the room until Alex clears his throat. "So it could be revenge killings over the attack?"

Mortlock nods at his question, worry lining his handsome face. "It would make sense why the bodies have been left out in the open —a statement to ASP."

"What do the other packs think?" Killian asks, his face severe.

"They're reluctant to meet again in a big group after what happened last time, but I've been in touch with a couple of the alphas. Everyone is worried this is going to end in war."

I have to agree with the alpha. War with ASP is the last thing we need when the Shadow Pack is still killing and abducting supernaturals.

"I need to go back to the Shadow Realm, speak with Em. It's about time I hear him out." I can feel Killian wanting to protest, to tell me it's not safe, to demand that I stay. I turn to look at him, gripping his hand in mine. "I'll be safe. I know how to protect myself," I assure him softly, pushing a little feeling of love down the bond, declaring I'll be safe, and I can feel him beginning to relent.

Alpha Mortlock nods, his face grave. "I hate to ask this of you, Ari, but I think you're right. We need answers, and I think only you can get those for us." Taking a sip of his coffee, he gives me a little smile. "What is the other matter you wished to speak of?"

My heart starts to pound in my chest, and I feel the guys around me sit up, looking for a threat when they hear my heart race and sense my apprehension. A small, nervous smile crosses my lips as I look at them before meeting the alpha's eyes.

"If it's still available, I would like to officially take my place within the pack."

I feel the shock of everyone in the room, but I keep my eyes locked on the alpha as a large grin fills his face.

"Well, it's about damn time."

"Why now?"

I stir from my place in Garett's arms and look up at his handsome face. After my conversation with the alpha, I'd called Garett to explain, and he immediately came over.

Now, sitting with all five of my guys, I soak up their company, enjoying the moment of peace before the ceremony tonight. Apparently, being accepted as an official member is a big deal, so the whole pack has been called together. Our allies have been invited as well, including Garett and Eric.

Sitting in Garett's lap, I shrug, keeping his arms wrapped tightly around me. I've missed him, and I'm making the most of this moment, knowing he'll probably have to go back to his pack after the ceremony.

"It felt right," I reply, struggling to find the words to explain the complex mass of feelings that's been sitting in my chest. "This place has felt like home for a while, and with everything that's going on, I don't want to die being the wolf that didn't belong."

"No talk of dying," Killian growls out from the other side of the room, his gaze locked on me as he combs out his long hair. "But even if you weren't welcome here, you would always have a home with us, even if we had to start our own pack." His comment surprises me. Not that Killian wouldn't leave Moon River, he's never fully felt like he belonged here, but the fact he would accept the others in a pack of our own is a big deal. He's mentioned it before, but I hadn't realized he was serious.

Having more than one alpha in a pack doesn't tend to work, as there is a constant power struggle for who's in control. But when Killian's pack was killed, Alpha Mortlock allowed him to stay if he agreed not try to take control of Moon River Pack. Because of this, he's always felt like an outsider. Not fully belonging, an alpha with no pack.

Frowning, I look around at the others. Surely they didn't feel the same? "I couldn't do that to you guys though. Alex is pack beta, it would kill him to leave the pack behind. And what about Seb? He wouldn't want to leave Jessica."

"I would though," Alex states, surprising me. "I'd leave if they didn't accept you. For you, I would give up being a beta, even if it meant I had to call this bastard 'Alpha,'" he jokes with a gesture at Killian, who in return, flips him off.

I shake my head at their antics, but I can tell they are telling the truth. They would leave everything behind for me. Thankfully, they don't have to, but it warms something inside me that they would do that for me.

"I also wanted everyone to have a home," I explain quietly, "in case anything happens to me." I know none of them want to think about that, but now that I'm pack, Garett and Eric will be offered a place with them if I die. Losing Tori has made me think more about what will happen to those I leave behind.

Feeling them all crowd around me, I savour this time we spend together, their scents filling my nose and making me feel safe. Need starts to build up in me as their hands touch my skin, all seeking to get closer to me. I see the moment they sense my arousal from the dilation of pupils and the hitch in their breathing, making me want them all the more.

A knock at the door has Killian and Alex snarling at the interruption, but Seb peels himself away and opens the door. I hear quiet voices from the doorway, and I know it's time for us to leave, but everyone seems reluctant to let go. My eyes pass over them and land on Eric, who's trying to school his expression, but he isn't quick enough to hide it—a look of pure happiness and peace. It may not have been how he imagined, but he's found a home here too. I make a note to spend more time with him. As the newest member of our relationship, I worry that he feels left out, but I'm still coming to terms with how he fits with us.

Seb re-enters the room and leans against the doorway, watching us with lust filled eyes and his signature smile. "I hate to interrupt whatever is about to happen here, but you're missing your party."

This causes the guys to chuckle as they start to untangle themselves from me. Unlike some parties where you're required to dress up, these ceremonies are the opposite. After the wolf is accepted into the pack, everyone shifts and takes part in a run, which makes clothing impractical. Instead, everyone is dressed in loose clothing, which will be easy to remove when needed. Even Eric will be shifting into his demon form, which I'm equal parts nervous and excited to see. I haven't seen that side of him before. Although, he's been more relaxed around me and recently allowed me to feel some of his otherworldly power.

We all leave the house in silence, walking barefoot towards the clearing in the woods where pack runs and other important ceremonies are conducted. The atmosphere is full of nervous excitement, and as I glance around, I see small smiles on the guys' faces.

Even Killian has lost his trademark scowl, and when I meet his gaze, a surge of love and something that feels like pride runs down the bond.

When we reach the clearing, we're greeted by a symphony of voices as many of the pack members call out to us with well wishes and congratulations. Even Garett is greeted by name from several of the younger male wolves he's been getting friendly with. Since he's been spending so much time here, he felt it was important to give something back to the pack and has been working with the young wolves, training them on strength and fitness. I even caught him playing a game of basketball with them the other day.

While I'd expected Garett to be welcomed, I wasn't as sure about Eric. Shifters don't tend to associate with other supernaturals, so I thought the pack would struggle to accept a demon, but it was the opposite. Sure, they'd been wary at first, since they had recently suffered from an attack, but they accepted him here for me. Once they began to work with him, and they saw him as a truly caring and talented doctor, they seemed to look past his species and accept him for the man he is.

A blur catches my attention before I'm tackled to the ground. Since I've accepted my wolf and my shadow powers, I've been able to feel and do things I never could before, so I know I'm not in danger as my wolf instincts don't react at all to protect me.

Grinning up at the little girl 'pinning' me to the ground, I wrap my arms around her, tickling her sides until she falls off me in heaps of giggles.

"Ari! Seb tells me you're becoming pack! I didn't understand what he meant because I thought you already were. See, Seb says that pack is family, and you already are part of our family," Jessica announces, her words coming out fast as she tries to tamp down her excitement. "But then he said that you're going to stay here and help protect us."

She stares up at me, and I see the vulnerability in her eyes, even though she tries to hide it. My heart aches, and without a word, I sit up and open my arms. She immediately crawls over from where she was sitting in the grass and climbs into my lap. Wrapping my arms around her, I bury my nose into her hair, inhaling her fresh scent. As I hold her, I realise she's right—I don't have to do this ceremony to become part of their family, since I already am. But I've made up my mind. I'm doing this for the guys and for Jessica, so she doesn't have to worry about losing any more of her family, but I'm also doing this for me. I want a place to truly call home.

"You're right—we already are family. But this means I get to stay here with all of you. I won't have to leave any more," I explain, pressing a kiss to her forehead, enjoying the wide smile that beams across her face. Climbing off my lap, she tilts her head to one side as if she's contemplating something, her little face screwed up in concentration.

"So, does this mean you can marry Seb now? Then we would be sisters and you can keep us safe!" Her voice is bright and full of hope.

Whoa, what?

The question fills me with panic, and I look around, wide-eyed, at the guys for help. Killian is scowling, Eric and Garett look like they're trying to hold back their laughter, and Seb falls dramatically to the ground next to me, wrapping an arm around my shoulders.

"Yeah, Ari! Are you going to marry me now?" he teases, his grin wide. The bastard is enjoying my discomfort.

"Um," I answer, completely lost for words until I look back at Jessica. Her face has fallen since she sensed my hesitation. She needs this, she needs my assurance that I'll stay in their lives. Gesturing for her to come closer, I kneel in front of her so we're face to face.

"Jessica, I will *always* try my best to protect you and keep you safe, whether I marry Seb later down the line or not. Family isn't made through marriage, it's made up of those who care about you." I press my forehead to hers as I've seen some wolves do with their pups in a gesture of love and trust. "I don't need a piece of paper to tell me that we're family."

Something resonates within me as I speak, like a fog has lifted, and I finally understand. Family is what we make it. Alpha Black and Shadow Pack may have sired and raised me, but they are not my family. My family is larger than I thought, not just made up of my guys, but their families too.

There is one thing I know for certain—I will do just about anything to keep the people I love around me safe, and I pity those who try to come between us.

Chapter Five

A change in the atmosphere signals the start of the ceremony. There is no announcement, no obvious sign that something is about to happen, except for a ripple of excitement that runs through the gathering crowd. Voices hush as everyone stands and turns towards the alpha. I'd expected Alpha Mortlock to stand near the front to direct to the group, but instead, he walks among us, barefoot and quietly greeting pack members with a smile or a touch on the shoulder as he weaves his way to the centre of the pack. Lena walks next to him, her hand brushing his as they walk side by side. Alex and Isa follow just a few steps behind them.

The stark contrast between Shadow Pack and the pack here throws me for a moment. I know it shouldn't, Moon River has proven over and over that they're nothing like my old pack, but it's not easy to forget what I saw in the years I grew up there. In Shadow Pack, the alpha would walk ahead of everyone, followed by his beta, gamma, and lastly, the female the alpha had claimed. By walking side by side with his mate, Alpha Mortlock is saying that Lena is as important as he is, that they share a powerbase. This says a lot about the pack I'm about to join.

Nerves run through me, but not because I'm doubting my decision. Being surrounded by my old pack was never a good thing, and

I have to fight against the memories pushing to be re-lived in my mind. Sensing my discomfort through our bond, Killian gives my hand a squeeze, dipping his head towards me in encouragement. The others follow his lead and step closer to me. Taking a deep breath, I let their scents settle me, my inner wolf humming with pleasure at being surrounded by her men.

Home.

Once in the centre of the gathering shifters, Mortlock looks around, his face proud as he takes in his pack. Alex stands just behind him, his eyes locked on me. There's a promise shining in them as a sly smile crosses his lips, causing my core to clench. I recognise that look all too well. The guys shift around me as they scent my arousal, their hands finding innocent ways to touch me. I don't think they even realise they're doing it half the time, but I find them gravitating towards me constantly—a simple touch of hands brushing against me as they reach for a glass or stroking my hair as they pass me.

Pulling my gaze from Alex, I look at my guys surrounding me. Killian's on my right and Garett's on my left, with Seb standing by his side. Eric is a little farther away with a blank expression on his face as he watches us. Catching me watching him, a smile lights his face, and I feel a little guilty at the distance between us. I still don't know how he fits in with us here, and I hadn't considered how he would feel being surrounded by shifters. I don't say a word, but he must sense something as he walks over and cups my face between his hands.

"Don't worry about me, Ari, this is your night. Enjoy this." His words are soft, but I roll my eyes. He's using his doctor voice. Typical, self-sacrificing Dr. Eric.

"You're going to be left out. There's no way you can keep up with us when we start running. Why hadn't I thought of this?" I turn to Garett to see if he has any words of wisdom, but Eric's laugh stops me from asking. Turning back to the incubus, I raise an eyebrow in question.

"Ari, thank you for being concerned about my feelings, but I have no intention of being left behind." His eyes light with an inner fire as his demon comes to the surface, and some of his otherworldly power washes over me. "I fully intend on shifting with you. Then we shall see who's left behind." His face is close to mine, and for a second, I think he's going to kiss me, but we're interrupted when Killian slings his arm around my shoulders.

"So, the demon is coming out to play, huh? You really think you can outrun a werewolf?" Killian snorts disdainfully, but the teasing glint in his eyes tells me that he isn't about to start a fight. I take half a step back, shaking my head as I watch the two males face off against each other, both unable to turn away from a challenge.

"Oh, I know it, wolf," Eric goads, his whole demeanour changing from calm doctor to playful young man as he teases the grizzly werewolf. Something within me warms as I watch them.

"Ari."

Glancing up when my name is called, I see Alpha Mortlock smiling at me, gesturing for me to join him in the centre of the pack. Taking a deep, shaking breath, I step forwards, pushing my nerves away. When I reach the alpha's side, he smiles kindly at me, patting me on the shoulder before his mate pulls me into a tight hug.

"I'm so glad you decided to join us." Her voice is strained, as if she's holding back tears, and she embraces me tighter. Startled, my arms hang by my sides for a second before I smile and wrap them around Lena, returning her hug. I marvel once again at how such a kind woman has remained in such a place of power.

Releasing the alpha's mate, I take a small step back, my face flushed at such shows of affection. Alex walks up to me next, his steps predatory. When he reaches me, he presses his forehead to mine, my wolf instantly settling at his touch.

"I know what this means to you. You've got this." His voice is quiet, meant only for me, but it doesn't take away from the power in his words. I would've been happy to stay in that position for far longer, but a wall of muscle walks to my side.

Pulling away, I smile up at the pack gamma, Isa, who greets me with a rare smile of her own. She pats me on the back with a force that has me stumbling, and the pack around us chuckles, having been at the receiving end of one of her shows of affection before.

"I'm glad you have finally decided to join the pack. It is good to have another strong female around to show these men who is really boss." Her thick German accent has me smiling again. Seb told me that while she is fair and mingles with the pack, she doesn't have many friends outside of the male German wolves that joined the pack with her. This is something we have in common. Other than Tori, I've never really had any female friends, so this fragile new friendship means a lot to me.

"Friends, pack mates, and guests. Thank you all for joining us. We have gathered here tonight for a very special reason." Mortlock's words fills the air around us, and although he doesn't raise his voice, our sensitive shifter hearing pulls our attention to him, his alpha power imbedded in his words. "We are here to welcome a new member to our pack, someone that many of you are familiar with. She's helped and protected this pack, even at risk to herself, first as our nurse, then as our friend. When we were attacked, when she was targeted by one of our own, she still fought for us." Mortlock pauses at the reminder of Marcus' betrayal.

When I first arrived at the pack, I beat Marcus in a formal challenge. I had refused to kill him when he lost the challenge, even though it's against what shifter law demands. He had been banished from the pack as a result and had joined forces with Shadow Pack, who later attacked Moon River. Seb's mother, Gloria, had been killed and several others wounded. The pack was still trying to recover from this betrayal.

Glancing across at Seb, I see his arms wrapped around a sombre-looking Jessica, but what surprises me is the look on his face. My submissive, playful wolf looks like a different person, his expression fierce, and the strange new sense of power is pulsating from him. If I hadn't been paying attention or looked at Seb in that moment, I wouldn't have noticed it, as it disappears in the next moment. Frowning, I look at the others to see if they noticed anything, but they're all focused on the alpha. All except Eric, who's frowning at Seb with a look of confusion on his face.

"Ari has decided to become part of our pack, part of our family, and as such, she and her mates are welcome to stay here indefinitely," Mortlock announces and turns to face me, his face sombre as he speaks the formal words that will bind me to the pack. "Ari, formerly of no pack, do you accept a place among Moon River Pack? In accepting this, you swear to heed by our rules and protect the pack to the best of your ability until your death or for as long as you remain with the pack."

The forest is quiet, even the breeze that had been winding through the trees seems to have stopped, as everyone holds their breath while they wait for my answer. My heart thumps in my chest like a frantic bird trying to escape as I feel hundreds of expectant eyes on me. A pull down the bond has my wide-eyed gaze meeting Killian's eyes, and a sense of calm washes over me, his haughty smile familiar enough to help settle my nerves. My eyes flicker over to Garett and Seb, my protective bear and playful wolf, and they smile at me in encouragement. Looking at Eric next, he dips his head at me, silently acknowledging me and supporting my decision. I feel a hand on my shoulder and know it's Alex.

Taking a deep, steadying breath, I turn to face Alpha Mortlock again and give him a slight apologetic smile. "I, Ari, lone wolf of no pack, hereby swear to live by the rules and protect Moon River Pack to the best of my abilities until my death or until I choose to leave the pack." As I speak the binding words, the hairs on my arms stand up as a tingle runs along my skin and a breeze picks up, blowing power through the clearing. The forest around me glows with an unnatural light as the pack's eyes start glowing with the strength of power that surrounds them. Several of the younger and less powerful shifters fall to their knees as they start to change into their wolves, unable to control the change with the amount of power that's filling the air.

"Welcome to the pack," Mortlock addresses me quietly with a large smile, before turning to the rest of the pack. "Let's run!" he announces to cheers as people begin undressing in preparation of shifting.

Alex takes hold of my arm, his smile wide as he leads me over my guys where they are waiting for us. Seb is struggling to hold a small wolf in his arms who's trying to get free. I laugh as she manages to escape his arms and lopes over to me. Kneeling down, I hold out my hand for Jessica's wolf to catch my scent before reaching forward to pat her head when she licks at my hand. I smile at her, rubbing between her ears before she jumps back at the sound of other wolf pups playing and yipping on the other side of the clearing. Spinning on all fours, she looks up at Seb, tilting her head in question, a small whine leaving her as she wordlessly pleads with her brother.

Rolling his eyes, Seb nods and gestures towards the other pups. "Fine, you can go with them, but you stay with the others, don't run off from Miss Jones like last time!"

I watch the whole exchange with amusement as Jessica yips in agreement and runs towards the group of wolf pups. Standing, I walk to Garett, who has his arms open wide. I snuggle into his hug and breathe in his comforting scent as he nuzzles my hair.

"Well done. I know what this means to you." His voice is rough as he presses a kiss to the top of my head.

"Come on, Ari, we need to shift," Alex calls, gently extracting me from my bear's arms, playfully winking at me as he starts to take off his shirt.

"Yes! Naked time!" Seb declares, his hands going to the buttons of his jeans. Suddenly, I don't know where to look as my guys start to undress around me. Not because I'm embarrassed, but because I'm having a very hard time keeping my hands off them.

"You too, demon," Killian chides, facing Eric as he removes his shirt. Eric just grins at Killian's challenge, unbuttoning his own shirt as he prepares to shift.

"Don't worry, wolf, I'm right behind you," Eric replies, chuckling slightly at Killian's impatience. I still as Eric undresses, my eyes following his hands as he unbuttons the cufflinks at his wrists. The crisp white shirt slides down his arms, exposing broad shoulders and a defined chest. I've never seen Eric other than in his smart, casual clothing or doctor's coat, and I find that I can't look away, even if I wanted to. His skin is paler than the others, but not quite as pale as mine. His chest is completely hairless, apart from a trail leading from his belly button down beyond the waistband of his trousers. I have this insane urge to run my fingers down his chest and see what the trail leads me to.

"Ari, you're drooling," an amused Seb teases before stalking over to me in only his boxers and playfully running his hands over his own chest. "What can I do to make you look at me like that?"

Rolling my eyes, I push his shoulder softly, but I can't hide the guilty grin that spreads across my face at being caught ogling Eric. They know how they affect me, I've shown them several times, but having them all here, surrounding me in various states of undress and their eyes only for me, is making a heat within me rise up. Scenting my arousal, they all take a step closer, their eyes glowing with their inner animal, or demon in Eric's case, with a small growl emitting from Killian's chest, the need to be with his mate riding him hard.

A howl brings my attention to those around us, many of whom are already in their wolf form or in the process of changing, with the alpha standing in the centre, watching over us all. A whimper has me frowning as I look through the crowd to find where the sound is coming from. A young woman, who I'd say was only about eighteen or nineteen, is crouched on the forest floor, her head in her hands as her skin seems to ripple. An older man and woman who have to be related to her crouch by her side, talking to her in low, reassuring tones, but I can see the pain in the older woman's eyes.

Feeling a hand on my arm, I pull my gaze away and see that Alex is by my side, wearing a concerned look on his face as he watches the young woman.

"What's going on? Why does she seem like she's in so much pain?" I ask quietly, my heart clenching as the girl lets out a mournful cry.

"We're not sure. Something seems to be affecting the younger wolves," he replies, his worry evident in the tightening of his eyes.

A chill runs down my spine at his words as I reach out, drawing his attention to me. "What do you mean 'affecting'?" My words are hurried, for some reason this seems really important. Alex looks at me and sighs, then runs his hand through his hair. I'm shocked when I see his face full on, he looks like a different person, the weight of this sitting so heavily on his shoulders.

"They can't seem to shift. They get stuck, their bodies trying to shift but unable to, just stuck in this agonising cycle."

I fall silent, the gravity of what he's saying sinking in. If wolves can't shift and are getting stuck during their shift, they're completely vulnerable, not to mention the agonising pain. Why did no one mention this before?

"What can we do?" I finally inquire. This is my pack now, part of my responsibility, there has to be some way I can help. My nursing side is screaming at me to go help her, and when I look around, I can see that Eric is frowning in the direction of the young woman, obviously desiring to help but not wanting to cross any lines.

"The alpha can help her, that's why he hasn't shifted yet. Look, he's going over now." Following Alex's outstretched arm, I see that he's right. Alpha Mortlock is crouched down next to the girl, his eyes glowing as he says something to her in a voice too quiet for me to hear, although I realise what he's doing when the girl's body convulses once before bursting into her wolf form.

"He's forcing her shift," I whisper, fighting against a shudder. Alpha wolves have the ability to make their wolves change forms, and the old Alpha of Shadow Pack used to enjoy using this as a punishment, forcing me between forms. He would spend hours trying to get me to shift, and I would always refuse to shift for him. He required complete loyalty, expecting his wolves to follow his every order, so it would piss him off when he had to result in using his alpha power to force me to shift, and I can still remember the pain it would cause. But as I watch Alpha Mortlock with the young woman, I realise he's helping her, pressing his hands on either side of her muzzle and stroking the back of her head until her back legs stop shaking and the terrible whine she was making begins to quiet. Letting go of the wolf, the alpha sits back on his heels, and a small smile comes to his weary face when the young wolf takes a hesitant step towards him, licking at his hand before turning back to whom I assume are her parents.

"How long has this been going on for?" I ask as I turn to face my group of guys.

"The first time was a couple of months ago, but it's happening more often now," Alex tells me and holds up his hands as if to fend me off as my face clouds over, anger growing in the pit of my stomach. This started around the time they asked me to help the pack, and no one told me about this!

"Ari, let's not talk about this now, it's time to celebrate. You're pack now!" Seb chimes in, his smile infectious.

Looking around, I see that Killian, Seb, and Alex have stripped down to their boxers, ready to shift, and I realise he's right—now is not the time for anger, especially as I'm surrounded by half naked men. Garett stands next to me fully nude, and when he catches me looking, he just winks.

"Bears aren't as squeamish as you wolves. Besides, it would get really expensive if I had to buy new underwear after every shift, have you ever tried to get boxers for someone my size? It's pricey," he explains, causing me to roll my eyes.

Pulling my shirt off over my head, I start to unbutton my jeans, acutely aware of their eyes on me, heating my skin as I remove my clothing, until I'm left standing in my underwear. Sure, they've all seen me naked before, and I've shifted with Garett naked before, but I'm still uncomfortable taking my clothes off in front of people I don't know. Except they aren't just people anymore, they are pack, family. Taking a deep breath, I slide my underwear off and unhook my bra, letting it drop to the floor next to my other discarded clothing. As if this is the symbol they were waiting for, the others drop to their knees and begin to shift. Kneeling on the ground, I close my eyes and welcome my wolf to the surface. I can almost feel her fur brushing up against me as she prowls under my skin.

When I open my eyes again, I know I'm in wolf form. Before I fully accepted my wolf, shifting was always an unusual, slightly unnerving experience, like taking a backseat while someone else drove your favourite car. However, it's different now. I'm fully in control of myself and share this form with my wolf, so it's exhilarating.

A large, grey wolf stalks up to me, the brutal scar on his face standing out against his fur. Killian is huge, his shoulders would reach my chest if I was in human form. Lowering his large head, he rubs his jaw against me, emitting an almost purring sound from his chest. Alex's wolf comes next, rubbing up against my side in greeting, only to be pushed out of the way by a very excited smaller wolf. Seb's wolf yips as he bounces around in front of me, causing me to bark out in laughter.

A huge shadow falls over me, and I instinctively spin around, crouching down into a defensive position until I realise who it is. Garett's bear form towers over me, his head tilted to one side as he watches me, waiting for my wolf to get used to his presence. Dropping to his hind quarters, he sits to make himself seem less threatening, but my wolf and I would recognise Garett anywhere in either form. Jumping up, I rub myself around him, enjoying the feel of his fur against my muzzle, a happy rumble coming from my chest.

A change in the air has me pulling away, looking around me for the source of power that's suddenly filling the air until my eyes lock on Eric. He's standing in just a pair of trousers, his feet bare as he calls his power. The air seems to crackle around us, making my hair stand on end as a bluish aura surrounds him. Throwing his head back and arms open wide, Eric seems to hover off the ground for a moment before he bows his head. He pauses, then he slowly lowers his arms to his sides and lifts his head. His blue eyes glow with unearthly energy as they instantly lock on me. He still looks like Eric, albeit slightly different with the glowing eyes and something that looks suspiciously like horns protruding from his forehead, but the amount of power he's throwing out is new. It's almost overwhelming, and several wolves around the clearing are cowering from the strength of it.

Eric warily walks towards me, as if worried how my wolf will react to him. I have to admit, I'm afraid of his power, but I'm not afraid of him. I hadn't realised until he changed into this form, but I can almost *see* the connection between us, a bluish line that seems to tie us together, the bond that he says makes me his mate so much stronger.

Reaching my side, he kneels so we are face to face.

"Hello, mate, I have been looking forward to meeting you." His voice is deeper, more guttural in this form, the words full of power, and I fully realise how strong he is. My kind, gentle doctor is gone, replaced by a powerful demon. As if he can sense my thoughts, he frowns and sits back on his heels. "I'm still Eric. I am him and he is me. He may hide my presence in his human form, but I am never far away, much like your wolf. You should never fear me in either form."

Although he says this with confidence, something in his eyes flickers, telling me he's worried about my reaction to him. Taking the last couple of steps closer to him, I press my head against his chest, feeling at home as the guys surround us.

Chapter Six

The sensation of running in my wolf form is the closest feeling to freedom I've ever had. Freedom from my past, my responsibilities, my fears. Even when shifting into my wolf form felt more like a punishment, running through the forest with the moon high above us always felt freeing. Right now, running with my new pack around me, it finally feels like I'm free, free to be the person I want to be without having to constantly look over my shoulder to see which of the monsters from my past are following me.

Glancing to my left, I see Seb loping besides me, skipping about as he chases moths as we run, his tongue hanging out the side of his mouth giving him a goofy expression. Alex is just behind him, watching our backs, like the good beta wolf that he is, protecting us at all times. To my right, Garett runs next to us in his bear form. He isn't as fast as some of the fully-grown wolves, but considering he stands over seven feet tall when on his hind legs, he is *fast*. Eric and Killian have run ahead of us, racing against each other, but they're never out of sight. I know they're both fast enough to run far enough away that we couldn't see them, but I catch the little looks they keep throwing my way, checking that I'm okay.

The pack seemed a little wary of Eric in his demon form, but not as much as I thought they would be, trusting that the Eric they have come to know wouldn't hurt them.

As a pack, we run deeper into our territory, remaining together as a group as we run. I've been on pack runs with Moon River before, but this feels different, like I'm seeing the land with different eyes. I'm not sure how long we run for, but everyone comes to a stop, and I realise we've made our way back to the clearing we started in. Mortlock walks over to me, huge in his wolf form, and gently butts his head against mine before throwing back his head and howling at the moon. The rest of the pack does the same until the air is filled with the sounds of our howling. Giving me something that looks suspiciously like a wink, the alpha turns around and lopes towards Lena's wolf before they both trot off into the woods. A couple of other wolves, including Isa, come and make the same gesture as Mortlock. The rest of the pack mills around, some changing back into human form, while others head off in small groups still in wolf form.

Turning my head, I see my guys have gathered around me, waiting to see what I want to do next. Usually, I would change back as soon as I could, but tonight, my wolf isn't ready to go back, she wants to play with her mates. Looking at the guys around me, I realise she considers all these guys as her mates—not just Killian and Eric, who we have a fated bond with, but *all* of them. I haven't really thought past living in the moment and haven't really considered what this could become or what any future with these guys would be like. Would society accept a wolf with five mates, two of which are a different species altogether? Do I care?

Shaking my head to rid myself of those thoughts, I give the guys a wolfy grin. I don't want to think about that now, I want to *play*.

Pouncing forward, I bop Garett on the nose with my muzzle, enjoying his shocked expression before a cunning guise crosses his face, which is an interesting look on a bear. Before he has the chance to retaliate, I spin on my paws and run deeper into the forest, glancing over my shoulder in time to see Garett knocking shoulders with Alex, bumping the shocked wolf over before Garett runs away.

A rough game of tag ensues, and by the end of it, all of us are panting for breath. Dropping to the ground, I let my wolf form drop, opening my eyes as a human once more, smiling as I see the others have done the same. Every one of them is grinning, even my grumpy Killian. Shuffling closer, we lay down on the forest floor, the guys each touching me in some way, with Seb's head resting on my stomach. We are all naked except for Eric, who's still in his demon form and loose trousers.

Enjoying being in their company and my body completely exhausted, I find that my busy, chaotic thoughts are quiet. It's beautiful out here, the moon hanging bright and low in the sky. I wish I could share this with Tori.

My heart thuds painfully, and my breathing hitches. For a moment, I had forgotten about losing her. What kind of friend am I? Running around in the woods when I should be out there hunting those who are behind her death. Sure, I killed the guy that shot her, but he had been following orders. I haven't forgotten the words he spoke into his microphone. *Target number four has been neutralised.*

"Ari, what's wrong?" Seb asks quietly, having sensed my inner turmoil.

"For a moment, I forgot about Tori. She would love this," I admit, my voice tight, but I won't cry. The bastards that took her from me don't deserve any more of my tears.

"Ari, Tori wouldn't want you mourning her. She would want you to get on with your life. I know what it's like to lose a loved one, and if you let it, it will tear you apart. The guilt, blame, and thirst for vengeance can take over you. I know you miss her, and that's only right, but you have to live. She would've wanted that." Killian's voice gets louder as he sits up and pulls me into his lap, the others moving in sync around us to keep physical contact with me, like magnets.

We sit like this in silence for a while, until the cool evening air starts to chill our skin, and eventually, I pull away, meeting each of their gazes.

"Thank you."

I don't explain why, and I don't need to, their gentle smiles let me know that they understand. Jumping to his feet, Seb offers me his hands, helping me up as Killian and Alex go hunt for our clothing.

"Ari, I need to go back to the city tonight." Eric's voice, deep from his demon form, still surprises me. Turning to face him, I study his face with human eyes. He still looks like Eric, just *more*. He even seems taller in this form, more imposing, but I guess that makes sense. He is a demon after all.

"So, what do I call you?" I inquire, the question suddenly coming to me, unsure whether he would have a different name or not. Sure, they are the same person, but they have such different personalities that it makes sense for them to have different names. He smiles at the inquiry, brushing a lock of hair behind my ear.

"My name is the same, just pronounced differently. Some choose to take a different name for their human form, but I chose to keep mine. I was born Eiríkr many, many years ago," he answers, putting more emphasis on the 'I' so his name sounds more like Er-iee-k with a hard 'K' sound on the end.

I'm quiet for a moment as I think over his words. "You have an accent in this form." It's slight, but certainly not the soft central American accent I'm used to from him.

"Yes, I was born in Norway, my accent stayed with me." My eyebrows raise at his comment. I hadn't thought that Eric was anything other than an American human for years. I've known he's part demon for a while now, but for some reason, the revelation that he's from Norway shocks me more than that he's a different species.

"So, Norway… Were you a Viking?" I joke, unsure what to say about these new pieces of information.

"No, I had left Norway by the time the Vikings were around."

"Whoa, how old *are* you?" Seb chimes in, making me laugh at the blunt question.

"I was born in the year 532 AD," Eric says with a sly smile.

"Wait, you're over fourteen hundred years old?" Seb mirrors my shock, but I'm glad he was the one to ask. Eric looks between the two of us, staring at him in open-mouthed shock, and bursts out laughing.

"Well, I'm a demon, we live long lives," he explains with a shrug of his shoulders.

I can't help but look at him in a different light. *Damn, he looks good for such an old man*, I think to myself, my eyes running up and down his defined abs.

Realising I'm staring, I drag my gaze away from his body, but not before catching the knowing look on his face.

"So you're leaving now?" I ask, trying to hide the tone of disappointment in my voice.

"Yes, there are some things I need to take care of." Stepping forward, he places his hand on my cheek. "Plus, I need to feed, and I don't think you're ready for that tonight, not with me in this form." I shouldn't find what he says sexy, but I can't help the arousal his words cause. A low growl leaves his throat as he takes a step away from me. "If I don't leave now, we may both regret what happens. While I want nothing more than to complete the mating bond with you, you're not ready yet." He walks back a few steps and tilts his head back as a blueish light seems to form around him, until he simply vanishes from view.

"Of course he can teleport," I mutter to myself, shaking my head as I turn to face Seb and Garett, who are eyeing the spot Eric had been standing in only a moment ago.

"Phew, that guy is intense in that form," Seb comments, pretending to fan himself, causing me to laugh. My attention turns to Garett, who has stayed silent during the whole exchange, his expression distant.

"Garett, do you have to go back tonight?" I call quietly, knowing I've kept him away from his pack and his brothers for a while. I can't help my pleased smile as he shakes his head, holding out his hand for me to take. Placing my hand in his, he pulls me closer, wrapping his arms around me.

"No, my attention is fully yours tonight." His tone lowers, and a glint in his eyes tells me exactly what he has in mind for us tonight. I wrap my arms around him, gripping his shoulders as he lowers his lips to mine, kissing me gently at first, slowly adding pressure against my lips until I'm moaning into his mouth.

"I guess I'll leave you guys to it," an awkward Seb remarks, and I pull guiltily away from Garett's mouth, dropping my face to bury it into his chest. I can hear Seb's footsteps as he starts to walk away, wanting nothing more to call out to him, to stop him, but I'm unsure of Garett's reaction.

"Seb, wait!" Garett calls, and I look up at him in surprise. "Ari, do you want Seb to stay?" He looks down at me, no judgement on his face, just the desire to please me. The only time someone else has been involved in our sex was with Killian when the two of them had some stuff to work out, and Killian had to learn that Garett wasn't willing to walk away. It hasn't happened again, and Garett hasn't shared me with anyone else since, and while I know he doesn't have a problem with me being with the others, I'm not sure how well he would take *seeing* me with them.

Glancing over at Seb, I see the hopeful look he's trying to hide. "Stay." The word leaves my mouth quietly before I've really thought it through. "If you're okay with it?" I murmur as I quickly look back up at my bear.

Answering me with a knowing smile, he leans down to kiss me again, letting out a low growl as I catch his lower lip between my teeth, biting down gently. I feel his erection pressing against my stomach, and I can't help the smile that crosses my face.

"Get over here, wolf," Garett growls out, his voice gruffer than it had been a minute before.

"Yes, sir!" Seb presses up against me, moulding against my back, giving stinging little bites and kisses against my neck, causing me to arch into Garett's chest more. I dig my nails into his back from the intensity of having two guys kiss and worship my body at the same time.

"Fuckkk," Garett mutters under his breath between kisses, his hand skimming down my side, cupping one of my breasts, and pinching my nipple gently in his fingers, making my breath hiss from my mouth.

The benefit of doing this straight from a pack run is not having to waste time removing clothing. Dragging my nails down Garett's back, I enjoy the feel of his muscles under my hands, knowing how strong he is, that he could stop me any time he wants, but he won't. I meet his gaze and see the truth of that reflected back at me, his love so easy to see shining in his eyes. There was a time where I would have run from a look like that, but now it only serves to turn me on even more.

Seb moves his hand from where it rests on my hip, dipping it lower until he finds my pussy. His finger circles my clit as he uses his other hand to pull back on my hip, keeping himself pressed against me. Sandwiched between two of my guys, I think I might have died and gone to werewolf heaven.

I drop my hand between us and reach for Garett, a small moan of pleasure slipping from my lips as I find him hard and ready for me. Kissing him deeply, I swallow his groans as I run my thumb over the head of his cock before slowly stroking the length of him. Seb distracts me, slipping a finger inside me, making it my turn to groan. My legs start to tremble under their ministrations, and they help me to the ground, laying me on my back with them on their knees on either side of me. I should probably be more concerned with the fact that we're in the middle of the pack forest. Anyone could walk by and spot us, not to mention Killian and Alex will be coming back any moment, but I can't find it in me to be bothered, in fact, it excites me even more.

Garett leans over me, pressing a kiss to my lips before trailing them down my neck, collarbone, and down to my breasts, before pulling my nipple into his mouth and twirling the hard bud with his tongue, then he moves to the other breast, paying it the same attention. I open my eyes as he pulls away, not even aware I'd closed them in the first place, just catching his appreciative look as he runs his eyes over my body. Movement catches my eye, and when I glance to the side, I see Seb is watching us with a hooded gaze, his hand tightly wrapped around his cock as he pumps slowly. For a moment, I'm worried he's feeling left out, but the cheeky wink he sends me tells me he's enjoying himself too much to mind.

"So beautiful," Garett murmurs, running his fingers softly along my leg, causing the hair on my body to stand up on end. His touch so different from Killian's, who is demanding and intense. Even Alex likes to take control in the bedroom, whereas Garett and Seb truly worship me. If pleasuring me meant that they didn't get to come at the end of it, they would still find pleasure in making me happy.

Gently parting my legs, Garett leans down and presses kisses against my core, paying particular attention to my clit, making my breath come out in pants, and I have to dig my hands into the ground, needing something to hold on to.

Seb hums in his appreciation. "You should see what I can see right now. So fucking hot."

Curling my finger at him, I gesture for him to come closer, wrapping my hand around his cock as soon as he's near enough as Garett continues to lick and kiss my pussy. Slowly pumping down the length of Seb's cock, I watch his face as he groans before leaning forward and biting at my breasts, nibbling at the sensitive skin there. It's an awkward angle, but neither of us care, completely lost in each other's bodies.

The pleasure of their touch has wound me up, pushed me, but not quite taking me over the edge. I need *more*.

"If someone doesn't fuck me soon, I'll find someone who will," I growl out, then gasp as Garett slides his fingers inside me, curling them up so they flick against that sweet spot within me.

"Huh, someone wants to be fucked, do they?" he asks as he pulls away from me, sharing a knowing look with Seb as he shuffles back. "We better not keep the lady waiting then, Seb."

They both move back to give me room, and I realise I'm in control here. I get to dictate how I want this to go. A grin fills my face as I sit up, feeling powerful as I run my gaze over them, both hard and ready for me.

"Seb, I want you in front of me, I want to taste you." I grin, enjoying his obvious pleasure at hearing me talk like this to him, watching as he eagerly comes forward with his cock gripped tightly in his fist. Glancing over my shoulder, I see Garett slowly pumping his cock, catching him admiring my ass as I talk to Seb. Winking at me, he doesn't try to hide that he was checking me out.

"Garett, I want you to fuck me." His eyes darken at my words as his bear comes to the surface, his chest rumbling with a growl as he stalks towards me. Some may worry about getting fucked by a bear shifter, thinking they might lose control, but not Garett, neither he nor his bear would ever hurt me.

Getting onto my hands and knees, I smile as I feel Garett move into place behind me, his large hand engulfing my hip while he uses the other to position his cock against my entrance. He slowly presses forward, entering me, and we both groan as he fills me fully, stilling for a moment as he waits for me to adjust to his size.

Looking up, I smile at Seb before I take hold of his cock, licking the head before taking his length into my mouth. Seb's cock isn't as wide as some of my guys, but what he lacks in girth he makes up for in length. Taking as much of him in my mouth as possible, I grip the base of him, caressing with firm strokes of my hand, savouring his moans of pleasure.

Garett uses this moment to start slowly moving, easing his cock out before sliding back in, causing me to moan around Seb's cock. Picking up speed, Garett starts to fuck me as I hollow out my cheeks, sucking Seb farther into my mouth. Seb's fingers thread into my hair, directing my movements as he gets closer to his climax. His body stiffens for a second, then he comes in my mouth, panting before he pulls away and drops to his knees. He kisses me hard while Garett continues to fuck me from behind. Pulling away, Seb leans against a tree trunk and watches us with pleasure filled eyes.

A cry of protest is pulled from my lips as Garett pulls out of me, but it's cut off as he spins me around and crushes his lips to mine. I lose myself in his kiss and follow him as he guides me until his back is pressed against a tree trunk and he lowers me onto his lap, letting go of me for a second to position himself so as I sit down, I impale myself on his length. I throw back my head and moan in pleasure, my hands finding their way to his shoulders as I start to ride him.

"As sexy as it is to fuck you from behind, I want *you* to fuck me." His voice is low, growling, as his large hand grips my hair, lightly tugging on it so my neck is exposed to him. Leaning forward, he kisses my pulse point, nibbling along my collarbone as I pick up the pace, feeling the hitch in his breath as I rock against him, dictating the speed of our fucking. Garett has always enjoyed having me on top, being in control, so I make the most of that now, digging my nails into the skin of his shoulder, causing him to thrust up into me farther.

I'm close, so close to the edge that when Garett bites my neck, harder than before, the slight pain only adds to my pleasure as it pushes me over the edge and into a bone-quaking orgasm, with him following quickly behind me.

Resting my forehead against his, we sit silently as we try to catch our breath, as a happy, sated Seb comes over to join us, curling up against the two of us. With Garett's help, I slip between Garett and Seb, my eyes closing as they put their arms around me.

"Looks like we missed out on something." Alex's amused voice stirs me from my dozing. I look over at Killian, the most jealous of my guys, but find he's smirking. Perhaps we can make this work after all.

Seb

I wake up in the middle of the night. I'm not sure what's woken me, and looking around, I can see that Ari and the others are still fast asleep. Walking over to the window, I look up at the moon, still high in the sky, and feel a pulse of energy jolt through my body.

What the hell was that?

Recently, I feel like I'm not in control of my own body. Strange waves of power roll over me, which shouldn't be possible. I know the others can feel it, I've seen their worried glances when they think I'm not watching.

I've been spending a lot of time with Jessica lately, making sure that she's okay since our mom died, but mostly because she doesn't seem to notice or care about these...power surges.

Sighing, I turn to look back over at Ari. She looks beautiful with the moonlight shining on her face, peaceful in sleep. Whenever she wakes, I can see the weight of her past settle on her shoulders, which is why I work so hard to make her smile—she doesn't smile enough. Tonight has been the first time I've seen her so carefree, running with the pack, her pack. Pride runs through me, knowing we are part of the same pack, and I feel that strange wave of power pulse through me again.

It seems to get stronger the longer I look at Ari, and soon, a loud cracking noise fills the room. Spinning around, I see that I've crushed the wooden windowsill with my hands. I hadn't even realised I'd been holding it. Splinters now cover my hands, but I can't feel anything over the pulsing of the power, so alien to me.

Ari moans in her sleep, and I panic. I need to get out of here, get away from them until I know what's going on, and if I'm safe to be around them. Hurrying to other side of the room, I pull on my clothes from earlier and go to leave the room, pausing at the door. Indecision fills me, I don't want to leave, but I need answers.

Glancing over my shoulder, I take one last look at Ari, the power throbbing painfully through me.

"Bye, Ari, I'll be back soon."

Chapter Seven

Waking up to the smell of freshly ground coffee brings a sleepy smile to my face as I sit up in bed, looking around to see I'm the only one in it. I frown and climb out of the bed before shuffling to the wardrobe and throw on some clean underwear, jeans, and a light blue jumper. Pushing open the bedroom door, I follow the scent of coffee. Walking downstairs, I try and scent who's in the house, but I struggle to pick any particular scent out over the strong smell of brewing coffee. As I enter the kitchen, I smile when I see a shirtless Killian at the stove, wearing only a low-slung pair of jeans as he cooks. My wolf stirs within me at the sight of our mate, and I watch in silence, enjoying the show as his muscles across his back bunch as he adds something to the pan.

"Are you going to come say hello, or just continue to stare at me?" he inquires, but the small smile he flashes me over his shoulder takes any sting out of his words. Thoroughly caught out, I chuckle and walk farther into the kitchen, grabbing my favourite mug, which is full to the brim with coffee, as I move closer to the stove to see what he's cooking.

"Guilty," I mutter, inhaling the scent of the coffee as I nurse the mug between my hands. "I didn't know you could cook."

"I was an alpha, remember? That involved providing for my

pack, and cooking is an aspect of that. My mother taught me," he replies, unusually chatty as he focuses on his task.

"What was she like?" I press, deciding to make the most of his open mood while I sip at my coffee, savouring the bittersweet flavour of the drink. Killian stills, going silent, and for a moment, I think I've pushed him too far.

"My mother was a very loving, very open person, the complete opposite of me. She was over the moon when I mated with Julie and couldn't wait to become a grandmother." A fond smile graces his lips. "From what I remember, my father was a kind man, but we never saw him. He was always away on pack business and died when I was young. So really, it was my mom who raised me," he explains, falling silent as the smile drops from his face.

Biting my lip, I ask the question that's hanging in the air between us.

"How did she die?"

"Mom died of cancer not long after Julie and I mated." His voice is low, and he lets out an unamused chuckle, running his hand through his hair. "She wouldn't recognise me now." He laughs bitterly, and I know he doesn't mean because of his scarred face.

Frowning at his comment, I walk up to him and press up against his back as I wrap my arms around him. Feeling him tense up under my arms, I simply rest my head against his back, waiting for him to relax into me. It doesn't take long before I feel the tension start to leave him, and he lets out a long sigh.

"What did I do to deserve you? You're too good for me." His tone is light, but I can hear the self-loathing and pain in his voice.

"Me? I'm about as damaged as you can get, Kill. Plus, I come with four other men and a list of enemies as long as my arm," I joke, but my words are true.

Reaching around him, I turn off the stove then spin him around in my arms so he's facing me. "Kill, you're not responsible for their deaths. You did everything to protect them, and you do everything to protect us now. Yeah sure, you can be a bit of an asshole at times, but I still love you."

His eyes are wide, and for a moment, I think he's going to say something, but then I realise this was the first time I've told him that I love him. I open my mouth to make a smart comment, but he beats me to it, pressing a firm kiss to my lips, demanding entrance. I quickly give in, returning his kisses and holding on to him tightly. We stay like this for a moment before the smell of food causes my stomach to growl loudly. With a laugh, Killian pulls away from me and turns the stove back on to finish cooking for us.

I grin and move away, knowing I'll struggle to keep my hands to myself if I don't. Picking up my discarded coffee mug, I frown as Killian dishes up our breakfast on two plates.

"Where is everyone this morning?"

"Garett had to return to his pack, there were some issue with his brothers. Alex was called early this morning to the main house, pack business," he answers with a shrug. "Not sure where Seb disappeared to, he was gone when I woke up."

I miss them all, but I feel Seb's absence the most. He's been the one constant since I moved in here, staying in this house almost every night, so the fact he left without saying anything concerns me, it's unlike him.

"Maybe he's with Jessica?" I half-heartedly suggest, but something inside me says he's somewhere else. Pulling out my phone, I tap through it until I find his number, quickly typing out a message.

Ari: Hey packmate. Everything okay? I miss seeing you this morning.

Pressing send, I look up to see Killian watching me, his face pulled into a frown.

"I'm sure he's fine—" Killian begins before my phone buzzes in my hand, cutting off anything else he was going to say as my attention turns fully to the message.

Seb: This is one of the best things you could have said to me this morning. I'm not sure when I'll be back, but it won't be too much longer. Miss you too, packmate.

The message makes me smile, but something still strikes me as odd, I just can't put my finger on it. What does he mean by 'not sure when he would be back,' where is he? Having nothing else to go on, I show Killian the message, and he just nods, gesturing for me to sit down at the table, where breakfast is waiting for me. Sighing, I put the phone down next to my plate and sit across from Killian, who's watching me with a raised eyebrow.

"Why are you so worried?" He doesn't have to explain what he means by that, I know he's asking about Seb.

"This is unlike him, to just go without saying anything." I try to put my emotions into words, but I know he doesn't really understand. "I just have a funny feeling, that's all."

Killian nods, acknowledging my comment before gesturing towards my food. "Now eat," he commands, picking up his own knife and fork as my phone rings. Ignoring his growl of frustration, I accept the call, pressing it to my ear without checking the caller ID.

"Good morning, Ari. How are you today after last night's... exertions?" Eric's smooth timbre greets me, and I can't help the smile that crosses my face. It's very obviously Eric and not his demon form calling right now. I can tell by Eric's central American accent and easy, soft tone that I like to call his doctor's voice, compared to the deeper accented voice of Eiríkr that set the hair on my arms standing up.

"Morning, Eric. I'm well, how're you?" I ask as I take a sip from my coffee as another thought comes to me. "And how do you know about my exertions?" The way he said the word tells me that he means more than just our pack run.

"Ah..." Realising he'd been caught, Eric pauses on the other end of the phone. "Well, we may not be fully bonded, but I still feel strong emotions from you." I can hear him moving around and closing a door as he explains this to me, his voice amused.

"Wait, so you have felt every time I—" Pushing up from the

table, I fight down the embarrassment and amusement that's warring within me. Killian smirks, obviously able to hear the conversation, thanks to his supernatural hearing. Spinning on him, I point a finger at him accusingly. "Shut it, wolf boy. Hang on, we're bonded, does that mean you can feel when I'm having sex with the others?" I demand, ignoring Eric on the other end of the phone.

"Yes, but you knew that already," Killian replies with a shrug.

Eric laughs on the other end of the phone, having heard our conversation. I remember a discussion we had early on, and realise he's right, but that doesn't mean I'm happy about it though.

"Is that weird? Doesn't it make you feel, I don't know…jealous?" The question comes out more unsure than I would've liked it to, but I can't imagine being able to feel one of my guys having sex with someone other than me. I'm pretty sure it would tear me up.

"No, Ari. I can't speak for Killian, but I find it a turn-on." Eric's voice deepens as he reassures me.

"Really?" I glance at Killian as I say this, finding it difficult to believe that he wouldn't get jealous. I watch with wary eyes as he pushes away from the table, his every step predatory as he stalks towards me.

"I find it difficult to say this, because the alpha in me doesn't like sharing what he considers his, and he *definitely* considers you his. But the human part of me knows there's something greater going on here, and I'm not going to risk losing you because I was a jealous dickhead. I know you are my second chance, and I intend to make the most of it." Taking the phone from my hand, he presses the call end button and places it on the table behind him, pushing me up against the cabinet. He dips his head and presses his lips to mine, growling as my phone buzzes again. Laughing into his lips, I push him away and answer the phone with a grin.

"Sorry, Eric."

"I need to come over, there's something I need to tell you." Dread lines my stomach at Eric's complete change of tone. I want to ask questions, but I know I would just be holding him up.

"Yeah, of course," I reply, urgency suddenly underlining my words. "I'll get the others together." Hanging up, I turn to look at Killian, who's already on the phone to Garett. I can hear the concern in my bear's words from here, and Kill assures him that everything is okay, that Eric needs us all together to tell us something.

Glancing at my phone again, I tap in a message to Seb.

Ari: Can you come back to the pack? Eric needs us all together to tell us something.

Killian calls Alex, asking him to come around, and I keep myself busy with making tea for him and Garett when they arrive. While we wait for Eric, I keep checking my phone to see if Seb replies. He doesn't.

A slight tugging in my chest alerts me that Eric has arrived. I say as much, stand up to open the door, and give him a tense smile as I see him walk up the porch steps. He looks healthy, his skin almost glowing as he hugs me close, his power pressing against me as if looking for a way to escape his human shape. He must have fed, it's the only way he can appear this healthy.

I remember when he first came clean about what he was—a pain feeding demon, a type of incubus, and that *I* was his mate. As some weird rule of fate, when an incubus finds his mate, he can't feed from anyone but his mate until the bond is accepted. The night Tori was killed, I let Eric feed from me for the first time. I wasn't ready to accept the bond, but somehow, it created a semi-formed bond. Since then, Eric has been able to feed off others, but it never lasts long before he has to feed off me again, describing it like drinking watered down wine, not as strong or potent as the real thing.

When Eric is like this, full of power, it's difficult for me to take my eyes off him, and I wonder how on earth I never knew that he was anything other than human, since it seems so obvious now. As if he knows what I'm thinking, he winces slightly, and all of a sudden, it's easier to breathe, and I look around to see what just changed.

"Sorry, Ari, I didn't realise how much power I was leaking. I'm usually so good at keeping it dimmed, but I haven't been as careful since I told you about what I am," he explains, pulling me in for another hug before walking into the kitchen where the others are gathered. "No Seb?" he asks with a raised eyebrow, glancing around the room before turning to me.

"No, I can't get a hold of him." My response makes Eric frown, and he runs his hand across his face. "What's this all about?" I question as I lean against the kitchen counter, all our eyes glued on the demon.

"Last night after I left to feed, I was in the city...looking for my next meal," he begins with a grimace. We all know what he means by that—he was hunting. Feeling the atmosphere in the room change, he rushes to add, "You know I don't hurt anyone. I simply find someone already in pain, and I syphon off power from their pain. I didn't even touch them."

"You're looking pretty healthy, Doc, practically glowing. You must have found someone in a lot of pain to syphon off that much power," Killian grumbles, his words sarcastic.

"That's what I need to tell you about." He looks around the room before his eyes settle on me. "I'm able to feel large uses of power, and in the city, I felt bursts of it, really strong, but unfocused, like the user didn't know how to use it. I followed the bursts, but by the time I got to the place the power had been used, the person had left, leaving behind a body."

"Someone is killing people in the city?" Garett inquires, his voice concerned, undoubtedly thinking of his family and pack who live in the city.

"That's the thing, the victim wasn't dead." Eric's reply is met with a chorus of swearing and groans. "That's how I was able to feed."

"But you shouldn't be that strong from one dying person... Shit. There was more than one?" Cursing, Alex pulls his phone from his pocket and starts tapping out a message to someone as Eric nods.

"There were four of them. The last one was more compos mentis than the others, and I was able to...ask a few questions. They were all ASP agents."

"Fuck. So this is the guy that killed the other ASP agents the other week?" Pushing away from the table, Garett starts pacing the length of the kitchen. "Do you think other supernaturals are safe?"

I shake my head at his question. "With Shadow Pack still around, no one is safe." Walking up to Garett, I put my hand on his arm, stopping his pacing. "We won't let your family get caught up in this. Did you manage to get any more information about the killer?" Aiming the last question at Eric, I turn to face him, keeping my hand on Garett, who in turn wraps his arms around me, pressing my back to his chest.

"No, I couldn't pick up much, but this feels like a baby demon."

"What do you mean?" Alex asks.

"Some of us are born demons, others are only part demon, they could go their whole life not knowing they weren't fully human, then one day, something triggers them and their powers start to come in. They are difficult to control at first, sporadic, and usually there is a trail of bodies following them until they learn to control it." Eric looks at me as he says this, and I feel my stomach drop, remembering what he said the other morning, that Seb's power outbursts felt a little like a demon coming into power. No, not Seb. Grabbing my phone, I press the home screen to see if he's replied to my text. Nothing.

When I look up, the whole room is watching me, obviously

picking up on my distress, but I'm not ready to share my theories with the others yet.

Feeling lost, I take a deep breath and focus on Eric again. "What do we do now?"

"We need to know more about the ASP killings," he responds.

"How are we going to do that? Just hang around street corners until an ASP agent happens to get murdered?" Killian drawls helpfully, and I restrain the urge to throw something at him.

Eric doesn't rise to his jibe and keeps his gaze steady on me. "Who do you know that would know about ASP, who works for them but trusts you?"

Shit. Em.

I haven't spoken to the lying bastard since I found out he'd been working with ASP, not to mention the fact he kept quiet about a group of Shadowborn after he let me believe I was one of the only ones left. I feel sick at the thought of talking to him again, but I know he'll have answers I need.

"I need to go back to the Shadow Realm."

Chapter Eight

My statement went down about as well as you could've imagined. The only person that semi-agreed with it was Eric. I've known I'd need to go back to the Shadow Realm sooner or later, but I've been putting it off. The thought of seeing Em again twists my stomach and makes me feel a little sick. In fact, the last time I saw him, I wanted to kill him. Tori had just died, and he told me that he worked for ASP, the very people who killed her in the first place. I knew Em had a secret, but I didn't feel it was my place to ask it, after all, I have hundreds of secrets, but the betrayal I felt after learning that he worked for them hurt me more than I thought it would. He'd become like a father figure to me, sure, a crazy Yoda type father figure, but the closest I've ever felt to having a dad.

Leaning back in my kitchen chair, I cross my arms and watch the four growling males in the room. Okay, so Eric isn't growling, he looks as cool and calm as he did before, but the others are struggling with my declaration. Garett is sitting at the table with me, trying to be supportive, but I know he really doesn't want me to go.

"Why should you give that traitorous piece of shit a single moment of your time?" Killian growls out as he storms across the room, pacing like a caged animal. "You're not going."

"Excuse me?" Pushing to standing, I brace my arms on the

table in front of me, uttering a bitter laugh in response to his order. "Oh come on, Kill, you know better than to try and order me around."

"Ari, I agree with him. I don't think you should go, and as your pack beta—" Cutting Alex off, I stalk towards him, my wolf prowling under my skin as I stand nose to nose with him.

"Don't even go there, Alex. I've been part of the pack for less than twenty-four hours, and you already think you can order me around?" My eyes glow with my inner wolf as I stare down my beta, my heart eerily calm as I wait for his response. "Have I made a mistake?" My tone is low but even, keeping my eye contact with him firm as the rest of the room falls silent.

"Fuck no, Ari, that's not what I meant, and you would know that if you hadn't automatically assumed the worst of me!" His anger causes me to take a step back in shock. "When are you going to learn that we. Are. Not. Shadow Pack!" His voice is loud, and it causes me to tremble slightly.

"Alex," Garett warns, but I put out a hand to stop him. Before, I would've turned and run, but I can't do that anymore. I look around the room and see the guys around me, my family, and know I need to try and explain, make them understand.

"No, you're right—I've been a lone wolf for a long time, my only experience of being in a pack was being tortured and treated like a piece of shit, but you knew that about me before you decided you wanted to be part of whatever this is." I gesture around the room, my stomach churning as I meet his heated gaze again. "I'm damaged. I'm broken, and half the time, I'm a complete mess. I'm trying, I want a better life, but you have to know that I'm going to make mistakes." My words come out in a rush. "I'm really trying." I can feel the others gathering around, their hands reaching out to comfort me, but I keep my eyes locked on Alex. There's something more going on here, something deeper I don't understand, but I need to show him that I'm not the person I was.

We stand there for a few moments, and I feel the pressure of lost seconds weighing on me. Seb's absence is like a void, an empty ache, a missing piece of me I hadn't known existed. The longer we wait, the more it hurts, and just as I think I'm going to break, Alex's eyes soften as he raises his hand to cup my face.

"I know," he says on a sigh, pressing his forehead against mine. "I'm sorry. I just still can't believe you're here, that you're mine. I keep expecting to turn around and find you gone. That was wrong of me. I'm sorry," he apologises and presses a gentle kiss to my lips. Heat sparks within me as I kiss him back, my skin igniting where the others touch me, the atmosphere in the room changing like the flip of a switch. A little part of me wants to carry on, to see where this would go, but without Seb here, it feels like something is missing.

Breaking away from our kiss with a sigh, I take a step away, needing some space while I try to figure out our plan of action. Killian's eyes narrow as he takes a step towards me, but I put a hand out to stop him.

"I'm not running away. I just can't think straight with all of you touching me." My smile is wry as I elucidate, and I see the moment he understands. His pupils dilate as he scents my arousal, his smile turning smug. "Now, can we have a conversation without one of you ordering me around?" I keep my voice light, but I mean what I say. I may be part of this pack now, but no one can stop me from doing what's right. I *need* to go back to the Shadow Realm.

"I don't like it," Killian grumbles, surprising the hell out of me. I'd expected more snarling and growling from him, demanding that I couldn't go, but instead, I'm met with this. "Are you sure this is what you need to do? I don't trust Em." His jaw is tight and his body posture rigid, so I know how hard he's trying to reason with me, which endears him to me all the more. My broody alpha mate is not known to compromise. But he's right—Em can't be trusted anymore.

"I don't trust him either," I respond, pushing away from the side of the room so I'm facing him. I rest my hand on his arm, ignoring the feeling of rightness at our touch and the heat that blooms in his eyes. "I need to do this. Em has answers, and we need them now. I'll be safe," I promise. Although the words are aimed at Killian, I look around the room at the others, making sure they understand. Garett opens his mouth to say something when a ringing fills the room. Frowning, he fishes his phone from his pocket before answering the call.

"Hello?" Turning from us, he walks into another room, although with our shifter hearing, we could hear him from the other end of the house. We make small talk while Garett finishes his phone call, trying not to listen, but I can't help hearing the worry in the tone. After a couple of minutes, Garett walks back into the room, his shoulders tight with tension and his brow furrowed with worry.

"What's happened?" I inquire as I step forward, the rest of the room on alert, searching for whatever threat has caused Garett to look like this.

With a sigh, he runs his hands across his face before facing me, looking grim as he speaks. "I have to go. Something's going on with the twins."

Concerned, I take a step towards him. "What do you mean?"

"They seem to have snapped. Losing Tori has done something to them." Garett's voice is heavy, like the weight of the world is on his shoulders. I knew his brothers were struggling, but I hadn't realised how bad it had become.

How could fate have been so cruel for Tori and the bears to find each other, their mates, only for her to be taken away within the space of minutes? I mourn Tori for the friendship we had, she was my best friend and the closest thing I had to family. She had a shitty past like me, she understood like no one else could. But the twins and Max, they never got the chance to know her, and now they mourn the future they will never have.

"Grief affects everyone differently," Eric says softly, placing his hand on Garett's arm in a comforting gesture.

"No, it's more than that." His voice drops to a growl as he paces the room, his frustration showing through his usual calm persona. "They're saying that they have to find her, they need to be with their mate."

"Is that normal?" Frowning, I look to the others for the answer. I've never been part of a normal functioning pack, certainly not one with true mates, so I don't know if this is to be expected. I try to imagine what it would be like if Killian, or even Eric, died. The bond between us is so strong that it would feel like a part of me was missing. Who am I kidding? If any of my guys died, it would ruin me, mate bonded or not.

Alex clears his throat and his expression has my heart dropping. "Often, when one part of a true mated pair dies, the other isn't far to follow. Their grief consumes them."

"No, this is more than that," Garett insists, although I can see the concern in his eyes. "They're acting like she's still alive and they need to find her. We've had to lock them in the compound, but they keep trying to escape. It's not safe for them."

The others share a look, and I feel grief clawing at my throat. "She's dead." The words rip from my throat, my eyes brimming with tears that I refuse to let fall. Screwing my eyes shut, I take a deep breath. "I saw her die. She was shot in front of me. She's dead." Arms wrap around me, and I know from the scent that it's Garett.

"I know. I'm sorry." His deep voice soothes me as I bury my face against his chest, my heart still raw and aching from loss, but these guys help make life without Tori bearable. "Maybe I should stay..." Pulling away, I shake my head at his words, giving him a strained smile as guilt eats at me from keeping him from his family.

"No, I'm fine. You should be with your family," I tell him, taking a step back to clear my head. When I'm in his arms, it's easy to be selfish, to ask him to stay.

Locking those intense eyes with mine, he stops me from retreating with a hand on my arm. "Ari, you're my family too." The conviction in his words hold more meaning than I want to explore right now, but my heart flutters in my chest at his statement.

Clearing my throat, I nod and smile fully at him this time. "They need you. We'll be fine, I won't be in the Shadow Realm long."

Just long enough to get the answers I need, I think to myself. I don't want to spend a second longer there than I have to. Garett continues to stare at me for a while until he sees whatever he's looking for. Pulling me into his arms, he presses a gentle kiss to my lips.

"I love you. Be safe, don't take any risks. I'll be back as soon as I can." Pulling away from me, he turns to the others, his gaze moving between the three guys. "Look after her."

The others nod in agreement, though I notice Killian bristle, his inner wolf disliking being ordered, even over something like the safety of his mate, but he stays quiet. I guess we're all growing and changing. Standing back from the guys, I watch with a heavy heart as Garett says his farewells, my gut telling me that this journey to the Shadow Realm is going to take me away from them far longer than I would like.

After Garett left, I didn't see the point in hanging around wasting more time, so I walked up to my room, followed closely by the others, with Killian practically biting Alex's hand off as he touched my shoulder. The tension in the room rose pretty high as my growly alpha became possessive, their concern about me returning to the Shadow Realm filling the air. With a bravado I didn't feel, I gave them a cheeky wink and lay down on the bed before closing my eyes and following that pull that's always beckoning, always calling me.

Even before I open my eyes, I know I'm back in the Shadow Realm by the feeling of nothingness that surrounds me—the absence of wind, scents, and sounds are all hallmarks of this lifeless place.

As I peel open my eyes, I'm greeted by the unchanged grey expanse of the realm. I turn my head and see the dark tree line of the forest, the trees extending for as far as the eye can see. I don't know why I always end up here when I visit, on the strip between the dark forest where the shadow beasts roam and the unending plains. Movement by the tree line catches my attention, and I can see the sifting, flickering shape of one of the beasts, and although I'm too far away to be certain, I get the distinct impression that it's watching me. The feeling of being hunted clings to me like a shadow, like no matter how fast I run, I will never be able to shake it. My arm aches from where the shadow beast scratched me the last time I entered the forest. Looking down at the wound, I see the ugly, shiny scar of a long-healed wound, but being here makes it ache like a fresh injury.

Pushing to my feet, I take another look around me. There is no sign of Em, but that doesn't worry me, he always seemed to know when I was here before, so I have no doubt he'll turn up today. There's something he wants from me. It took me a while to work it out before, why he would keep turning up and offer to train me. I thought it was out of the goodness of his heart, and then I learned that he worked for ASP and I was reminded again that nobody does anything for free. You'd have thought I'd have learned that by, now given my history, but I guess I'm a glutton for punishment.

I begin to walk, and the slight changes in the twisting tree line to my right are the only indicators that I'm moving—the unending plains to my left unchanging, the strange mist eddying around me as I go. After what could have been minutes or hours—time moves strangely here—I feel a change in the atmosphere and I know Em has arrived.

"How did you know I was here?" I keep walking, my footsteps steady and quiet against the dull grass, my gaze straight ahead, not wanting to look at him just yet. I'm not ready to see his face. Will he even feel guilty about everything that's happened?

There's a pause, as if he's surprised by my question, but he isn't quiet for long, he never is. "Shadowborn can feel when there's a change in the Shadow Realm, that includes someone entering it."

"So you knew every time I came here." My words are more of a statement than a question, but he answers anyway. I had suspected, but now I have confirmation.

"Yes. The first time I met you, I wasn't going to come, I was going to leave you alone, not draw attention to you." He sighs, and I finally turn to face him. He looks the same, not that I can fully make out his features, thanks to the glow that always surrounds him. "But I felt your fear that day when you went into the forest, and I couldn't stay away." A weight seems to settle on his shoulders as he speaks, but I'm not about to try and make him feel better about it, not until I get the answers I need.

"Why're you always glowing, why aren't you in full form like me? And what do you mean you didn't want to draw attention to me?" The questions fall from my lips with my impatience. I've had enough of his secrets and I need answers.

"I'm just projecting an image of myself, I'm not fully here like you are. I'm still fully conscious in my body. But you, you throw your whole self here, your soul has left your body, which is why your body reacts like it does. Without your soul, you can't function fully," he explains as I continue to walk through the realm. "Like I said, all Shadowborn know when someone enters the Shadow Realm, especially with how much of a commotion you cause when you enter," he says wryly with a roll of his eyes. "Remember, we're in hiding, they have lives and families they're trying to protect." The prospect that other Shadowborn are out there, with families and normal lives, makes my stomach churn from frustration, since I seem to have been excluded from this secret Shadowborn society. I hold down my anger, there's nothing that can be done about my past now, and with a father like mine, there was never any way I was going to have a normal life, Shadowborn or not. At least I've learned how to protect myself now. It's not fair to those who have managed to fight for a life if I hold it against them. It's exactly what I would have done if I was offered a chance at peace. That doesn't stop me from being mad at Em, though, or from feeling bitter at the life I missed out on.

"My every move is being watched, if I entered the Shadow Realm to help you, then they would know, and it would bring attention to you. Which is why I left it so long," Em continues, unaware of my internal turmoil, and I get the feeling he's trying to apologise, to get me to understand. Well, he has a lot more to explain before I even consider taking his apology. Narrowing my eyes, I pick up on a particular word.

"What do you mean 'they'?" He can't be talking about the other Shadowborn, and I've noticed he's said this before, but I never questioned him on it. Who is this mysterious 'they' he seems to be hiding from?

"ASP." My eyes narrow in confusion as he speaks, not sure that I understand what he's saying.

"But-but you work for ASP, you said so yourself," I point out, getting frustrated at the circles he's talking around me.

He sighs, running a hand through his hair before he starts speaking. "It's time I told you more about myself, but I don't have much time." There's a pause as he gathers his thoughts, and for a moment, I don't think he's going to say anything until he turns to face me. "About twenty years ago, I was arrested by ASP. They were going to terminate me, as was protocol at the time. All Shadowborn were killed immediately, without trial, not to mention what I was caught doing wasn't particularly legal." He grins, and a shudder runs down my spine. "There's a faction within ASP. They saw how corrupt the organisation was and how shifters, in particular, were being persecuted. They proposed that I work with them, to help them, and to protect other Shadowborn. They faked my execution and gave me a new name."

"Em," I mutter. I had always thought the name was strange, perhaps a nickname, but I never questioned it.

"Yes. My real name was Emanuel. I convinced them to let me change it to Em. Not very original, I know, but it meant a lot to me to keep that part of myself."

My mind is spinning from his revelation. I'd always thought that ASP was corrupt, with the recent shifter disappearances and deaths being the nail in the coffin, but I hadn't realised the depth of what was going on. "I don't understand. How does ASP not know you're alive?" This is what I find difficult to understand. ASP knows everything, how would they miss that a Shadowborn was working for them when they had ordered him to be executed?

"As part of the deal, I have to stay within ASP headquarters, under house arrest." His mouth twists as he speaks, and I can tell that the fact he can't leave the ASP headquarters is something he hates, but I don't say anything. I need to know more before I can make any decisions. "According to ASP's official paperwork, I'm a warlock's great nephew, and I witnessed a dodgy deal, so I was offered protection if I testified against my 'uncle.' They leave me alone, and I can help the splinter group of ASP, keeping Shadowborn safe and giving them a heads up when a new Shadowborn emerges so they can get in there and help them hide their gifts before someone else notices. The whole family will simply disappear, and because Shadowborn powers are more often than not found in shifters, ASP doesn't go investigating the disappearances. They've always been discriminatory towards shifters, but it has become worse the last few years. Whole packs are being eradicated, and females are struggling to get pregnant and carry to term, but they don't bother to investigate." Anger laces his words, and I can see now that he truly wants to help us.

"Are you a shifter?" Curiosity runs through me. Em has always been a bit of an anomaly for me. He doesn't smell or feel like a shifter, but what he says is true—Shadowborn powers tend to predominantly turn up in shifters. I once heard rumours that the merfolk had a Shadowborn, but that's all it was, rumours.

Em smiles gently at my question. "No. I'm distantly related to the fae, but I only have very weak earth magic, my shadow powers far surpass my fae magic."

Huh, I wouldn't have guessed he was fae, but now that I think about it, he does have the tricky nature of some of the fae races. A question burns within me, and my gut is telling me it's important I ask this. "Why were you arrested in the first place?"

He sighs, finally bringing his eyes back to mine. "I was trying to get to you."

Silence fills the space between us, my eyes wide as his words sink in. "What do you mean?"

"I sensed a new Shadowborn. Young, the strongest I'd ever felt, but so confused and in pain. So much pain..." He trails off, his eyes on mine but not truly seeing. "I was young and impulsive. I was trying to find a way to get to you, especially when I found out you belonged to Shadow Pack, but you were so far away, across the ocean. Even back then, Shadow Pack was notorious, and I knew I had to get you away. But I failed, I asked too many questions, attracted attention to myself, and got caught," he finishes, his eyes brightening as he comes out of his memories.

My heart beats painfully in my chest, desperately wanting to believe his words but struggling to push past the distrust that's ingrained within me. For a moment, I let myself think of what my life would have been like if Em had managed to help me, to get me away from Shadow Pack. I could have been a normal child and had a happy childhood without pain, fear, and loneliness. Shaking my head, I push away those thoughts. Em would only have gotten himself killed, there was no way he would have got past my father, the alpha. He would've killed his way across the world until he got me back, his little weapon.

"I never intended for you to feel so alone. I tried, I promise." Em's words are full of pain, and for the first time, I believe him.

Letting go of the pent-up breath I hadn't realised I was holding, I sigh and come to a stop, running my hand through my tangled hair as I try to come to a decision. Do I trust him? Scratch that, *can* I trust him? He lied to me, but I believe he had nothing to do with Tori's death and that he wants to help me. I'm so used to facing problems alone that trust has become difficult, but through the love of the guys, I'm beginning to see that I don't have to face everything alone anymore. Turning to face him and seeing the hope in his expression, I come to my decision.

"So, what do we do now?"

Chapter Nine

Walking down the high street, I spot the sign I'm looking for and head towards the coffee shop, my entourage of guys following closely behind me. Usually, I'd be daydreaming about the coffee I'm about to consume, my thoughts on my next caffeine hit, but not today. Coming to a stop just outside the door, I take a deep breath, readying myself for the meeting ahead. My stomach is a bundle of nerves, not that I would let anyone know that, my expression calm and closed off as I eye the shop behind my dark sunglasses, my hands in the pockets of my leather jacket. Seb takes a step closer, and as I bring my eyes to meet his, my stomach twists again, but for a different reason this time. He'd turned up in the middle of the night and crawled into bed next to me. When I'd questioned him this morning, he just shrugged off my questions with a smile, but I know something's going on, we all do.

A hand on my shoulder brings me out of my thoughts, and I turn my head to see who the hand belongs to. Garett. I guess I'm not as good at hiding my feelings as I thought I was, or perhaps it's just them?

"Are you okay?" he asks quietly, and I know all I have to do is say the word and they will take me away from here. Pausing, I mull over my answer, but the guys step closer to me, surrounding me with their strength, taking my silence as a sign of uncertainty.

Alex takes my hand, drawing my attention to him. "You don't have to do this."

"I still think it's too risky. We don't need them," Killian announces, crossing his arms as he glares at the coffee shop. He's right—this is risky. I could be walking straight into their hands, and to be honest, I want to stay as far away from ASP as possible. However, we need answers and we need Em—ASP has both of these.

With a sigh, I shake my head and start walking towards the door. "Let's get this over with," I mutter under my breath, but I know they can hear me.

Stepping inside, my inner wolf winces at the barrage of noise that greets us as we walk through the groups of humans ordering their coffees and chatting in groups around the circular tables. It doesn't take long for me to figure out who we're meeting, they stick out like a sore thumb. Sure, they are dressed in casual clothing to try and blend in, but they sit there with a stillness only a supernatural could possess, and although they are simply watching the humans around them, there is something that screams predator when you look at them. Their eyes lock on mine, and I realise why they seem familiar to me. I've met them before. Ryan and Aiden Cross, the shifter cousins who tried to convince me to join ASP before, although now I wonder who they were asking for—ASP or the faction group?

I think over what I know about them already. Ryan is a wolf, and the feistier of the two, quick to anger but powerful. Aiden, the quiet and thoughtful bird shifter, didn't say much at our last meeting, but he did warn me that something was coming, and he was right, that was when the Shadow Pack attacked us and I nearly lost everything. Can I trust them? My gut is saying yes. Deciding to trust that instinct, I walk over to the table in the corner of the room, the two agents standing to greet us. They aren't in uniform, so this obviously isn't official ASP business, but other than that, they look the same as they did before. Ryan narrows his grey eyes on me, his stubbled jaw clenching as I reach their table. This obviously wasn't his idea then.

Aiden ignores his cousin and smiles at me as he offers his hand to shake. "Ariana, thank you for agreeing to meet us."

"Call me Ari, please." Wincing at the name, I pull my hand away from his as soon as I can. I don't bother to offer to shake Ryan's hand. No one calls me Ariana anymore, the only person who used to was my father, and he's dead now. "Enough of the niceties, why did you want to meet me?" I demand as I take a seat opposite them, the guys pulling over spare chairs and sitting close, forming a protective ring around me as I chat with the two agents.

"I'm sure Em has explained about us," Ryan drawls as he sits, confirming what Em said about working for this group.

Dipping my head, I turn my full focus to the wolf shifter, daring him with my eyes to press the issue further, pushing a little alpha power into my words. "Yes, but I want to hear it from you."

Ryan snarls, and I feel his power whip out in response, testing me, feeling for my strengths and vulnerabilities. We're actually fairly evenly matched, he's stronger than I'd thought, but I also have three wolves, a bear, and a demon at my side, all of which dislike Ryan's blatant challenging behaviour. The atmosphere around us changes, the hairs on my arms standing on end as Killian and the others turn their attention to the wolf shifter. Glancing across at Killian, I worry he might lash out like he would've when I first met him, but he simply keeps his gaze locked with Ryan's as he takes my hand, the others doing the same. It's simple, but makes a powerful statement. I'm theirs and they're mine. I'm the centre of the group, and they will protect me from any threats.

Aiden clears his throat, throwing a glare at Ryan before raising an eyebrow at me. "We aren't here to threaten you, we just want to talk. We didn't realise you had taken on several mates."

"That is no concern of yours. Say what you came here to say," I command, tired of the games they are playing.

"Fair enough," the bird shifter concedes, shifting in his seat. "For years, we've noticed the way that shifters are treated as lesser beings by ASP. It started small, taking longer than necessary to investigate shifter cases, only allowing shifters to have low positions within the organisation, but over the last few years, it has grown worse. They're completely ignoring missing person cases, packs disappearing, attacks on shifters are not investigated, and we recently discovered that ASP might be behind the drop in shifter pregnancies," Aiden explains, and for the first time, I get a wave of his power as he gets frustrated, he feels just as powerful as Ryan, if not more so.

"What? How would they have anything to do with the pregnancy rates?" Eric questions, speaking up for the first time.

"Why is the human here?" Ryan narrows his eyes at Eric, and I realise the first time ASP came to speak to me, I was meeting with Eric in a coffee shop much like this. They had thought he was human then, back when I was trying to work out exactly what he was. They must still not be able to sense what he is.

"That's irrelevant. Answer the question," Killian challenges, avoiding the question.

"Magic." The answer doesn't tell us much, but my stomach drops all the same. If the magic users are involved, then this is much bigger than one corrupt organisation. Aiden drops his voice as he speaks so the humans can't overhear us, and I realise that them agreeing to meet in public is just as much to protect them as it is to protect me. "This separate group within ASP, we make sure that shifters are protected, investigate the cases that the other agents won't. We want you to join us, to help us. Your...unique talents will aid us." Unique talents, I guess that's one thing to call my shadow powers, but I also understand why they wouldn't want to say it out loud.

I hold their gazes, my body stilling, not giving anything away. Sure, Em has probably told them I'm Shadowborn and they suspected before, but I'm not going to admit it to them, not when I've been hiding it my whole life. "Why should I trust you?" My eyes flick to Ryan as I speak, but it's Aiden who answers me.

"I understand ASP doesn't exactly have a great reputation, but that's why we need you, you can help us, help people like yourself," Aiden states plainly, his face not giving anything away, but I can feel how much this means to him, and I hate to admit it, but something stirs to life within me. Could I use my powers to help others? The reason I became a nurse was to assist others in the only way I knew how, those who had suffered and been abused their whole lives. What if I could do something to help stop that from happening? I push these thoughts away and clear my throat before asking my next question.

"So, what're you saying? You want me to become an ASP agent?" The thought of me working as an agent makes me want to laugh, and the lilt at the end of my question makes it clear I find this proposition amusing.

"Yes, you would be assigned to our team, and then you can help us. We'll help you keep your...other powers under wraps, Em can teach you how to control them." Aiden's voice is calm as he ignores my amused smile.

It's at this point, I realise how serious they are about this. Shit. Me, an ASP agent? Can I really imagine myself in the ASP suits? It would feel like I'm betraying everything I am, but at the same time, I'd be able to help so many people if I accepted their proposal. Realising I'm leaning forward, I sit back, crossing my arms over my chest, hoping they can't hear the pounding of my heart in my chest.

"What if I say no?" The two agents shift in their seats as I speak, which is the only indication I get that they don't like my question.

"You can still help us, give us information, and in return, we'll help you when we can," Aiden replies, his voice completely business-like once more, his face back to a professional mask, and I know they're disappointed.

I turn to look at the guys. They've been peculiarly quiet, and I know that they will have plenty to say once we get out of ear shot, but for now, I push to my feet and smile at the agents.

"I'll think on your offer."

Ryan jumps up, his chair falling to the ground with a loud clatter. "You can't be serious," he demands loudly, not seeming to notice the coffee shop has gone quiet to see what the commotion is about. "You're in danger, we all are, and you're turning us down?"

Aiden stands and places his hand on his cousin's shoulder, trying to calm the situation, and I'm aware of several sets of human eyes watching us. "Ryan, now is not the time—" he begins, but I interrupt, needing to explain my reasoning. I don't know why, but I don't want them thinking that I don't want to help people in need. Since when did I care what ASP thinks? Or perhaps it's not ASP I care about, but the agents who dream of a better life for us all.

"I've learned that ASP are the bad guys, the ones who will dole out justice as it suits them, and ignore those of us who are truly in need, and I can't just forget that. My trust is not easily given." I feel the guys gather closer behind me as I speak, their hands touching me so I know they're there, that they support me. Taking a deep breath, I give them a small smile as I continue, "This isn't a no, just give me some time to talk to my family."

There is a pause as my words sink in before Ryan nods and leaves without another comment, leaving Aiden watching after him as he storms out. Aiden is silent for a moment before his gaze returns to mine, his grey eyes apologetic. "Thank you, Ari, I'm sorry about Ryan. I hope we can meet again soon," he says as he finishes the last of his coffee, returning the empty mug to the table. My guys take the cue and start to file out, walking towards the door, but something stops me from following them. Turning, I stop Aiden with a hand on his arm.

"Who did you lose?" My words are quiet, so even those with supernatural hearing would struggle to hear what I'm saying.

His eyes narrow in confusion, but I know he knows what I'm

asking. "What do you mean?"

"Earlier, when you were talking about helping those who need it most. I know that look you had in your eyes, I've lived it. You lost someone." A stubborn spark enters his eyes, and for a moment, I think he's going to brush me off and tell me I'm barking up the wrong tree, but he drops his gaze and lets out a long sigh.

"I didn't have the easiest upbringing. I was stolen from my family as a youngling by a group who trafficked shifter children. I was strong and the other kids looked up to me, so I was kept around longer. A young fox shifter and I became close, she was like a sister to me..." He pauses, and my heart aches, knowing what's coming next. "Anyway, she was killed. ASP eventually had to investigate the disappearances of shifter children, and we were rescued. They couldn't find my parents, but they managed to track down Ryan's family, who were the closest thing. Turns out, there's some wolf blood in my ancestry somewhere," he explains, and I have to fight the urge to wrap my arms around him.

"How long were you there for?" I don't need to explain where 'there' was, he knows what I'm asking.

"Six years." I close my eyes briefly as he speaks, anger running through me. He was with those bastards for six years, and ASP did nothing. I may not know him well, but I wouldn't wish that life on anyone. When I open my eyes, I have one question.

"Are you happy now?"

He finally smiles at me. "Yes, Ryan's like a brother to me, and his mother treats me like her own. As for work, I find pleasure in helping those like me—like you."

I meet his eyes and see understanding there. He knows what it's like to not know who you can trust, but he has battled it and come out on the other side.

"Ari?" I turn to see who called me and see Seb waiting for me with a confused smile, the rest of the guys standing just behind him. Except someone is missing. Saying my goodbyes to Aiden, I walk over to the guys, looking around the coffee shop in the process.

"Where's Garett?" I ask, my nerves on edge without my bear here. I've become so used to having him around.

"He's just outside, he had to take a call," Alex replies, just as the door opens and my bear walks towards us. The smile that had begun to form on my face drops when I see his frown.

"What's wrong?" Everyone is on alert at my tone, looking around for any threats, but my eyes are firmly locked on Garett, who sighs, his body seeming to deflate in the process. This has me more worried than anything else. I've never seen my positive Garett like this before. "Garett?"

He avoids my eyes as he looks around at the others. "I hate to ask this of you, Ari, but I wouldn't do it if it wasn't important."

I try to stay calm, but he's making me nervous with his blatant avoidance of answering the question. "Anything. What's going on?"

"It's my brothers, we need to go over to my pack," he answers, and I feel a sense of relief fill me. Why was he so worried about asking me this?

"Of course, but why're you so stressed?"

"It's my brothers. I need you to help calm them down, they don't believe that Tori's dead. They won't listen to anyone else. We need you." The ever-present pain that appeared after Tori died flares in my chest, almost taking my breath away. It hurts so much that I see Eric and Killian rubbing their chests, feeling the pain through our bond. Killian steps forward and positions himself in front of me, as if to protect me from Garett.

"Stop. You're upsetting her—" Killian growls, but I cut him off.

"It's okay, Kill, I'll go, I want to help." There is some grumbling, but the grateful look on Garett's face is enough to help pull me through the pain-induced fog of Tori's death. Will this pain, this grief, ever leave? Or will I forever be torn, the fractured, gaping hole that Tori left behind defining the rest of my life? I can only hope I'll learn to live with it and that I don't let it consume me.

Chapter Ten

The journey over to Long Claw Pack is quiet and tense. No one's quite sure what to expect, except Garett, but he isn't telling me much. I'm sure it's to protect me, but I'm going to find out soon enough. Sitting in the back of the large town car that was sent over by the pack alpha, I hold on tightly to Seb's and Killian's hands. I would've been fine sitting alone, I'm used to caring for myself, but they wanted to comfort me, and shifters tend to find comfort in physical touch. Garett and Alex sit in the seat opposite us. Alex's gaze is focused on my hands, his look of longing making it clear he would prefer to be the one sitting next to me, but I'm grateful that they have allowed Seb to sit next to me. As Seb is the lowest member of our little group, if we were to follow pack rule and hierarchy, then he would be far away from me, even though out of all of us, he would benefit the most from being close to me, both physically and emotionally. Lower members of the pack need and rely on those with more power, it helps sustain them, which is why you only ever see alpha level lone wolves, those with lesser power just wouldn't survive on their own.

I glance across at Garett, who stares out the window, completely silent as we travel the short journey across town to the gym that acts as the pack headquarters. His expression is troubled, which only serves to make me more nervous about what might greet us when we arrive.

The only person from our group who isn't joining us is Eric. When we were waiting for the car to arrive, he started acting strangely, his features sharpening as his demon started pushing for control. The thought of a demon as old as Eric losing control is scary, so when he made excuses and started backing away, no one questioned it, giving him the space he needed. However, now that he's gone, I can't help but worry.

"Do you think Eric's okay?" My question breaks the silence in the car, bringing several sets of eyes to mine. "He was acting strange," I clarify, but Alex just shrugs.

"He seemed okay to me, just distracted. He said he had something to check out. I'm sure he'll be fine."

"Yeah, he would've told you if there was something wrong," Seb chimes in, "Besides, he's like a thousand years old, right? I'm sure he can look after himself," he jokes, running his hand up and down my arm, and I force myself to nod.

That's strange. They obviously didn't feel the little bursts of his power or notice the change in him as his demon surfaced like I did. Is that because I know him better, or because of our bond? Leaning back into my seat, I close my eyes, feigning tiredness as I focus on the sliver of a bond that Eric and I share. It's not like the gleaming silver bond Killian and I have, more like a pull, a feeling of electricity within me that draws me like a moth to a flame. I don't know if it feels so different because Eric is a demon, or if it's because we haven't completed our bond yet.

Taking a deep breath, I grasp at the bond and can't help the gasp that escapes me as a feeling of electricity rushes through my body. I can distantly hear the guys calling my name, but it's like they are yelling from far away. My limbs feel like they are charged and full of energy. I've reached out to touch my half-formed bond with Eric before, but it felt more solid, more human, but this, this feels completely different. Nothing about this bond feels human right now, and I realise that Eric is in his demon form. At first, he doesn't seem to feel that I'm there, his attention fully focused on something else, and when I realise what it is, shock runs through me.

He's hunting.

He must sense my shock, as surprise runs through him and he stumbles to a stop, followed by a begrudging admiration.

My little wolf. I can't hear the purring words, but I can *feel* them, my whole body warming as arousal fills my veins to the point that my need is painful, and I can feel my body gasping as bolts of energy run through me. *I'm impressed you were able to reach out to me in this form. Just another affirmation that we are made for each other.* There's a pause, and I can almost feel his claws lightly running down the skin on my arm, which should be impossible since we are miles apart. *Eric has been trying to keep me away from you, but it is only a matter of time.*

"Until what?" I gasp out, and I can't help the groan that escapes me as he chuckles, washing waves of arousal over me, that line between pleasure and pain blurring.

Until I get my hands on you. That day will come soon, and when it does, I will make you mine.

With all my strength, I rip my mind from his hold and am thrown back into my own body. I open my eyes and meet the glowing gazes of four barely in control shifters. The scent of my arousal fills the car, and my breath comes out in gasps. Aftershocks of electricity seem to run along my limbs, causing a pleasure that borders on pain. I can see why it's frowned upon to take a demon lover—that kind of power could be addictive. Already, my body aches for more.

"What the fuck was that?" Killian's voice is low, almost a growl as he grabs my shoulders, turning me to face him, which in the confines of the car has me almost in his lap.

"You felt it too?" I breathlessly ask, turning my head to see if the others are as affected as I am, but I'm stopped when Killian tightens his grip on my arms and growls low.

"Unless you want me to completely lose control, don't look at anyone else right now." Freezing in place, I keep my eyes on his, not taking his warning for granted. I know all too well the look of an alpha about to lose control of his wolf. "What happened?"

I wouldn't usually let Killian speak to me that way, or I'd give him a hard time for acting like an overprotective alpha, letting his instincts control him, but right now, I don't think it's wise. "I was worried about Eric, so I tapped into our bond. He was in his demon form." Cursing follows my words, and I have to focus on taking a deep breath as I push away the memory of what it felt like, how powerful I felt. "He's not the same Eric in that form. He was giving me a...taste of what it will be like when I meet him fully."

"Fuck that. If that's how you react, he isn't getting anywhere near you! You looked like you were in agony. He's a pain demon, Ari! The only reason I let Eric anywhere near you is because he has such good control over himself!"

"You don't *let* me do anything. *I* am in control of what I do or don't do." My voice deepens into a growl, my wolf prowling under my skin. With so many dominant personalities and the scent of my arousal in the air, it's aggravating all of us, stirring up our animals and bringing out Killian's possessive alpha tendencies. A movement across from me catches my eye. Turning my head, I see Garett leaning towards me as if he's going to pull me over to him, desire and something that looks like pain clear to see in his eyes, but he doesn't move any closer.

The car pulls to a stop and I see that we are outside the bears' headquarters, but no one moves, the tension in the car high. I start to slide away from Killian, but his arms tighten around me, a low growl rumbling from his throat. Turning my attention back to him, I put my hands on his chest and meet his eyes, staring him down. Rule number one of dealing with an angry alpha—don't look them in the eyes unless you want to challenge them. For a moment, I see

Kill's eyes narrow as he senses the challenge, but he manages to gain control over his wolf.

"Now is not the time for this. Garett and his family need us."

"I'll let it drop for now, but this isn't over, Ari." Killian's words sound threatening, but he sends me a glimpse down our bond of how he plans on resolving the issue, and it causes desire to flare in me again—flashes of pinning me to the bed while he fucks me, calling him Alpha as I submit to him. Raising an eyebrow, I send him an image right back, his arms tied behind his back as I worship him with my mouth, him unable to touch me, unable to direct me as I do exactly as I please. His pupils dilate, and a groan fills the car.

"Well, this isn't awkward," Seb comments from my other side, and I can't help but laugh, breaking the tension as the others join in with low chuckles.

"Will you guys wait outside for a moment? I want to have a word with Garett." The guys nod in response to my question, filing out of the car with a few hot glances sent my way until it's just Garett and me left. The silence stretches as I wait for him to start talking, to tell me what's going on. After a tense minute, I sigh and climb out of my seat, with Garett tracking my movements until I sit in his lap and his arms wrap around me, a content little sigh leaving him as he breathes in my scent.

I tell myself I'm doing this to comfort him, but in all honesty, I find just as much comfort in this as he does. My bear shifter has always been my source of comfort and protection, even before I knew that I loved him, back when we were just friends. "You okay?" I keep my words soft as I nuzzle into his chest, feeling his hands rub small circles on my back.

There's a pause before he speaks as he puts his thoughts in order. "I... I'm just worried about my brothers, and sorry that this is going to cause you pain."

Typical Garett, worrying more about me rather than the situation at hand. Pulling my face away from his chest, I look up at him, smile softly, and put all the warmth I can into my voice. "They're your family, so they're also my family. I'll always do what I can to help my family." His responding smile is like that of a man who has everything he ever wanted, and it makes my heart stutter in my chest, lighting the whole car with its warmth.

"What did I do to deserve a mate like you?" he whispers, his voice the happiest I've heard in a long time as he presses his forehead to mine, and I suddenly feel like the worst person in the world. This is all it took to make him happy? Garett has always been there for me, our relationship has always been easy, even when we were just friends. He always knew when to refrain from pushing me for more. Am I that selfish that just telling him something so simple makes him act like I've given him everything?

"You mean a damaged, selfish, pain in the ass mate who was oblivious to your feelings for years?" Voice cracking, I try to pull away from his embrace, but he stops me with a hand on my chin. I avoid his eyes, and his bear lets out an unhappy grumble that rumbles through my body. It's a common misconception that bear shifters are just rough, brutish creatures. Sure, they can be, but they're also incredibly compassionate and protective to those they consider family, not to mention they revere their mates above all else.

"Ari, look at me." Holding on to my chin until I meet his eyes, he watches me with a frown marring his face. "I'm not sure where this is coming from, but I don't think you're any of those things. What Shadow Pack did to you was evil and would have broken most people, but not you. You came out of it and made a life for yourself, and not only that, but you help people on a daily basis with your work!" He starts caressing my cheek with his thumb as he continues, "I know trusting people is hard for you. I've known it from the start, and honestly, after everything you've been through, I'm amazed at your capacity to love and care as much as you do. I'm constantly thanking my stars that you love me in return, even if you made me wait for it." A wry smile crosses his lips, and I can't help the chuckle that escapes me.

I don't have any words for him, my heart full from his words, so I say the next best thing. "I love you."

He stills in a way that only a supernatural can, and I feel his bear pushing to the surface, his eyes glowing as a rumble of pleasure emits from his chest. "I love you too, Ari, more than words can say."

Reaching up, I thread my hands through his hair, loving the feeling of the silky strands, and use it to pull him towards me. Garett makes a startled noise at my sudden action, but eagerly leans into me, our lips pressing together in a passionate kiss. His hand moves from my face, and he wraps his arms around me, holding me close.

A knock on the window startles us, both of us pulling away and looking around guiltily. "Fuck's sake, guys, I thought we were here for some sort of family crisis." Killian's muffled voice sounds from outside the car, getting quieter as he moves away. Meeting Garett's eyes, we both start laughing like guilty school children as we untangle from each other, but I soon see the happiness drain from Garett as he remembers why we're here. Reaching forward, he opens the door for me, and I smile at him in thanks as I step out to join the others. Alex wiggles his eyebrows as I straighten my clothes after my impromptu make out session in the back of the car. Flipping him off, I turn to face the gym, ready to take on whatever is waiting for us inside.

Looking at the building before us, you would never know it was anything other than a gym and fitness centre, but it holds space for pack meetings and additional training rooms designed for shifters and their supernatural strength. A sense of guilt fills me. I promised Max I would help him and his brothers, but since then, I've barely seen them, their grief so raw that it hurts to be around them. I've been so caught up in trying to find out what ASP is up to that I forgot those who are suffering.

A shadow falls over me, and I glance up to see Garett's grim expression. Reaching over, I take his hand and lead him into the building, knowing that the others will follow us in.

"Ari, Garett. Thank God you're here," Alpha Phillips calls out as he walks towards us through the gym, shaking Garett's hand before pulling me into a one-armed hug. Nodding his greeting to the guys, he leads us through the gym to the rooms out the back reserved for pack. I've never seen the place so quiet before, the space is usually buzzing with life, but today, it feels heavy with grief. As we make our way through the corridor, I nod in greeting to the few pack members we see, all of whom have grim expressions. Rounding a corner, I see Max, looking much the same as the last time I saw him, the only difference being he's wearing clothing this time. He smiles as he turns to greet us, but I can tell he's worried from the tightness around his eyes and the tense way he holds his body. His hair is longer than the last time I saw him, making him look almost identical to Garett.

Striding towards us, he grasps Garett's hand and pulls him into a hug, the two large men taking comfort in each other's touch like only family can. Max pulls away and looks over at me before pulling me into a hug, surprising me. Of all Garett's family members, Max has been the most distant, but I guess grief changes people. "Ari, thank you for coming. I wouldn't ask this of you if we weren't desperate."

Pulling away, I give him a small smile and shrug my shoulders, brushing off how much it means to me that he seems to have accepted me as family. "Of course," I reply, hoping he can hear the sincerity in my voice. "I'll always help when I can. What's going on?"

Max sighs, running his hand through his hair in a gesture that reminds me of his brother. "You managed to reach me when I lost all control, so I thought maybe it would work with them as well..." He's rambling. Max, the strong Gamma of Long Claw. It must be bad, I've never seen him like this, and as I glance over at Garett and see his concerned expression, I know I'm right to be worried.

"Max, stop stalling. What happened?" I demand, the time for niceties having long passed.

Max looks over to his alpha, who's been watching our exchange from a distance. "It's the twins. The loss of Tori seems to have broken them," Alpha Phillips explains pragmatically, but I can tell that seeing his bears in such a state is affecting him. His choice of words makes me frown though. Broken?

"You mean they've lost control of their animal?" I question, not sure exactly what he's trying to tell me.

"If only it was that simple." Max lets out a humourless laugh. "They were doing okay, but then something in them snapped a few days ago. They keep trying to escape, and I don't know how to reach them. To make them understand."

Frowning, I look at the others to see if they understand any more than I do, but I'm met with questioning expressions and shrugs. "But where would they go?" I don't understand why the twins would leave the safety of the pack.

"That's the thing. They're trying to find her." He doesn't need to elaborate, I know exactly who he means, and a feeling of dread fills my gut, like I've been punched in the stomach.

"But she's dead." My voice is hoarse, and my eyes burn as I fight against the memories of holding her stiff, cooling body in my arms.

A hand on my shoulder has me looking up at Max's pained gaze, and I know he's reliving the same memories as me. "That's the thing. They think Tori's still alive."

Chapter Eleven

Standing in front of the huge metal door, I flinch at the loud sound of the locks being pulled back. I'm not sure what to expect and keep having to remind myself that these are Garett's brothers. They need me. Taking a deep breath, I reach forward, grasping the handle as I feel a familiar presence behind me.

"You don't have to do this." I would've known it was Killian, even if he didn't say a word, the little part of me that's connected to him warming as soon as he's near.

"I can handle them. I know how to protect myself." My words sound defensive, but they aren't, I simply state them as fact. Standing still, I feel the hairs on my arm stand up as steps closer to me. I don't turn around, my hand still on the door. All I have to do is push it open, but I don't. Instead, I wait, listening to the soft sound of his shoes on the carpeted flooring, the only indication he's coming closer. I can feel the warmth radiating off him, and I have to resist the urge the lean back into him, my wolf feeling comforted just by his presence.

"It's not your fighting skills I'm worried about. I'm more worried about what this is going to do to you." My hand drops from the door as I turn to face him, not because of what he's saying, but because of *how* he's saying it. "I can't risk you disappearing into the

Shadow Realm again. Every time you go, I feel like part of me has gone with you, and I'm never sure if you're going to come back." My heart pangs in my chest as his voice cracks. When I glance up, his eyes are dry, but I can feel his pain through the bond. No matter how hard he tries to hide it from me, he will never be able to conceal his feelings from me.

There are many things I could say, explanations and justifications, but I don't need to, with Killian, I never have. Instead, I lean forward and press a kiss to his lips, resting my hands against his chest as I send him my feelings down our bond. "I will always come back," I whisper against his lips.

We stay like that for a moment, and when I open my eyes again, Killian is staring down at me intently. With a nod, he presses another kiss to my lips and pulls away, turning and walking back down the corridor without another word. Facing the door once more, I reach for the handle and push it open, not hesitating anymore.

I see Jake as soon as I enter the room, but that isn't hard. The large square space is mostly empty, the same room I had seen Max in not long ago, with just a bed and a small table in one corner. The large mirror against the wall behind me is actually a one-way window, and I know Killian and the others are watching, ready to burst in if they are needed. The twins had been separated once they snapped, since they hadn't been able to control both of them together, but my heart clenches when I see him.

Pacing up and down the room, Jake is obviously agitated and hasn't noticed me yet. The twins are older than Garett, but they never acted like it, their excitable energy so infectious, you would smile whenever you shared a room with them. The feeling now couldn't be any more different. His desperation and determination are so strong, I can feel it seeping into my pours. The twins are large in build, like their brothers and other bear shifters, but Jake looks skinny, his skin pale and bruised, like he's been trying to escape the room, and as I look around, I can see scuffs on the wall proving my theory. He looks like a caged animal.

"Jake?" Keeping my voice low, I move slowly towards him. His head shoots up as I speak, and a beautiful smile crosses his face, pushing back the madness that lingers around him.

"Little sister!" Speeding towards me, he wraps his arms around me, enveloping me in a huge hug. "I missed you," he murmurs into my hair, placing a kiss on my forehead as he takes a step away, excitement filling his face. "Did you come to help me find her? They locked me in here, they don't believe me, but you believe me, don't you?" Speaking fast, he bounces on the spot like he longs to be running round the room, and I blink and struggle to keep up with what he's saying. Taking a deep breath, I try to decide how I'm going to handle this.

"Jake, find who?" I ask gently, but I know exactly who he's talking about. However, that doesn't stop the despair that washes over me as he answers.

"Tori of course!" My stomach drops at his words, his eyes shining with a madness that breaks my heart.

"Jake, Tori is dead. You were there, you saw it." No matter how much I try, despair still marks my words. Taking a step away from me, I see the hurt in his eyes as he realises I don't believe him.

"Yes, yes, yes, *I know*. But she's *back* and she's hurting, and they won't let me out!" He bellows the last part, hurling himself at the one-way mirror, pounding his fists against it like a man possessed. I want to believe him, I would do *anything* to have Tori back. But it's hopeless, she's gone, there is no coming back from death.

Watching him and seeing the full effects of what losing your mate can do to a shifter breaks my heart. I shudder at the thought that this could have been one of my guys.

Walking towards him, I try to call out to him, desperate for him to stop. "Jake, stop—you'll hurt yourself." When I reach his side, I leave plenty of room between us so he doesn't feel trapped as I approach him. Hearing my voice, he suddenly stops, surprise lighting his features as he sees me, and a happy smile spreads across his face.

"Little sister! When did you get here? Are you here to help me find Tori?" His delighted words make me sad beyond reason as I reach for his clenched fists, checking them over for wounds. "They locked me away, they think I'm crazy." His voice drops as he looks over his shoulder at his imaginary foes, baring his teeth. "We need to get out of here." He turns his frenzied eyes on me again, and I have to fight the tears clogging my throat. They were right—losing Tori has broken him, and I'm not sure I can cope with seeing the same thing in Ben.

"I—" My words cut off, and I have to clear my throat as agony, loss, and despair claw at me, but now is not the time to lose it, the twins need me. "Jake, I'm going to speak with the alpha. I'll be back, okay?"

Jake has gone back to pacing the room, but as I speak, he stills, and a feral edge enters his eyes as he looks up, turning his smile from something comforting to a disturbing sight.

"Take me with you. We need to find Tori." His slow, stalking steps towards me remind me of a wolf hunting its prey, the happy, playful person I know gone. Shifting into a defensive stance, I take a slow step back towards the door, raising my hands in a calming gesture.

"I can't let you out just now." My words are firm, and I continue my slow retreat as his face twists in anger.

"You're just like them, locking me away, trying to keep me from Tori." Jerking towards me, his stride lengthens, his nails elongating into claws, but his eyes never leave my face.

"Jake, Tori is dead. I held her in my arms as she died, you were there, you saw it." Keeping my voice low, I try to reason with him, but I know it's useless, he's past the point of reasoning, his grief stripping away his good qualities until all that's left is hate and anger.

"I know!" he roars, his voice guttural as he drops to his hands and knees, fighting the change that's trying to take over his body. "But she's back, I can feel it." The agony in his face breaks my heart, and for a second, I see his eyes clear. "Ari, you need to leave, I can't hold back the—Ahhhh!"

He cries out as the shift finally overpowers him, his body shaking as it starts to change. Holding back a shift is agonising, and the pain in his voice is obvious. Continuing to back away slowly until my back hits the door behind me, I twist my hand until I can grasp the door handle, then let out a curse when I realise it's locked behind me. Knocking against the door, I don't take my eyes off Jake, who has now fully shifted into his bear form.

The bear shakes his head and sniffs the air, looking around the room until his eyes land on me. His lips pull back over his muzzle, exposing his rows of sharp teeth, releasing a roar aimed in my direction. I don't think he means to attack me, but I can see the agitation in his movements as he steps towards me. Time seems to slow down as I hear someone scrambling to unlock the door behind me, voices shouting from the room behind the mirror, not to mention Killian's anger and fear pouring down the bond. All of this only seems to agitate Jake's bear as he aims another roar in my direction and stands up on his hind legs. His bear form was big before, his head coming up to my shoulder, but on his hind legs, his ears almost touch the ceiling. I realise in that moment that he's going to attack me unless I do something.

Calling on the power within me, I let my wolf rise to the surface, my skin prickling with the strength of my alpha power. I rarely use it, I hate forcing others to do my bidding like it was forced upon me so many times during my time with Shadow Pack, but this is the only thing that Jake's bear will respond to right now.

"Stop." The command falls from my lips, and although I know the bear can't understand what I'm saying, the strength of my alpha wolf is imbued in my words. He may be a bear, but I'm still strong enough to make his steps falter. I know it won't last long, but it should give me enough time to escape from this room. The lock finally gives, and the door swings open slowly behind me. Jake's bear moves his attention from me to the open door, sniffing at the air as he takes a step forward. "Stop," I command again, his roar filling the air as I take a step back over the threshold, but it works, the bear halting.

Keeping eye contact for as long as possible, I walk backward, my hand brushing along the length of the door until I feel the edge of it. I grasp it and quickly slam it shut, locking the door as an almighty roar seems to shake the building when Jake realises he's trapped again.

My breath comes out in rapid gasps as a set of hands lands on my shoulders, and I know who it is without having to turn around— Killian. Frustration is radiating off him, and I know he's fighting against the urge to go tearing into the room I've just escaped. I turn around and meet his gaze, watching as some of his anger releases as he runs his eyes over me, checking for any injuries. I don't bother to stop him, knowing he needs to do this to calm his wolf's instincts.

Over his shoulder, I see Garett watching with concern etched deeply into his features. "Ari, I'm so sorry—" he starts, but I cut him off with a narrowing of my eyes before walking past Killian, who simply stands to the side, letting me pass.

"No. You don't apologise for this. This is not your fault, this is ASP's fault. They're the ones who killed Tori and ripped away their future," I growl out, my voice deepening with anger as I jab a finger back at the locked room, where I can still hear the growls and thumps of Jake's bear trying to escape. Sighing, I walk towards Garett, grabbing his hand and pulling him along as I go to the room behind the one-way mirror, with Killian stalking silently behind us. Alex and Seb are watching grimly as Jake's bear tears through the remaining furniture in the room.

"Is that what would happen to Killian if Ari died?" Seb's horrified question makes me pause and glance over at Kill, who's wearing a sullen expression. He nods once, causing horror to run through me.

"The bond that true mated pairs share binds them together," Alex explains, keeping his sorrowful gaze on the rampaging bear through the mirror. "Most die when the other does, their soul unable to exist without their pair. Some of the stronger shifters have been known to survive their pair's passing, but it breaks something within them. Either they live a half-life, or something like this happens." The room falls silent as Alex talks, a heaviness filling the space between us.

Shouting comes from somewhere in the building, and without a word, Garett hurries out of the room, leaving the rest of us frowning.

"What—" My question is interrupted as Garett hurries back in the room, his expression grim as he scans the area before his eyes settles on me.

"Ben attacked the alpha. He escaped."

Chapter Twelve

You'd have thought tracking down a rampaging bear shifter would be easy, just follow the trail of destruction, right? Except Ben seems to have completely disappeared. Sighing, I brush my long hair from my face as I exit the alleyway, looking around the empty streets, but I only spot my search partner, Max, who's leaning against the wall with fatigue crossing his face.

We've been searching for hours now with no sign of Ben. Once we learned that the bear shifter had escaped, Alex quickly made a call to Moon River Pack for additional assistance. Isa and a couple of our other pack mates turned up to help, splitting off into different sections of the city, each partnered up one of the Long Claw bears. My guys hadn't wanted to leave my side, but we can cover more ground this way, so they eventually agreed if I went with Max.

The sun had set a couple of hours ago and most of the search parties had returned to the gym, but Max wanted to keep going. Glancing across at my search partner, I frown as I walk over to him and place my hand on his shoulder.

"Are you okay?" It's a dumb question, he lost his mate and now one of his brothers has disappeared, but I had to ask. His face is marred with lines, and a grim hopelessness seems to cling to him.

Glancing up at me, he grimaces before straightening and shaking off my hand, rubbing his palm roughly across his face.

"I'm fine, just tired." I raise my eyebrows at his response, calling bullshit, but I don't say as much out loud, simply leaning against the wall next to him and crossing my arms as I look up at the moon.

"We can go back, rest for a bit." My suggestion is met with a growl as he pushes away from the wall, turning his glare on me.

"What, just give up? Would you go back if it was your family? Oh wait, you don't have one." Bitterness laces his words and I feel them twist into me like a knife, but I'm careful not to show it, simply raising an eyebrow. He seems to realise he's out of order as soon as the words are out of his mouth, regret lining his features as he takes a step towards me, his hands out in a placating gesture. "Ari, I'm sorry. That was wrong of me."

Continuing to lean against the wall, I keep my face blank. He's right—he was out of order, but his comment was true. I don't have a family, not in the sense of blood relations. I never really knew my mother, and my father was my tormentor for years until I ran away. As far as I'm concerned, I didn't have any family until I met Tori, and she taught me that blood doesn't define you. Tori was my family, and then slowly, over the last year, my family has grown, more so than I ever would have thought. It's overwhelming sometimes, but they know to give me space, to back off until I need them, then they come right back.

Opening my mouth to reply, I freeze as a wave of power washes over me. I glance over at Max's puzzled face, and I know he felt it as well. Pushing away from the wall, I look around, trying to find the source of the strange power wave when I'm hit by it again, except this time it's much, *much* bigger.

"Whoa," Max mutters, his eyes glowing with his inner animal as he presses a hand against the wall to steady himself. "What the hell was that?"

All my senses are on edge as I scan the area around us, none the wiser of where the power came from, but whatever it was, it was strong. My phone starts to ring, and I raise my eyebrows at the name that comes up on the screen.

"Eric, everything okay?" Taking a few steps away from Max, I wait for the demon's reply. Kill and the others had been constantly sending me texts the last few hours we'd been separated, so Eric was the last of the guys I expected to hear from.

"Yes, I'm fine. Are you okay?" His soothing doctor voice greets me over the phone, the type of tone he uses when he has to break bad news to his patients, and it instantly makes me nervous.

"Yeah. What's going on? There's something strange happening in the city, did you feel it?" My skin still tingles from the memory of the power. Whatever it came from was potent, and I get the feeling it has something to do with why Eric was calling me.

There's a pause as Eric processes my words. "Yeah, I felt it. Where are you?"

I look around, not a hundred percent sure where I am, so I give him a description of the area. "I'm out looking for Ben, Garett's brother. He's gone a little crazy, thinks that Tori is still alive and escaped the bear compound." Glancing over, I send Max an apologetic look as he grimaces at my words. *Well said, Ari, very sensitively put*, I chide myself. Eric's next words have my turbulent thoughts coming to a stop.

"I don't think you need to worry about that now." The sureness of his words is what makes me pause, like he *knows* more than he's letting on.

"What do you mean?" A strange feeling runs through me, one I can't quite place as I wait for his response like it's is crucially important. He sighs, and I can almost feel his careful, professional mask dropping as urgency slips into his voice.

"I need you to come to me, I have something you need to see." Frowning, I run my hand through my hair, pushing the frustrating strands from my face as he speaks.

Well, that was as clear as mud, I think to myself before speaking again. "Eric, what are you saying?" My frustration is obvious, and I can almost feel his grimace.

"Just trust me, please." His response sends a ripple of nervousness through me. He either *can't* tell me, or he *won't*, and I'm not going to find out until I go to him, that much is clear.

Letting loose a small growl, I push back my wolf as she becomes more frustrated, wanting to shift and *make* Eric tell me. "Okay, fine. Where are you?"

After my call with Eric, I called the others, giving them directions to the industrial estate where I'm supposed to meet Eric. Max hadn't been keen to give up the hunt for his brother, but I had a strange feeling that he needed to come with me, call it fate or intuition, whatever, but he needed to accompany me. It felt important.

Alex was already there when we arrived, being the closest to the industrial estate, but he was alone. His bear shifter companion had already headed back to their pack. Taking one look at me, he steps forward and wraps his arms firmly around me, holding me close for a moment before moving back, his thumb tracing my concerned frown. Silently, he takes hold of my hand as we wait for the others, while Max impatiently scans the area around us. Another wave of the strange power runs over me, and I realise why I recognise it. It feels like Eric's power.

While it's not exactly the same, it has the same...flavour to it, a demonic edge that feels void of humanity. Something hums in my veins, urging me forward, and my feet take a few steps before I even realise I've moved. Turning to Alex, I meet his frowning gaze, my stomach reeling as I resist the urge to follow the waves of power that are beckoning me.

"I need to go." My face twists, I *need* him to understand. I can't explain where these feelings are coming from, but it's really important that I go. Taking a few more steps, a confused look crosses his face as he reaches out to grab my arm, missing by an inch.

"Ari, wait. We're going to wait for the others. It could be a trap!" I hear the confusion in his voice, and I wish I had the time to explain, but I can't put it into words.

"I know, I can't explain it and I'm sorry, but I need to go *now*, it's important."

The sound of footsteps has me turning, and I see Max running between the buildings towards the area where the power seems to be coming from. Turning, I start to follow the bear shifter, throwing a look over my shoulder at an agonised Alex.

"I *have* to go. Come find me when the others arrive!" I shout before breaking into a flat-out run towards the source of the power.

"Ari! Shit—" Alex's footsteps follow me, and I hear him on the phone, then his voice soon fades out behind me and I know he's calling the others, but he can't keep up with me.

When I think back on this later, I'll be amazed I was able to navigate the maze of the industrial estate with ease, that I knew *exactly* where I was going, the tug within me guiding me exactly where I needed to be.

Rounding a corner, the first thing I see is Eric standing by the edge of a building, except he isn't the Eric I know. The imposing figure turns, and his glowing blue eyes lock on to me. His grin turns feral, revealing a set of menacing fangs, and I notice a large set of horns protruding from his hair, with a second, smaller set snugly fitted against the first. His usually perfect blond hair seems to float around him, like it's dancing with static. Glancing down, I see that instead of his neat shoes, he has a set of black hooves. He still looks like Eric, just so much *more*. You would be stupid to mistake him for human, even without the horns and hooves, the amount of energy he's throwing out screams demon. Raising a clawed hand, he crooks a finger and beckons me closer.

I step forward slowly, my trepidation building as I see Max on the ground as I get closer, staring down the alley between two warehouses. The corner of the building is blocking my view of what he's staring at, his eyes wide as tears slide silently down his face. Frowning, I stop, my senses returning to me as a rising sickness fills me, not sure that I want to see what's behind the wall that has brought Max to his knees. There's a flash of light and a shift in the energy that's surrounding us, but my eyes stay locked on the kneeling shifter.

"Ari." My head snaps up as someone calls my name, and a very human-looking Eric stumbles towards me. Running my eyes over him, I try to work out why he seems different. His clothing is a little torn and he looks tired, but his skin is glowing, like the supernatural energy is still running through his veins. When he reaches my side, he stretches a hand out to me, and when I don't flinch away, a small smile crosses his lips before he pulls me closer for a hug. Enveloped in his arms, I allow myself a brief moment of comfort, breathing in his comforting scent, although he smells different today. Still Eric, but...more. Like the smell of rain on tarmac, a slightly fresh, metallic scent. I pull away and meet his blue eyes, then shake my head.

"What's going on, why am I here?" The question is simple, but I have so many more. Why was I so drawn to this place? Why is Eric here? What's going on with Max? The questions go on and on, and Eric seems to understand that, his hands coming to my arms again.

"There have been some strange energy surges in the city over the last week or so. I ignored them, I tend not to get involved in other demons' business, but they have been increasing over the last few days. They felt fresh, new, like a new demon had come into being."

My mind whirls as he speaks, remembering what he said about Seb's strange power surges, and my eyes widen in shock, his name on the tip of my tongue, but Eric is already shaking his head at my unasked question.

"No, not Seb. So I decided to investigate. Then earlier today, I felt a huge power surge. I tracked it down, and I found the source of the power," he continues, and although he's smiling, the smile takes on a sympathetic edge. This only makes me more nervous.

"What? What are you not telling me?" I demand, shifting my feet, fighting against the sickening pull that's drawing me towards the glowing light behind the other buildings.

"I wanted to be in a form you recognised for this moment, but I'm struggling to keep my demon away with all this power around," Eric says, avoiding my question with his doctor voice in full swing, but I don't want to be placated, the energy that's being flung around makes me jittery.

"Stop stalling. Tell me." Narrowing my eyes on him, Eric sighs and gestures towards Max. He's still kneeling with his eyes glued to whatever is causing all of this.

"See for yourself."

Taking a deep breath, I walk towards the intersection, the waves of power that are rolling over me enough to make my stomach turn. It's an odd sensation, everything about the power is warning me away, pulsing cautions, enough to scare away even the most non-magical of beings. You ever get a feeling that you shouldn't be somewhere, you can't explain it, but you can't leave? That's exactly the feeling I'm experiencing.

Except I also feel it calling to me, like it's whispering my name into the wind. This feeling could be addictive, a power high that makes me feel invincible. It causes an uncomfortable war within me. My instincts scream at me to run away, to leave whatever is behind that wall alone, but I'm unable to resist the call.

With slow, heavy footsteps, I walk towards the light, keeping my eyes on Max, who hasn't moved as silent tears track down his face.

"Max, are you okay?" I call out, hovering at the edge of the light, using the corner of the building to shield me from the source of the power, not ready to face whatever it is just yet.

He doesn't respond, and I become aware of someone else just

beyond him. Ben, the runaway twin, is also kneeling on the ground, staring up with rapt adoration on his face. Confusion, dread, and something that feels suspiciously like hope runs through me.

"Ari?" a voice calls out, freezing me to the spot. The voice sounds different, full of power, but I would recognise that voice anywhere.

"No." I round on Eric, my eyes wide, my stomach twisting as he slowly nods. Breaking out of my stupor, I hurry the last few steps it takes me to round the building, only to stop dead as my gaze falls on another person.

Hovering above the ground, surrounded in a purple light that seems to pulse around them, is the source of the power, and I don't know how any single being can contain that amount of power. Where you would expect her feet to be are a shiny set of hooves attached to smooth, ebony legs. Her body is cloaked in twisting, pulsing magic, covering her body, but somehow exposing enough of it that you know she's curvy and generously endowed. I almost don't want to continue staring, since I know that when I look at her face, I'll have to fully accept what I hadn't thought possible, but I have to know. Lifting my gaze, I see a familiar face, one I could draw with my eyes closed—familiar full red lips, high cheekbones, her dark, curly hair falling around her in luxurious waves, floating with the power that surrounds her, and even her eyes are the same, but glowing with an unnatural purple light. Poking out the top of her hair is a curling set of horns, lighter and more delicate than Eric's. On her forehead, right in the centre, is an intricate twirling tattoo, marking the exact spot where the bullet had hit her.

"Ari, you came." Her voice washes over me, and my legs can no longer hold me up.

Falling to my knees, I look up at the impossible sight before me as I gasp out her name like a prayer. "Tori."

Her face lights up into a smile, and I feel her power start to ebb, her body lowering to the ground. Max and Ben run forward to catch her before she hits the concrete, lowering her down gently.

Leaning against Max, Tori's eyes flutter closed as the strange, overwhelming power seems to disappear. Her eyes open again, and her gaze seek me out. When she sees me, an exhausted smile lights up her whole face.

"You came." Her words are quiet, almost a whisper, but I feel them somewhere deep within me.

My eyes sting as I fight against the emotions flooding my system. I give her the grin I always saved for her. "Always."

Chapter Thirteen

After that little revelation, Tori passed out.

She always did have a dramatic flare, I think to myself as I watch her sleep. She would find the fact that I was watching her sleep hilarious. I can almost hear her calling me a creepy peeping Tom.

We're back at the Moon River compound now, as we had deemed it safer than the Long Claw gym. Being in the centre of the city makes it easy to access, but also makes it more difficult to hide things, like carrying an unconscious woman without attracting attention. The Moon River compound is in the middle of the woods and well-guarded, so there is less chance of prying eyes discovering something they shouldn't.

It'd been difficult getting Tori back here. Max and Ben's protective instincts had been riding them hard, and they wouldn't let me anywhere near her for some time, especially when my guys turned up to assist. Eventually, I convinced them to help me move her, and we managed to get her back here.

Now, she's safely in one of the spacious meeting rooms, stretched out on one of the comfortable sofas, her head resting in Max's lap as he runs his hands through her curly hair. His eyes watch the corners of the room suspiciously, like his enemies are hiding there. Ben is sitting at the other end of the couch with Tori's legs resting in his lap, his adoring gaze never once leaving her face as he waits for her to wake. Curled up on the floor in his bear form is Jake. From what Alpha Philips told me, he's been in his bear form since I saw him earlier, and they haven't been able to coax out his human side. They had to tranquilize him to transport him here, and I know there had been some murmurs about not letting him in the room with Tori while he was in his bear form. Killian had stepped in then, explaining that a mated pair would never harm their mate, it would be like harming themselves, and separating them would only make things worse.

Standing at the window, I stare into the room, still sure what I'm seeing is a dream. Knowing she's back here and safe is just starting to hit me. Tori was dead, she died in my arms, I saw it, so how is it possible that she's here? She's obviously something *other* now, but she's still Tori, right?

Turning, I smile as I see my guys on the sofas in the communal area. Alex and Seb are fast asleep, leaning against each other. A grouchy-looking Killian is trying to stay awake, but I can see his heavy eyes closing, only to startle awake a moment later. His gaze lands on me, then the pattern to repeats every few seconds. Garett stands next to me, his eyes locked on his brothers, his body stiff with tension. Slipping my hand into his, my eyes fall on Tori again and I shake my head, my calm starting to slip.

"How's this possible?" My words are whispered, but Eric hears them and pushes away from the wall he's been leaning against. He hasn't said a word since I first saw Tori, giving me space as I processed, but I need answers. Turning to face him, I see he's watching Tori with a frown.

"Tori must've been part demon," he concludes, pulling his eyes from my sleeping friend and stepping closer as he feels my distress down our bond.

"What do you mean, must've been? Can't you sense this sort of thing?" My frustration and confusion are easy to hear, and I wince, realising I'm taking it out on Eric. "Sorry, I just...I'm so confused."

Brushing away my apology, he steps even closer, pressing up against my side, and rests his forehead against mine. His hand rubs soothing circles against my back. "Don't apologise. You're right—usually, yes, I would be able to sense if someone was a demon. But one of her parents must have been a death demon."

I rub my brow to ease the ache that's settled there as I try to work through my thoughts. What the hell is a death demon? Weren't they all involved in death one way or another? "I don't understand," I admit with a sigh, my eyes landing once again on my sleeping best friend. The friend that, until an hour ago, I believed dead.

"Death demons look like me and you, but they collect the souls of the dead. You've probably heard of them as reapers." Eric's tone has taken on that of a teacher as he explains, as if he isn't talking about my best friend.

"As in the Grim Reaper?" The exclamation is out of my mouth before I can stop it as I spin around to face him, startling the others awake in the process.

"I thought reapers were a myth," Garett murmurs, rubbing his hand across his face as he tries to chase away his exhaustion. I can tell he's happy that his brothers have found their mate, but finding out that said mate is a death demon is worrying him. I'm not so worried about them, I know Tori would never harm them, but I have very little knowledge on demons and I've never even heard of death demons before.

"There haven't been any for hundreds of years. The thing with death demons is that their powers don't fully come in until they die. Their human side has to die for the demon to be born. Tori is a completely different matter, since she was a witch. She already had magic. Did she ever show skills that were unusual for a witch to possess?" Listening to his explanation makes something within me click, and I think back to her summoning hellhounds and how the other witches tended to shun her. It all made so much more sense now.

"So, she did die? They did kill her?" My words are quiet, void of emotion as an inky rage starts to build up within me.

"Yes, the human part of her died, and then the demon side was born." Like a phoenix rising from the ashes.

Shaking my head again, I look over at Tori's sleeping form. "What does this mean? Is she still the same Tori?"

"Will she be dangerous?" Killian asks, pushing up from the couch, fully involved in the conversation now that the question of my safety has come up.

Sighing, Eric shrugs. "This is new to me, I've never met a death demon, especially not one who was part witch. I didn't even know that was possible. I was born a demon, this is all I've ever known." Looking over at her, he tilts his head to the side as he considers something. "I've known of a few half demons coming into their powers though, and helped them adapt. She'll need to learn how to control her powers, sate her new appetites."

An unhappy grumble comes from the male next to me. "Appetites? What do you mean? Will my brothers be safe?" Garett inquires with a frown.

"Well, demons don't eat food to feed..." Suddenly feeling awkward, Eric shrugs, avoiding my bear's piercing gaze. "Your brothers will help anchor her, they will help her regain control and feed her...other appetites." My eyebrows shoot up in surprise. I know exactly what he means by that, but apparently, not everyone else does.

"What the hell does that mean?" Garett demands, seeming to fill the space as he gets frustrated. Placing my hand on his chest, I murmur softly to help calm his bear, and while he doesn't look at me, I can feel him relax a little under my palm.

"Demons have a rather high sex drive. If they can help curb that, then it will help her overcome the urge to satisfy her other needs." I can only guess that since Tori is a death demon, her 'other urges' will involve death.

"Wait, is she the one who was behind the death of the ASP agents? You said it felt like a baby demon was behind the power surges." I don't mention the odd feelings Seb has been throwing out recently, but I know he wouldn't be able to kill those agents though. But this new Tori?

Grim faced, Eric nods. "Her power signature matches the one found on the bodies. She probably doesn't even remember doing it, her demon would have been fully in control, acting purely on instinct."

Shuddering, I take a step away from everyone, suddenly feeling crowded. My gaze once again falls on my sleeping best friend. Looking at her, you would never know she's anything other than human. "I feel like this is some sort of fucked-up dream, and any moment, I'm going to wake up."

Seb pushes up from the couch, walks over to my side, and wraps his arms around me before pulling me into his chest. "You've got your best friend back, that's good, right?"

I hide my face, burying it into his chest. "Do I? Is she still the Tori that I knew and loved?"

"Isn't it better that you get that chance at all?" Seb counters softly, and I know he's right, feeling guilt eating at my insides. I just started to accept that she's gone, and then she comes back, but she isn't who I thought she was. Sighing, I pull away and look up at him, his usual grin absent.

"When did you get so smart? It's...just difficult to get my head around," I divulge, but I know I don't really need to explain it to him. Seb would never judge me.

I look around the room, seeing the guys leaning against the walls, yawning, and I glance down at my watch and let out a curse. It's almost two in the morning. We had been out all night, not to mention that we met up with ASP this morning. No wonder we're all exhausted.

"Come on, guys, we all need some sleep," I suggest, and they all nod in agreement. I watch as my three wolves all head towards the door, then turn and see Garett making himself comfortable on the couch facing the window on the room Tori and his brothers are in. "You coming?" I ask with a small, knowing smile.

As he shakes his head, I walk over and kiss him goodnight, running my hands through his hair as I pull away. "No, I want to stay, make sure they're okay," he replies, squeezing my hand before I start to leave the building, wishing him a sweet dreams as I leave.

Following behind the guys, I notice as Eric breaks off from the others, heading towards the building he now calls his own. Frowning, I send a thought down the bond to Killian, telling him not to wait up, and from the sleepy feeling of agreement he sends in return, I know he won't be waiting up for me for too long.

Eric's house isn't far from where I live in the medical building. As the pack's doctor, he wanted to be close in case of any emergencies, but hadn't moved in with me or the other guys yet.

I'm sure he's heard me following him, I haven't made any effort to hide the sounds of my footsteps, but he makes no indication of it or slows his steps. Reaching the small porch to his house, he climbs the stairs and finally turns to face me. His face is guarded, like he's about to deliver bad news. My steps falter and a frown crosses my face at his expression.

"Eric?" My voice is quiet as an irrational fear twists through my mind that Tori is better suited to him, that he's going to tell me he's leaving.

"I'm sorry." His response makes me feel sick, but I won't let him see that.

"What for?" My question is curt, my body vibrating with tension as I wait for his answer. His face falls, and he takes a small step away from me, like he's expecting a bad reaction from me. I've never seen Eric act this way, and it's confusing me. What exactly is going on here?

"I know this isn't the life you wanted for Tori, to be a demon like me, but I promise I'll try and help her in every way I can," he states with his doctor's voice, and I wait for him to give me the bad news. There's always bad news when he uses that tone.

"Thank you, I appreciate that," I respond, still standing at the bottom of his porch steps. Eric waits, as if expecting me to say something else, and a soft frown crosses his face when it doesn't come.

"So," he starts, and I brace myself for his rejection. "You're not bothered that Tori's a demon?"

Wow, okay, not what I was expecting him to say. I pause for a second and think about his question. "Look, it's not what I expected, but I have a chance to have Tori in my life again. That's something I hadn't thought possible. I know things are going to be different, but I'm going to make the most of it," I reply honestly. I have no idea what Tori's future is going to be like now, or if she will even still be the Tori I knew, but I'll be damned if I'm going to abandon her now when she needs me the most.

Eric smiles, his face warming as he takes a small step towards me. "You're a good friend. I know many people that would turn away a demon, even if it had been someone they knew and loved before."

"She's family," I say with a shrug, as if it's as simple as that, and truthfully, it is that simple. She was the first person to see me for who I was when I arrived here, to look past my hard exterior. She didn't turn her back on me then, and I won't do that to her now.

Shaking his head, Eric smiles at me as I start walking up the porch steps towards him.

"You're amazing." His smile is still there, but I can hear a hint of awe in his voice that makes me feel uncomfortable. Shrugging, I take the last few steps between us until only a few inches separates us. I turn away and lean against the porch railing, looking out into the woods that surround us.

"I thought you were going to tell me you couldn't be with me anymore." The admission makes my cheeks flush when I realise I sound like a teenager. It's not like Eric and I had even taken steps towards that type of relationship yet, but for some reason, his next response feels like it's really important.

"What? What gave you that idea?" I can feel him turn towards me at his exclamation, his eyes boring into the side of my face, but I refuse to turn around, keeping my eyes locked on to the trees. "Is that why you looked so uncomfortable?" His question has me shrugging nonchalantly.

"Well, now that Tori is here and she's the same as you... She's so beautiful and powerful," I murmur, like the words aren't tearing me up as I speak them.

"She is powerful," he agrees, his hand landing on my shoulder as he spins me around to face him. He places a gentle hand on my chin to bring my gaze up to meet his. "But I don't have a bond with her, I have a bond with *you*." His blue eyes start to glow with his power, and my skin tingles as he runs his hand up and down my arm. Little sparks of electricity leap from his fingers onto my skin. "It's you I want, and not just because some mystical bond is telling me to."

"Is it possible to reject the bond?" My voice is breathless as I speak, my body tingling with the promise of his power.

"Yes, it's not pleasant, but it is possible," Eric answers, and I can see his focus narrow on my flushed face before his eyes drop to my neck, where he can undoubtedly see my pulse pounding under my skin.

I don't know if it's the stress of the day or the shock of finding Tori, but I need physical comfort, to feel someone holding me. Turning from the woods, I face Eric, taking a final step towards him and closing the gap between up. I raise my arms and drape them over his shoulders, my chest pressing against his. His eyes heat with desire, and I feel another wave of his power roll over me.

"I don't know if this is a good idea. My demon is close to the surface tonight, I don't know how much I can control him if we..." He trails off, his eyes falling to my lips.

"You won't hurt me." My voice is sure and certain, but he snorts at my words.

"Ari, I'm a pain demon." His face twists as he speaks, but I can still see the desire in his eyes.

"I trust you."

For a fraction of a second, I think he's going to turn me away, but he surges forward, melding our lips together with a soft groan, his hands pulling me close. Like a woman drowning, I return his kisses, the desire and need building up until it's like a roaring fire beneath my skin. We've been denying our feelings and lust for each other for so long that it's like we have finally broken the dam, and the more I touch him, the more I *need* him. It's been building within me since I discovered that we had a bond. Sure, I've always thought he was good-looking and he may have entered my fantasies, but I never thought he was an option for me.

Pulling away, Eric holds me at arm's length, his eyes glowing blue with the power of his demon. "If we keep going, I'm not going to be able to stop, my demon won't let me."

"Don't stop," I whisper with a shudder of pleasure.

This seems to break his control, and he pulls me into his arms again. At some point, we move into the house and make it upstairs, a tangle of limbs as shoes and clothes are stripped off. Reaching the doorway to his room, I pull away and cross the threshold, staring at the neatly made bed.

Standing in just my underwear, I can feel as he steps behind me. The heat of his body reaches mine as he steps closer, the little hairs on my skin standing on end as I feel the crackle of his power touch me.

"Don't move," he instructs, his voice deep, and I know his demon is taking control right now. A single finger touches the back of my neck and slowly drags down the length of my spine. With me facing away from him, I have no idea what he's doing behind me, and that turns me on all the more as his nails drag along my flesh. His large, warm hands come to my shoulders, his nails scraping down until he reaches the strap to my bra, slicing it open with a claw. The bra falls away and exposes my full breasts. An animalistic groan leaves his lips as he presses himself against my back, kissing along the length of my neck as his hands slide around to cup my breasts. My head falls back, and a breathy moan leaves my lips as he gently bites down on my shoulders, the slight prick of pain only turning me on more.

Suddenly, he steps away from me, and I feel the loss of his touch tear through me as a keening sound tries to work its way up my throat.

"Lay on the bed," he commands, and I turn my head to look over my shoulder, quirking an eyebrow at him. I've never followed orders well, but seeing the little smirk on his lips and glowing eyes makes me shiver with pleasure. He hasn't changed into his demon form, but his nails and teeth look sharper, and the most telling sign he's close to losing control is his glowing eyes and strong waves of power that keep washing over me.

Deciding to do as I'm told, I walk over to the edge of his large, king-sized bed, crawling up onto all fours as I make my way to the headboard, fully aware of his eyes on my ass as I move. Making sure my movements are exaggerated, I pull up the pillows before turning around and settling myself at the top of the bed, crossing my ankles as I smirk at him, waiting for his next move.

Stalking towards me, Eric undoes the leather belt that's holding up his denim jeans and wraps the belt around his fist before pulling the length of it, as if testing its strength before placing the belt on the bed. At some point, he lost his shirt—most likely it's been discarded with the other clothing and shoes on the way to the bedroom—so I'm able to watch his abs bunch up as he leans down to slide off his jeans. Eric isn't the most muscular of my men, but you can tell from the definition of his six-pack that he works out. He stands at the end of the bed in only his boxers, then climbs up and crawls towards me, looking every inch the predator hunting for his next meal.

As he reaches me, I lean forward to press a kiss to his lips, but he stops me with a hand on my shoulder, pressing me back down onto the bed. Hovering over me, he leans down, and I get the kiss I wanted before he pulls back, biting down on my lower lips before he begins kissing a trail down my chin to my neck and then down to my breasts. He settles himself over me and snakes one hand up to my breast, his fingers finding my nipple, twisting and pinching it into a stiff peak. His touch is almost painful as little sparks of his power flutter against my skin. His mouth descends on my other nipple, his tongue flicking over the sensitive nub. Before long, my skin starts to get overly sensitive, but before I even finish my thought, Eric is pulling away, moving down my body and grasping my underwear with his fingers, pulling them down as he moves. His nails gently scrape down my legs as he removes them, the pressure almost at the point of pain, but he always pulls away just as I think the feeling is too much.

He settles between my legs and pushes them apart, his glowing eyes staring appreciatively before he lowers his head to my core, pressing kisses to the inside of my thighs as he works his way up. I can't hold back the contented sigh as he kisses my clit, his tongue flicking against it in a fast motion. My hands fist the bedsheets to keep myself from reaching out to Eric—to stop him or encourage him, I'm not sure. The movement causes Eric to look up from between my legs, his eyes narrowing as he licks his lips.

"Don't move." It's easy to hear the order for what it is, his voice firm and authoritative. The rebellious voice in me says I never usually do what I'm told, so why start now, especially when I already followed his earlier command? However when he presses his mouth back to my clit, flicking it with his tongue, the will to fight leaves me, my bones turning to jelly as pleasure runs through me.

A gasp of pleasure escapes me as he slides a finger inside before curling it up, flicking that sweet spot before pulling it out slowly.

He continues this with excruciating slowness, causing a growl to leave my lips as he laughs.

"Greedy," he admonishes, but slides in a second finger, alternating between kissing, licking, and nibbling at my clit. The building pressure is driving me crazy, Eric's administrations to my body slow and teasing. Another growl leaves my lips, my wolf close to the surface, and I raise my hand to my breast. Pulling away, Eric tuts, his face disappointed, but his eyes are alight with excitement.

"I told you to stay still," he scolds, his hands going to my hips and flipping me on the bed. His hands grab my arms, and he wraps his belt around my wrists.

"You don't want to do that," I warn, but he just chuckles as he tightens the leather around my arms. Feeling him step away, I test my new bindings. They're tight and firm, but not tight enough that it's cutting off circulation.

"Yes, I really do. I did warn you." His voice deepens as I feel another wave of his demon power. Something about it stirs my wolf. I'm not sure if it's because of his demon magic or if it's because we have a bond, but it's making her restless and I can feel her pacing beneath my skin.

I feel him position himself and know he's going to enter me from behind. I've done doggy style before, but for some reason, my wolf wants to be on top, to see the demon that's about to claim her as his, pushing my dominant side to the surface. With a growl, I access that supernatural strength and pull at my bindings. In one sharp move, I break the belt around my wrists, knowing that if I was human or even a lower-level wolf, I wouldn't have been able to do this, or at least not without hurting myself.

Spinning around, I grab him by the shoulders and twist, throwing us both onto the bed with me landing on top of him. I can see my glowing eyes reflected in his, so I know my wolf is close.

Eric briefly looks shocked before a grin appears on his face. "Oh, so we're going to play it that way?" His eyes dance with mischief as his arms tangle with mine, then he locks his legs around me so our bodies are pressed together before flipping us over and pressing his lips to mine as his hands skim my body. Moving my hands to his back, I run my nails down his bare skin, enjoying the shudder that runs through him as his kiss deepens. His hand moves down between us as he positions himself and slides into me in one smooth move, both of us groaning as he fills me completely. Pulling back, he rolls his hips as he moves within me, his eyes on mine as a wave of his power washes over me. I should be used to his power by now, but this feels different, and each time he pounds into me, my skin tingles. But it's more than that, like electricity is dancing along my skin, and I look down at my arm, half expecting to see little blue sparks, but it looks normal.

"Eyes on me," he calls out, and my eyes snap to his. Not because he demanded it, but to narrow my gaze at him for thinking he can order me around. I open my mouth to comment, but just at that moment, he picks up his pace and the little zapping on my skin increases with his movements, almost to the point of pain, but not quite enough for me to shout out.

Wrapping my arms around him again, I throw my weight and spin us so I'm pinning him to the bed, my wolf pleased that we are once again in charge. For the moment at least. Eric just grins and reaches his hands back, grabbing on to the headboard as I start rocking my hips, pressing my hands onto his chest as I move over him. Soon enough, his grin drops and we're both panting as we near our releases. Need builds within us, and the sting of the electricity running along my body almost becomes too much, but as I throw back my head and my orgasm hits, the sparks only heighten my pleasure. Eric follows quickly after, shuddering below me.

Panting, I push up from Eric's chest and laugh at his sleepy smile as I climb off him, walking over to the bathroom to clean up. While I would just love to fall into bed and cuddle up, I'm all sticky and I know I won't be able to sleep until I do.

After I've done what I need to in the bathroom, I face myself in the mirror, splashing my face with cool water before glancing at my reflection again. I feel different, but I don't look any different. Then I realise why I feel odd. A weird fluttering in the back of my head makes me frown. I reach up, trying to find it, until I realise that it's *inside* my head. Closing my eyes, I look inside myself and follow the fluttering until I find what feels like a ball of energy. I inspect it, expecting it to hurt, to zap me like Eric's powers usually do, but I find it welcomes me, and a warm feeling and a sense of Eric's personality fills me.

"It's the bond," he says behind me. He moved silently, so I should've been surprised, but I wasn't. I *felt* him walking towards me, like a little compass within me directing me straight to his whereabouts. Turning to look at him, I run my gaze over his body, noting sadly he's wearing underwear now, but that doesn't stop me from ogling his chest, making me aroused again. Eric must feel my confusion because he laughs, then holds out his arm to me.

"That's also the bond," he informs me with a grin, and I can already see his cock hardening through the thin material of his boxers. "Come to bed, mate."

Chapter Fourteen

"Hang on, how come you get to walk around looking like God's gift to humans and I have to look like this?" Tori's outraged voice brings a smile to my face as I walk through the kitchen to the living room. I'm clutching mugs of coffee in my hands, and pressing a packet of chocolate digestives to my chest as I try not to drop everything.

"Well, I'm a full demon," Eric explains, his face lighting up as I walk into the room. Perched on the end of the dining room table, he tries to teach Tori about her powers, while Jake and Ben watch on silently.

It's been a few days since we found her, and things had been a little...unsettled. Tori had woken up surrounded by her bears and freaked out, demanding that they call me, with no idea as to what was going on. Since then, she's been staying with me in the medical building. I have a spare bedroom, but it's been untouched. The first night she stayed here, she snuck into my bed and has been there every night since. Her bears have been taking it in turns sleeping on the couch downstairs, even though they've been offered lodgings by the alpha, not wanting to be away from their mate.

Looking around the meeting room, I walk over to the small coffee table, place Tori's drink down, and move to the couch. Eric and Tori are standing to my right, but while Eric looks calm, dressed in his usual slacks and white button-down shirt, Tori is pacing the length of the room, her dark, curly hair bouncing as she walks. Her frustration is evident as her power seems to pulse around her in a purple glow, and her hooves make a clacking sound against the wooden floor. I find of all of it—the horns, the power, the glowing mark on her forehead—the hooves are the hardest for me to come to terms with.

Jake and Ben are sitting on the opposite couch and each give me a distracted smile before their gaze is drawn back to Tori. Fighting to suppress my sigh, I lean back in the chair, opening up the biscuits and biting down into the chocolatey goodness. I love having Tori here, but that means her bears are here too. That wouldn't be a problem, but she doesn't seem to want anything to do with them, and they refuse to leave. Eric assures me it's because Tori's had a massive shock and is trying to reject the bond since she doesn't understand it. My gaze lifts to the twins and I hold out the biscuit packet in offering, but they barely look at me as they shake their heads, their eyes following Tori's agitated movements.

They've been staying in the small house Eric's been living in, using it to shower and change in before returning here, never being away from Tori for long. I offered for them to stay with me, seeing as Tori's been in my bed, but Tori refused, saying she needed space. Max seems to be struggling the most with Tori's indifference. As the Long Claw gamma, he's strong and his bear will be demanding that he be with his mate to protect her, especially now that he has a second chance. He'd been called away today on pack business, but I know he's been checking in with the twins via phone.

"And I'm not?" Tori demands, stopping her pacing as she spins and glares at Eric. "I died. I'm not *me* anymore, I'm a demon." She gestures to herself, then flings her arms out in a frustrated gesture before she resumes her pacing.

Eric pushes away from the table and walks towards her, his voice soft. "Tori, you're still you. You've always been part demon, you just needed your human side to die so your demon half could come through."

"But I don't want this, I didn't ask for this." My heart aches as she speaks, the pain easy for us to hear. The bears shuffle in their seats as they fight against their instincts to comfort their mate. All is quiet for a moment before she narrows her eyes on Eric. "So I *am* a full demon now then."

Sighing, Eric shakes his head. "No, it doesn't work like that." Tori makes a rude noise before stomping over to me, stealing the biscuit packet, then sitting on the arm of the couch as she shoves several chocolate biscuits into her mouth. "You were born part witch, part demon, and the witch part of you, the human part, died. You've been reborn, but you will always be part demon. Half demons are weaker and have limited powers compared to a full-blooded demon," Eric finishes, running his hand through his neat hair.

"So why can't I wear my human form like I did before? I mean, you look like a human. I look like Mr. Tumnus' love child." I fight back the laugh that threatens to come out as Tori rants, throwing her arms up in the air before shoving more biscuits into her mouth.

"You look beautiful," Jake comments helpfully, but Tori just rolls her eyes.

"Shut it, bear. I have fucking horns. Horns! And look at my feet! I'm never going to get shoes that fit," she laments, then groans and sinks into a chair with her head in her hands. I glance over at Jake to see if he's offended by Tori's words, but there wasn't real heat in her voice, just frustration.

"I like the horns." Ben's words have Tori spinning towards the two of them. She wears a glare that's made all the more uncomfortable by the purple glow that seems to surround her. Neither of the bears appear bothered, in fact, they are leaning forward towards Tori, like they're being pulled towards her. Seeing their expressions, she turns away from them to face Eric again.

"I can't access my magic." Her words are quiet, her body stiff as she waits for Eric's response, as if she's preparing herself for bad news.

"No." A sombre expression crosses Eric's face as he contemplates the young demon before him. "Like I said, your human side died, and with it, so did your magic."

She crumples before my eyes, and I jump to my feet, guiding her to the couch as all the energy seems to leave her body. She collapses into the chair, and my heart breaks as I watch her sorrow. "I'll never be able to use my magic again? That was all I've ever known."

"Not your witch powers, no." The doctor voice is back as Eric takes a step towards us, stopping as the twins growl from their place on the couch. His brow lowers into a frown as he glances over at them before addressing Tori again. "But I can teach you to access your demonic powers."

She seems to sink into the chair, and the bright and bubbly Tori that I knew disappears. I've only ever seen her like this once after she had walked in on her ex messing around with another woman. Taking her hands in one of mine, I use the other to reach out, cup her chin, and raise it to meet my gaze. Her eyes are focused on her hands in my lap as she avoids my eyes.

"Tori, you're alive. I know this is a shock and isn't what you wanted, but I got you back and I'll forever be thankful for that." As I speak, her eyes well, but she raises them, and I smile at the strength I see there. "I love you, horns and all." This makes her laugh and shake her head, her curls bouncing around said horns. I'm not going to say as such, but they are beautiful, curling up in ebony spirals that stand out against her golden skin. They are far more delicate than Eric's horns, and I reach up to touch them, marvelling at the smoothness of them. Tori coughs and shifts in the seat.

"Um, Ari, can you stop touching them please?" Her voice is tight as she leans away from me. Frowning, I pull my hand back swiftly, looking up at Eric, who's trying to hide his grin. Have I just broken some unspoken rule?

"Our horns are very sensitive and are used during mating. You probably don't want to touch another demon's horns, especially not a male's, unless you want to...become intimate with him." I gape up at Eric as he finishes his explanation before turning to Tori, who's still shifting in her seat.

My shock turns to amusement and I grin at my best friend. "Did I just turn you on? You got the hots for me?" I tease, feeling elated as she grins back at me, nudging my shoulder with her own.

"You wish, you big, hairy mutt." Her harsh response is undermined by the grin that spreads across her face and I laugh, used to her calling me this and much worse in the past.

Leaning towards her, I pucker my lips, grab her face, and pull her towards me. "Go on, give us a kiss."

"In your dreams, dog breath." She laughs her signature, full-bellied laugh, and something lights up within me, something I thought had been lost when she died. My throat dries, and I have to fight against the tears that are threatening to spill, my eyes stinging as I blink them back furiously. Seeing the change in my face, Tori's happy expression drops a little. "Ari," she starts, but I shake my head and force a grin.

"Don't make me tickle your horns again," I reply. My voice cracks a little, but I hide it behind some bravado, except she knows me too well and sees right through me, pulling me into a hug. The twins laugh as I untangle myself from Tori's arms, but when I look up at Eric, he has a sympathetic look on his face, and I remember our bond. He's feeling everything I am right now.

Turning away from him, I lean forward to pick up my coffee mug. It's too early for this kind of emotional turbulence. I sip my coffee and let out a contented sigh, then smile when I see Tori is doing the same. Seems even death can't cure Tori's caffeine addiction.

As we sit and drink our coffee, chatting about nonsense and

ignoring the issue of Tori and her new powers, I feel a sudden shock of alarm shoot through me. Jumping to my feel, I look around for the threat, my powers surging to the surface as I scan the room. Tori's staring at me like I've lost my mind, while the twins are playing it cool, glancing around the room, but I can see the tension in their muscles as they ready themselves to protect their mate if needed. Eric is still leaning against the table, his posture relaxed, but he's frowning at me, appearing confused.

I can't see any threat, so why do I feel so...alarmed?

I blink dumbly as I realise what's going on. The thought isn't mine.

"Ari, what's up? I can feel your anxiety, but it doesn't feel like you." Eric takes a step towards me, rubbing his chest absent-mindedly.

"The bond. Somethings going on with Killian," I announce, feeling stupid that it took me so long to realise what I was feeling.

"What? Is he okay?" Tori asks, pushing up from the sofa so she's facing me. The twins are staring at each other in confusion, but look ready to jump up at a moment's notice.

Frowning, I rub my temple, fighting against the headache that's threatening to form. Blowing out a frustrated breath, I shrug and glance over at Eric. "I don't know. I *think* so. I can't tell."

Eric walks over and crouches in front of me, placing his hands on my knees as he explains, "Look inside yourself where the bonds sit. Find his and follow it, you should be able to tell if he's okay." My trepidation must show on my face, because he squeezes my leg and smiles softly. "If he was hurt, you would know."

Feeling reassured, I close my eyes and follow Eric's instructions, looking inside myself for the bonds. I've always struggled to understand this concept. Sure, none of this is new, I've had the bond with Killian for a while now, but there is no manual on how this all works. How does one look *inside* themselves, and how does something like a bond, something that's metaphysical, reside inside me? But they were right—sure enough, I follow my instincts and find the place where my bonds lay. I reach out and grasp them, giving them a tug, but I soon lose my concentration as Eric lets out a grunt. My eyes shoot open, and I see he's rubbing at his chest and smiling wryly at me.

"What happened?" I inquire, confused.

"It felt like you grabbed the bond and yanked." He laughs. "You certainly got my attention."

"Oh shit. Sorry," I apologise, biting down on my lip before taking a deep breath and closing my eyes again.

Finding that place within me once more, I contemplate the bonds. I've felt stuff from Killian previously, and even Eric to an extent before the bond was fully formed, but now I've got *two* fully formed bonds and it's difficult to make sense of everything. I can understand why the guys were concerned when they found out I had two bonds. They seem to be pulsing and writhing, like they are fighting for space. I gently touch one of the bonds, and I immediately get a sense of Eric, his calming presence but with a little electric spark that hints at his power. Reaching out for the other, I can't help but smile as I sense Killian. This bond feels completely different from the other with a grumpy exterior, but once I push through, I'm enveloped by love and an urge to protect me. Sensing that he's not hurt, I pull away as the bond tugs gently at me, my internal compass telling me that he's on his way over.

"Killian's on his way here," I say, reaching forward for my coffee cup once again. I'm going to need caffeine for this conversation, but before I can even lift my cup to my lips, the door slams open, causing me and the twins to jump to our feet as a frustrated Killian storms in.

"What the hell was that?" Kill demands, marching right up to me.

"Sorry, I—" My explanation is cut short as he reaches me, his hands reaching out to grab my arms as he checks me over for injury.

"Are you okay, are you hurt?" His words are muffled as he

turns me around, and I know he's not going to believe me until he's fully checked.

"I'm fine! I felt your alarm, and I was checking that you were okay."

His expression softens. "If you wanted my attention, all you had to do was call me," he jokes, his frown turning into a grin as his hand reaches up and cups my cheek. He looks me in the eyes, and I can see the tension he's trying to hide from me. "It felt like someone was tearing my heart out. I was worried." I'm about to accuse Killian of going soft when several sets of footsteps on the wooden porch alert me that others are joining us.

Eric pushes away from the table once more and walks over to the door, and I can hear him greeting someone in the hallway. Glancing over, I see Alpha Mortlock and Alex walking into the room, with Isa following closely behind. I go to stand up to welcome them, but the alpha just smiles and waves his hand.

"Ari, don't worry about formalities, it's just us. Sit down," he says, and I can't help the surge of warmth that fills me, wishing I had grown up under an alpha like him. Leaning back into the seat, Tori shuffles uncomfortably next to me, unsure how to act around the alpha.

Alpha Mortlock turns his attention to her and he smiles gently. "Tori, we were shocked, but also very pleased to hear of your... recovery." The pause only lasts for a couple of seconds and he covers it well, but Tori shifts awkwardly in her seat again. "I know Ari was lost without you," the alpha continues, and a couple of low laughs fill the room.

"Yup, I'm not sure how she survived that long without me, to be honest," she quips, but her tone is off and I know she's still uncomfortable about her rebirth and struggling to come to terms with the idea.

I see a flash of understanding in the alpha's eyes, and he turns to the bears, who jumped to their feet when they realised that the alpha had entered the room. Holding out his hand, he nods his head and firmly shakes their hands.

"You are welcome here as Tori's mates for as long as she wants you here. Please pass on my best wishes to your alpha," Mortlock declares formally, and I realise the significance of what he's saying. By phrasing it this way, he's making Tori pack, which means she will be protected by Moon River just like any other pack member.

Tori, on the other hand, is focused on something else. "Wait, does that mean you can make them go?" Eagerness fills her tone.

"You don't want them here?" Confusion fills the alpha's face, he certainly hadn't expected this reaction from her.

"No! They won't leave me alone!" she cries out, throwing her arms out as she gestures around her.

Frowning, the alpha takes a step towards the bears. "Then you must leave." He sounds genuinely sympathetic but firm in his resolve. If Tori doesn't want them there, then they must leave.

"Tori," I comment softly, but she turns her head and looks at me accusingly.

"I didn't ask for this, Ari, none of it! Especially not coming back from the dead as a fucking demon! I didn't get a choice about that, or losing my magic. It's nice to have a choice about the men that keep hanging around, expecting me to fall into their fucking arms like a damsel in distress!"

My heart breaks for her, and I pull her into my arms, being careful of her horns after what happened earlier, and gently press her face to my shoulder. Looking over at the twins, I can see their expressions are torn. They want to be with their mate, to comfort her, but their presence is also causing her pain, which is abhorrent to them.

"Maybe you guys should just wait outside for a bit?" I suggest gently, knowing that Tori will feel the loss of them once they've gone and that will only make things harder for her. I feel bad for the bears, but Tori is my top concern and she needs me. Their shoulders slump as they walk from the room, and it's not long before I hear the roar of a bear in the woods behind the house. I wonder if this is how Killian and Eric felt when I denied our bonds and kept walking away? I would have to call Garett later and make sure he comes around to speak with his brothers. My bear had also been called away to the same business as his older brother Max, and I was feeling his absence keenly. We don't have the same metaphysical bond I share with Killian and Eric, but it is just as special, a bond made of love and not forced on me like the fated mate bonds. Seb and Alex also.

Tori abruptly pulls away from me now that the bears have gone and scowls at me. I'd expected to see her face red and streaked with tears, but it looks just as perfect as it did before.

"I can't even fucking cry now!" Her frustration is easy to hear as she jumps up from the couch and paces across the living room, her hooves clopping against the wooden floor.

"Demons don't cry," Eric responds with a twitch of his upper lip. "It would wreak havoc on our reputation." Tori lets out a startled laugh in reply and shakes her head before letting out a deep breath.

"I'm going to need to talk to them, aren't I?" Her voice sounds resigned, and Tori avoids eye contact as she braces for the answer.

Pushing up from the couch, I walk over to her, making sure I don't touch her. I know she needs space, but she also needs to hear this. "Yes, but that doesn't have to be today."

The room is silent for a moment until the alpha clears his throat, bringing our attention back to him. Facing the alpha, I frown as I realise Alex and Isa are standing formally just behind him, enacting their roles as beta and gamma. Usually, Alex would be by my side, and I raise an enquiring brow to him, opening my mouth to ask what's going on, but he just shakes his head. Closing my mouth, I frown once again, looking at Killian, who has gravitated to my side, his eyes locked on me.

"Why don't we all sit down," Alpha Mortlock suggests as

apprehension and dread rises within me. Something has happened, that's the only explanation for the formalities.

I take a seat back on the couch and look up at Tori expectantly, but she hovers in the centre of the room, glancing between the alpha and me. "Do you need me to leave the room?" Seeing the alpha shake his head, she frowns and presses, "But isn't this pack business?"

The alpha's formal façade drops as he gives her a welcoming smile. "Tori, for as long as you need us, you are pack. Besides, this will affect you too." Although he had implied it earlier, he's now formally announcing it. Something about her must have impressed him, and I can see the surprise and gratitude written across her face. Nodding her head, she walks over and sits next to me silently, taking my hand in hers and squeezing it once. Something inside me settles. We'll be okay, we'll get through this.

Looking up expectantly at the alpha, I smother a smile as the alpha sits in the centre of the room, Alex and Isa standing just behind him. I must not smother it quickly enough though, as Alex meets my gaze and narrows his eyes slightly. Uh-oh, I'll pay for that later. I have to hide another grin as the various ways I can make it up to him flash through my mind.

Clearing his throat, the alpha begins, "We have just learned of an attack on a group of shifters." He pauses as we absorb this, my stomach dropping. Not again.

"Who was attacked?" My voice croaks as I struggle to get the words out, almost as though if I can't voice the question, then I don't have to know the answer. But I have to know.

Mortlock's sombre eyes meet mine. "The lions." The room falls silent as the implications run through our minds. I can see now why Killian was shocked enough that I felt it through the bond. The local lion pride attended the meeting that ASP stormed, the meeting where Tori was killed, but they did so with extreme reluctance. They made it clear that they weren't going to take sides, that their feelings towards ASP were neutral, and the only reason they had attended was to listen to what we had to say.

"Wait, the lions? Why would they be attacked?" Eric's astounded tone fills the room, but I only have one question.

"Who was the target?"

The silence lasts long enough that I know the answer is bad, not to mention the tight expression Isa is wearing as she shifts from foot to foot, as if she's wanting to take action. Alex keeps his gaze trained on me, as if he's unsure what my reaction is going to be. Turning my attention back to Alpha Mortlock, I can see anger simmering in his eyes, along with a deep sorrow, and that alone tells me the answer before he's even said the words.

"The whole pride. They were eradicated." His tone is even, as if he's telling me the cricket scores, but I can tell from his formality and stiffness that this is hurting him. He wants action, but he has to keep his cool, not wanting to risk his pack.

"There were no survivors," Isa bites out in clipped tones, her German accent stronger than usual with her anger. "Even the cubs were murdered." The room falls quiet as the news sinks in.

"Who did this?" I inquire, a deadly calm running through me, the darkness that resides within me threatening to envelop me as I wait to see if my suspicions are confirmed. Shadows appear on my skin, flickering along my arm like a living animal until my whole body seems to be embraced by the darkness.

"We believe it was the Shadow Pack, but disturbingly, we suspect ASP's involvement," Alex finally speaks up, and my power flares at the mention of Shadow Pack, the shadows rippling around my body. Tori leans back on the couch, watching my shadows warily as they seem to try and stroke against her.

Alpha Mortlock nods in agreement, explaining his reasoning. "The lion pride's exact location was a secret, one that they guarded very closely, the only people that knew its location was ASP and the members of the pride."

What he says makes sense, but that doesn't prove that ASP was involved. I'm sure ASP participated, but we can't do anything without proof. "That doesn't mean ASP was involved," I begrudgingly admit, then voice a question that's been bugging me since I heard who the target was. "Why would they attack the lions? They wanted to trust ASP."

"It could be a message?" Isa muses. "To show that no one is safe from them."

Mortlock shakes his head. "There were other signs too. Not to mention this attack was the same as all the other murders and disappearances. It was reported to them, and they've done *nothing*." His voice cracks, and I realise he's mourning, remembering that he had a contact, a friend, in the lion pride.

"What do we do now?" My question breaks the heavy silence that's fallen over us, but I've had enough, now is the time for action.

"This can't go on," Killian chimes in, adding his piece for the first time. He's addressing the room, but his eyes are locked on me.

"What I don't understand is why Shadow Pack is working with ASP. ASP seems to hate shifters, so why work with them?" Eric ponders, his brow lowered in confusion, and the others share similar looks.

"To get what they want." Everyone turns to look at me in question. They don't know Shadow Pack like I do. "They want to cause as much disruption and chaos within the shifter population as possible. Shadow Pack will happily kill and maim if it means they prove their superiority. They're trying to harm me by harming others. ASP hates shifters. This way, shifters are dying, but they can blame it on someone else, and not just that, the killers are shifters, thereby proving their point about us and causing distrust between us at the same time."

"So, we attack them," Isa announces, and I turn to her in alarm and dismay.

Shaking my head, I meet her fierce gaze. "No, not until we know for sure that ASP is involved. Just rushing in will get us killed," I reason, but I can feel the anger building in the room and I know I need to try and calm everyone down.

"We can't just keep sitting here doing nothing while they are killing children!" Isa shouts, her eyes rimmed with tears, and this is when I realise they're winning. If we run in and attack them, we're doing exactly what they want us to. If we attack Shadow Pack, then we're just ridding them of another shifter pack.

I explain this to the others, and they sit back and contemplate my words, even Isa seems to have accepted what I'm saying, although she doesn't look happy, her simmering anger clear to see in her rigid posture.

"What do we do then?" Eric asks again, and my stomach drops as everyone turns to me.

"Don't look at me! Ask the alpha!" I exclaim, throwing my hand in his direction. No way, no way am I making a decision this monumental, not when it involves people's lives, that's a job for the alpha.

"Ari—" he starts, his voice cajoling as he takes a step towards me, but he stops when I hold up my hand.

"No. Sorry, bossman, but I'm not making that decision." Tori raises her eyebrows at my audacity, but I refuse to have that responsibility on my shoulders.

He meets my gaze and contemplates me for a moment before dipping his head in acknowledgement. "I'm not asking you to make the decision. I'm asking you what you think we should do." Silence fills the room as everyone turns from the alpha to look at me, and if the situation wasn't so important, I'd be laughing at their yo-yoing between us. I lean back against couch and contemplate what he said, running the options through my mind.

"I think we need to speak to the splinter group and accept their help. We need to know what's going on inside ASP, we can't risk attacking until we know more," I suggest, hoping they understand the risks of attacking an agency like ASP, especially if we're wrong. We would be wiped out as an example to the rest of the shifters. "I don't like it, but I think it's our only viable option. Isa's right—we can't just sit back and let more shifters die."

Looking at said shifter, I watch as she nods her head at me in thanks, while the alpha considers what I've said before letting out a big sigh. "Can we trust this splinter group?"

I almost laugh out loud. I'm the last person to ask about trusting people. *I trust no one*, I think before frowning as I look up at the people around me and realise that's not true. It might have been true once upon a time, but now I have a family, a pack, friends, and even mates. I never thought this was a life I could have.

I consider his question again, and decide to trust my instincts, they haven't lead me astray so far. Nodding my head once, I reply, "Yes."

Alpha Mortlock holds my gaze, and I feel the weight of his alpha power on me as he contemplates my answer. Frowning, he lets out a long breath. "Okay, let's get in touch with them." He glances at Alex, who nods and leaves the room, with Isa following after him. Pushing to his feet, Mortlock looks at me once more. "I really hope you're right about this."

As I watch him leave the room, a sense of foreboding fills me.

"So do I."

Chapter Fifteen

The next couple of weeks pass by in a blur, and we all fall into a routine. After that day with the alpha, we'd been in touch with Aiden from the ASP splinter group, passing information between us as we discovered it. Thanks to their information, which in some cases were just whispers, we'd been able to warn a couple of packs that they might be targeted, and they were then able to take extra precautions.

It's been suspiciously quiet recently. Whether that's because we've managed to thwart some attacks or because of other unknown reasons, it's difficult to tell. The other option is that they knew we had people on the inside and were holding off on their attacks to lull us into a false sense of security. Whichever it turns out to be, I'm walking around in a constant state of tension, waiting for my decision to bite me on the ass.

"Ari, is everything okay?" Jessica queries, her little voice tight as she looks up at me. Mentally slapping myself, I smile at Seb's little sister and carry on dressing the wound on her head.

"Sorry, sweetie, I was miles away. Yep, make sure you keep this clean and dry, and come see me again in two days, I'll need to remove the stitches," I instruct, using my nurse's voice, as Seb likes to call it. The small, neat line of stitches would usually be in longer if Jessica was human, but her shifter genes come with faster healing. "Remind me how you did this again."

A guilty look crosses her face as she glances up at Seb. "I was playing with Tom out by the edge of the pack boundary on the big boulders, and I slipped."

"You know not to go out that far, it's dangerous. Plus, I told you not to play with Tom, he's a bad influence, play with boys your own age," Seb chides with a frown, but I see him softening as soon as Jessica turns her puppy dog eyes on him. Smiling, I tidy up the medical room, disposing of the needle and bloodied gauzes and cleaning down the surfaces as they continue to talk about playing with boys who are much older than her. Seeing this side of Seb always makes me re-evaluate him. He's always so playful around me and the others that it's easy to forget he's the head of his family now, he has responsibilities just like the rest of us.

The life of a nurse in the pack is much slower than that of a hospital nurse, but moments like this make it worth it, and I'm pleased I can still help people, even if it's not as often or in the way I would like. Now that Eric lives here, the pack has a full-time doctor, and he's been looking into hiring another full-time nurse to assist him. I'll have to move out of the apartment above the medical rooms eventually, and I know that the alpha will give me, us, one of the empty couples houses on the edge of the property to move into, but I struggle with the idea. I've always had to work hard for what I've got, and to simply be given the property doesn't sit well with me. I know it's one of the benefits of being part of a pack, but something about it bugs me, not to mention it will never be a home for all of us, not truly.

While Eric was been welcomed into the pack, he'll always be an outsider. He says he doesn't mind, that he has wandered the Earth for many lifetimes and says anywhere with me is his home, but it matters to me. Garett, as a bear, can't join Moon River for obvious reasons, and as such, will still always owe allegiance to Long Claw, and while he can stay with us, it will never be his home. During lazy morning conversations curled up together in bed, he's offered to leave Long Claw, to belong to no pack, but I won't let him do it, it's not fair to him.

Speaking of being curled up in bed together...there hasn't been much of that recently either, thanks to the constant presence of my best friend. I love Tori, and I would never say as much to her while she still needs me, but she's a bit of a buzzkill.

After the first week, she moved into the spare bedroom to give me and the guys a bit more space, but she keeps waking up in the middle of the night screaming. Since that first night, when I'd walked into the spare room and found her curled into a trembling ball, I've been spending most nights checking up on her, unable to sleep myself. She won't tell me what she dreams of, but I can imagine. I know a thing or two about bad dreams. A couple of times, Max or the twins have tried to storm into her room, feeling her panic through the bond from across the pack compound, and things are starting to get a bit difficult.

As if able to sense that I'm thinking about her, she appears in the doorway of the medical room, her curls bouncing slightly as she walks, the clipping sound of her hooves on the floor announcing her presence.

"Everything okay in here?" Leaning against the doorframe, she smiles at Jessica, who's sitting in the examination chair, her little legs swinging as she waits for me to finish clearing up.

"Tori!" Jumping down from the chair, she rushes over to the demon, proudly showing her the stitches in her head. I'd been worried that the horns and hooves would scare the little girl, but she merely shrugged and took Tori by the hand to the table where she proceeded to show her the drawings she'd been working on that day. Since then, they'd been fast friends.

"Hey, monkey!" Kneeling down, Tori has a look at the wound and nods sagely. "Got your head stitched up so your brains can't fall out?"

Jessica looks at her with wide eyes, her expression in a half-smile as if she can't quite decide if Tori's joking or not.

"She's joking," Seb comments, his voice calming and far different from the playful Seb that I know, but I can see a little sparkle in his eye. "Are you coming to the BBQ?" He looks up at Tori, directing his question at her.

We had all been invited to a BBQ Lena was throwing over at the alpha's house. It wasn't an official pack meet, but the whole pack was invited and would likely turn up, especially if they knew Tori and the bears were going to be there. Turns out that werewolves are huge gossips. I've left the decision up to Tori. If she doesn't want to go, then she doesn't have to and I'll stay with her, even if the pack elders would frown upon it, plus Alpha Mortlock would understand.

Glancing over at my best friend, I see her face twisted with indecision, and then her eyes flick to me. I hope my expression conveys my feelings, that I don't mind either way if we go or stay, but something seems to make up her mind as she turns to Seb with a small smile and a curt nod.

"I guess I should show my face, especially when the alpha and his wife have been so kind." Her voice sounds sure, but I know her better. She's nervous, and I don't blame her.

The three of them continue with small talk as I finish wiping down the surfaces and locking up the medicine cabinet. Glancing around once more to make sure everything's in place, I grab my keys and usher them out of the room, locking it behind me.

"Meet you there?" I ask Seb, smiling as he nods and leads Jessica out of the building. Linking arms with Tori, I lead us towards the stairs that go to our rooms, eager to get out of my work clothes. "Let's get changed."

Up in my rooms, I frown at Tori's back as she rifles through my sparse wardrobe, throwing items of clothing onto the floor in disgust. I've never been big on fashion. For years, I lived lightly, so if I needed to run, I wouldn't need to leave anything behind. It was only when Tori and I had been settled for a few years in our apartment that I let her convince me to buy some more clothes, but even then, my collection was far smaller than hers. Some habits are hard to break. Besides, when you work in a hospital with scrubs as a uniform, you learn to love comfortable clothing. Many of the things Tori wears, while looking amazing, also look horribly uncomfortable and tight, so naturally, she dislikes my clothing.

Pushing up from the bed where I've been sitting and watching Tori, I gently push her out of the way to survey the wardrobe. I shift through a couple of the clothes hangers then reach in with a smile, pulling out a purple maxi dress. The length will hide her legs and the colour will suit Tori, the elastic in the dress will also make it easier to fit around her ample bust better than most of my clothes. Handing it over to her, I roll my eyes at her expression.

"Just try it on!" I demand, turning my back to look in the wardrobe again, picking out my favourite pair of jeans and light blue button-down shirt.

"Hey! If I'm having to wear a dress, so are you!" Tori argues as I spin to look at her. I was right—the dress suits her. The elastic waist hugs her curves and the fabric cascades down to the floor, completely covering her lower legs and hooves, which I know she's self-conscious about.

My mouth pulls into a smile at her comment. I can count the number of times I've worn a dress on one hand. "Tor, I'm not wearing a dress."

"Well, you're not wearing that." Her voice is disgusted as she points to the clothes I clutch in my hand. "We're going to a BBQ, not work. Fuck me, your clothes are boring." My mouth drops open in mock outrage at her comments, but I'm used to Tori's dislike of my clothing, so I don't take it personally. Plus, I'm enjoying being with her, just like old times. It feels like the events of the last few weeks were all just a bad dream. Well, if you can ignore the horns poking through my best friend's hair.

"They're not boring, they're practical!" I retort, defending my clothing choices, but a smile curls my lips as she strides back to the wardrobe, her head buried from sight as she hunts for the perfect outfit for me.

"Aha!" Her muffled cry reaches me before she pulls back, but she has to stop when she gets caught up in a strappy top, the tip of her horns going through the strap. The more she moves, the more tangled she gets. "Fuck's sake. Ari, will you wipe that smile off your face and help a girl out?"

With great effort, I rid my face of all emotion as I go to her side and slowly try to untangle the clothes and hangers from her horns, avoiding her gaze since I know I won't be able to hold back my laughter if she looks at me.

Finally free, Tori shakes her head, and her brown curls fall into perfect ringlets around her face. She blows out a breath and throws a dirty look at the wardrobe before handing me the hanger I hadn't realised she'd been holding earlier.

"Put this on." Her demanding tone has me raising an eyebrow, before lifting the dress to have a better look.

"I didn't even realise I had this," I admit, wondering when I'd have bought something like this. It's nice, really nice, but it's not something I would've bought for myself.

"I bought this for you two years ago! You said you loved it!" Tori says indignantly, causing me to wince. Oops.

"I did love it! I mean, I do love it!" At her disapproving glare, I throw my hands up. "Come on, Tor, it's a dress, when do I have the opportunity to wear a dress?"

"Right now," she counters with a grin, and I realise I've walked right into her trap. Sighing, I walk into the en suite, pulling the door closed behind me as I hang up the dress. Removing my clothing and standing in just my underwear, I reach up for the dress, running my hands over the soft fabric as I reach for the zipper at the back. I slip the fabric over my head and thread my arms through the sleeves, then pull the dress into place. Looking in the mirror, I have to admit that Tori's pick perfectly fits my body. The sweetheart neckline shows off my generous bust without revealing all to the world, and the cap sleeves help cover the myriad of scars that cross my body. Tor knows how much I hate showing them off, which is part of the reason I hate wearing dresses, but she's done a good job with this. The waist cinches in, showing off my figure before falling to my knees. Letting out a breath, I shake my head at my reflection. It's very pretty, but my reflection looks nothing like me.

"I can hear you sighing, come out so I can see you!" I hear my demanding best friend call out, and I smother a smile as I push open the bathroom door and walk towards her. Tori grins when she sees me and twirls her finger, gesturing for me to spin. I roll my eyes but spin anyway, secretly enjoying the way the skirt flares out with my movement.

"Happy?" I demand, half hoping she says no so I can take it off, but those hopes die quickly when I see her expression.

"I have such great taste in clothes," she says, congratulating herself as she walks over to me and pulls one of the sleeves into place before playing with my hair.

"Tor, I'm not doing anything with my hair, so don't even start."

My warning makes her purse her lips before she reaches out to touch my hair again. "Not even some little curls—"

"No." I point a finger at her, narrowing my eyes in warning. "I'll brush it, and that's it. I'm going to look out of place in this thing anyway without you playing hairdresser." Gesturing to the dress, I shake my head as I catch my reflection in the mirror. I mean, I look good and the guys aren't going to know what's hit them, but I'm much more comfortable in my normal clothes, the ones that cover me up.

"Stop fidgeting. I can barely see your scars," Tor admonishes, but her voice is soft.

"I'm not worried about them." *Liar*, I think to myself, and Tori just nods before walking up to me and wrapping an arm around my shoulders.

"Uh-huh," she responds, sounding completely unconvinced.

Standing together like this, her just behind me with her arm around me, resting her head on my shoulder, makes me think of old times, before the guys turned up in my life and before Shadow Pack tracked me down, better times. But no, it wasn't better. Packless. I was so lonely, and I didn't even know it, afraid of my own shadow, literally, and that my past was going to catch up with me. Now, I've met the guys, and I wouldn't want life any other way.

Obviously thinking along similar lines, Tori squeezes me slightly, tightening our hug before kissing me on the cheek and walking back towards the wardrobe.

"Now, what are we going to do about shoes?"

Groaning dramatically, I throw myself down onto the bed face first. We could be here for a while yet.

We're late to the BBQ. Thankfully, it doesn't seem to matter as people are coming and going from the alpha's house. The guys had gone on ahead, so it's just the two of us as we walk the short distance across the forest, following the sound of voices as we reach the house.

I feel people's eyes on me, but I know Tori feels the same when she reaches out for my hand, squeezing it tightly, her long nails biting into my palm.

"I told you the dress was a bad idea," I mutter behind a smile, but her attention is focused on something else completely. Glancing across the garden, I see that her gaze is locked on her mates, all three of her bears, standing awkwardly to the side with a beer in each of their hands. Their gazes locked on Tori as soon as we rounded the corner, their posture straightening, and their conversation with Garett forgotten as soon as they spotted her. Confused, Garett turns to see what's taken their focus, and his eyes instantly find mine. His smile makes his face glow, although as his gaze drops to see what I'm wearing, his eyes heat. Taking a step forward, I start towards him, only to be yanked to a stop by the demon at my side.

"Christ, Tor, you nearly ripped my arm off." I rub my shoulder and roll my eyes at her. "You're much stronger now, remember?" My admonishment is met with a flippant wave of her hand, her gaze still on the bears.

"Yeah, sorry. Why were you going over there?" She glances at me as she asks this, but I can tell she isn't really looking at me, simply using me as a barrier so she can still sneak peeks at the guys behind me.

"I was going to see Garett." I shrug before narrowing my eyes on her, realising exactly what she's doing. "Tor, they're your mates, you can't ignore them forever."

Silence meets my words as she drops her eyes to the ground, fiddling with the skirt of her dress. Frowning, I place my hand on her arm. I've never seen Tori like this before, and I realise this is more than her just being stubborn. "What if I don't want to be their mate?" Her voice is low, and it's the note of uncertainty that hits me.

"Then you don't have to do anything. We can leave right now if you want." I make my voice firm. No one will make her do anything she doesn't want to, not even if that's to see her fate chosen mates. Fate can go fuck itself.

Taking a deep breath, she shakes her head. "No, it's fine. Their brother is one of your mates, I can't avoid them forever." She mirrors my words from earlier. Straightening, she throws back her shoulders and brushes an invisible piece of lint from her dress. "How do my horns look?" she asks quietly, and I don't bother hiding my smile.

"Fierce," I assure her, and she finally smiles, linking her arm with mine.

"Then I'm ready."

As we start to walk over to the bears, I look around to see who else is here. I smile when I see Seb entertaining the children in the corner, undoubtedly playing some silly game. Alex is with the alpha, who's talking with Eric, who's looking causal and relaxed. I can't see Killian, but I can *feel* him through our bond. I really need to do some more work on building this bond. I still don't really know how to use it, but I've been assured that I will learn with time.

A flash of amusement trickling down the bond has me throwing a look over my shoulder. I see Killian at the grill, cooking some of the meat while talking with one of the other nomad wolves, Michael. I'm surprised to see him here, to be honest. Killian once told me about him and how he came to be here. He wouldn't tell me much, but what I heard made my heart go out to him. Like Killian, Michael was one of the outcast wolves, living on the edges of the pack and not taking part in any pack gatherings. He isn't officially part of the pack, so he doesn't have to, but the alpha allows him to live here because of the person he is, and although the pack is friendly, the outcast wolves tend to stay very separate. I don't think I've ever seen Michael in public before. The one and only time I met him was when he was leaving Killian's hut as I was walking over to meet my mate.

Looking at him now, I can see he looks uncomfortable as he shifts from foot to foot, but he laughs at something Killian says, and I feel a flash of love for my mate. Before we met, he never would have come to something like this, let alone encourage the other nomad wolves to join in, and although he's still my grumpy Killian, something has opened up in him, allowing him to be more compassionate to others. Not that he would ever admit it.

Reassured that all of my guys are here and safe, I look back at my bear. My smile widens as we reach him, and his arm stretches out and pulls me to his side. Leaning up on my tiptoes, I press a kiss to his lips, lingering for a moment until someone coughs, reminding us that we're in public. Grinning, I pull away, not at all ashamed. Garett has been helping out at Long Claw much more recently, taking on a lot of the roles that the twins and Max usually do. They've been taking it in turns to stay here with Tori, but when they are away, they're distracted, so Garett has stepped in to fill those gaps, but that means he's been away a lot and I've missed my bear.

Reluctantly pulling away from Garett's hold, I look over at Tori to see she's making awkward conversation with her bears. The twins are trying to engage her in a silly story, and I can see the corner of her mouth turning up as she fights a smile. Max stands next to them, silently staring at her until her patience finally snaps and she spins to point a finger at him.

"Will you stop staring at me? What is your problem?" Her shout silences the garden around us as people turn to stare at us. Max's eyes narrow before he looks briefly at me before storming away.

"Well, that went well," Ben comments, breaking the awkward silence. At least, I think it's Ben, I still haven't gotten to know the twins well enough to where I can tell them apart yet.

Garett is frowning as he watches his older brother stalk off. "I should go check if he's okay." Sighing, I nod at him. I don't want him to go, but I know he won't be happy until he's checked up on Max.

I can see the strain he's under, knowing these last few weeks are taking their toll, and I'm pretty sure I can see a couple of grey hairs, not that I'll tell him this. If I'm being honest, I find it attractive. Running my hands through his hair, I simply nod and ask, "Will I see you later?"

Wrapping me in his arms again, he presses his forehead to mind. "Yes, I'll come back, but I can't stay tonight." Regret lines his words, and I can't wait for a time that we can all stay together in the same house.

"Okay, I'll see you later. Love you."

"Love you too." Sealing his words with a long kiss, he pulls away before grinning at Tori and his brothers. "See you in a bit, guys."

Turning to watch him go, I become aware of someone watching me. I follow the feeling and find Tori staring at me with a knowing grin. "I still find it weird when you do that," she comments, taking a sip of the drink one of the twins handed her.

Frowning, I scratch my head, brushing my hair into place. "Do what?"

"Tell Garett that you love him," she replies, taking another sip. "He's been in love with you for years, and you never seemed to notice, didn't want any sort of romantic relationship at all, and now you have five men devoting themselves to you!"

"Yeah, well, I didn't think my kind of life allowed for love. They would just end up being something for Shadow Pack to use against me." Tori sobers at my words, walking over to me and sliding her arm around my waist.

"Well, I'm glad things worked out this way." Her smile is warm, and I know she means it. She'd always been worried about me and how I kept people at a distance, so the fact that I now have five men in my life who all dote on me must make her giddy with happiness. I start to smile, to agree with her, but then I remember why I kept my distance in the first place.

"Shadow Pack is still out there though," I reply, my gut clenching as I think of Terrance and the rest of my old pack hunting me down, but determined to take others out with me at the same time.

"I know." Her voice is sombre as I feel my old fears coming back to me, winding themselves around me in a tight band. Taking a deep breath, I focus on all the good things in the life I've built for myself here and reach for the bond I have with my men. I feel Killian's gaze on me, and when I glance over his eyes bore into mine, and I can feel his question down the bond.

Are you okay?

I can't hear the words, it's more of a feeling, but I nod, taking comfort in the strength I feel in the bond. Eric is also looking at me with a sympathetic expression on his face as he sends me a feeling of safety through our bond. Although I don't have a metaphysical bond with my other mates, they seem to sense something isn't right as they all watch me. Giving them a smile, I reassure them that I'm okay, and I can feel Tori staring at me with interest, then she shakes her head with a knowing smile as I turn to look at her again.

"It makes me nervous that we've heard *nothing* from them." Voicing my worries, I tell her what's been playing on my mind. Over and over, I've envisioned them attacking us here, but so far, only other supernaturals have been attacked.

"Maybe they're licking their wounds, you did kill their leader," Tori comments, clearly fed up with this conversation, frustration evident in her tone. "Don't worry, we'll find them. I still have to pay the bastards back for killing me." She smirks as she reaches up and taps the swirling, tattoo-like mark that shows the place where the bullet hit her in the forehead. The familiar feeling of guilt I carry around like a lead weight at Tori's death rises, but as I look at her now I find that it's changing. I no longer feel guilty that I couldn't save her. I know that I did everything I could, but fate stepped in, bringing her back to me. However, I *do* feel guilty that I brought her into this and she got hurt in the process. She may be stronger than she had ever thought possible, but her whole life has changed and she's not who she thought she was.

Reaching out, I pull her into my arms for a tight hug, her body stiffening at the sudden body contact. "I love you, Tor." My throat gets tight as the thought of how close I was to losing her grips me. "Horns and all," I joke, trying to blink away the moisture gathering in my eyes.

Snorting at my comment, she relaxes into my arms, returning my hug before finally pulling away. "Love you too, dog breath." She grins, but she can't hide the catch in her throat as she speaks or the tears I see gathering in her eyes.

Chapter Sixteen

The BBQ goes on for a couple of hours and I get the opportunity to speak with some of the wolves that don't tend to mingle other than at pack meets. I have an awkward conversation with Michael, but after a couple of minutes he loosens up a bit and tells me some stories about Killian that have me howling with laughter. I don't think we're quite friends yet, but I hope that in time, he'll come to think of me as one. After an hour or so since I arrived, Michael has enough of being social, and both him and Killian leave, the two of them having a guys' night, which I learned from Seb is just the two of them shifting and hunting deer.

Leaning back in one of the wooden benches, I take a sip from my beer as I watch those around me. A happy, settled feeling fills me as I take in my pack mates. It still seems strange to say after being a lone wolf for so long, but it feels good. The bench shifts slightly as someone sits next to me, and I can tell by his scent who it is before I turn to look at him, his arm sliding over my shoulder.

"Hey, Seb." My smile is content as I lean into him.

"You look happy."

"I am."

"You know, that's pretty sexy."

Raising my eyebrows, I look at him dubiously. "Me being happy is a turn-on for you?"

"It's not so much that you're happy, although that's part of it," he explains. "It's that you have found your place, and since then, you have been so much more confident. You've claimed us. Now *that* is a turn-on." His eyes glint as he talks, leaning in closer as he lowers his voice, his body pressing against mine on the bench. My wolf has always craved Seb. As one of the lower wolves in the pack, he's completely submissive, both in and out of the bedroom. Having that unquestioning, trusting person to do with as I like is a refreshing change from my other, more dominant mates, not to mention my grumpy alpha wolf. Right now, my wolf wants Seb, and I can feel her pressing forward, the hair on my arms rising as my power surges.

"What are you two whispering about? Planning world domination?" Alex's voice has me looking up, his eyes going from me to Seb and back again. He must have felt my power. Smirking, I place my hand territorially on Seb's leg, feeling my wolf rise to the surface, not pleased at the interruption.

"Yeah." My voice comes out in a growl. "Want to join us?" I tease, knowing what his answer is going to be.

His eyes heat as his expression becomes serious, and his body stills as his wolf comes out to play, his powers rubbing against mine. With what looks to be immense effort, he manages to pull back his inner wolf, but the hunger and longing is still there.

I stand up, and Seb jumps to his feet next to me, taking my hand in his as I stalk towards Tori. She raises her eyebrows when she sees me and Seb with Alex following behind like a wolf stalking his prey, then she grins and waves a hand at me.

"I'll be staying with Eric tonight," she tells me before I've even said anything. I'm surprised she's agreed to stay anywhere other than with me, not to mention the fact the bear twins are staying there at the moment. Eric seems just as shocked as I am, but he covers it quickly.

"Oh yes, of course," he replies with a smile before sending me a feeling down our bond. He'll keep an eye on her and the twins. Nodding at him, I send him feelings of gratitude before I turn back to my best friend.

"You sure?"

"I'm a big girl, Ari. Besides, I really don't want to hear whatever you've got planned for tonight," she teases as Alex walks up behind me and wraps his arm around me as if to prove her point. "Girl, go get some." Her wink makes me laugh as Seb and Alex try to lead me away, my traitorous feet taking the steps, even as I turn back to look at her.

"You know where I am if you need me," I call out, feeling guilty at leaving her, but I know Eric will look after her.

The walk back to the medical building doesn't take long, but we're silent the whole time. My steps up the porch stairs are sure, and I sense the guys hovering behind me as I unlock the door, not stopping to wait for them before I walk upstairs towards my bedroom. Pushing open the door, I step over the threshold to my room, feeling them stop behind me, their instincts making the decisions for them. Someone steps up to my back, reaching a strong hand around and holding on to my hip to anchor himself to me—Alex. My pack beta, who has alpha power, holds me tightly as he leans forward, his breath tickling me as he kisses along the length of my neck. Leaning back my head so he has full access, I hear a breathy moan escape my lips as someone presses their body against my front—Seb.

Being sandwiched between two of my mates is the perfect way to spend the evening. I open my eyes and smile as I see the look on Seb's face, like he's found the holy grail.

"I'm going to change. Make yourself comfortable." My voice comes out breathier than I would have liked, but they both pull away and make their way to the bed. Alex keeps his eyes on me the whole time, like he's watching his prey, smirking at me as I reach the en suite.

"Don't take too long." His voice has deepened, and I can see the large bulge in his jeans. Another wave of alpha power washes over me as a low growl leaves his lips at my hungry look.

Walking into the bathroom, I shut the door behind me and take a deep breath, trying to clear my head of the heady power Alex gives off. I don't think he has any idea how strong his power is, and combined with Seb, it's easy just to let my wolf take control, but I want to be in control today. Alex's power is so different than Killian's alpha power, and I think that's because of how they use it. Kill knows how to wield it and when to use it, while Alex seems to ooze that power.

Looking in the mirror, I can't help but smile at what I see, the heat in my eyes and the happiness that seems to emit from me. Reaching for the hem of the dress, I pull it over my head and drop it to the floor so I'm only standing in my dark bra and matching knickers. I didn't need to leave the room to get undressed, they have seen it all before, but I wanted to take back some control, let them imagine me getting undressed behind the door. Grinning at the thought of them waiting for me, I saunter over to it and push it aside, leaning against the doorframe.

My pussy clenches at the sight before me. Seb is sprawled out at the foot of the bed, naked except for his boxers, which sit low on his slim hips, and one arm props him up as his eyes meet mine. Behind him, Alex sits at the head of the bed, leaning up against the headboard, completely bare as he lazily strokes his hard cock, waiting for me.

I step forward and crawl up onto the bed, leaning over Seb so I'm pressed against him as I kiss his lips. Opening them, he kisses me back, keeping his hands completely to himself as I take the lead, biting down on his lip hard enough to hurt as I pull away. Groaning, Seb pushes up and wraps an arm around me as he tries to tug me back to him.

The bed shifts as Alex crawls up behind Seb, his large, muscled arm wrapping around his chest as he pulls the smaller man away from me. "Hogging our mate, Seb?" There's a note of warning in his voice, but I can see a glint of amusement in Alex's eyes, so I know he's not really offended. Seb's breathing has changed, and I can see from his dilated pupils that he's enjoying every second of this.

"Hold him," I demand, and Alex's face immediately spreads into a grin as he moves his grip so he's holding both of Seb's arms behind his back.

"Yes, mate."

Keeping my eyes locked on Seb, I slide my body against his, pressing a kiss to his lips once more. He immediately responds and returns the kiss, and I can feel him fighting against Alex's hold as he tries to reach me. Making a *tsk* noise, I pull my lips from his and place my hands on his shoulders, then call my power to change my nails into claws. I gently drag them across his skin as I skim down his chest, and his breath hitches.

"More, harder," he pants, and I obey, slowing the path of my razor-sharp nails, pressing them into his skin hard enough to leave a mark, but not enough to break the skin. When Seb and I started playing like this, I was worried about hurting him, but I learned fairly quickly that he likes this, and we have learned to compromise. I refuse to hurt him enough so it draws blood or will bruise, so we found ways to satisfy this need.

Seb shudders in Alex's grip as I dip lower to his waistband. Pulling my claws back on one hand, I slide that hand down into his boxers, wrapping my palm around his already hard cock. Stroking, I slowly slide my other hand between him and Alex, pressing my claws into the soft skin of his back. He jerks forward and almost rips out of Alex's strong hold, his power emerging out of him in stuttering waves of various intensity. Sharing a look with Alex, I pull away, then smile at Seb as his heavy lidded gaze rises to meet mine.

"Sit down, Seb. Alex, I want you behind me," I instruct, looking at Seb before flicking my gaze to my beta.

"No." A flare of power surges the room as Seb speaks, and I

realise with shock that it's coming from him. "Alex, lie down." The demand is followed with a wave of alpha power, and shockingly, Alex does as he's ordered with a confused look on his face.

Alex sits back at the head of the bed where he had been before. I crawl over to him, straddling his legs as I lean forward and press a kiss to his lips, groaning into his mouth as he kisses me back. The bed dips behind me, and I feel Seb's chest brush against my back, his hard cock pressing against me as his hands slide around my body, almost in a mirror of what Alex had been doing. I continue kissing Alex, finding this new dominant side of Seb a major turn-on. I don't know where it's come from or how long it's going to last, but I'm going to enjoy it for now and worry about it later. Pulling away from me slightly, Seb's hands gently undo my bra and slide the straps off my arms before his strong hands seek my breasts. He cups my breasts before tweaking my nipples sharply at the same time as he bites my shoulder. He doesn't bite down hard, certainly not enough to break the skin, but with him behind me, I have no idea what he's going to do next. The pleasure-pain of both the bite and his hands on my nipples makes my pussy clench as I groan into Alex's mouth.

Pressing light kisses against the place he bit, Seb moves one of his hands, sliding it down my body and past the waistline of my knickers. His fingers seek my pussy, his groan letting me know that he found me wet and ready for them. Finding my clit, he starts to circle it, pulling away every couple of seconds just as I'm getting into it. I pull my mouth from Alex's as I push him against the headboard and shuffle back a bit. Seb moves with me as he refuses to let go, his hand tightening on my breast as he buries a finger inside me.

"Seb, you're going to have to let me go for this," I murmur around a gasp, my words breathy, and with a satisfied growl, he pulls away, letting me reposition myself on all fours. Without saying anything further, I lean down and take Alex into my mouth. His satisfied male groan makes me want to smile, but I continue to suck him, gliding up and down his length. Seb repositions himself behind me, his hands running over my hips before moving one of them to cup my pussy as his index finger flicks my clit, my moan muffled by Alex as I continue to suck him.

Behind me, I feel Seb shift his weight, and then he slowly pushes himself inside me, each glorious inch until he reaches the hilt, and I savour the stretch, wanting more. Pulling back out, he slowly begins to thrust in again, and my wolf pushes to the surface, not happy with the tortuously slow movements—she wants to be fucked, and hard. Pushing my hips back with a jerk, I impale myself on his cock, closing my eyes in bliss. Hands grip my hips, hard, and a slapping sound fills the air, my ass stinging from where Seb just spanked me. A wave of arousal runs through me at the thought of my submissive wolf taking control. We've never done anything like this before, and to be honest, I didn't think I was the kind of woman who would be into that, but something about Seb doing it is a real turn-on.

"No," he growls, telling me off for trying to take control. His voice is deeper than I've ever heard it as another strange wave of his power rolls over me. His hands tighten on my hips as he starts pushing into me again, his pace slow, purposeful, and agonisingly good. Thankfully, after a few minutes, he starts to pick up his pace and some of his control begins to slip, his careful movements becoming fast and hard.

Moaning around Alex's cock, I also pick up the pace, taking him deep into my mouth, hollowing out my cheeks as I suck him. Alex makes a pained sound, and I flick my eyes up and see his face set in concentration, and I suddenly realise what he's doing—he's trying not to come. If I could smirk right now, I would be.

Not happy with my attention being taken away from him, Seb slips a hand around and starts flicking my clit again, moving in time to him pounding into me. This is all it takes to push me over the edge, and I pull away from Alex to throw my head back as ecstasy runs through me, pulling Seb into his orgasm as he stills inside me, my pussy milking him as we pant our way through our orgasms.

As Seb pulls away, I look back at Alex with a smirk, his eyes gleaming with an emotion I don't recognise. Opening my mouth to comment on it, I watch as a wicked grin spreads across his face, then he grabs me and spins us, so my back is pressed against the bed and he's above me.

"It's my turn now that the cub has finished." He grins as he looks over at Seb, who's lounging back, his eyes hooded with pleasure as he throws us a sleepy look, back to my submissive Seb.

"Attention on me," Alex commands, his hand gripping my chin as he guides my attention back to him. A spark enters his eyes, and I can't help but smirk. I've seen that look before.

"Possessive alpha babies," I comment, and as his eyebrow rises. A glint enters his eyes, and I know I'll pay for that remark. Leaning down, Alex starts kissing along my collarbone, following the path down my chest and to my breasts, occasionally nipping at the skin before kissing away the sting of his bite. When he reaches my nipple, he sucks it into his mouth, running his tongue over the bud before gently biting it, my gasp making him grin and urging him on all the more. Alex slides a hand down my body, and I let out a small gasp as he finds my tender clit, gently circling it, and soon, I'm moaning as he switches to my other nipple, kissing and licking at the sensitive skin. Removing his hand from my clit, he lines himself up and enters in one smooth stroke, our moans of pleasure mingling as we kiss, his thrusts coming fast.

A noise at the side of the room catches my attention, and when I glance over, I see Seb watching, his cock in his hand, slowly stroking with a lazy smile.

"What did I say about eyes on me?" Alex pants, picking up the pace as he pounds into me, his kisses become bruising, and I can feel my core tighten as I reach my second orgasm of the night. I cry out as I come, with Alex finding his release close behind me as we climax, and from Seb's groan, I'm guessing he finished too. Laughing, Alex leans down and presses a kiss to my lips before collapsing into a pile of limbs.

That night, after we have cleaned up and showered, we fall asleep in a puppy pile, reminding me of the first time I woke up in one. With the memory fresh in my mind, I fall asleep with a smile on my face.

Chapter Seventeen

Looking up at the clear blue sky, I let out a sigh of contentment. The rays from the afternoon sun warm my skin as I lie back and enjoy a quiet afternoon. Feeling a squeeze of my hand, I turn my head to smile at the man lying next to me, squeezing his hand back in return. Garett opens his eyes when he feels me looking at him and gives me the smile that always makes my breath catch. It's the look in his eyes that gets me, the look that says I'm everything he needs, the look that says he would do anything for me. If I turned around and told him to get me the moon, he would do everything in his power to get it for me. Sometimes that scares me, knowing he loves me so much, that his happiness depends on me, but then I remind myself that I've changed, I'm different than the flighty, scared, lonely girl I was when I first met him. Sure, I still get fearful, I still have commitment issues, but I'm working through them, and it's okay that I'm not perfect, it's okay I'm not okay every day, and Garett was one of the guys to teach me that.

Lying side by side in the park, holding hands and watching the world go by, we simply enjoy each other's company. Having five guys all vying for my attention makes it difficult to ensure no one feels left out, and for my bear, I know it's hard staying with me at the wolf pack all the time where he doesn't fit in. Especially recently with all the time he's having to spend at Long Claw, and I know that it's causing him stress, even if he won't admit as much.

So I decided we should spend some time together, just the two of us, away from the packs and our responsibilities, just two people going on a date together. Glancing back over at Garett, I smile softly as he closes his eyes again, basking in the sun. When he's like this, he looks so peaceful, the stress and tension leaving his face, and it reminds me of when we first met all those years ago.

"Cut it out," he grumbles, his arm is draped over his eyes, but he tilts his head slightly towards me.

Frowning, I glance around us for my supposed crime. "Cut what out?"

"I can feel you staring at me." Hearing the smile in his voice, I can't help the smile that spreads across my face.

"I can't help it, you're too good-looking." Garett snorts at my joke, and I laugh, rolling onto my side and propping my head up with my hand. "You look peaceful, what are you thinking about?"

"You," he responds in typical Garett fashion.

It's my turn to snort as I roll my eyes and wait for his real answer. "No, really, what are you thinking about?"

Opening his eyes, he rolls onto his side, mirroring my position so we're almost nose to nose. "I'm always thinking about you, is that so hard to believe?" He smiles as he says it, reaching out to brush a strand of my hair behind my ear, but I can tell he's waiting for my rebuttal, for me to retreat from his affections. Shock rolls through me as this realisation hits me. It's true, my first gut instinct is to roll my eyes and tell him not to be stupid. Not anymore. I'm broken, but I think these men might be fixing me.

Letting out the breath I hadn't realise I'd been holding, I give him a shaky smile.

"I love you," I reply, the only response to his comment that seemed appropriate, and I mean every word.

His smile gets wider, and his eyes heat. "I love you too."

Heart swelling, I lean forward and press my lips against his as he meets me in the middle. It's a slow, soft kiss, not like the firm, commanding kisses from Killian, or the electric, tingling kisses from Eric. This is a kiss completely unique to Garett. Our lips move together, and I can feel the moment things start to get a bit heated as Garett throws an arm around me, pulling me towards him so I'm flush against his body.

Drawing away, I gasp for air, both of us laughing as he does the same before brushing a hand through his now mussed hair with a wry look on his face. I take in his flushed face and heated eyes, and I can feel the evidence of his arousal pressed against me. I'm toying with the idea of getting up and heading straight back to my place when he laughs at my expression.

"As much as I'd love to do that, I'd rather spend more time with you here, where I get you all to myself," he tells me, pressing a kiss to the end of my nose before sitting up.

"How did you know what I was thinking?" I ask as I look up at him, admiring his form as the sun shines down on us, framing his strong jaw as he smiles at me.

"It was all over your face."

"Oh." Pushing up into a sitting position, I grin at him as a thought crosses my mind. "Okay, do you know what I'm thinking now?"

Laughing, he shakes his head, his voice playful as he waits for my response. "No, tell me."

"That it's time for ice cream." Reaching for my purse, I begin to stand up, but Garett puts his hand out, stopping me before gesturing for me to sit back down.

"I'll get it, you stay here with our stuff," he offers, and I know better than to try and argue with him. He may be a bear shifter, but he's as stubborn as an ox.

"Fine, at least let me give you some money for it." Rooting through my purse, I grab some curled-up notes and hand them over, my expression telling him not to bother arguing with me. He rolls his eyes and takes the notes from me, then leans down to press a kiss on top of my head.

"What flavour do you want? A Garett special?" he inquires with a grin, and I can't fight the laugh as I nod. A Garett special is basically a potluck, where he chooses a random mix of flavours. Sometimes I get lucky, other times, I end up with some really weird combinations.

Watching him walk through the grassy ground towards the small café that sells the ice cream, I can't help the dopey smile that crosses my face.

"Ah, young love."

My wolf surges to the surface as I bound to my feet, spinning to see a smiling gentleman just behind where I was sitting.

"It's okay, Ari, I mean you no harm." He holds his arms out to the side in a gesture of peace. I run my eyes over the stranger, taking in his calm appearance. He's tall, about the same height as Garett, but smaller in build. His greying dark hair and the fine lines around his eyes tell me he's in his forties, but if he's some sort of supernatural, he could be much older than that. My wolf is demanding that I let her out, something about this stranger making her vicious in a way she hasn't been since I met the guys. My skin ripples as I fight the change.

"Then why is my wolf acting this way? She doesn't trust you." My voice is more like a growl, but the stranger doesn't bat an eye, his smile staying fixed in place. Sniffing the air, I try to get a read on what he is, and I frown as I scent...nothing. He's definitely supernatural, but I can't tell what.

All supernatural races have a scent. Shifters have a woodsy smell to them, and if you have good senses, you can usually get a sense of what type of animal they are. Witches have a tangy smell that reeks of magic, vampires scent of, well, death, and the fae smell like the forest, but this guy doesn't seem to belong to any race, at least not one I've come across before.

"What are you?" I question, my brow furrowing in confusion.

The man opposite me smiles, and a cold feeling crawls down my back. Something about him reminds me of a predator enjoying the hunt for his prey, which in this case, is me.

"My name is Hunter. I've been trying to get a hold of you for a while now, Ari."

Crossing my arms over my chest, I try to adopt a more casual stance so he doesn't know how much he's affecting me, when all my wolf wants to do is tear him apart. He's clever, this one, a master at twisting words and not answering the question. He'd make a good politician. "You didn't answer my question. I said *what*, not who."

His eyes light up as he looks over me again, his expression appreciative. I'm used to guys eyeing me up, but I don't get that vibe from this guy, it feels more like he's appraising me. "You have good senses, Ari. I have some friends who help protect me, and one of the side effects is it wipes my scent." My eyebrows shoot up at his response before I have a chance to school my expression again. Witches, it has to be, they're one of the only races of supernatural that could do something like that. His gaze goes distant as he starts speaking again, more to himself than to me. "I wonder if your fine senses are from your wolf or your other abilities?"

My entire body stiffens as panic courses through my body, but I force myself not to react, to do so would be a death sentence. My inner wolf is urging me to kill him, to jump forward and swipe my claws across his neck. We can't risk him knowing about me. "What are you talking about?"

"Your Shadowborn powers of course."

I force a laugh, but it sounds flat and forced. "Buddy, I think you've smoked one to many fae pipes. The Shadowborn are a myth, a scary story told to children to keep them in line."

"Don't treat me like a fool, I know what you are." His voice rises before he smiles again, his stance relaxing, revealing a brief crack in his calm exposure and allowing me to see the real Hunter beneath. "You see, Ari, I'm the Director of ASP, and I've been watching you for a while now." My whole body has frozen. I can't move, even if I wanted to. My lungs burn as I try to take deep breaths to calm myself, my thoughts screaming as they spin round in my mind.

No. No, no, no, this can't be happening. He's found me. He's going to kill the others who protected me, not just the guys, but the whole pack. Stay calm, Ari, don't give anything away.

I repeat the mantra to myself, not believing I have the fucking ASP director casually chatting with me in the middle of a park. He doesn't seem to notice any changes in me as he carries on talking. "Back when you were a lone wolf, I wasn't so sure. I knew there was a Shadowborn in the area, I could sense it, but you were just one of my suspects."

The idea that he can sense Shadowborn is both shocking and terrifying. I've never heard of an ability like it, and its bad news for those of us who are trying to get away from people like him. A slow realisation comes to me as I think over his words.

"The missing shifters...that was you?" We'd suspected it was Shadow Pack and had wondered about ASP's involvement, but now I know they were searching for Shadowborn. "What was Shadow Pack's involvement in all this?"

"To start with, it was to find Shadowborn and keep an eye on you. Your old pack was useful, abducting those we needed, and when they went feral and started picking off extra shifters, killing them, we could easily blame it on them, keeping a distance between ASP and them. It was win-win, fulfilling our tasks and ridding the world of extra shifters." His explanation makes me feel sick, I don't want to hear any more, but I need to know.

"Then what changed?"

"There is so much more going on than you understand." His smile widens as he speaks to me, like he's trying to explain something complex to a child.

"Then why don't you tell me?" He seems to be in a sharing mood, so I encourage it. I want to get as far away from him as possible, but I need to hear this.

"ASP has a vision, a world where the races don't fight, where we can all coexist peacefully." A blissful, faraway expression crosses his face, and I realise how he got into power. He's very charismatic, I'll give him that, and my first impression of him was right—he would make a great politician.

"Do we not have that now?" I ask carefully, trying to keep my tone neutral, knowing that if I anger him, he might stop talking.

"No! Shifter packs are constantly challenging each other, eradicating other packs. They can't control their animal urges. They've grown so much, there's triple the number of shifters than any other supernatural group. We need to change that, they're a threat to the other races, and we need better control over them, but they won't comply to any new rules we give them," he rambles, spittle collecting in the corner of his mouth as a hint of madness enters his eyes. It's at this point I realise how dangerous this man is. Not only is he in a position of power, but madmen are so much more dangerous. He truly believes in this vision of his, and he won't stop until it comes to pass.

"Have you even asked them?" I can't stop the question, my frustrations making me act beyond my better judgement. My question seems to awaken him from his trance-like state, and that intelligence I saw earlier appears, a wry smile in place as he raises an eyebrow at me.

"Come now, Ari, I'm not stupid. Do you really think they'll comply with any new rules we put in place about curfews, when they can conceive, and decide who they can and can't accept into their numbers?"

He's right—they would never accept those rules. Even the thought of them trying to restrict us, culling our numbers, controlling when we can have our own children makes a hot rage boil in my stomach. We were right—they *are* behind the pregnancy rates and the difficulties the shifters are having carrying their pregnancies to term. I don't know how they're doing it, but magic has to be involved.

Shifters are a prideful lot, they would never comply to being restricted so, to acting like lower-class citizens so the other supernaturals can feel validated and more powerful. I ask the question that's been plaguing my mind since he started talking.

"You talk about shifters as *them* and *us*. Why am I any different? I'm a shifter too."

"Ah, but you are different, Ari, you are so much more than *just* a shifter." His last words drip with disdain, and I fully understand what's going on. This isn't about shifters being more powerful or having greater numbers, this is about one man's hate for a race of supernaturals.

"What did they do to you?" My words aren't accusatory or judgemental, I simply want to know. This kind of hatred is born from somewhere. He pauses, watching me with a calculating look as if trying to decide whether or not to tell me. The silence stretches, and for a moment, I don't think he's going to answer me.

"An alpha claimed my sister. He was not all unlike your father." I wouldn't wish treatment like that on anyone, and if this alpha was anything like my father, then her life would have been a living hell. Seeing my grimace, he nods. "Yes, exactly. She wasn't strong like you are. Once he'd used her, he returned her body to us." Although his voice doesn't change as he speaks, I notice that his smile, which has been present throughout our conversation, has dropped.

Nodding my head in acknowledgement, I see him dip his head in return. I'm not going to apologise for the treatment his sister received, but I am sorry it happened to her. We are silent as I mull over our conversation, but something he said earlier sticks with me. "What did you mean that I'm more than a shifter? How do I fit into all this?"

"You're a Shadowborn." His tone is hushed, reverent as excitement lights his eyes, the madness returning. "All of this," he waves his hands around, and I know he's talking about the rules he wants to impose on the shifters, "is nothing to do with you. ASP has no interest in you other than you're a shifter."

"I don't get it. If I'm so unimportant, then why are you here speaking to me now?" Confusion runs through me as I try to link everything together.

"I have a personal interest in you, and my position in ASP allows me powers and privileges I wouldn't have otherwise." Dread fills me at his words, and my wolf tries to take control of my body, the skin on my arms rippling as she tries to break out, and I have to grit my teeth to stay in control. I need to get out of here—no, *we* need to get out of here. Scanning the area, I look for Garett, he's been gone a while, longer than he should've been. Fear starts invading my thoughts as visions of Garett being hurt play through my mind. I must send some of these images down the bond I share with Killian and Eric, as I feel alarm that isn't mine being sent back through. Taking a deep breath, I push the bond as far away as I can, shutting it down so I can focus on what's happening here and now.

Hunter watches this all with a little smile, his cunning eyes observing my every reaction. "Let's go for a little walk, and don't make me threaten to hurt your bear." He shudders at the thought. "I'll return him unharmed once we've had our talk."

They've got Garett.

I know what I need to do.

"Okay, I'll walk with you, if you promise you won't harm him." My voice is calm, controlled, but inside, I'm a mess. However, the skills I've gained over years of being on the run and learning to control my feelings comes to my aid.

Hunter nods and gestures for me to follow him. Walking up to his side, I have to fight not to cringe away from him. Half of me is scared of him, my wolf wants to kill him, but the other part of me, the calm, logical part, knows that I need to stay in control, get more information out of him so I can find a way to get us all out of this.

Reaching the wooded part of the park, we start to walk through the trees, climbing over fallen logs and branches, the untamed brambles pulling at our clothing, but we don't stop. The sunlight can just about reach us here, the canopy of branches and leaves filtering the smallest rays of light.

"I'm aware there's a small faction within ASP who don't agree with me about the shifters." His comment almost causes me to stumble, but I force myself to keep walking. His little smile tells me that he saw my reaction, but I don't say anything, just keep walking and wait for him to start again.

"They don't believe I know about them, so I can continue to keep an eye on them. They aren't causing many issues at the moment, and them working with you works in my favour." His voice is calm and casual, like we're talking about the weather and not a rebellion group within his organisation. "They're protecting you, and you pass on to the packs that they are helping you, which stops an all-out war."

"That's not what you want?" I don't have to fake anything when I ask this, I'm confused by his motivations.

"Ari?" My body freezes as I hear Garett call out my name from behind, from the direction we just left. He sounds confused, but not worried. I've been tricked. Turning to glare at Hunter, I wait until he realises I've stopped following him, but as he spins to face me, he seems too focused on what he's been saying to comment on the fact I'm not walking with him anymore.

"No! Didn't you listen?" That hint of madness enters his eyes again as he throws his arms out. "I want peace, and the only way to do that is to control the shifters. They won't comply, so we will force them."

"So, you will kill innocent shifters to reach your vision?" I have to fight with the anger his words stir in me, but I can't hold it back as I spit the words at him. Figures appear behind him, dressed all in black, their faces covered, and movement from the corner of my eye tells me that we are surrounded. My eyes flick around to look for a way out, realising that this was an ambush. Sniffing the air, I notice their scents are also hidden from me. I curse my stupidity and fall into a fighting stance, dropping all pretence that I'm interested in what he has to say. Seeing the change in me, he finally drops his smile and a look of disappointment crosses his face.

"If that's what it takes." Even his voice changes, and I can see why he's the head of ASP, his tone commanding.

"That's genocide," I snarl, furious.

"Ari!" Garett calls out again, a note of panic is his voice as he realises something is wrong, causing my heart to break. I want to shout out to him, to tell him to run, to leave without me, but I know he would never listen to me.

"I think that's the end of our talk today, Ari." The Hunter I'd previously been talking to is completely gone, replaced by the commanding Director of ASP. Arms grab me, and I try to rip away from them, but more hands grab me, their strength greater than it should be. I've fought bear shifters and managed to beat them in a fight, but I can't even get these guys to move an inch, their hidden faces and scentless bodies making me realise that we are all in much deeper shit than we had realised. The hands on me tighten as they start forcing me forward. Hunter has a grim smile on his face when I have no choice but to stumble forward.

"Wait, where are you taking me?" My voice is low, demanding, as my wolf tries to come forward to protect me, only to find she can't. It's like we've been disconnected, and I can't feel her anymore. Panic starts to set in.

"I'm taking you in for your own safety," he answers me, his smile widening, and I know his answer is total bullshit. He wants something from me and he knows I won't give it to him, so he's going to take it.

"Why? Why me?" There's no pause, his answer immediate.

"You're Shadowborn, I need you."

"Ari!" Garrett's pained shout fills my ears, and I know he's trying to find me. A part of me wants him to, while the other part of me is terrified he's going to get taken also.

I throw my weight into the masked figure to my left, and they have to stop the steady procession we were taking, but no matter how much I struggle, I can't get free. Desperate, I reach for my shadow powers and find that I can still access them. I close my eyes with a grin and call them forward, my limbs starting to turn into shadow. Opening my eyes, I meet Hunter's gaze that's watching me with unhidden longing, which makes me pause. A sudden hit to the back of my head causes stars to appear in my vision as darkness starts to swallow me up, and the last thing I hear is Garett's roar as his bear breaks through his careful control.

Garett

Clutching the ice creams in my hands, I smile as head back towards my mate. I may not have the mating bond with Ari, but I love her just as fiercely as if I did, and she never lets me feel like I'm anything less or different than the others. Killian may be a dickhead, but Ari loves him, and he treats me like a brother, so I can't complain. Since he has a true mating bond with Ari, according to shifter law, he could force me away, but he doesn't. I'm still not quite sure how Eric fits into it all, but he's a good guy, well, demon. I've never had any problems with Seb and Alex. They're in the same situation as me, so we stick together. Even if we didn't get along, I would go to the ends of the Earth for Ari.

I may not be bothered by the fact that Ari has multiple mates, but we do need time just for the two of us. Staying with her is my favourite part of my week, but living with four other guys can be a bit overwhelming.

Today is just what I needed. I was finally able to take Ari out on a date like a normal couple, no fighting with other people or asserting my dominance, purely time with her. I've loved her since I first saw her in my bar when we initially met. She was skinny and scarred, hating everyone, but I saw through all that.

Reaching the edge of the pathway that leads back into the park,

I frown as I look around for Ari, not seeing her. I walk towards where our jackets are lying on the grass.

"Ari?" I call out, confused. Turning in a circle, I look for my mate.

Perhaps she's gone to the bathroom? I wonder to myself, before shaking my head. I would've seen her if she'd done that, she would have had to walk past the café where I'd gotten the ice cream.

Reaching for my inner bear, I focus on scenting the air. Ari, like all wolves, has a distinctive smell, but hers is unique, one that I love. My bear obediently comes to the surface, and I know my eyes must be glowing with his power. Catching onto her scent, I let out a happy grumble, my bear pleased to be finding his mate as I follow it. I scowl when I reach the edge of the wooded part of the park and a bad feeling washes over me. The closer I get, the more that feeling increases. Using my free hand, I reach into my pocket to fish out my phone, dialling Killian. He picks up after one ring.

"Is Ari okay?" he asks immediately, not bothering to greet me.

"I don't know where she is, I went to get ice cream and when I came back, she was gone," I explain, guilt and dread building the more time ticks on, increasing as Killian curses.

"I felt her fear down the bond, something is going on. She's really angry right now."

"Shit," I curse, starting to pace at the edge of the tree line

"Where are you?"

"The park." I rattle off the address. "Be careful when you get here, witches are involved, there is some sort of spell at the edge of the woods to turn people away," I instruct and then hang up, knowing backup is on the way. Killian had been shouting at me to wait for them, but I can't wait, knowing that Ari is in danger.

Pushing past the feeling of dread, I stride into the forest, trying to scent Ari, but I can't, it's like her scent has been erased. Real fear starts to run through me.

"Ari!" I call out, not ashamed to admit that I'm scared, my worry and fear easy to hear in my voice. Part of me wishes that she's just going to pop out from behind one of the trees with a grin on her face, happy that she's pulled off a prank, but I know better. Ice cream forgotten, I drop them on the ground and hurry forward.

As I continue to walk, the canopy makes everything darker, but thanks to my bear's eyesight, I can easily see, and that's when I notice broken branches and footprints of other people. My usually compliant bear surges up within me, and I have to close my eyes for a moment to fight against him. I need to keep my cool right now. Except that I can't, something is really wrong.

One of the pairs of footprints on the ground starts to look dragged, the dirt and bits of grass disturbed, like someone was being moved against their will.

There. I can see her just ahead, and she's surrounded as she tries to fight those holding her.

My will snaps, and my bear finally takes control.

"Ari!" I bellow as I'm fully consumed by my bear.

Bounding forward in my bear form, I lot out a loud roar, but just as I reach the clearing where they're gathered, they disappear. My bear stops, my paws skidding in the loose dirt from my sudden change of movement as I look around, struggling to work out what just happened. Seeing a mark on the ground, I hurry over, sniffing at the strange symbols I can't understand in this form, but the strong tang of magic tells me exactly what's going on—witches.

For some reason, the witches have taken my mate, and for that, they will pay. Sitting back on my haunches, I throw back my head and let out a bellow, my despair loud and clear for all to hear.

Chapter Eighteen

A bright light shines in my eyes, making me moan and bat away the cold hands that are touching me. My head pounds and my stomach churns as I try to pull away. I feel like I was hit by a truck before going on a drinking binge. Thankfully, the cold hands pull away, and I hear the sound of heels clipping on the hard floor, then a door opening and closing before soft voices reach me.

"Will she be okay?" a deep male voice asks. He sounds concerned, but in a detached way. I recognise the voice, but I can't think of where I know it from.

"She'll be fine, sir, just be gentle with the interrogation today." A woman's voice this time.

"They shouldn't have hit her so hard," the first voice grumbles, but I can't hear the woman's reply as they move farther away.

Turning my head, I press my forehead against the cold wall I'm leaning against, the cool material helping to sooth the pounding in my temples. The hard floor beneath me is unforgiving and biting into my skin.

Where am I?

Peeling open my eyes, I gingerly look around, confirming my suspicions. I'm not back at the pack. I'm in a small, white room. A door and mirrored window are on the wall opposite me, and just in front of me is a table and two chairs. I think back to what the woman had said. *Interrogation.*

Memories flood back, and I lean forward with a groan, lifting a hand to the back of my head. I suck in a sharp breath of pain as I feel the tender lump. Fucking ASP. My inner wolf is snarling, wanting to be let out, to kill those who threatened us and our mate. Relief floods my system when I realise I can feel her again, I hadn't realised how lost I would be without her, how integral she is to me. I've always hated being a shifter, begrudging my wolf and my Shadowborn powers, but have learned to embrace her. My wolf is part of me, just like I'm part of her, and right now, we want to get out of here.

I push against the wall, using it to help me stand, and curse at how unsteady I am on my feet before looking around the room again in search of an escape route. Trailing a hand against the wall, I feel for any weaknesses, but the walls are all made of stone. Even at my strongest, I can't break through that. The door is cold to the touch, metal, and I'm sure it's heavy duty, designed to keep shifters and the stronger supernaturals at bay. The mirrored glass is undoubtedly a one-way mirror. Stalking up to the glass, I stare at my reflection, my eyes glowing with the power of my wolf.

I'm not sure how much time has passed when there's a noise on the other side of the door and something changes within the room, my connection with my wolf suddenly lost like it was in the park. Looking around, I search for any signs of what's causing this, and I curse myself for not thinking of it. Metallic noises tell me that someone's about to come through the door, and as it swings open, I snarl at the person standing in the doorway.

"Hello, Ari," Hunter greets me with a smooth smile, walking into the room like he owns it. "Sorry about our little...miscommunication earlier."

Miscommunication my ass.

Narrowing my eyes at Hunter, I back up against the wall,

making sure to keep him in my sights. I'm not going to get caught off guard by him again.

"You kidnapped me," I accuse, trying to keep my voice even. If I learned anything from him earlier in the park, it's that he needs to feel in control, and I don't want to see what he would do if he loses that control.

Frowning at my accusation, he picks an imaginary piece of lint off his suit. "Kidnapped. That's such an ugly word."

"What do you want?" I ask as he walks farther into the room, sitting at the table and looking up at me expectantly.

"I want you to work with me, that's all."

"Do you hit all of your potential work colleagues over the head and lock them in a cell? If so, you need to work on your recruitment strategies." I'm supposed to be hearing him out, keeping him calm, but I can't keep the sarcasm from slipping out. He stills, his face tight, and for a moment, I think I've blown it until he dips his head towards me in acknowledgement.

"We were a little heavy-handed, but we were about to be interrupted." His voice is smooth again as he justifies the abducting of another person to himself. My heart clenches painfully as I think about the 'interruption,' hoping Garett is safe and made it back to the pack. I'm pretty sure they were lying to me when they said they had Garett. He'd be devastated, and I know he'll be blaming himself. I want to ask if he's okay, but I don't want them to know how much I care for him, that's just exposing another weakness. They already suspect, Hunter said as much when he called him my bear, but I won't hint that he's anything other than a friend.

"Sit down, Ari."

I want to resist, tell him to go fuck himself, but a strong compulsion falls over me, trying to convince me that I actually *do* want to sit down. Horror courses through my body, but I keep my face in a mask of disgust.

"What the fuck have you done to me?" I spit, my body

betraying me as I pull the chair back and slide into it. I grip the edge of the table in front of me as I settle back in the chair.

"This is just to ensure our safety, both mine and yours. We wouldn't want you to hurt yourself, would we?" Leaning back, he smiles lazily at me as he continues, "See, I know you, Ari, you wouldn't want to hurt me, but your wolf, she wants to kill me. Am I wrong?" I open my mouth to speak, to tell him I would happily kill him, but my throat constricts, blocking all air entry. Panic sets in as I raise my hands to my throat, clawing at the invisible band that's squeezing my airway. "See, it's your instincts, that's what makes shifters so dangerous," he adds, waving a hand towards the window, and the tight band around my neck disappears. Slumping forward against the table, I take in large, noisy gasps as I try to settle my breathing. His gesture tells me all I need to know—there is someone behind that window who's behind the compulsion. Narrowing my eyes at Hunter, I sit back in the chair.

"But I'm able to control those instincts. That's the difference, we are not controlled by our animals." My voice is rough and raw, but I mean every word I say. If I've learned anything in this last year, it's that control is key.

"So many are though. Besides, that's not what I wanted to talk to you about." He pushes our conversation away so fast that I'm frowning, trying to work out what's going on here. "How do your Shadowborn powers work?" The madness has entered his eyes again as he leans towards me, his words fast and excited. "How did you get them?"

I have to fight my groan. Not this again.

We're taught that Shadowborns are executed on sight, even when there's no proof, so why am I still alive? I know he has Em, a Shadowborn already, so he might not kill me. The thought of ASP having another Shadowborn at their disposal is scary, especially as they seem to be able to force me to comply with their demands.

"I don't know what you're talking about."

"Don't lie to me!" Hunter shouts, his fists slamming down onto the table with a bang, causing the wood to fracture from the force of the blow. Pushing up from his seat, he leans towards me, his voice low with menace as he begins to lose control. "I know what you are, Ari. Tell me what I want to know."

"So you can kill me? We both know that would be a death sentence."

"You don't understand! I don't want to kill Shadowborn, I want to work with you, there is so much I want to know!" he says hurriedly, trying to reassure me, his personality flipping again.

"What do you want to know?" I finally ask, neither admitting nor denying his claim. If I can get him on side, make him think I want to help him, I might be able to use that to my advantage.

"How did you get your powers?"

"Shadowborn are born with their powers," I answer with a frown. Surely he knows this? According to legend, we are descendants of an ancient God of Shadow and Deception. Other myths say we were cursed to walk in the shadows for a sin from a past life, never able to fully enjoy the sun. I'm not sure I believe these stories, and I don't know where these powers have come from, but all I know is I've had them since I was born.

"No, there must be another way to get them." Hunter's frustration is evident as he pushes away from the table, striding up and down the small cell.

"I've never met a Shadowborn, so I don't know for sure," I answer honestly. Other than Em, who I've never actually met in person, I don't know any Shadowborn, but the clue's in the name—Shadow-*born*.

Hunter stops his pacing and turns to face me, his face set in a snarl as he darts forward, his hands clutching the top of my arms. That heavy weight settles over me again, and I can't move, like I've been bound to the chair, my heart racing as I see the madness fully descend.

"Liar!" he screams in my face, spittle spraying as he completely loses control, his grip bruising as he shakes me. "How do I become a Shadowborn?"

My eyes widen as I fully realise what he wants. I was wrong—he doesn't want Shadowborn to build his own army, he wants to *become* Shadowborn. I can't stop the laugh that builds up in me, spilling out until my eyes are watering. I know this will only make everything worse, but I can't seem to stop. His expression darkens, and before I know it, he's pulling back his fist and a hard punch hits me in the jaw. My head snaps back until whatever magic is holding me pulls it back forward. My neck screams out in pain at the whiplash effect the binding magic is having on me.

I stop laughing, my head bowed and my breathing heavy as I try to think through the pain. I can taste blood in my mouth, and I experimentally move my jaw, and while pain shoots through it, I don't think it's broken. Lifting my head, I see he's sitting back in his chair, rubbing at his fist. Looking at him like this, I feel pity for him. Sure, I still hate him, but this insane desire to be Shadowborn is useless.

"There is no way to become Shadowborn." Leaning forward as much as the binding magic will let me, I implore for him to listen so he'll stop this mad search.

His face shuts down as he pushes away from the table, his face becoming a mask as he straightens his suit as he walks towards the door, knocking twice before the door swings open. Just as he steps out of the room, he throws me one last look, and this scares me more than anything else that he's said or done so far.

"Yet." The surety in his tone is what frightens me the most. Shuddering at his parting word, my invisible bonds dissolve at the same time the door slams shut behind him. Surging up from the chair, I hurry to the door, pressing against it to test for any weaknesses, foolishly hoping that they would have forgotten to lock it. No such luck. I have no idea how long they will leave me here for, and my stomach growls, clenching painfully, letting me know it's been a while since I was taken. I realise then that although I'm able to move and feel my wolf, I still can't access her, like there's a wall between us.

Suddenly, the locks in the door make a loud clunking noise, which makes me jump back and press into the wall as several ASP agents all dressed in back surge into the small room, their faces obscured and their guns trained on me. Dropping into a defensive crouch, I snarl at the agents filling into the room.

"At ease, I've been sent to take the suspect to her cell," a familiar voice calls from behind the wall of agents who shuffle awkwardly. Frowning, I wonder what has caused the sudden tension in the room, and why is that voice so damn familiar?

"Sir, I'm not sure—"

"The director has ordered it." A steely tone enters the voice, and the agents straighten themselves. So whoever this is must be fairly well-respected if they react like this. "Besides, I can handle a little shifter." A low chuckle fills the room, and it makes my hackles rise. Thanks to their faces being covered, I can't tell who or what these agents are, but I'm betting that none of them are shifters. There may be rivalry and dislike amongst some of the shifter groups, but wolf shifters are respected for their strength and ferocity. Being referred to as a 'little shifter' would make any self-respecting shifter furious, and maybe that's why they said it.

The agents finally stand aside, and I fight to keep my face straight as Agent Ryan stalks into the room like he owns it. I always disliked him most of the two agents who've been helping us, but I don't think he would betray me. These two agents form the leadership of the faction group within ASP, and the information they have been giving us has helped us inform packs of any planned ASP raids or rumours of movement by the Shadow Pack.

The faceless agents start to file from the room until it's just Ryan and me. Straightening slowly from my crouch, I keep my distrustful glare, eyeing the distance between me and the open door behind him.

"Don't even think about it," he drawls, my eyes flashing back to his.

"Think about what?"

"There are twenty armed agents down this corridor and six doors that require fingerprints to open them before you would even reach the street. Save me the hassle of cleaning up your mess." Crossing his arms, he waits for my response, his body language showing me that he's not worried about an escape attempt, his arrogance showing through.

Tilting my head to one side, I make it look like I'm contemplating something. "I could always chop your hand off," I suggest sweetly, taking a step towards him.

Snorting at my comment, I see his body stiffen as I move, his eyes narrowing on me, and a slight shake of his head so miniscule, I nearly missed it. "It's been tried, the hand has to have a blood supply going through it. We have the best technology in the world built into our systems. I wouldn't do it, sweetheart." He may sound like he's being a dick, he usually is, but he's also telling me something. He's warning me that I'm not getting out of here by force.

"Face the wall." The sudden order makes me narrow my eyes as he goes from a sarcastic dick to ordering me about. I'm about to do as he says, unsure who to trust anymore, when I see something flash in his hand and his head shake a minuscule amount. Remembering what Hunter said makes me pause. *I'm aware of the little faction group within ASP.* If that's the case, these guys are in just as much danger as I am.

A flicker catches my attention again, and I look back at his hand. When I do, I have to force myself not to rush forward and snatch the item from him, a thousand questions on the tip of my tongue. Eric's watch. He wears it everywhere, and I've never seen him part with it. My heart speeds up as I contemplate why Agent Ryan would have it. Is it a gesture of trust? Has Eric been captured too? Is he a prisoner here?

No. Think, Ari, I berate myself as I try to focus my thoughts. If

ASP had Eric or any of my other guys, then they would be rubbing it in my face. They had the opportunity to take Garett too, but they didn't seem to want that confrontation. Taking a deep breath, I meet Ryan's gaze and decide to take the risk.

"Where are you taking me?" I demand, not moving an inch as his face turns into a scowl.

"I said, face. The. Fucking. Wall."

"Fuck you," I snarl, seeing a look of approval before Ryan rushes forward and grabs my arm, twisting it behind my back and slamming me face first into the wall. I struggle against him, my cheek biting into the rough surface of the wall as he pins me there. My supernatural strength and speed is muted, making my struggle look pathetic against him, and I realise I have no idea how to fight without my wolf and vow to train harder. Against a human, I would probably still win, since I've been training in fighting and self-defence for years, but always with the benefit of my supernatural strength.

"We don't have long, we're being watched. Your mates are safe and are working on a way to get you out." The words are so quiet, I could've missed them, but my body sags with relief. They're safe.

"How's the wall taste, bitch?" he sneers, obviously for the benefit of whoever's watching us. Disgust and amusement lace his tone as he presses me into the wall. He leans his shoulder into my back as he binds my hands together behind me. "Make it look like you hate me," he whispers to me again, before the weight of his body is removed from my back.

That's easy enough, I think wryly to myself as I'm hauled upright and stumble into him.

"Get the fuck off me," I snarl, wishing I could growl right now.

Moving behind me, he grabs my hands and pushes me forward with a shove to my back. Suddenly, I don't have the ability to talk as I have to fully focus on placing one foot in front of the other, my vision swimming as the gravity of the last few hours weigh on me. The head injury probably isn't helping either.

"You're almost there," Ryan whispers, encouraging me in the only way he can, slowing his punishing march as he realises I'm struggling.

Huh, I think to myself as I try to keep my walk steady, *maybe he's not as much of an asshole as I'd thought.*

As we walk down the corridor, we stay silent, and I get the sense that this is a test, that Ryan has been sent to me on purpose, and I wonder if they're aware that Hunter knows there are moles in the organisation. My stomach clenches at the thought, and I rack my brain to see if there is any way I can warn him. I might not like the bastard, but he's been helping us, and I wouldn't want him to get hurt because of me. However, I don't get the chance to warn him as the hallway is suddenly swarming with agents who rip me from his grip.

"What are you doing? I was ordered to take her to the cells!" Ryan shouts, his voice loud and authoritative as he glares at the masked ASP agents who are holding me in a tight grip, their hands biting into my skin.

"Change of plans." A new voice fills the corridor as a man in a suit steps past the wall of agents, walking directly up to Ryan, his eyebrow raised as if to dare Ryan to protest. This guy is scary-looking, and his body language is screaming violence. His grey hair is short on the sides and slightly longer at the top, and he has a neatly trimmed beard, which makes him look distinguished. Ryan straightens as they come toe to toe, the newcomer obviously outranking him if his blank expression and 'to attention' stance is anything to go by.

"Director Hunter instructed me himself."

"Like I said, there's been a change of plan." The new guy crosses his arms, his face expectant as he waits for Ryan's response. I can tell he doesn't want me to go with the new guy, but without giving himself away, there's nothing he can do.

"Fine. I don't give a fuck, as long as I don't have the director up my ass for not doing my job." Throwing his hands up in the air,

Ryan spins away and pushes through the agents that are blocking the corridor, his shoes clipping against the flooring as he stalks away. The new guy finally turns his attention onto me, eyeing me from head to toe, and I shudder in disgust. I'm used to people checking me out, but none of them have ever looked at me that way before. I can't name the expression, but it scares me.

With a nod to the guys restraining me, they begin to shuffle me away, taking me down a side corridor I hadn't seen as we walked down it. The smell of medical grade bleach reaches my nose as I'm dragged through an open door. Digging my heels into the floor, I begin to fight against the agents holding me with earnest. The agents curse, but no matter how much I fight, I get hauled farther into the room, towards the awaiting chair. The room looks like that of a dentist's office, with a reclining chair in the middle of the room, except in this room, the chair has strong leather straps attached to the arm and leg rests. A metal trolley full of gleaming tools are laid out on display, and my stomach churns.

Suddenly, my hands are free as they untie me to undoubtedly try to strap me into the chair. Fuck that. Dropping to the floor, I twist to try and rip my arms from the agents' grips, sweeping my leg out in an arc. My leg connects with one of the agents who falls to the ground with a thud, but other agents are on top of me before I know it, pushing me down into the chair. Arching my back, I refuse to sit, but without the strength of my wolf, I can't out power them and my arms and legs are roughly strapped into the chair. The agents file out of the room and I use this opportunity to fight against my restraints, growling as the leather bites into my skin, but not budging. Movement by the door catches my attention and as I look up, I see the grey-haired man watching me with a small smile on his face.

"Hello, Ari. We haven't had a chance to be introduced." His voice is cultured, his accent telling me he's not originally from the US, but I can't place it. Trying to calm my pounding heart, I give him a curt smile.

"I can't say I'm sad about that," I bite out, pulling at my restraints, even though I know it's pointless.

"No, not many people would." He laughs, running a hand through his hair as he stares at me hungrily. "You see, I don't get the opportunity to leave headquarters very often. I have a particular skill set that makes me very valuable to ASP. My name is Rutgar, but I'm known as the Butcher."

Well, that's not promising, I think to myself as I watch him closely, panic rising as I try to steady my breathing. I've been through hell and back when I was in Shadow Pack and came out the other side, so I can do this.

As if able to sense my internal monologue, his smile widens. Walking farther into the room, he shuts the door softly behind him. Everything about this man is quiet, even down to his footsteps on the floor. His eyes flick from me to the silver trolley to my left, and a gleam enters his eyes. I've refused to look at the trolley and the items carefully laid out there, but bile rises in my throat as my mind starts to imagine the worst. Incapable of bearing the suspense, I glance over, unable to see most of them since Rutgar is blocking my view, but as he turns around, I see a knuckle duster in his hand before I raise my eyes to meet his.

"I think you and I will get to know each other very well."

Alex

Ari's been gone for a day, and as the hours tick by without her, I feel a little piece of my humanity slip away. As pack beta, it's my job to protect the pack, and even if that's all she was to me, I would still feel like shit that she was taken, but she's my mate and there was nothing I could do to stop her from being taken.

Garett's a complete mess, blaming himself for Ari's kidnapping. I've never seen him like this, the usual calm and collected bear is livid, wanting to storm ASP headquarters. He was acting like...well, Killian.

Killian, on the other hand, has retreated in on himself, getting quieter and more distant the longer time goes on without her.

When that dickhead Ryan turned up at the pack boundary, it was Isa who brought him in, taking him straight to the alpha. He then explained that ASP had her, that they knew she was Shadowborn. We were ready to storm the headquarters, even Alpha Mortlock offered wolves to assist us, and I know we would have the backing of the bears, but Ryan stopped us. Let's just say it took a lot of convincing, but he explained that we would never get past security to get to her, it would be putting her at risk if we were to rush in. So instead, we're waiting, waiting for Ryan to put his plan into place, and then he'll call us in. Until then, it's business as usual at the pack, and I have to put on a brave face and continue my beta duties.

All I can say is that Ryan had better figure out a plan soon before we just storm in. We need our mate back, she completes us, and if we were to lose her, I feel we might not survive that.

Chapter Nineteen

Rutgar was right—we did learn more about each other, I also learned some new things about myself. I learned that he favours his right side when punches and that he gets a sick pleasure from hurting people. I learned that he hates it when I swear at him, and he always punches harder after that. I also learned that this was only the start of it. He wanted me bruised and bloodied for some reason, and only used the knuckle duster and his own fists. The knives and instruments were for show, to scare me, but I know that sooner or later, he'll begin using them. If he truly wanted to hurt me, there are ways of doing so without leaving marks on the body. This is a message, I just haven't figured out who that message is for yet.

Leaning forward in the chair as far as my restraints will let me, I breathe deeply, my face aching as my chest rattles with each breath I take. I'm sure my ribs are broken, and without my wolf, my healing will be slow like a human's. Rutgar is currently sharpening a knife in the corner of the room, but I pay him no attention, since that's exactly what he wants. He craves the feeling of being in control. Footsteps sound outside the room before a knock breaks the silence.

"I think our time together is over for now, Ari," he remarks with a wistful sigh as he walks over to the door and pulls it open to allow two agents into the room. They don't bother bringing a whole group of them, they know they won't need to, I'm too weak. I'm not sure how long I've been locked away with Rutgar, but it feels like days, each second ticking by agonisingly slowly.

From my slumped forward position, I can only just see them through a layer of hair, but they can't see my expression, which is probably a good thing since I'm sure it's pretty feral. Hands land on me, and I throw back my head, growling at the guard who dared touch me. Jumping back, the guard eyes me warily before looking over at his colleague, obviously not expecting a fight from me.

I may be cut off from my wolf, but those instincts are still there, and right now, I don't have words. The civil part of me has been driven away by pain, and my instincts are the only thing I have left to protect me. Whatever, whoever is blocking my connection with my wolf is dangerous and needs to die. They seem to have figured out a way to block my shadow power too. In desperation, I had reached for them, trying to escape from Rutgar's brutal brand of questioning, but had found them sluggish and unresponsive, like they were just out of reach.

"Didn't break this one in yet?" The guard's voice snaps me out of my daze, and I force myself to sit up in the chair, as much as my bindings will allow. He's right—he's not broken me. I've been through worse. You don't grow up in a pack like Shadow Pack without scars. I survived that, I can get through this, plus, I have my mates I need to get back to.

"Ari is special." Rutgar's voice comes from behind me, and I have to fight a flinch as his hand lands on my shoulder. I won't give the bastard the satisfaction. "Today was just a little welcome and a taste of what's to come. Isn't that right, pet?" he says with a smile as he walks around to face me. His use of the endearment makes me growl, and his smile widens, knowing full well that it bothers me. Back in England, 'pet' is used as a term of affection, but I know he's using it not only because he knows this, but because I'm a shifter and we hate being treated like animals. Truthfully, it doesn't bother me much, words can't hurt me, but I would prefer he thinks this bothers me rather than move on to something else.

Hands land on my arms, and my growling doesn't have the same effect, they simply tighten their grip as they release my bonds, hauling me up between them as my legs give way. At one point, my pride would have been damaged at being dragged out of the room, but I'm just so happy to be taken from that place that I don't give a damn about bruised pride.

With their arms under my shoulders, I'm hauled unceremoniously down the corridor, my legs dragging behind me. My shoulders are screaming in pain from being pulled like this, but the pain in my face and abdomen overrides the other feelings in my body. Stopping briefly at a locked door, the guards fumble with a security pad, but I keep my head bowed, since there's too much pain running through me to look up. As we wait, a drop of blood falls from my face, splashing onto the perfect white tile beneath me, and I watch it with a numb detachment. A mumbling catches my attention, and I realise the guards are talking to one another.

"He did a number on her face. Fucking Butcher, fucking up the only pretty face we've had around here for months," the guard on my right grumbles quietly, and I get the impression he doesn't want to be overheard. Movement on my left tells me that his colleague is trying to get a better look at me.

"He doesn't usually leave them looking like this."

"No, he has other, more subtle ways of causing them pain. I watched once, it's fucked up what he can do." Disgust lines his voice and a flash of hope fills me. If he disagrees with what's happening here, then could he be a potential ally?

"Then why do this to her? What did she do?"

"He's a fucking psychopath, who knows what goes through his head."

The door buzzes and the guards fall silent again as they pull me through the open door. This part of the building is different than where we were before, it looks the same, but it has a different feel to it, like all the hope has been sucked out of the room. Through the curtain of hair that has fallen over my face, I can just make out rows of cages, their cold metal bars lined up next to each other and sad, huddled figures pressed against the wall at their backs.

"They want her in that one," the first guard suddenly says as they move through the room, my shoulders screaming.

"But they never put anyone in that cell, it's reserved, right?"

"Yeah, for *her*." There's a pause as the other guard realises what this means, and I can almost feel him reassessing me.

"Shit, she's one of them?"

"I guess that's what the Butcher's trying to find out."

The soft beeping of a keypad, followed by a metallic clicking, tells me they've opened one of the cells, and I'm unceremoniously thrown forward, and the loud banging of the door behind me has me flinching away from the noise. As soon as the door locks behind me, my skin starts to ripple. I fall back as pain races across my body as my wolf is suddenly released from whatever magical binding was holding her. The sounds of footsteps fade as the guards leave the room, the outer door locking behind them, and I finally let go of the pent-up breath I've been holding on to. My ribs scream in agony as the fractures move with my deep inhales, and I can't help the grunt of pain that escapes me as my wolf tries to force me to change forms so I can heal quicker. My pained noises must have disturbed my neighbour in the cell next to me, as movement out the corner of my eye catches my attention, although I quickly focus back on trying to calm my wolf. I can't risk shifting. If I can access my wolf, then I'm betting my bonds with the guys are back, and if all they feel is fear and pain, then they will come storming down to the headquarters to get me, and there is no way the five of them alone would get me out. I need to get control, to focus, but it's difficult when I'm in so much pain.

"No," a croaking male voice calls out, the tone rough and unused, but I pay it no attention until a flashing light has my head whipping around to look at the huddled figure by the side of my cell. "Ari?" His voice is pained, like I'd just told him terrible news, and he's holding his hand like he's been burnt, the bars still smoking where he'd obviously tried to touch. Dread pools in my stomach. Does ASP have someone I know? Shuffling closer, I try to see through my swollen eyelids, my vision blurry as I focus on the figure in the cell next to mine. Shock and realisation rock me to my core as I stare at the haggard figure.

"Em?" I'd only ever seen him in the Shadow Realm and I've never been able to see his full features due to the glow that would cling to him, but seeing him here, he looks like he's aged twenty years. His body is frail and battered, and cuts and bruises mar the skin that's on show.

"They got you." His voice cracks, and for a moment, I think he's going to cry, the weight of the world seeming to settle on his shoulders. "I worked so hard to make sure you were never found."

"What's going on? I thought you were being protected. You said you worked for ASP." The questions keep coming, my mind frantically trying to keep up with the revelations from the last day.

"Things changed." His voice is weary as he rubs his hands across his haggard face. "ASP worked out that there was a faction group and have started randomly interrogating their agents. One of the weaker agents let it slip that I was Shadowborn, and I ended up in here," he explains, and I feel fury start to build in me that Em and the others were put at risk because someone couldn't keep their mouth shut. "I don't blame him, his family was being threatened, and now it's taken some of the pressure off the other agents who are still undercover."

Sitting back on the cool floor of the cell, I reassess Em and what I know about him. I'm still not a hundred percent certain that I trust him, but I can't deny that a part of me cares for him and doesn't want to see him hurt, like a crazy uncle you don't see often and you're never quite sure what he'll do next. Whether I like it or not, he's tangled in my past. He tried to save me as a pup, and in return, he was captured by ASP, and I had no idea he even existed.

"What happened to the agent who told them about you?" My face screams in pain as I speak, my wounds pulling. I suspect I already know what happened to the agent, but I need to know. ASP isn't known for its forgiving nature.

"He was branded a traitor and publicly killed."

Closing my eyes, I take a deep breath as I try to calm myself. I didn't know this agent, he betrayed Em and the other agents in the faction group, but I'm just so tired of all this death. A wave of love hits me in the chest like a physical blow, the sense of Killian and Eric so strong, it's like they're in the room with me, and I have to lean forward as my wolf tries to take control. She wants to be with her mates, to shift forms so she's not hurting anymore, but I fight her, I need to be human right now. Closing my eyes, I focus and return the feeling, opening my heart to them and showing them how I truly feel. It hurts and it's raw, but I let them see my feeling for them, broken pieces and all. I also try to send a thought to them, telling them not to come after me. I know Killian will object, he'll want to fight to get me back, but I hope Eric can stop him. He's more sensible and can reason with Kill. If they come now, it will only lead to their capture and deaths, and I can't live with that.

"I'm sorry." Em's voice pulls me out of my musings, my heart still raw, but I'm feeling a bit lighter now that I've been able to let my mates know I'm alive.

"What are you apologising for?" I ask, curious. There are many things he could be apologising for, not that they are his fault, but I want to know what's causing that pained look he's giving me.

"They did it on purpose to hurt me." Shaking my head at his words, I wince at a bolt of pain the moment caused.

"What are you talking about?" The words are forced out through gritted teeth, pain and exhaustion driving my wolf close to the surface, and I'm sure my eyes are glowing with my power.

"Your face. They have creative ways of causing agony without leaving a mark, he hurt you like that to get to me."

"I'll heal, I've had worse." In fact, I can feel myself healing already. I may sound full of bravado, and it's true, I've had worse, but I'm terrified of what Rutgar has in store for me. My only blessing is that my connection with my wolf and the guys is cut off in that room, otherwise they would be living it through me and there is no way they would be able to hold off attacking ASP then. Uncertainty washes through me, would the guys really just sit back and let this happen? If the situation was reversed, I know I would stop at nothing to get my guys back. I need to get out of here and quickly, before they do something stupid. "What's our plan?"

"You think you can escape?" His dull laugh echoes around the room, mocking me. "Our shadow powers don't work in here, there's something blocking it. There's no way out, we're stuck here."

The hopelessness in his voice and dull look in his eyes tells me he's given up. The thought of never seeing my mates again, my new pack, Tori, sends a ripple of pain, both emotionally and physically, through me as my wolf takes control of my body. I'm not strong enough to stop her this time, and my cry of pain turns into a mournful howl as my broken bones shift and stretch.

The shift was painful, it always is when my human form is so damaged, but it's a relief to be in my wolf form. Strange whining noises catch my attention from my curled-up position, and as I lift my head, I blink as I look around the cells we are contained in, my muzzle sniffing the air as I try to see who's in such pain.

"Ari." My ears flick towards the familiar voice, which is full of pain and sadness. Turning my head, I see the man that human-Ari thinks of as family. He looks exhausted, and his face is contorted as if he's in great pain. "Come here, little one," he calls out, his hand outstretched towards me. That's when I realise it's me making the noises. I'm in pain and this place is strange, full of worrying smells and odd sounds. The bars around my cage seem to buzz with an unseen barrier that I know will sting me like the time I tried to eat a bee as a cub. I'm a fierce, strong wolf, as strong as any male alpha, but right now, I'm scared, my ears flat to my head and my hackles raised. The only familiar thing in this room is the man on the other side of the bars. Standing up on shaky paws, I make my way slowly to the man, snarling at him as he reaches for me. He hastily pulls back his hand, bowing his head to me in reverence. Seeing he's paying the proper respect, I drop down next to the bars that separate us, curl up and wrap my tail around me, resting my head on my front paws. After a few minutes, I feel a tentative hand land on my back, stroking my soft fur, and when I don't snap or bite him, he continues, the touch comforting in a place full of fear.

At some point, I must have fallen asleep while I was in wolf form. Memories of Em's large, warm hand on my back, comforting my wolf, are fresh in my mind. Back in human form, I look around, finding a ratty sheet covering my bare form. Remembering my quick shift yesterday, I realise I must've ripped my clothes, so when I changed back during the night, I would have been naked. I frown and clutch the sheet to my chest, not sure how I feel about Em seeing me naked, but it's a hundred times better that he was able to throw the cover over me.

Glancing over at his cage, I see he's not there, and I wonder when they took him away and how I managed to sleep through it. I know that healing so quickly can cause some shifters to fall into a deep, coma-like sleep while they heal, but I find it hard to believe I didn't hear *anything*. Lifting a hand gingerly to my face, I press against the skin, surprised to find that I only feel a little discomfort. I lift the sheet and look down at my abdomen, which was covered in black bruises and cuts yesterday, but is now only marred with greenish, fading bruises. Working with humans for so long makes me underestimate the strength of our inner animals and the healing of shifters. I'm sure I still look like shit, but at least I can move around without worrying about puncturing a lung.

A black object catches my eye, lying just outside the front of my cell. Frowning, I crawl over slowly, still clutching the sheet to my chest. I'm not usually modest, but I don't want these bastards seeing me that way. As I reach the pile, I realise it's clothing. Why would they do something like this for me? I lift the loose male shirt and something falls to the ground as I unfold the clothing. Reaching down, I see that it's a feather, like that from an eagle, and suddenly it makes sense—Aiden.

Glancing between the clothing and the sheet I'm clutching to myself, I look around the room, catching a glimpse of movement in the corner—a camera, zooming in on me. Sick bastards. Am I going to let them watch me cower behind a dirty sheet as I get dressed? Fuck no. Giving them the middle finger, I carefully stand, wincing with the echo of pain from my injuries, and drop the sheet, baring myself as I start to get dressed. The clothes are too large for me, and all men's clothing, but I don't care, I'm just grateful to be wearing something again. The clothes smell like bird, and I realise they must be Aiden's. My wolf isn't happy about wearing another male's clothes, but beggars can't be choosers.

My muscles feel sore and stiff, so I gently start to stretch out in the space the cramped cell allows me. My newly healed muscles protest at the movement, but I need to keep myself warm. I have no intention of staying here, and I won't have much hope of escaping if I'm out of shape.

The sound of footsteps makes me pause as I wait to see if they come this way, and the beeping on the keypad confirms my suspicions as four guards march into the room. Normally, I'd feel offended at that they think four guards could contain me, but after how they controlled my wolf yesterday, I'm not so sure.

The guards' faces are all covered as before, but as one of them steps forward, I see a mark on the top of his uniform that the others don't have. I guess this one is in charge then. Leaning back against the wall behind me, I cross my arms and smile at them with a bravado I don't feel.

"Morning, boys, what delights have I got in store for me today?"

"Shut the fuck up and come with us," the one in charge growls out as he steps into my cell, the others following closely behind. The space so crowded, I can hardly move without brushing into one of them. Hands grab me and I'm quickly bustled out of the cell, and as soon as I step over the threshold, my connection with my wolf is cut off. Interesting. Two guards take hold of my arms, the other standing behind me as the leader takes his place in front of us as we begin to head out of the room.

"My, such foul language, your mother would be so ashamed." I tut, shaking my head in mock disgust, my lips twitching in amusement at his growl. Spinning around, he raises his arm and smacks me across the face, the blow sending me barrelling into the guard on my left.

"I said shut. Up," he snarls in my face. The guard holding me up on my left shoves me off him, and I taste blood in my mouth, my head ringing from the sudden blow. Looking at the faceless dickhead, I spit at him, wishing he wasn't wearing a mask so I could see his expression.

"You little bitch—" His arm is raised and I brace myself for another blow, but someone comes to my rescue.

"Ace, what's the hold up? They're waiting for her, you wanna keep the Butcher waiting?" I would groan at hearing Ryan's snide voice, but the thought of seeing Rutgar again makes my blood freeze and I have to fight to keep myself standing up.

The guard in charge, Ace, drops his arm and turns his attention to Ryan, nodding his head in respect. Interesting, so Ryan and Aiden are higher up in ASP than we had thought.

After that little show, we are quickly led back towards the room I'd been in yesterday, and no matter how much I fight it, I can't stop the tremble in my limbs as I see the open door to Rutgar's room.

"There's no point in resisting anymore, Em, you might as well give me what I want. Just tell me what I need to know, and I'll call Rutgar off." I recognise Hunter's voice as we near the doorway, and as we step across the threshold, I'm surprised to see the room so full.

Em is strapped into the chair, his arms bleeding from multiple cuts as Rutgar leans over him, dragging a knife through the wounds, prolonging the pain. It hurts so much more to cut an already open wound than to cause a new one, and the Butcher knows this if the sick, serene smile on his face is anything to go by. Standing in the corner of the room is someone I haven't seen before, but the intense way he's looking at me makes me feel like I should know him. I try to figure out what he is. There's something strange about him, and I realise it's a void, a nothingness around him.

"Oh good, Ari, you're here." Hunter's voice breaks me out of my staring match with the stranger in the corner.

"No, leave her out of this!" Em shouts, his voice ragged and broken, like he's been screaming. My heart breaks, and I try to pull my arms from the guards, to help, to do *something*, but no matter how much I pull, without my wolf, I'm not strong enough against two shifters holding me in place. I can deal with a lot, hell, beatings were a pastime in my old pack, but I'm not sure I can cope with watching them inflicting torture on Em.

"Then give me what I want." Hunter's voice is light, like he's only asking a reasonable question.

"You're a fucking lunatic! I can't give you what isn't possible."

"Is that so?" Hunter's voice darkens, and as he turns to me, my blood freezes again, my stomach dropping as I realise what's about to happen. "Ari, I'm afraid our friend here isn't cooperating, and you're going to have to bear his punishment."

"No! You fucking bastards!" Em screams, thrashing against his restraints, but whatever nullifying force they're using on us combined with hours of torture makes him weak as they drag him from the chair.

"Just tell me how I become Shadowborn. That's all I'm asking."

Hands start to push me towards the chair, and bile starts to rise up in my throat. Digging my feet into the floor, I try to hold my ground, pulling and thrashing to stop my descent towards the chair. Dehydration, lack of food, and a day full of torture has made me weak, and even with my wolf, I would struggle with these odds. If only I could access my shadow powers...

Em weakly struggles against the man who's pulling him away, his frail body looking tiny and weak next to the guard. All of a sudden, he drops from the arms of the guard and stumbles into the trolley full of gleaming knives. Shouts rise in the room as guards rush towards him, but they aren't fast enough as Em uses a hidden strength and hurls a large blade at stranger in the corner. Eyes wide, the stranger stares down at the blade sticking from his chest before falling to the ground, and as soon as he does, my wolf returns, the block over me released.

"Ari, run!" Em's pained voice kicks me into gear, my shadow powers already turning my body to mist. Guards try to grab me, but their hands sink through my body as I turn to see if Em is following me.

"No!" I cry, as I see Em's body crumpled on the floor, the Butcher crouched over his form as he stabs a gleaming knife into his chest. Em doesn't seem surprised, in fact, his expression is peaceful as he watches my shadowed form.

"Go," he mouths, and fighting back tears, I allow my body to fully turn to shadow as I run through the building. The walls and barriers are no longer a problem for me, the magical barrier dropping the moment the stranger died.

With my heart breaking and covered in blood and grime, I leave behind the closest thing I had to a father figure and run back to my pack, my family, and the guys waiting for me there.

Chapter Twenty

They meet me at the pack border.

I'm trembling. I've never used my powers for so long before, and my body pulses with the shadows that writhe across my skin. I don't know how they knew I was coming, I guess Killian or Eric sensed me through the bond, but I was too busy escaping at the time to send them any feelings through our connection.

As soon as I see them standing there, I freeze just on the other side of the pack lands from them, and the tears start rolling down my cheeks. Are they still going to want me when they know what I did? When they know that I'm part of the reason for the shifter deaths?

"Ari?" Seb calls out, taking a hesitant step towards me.

I'm sure I look a right mess. My hair seems to have a life of its own, my skin is coated in mud, and my arms are covered in criss-cross cuts from where I've run through the forest. Not to mention the fading bruises that cover my face or the rolling shadows that caress my skin, embracing me in their hold. I may be in my human form, but my wolf is controlling my actions, protecting me from the emotions trying to overwhelm me.

A low growl from Alex has me flinching, the fear of their rejection in the forefront of my mind. My eyes flick across them, judging their expressions and weary looks.

"Look at her! Look what they've done!" Alex shouts, making me wince again, his voice hurting my sensitive hearing. Killian spins and throws Alex a deadly look, his tone low with a barely concealed growl.

"Stop it. You're scaring her."

Eric shakes his head and takes a step towards me, but stops as soon as he sees my hasty retreat. "No, it's not that." Frowning, he rubs at his temples, and I can feel him reaching out through our bond. "She's feeling...guilty?"

The guys share looks of confusion and worry.

"Ari," Garett calls out, my head snapping towards him as I see him take a slow step forward. The guys freeze, expecting me to retreat, but I simply eye him warily. He takes another step towards me, and the tears start to flow faster down my face. I don't sob, I don't make a sound, I simply watch him. "I love you. *We* love you, and no matter what, whatever they made you say or do, we still love you and we'll deal with it." His low, steady voice calms my wolf as we register what he's saying. "Whatever happened, it won't change the way we feel about you."

The guys mumble their agreement, and I flick my eyes across them, taking in their sombre and sincere expressions. Self-loathing and regret are making me feel sick, but as I watch Garett's expression, that feeling starts to recede. Taking another step towards me, he pauses, but after seeing I'm not retreating, he takes another step until he's toe to toe with me. He raises his hand and places it gently on my face, his expression darkening when I wince, and he opens his mouth to say something when a shout has us spinning around, looking for a threat.

"Fuck! Fucking woods, can't you guys live somewhere more original?" I can't stop the small smile that crosses my face as I hear Tori's ranting. "Where did you all fuck off to anyway? I thought we were meeting to come up with a rescue plan! If I scuff a hoof, then

I'm going to kick someone's ass." Tori keeps up her rant as she picks her way towards us, her eyes trained on the ground in front of her, concentration pulling her face into a frown. A small chuckle leaves me, and her head whips up, her eyes wide as surprise stuns her into silence. A noise like a sob is ripped from her chest as she runs towards me, her figure blurring as she barrels into me.

"Careful she—" Seb calls out, but I'm already in Tori's arms, her face buried into my neck as she sobs loudly, her shoulders shaking with her emotions. My heart races at the impact, my instincts telling me to push her away and run, but I close my eyes and take a deep breath, my body stiff and arms out to the side as I breathe in her familiar scent.

This is Tori, she would never hurt me, I think to myself, repeating the mantra until my heart settles and my limbs unfreeze, and I'm able to wrap them gingerly around my sobbing best friend.

"I thought you couldn't cry now that you're a demon." My voice is raw and cracked, like I've been screaming, but I know they all heard me from the quiet sighs of relief and low chuckles. Tori's shoulders immediately stop moving, and she pulls away. Her face is completely dry, but her expression is devastated, especially when she sees my face. Raising a hand to my cheek, she gently examines my face.

"Oh, Ari, what did they do to you?" The pain in her voice makes my throat tight, and I have to pull away from her embrace. She's never looked at me that way before, even when we first met and I was a starving wreck. The guys slowly walk over, their eyes watching me warily as if I'm going to run away, but my gaze flicks back to Garett, and the love in his expression calms something within me. Eric appears just behind him, smiling softly, and I realise he's using his doctor voice on me, which makes the side of my mouth quirk up in a smile.

"Let's go inside, I want to check you over."

Nodding my agreement, I start walking towards the pack boundary, and as soon as I cross it, my shadows drop and the guys fall into step with me. We walk in silence, but it's not the tense silence from before when they were worried I was going to run, but a comfortable, companionable silence.

We reach the medical building, and I try to head straight upstairs to the rooms I've been staying in, but Eric reaches out and snatches my hand, shaking his head as he leads me into one of the examination rooms.

"Eric, I just want to go to bed." I hate the whining sound my voice makes, but I'm tired and emotionally drained.

"You've been gone for three days, and we could do nothing to get you back. I want to check that my mate is all right. Just humour me, okay?" I recognise the strict tone of voice he uses with our more difficult patients, and I'm about to comment on it, but I see the tension around his eyes and the stiff way the guys are standing around the room.

"Okay." My voice is rough as I pull off the ruined shirt, fully expecting the growls and hisses that fill the room when they see the full extent of bruises and wounds covering my stomach. There was no point in hiding it, they were going to see it sooner or later. "The light makes it look worse," I defend as I stand up straight, the fluorescent bulbs making my bruises stand out all the more, but I refuse to cower or try to hide them, letting the guys see me as I am. Sliding off my borrowed, ripped trousers, I walk over to the examination table and climb up onto it.

"You smell like another man." Killian's stiff voice fills the room, and I can see his eyes glowing slightly as he glares at my discarded clothing.

"My clothes ripped when I shifted. One of the agents found me some clothing."

The room is silent as Eric descends into doctor mode, flashing his pen torch into my eyes and checking the bones in my face.

"Most of the damage seems to be centred around your face and abdomen." His fingers walk up my jaw, gently pressing on the bones. He gives me a sympathetic look as I wince. "Since shifters heal so quickly, I need to check that your bones are healing in the right place, otherwise you could have issues later on," he explains, and I nod in response, but I know his explanation is for the guys' benefit. Finished examining my face, he moves onto my abdomen, frowning at the blotchy patterns of bruises. I know I'm not seriously injured, my wolf has healed the worst of it, but I understand Eric needs to check.

"Em's dead," I say into the silence. Eric's hands fall away from me, his expression sympathetic. My eyes sting as tears threaten to fall again, finally spilling over as Seb pushes his way past the others and climbs up onto the table next to me, wrapping his arm around me and pulling me into his embrace. "He sacrificed himself for me." The words are quiet and broken.

Suddenly, I'm surrounded, the guys wrapping me in a cocoon of safety. I wear them like armour, every inch of my exposed skin covered, and I use their strength to keep going when all I want to do is fall apart.

I don't know how long we stay like that for, but eventually, I'm wrapped up in Garett's arms as he gently carries me upstairs. The rest of the guys follow behind silently, knowing I need to be surrounded by them tonight. Tomorrow, I'll be strong again, but tonight, I need to be weak, I need them. Tori presses a kiss to my forehead and promises to return in the morning before she heads away.

I can hear Alex and Eric downstairs, talking to Alpha Mortlock, explaining what they know and promising to explain more tomorrow. I close my eyes and snuggle closer into Garett's chest at the thought of having to relive everything, but I know I can't put it off forever, they need to know what's happening.

We enter my bedroom and Garett goes to put me down on the bed, but I cling to his chest, not ready to let go, finding his warmth comforting. Without saying a word, Garett simply climbs onto the mattress, kicking his shoes off before knee walking into the centre of my large, king-sized bed. Settling down, I raise my head from his chest to look for my other guys. Seb is already shucking out of his clothing, climbing onto the bed in only his boxers, and laying on his side so he's pressed up against Garett with his head resting on my hip. I slip my fingers into his hair, playing with the blond strands and smiling at the purring noise he makes deep in his throat. Looking up, I see Eric and Alex in the doorway. There's a predatory look on my beta's face as he stalks in, pulling his shirt off before climbing into bed.

Eric's soft voice catches my attention, and I see he's talking to Killian, who's standing in the corner of the room, staring at me with a heated expression, but his brow furrows with a severe frown.

"Kill?" My voice sounds weak and unsure, and I hate it as soon as I say his name. My other guys move in closer, their instincts to comfort their mate riding them hard.

"I thought I'd lost you, *again*." His words end in a snarl as he stalks towards the bed.

"I'm sorry—"

"Don't apologise," he spits out, his expression murderous. At first, I think that he's angry with me, but all I feel down the bond is self-loathing. "They took you, they hurt you, and I could do *nothing*." His eyes glow and the strength of his wolf fills the room, his alpha power stroking against mine, calling my wolf to the surface. Seb bows his head under the strength of the power, and even Alex has lowered his eyes. "Do you know how hard it was to just trust you? I felt it down the bond, you wanted me to wait, but I was ready to tear the place apart. They. Took. My. Mate."

I realise then how difficult this must have been for all of them. Garett because I was taken when I was with him, but especially Killian. Both him and Eric have the bond with me, but Killian is an alpha, which means he is often ruled by his instincts, not used to bowing to the wishes of others. "But then I felt it, your strength, and I knew I had to wait. It nearly drove me mad, but I trusted you." Climbing up onto the bed, he crawls towards me on all fours, straddling Garett in the process of getting as close to me as possible.

"My strong, powerful mate. They haven't broken you. You are not weak. Feeling sad because you lost someone is not a weakness, you taught me that."

The atmosphere in the room changes as the shifters in the room scent my arousal. Knowing that my guys trusted me to take care of myself but were still ready to rescue me if I needed help, and that my alpha mate deferred his decision to me, is a major turn-on.

Garett rumbles in agreement, gently turning me in his arms so I'm facing him and my legs straddle his hips. Killian shuffles up behind me, pressing his chest against my back as the others move in closer.

"I agree with Killian," Garett starts, placing a hand on my hip and rubbing small circles on my skin with his thumb. "When you were taken, I felt like my heart had been ripped from my chest. They took you from me, I should've been able to stop them." I can hear the self-loathing in his voice, so I lean forward and press a kiss to his lips to silence him. I won't have any of them blaming themselves. Pulling back, I can see the relief in his eyes and realise he was carrying the blame for me being taken on his shoulders.

"Stop. This wasn't your fault. I was stupid. He said they had you, so I went with him to hear what he had to say. When I realised they didn't have you, they did something to knock me out, and they have a way to nullify our powers." They all make noises of anger or shock at my words as questions form on their lips, but I shake my head. "I can't talk about that tonight. I just need to be with you guys." I know they can hear the tension in my voice, and I see the moment they decide to let it drop. A sigh of relief leaves my lips as Alex presses against my side, trailing kisses along my arm and up to the top of my shoulder.

"Let us help you forget," he whispers, pushing me down into Garett's lap so my centre is pressing against his growing erection, both of us moaning at the contact. Garett leans forward, pressing soft kisses against my lips, but I quickly deepen them, taking the lead, which he happily to gives me. Killian, never one to be left out, growls into my ear as he presses himself against my back, one arm coming around my stomach and the other over the top of my shoulder so it lies across my chest, his hand resting at the base of my throat. My pulse flutters under his fingers, and I can't stop my moan as he takes control of my body. I continue kissing Garett as Killian lowers his head and starts gently biting and kissing along the left side of my neck. Alex comes up to my right side, mirroring Killian's actions as he kisses and bites my neck.

Pulling away for a deep breath, I glance around and see Seb leaning back against the headboard next to Garett, with one arm behind his head as he stretches out, and his other hand down the front of his boxers as he strokes his cock. Rolling my head to the other side, I see Eric sitting on the edge of the bed, desire in his eyes, and his hands tightly gripping the sheets as he watches us. I close my eyes and reach for our bond, the tingle of electricity flooding my body as we connect, and I push my feelings, my love for him, my desires, my needs towards him. Opening my eyes, I meet his heated gaze as he crawls over to me across the bed, before grabbing my chin, pulling me across, and pressing bruising kisses to my lips. As I pull away, I swear my lips tingle with electricity, and he winks at me as he leans back on the bed, happy to watch the show as Killian's and Alex's hands start to explore my body, and little gasps leave my lips as they tweak my nipples.

I lean forward to kiss Garett again, and I feel Alex slide his hand across my hip and into the top of my underwear, his fingers circling my clit. My body is overstimulated, and it's almost too much, especially knowing Eric and Seb are watching me, but I know they won't let it get too far. They will take me to the brink, but would never push me beyond my limits.

"I need you." My words are mumbled against Garett's lips, but I know the others hear me as Killian and Alex sit back, the latter holding out a hand to help me climb off the bed. My skin feels hot as I slip off my underwear, feeling five sets of eyes watching my every move, tracking my movements in ways only predators can. Crawling back onto the bed, I move up to Garett, pressing kisses against his lips before dipping down, and kissing a trail down his neck, chest, and down to his hips, licking along his delicious V lines that form his Adonis belt. I unbuckle his jeans and push them down to expose his cock. The bed shifts as someone moves behind me, and I assume it's Killian or Alex about to fuck me from behind, but I let out a surprised laugh when Seb starts to wiggle between my legs, pulling me down so I'm practically sitting on his face.

"Seb, I'm going to suffocate you!" I protest, but bite down on my lip as he starts kissing along my inner thigh to my clit, his tongue flicking out.

"I get the feeling that doesn't faze him," Alex replies, his face stretched into a grin as he palms his cock. Seb mumbles his agreement, the vibrations from his voice making me squirm. Leaning forward, I take hold of Garett's cock and stroke the length a few times, enjoying the velvety feeling of his skin over his rapidly hardening cock. Kissing from base to tip, I lick the head, and the salty taste of pre-cum touches my tongue before I take him into my mouth. Hollowing out my cheeks, I swallow him as deeply into my mouth as I can, gripping the base of his cock as I suck.

Seb continues to kiss and lick my clit, his hand gliding up as he slides a finger inside me, curling it to hit that sweet spot and timing his movements with my bobbing head. Moaning around Garett's cock, I watch when he grips the bed sheets tightly as the vibrations from my moan intensify the sensation. I feel Garett's cock stiffen, and he comes in my mouth, his length pulsing as I swallow his cum. Pulling away, I lick my lips just as Seb slides another finger inside me, pushing me over the edge. I throw my head back and cry out as my orgasm ripples through me, enjoying the feeling of everyone's eyes on me. Usually, I'm not into voyeurism, but having my guys here, watching me take my pleasure from them, is a huge turn-on, especially as they seem to find it just as arousing as I do.

Climbing off Seb, I fall back onto the bed with a sleepy-looking

Garett running a hand through my hair. Alex grabs my ankles and pulls me towards him, causing a startled laugh to escape my lips. He settles between my legs, pumping his cock a few times before he presses it into my centre, a breathy moan leaving my lips as he starts to move slowly inside me. I'm used to Alex taking what he wants, his commanding attitude leading me towards orgasm, but not today. Today, his hips gently roll as his eyes lock with mine.

"Ari, I think Seb deserves a thank you for what he just did for you." Killian's voice breaks my eye contact with Alex, and as I look over at him, I raise my eyebrow, seeing that alpha Killian is still with us. I see what he's doing. Rolling my head to the side, I see Seb is lying next to me with a beatific smile on his face.

"Thank you." My voice is breathy as pleasure rolls through me with each of Alex's thrusts. Seb brings his face up to mine, and we share a gentle kiss.

"Show him how grateful you are," Killian instructs. He isn't pushing his alpha power into his words, so we could easily say no, but there is something quite freeing about being told what to do—not that I'll ever tell him that. My hand snakes out, and I grip Seb's long cock, grasping the base firmly as I stroke in time with Alex's movements.

"Eyes on me," Alex calls out, and I swing my head back to look at him, his gaze heating as he watches me writhe beneath him while I'm stroking Seb's firm length. There's a shift in the atmosphere and the smell of fresh rain on concrete fills the air, dragging my eyes over to Eric, whose eyes are glowing with his power. One hand is wrapped around his cock, pumping slowly, and when he sees me watching, he gives me a smirk and reaches out, placing a hand on my shoulder. Immediately, my skin feels like it has electricity running through it. It should be too much, too intense, but Eric seems to know how much to use. Closing my eyes, I realise that he's using the bond to feel what I'm feeling.

Eric's hand glides across my collarbone and moves down to my breast, cupping the mound of flesh before circling my nipple with his fingertip. I watch with hooded eyes as he sends little sparks of electricity into my nipple. Arching my back, I gasp in pleasure. It should be painful, but it's not, bordering just on this side of pleasure. Hearing a gasp to my left, I glance over and see Seb close his eyes, his face slack with pleasure as his cock stiffens in my hand, finding his release as I give him a few firm strokes. Alex starts to pick up his pace, and before long, I feel the pleasure build up into a blinding orgasm, my pussy clenching down hard on his cock as he finds his own release. Eric groans, and I realise he also came alongside me, feeling my own release through our bond.

Out of breath and thoroughly exhausted, I look over at Killian, who is watching me with intense eyes. I waggle my eyebrows at him in question, but he just shakes his head, the side of his lips curling up in a semblance of a smile. Climbing up off the bed with a groan, I head towards the bathroom to clean up, but he catches me with an arm around my waist.

"You missed out. Don't you want to..." I wiggle my eyebrows again, and this time, he chuckles out loud as he pulls me closer to him, resting his forehead against mine.

"Having you back is enough." His voice is low so as not disturb the others, but the atmosphere in the room changes when they hear him. Pressing a gentle kiss to my lips, which is very unlike my usually demanding alpha, he lets go of me and heads over to the bed.

After cleaning up, I walk back into my bedroom to find the guys piled up on the bed with an Ari sized space in the middle. My chest warms, and I have to fight the tears that prick my eyes.

I'm so lucky, I think to myself as I climb up onto the bed and fit into the gap they saved for me. Sleepy smiles are thrown my way as they all reach for me, their arms and leg piling on my body as I fall asleep with a smile on my face, remembering the first time I woke up in a puppy pile.

The sound of running water pulls me from sleep. I peel my eyes open and see a light shining from underneath the bathroom door. Pushing myself up into a sitting position, I glance around the bed to see who's missing. I feel a sleepy smile spread across my face as I try to work out who is who from the tangle of limbs on the bed, especially when I see Seb completely buried with just a tuft of his blond hair visible, sticking out of the side of the bed.

Untangling myself from the puppy pile, I climb off the bed and grab a blanket from the corner of the room as the chill of the night causes goosebumps on my skin. Knocking softly against the door, I push it open without waiting for an answer, seeing Killian in his full, naked glory in the large shower. He's leaning his arms against the wall and resting his head on his hands as the water cascades down his body, his long hair plastered against his skin. He turned his head towards me as soon as I walked into the room, but otherwise, he hasn't moved, his grey eyes boring into mine. He doesn't say anything, and he doesn't need to. Dropping the blanket, I step into the shower, throwing my head back as the hot spray soothes my sore muscles. It hadn't bothered me earlier, and I'd freshened up before we went to bed, but I can still feel the dirt on me from my time in the cells at ASP. Suddenly, it's really important for me to wash them from my skin.

I reach forward to grab the soap, but Killian stops me with a hand on my shoulder. He pushes away from the wall, then guides me so I'm standing directly under the shower spray. The hot water works on the knots in my shoulders I hadn't realised were there, and as I feel Killian's soap-slicked hands gliding over my body, I let out a relieved sigh. His hands are firm as he works the sweet-smelling soap into my skin, his talented fingers kneading my aching muscles. Guiding my head back, he wets my hair before pouring a generous heap of shampoo into his hands and working it into my scalp. My groan of pleasure echoes around us, the glass walls of the shower amplifying the sound as I melt under his touch. Gently, so gently, he rinses my hair, and I finally feel clean.

I turn in his arms and look up at him, and realise he needed this just as much as I did. He presses his forehead to mine again, his eyes closed tight.

"It nearly drove me crazy." His voice is pained, and while he doesn't explain *what* he's talking about, he doesn't need to, I can feel his pain through the bond.

"I know."

"If you hadn't managed to get away..." He trails off, his eyes opening as he examines me, his gaze catching on the healing bruises on my skin. "They hurt you."

"Yes, but I escaped," I reassure him, sliding my hands up his chest, then wrapping them around his neck as he places his hands on my hips. "I didn't tell them anything," I tell him, but his eyes narrow on me, and I get the feeling he wants to tell me off, but something changes as he leans forward and presses kisses against my lips.

"My strong, beautiful mate," he whispers between kisses. His hands roam over my skin as he pulls me close, his erection firm as it presses against my stomach. "I love you," he murmurs into my mouth, and excitement blooms in my stomach as he says it. I still can't help but get excited when one of the guys says it, but especially from my surly alpha.

"I love you too," I whisper back, biting down on his lower lip just hard enough to sting. Growling low in his throat, he presses me against the cold wall of the shower and pins me with his hot, wet body, while pressing bruising kisses against my lips. Sliding my hand between us, I grab his cock, stroking it firmly, until the shower is practically vibrating with his deep growl. Holding my ass, he picks me up and impales me on his length, my shocked gasp soon turning into moans of pleasure as he begins moving inside me. It's fast and rough, but it's exactly what we need, our sounds of pleasure echoing around us as he guides my hips with his strong hands. Pleasure builds up, and soon, I'm crying out, my nails biting into his shoulders as my orgasm burns through me, my pussy milking his cock as he follows, finding his own release.

We stand, panting in the shower, the water still raining down on us as he presses our foreheads together again, his eyes watching me carefully as if I'm about to disappear.

"You're back," he whispers, and I suddenly understand. Wrapping my arms around him, I tilt my chin forward and press a soft, tender kiss to his lips.

"I'm back."

Chapter Twenty-One

"Director Hunter is dead," Aiden informs us, his face stoic as my mouth drops open in shock at his declaration.

"Wait, what? How?" I demand, leaning forward in my chair in the busy coffee shop, not caring that we could be overheard by humans. I just need to know who stole my kill. It may sound dark, but that bastard was behind the kidnapping and murder of shifters, and the reason shifters were being unfairly prosecuted. Not to mention, he wanted to put harsher restrictions on our movements. I'd later learned that Hunter had an ulterior motive. While he believed all the crap he spouted about shifters, he truly wanted a Shadowborn. Not as an assassin, as most would think, but because he wanted to *be* a Shadowborn, and since shifters produce more Shadowborn than any other supernatural race, it was fair game on shifters.

When Alpha Mortlock had received the call this morning, we debated for a long time about whether I should meet with Agent Aiden. While we trusted Aiden and Ryan, they still belonged with ASP, and after their blatant and illegal abduction of me, our trust is a little thin. When he suggested meeting in the coffee shop—a neutral, open place with plenty of humans around—I argued that we should hear him out. The pack was outraged with what they had learned, and I was humbled when I'd found out that they were ready to mount an attack on ASP to get me back. Thankfully, due to the link I had with my mates, they knew I wanted them to hold off on rescuing me, which they'd passed on to the pack. I dread to think what the outcome would have been if they had.

If they had, Em might have survived. I can't help but wonder if he could have been saved if they had ignored my insistence that they hold off, and another wave of grief falls over me like a storm cloud. I can't think that way, there *would* have been casualties if Moon River had attacked the ASP headquarters, and Em never would've wanted that. I know being locked away the last twenty years had been difficult for him and that I was the reason he was locked up in the first place. The idea that he died trying to save me, completing his task from twenty years ago, is quite fitting, and I know it's something he would have wanted, even if I'll take that guilt to my grave.

A wave of compassion and concern reaches me through the bonds, and I feel the guys gather closer around me in comfort. Mortlock, who's sitting to my left, frowns as he sees the guys' reaction, and he meets my gaze with a hardness that shocks me.

"We can leave if this is upsetting you, Ari." A wave of his power follows his words as he looks over at the ASP agents, and I see the moment they feel it, their eyes glowing slightly in response. I realise then that Mortlock's anger is not at me, but as an alpha protecting one of his pack from a threat. Warmth blooms in my chest, and I reach over to place my hand on top of his, waiting for him to drag his eyes back to mine.

"Thank you, Alpha, but I'm fine." I wouldn't usually address him so formally, but since this is an official meeting, I thought it was best to keep up appearances.

Mortlock's gaze softens as I speak, and he squeezes my hand slightly before turning back to Aiden and the other agents. Ryan's face is tight and pinched as he sits back in his chair, and I wonder what's crawled up his ass. I know he's never been a fan of me, but I thought I'd earned his begrudging respect.

"Alpha Mortlock, Ari, let me introduce you to Agent Thomas, she will be taking charge of ASP in the interim." Aiden's voice distracts me from my musings, and I realise why the agents are acting so stiff and formal when Agent Thomas takes a step forward. She doesn't bother sitting, preferring instead to stand and look down at us, her hands clasped behind her back. None of them have uniform on, so they blend in within the open setting, but there is no mistaking her as a normal civilian by the way she acts.

"Alpha," she addresses Mortlock, giving him a curt nod before turning her sharp gaze on me, and if looks could kill, I'd be in deep trouble. "So you are the one Hunter destroyed our organisation over."

Low growls fill the air as my mates react to her slur. Humans look around the coffee shop, trying to identify the sound, and I even hear a few mutter about thunder. Killian pushes up from his chair, his teeth bared as he leans over the table towards Agent Thomas. The others curse and shift positions in their chairs in case they need to jump up and stop him, but I wave them away. I trust Killian, he's not the man he used to be.

"How dare you insult my mate." His voice is low, his eyes locked on her as he defends me. Reaching out, I clasp his hand, stroking my thumb over his palm in a calming gesture.

"Kill, it's okay." I can feel his indecision down the bond. He wants to defend my honour, but he also knows I'll be pissed if he makes a scene in a human coffee shop.

"Killian, my friend, it's not worth it." Mortlock's steady voice cuts through the tension, and Killian finally looks away from the agent before nodding his head in agreement and returning to his chair, but not before pulling me closer to him, his inner wolf demanding that he protect me. "Ari did nothing wrong other than exist," Alpha Mortlock states, addressing the woman, his words clear and leaving no room for disagreement. There is a pause as her steely gaze moves from me to the alpha.

"We will be undergoing a full investigation of what has been going on under Hunter's leadership." Her words are clipped and to the point before her eyes narrow on me again. "If I had my way, I'd be bringing you in for questioning, however, testimonies from agents have saved you." An unsaid 'for now' hangs in the air, and I know I'll have to keep an eye on her in the future. "I shall leave Agent Cross to answer any questions you may have. I'm sure we will cross paths again, Ari." Narrowing my eyes on the woman, I hold her stare until she looks over at Mortlock, giving him a curt farewell. "Alpha Mortlock." Bowing her head briefly, she straightens her pantsuit before stalking out of the coffee shop, her entourage following her, leaving only Aiden and Ryan sitting awkwardly in their chairs.

"What a bitch," Alex mutters, his eyes narrowed on the door Agent Thomas just walked through.

"Tell me about it," Ryan replies, sliding off his suit jacket and unbuttoning the top button of his shirt now that his superior has left. Seeing Aiden's disapproving look, he shrugs. "What? You think it too."

Smothering a smile, I rethink my impression of Ryan. He may be an ass, but he says it how it is, which is refreshing.

"Agent Cross, what can you tell us? Is Ari in danger?" Mortlock inquires, shifting the focus and getting down to business, looking at how he can protect his pack.

"Please, we can drop the formalities, Alpha? I'm Aiden and this is Ryan," Aiden responds, gesturing from himself to his cousin, who is watching the humans around us with interest.

"In that case, call me Mortlock," he replies with a nod of his head. "Now, what can you tell us?"

Aiden pauses as he looks over at me, and I get the impression that while he's talking to all of us, it's me he's really addressing.

"After Emmanuel, formally known as Em, killed the witch, Ari was able to escape." He tries to hide it, but I can hear the note of pain in his voice. It's not just me mourning Em. I'd forgotten that Em was working with Aiden and Ryan, so they would have known him well. "As you know, the Butcher stabbed Emmanuel, but before he died, he called on the last of his power to...shadow himself over to Hunter," he explains, stumbling over how to describe the ability, looking at me to confirm he explained it in a way that made sense. Heart aching, I nod my head, it makes too much sense.

"How did he do it?" My voice is quiet, but they hear it and understand what I'm really asking. *How did he kill Hunter?*

"He pulled the knife from his chest and stabbed Hunter with it. He died shortly after," Ryan answers in his usual blunt manor, but surprises me when he leans forward, lowering his voice. "There was nothing you could do, it was a fatal injury."

Leaning back in the chair, I nurse my coffee, mulling over the information they've given me. None of it's a real shock, other than Hunter died, but I find a sense of satisfaction knowing Em managed to take him down. While I'm pissed that I wasn't able to do it, Hunter had tormented Em for far longer than he had me.

"What happened to the body?" I ask Aiden, who glances at Ryan. They seem to have a silent conversation before Ryan answers.

"We were going to ask you what you would like us to do with it."

"Can we take him back with us, bury him in the pack forest?" I request, glancing at the alpha for permission, then smiling at his nod. Em had been locked away for over twenty years, he would want to be buried outside. Plus, with his earth magic, I figured he'd want to be around nature.

"He would've liked that," Aiden says softly, and we pause for a moment in respectful silence. I know none of the guys ever met Em, but they know he meant a lot to me, even when I thought he had betrayed me by working for the organisation that killed Tori.

Thinking over everything I've learned so far, something sticks in my mind, and I lean forward, placing my coffee back on the table between us.

"The witch. Who was he?"

"We don't know." Ryan's curt response makes me frown and glance over at his more open cousin.

"What do you mean, you don't know?" I'd aimed the question at Aiden, but surprisingly, it's Ryan who answers.

"Exactly that, there's no record of him. We've only seen him around a few times, and he was always heavily guarded. But there was something off about him," Ryan explains with a shudder, like even the thought of the witch was enough to disturb him. Leaning forward, he drops his voice, shaking his head as he clarifies, "A normal witch shouldn't have the power to do what he did, to neutralise not only a shifter, but *any* supernatural."

Aiden nods and takes over from his cousin. "Retaining supernaturals is dangerous, and we have rooms designed to hold different supernaturals based on their skill set, but never to completely take away and nullify their powers." A shudder runs through me that any one person has that amount of power, and I can tell from the shifting of the guys around me that they feel the same. "He was brought in about a year ago and has been working with a special task force. That's all we know about him, but we do know there are more like him."

Everyone falls silent as they digest this. Not only is there someone who can take away our connection with our wolves, but there is more than one of them. My mind, however, is caught on something else he said.

"This special task force...is that the one that killed Tori?" I ask, remembering the words the agent said when they shot her. I hear those words in my sleep.

Target number four has been neutralised. The words echo through my head as I relive the bullet piercing through Tori's forehead.

"Ari." A hand on my shoulder brings me back to the present, and I lean back into the comfort of Garett's gesture.

"I'm okay." Glancing over my shoulder, I smile at him, waiting for him to smile gently in return before I turn back to the agents. Aiden's wearing a sympathetic look, while Ryan just appears bored, and it's his total lack of empathy that makes me snort. I nod to Aiden to start again.

"We believe so. We're still going through the records, but there's a list of high priority targets that were being watched. There were also instructions that if the opportunity arose to…neutralise those targets in a way that wouldn't tarnish ASP's reputation, then they were to take it." He struggles to word it in a way that doesn't upset me, but also accurately conveys what he's saying.

"Like during a raid." I can see them justifying the death of a witch during a raid. *It was an unfortunate necessity, a dangerous witch who was trying to hurt the agents.* Except she wasn't, she was trying to escape unscathed, but that's not what the general public would think if this was ever brought up, but those who were there know the truth.

"Why was Tori a target? Who else was on the list?" Alex questions, and I throw him a grateful look. I should've thought to ask that, but I'm just thinking that I'm really fucking glad we didn't let Tori come with us, making her stay behind at the pack.

"You were number one, but yours specified only to kill you if there was no other way to bring you in." Blowing out a breath, I lean back in my chair. Of course I was target number one. I'm not surprised, especially after what I learned about Hunter. He would have stopped at nothing to get me. "I wanted to bring the other files to see if you recognised any of the other targets since we didn't know them, but my request was denied." Frustration is evident in his tone, and I can guess who that order came from. "In Tori's case, at first, I thought it was because of your association." A familiar sense of guilt starts to rise, but as if sensing it, Aiden shakes his head. "However, none of your mates, except for Seb, were targets, so it didn't make sense. The only documentation in her file marked her supernatural status as 'unknown' and branded her as highly dangerous."

A stunned silence falls over us as we share confused looks, our focus settling on Seb, who leans back in his chair. His trademark smile is gone, and his worried eyes meet mine.

"What?" Killian surprises me by speaking first, his growl low and threatening, as if daring anyone to try anything. Looking over at the alpha, I see his brow furrowed as he clears his throat to gain attention.

"Seb was a target?"

"I'm not a threat to anyone! Why would I be a target?" Unable to contain himself, Seb stands and starts pacing among our chairs, but never far out of reach. His worry is palpable. Mortlock and Killian scan the area and watch his route with a determined gaze, so I know Seb won't be in any danger, his every move monitored. It's Killian's behaviour that surprises me the most. I know he cares for Seb like an annoying little brother, but he's acting like he's an alpha and Seb is one of his wolves.

Interesting, but I don't have time to think about that now, I think to myself, turning my attention back to the agents.

"Your file instructed to observe only. The only instance they were to bring you in was if you started to display 'unusual behaviour.'"

At the words 'unusual behaviour,' I share a look with the other guys. Eric's face pulls into a frown, and I know he's thinking the same thing I am—Seb's unusual power bursts. What did ASP know about them? Were they behind them?

"What happens now? Will the attacks on shifters stop?" Garett asks, sipping his coffee, his body language relaxed, but I can tell he's worried from the tension around his eyes. Reaching out, I grab his hand, squeezing it before turning back to face the agents.

"There's evidence all over the organisation of internal corruption. Director Hunter will be branded a traitor, and all ties with

Shadow Pack have been dissolved. A public statement is being prepared," Aiden explains, and I can't hold back my snort, shaking my head. Of course they are cutting all ties, no one is prepared to take responsibility. I'm not the only one to feel this way, if the rude noises from the guys around me are anything to go by.

"ASP is dead now. As soon as the public hears about us, they won't trust us. The organisation will fall," Ryan states bluntly, and I rock back in shock. Is that really what it will come to? I don't like ASP, but they are necessary. Without a governing body or anyone to police the supernaturals, crime rates will soar.

"ASP was flawed, but it still protected us. What will happen without it?" Alpha Mortlock questions, voicing the question that's on all of our minds.

"Something new will rise. There is already talk of a new organisation." Aiden tries to reassure us, but I don't think it will be as easy as he thinks.

"There is a lot of distrust among the shifter community, you'll have your work cut out for you," Eric responds, pulling the agent's attention onto him.

"I know." Silence follows his words, and I lean back in my chair, glancing out the window as I watch the humans hurry about their lives. I know this is a good thing, that Hunter can't torment us anymore and that the group of elite agents has been disbanded, but I can't fight the feeling that something bad is going to happen.

"This won't be the last we hear from Shadow Pack, they will be planning something, Terrance is still out there." The guys shift around me and search the café for any threats.

"We won't let him hurt you," Killian reassures me, and I nod before standing and walking over to his chair, then climb into his lap. Humming with pleasure, he wraps his arms around me and rests his chin on top of my head.

Alpha Mortlock watches us with a smile, and I'm reminded that they are old friends. Nodding at me, he turns his attention to the agents.

"What's going to happen regarding the other witches?"

Aiden and Ryan share a look, which makes me nervous. If there's no ASP and they haven't sorted out a new governing body, things might get messy for a little bit, especially if there are rogue witches running around with more power than they should have.

Aiden clears his throat and looks directly at me. "I was hoping to talk to Tori, see if she knows anything, if she's heard any rumours of witches with powers stronger than they should be."

Frowning, I shake my head, my first instinct to say no, to protect my friend who has been through so much. I know she would want to help if she can, but she's still traumatised about everything that happened.

"I'm not sure, Tori's been through a lot, I would have to ask—" I'm cut off as Mortlock and Ryan's phones go off at the same time. A sinking feeling settles in my stomach. Something is happening, something bad.

"Isa?" Mortlock answers with a frown. Why would Isa, the pack gamma, call? Unless the pack's safety was compromised, she wouldn't interrupt us. "What? We're on our way." His voice suddenly changes, and I can hear the alpha power in his words. I catch Isa's response, and just before he hangs up, he turns away and I hear his desperate words whispered down the phone. "Please keep Lena safe."

"Fuck," Ryan swears into the phone, pushing out of his chair as he gestures for us to follow him out of the coffee shop. "Understood," he replies curtly before hanging up.

"What the fuck is going on?" Killian growls, his wolf prowling under his skin, his control fraying under his frustration.

"Shadow Pack is attacking Moon River." Alpha Mortlock's tone is grim as he hurries from the shop, and we follow behind with curses.

"That's not all," Ryan calls out as he and Aiden hurry after us. "ASP isn't going to help, we've been ordered back to headquarters."

Chapter Twenty Two

The journey back to Moon River is tense. Thankfully, Aiden and Ryan told their superiors at ASP to go fuck themselves, so they're following us in their black Jeep. Alpha Mortlock, Seb, Eric, and Alex are travelling in one car, with Garett, Killian, and me in the other.

Driving one of the pack cars, Killian is cursing under his breath as he weaves through the vehicles that seem to be driving at a snail's pace. I utter a curse, gripping tightly onto the door handle as we bank a corner tightly, if he keeps driving like this, we might not even get there. Garett obviously feels the same and places his hand on the driver's seat to lever himself forward.

"Fuck, Kill, we can't help anyone if we're dead," Garett bites out. The tension in the car is high, my mind stuck on the thought that every moment we're away, another one of my friends could be dying.

"They planned this. They waited until we left, until the alpha and beta were gone, until some of the strongest wolves left the pack, before they attacked." Killian's voice is almost a growl as his hands tighten around the steering wheel, the skin between his knuckles whitening as his wolf tries to push through his control, the points of claws pressing against the skin. The images of Jess, Lena, and the other weaker members of the pack flash through my mind. We should be there to protect them. My wolf agrees and pushes against the boundaries of my control, my skin rippling as she tries to force the change. Closing my eyes, I focus on the lessons I've learned from being with Moon River and the control trainings I've had with Em. I'm not going to let everything he taught me go to waste.

No. I'm in control of my wolf, I remind myself, taking a deep breath as I feel my wolf start to recede. *I am alpha, I'm in control here.* Garett places his hand on my shoulder, rubbing soothing circles on my skin, helping to ground me. Reaching up, I place my hand on top of his and give it a grateful squeeze as I open my eyes.

"We left Isa behind, and she's been training up some of the other wolves in combat since the last attack. They're stronger than you give them credit for," I say, rationalising it more for my sake than his, and from the tension in his jaw, he knows it.

"We should be there."

Nodding in agreement, I lean across and put my hand on his shoulder, pushing my feelings down our bond, feelings that I can't put into words. Love, fear, acceptance, and a sense of togetherness, that with all of us, we will finish this, for better or worse. "I know."

The rest of the drive passes in tense silence, until we enter the forest the pack calls home. Parking the cars at the edge of the trees, we all pile out, gathering together as the guys in the other vehicles park. Alpha Mortlock walks over to us, the others following close behind.

"Alex, Seb, I want you in wolf form. Killian, Ari, stay in human form for now, but change if you need to," Mortlock orders, nodding as Seb and Alex peel away to start removing their clothing. Turning to the others, he sighs and runs his hand through his greying hair. "You aren't pack, so I can't ask you to fight for us," he starts, but Garett is already shaking his head.

"Pack Long Claw is yours, my twin brothers are already with the pack with Tori, and they called Max as soon as the attack started. My father and our strongest fighters are on their way to help protect your pack," he explains, and I can see the effect of his words on the alpha.

"I can't ask that—"

"You didn't have to," my bear interjects, my heart aching at the gesture of the bear pack. To fight for us, to put themselves at risk for not only another pack, but another species, says a lot about them.

"I, too, will be fighting with the pack." Eric steps forward and clasps the alpha on the shoulder. "You offered me not only the chance to be close to my mate, but a job and a home. That's something I haven't had for a long time," he says, and I have to bite my lip at the feelings he's sending down the bond, the feelings of loneliness that disappeared, a feeling of belonging he felt with us, with me, that he hasn't felt before. "I'll change into my demon form. I don't want to scare any of the cubs, but I can protect them better that way." Mortlock just nods in agreement, his eyes wide at the show of support.

"Myself and my cousin will also fight with you," Aiden chimes in, taking a step forward as he gestures to Ryan, who's nodding. "I'll shift and fly ahead, scout the area so we aren't going in blind."

"Thank you."

Nodding at the alpha's gratitude, Aiden takes a step back, pulling his cousin with him as he speaks in a low voice, then tugs at his shirt as he starts to shift. Turning my gaze, I look around the circle of people who mean so much to me. Nervous energy runs through everyone as we wait for orders.

A high-pitched bird call signals Aiden's departure as he flies off into the forest, and I can't help but glance over at the dark wolf who watches the path of the bird until it's out of sight.

Time seems to drag on as we wait for Aiden's return. Ryan's wolf wears a path into the grass as he paces back and forth, a high-pitched whine occasionally drawing my attention to him. Alpha Philips and the bear shifters arrived about five minutes ago, and Alpha Mortlock has been discussing the plan with them and filling them in on what we know.

The nervous energy in the air is making people crabby, namely Killian, as he snarls at anyone who comes near him.

"Why are we waiting? We should be fighting those bastards!"

Mortlock sighs and rubs his face in frustration, and I can tell how difficult waiting is for him when his pack might be getting slaughtered. "Killian, we've discussed this. Shadow Pack wants Ari, they won't start fighting until she arrives. We need to know—" A bark from Ryan stops the alpha in his tracks as we all look over to the wolf, who's running over to a naked Aiden, who's hurrying towards us.

"A couple of the stronger wolves are tied up, and someone who I'm assuming is your gamma is fighting three wolves double her size. She's protecting some of the female and cubs," Aiden explains, running his hand through his hair, his chest heaving as if he just ran here. A ripple of pride runs through me as I think of Isa fighting three wolves at once—that sounds like our gamma. "Other than that, no one seems to be badly hurt, they seem to be waiting for something." I feel the weight of everyone's stares on me, but I don't meet anyone's gaze. I know I'm the cause of this, but I won't feel guilty. I didn't ask for this.

Mortlock nods at Aiden's assessment, reassured that no one seems to be badly hurt, and I can see the wheels turning in his head. "Same plan as before. Anyone who doesn't want to fight, now is your time to leave, I won't force anyone to fight." Looking around, he meets everyone's gazes, nodding when no one leaves, a grateful glint entering his eyes. It doesn't last long, because a steely, determined expression takes over as he claps his hands together. "Those of you who are shifting and haven't done so yet, now is the time."

Everyone steps away and moves into small groups as they prepare for the fight. The guys gather around me, Seb and Alex in wolf form, brushing their large heads against my legs. Killian's intense look pierces me as he stalks towards me.

"No rash, self-sacrificing today. I mean it, Ari, we do this together," he orders, my wolves yipping their agreement at my side.

Something bumps into my legs, which nearly pushes me over, and as I turn around, I see my grizzly bear sitting back on his hind quarters, his tongue lolling from the side of his mouth, and despite the nerves running through me, I can't help the smile seeing him brings. A rush of electricity shoots through the bond, alerting me to Eric changing into his demon form. I follow the bond and smile when I see Eric's demon. I can see why someone would fear him, in fact, some of the shifters in their animal forms are shying away from him. Taking a deep breath, I release it on a shaky exhale.

"Ready to go zap some people?"

His face transforms into a smile that scares even me as his body seems to grow, and blue crackles of electricity bounce off his body. Thanks to our little love making session last night, my demon is more powerful than I've ever seen him. "Yes, my little mate."

The forest is eerily silent as we make our way towards the pack, even the birds in the trees are quiet, the only sound from our feet on the undergrowth. Alpha Morlock is at the front of our group. As the alpha of the pack, it's only right that he leads us. Alex, as beta, takes the position to the alpha's right in his wolf form, and to the left in the gamma position...is me. When Mortlock suggested it, I had initially refused. I'm the reason behind this attack, after all, but he had insisted. I'd worried that some of the other wolves would be upset that I was in this station, but everyone had agreed, including Killian, who rightfully should have been offered the position. He was just as strong, if not stronger than me, but had also been a friend of the pack far longer than I had. I'd eventually agreed, but only on the insistence that I was holding Isa's place for her.

We walk fast, not bothering to hide the sound of our footsteps. We had decided against running, wanting to show a united, calm front. Shadow Pack would know we were coming either way, and

I've noticed a few scouts in wolf form run ahead as we make our way through the forest.

The guys fan out behind me, Killian on my left in human form, followed by Seb's and Ryan's wolves. Garett is just behind us, his brother and other bears following closely. Their alpha is still in human from in the middle of them all. Eric stands off to the side of the group, watching our sides and rear, trying to avoid spooking any of our animals.

Aiden is once again in his eagle form, flying high above us. I had pulled him aside before he changed again and had asked if he'd seen Tori—surely he would have seen a demon and her raging bear mates causing hell? He explained that he hadn't seen them, but had seen evidence of hurried paths away from the pack buildings.

Pushing aside the gnawing fear that she's been taken, I take a deep, calming breath. No, she wasn't with those tied up, and if she had been taken, there would be obvious destruction, not only from her mates, but from her. This makes me think that they're hiding out, waiting for us to return. Besides, Max would be going apeshit if anything had happened to her. I just can't shake the guilt that she's been brought into another fight. I can't cope with losing her again.

Finally, we reach the edge of the pack. Some of the outer buildings peek out from behind trees as we walk by, heading towards the centre of the land. The farther in we get, the more densely populated the area is with buildings, but where we would usually see people coming and going, the space is empty. The centre of the pack land is kept clear, other than the alpha's house facing it, so pack gatherings can take place there.

Low and behold, as we come up to the clearing, Terrance is lounging on the porch of the alpha's house, watching us with a smug smile as we make our way closer. His eyes narrow a little when he notices we've brought backup, but his whole face lights up when he sees me at the alpha's side. Scanning the clearing, I see several of our wolves pinned to the ground, and a furious Isa snarling at three wolves who have pinned her in a corner. She's bleeding from a cut on her ear and seems to be favouring her left side, but otherwise, she looks unharmed. Inside the alpha's house, I can hear a child crying, so I assume that's where they're keeping the children. Glancing at Eric, I push my feelings down our bond, and he nods his head slightly in agreement, obviously thinking the same thing. He'll focus on protecting the children and those who can't fight.

Terrance glues his eyes onto me, jumping up from the chair and practically bouncing to the front of the porch. His other wolves look at our numbers and shift their weight uneasily. They probably thought this would be an easy takeover, but their numbers have been thinned since they last attacked us. Scanning the row of wolves, I run some figures through my head. There are more of them than us, and the training they go through makes them ruthless fighters who would rather die than lose, which makes them dangerous, but they haven't outright killed our pack, so there is something that's more important to them here.

"Ari! You decided to join us!" Terrance crows, knowing full well that not addressing the alpha first is a slight. Mortlock, however, doesn't rise to it, instead, he nodding at me, happy for me to take the lead. "Not running away anymore?" Rolling my eyes, I cross my arms over my chest.

"Fuck off, Terrance."

Mortlock grins at me in approval before taking a step forward, raising his power so it fills the air around us. The hairs on my arms stand on end as he calls our wolves to the surface. "You are trespassing on my land. Leave now, and you will remain unharmed." He doesn't raise his voice, he doesn't need to, his power carries the weight of his words.

"You know what? Now that ASP isn't ordering us around anymore, I quite like the idea of settling down here," Terrence replies, calling forth his own alpha power, but it feels weak, forced, as he calls his wolves to him. "We need a new home now, and I've got my sights set on a mate fit for an alpha." His eyes narrow on me again, and I can't hide the shudder of disgust his words cause. The wolves around me growl, taking a step towards me, their hackles raised at the threat.

"My answer was no then, and it's a fuck no now."

"That's a shame," he responds, before his eyes glow bright and he gestures towards us. "Don't kill the girl, the rest can die."

The answering snarl from our shifters is deafening, and before I know it, they are running towards the Shadow Pack. Mortlock and Alex race to help Isa with one of the bears assisting, as we had planned. I see Eric walking calmly over to the house, his body practically vibrating with energy as he zaps a wolf that dared get in his path.

My job is Terrance. When we were coming up with the plan, that was my one condition—I get to kill the man who helped torment me for years.

Glancing around, I try to find the Shadow Pack alpha, cursing when I don't see him. A shout from Killian brings my attention back to the fight as four wolves run towards us. Focusing, I call on my shadows, their cool embrace surrounding me as my limbs flicker in and out of this realm. Killian tilts his head back as he shifts into his wolf, his huge grey form impressive, but I don't have long to admire it before he's throwing himself into another wolf. Seb remains at my side, teeth bared as the other three wolves circle us. Calling my shadows, I dart forward, pouncing on a wolf and taking him by surprise. I surround us with shadow, covering him completely and snapping his neck with one sharp movement. Pulling away, I see the other wolves watching me carefully, and I know that trick won't work again.

A lady's scream comes from inside the house, and before I know it, I'm running towards the front door, leaving Kill and Seb behind. I know they will be okay, but my heart is pounding, torn in different directions.

Entering the house, I see Eric fighting several wolves with a group of crying children and wolf pups cowering in the corner, being cradled by some of the weaker shifters and those unable to shift. Lena stands in front of them, brandishing a kitchen knife in her shaking hands.

"They've got Jessica!" she cries out, tears running down her face as she points to the open back door. My heart drops but I nod at her with a small smile.

"You did good. I'll get Jess back," I reassure her, turning to give Eric a hand just as he kills the wolf with his electricity, his eyes glowing as he absorbs the pain from the dying wolf, fuelling his power all the more. "You good?" I ask him as I hurry out the door, feeling his confirmation through the bond.

I know I'm going against the plan, that this is risky, but a little girl's life is at stake. I would never forgive myself if I let her die because I was waiting for a bunch of guys to come and help me. Following the trail out of the house, I scent the air to see if I can follow her. A flash of colour ahead has me running to catch up, and as I run farther from the fight, I know I'm entering a trap. Seeing the medical building in the distance, I know that's where I'm being led.

I step into the building, not bothering to hide my footsteps, and follow the sound of Jessica's sobs.

"Don't worry, Jess, I'm coming," I call out, the building eerily quiet as I walk into the large reception room. Jess is sitting huddled in the corner, she's crying, but looks unhurt otherwise.

"Ari!" Her little face lights up when she sees me, but she doesn't leave the corner of the room. Terrance steps out of the other corner, suddenly appearing with a smile on his face. He always had a flare for the dramatic. Taking a step towards me, he smiles even wider when he notices I didn't bring anyone with me.

"You came." His voice is almost delirious with glee as he starts to circle me. I mirror his moves and drop into a defensive position.

"Of course I did, you fuckwit, you took someone I care for. I've come to get her back."

"You came alone, some things never change." He grins, and I

feel like an idiot for walking into his trap, exactly like he planned it, but then a surge of defiance pulses down the bond, and I realise I'm completely different from the person I was. I didn't leave everyone behind because I didn't trust them, I left them because I trust them to take care of themselves, and most importantly, I trust myself.

"A lot has changed about me," I warn, a smile finally starting to spread across my face. "I can do this now." Calling my shadow again, I make it flicker around me, and I see a flash of doubt in his eyes.

"Have you accepted your fate?"

"I would rather die than be your mate," I spit, his eyes narrowing at my rejection.

"Then you die." Stepping to the side, he calls out and a large black wolf appears in the doorway. Cursing myself for letting Terrance distract me, I allow my wolf to finally take control.

I shift too late. The black wolf is already charging towards me as my shift starts, biting into my shoulder. Its sharp fangs rip through my skin, and I cry out, but it can't keep hold of me as my bones shift and shape into my second form. Finally in wolf form, I whine at the pain in my shoulder, but I can't focus on that for long as the wolf goes in for a second attack. Dancing back, I try to call on my shadows to help me, but it's much more difficult in this form, and the pain from my shoulder is making it harder for me to concentrate. I snarl at the wolf and dart forward, swiping my claws at him, but he dances out the way.

Roaring outside the house reaches my ears, and I hope that the bears are on their way to protect Jess from Terrance. Backing me into a corner, the wolf snarls at me again, about to attack, when a burst of purple smoke fills the room.

"Oh fuck no. We're not having that." Tori's voice fills the room, and I try to squint through the purple fog, seeing her standing there with her hands on her hips as the twins pin down the wolf that was trying to attack me. "I'm assuming this guy is with Shadow Pack?" she asks me, familiar with my wolf form. Making my large head dip in agreement, I watch as a wicked smirk crosses her lips as she throws herself onto the wolf. "Let's take a little trip," she whispers into his ears, before laughing madly and disappearing in a puff of smoke, taking the wolf with her.

Stunned, I stare at the spot she had just been before calling my wolf back and groaning as my human form reappears. Rubbing my shoulder, I grimace as I stand up. It healed during the shifting process, but it's had to heal much more rapidly than usual, so it's still sore.

"What the fuck was that, and where the fuck has she gone?" I ask, dumbstruck, as I look between the twins. They share a proud grin before looking back at me.

"It's one of her powers. She takes them to the Death Realm," Ben replies, as he shrugs off his T-shirt and holds it out to me. I'm not bothered by nudity, but fighting with your tits waving around is a little distracting.

Pulling the T-shirt on, I'm pleased to see it almost comes down to my knees as I look at them in shock. "There's a Death Realm?"

"Apparently," they answer in tandem as Tori arrives in a puff of purple smoke again, setting me off into a coughing fit. The twins immediately surround her, reaching out to touch her, but she awkwardly shrugs them off before looking around with a frown. They hide their hurt expressions quickly, but I still saw them. Hmm, she's still not accepted them as her mates yet, but I don't have time to think about that now.

"Right, let's deal with this Terrance fucker. Where is he anyway?" she inquires, eyeing up my new outfit before holding out a hand towards Jessica, who eagerly runs over. "Hey, hun," she murmurs to the little girl, pressing a kiss to her forehead.

"We're going to have words later," I point at her, rolling my eyes at her 'who, me?' look.

"Ari, I've got something for you," Killian calls from outside the house. Tori and I share frowns, but the smug feeling Killian is sending down the bond has me hurrying outside.

A grin spreads across my face when I'm greeted by Killian, the rest of my guys, the alpha, the bears, and several of my packmates all forming a circle, and inside that circle is Terrance in wolf form. Snarling, he's trying to break out of the circle, pouncing towards one of the shifters, only to be batted back by several of the others in the circle.

Any one of these people could have killed him, but they knew I wanted that job. My heart glows as I see that all of my guys and most of the pack are here, alive. Sure, some of them are injured, but those injuries will heal. Looking around, I can see the bodies of several wolves lying around, but I don't recognise any of them as one of ours. Turning my attention back to the circle, I see Mortlock nod towards Terrance.

"This is your kill if you want it."

I'm grateful that he offered this to me, knowing that as alpha, he could order anyone to do it. Nodding, I step forward, stopping only when Tori's hand touches my shoulder.

"Go fuck him up."

Taking a deep breath, I step through the circle. I don't shift into my wolf form, even though I'm breaking some rule in shifter etiquette, not that I give a shit. I've imagined how I'm going to kill him for a long time, but now that it's actually time to do it, I find myself hesitant. Looking at him now, he just looks pathetic, and I find myself feeling sorry for him. He snarls and lunges towards me, but I simply turn to shadow and step through him. Whirling around, he tries to track me, growling when he sees I'm now the other side of the circle, and that's when I realise how I'm going to win this.

I drop to my knees, place my hands on my lap, and simply wait. I feel Killian's confusion and worry at the same time Tori calls my name, but I don't have time to respond, to tell them it's okay, because Terrance takes this moment to charge me. A second before he barrels into me, I open my arms wide, grab on to him, and focus my will on turning to shadow, dropping straight into the Shadow Realm. Except this time, I drag him with me.

I've never taken anyone with me before, and I can feel the shadow ripping at my arms as I go, my body burning, but I force the shadows to my will. *I am in control, not the shadows.*

I feel the moment we arrive, the lifeless grey plains the same as always. A cry has me turning around, and I take a step back from Terrance's writhing body. He's been forced back into human form, and the shadows do *not* like that he's here. In fact, they seem to be ripping at his body, surrounding him. He screams again, and I feel a little guilty for all of four seconds, until I remember all the things he did and put me through, all the innocents he killed while in charge of Shadow Pack.

"Goodbye, Terrance," I call out, watching as he realises I'm going to leave him here as he reaches out to me.

Closing my eyes, I call on the shadows once more and think of my family waiting for me, before following the glowing bond that leads me home.

"Ari," Seb calls, and I know I'm back, feeling a soft wind caressing my cheek as I open my eyes. I'm still on my knees in the middle of the pack, but the circle has broken up. Everyone is huddled in little groups, hugging loved ones and tending to the wounded. I'm surrounded by my guys, with Tori standing just off to the side, winking at me before turning to talk to Max.

"You did it," Garett grumbles, his voice still deep from changing into his bear form.

"Of course she did, she's our badass mate." Alex smirks, his pride clear in his voice.

They shift around me, and Killian steps forward to help me up, pulling me into his arms once I'm standing, and before I know it, I'm surrounded in a huddle of guys since he refuses to let go of me. A thought distracts me, and I pull away, looking for Jessica, and I see her clinging to Seb's leg. I smile and let out a sigh of relief before biting my lip, not wanting to ask the question in case I jinx it.

"Is it over? Did we win?"

Killian's hard gaze softens as he leans over and presses a kiss to my forehead. "Yes, it's over."

I smile at his reply, but I can sense the unspoken words he left of the end of his sentence. "Yes, it's over, for now." His trepidation is trickling down the bond, but as I gaze around me and see the looks of relief and the sense of happiness around us, I decide not to question it. I know the past will catch up with us, but for now, I'm going to enjoy the time we have together.

Epilogue

SIX MONTHS LATER

Of course it wasn't over, the Butcher was still on the loose, along with the witches that worked for Hunter. We've been working with Director Thomas and what's left of ASP to try and track them down, but the whole system has collapsed. Shifters are demanding more say in the election of the new governing body after what happened last time, and it's causing a rift between the other races. But mostly, things have settled down. There haven't been any attacks, the witches are helping to find the rogues, and a tentative peace has fallen over us.

After the attack, many of the pack buildings needed repairing, including the medical building I'd called home. Killian had been the one to suggest we build a new house at the edge of the pack property, one big enough for all of us, including the bear and demon who make up part of my family. They couldn't keep being pack guests, no matter how welcoming the alpha is. Ryan and Aiden are also staying with us, since they couldn't return to ASP after they ignored direct orders. So we bought some land from Mortlock, and we are making our own pack. It's a ragtag group, but it's home.

Tori has her own room and will for as long as she needs it. She's still rejecting the bond with the twins and Max, but I suspect they are wearing her down, she's just not ready yet.

"You need to lift it more on the left," Seb calls out, bringing my attention back to the task at hand. Raising the picture frame higher on my side, I smile as Alex lets out a bored sigh.

"That's perfect!" Jessica shouts, jumping up and down with excitement on her bed, clapping her hands together. "I love it."

Stepping away from the picture now successfully hanging on the wall, I admire the photo which was taken last month at the last pack meeting. Everyone was there, including Tori and her bears, Ryan, and Aiden. I grin as I watch Seb spin his little sister around, her giggles following me out of the room as I head into a quieter part of the house. My gut twists slightly as I look at Seb. We still don't know what caused his power to...change, but it's settled down since ASP disbanded. Alpha Philips told me that something similar happened to another bear pack, so I'm sure it's going to come back to bite us on the ass. However, for now, we're happy.

I can hear Garett talking with Eric somewhere in one of the rooms, probably the library, where my demon likes to spend most of his time. One thing is for sure, it's busy living with this many people.

Following the hallway, I walk into the large room that takes up the whole upper back side of the house, with a large bed taking centre place. The whole end wall is made of glass, which opens up onto a wooden balcony. This is my favourite room in the house, and seeing Killian on the balcony outside brings a smile to my face.

Brooding as usual, I think to myself, and I know he senses my thoughts down the bond since the corner of his mouth twitches up, but otherwise, he doesn't move. I push the double doors open, and he finally breaks his statue impression and holds his arms open for me as soon as I step onto the decking. Smiling, I walk over to him, enjoying the feeling of having him wrapped around me. I stare out at the view of the forest, and a feeling of contentment fills me.

"Everything's going to be okay, isn't it?" He phrases it as a question, but I get the feeling he's just realised this for himself, that we can finally live our lives together. As he places his hands on my stomach, I feel a flutter of nerves, but can't stop my smile as I think of the little life growing inside me. Tilting my head up, I smile as the door to the balcony opens, and as if called by my happiness, the others join us.

"Yes, it is."

Seb

Seeing her smile settles something within me, that strange, twisting anger that makes me feel like something *other*. I've seen their worried looks, but I paste on my smile and don't let them see that it bothers me. Sure, there have been no more...episodes with my power since ASP disbanded, but something has been awoken within me, and I'm not sure how much longer I can keep it hidden.

But for Ari and our family, I'll work my ass off to make sure they are safe and happy, even if it means hiding that part of myself from her.

Somewhere deep in the city

Sliding into the dark booth in the dingy pub that was chosen for this meeting, the hooded figure grimaces as her hands land on the grimy faux leather seats. However, she understands the importance of choosing somewhere discreet, so she bites back her seething comment. Since ASP fell apart, they couldn't be seen together, so they had been forced to skulk around in places like this. Three other hooded figures are already waiting for her, with untouched drinks before them on the sticky table.

"You're late," a deep male voice states from beneath his dark hood. Scowling, she merely dips her head in his direction. She never did learn the name of the powerful witch who'd pledged his coven's help with their mission, but she'd seen his power in action and didn't want to be at the receiving end of *that*.

"I was being followed," she replies simply, not bothering to explain her suspicions or how she lost her follower. "We have a problem. There is no way we can get to Ari, she's too closely guarded with those mates of hers. Especially now that she's pregnant, they won't let her out of their sight." Her voice is bitter as she remembers the scene she'd witnessed from her hiding spot, of them all huddled together on the balcony. It made her feel sick with jealousy.

"Forget target number one," the witch growls, the two hooded figures on either side of him straightening in their seats as his power seems to pulse out of him with his anger. "This is so much bigger than her. I never understood Hunter's obsession with her, and in the end, it got him killed. We move on to the others." He pauses and lifts his head, his glowing, silver eyes boring into hers as his mouth pulls up into a predatory grin. "We move on to the next phase."

The End

Tori and her bears will be returning in Demons Do It Better, coming Spring 2021.

BONUS SCENE

The moment Ari discovers she's pregnant

Ari

"Holy shit."

Tori's sentiment fully sums up how I'm feeling right now. The two of us are locked in the master bedroom of the huge house we're building on the edge of the Moon River Pack territory.

Clutched in my shaking hand is a pregnancy test.

I've not looked at the result yet, but if I'm being honest with myself, deep down, I already know the answer. Tori watches me with wide eyes, and I step towards her, thrusting the test toward her. "Tori, you do it. I can't look."

Screeching like a banshee, she backs away like the thing could impregnate her just by touching her. "Don't brandish that thing at me! You've peed on it!" Scrunching her nose in disgust, I know she's trying to make me laugh, and usually, this would work, but I'm too nervous. No, nervous doesn't even begin to convey what I'm feeling right now. Terrified, excited, scared, hopeful... The list goes on.

"Tori," I plead, my heart pounding in my chest. Her face softens as she finally realises just how scared I am, seeing the shaking of the dreaded stick in my hand.

"Fine." Blowing out a breath, she steps toward me and reaches out to take the test from me. Pausing right before she takes it, she raises her eyebrow and quirks her lips in a typical Tori smile. "But if I get your pee on me, I don't think we can be friends anymore." I huff out a broken laugh, stepping back as she takes the test from me, suddenly free from the spell that had me frozen in place. I can't look at her as she looks at the little plastic stick that will determine my future, pacing the length of the room.

I hear the intake of her surprised breath, and I know what she's going to say before she even says the words.

"You're pregnant."

I slow and come to a stop in front of the floor to ceiling wall of windows that overlooks the forest, her words ringing in my ears. *Pregnant.* Instinctively, my hand moves to my stomach. I'd noticed some changes recently, feeling sick in the mornings and feeling tired all the time, and I'm sure my wolf had known long before I'd suspected. A baby. Fear floods my system. I fought my father and my old tormentor to the death, no problem, but a baby? That is a whole other matter. I can barely look after myself, let alone a baby. However, the idea of a tiny Killian, Alex, or Seb running around fills me with a fierce sense of adoration. I know that Garett and I will never be able to have a baby together, and we're still not sure about interbreeding with demons and werewolves, but I assume the baby will be a wolf shifter...

"Ari?" Killian's deep voice calls out from somewhere in the house, followed by hurried footsteps as he makes his way to me. I can feel him tugging at our bond, trying to find out what's caused such a dramatic swing in my emotions. More pounding footsteps fill the house, and I spin to face Tori, my face set in a panicked expression.

"Uh-oh, mates incoming." Tori groans. "Need me to run interference?" Hurrying over to the door, she leans against it, seeing my reaction and knowing I'm not ready to tell the guys yet.

There's a thump as someone bounces off the door, followed by a low growl. "Ari?!" Killian pounds on the door with his fist, and I have to admire Tori's strength as she managed to hold back a fully grown alpha male werewolf trying to get to his mate.

"Killian, we're dealing with girl stuff, piss off for a bit," she grinds out, gritting her teeth as she pushes back against the door, her hooves digging in as she tries to keep him out. With a final push, Killian manages to shove the door far enough to squeeze through, except with a speed I didn't know she possessed, Tori is blocking his way.

Narrowing his eyes, Killian snarls slightly but doesn't touch the demon blocking his path—he learnt the hard way not to mess with Tori. "Something's wrong with Ari, I need to check on her." Stepping to one side, he tries to walk around her, but for every step he takes, she matches it.

"Don't make me smite you, wolf," she taunts, and I have to fight my groan as the two of them face off. The last thing we need is these two to start another feud.

Closing the distance between him and Tori, Killian growls as his alpha power starts to fill the room. "Don't test me, *demon*."

Seb, Garett, and Eric choose that moment to join us, the three of them filling the doorway. "What's going on, is Ari okay?" Garett immediately asks, his eyes skimming straight over Tori and Killian and going straight to me.

"Tori, is that a pregnancy test?" Seb asks loudly, spotting the test still clutched in Tori's hand. "Are you pregnant?!"

Everyone's attention turns to Tori. She narrows her eyes on me, and I can tell exactly what she's thinking. Before I can say anything or tell her not to, she sighs and turns back to address the room. "Yes. I'm pregnant."

Killian steps back and stares at her, the room completely silent for a few moments before everyone starts talking at once. Dumbly, I watch as they ask her questions. Who's the father? How far along is she? And I realise that she's fully intending to go along with this until I'm ready to tell them. *No, I can't let her do this. I have to tell them.*

"No, wait, stop!" I call out, waiting for everyone fall quiet and look at me. Taking a deep breath, I look between the guys, wishing Alex was here too, my other alpha mate on duty with Moon River Pack.

"Tori isn't pregnant." Pausing, I push back at the nausea that's threatening to take over. *What if they don't want this? What if they're not happy?* My inner thoughts plague me with doubt, but I force them aside. These guys are my mates and have been with me through some really tough times, they will be with me through this too. One by one, I meet each of their gazes, finally coming to land on Killian, who's practically rippling with tension. "I'm the one who's pregnant."

Although I whisper the words, you can see the moment the guys hear them, the effect instantaneous. They rush over to me, and I'm surrounded by their love and warmth, gentle hands reaching out and touching my stomach and arms wrapping around me. My fear evaporates. Sure, I'm still worried about my own inadequacies, but with five mates who will dote on me and the baby, we can't go too far wrong. Everyone is talking at once, in high, excited voices, and I can't help but laugh as I look between them. That's when I realise that Killian isn't here with me. Frowning, I look past the others and see that he's still standing by the door, staring at me in shock.

"You're pregnant." His voice is barely a whisper.

Swallowing the sudden lump in my throat, I nod my head and slowly walk towards him. When I reach him, his eyes drop to my stomach, and his hands reach out, pressing against the slightest curve that's beginning to show. Lifting his head, a beaming smile spreads across his face as he leans in and presses a kiss against my lips. Returning his kiss, I moan into his mouth, but then he's gone. Kneeling on the floor and lifting the hem of my top, he presses his lips against my stomach.

"I will never let anything happen to you," he whispers against my skin. "Either of you." He looks up, meeting my gaze. My eyes fill as I remember how he lost his first mate and how bittersweet this moment must be.

"Um...I'm just going to go now," Tori calls out awkwardly from the back of the room as the rest of the guys surround Killian and I. Smiling, I know as soon as the guys have gone, she'll have thousands of questions for me, but for now, I'm grateful she's giving me time with my mates.

We don't say anything, there will be time for talking and questions later, but for now, the five of us just stand pressed together, enjoying the physical contact and small, excited smiles.

Pounding footsteps breaks our calm, and as I look up, I see Alex jogging up the stairs. Practically falling through the open doorway, he raises an eyebrow as he sees us all cuddled together. "Not that I'm complaining, but Tori said I was needed upstairs immediately." Reaching up, he pushes some of his hair from his face, his expression turning apprehensive as he takes in our shared smiles. "What did I miss?"

BONUS SCENE

The inner musings of Doctor Eric Daniels

Lowering my medical journal, I glance over at Ari as she shifts on the couch next to me. Her feet rest in my lap as I gently rub her swollen ankles with one hand. At four months pregnant, she's starting to show now, her stomach swelling gently, and in my eyes, she's never looked more beautiful. Of course, she thinks the opposite, so the others and I have make it our mission to shower her with our affection.

Running my eyes over her now, I take her in as she reads her magazine, one hand resting on her growing bump.

Mate, my inner demon growls with satisfaction, and I fully agree with him. As a full-blooded demon, I have both a human and a demon form, a little like a shifter. Many demons choose not to use their human form, succumbing to their demon side fully. I, however, choose to be more than what my baser instincts try to force me to be—a pain-feeding demon. While I have to feed to live, I refuse to cause pain. As a doctor, I'm able to help people, to save them, but no matter what I do, I can never completely take away their pain. It seemed like a win-win, I can feed on their pain without causing it, *and* still save lives.

Sensing my gaze on her, Ari looks up from her magazine and smiles at me.

Protect. For once, myself and my demonic side are in agreement. Ever since Ari told us she was pregnant, when it comes to her, it's been much easier to control that side of me. The strongest urge within me is no longer the one to maim or hurt, but to shelter and defend the woman bonded to my soul who could be carrying my child.

We've all agreed that although biologically, the child will only have one father, we will *all* be its father. I don't care if it turns into a wolf or if he or she turns out to be part demon, I will love them fiercely either way.

With my demon hearing, I can detect the others moving around in the house, ever close by. They never leave Ari's side for long, being just as protective of her as I am. Happy sounds of a child playing reach me, so I know that Jessica and Seb are home. Tori's out in the city somewhere, that's another little worry we still have to contend with, but we'll deal with that another day.

Ari must sense my concern through the bond as she lowers her magazine and places her hand on my arm. "Is everything okay?" Her brow creases slightly, and I want to lean across and press a kiss there until she stops frowning.

A sense of joy fills me, my demon humming in the back of my mind as I run my eyes over my pregnant mate once more. I don't know what I did to deserve fate rewarding me with a mate such as her, but I shall be forever thankful. There's still a lot of uncertainty, a lot of unknowns, but right now, I'm consumed with contentment. Smiling, I take her hand in mine, squeezing as Alex and the others bustle into the room, breaking the quiet of the moment. "Yes, everything's perfect."

Acknowledgements

I can't quite believe that this series has been popular enough to warrant becoming an omnibus! When I first wrote Hunted by Shadows, I had no idea what I was doing and I though I would sell about ten copies, and most of them would be to my mum. But here we are!

Thank you to everyone to took a risk and bought a copy of the books, either the originals or this updated version. Thank you to the amazing team of people who push me and help make my books better. My Alpha and Beta teams, my PA Courtney, my author tribe, especially Katie who's like a sister to me. Let's not forget my editor, Jess, and my proof reader, Meghan, for making everything make sense, and my cover designer Harley, and the formatter Queen, Kaila.
I couldn't do this without any of you.

ALSO BY ERIN O'KANE

The Shadowborn Series:

Hunted by Shadows

Lost in Shadow

Embraced by Shadows

The War and Deceit Series:

Fires of Hatred

Fires of Treason

Fires of Ruin

Fires of War

Erin O'Kane and K.A Knight:

Her Freaks Series:

Circus Save Me

Taming the Ringmaster

The Wild Boys:

The Wild Interview

The Wild Tour

The Wild Finale

Erin O'Kane and Loxley Savage: Twisted Tides

Tides that Bind

Printed by Amazon Italia Logistica S.r.l.
Torrazza Piemonte (TO), Italy